TIMELINK

AN UNOFFICIAL
AND UNAUTHORISED
EXPLORATION
OF DOCTOR WHO
CONTINUITY
VOLUME TWO

TIMELINK

AN UNOFFICIAL
AND UNAUTHORISED
EXPLORATION
OF DOCTOR WHO
CONTINUITY

VOLUME TWO

Jon Preddle

First published in England in 2011 by
Telos Publishing Ltd
17 Pendre Avenue, Prestatyn, Denbighshire, LL19 9SH, England
www.telos.co.uk

Telos Publishing Ltd values feedback. Please e-mail us with any comments you may
have about this book to: feedback@telos.co.uk

ISBN: 978-1-84583-004-5 (volume 1)
ISBN: 978-1-84583-005-2 (volume 2)

Timelink: An Unofficial and Unauthorised Exploration of Doctor Who Continuity ©
2011 Jon Preddle

Parts of this book were published as *Timelink: An Exploration of Doctor Who Continuity*
by Jon Preddle in 2000 by TSV Books.

The moral right of the author has been asserted.

Internal design, typesetting and layout by Arnold T Blumberg
www.atbpublishing.com

Printed by Good News Press

1 2 3 4 5 6 7 8 9 10 11 12 13 14 15

British Library Cataloguing in Publication Data.
A catalogue record for this book is available from the British Library.

CONTENTS

PART FIVE
ADVENTURES
IN TIME
AND SPACE

DOCTOR WHO STORYFILE

All television stories spanning 1963 to 1989, 1996, and 2005 to 2008 are examined in this chapter. The stories are arranged in broadcast order – as this is generally accepted to be the same order in which they take place in the Doctor's timeline. And although the continuity between the stories of Season 25 is best viewed in the order originally intended, I have still used the broadcast order. Stories with special significance, such as the multi-Doctor adventures 'The Three Doctors', 'The Five Doctors' and 'The Two Doctors', and 'The Trial Of A Time Lord', have multiple entries for each of the Doctors positioned in the places that I believe work the best in terms of overall continuity. My reasons for placing them in these positions are explained fully under each story.

The following guide explains the various headings used and the section layout:

THE TITLE OF THE STORY

STORY LINK

Under this heading I examine the Link between the story in question and the television story that preceded it, with the objective of ascertaining whether or not the two stories are consecutive. Links to other stories and significant events in the Doctor's life are also examined where applicable. A + next to the heading indicates that the story and the one preceding it are consecutive.

(OTHER) LINKS

Links sharing a common theme, the Cybermen, Daleks, Gallifrey, the Master, and UNIT HQ are examined here when applicable, with particular focus on the events that have transpired since their last chronological appearance on-screen. The headings have been placed in alphabetical order.

UNIT HQ

Each time we see the interior or exterior of UNIT HQ during the third and fourth Doctor's eras, it is radically different from its last appearance. This suggests that there is actually more than one site used by the British division of the United Nations Intelligence Taskforce as its base of operations (which is hardly surprising given UNIT's desire for secrecy). There is of course a certain degree of similarity between some of the buildings – particularly the interior walls that are predominantly brick, painted a dark green along the bottom half and cream along the top half. This colouring could be UNIT's official colours, and so it could be that every building is coordinated to have matching decor.

From a production point of view, it appears that it was intended that there are different HQs; otherwise the same exterior location would be used, as well as the same permanent standing sets. By my own reckoning, seven different sites have been used by the UK division of UNIT: three in Central London, two by the coast, and two in rural areas. The HQ that appears in each story (where relevant) is noted.

OBSERVATIONS

Observations and notes about continuity or other items of interest are examined here. I give my own theories to explain some of the continuity anomalies.

LANGUAGE

This heading looks at Language (as examined in the chapter THE N-SPACE UNIVERSE), taking into account any anomalies surrounding the use of the Time Lord 'gift' of languages.

TIMELINE DATES
YYYY, MM DD *

This box contains my explanations and justifications for the dates I have used in the TIMELINE. A * next to a date indicates that the Doctor is actually present at that event in time.

Dates surrounded by << >> indicate events that take place in alternative timelines or dimensions.

HISTORICAL COMPARISON

This section only applies to historical stories. As the heading states, an historical comparison is made between the 'true' events in *Doctor Who* and the corresponding events of our own history.

DURATION

Duration covers the 'real-time' duration of the adventure as experienced by the characters during the course of the television episodes, breaking down the story into its number of days.

UNSEEN ADVENTURES

As noted under NAME-DROPPING, there are several untelevised adventures that are known to take place during a particular Doctor's era. These are recorded here as UNSEEN ADVENTURES, and have been placed at the most likely gap between TV stories. The three adventures that make up 'The Trial Of A Time Lord' have also been treated as UNSEEN ADVENTURES because we do not see the actual adventure – only a projection that might not even be the true record of the actual events.

UNSEEN ADVENTURES

PRE-1963

At the start of the series very little is revealed about the Doctor and Susan's origins, other than that they are 'wanderers in the fourth dimension … exiles … cut off from our own planet' (see LIFE ON GALLIFREY for an exploration of the Doctor's life prior to '100,000 BC'), but before arriving in 1963 we know they had been to various planets and time periods, including:

- some of the other off-screen adventures listed in the chapter NAME-DROPPING.
- many moments in Earth's past, hence Barbara's interest in Susan's advanced knowledge of Earth history ('100,000 BC')
- the French Revolution ('100,000 BC')
- England when decimal currency was in use ('100,000 BC')
- seeing Red Indians and the first steam train ('100,000 BC')
- a time when the TARDIS took on the form of a sedan chair ('100,000 BC')
- Greece or a Grecian colony, where the TARDIS appeared as an Ionic column ('100,000 BC')
- a place where Susan encountered snow ('Inside The Spaceship')
- the planet Venus, where Susan saw metal seas ('Marco Polo')
- Susan knows that the Himalayas are called the Roof of the World ('Marco Polo')
- an encounter with telepathic plants on the planet Esto ('The Sensorites'). Susan mentions having before heard the sound made by the whispering plants on Marinus ('The Keys Of Marinus'); it is possible that this was on Esto.
- a meeting with King Henry VIII long before the Doctor and Susan met Ian and Barbara; the TARDIS was in the Tower of London ('The Sensorites')
- seeing Zeppelins during an air-raid ('Planet Of Giants')

- visiting an old goat farm (although this could have been while Susan was living on Earth in 1963) ('The Dalek Invasion Of Earth')
- their adventure on the planet Quinnis in the Fourth Universe, which was 'four or five journeys back' ('Inside The Spaceship'). When taking into account that three of those journeys were to 1963, '100,000 BC' ('100,000 BC') and then Skaro ('The Daleks'), this makes the Quinnis adventure the first of the two immediately prior to the 1963 London landing ...
- the adventure in which the Doctor obtains the Hand Of Omega. As covered under MORE THAN TIME LORD? and 'Remembrance Of The Daleks', it is likely that the Doctor came into possession of the Hand Of Omega in the adventure immediately prior to '100,000 BC' (but not likely to be the one on Quinnis).

100,000 BC

STORY LINK

The Doctor has a notebook that contains 'notes of everywhere we've been to' (including all the unseen stories above, and no doubt many of the adventures listed in NAME-DROPPING). The Doctor shows concern that Ian and Barbara have found him and Susan: 'I knew something like this would happen if we stayed in one place too long'. Perhaps the Doctor was worried that the Time Lords would locate them if they did remain in one space / time location for any length of time.

The reason for the Doctor and Susan's long-term stay in London of 'five months' could be a combination of factors: the TARDIS needed repairs (the Doctor says he has 'managed to find a replacement for that faulty filament. Bit of an amateur job but I think it'll serve.'). It may have taken him many months to find suitable replacement parts that were compatible with the TARDIS systems. Also, the Doctor may have taken time to find a suitable place in which to hide the Hand Of Omega (see 'Remembrance Of The Daleks').

There is no reason to presume that the TARDIS actually landed in the Totter's Lane junkyard. Given its outward appearance of a police box it probably originally materialised on a street corner (where police boxes were usually located, as stated by Ian) and it was moved (by truck?) to the yard at a later date. If it landed in the junkyard it would have presumably taken on the appearance of an object more suited to the location, such as a wardrobe (as it did in 'Attack Of The Cybermen'). By this notion the TARDIS could have landed anywhere in the greater London area. The Doctor does say 'I knew something like this would happen if we stayed in one place too long' (but he could just as easily be referring to 1963 as opposed to just the Shoreditch area (see 'Remembrance of the Daleks')). In 'Marco Polo' Susan uses phrases such as 'fab' which she says is 'a word we often use on Earth', which demonstrates that in the time she has been in London she has picked up local slang.

The Doctor is not I M Foreman (when Ian calls him 'Dr Foreman' he replies 'Eh, Doctor who? What's he talking about?'), but Susan has adopted the surname to use in her school records. We can take it that the Doctor had permission from I M Foreman to stay at the junkyard, probably as a caretaker. It certainly isn't an abandoned property, as I M Foreman is still apparently the proprietor of the yard 22 years later in 1985, as seen in 'Attack Of The Cybermen'. The fact that the Doctor appears familiar with some of the objects in the junkyard shows clearly that he has some limited involvement in actually running the business. He may even have taken up the job to provide income with their living expenses while on Earth – he needed to pay for the new filament. She has her own transistor radio, and must have pocket money as she is seen eating something (sweets?) on her way home to the junkyard.

LANGUAGE

Susan can read and speak English (Barbara says 'You sound like us'). The real Neanderthal did not have a complex language structure, so either the Doctor's Time Lord 'gift' is working to the point of overload, or in this Universe the Neanderthal really did speak English. An oddity is that they speak 'English' before the Doctor arrives at their cave. Another oddity is that even though Kal is from a different tribe, he speaks the same language as Za's tribe. In reality the cavemen would speak in grunts and hand gestures yet here they have a complex sentence structure. The tribe also has a wide vocabulary of nouns (they sometimes speak in a very poetic sort of way: 'You should lie on the old stone 'til your blood runs into the earth'), and yet on hearing the word 'friend' they think it is Ian's name. In the TARDIS the Radiation meter is marked by a large sign saying 'RADIATION', and it has a segment marked 'DANGER'.

TIMELINE DATES

1963. October 15 ·

Susan says 'We've left 1963'. The year is also specified in later stories.

No month is specified, but 'Remembrance Of The Daleks', which is a follow-on from '100,000 BC', is set in November 1963. In 'Remembrance Of The Daleks' Reverend Parkinson tells the Doctor 'the grave's been ready for a month', to which the Doctor adds 'I had to leave suddenly', being a direct reference to the events in '100,000 BC'. This suggests an October setting for '100,000 BC'. It is dark when Susan leaves school ('Good night, Susan'), indicating that it is near-winter as the days get shorter at that time of year.

A notation on Ian's blackboard can determine the day of the week: 'Homework Tuesday'. 'Remembrance Of The Daleks' has been set over 15 – 17? November, so '100,000 BC' can be set on Tuesday 15 October 1963.

'100,000 BC' (late autumn) ⁕ ▨ ▨ ▨ ▨ ▨ ▨ ▨ ▨ ▨

The Doctor studies the console and says, 'Zero? That's not right. I'm afraid this Year-o-meter is not calculating properly'. There is nothing on-screen that indicates that this adventure actually takes place on Earth, however in 'The Sensorites', Ian refers to their trip 'back to prehistoric times', so it appears that as far as he is concerned it was Earth. On this basis given the title of the story, '100,000 BC' is the most likely date. From an historical point of view it is quite accurate (see below).

The Tribe are preparing for the arrival of winter (they speak of how Kal's tribe 'died in the last cold'), so it must be late autumn.

It is not clear where the tribe lives in terms of location. One would expect it to be Africa, as this is the historically recorded location of the Neanderthal. Near the caves there are mountains, a forest with a stream, a desert, and a plentiful supply of food; meat, fruit and roots.

HISTORICAL COMPARISON

The tribe appears to be Neanderthal, who existed from around 110,000 BC to 35,000 BC in our history (in the N-Space Universe they were wiped out when homo sapiens arrived on the scene, thanks to the intervention of the Dæmons, see 'The Dæmons'). The Neanderthal used fire, lived in caves, used basic tools, and was known to bury their dead. There are a few oddities in this story. Language is one (see Observations). And although they worship the sun ('Orb'), they have a curious understanding of what blood is.

600 BC ⁕ ▨ ▨ ▨ ▨ ▨ ▨ ▨ ▨ ▨ ▨ ▨ ▨ ▨ ▨

Susan says the TARDIS has been 'an Ionic column'. This form of Grecian architecture originated around 600 BC.

1581 / 1650 – 1750 ⁕ ▨ ▨ ▨ ▨ ▨ ▨ ▨ ▨ ▨ ▨ ▨ ▨ ▨

Susan says the TARDIS has been 'a sedan chair'. This mode of transport was first used in England in 1581, becoming more common from 1650 to 1750.

1865 ✴ ▨ ▨ ▨ ▨ ▨ ▨ ▨ ▨ ▨ ▨ ▨ ▨ ▨ ▨

The first railroads were built across the United States in the years after the Civil War, and by 1865 the network stretched from the West to East Coasts, driving the Indians from their territories.

1963, May ✴ ▨ ▨ ▨ ▨ ▨ ▨ ▨ ▨ ▨ ▨ ▨ ▨ ▨ ▨

Susan says 'the last five months have been the happiest of my life', which would give their arrival in this area in May. Of course, as covered above, the TARDIS might have arrived elsewhere in England much earlier.

1963, September ✴ ▨ ▨ ▨ ▨ ▨ ▨ ▨ ▨ ▨ ▨ ▨ ▨ ▨

With the new school term commencing in England in September and the school sequence set in October, Susan has most likely only been at the school for a month. This much is apparent given Ian and Barbara's comments about Susan behaviour. We can assume that after spending several months hanging around the TARDIS while the Doctor repaired the ship, Susan probably got bored and made contact with some of the neighbourhood children during the school summer break, and then once they all went back to school, she convinced the Doctor to let her to go the school.

1963, October 8 ✴ ▨ ▨ ▨ ▨ ▨ ▨ ▨ ▨ ▨ ▨ ▨ ▨ ▨

Ian tells Barbara of two instances that happened 'the other day' in which Susan questioned his teaching assignments. In both 'flashbacks' the blackboard reads the notation of 'Homework Tuesday'. Susan is wearing the same clothes in both flashbacks so we can take these to both be on the same day, being the previous Tuesday, 8 October.

Post-1971, February 15 ✴ ▨ ▨ ▨ ▨ ▨ ▨ ▨ ▨ ▨ ▨ ▨ ▨

Susan confuses time periods when she mistakenly thinks that England has a decimal coinage system ('Of course, the decimal system hasn't started yet'), indicating that she has been to England after the decimal system was introduced, which was on 15 February 1971.

DURATION

⇨ **Day One (1963) (Ep1)** ▨ ▨ ▨ ▨ ▨ ▨ ▨ ▨ ▨ ▨ ▨

The policeman investigates the junkyard at 3.00 am (a clock chimes three times). It is early evening after school when the TARDIS leaves London.

⇨ **Day One ('100,000 BC') (Ep 2-4)** ▨ ▨ ▨ ▨ ▨ ▨ ▨ ▨ ▨

The travellers arrive during the day. They are locked in the Cave of Skulls but escape after night has fallen. It is still dark when they are recaptured outside the TARDIS.

⇨ **Day Two ('100,000 BC') (Ep 4)** ▨ ▨ ▨ ▨ ▨ ▨ ▨ ▨ ▨

The travellers spend the whole of the next day locked in the Cave of Skulls. They make their escape again after night has fallen.

THE DALEKS

+STORY LINK

'The Daleks' follows directly on from the end of '100,000 BC', with the TARDIS landing on the radioactive planet Skaro.

DALEK LINK

As covered under DALEK HISTORY, 'The Daleks' is their second appearance on TV. Centuries after the events of 'Genesis Of The Daleks', the Daleks are aware that the Thals have survived in the wastelands. In 'Genesis Of The Daleks' the Doctor says 'the Daleks are programmed to wipe the Thals from the face of the planet'. Given the events in 'The Daleks', it appears that the Daleks did eventually attempt to fulfil this order when they triggered the neutron war. 'The Daleks' takes place 500 years after that second war.

OBSERVATIONS

- The Doctor does not know of the Daleks, and yet in 'The Five Doctors' he says 'you know our legends well enough. Even in our most corrupt period our ancestors never allowed the Cybermen to play the game. Like the Daleks, they played too well', which suggests that he has always known of them. (In 'The Daleks' Master Plan' the Monk knew of them 'by reputation' only – possibly from the same legends that the Doctor knows). It is unlikely that the Doctor is lying about not knowing them in 'The Daleks'. We can assume that the 'legends' the Doctor speaks of in 'The Five Doctors' didn't actually name the creatures as being Daleks, so in 'The Daleks' the Doctor simply didn't make the connection. It isn't until much later in his travels that the Doctor makes the connection between the 'robot' creatures in the Time Lord legends and the Daleks.

The dials on the TARDIS food machine are English (J62L6 is 'English bacon and eggs'). 'K7' on the fault locater is the fluid link. The Geiger counter in the Dalek city is marked 'DANGER'. The letter Susan writes to the Thals is in English. The Daleks have the cell bugged and listen in to the travellers' conversation. The Time Lord 'gift' cannot possibly work via this means, so the Daleks must speak English. Even their countdown is in English.

TIMELINE DATES

900 ＊

In 'The Dalek Invasion Of Earth' the Doctor says their adventure on Skaro happened 'a million years ahead of us in the future. What we are seeing now is about the middle history of the Daleks'. 'The Dalek Invasion Of Earth' is set in 2174, which would mean that 'The Daleks' was set millions of years beyond that date. In 'The Daleks' Ganatus knows of the Earth custom 'Ladies first', which suggests that other humans have visited Skaro, which would place 'The Daleks' in the future also, but I prefer to explain this slip by his having heard Ian use it off-screen at some point. In 'Planet Of The Daleks', set in 2540, the Thals talk about the Doctor and his companions Susan, Ian and Barbara being on Skaro at the time of 'the Dalek war' which was 'generations ago'. This places the events of 'The Daleks' (and indeed 'Genesis Of The Daleks') long before 2540.

It is impossible to factor all these dates in. I prefer to say that the Doctor simply does not know what time zone they are in (just as he does not know what zone they are in, in '100,000 BC'), and that he is only guessing the nature of Daleks' history in 'The Dalek Invasion Of Earth'; after all that is only the second time he has encountered the Daleks and does not know their full history yet.

The background to the Dalek and the Thal history is different to that seen in 'Genesis Of The Daleks'. There are many anomalies, such as the name Dal in 'The Daleks' and Kaled in 'Genesis Of The Daleks' actually referring to the same race. There was a neutron war in 'The Daleks' and the atomic war in 'Genesis Of The Daleks'. In 'The Daleks' the Daleks created their casings to protect themselves from radiation fall-out, whereas in 'Genesis Of The Daleks' Davros created them.

In order to fit both 'origin' stories into the one single history it is necessary to 'ignore' certain facts and to reinterpret others. To place 'The Daleks', I have worked backwards from other Dalek stories. In 'The Power Of The Daleks', set in 2120, the Dalek capsule has been buried in the mercury swamp for 200 years. That places its crash at around 1920. Those Daleks are still reliant on static electricity on Vulcan, placing the time of the crash at a point early in their history when they were still reliant on that mode of power (as they are in 'The Daleks', 'The Power Of The Daleks', and 'The Evil Of The Daleks'). The Daleks probably had space travel for several years by then, so let's use 1900 as a focal date for when they had developed space travel. The capsule contains an incubator, and so I believe it is a Dalek colony ship. The capsule is dimensionally transcendental, which seems to imply that it is time-capable, but this is never referred to, so I do not think it is a time-ship. This technology would take quite some time for the Daleks to develop, so let's say 1000 years have passed since 'The Daleks'. Therefore, 'The Daleks' would be set about 1000 years before 1900, so I have selected the year 900.

500,000 BC
The Doctor says the Thals' history goes 'back nearly half a million years', but he could be only guessing.

400
With 'The Daleks' set in 900, the war (which lasted 'one day') was '500 years ago'.

898
Susan is told about the five-year rain, which failed to fall 'two years' ago. Ganatus says it was 'over a year since we left our own plateau'.

DURATION

⇨ **Day One (Ep1)**
It is day when the ship lands (the clock in the TARDIS reads 5.15 for the ship's internal time). It is 'getting dark' when the travellers see the Dalek city for the first time.

⇨ **Day Two (Ep1-3)**
They spend the night in the TARDIS and venture out to explore the city 'at first light'. Susan is sent back to the TARDIS to get the drugs at night.

⇨ **Day Three (Ep3)**
By morning Susan has returned. The trap is set for the Thals. Food will be left for them to collect 'tomorrow'.

⇨ **Day Four (Ep3-5)**
(Although there is no apparent night scene following Susan's return and the ambush, another day has to pass for the simple fact that the Thals were to collect the food from

the Daleks the following day). The travellers escape and the Thals are ambushed the following morning. The travellers spend the night at the Thal camp.

⇨ **Day Five (Ep5)** ▨ ▨ ▨ ▨ ▨ ▨ ▨ ▨ ▨ ▨ ▨
The TARDIS crew spend the whole of the fifth day at the Thal camp planning their next move.

⇨ **Day Six (Ep5)** ▨ ▨ ▨ ▨ ▨ ▨ ▨ ▨ ▨ ▨ ▨
On the morning of the sixth day the plan to attack the Daleks is discussed, and that afternoon Ian and Barbara leave with the expedition. They camp by the Lake of Mutations that night.

⇨ **Day Seven (Ep5-7)** ▨ ▨ ▨ ▨ ▨ ▨ ▨ ▨ ▨ ▨
Elyon is killed the following morning. The expedition reaches the cliffs that night and the ordeal through the caves begins.

⇨ **Day Eight (Ep7)** ▨ ▨ ▨ ▨ ▨ ▨ ▨ ▨ ▨ ▨
The expedition enters the Dalek city that morning and the Daleks are destroyed.

INSIDE THE SPACESHIP

+STORY LINK

This story takes place immediately after 'The Daleks' – the console appears to explode soon after leaving Skaro. The crew all wear the same clothes from 'The Daleks' at the beginning; Ian's cardigan is ripped and Barbara still has her Thal leggings and has the cloth given to her by Ganatus around her neck.

Susan says the TARDIS was nearly lost on the planet Quinnis 'four or five journeys back'. The previous three journeys made by the TARDIS were to Skaro, '100,000 BC' and 1963, which means that the adventure 'in the Fourth Universe' was shortly before the TARDIS landed in 1963.

OBSERVATIONS

- It takes the full duration of this story for the TARDIS to travel back billions of years in time. In 'Castrovalva', the TARDIS makes a similar but longer journey back that takes a long time, however in 'City Of Death' the trip to 140,000,000 BC appears to be instantaneous. In 'Image Of The Fendahl' it takes about 20 hours for a round trip back 12 million years. In 'Frontios' the TARDIS drifts over 10 million years into the future.

- The Doctor points out that the heart of the TARDIS is under the column in the console, and if it were to be removed, the entire energy of the ship would be released. He also states that it would take 'the force of a total solar system to attract the power away from my ship'. When the console opens in 'Boom Town', Blon Fel Fotch Passamer-Day Slitheen looks into 'the heart of the TARDIS' / 'its soul' and is reverted back to an egg, while in 'Bad Wolf', Rose looks inside and absorbs the energy of the Time Vortex within. However in 'Doctor Who (The TV Movie)', it is said the Eye of Harmony is 'the heart of the structure' (which I understand to mean the ship's main power source; its 'engine'), and given what happens when the Eye is left open for over three hours in that story, it is clear that the Doctor has a good reason to be concerned about potential energy losses from the time ship.

LANGUAGE

The TARDIS food machine uses Earth alpha numerics and has a flashing light marked 'EMPTY'. The fault locater readout is in Earth alpha numeric (it scrolls from A12 to A17 at one point). The Fast Return switch is labelled by what appears to be felt tip pen. The Doctor and Susan both measure time in 'seconds' and 'minutes'.

TIMELINE DATES

5,000,000,000 BC ◆

The Doctor discovers that they have travelled far back in time and they are now 'at the very beginning. The start of a new solar system ... a new birth of a sun and its planets'. The warnings seen on the TARDIS scanner show their journey from Skaro, which the Doctor (incorrectly) states was 'in the future', to 'reach planet Earth'. Therefore the TARDIS has travelled back in time within Skaro's solar system, or Earth's. I assume it is the latter.

Modern science has estimated the age of our own solar system to be about five billion years old. It is logical therefore to apply the same time scale to Skaro's system. The actual location of the TARDIS notwithstanding, they are still billions of years in the past.

1890 ◆

Gilbert and Sullivan worked together from 1870 until 1900 when Sullivan died. The Doctor probably visited them at the height of their partnership, around 1890.

???? * ▪ ▪ ▪ ▪ ▪ ▪ ▪ ▪ ▪ ▪ ▪ ▪ ▪
Susan mentions their visit to the planet Quinnis in the Fourth Universe.

DURATION

(TARDIS) Day One (Ep1-2) ▪ ▪ ▪ ▪ ▪ ▪ ▪

The story lasts for no less than 50 minutes. There are two points of indeterminable duration – one at the beginning after the explosion when the crew are knocked out, and the other when the Doctor drugs the others. At one point, Ian's watch shows 9.10, but since the hands and face have melted, this is not clear enough to place a precise time. The hands of the ormolu clock in the ship are also unreadable.

MARCO POLO

+STORY LINK

'Marco Polo' continues directly on from the closing moments of 'Inside The Spaceship', with the TARDIS landing in Tibet. The Doctor says 'I directed the ship towards Earth and it looks as though I've been successful'. There is no possibility for another story to take place between 'Inside The Spaceship' and 'Marco Polo'; in 'The Sensorites' the travellers recount all of their adventures and although they miss out 'Inside The Spaceship', no other untelevised stories are mentioned.

LANGUAGE

Presumably everyone is speaking the local languages of China and the Mongol hordes. Marco Polo himself would have spoken Italian as well as a Chinese dialect. Kublai Khan speaks with a non-Asian accent. Oddly, Ian has to translate the meaning of 'Hashashin' to Susan. The term 'Shah-Mat' (The King Is Dead / checkmate) is not translated for Ian.

TIMELINE DATES

1289, April – September 1 * ▪ ▪ ▪ ▪ ▪ ▪ ▪ ▪

Polo says the year is 'Twelve Hundred and Eighty Nine'. When they arrive in Cheng Ting, Wang-Lo says the city 'is so delightful at this time of the year'. We can assume that it is spring or summer at that point in the long journey. The Khan is at his summer palace, so it is clearly summer at the end of the adventure.

HISTORICAL COMPARISON

Marco Polo was born in Venice in 1254. He joined his father on his second trip to China in 1271, where he would spend the next 20 or so years serving as an emissary for the Khan. It took the Polos about 120 days to travel from Pamir to Peking. Polo returned to Venice in 1295. The fact that his father and uncle do not appear in the serial (they are only mentioned in passing) is historically inaccurate. The journey with Tegana to Peking is fictitious, but elements of the narrative have been taken from several of Polo's actual journeys. It is historically recorded that the Khan always left Shang-Tu on 28th August every year and it took five days to reach Peking. This places the final day of the adventure to be 1 September. Taking into account the time it took the real Polos to travel from Pamir to Peking, the Duration of the serial (see below) is some 120 days, which places the month that the TARDIS first landed as being late April or early May.

327 BC

Polo mentions Alexander the Great, who lived 356 BC to 13 June 323 BC, and ruled Mesopotamia from 336 BC to 323 BC. The Doctor appears to have met him. Alexander was in India in 327, accompanied by Pyrrho, whom the Doctor has also met (see 'The Keys Of Marinus') so it is most likely the Doctor met both men during the same expedition (see also 'Robot').

218 BC

Polo mentions Hannibal, who lived c247 BC to 183 BC. Hannibal began his historical march across the Alps in 218 BC. The Doctor probably met him once – see 'Robot', also 'The Dalek Invasion Of Earth'. (Hannibal's act of melting rocks with vinegar is mentioned in 'Aliens Of London'.)

1264

Polo and Ian discuss the Crusades. To Ian, the Crusaders 'lived 700 years ago', which would be 1263. Polo says they 'were in the Holy Land 25 years ago', being 1264. This is slightly inaccurate: the Seventh Crusade ended in 1254, and the Eighth didn't start until 1270 (see 'The Time Warrior').

1266
1269

The Hashashins were killed '20 years' ago, after 'three long years in siege'.

1253
1271
1275
1277
1287 ▦ ▦ ▦ ▦ ▦ ▦ ▦ ▦ ▦ ▦ ▦ ▦ ▦ ▦

Polo says 'I left [Venice] in 1271. The journey to Peking took us three and a half years. When I arrived at the Khan's court I was 21' (1275, making his year of birth 1253). 'On my 25th birthday I was given an appointment in the Khan's service,' which Barbara establishes was in '1277' (but the maths shows this could also be 1278). It was 'two years ago' that Marco asked the Khan to return to Venice (1287).

???? * ▦ ▦ ▦ ▦ ▦ ▦ ▦ ▦ ▦ ▦ ▦ ▦ ▦

Susan tells Ping Cho about 'the metal seas of Venus'. Presumably this is where the Doctor picked up his ability to use Venusian Aikido, where he learnt Venusian lullabies ('The Dæmons', 'The Curse Of Peladon', 'The Monster Of Peladon'), and played Venusian hopscotch ('Death To The Daleks'). He knows how to convert Venusian miles ('The Time Monster'). The Doctor has Venusian spearmint toothpaste in 'The Shakespeare Code'. Venusians have large feet and at least three eyes

DURATION

This is the longest story in terms of 'real time' for the TARDIS crew. In historical fact the journey to Cathay would have been around 120 days, but only 18 days are actually depicted on-screen, with many others alluded to through Marco Polo's narration; 102 days therefore pass off-screen.

In the following Duration list the days indicated by a '⇨' are those actually seen on-screen; those marked by '🕒' are only alluded to in Polo's narration:

-(Ep1) ▦ ▦ ▦ ▦ ▦ ▦ ▦ ▦ ▦ ▦ ▦ ▦ ▦ ▦

⇨ The TARDIS arrives late afternoon. Ping Cho and Susan talk about Ping Cho's husband that night.
⇨ In the morning the caravan sets off again on its journey.
🕒 It takes several days to get to Lop.
⇨ On the first night at Lop, Polo tells the story of his life. Tegana meets with a Mongol soldier.

-(Ep2) ▦ ▦ ▦ ▦ ▦ ▦ ▦ ▦ ▦ ▦ ▦ ▦ ▦ ▦

🕒 It takes three days to cover only 30 miles across the Gobi desert.

⇨ On the night of the third day Susan and Ping Cho are lost in the desert.
⇨ Ping Cho and Susan are found. The caravan moves on 'at dawn'. They cover 15 miles before they make camp. Tegana sabotages the water bags that night.
⇨ The broken water gourds are discovered the next morning. Tegana rides ahead to the oasis. The caravan manages 20 miles.
⊕ The caravan manages 15 miles on the second day.
⊕ The caravan covers 10 miles on the third day.
⊕ The caravan covers 8 miles on the fourth day.
⇨ Only 2 miles are covered before the caravan stops. Tegana arrives at the oasis …

-(Ep3) ▦ ▦ ▦ ▦ ▦ ▦ ▦ ▦ ▦ ▦ ▦ ▦ ▦ ▦
… The caravan heads for the oasis during the night.
⇨ By morning the travellers have found that condensation had formed in the TARDIS. They arrive at the oasis.
⊕ They leave the oasis 'the following day' and head for Tun-Huang.
⇨ After an unknown period of time, the caravan arrives in Tun-Huang. Ping Cho tells the tale of Ala-Eddin that night. Barbara is trapped in the Cave of 500 Eyes.

-(Ep4) ▦ ▦ ▦ ▦ ▦ ▦ ▦ ▦ ▦ ▦ ▦ ▦ ▦ ▦
⊕ The caravan progresses for a further undefined period.
⊕ They follow the Yellow River for three days.
⇨ On the third night they stop at Sinju. The Doctor completes the repairs to the TARDIS.
⊕ Two days later they cross the bamboo forest.
⇨ On the second night through the bamboo forest (there is a full moon) they are attacked by bandits.

-(Ep5) ▦ ▦ ▦ ▦ ▦ ▦ ▦ ▦ ▦ ▦ ▦ ▦ ▦ ▦
⇨ 'At sunrise' they bury the dead and move on. But by 'midday' they stop again. Ling-Tau arrives and the travellers continue by horse-back to Shang-Tu.
⊕ For five days they ride.
⇨ 'On the sixth day' of their journey they arrive in Cheng-Ting. The TARDIS crew try to escape that night but are stopped by Tegana.

-(Ep6) ▦ ▦ ▦ ▦ ▦ ▦ ▦ ▦ ▦ ▦ ▦ ▦ ▦ ▦
⇨ They leave Cheng-Ting 'at dawn', and 'by dusk' have covered 40 miles. They stop at an inn. Ping Cho slips away that night and returns to Cheng-Ting.
⇨ Ping Cho is discovered missing the following morning. Ian heads back to find

her. The others continue on to Shang-Tu.

🕐 They continue for three days.

⇨ On the 'fourth night' the riders stop at an inn 50 miles from the palace. Polo sends Tegana back to Cheng-Ting.

⇨ The travellers arrive in Shang-Tu the next day and meet the Khan.

-(Ep7) ▨ ▨ ▨ ▨ ▨ ▨ ▨ ▨ ▨ ▨ ▨ ▨

🕐 It takes five days for the Khan's entourage to reach Peking.

⇨ The travellers arrive in Peking with the Khan. The adventure ends later that day.

THE KEYS OF MARINUS

+STORY LINK

Ian is still wearing his oriental court robe from 'Marco Polo', while the others, bar the Doctor, have changed into other garments. In 'The Sensorites' the crew discuss the adventures they have had since they met in 1963 ('100,000 BC'), and they only mention the adventures seen on-screen, so it is likely that 'Marco Polo' and 'The Keys Of Marinus' are consecutive. The Doctor has the new walking cane given to him at the Khan's court. (This walking cane apparently makes its final appearance in 'The Massacre Of St Bartholomew's Eve'.)

OBSERVATIONS

• Apart from their oddly-shaped heads, there is nothing to suggest that the Voords are alien beings. Mention is made of there being different 'races of men' on Marinus, it shouldn't be inferred that this description applies to other species as well. With the exception of the brains of Morphoton and the frozen soldiers in the mountain cave, the origins of which are never revealed, the main populace of the planet are humans. Therefore, the Voords are probably humans too. The fact that they are wearing protective rubber suits supports this. I would therefore suggest that the Voords' heads are in fact helmets that incorporate Yartek's 'immuniser' device. The helmets each have different shaped antennae – or in Yartek's case none at all. The immuniser is probably elsewhere on the planet, and transmits its operating signal to the helmets via the aerials.

LANGUAGE

Ian is able to read Darrius' journal. The chemical formulas use Earth notations: 'NH4NO3', 'DE3O2'.

TIMELINE DATES

????, (Winter) ◦

Sabetha has not heard of Iceland (which Ian says is 'far away'), so we can take it that Marinus is not an Earth colony in the far future. There are no dates with which to establish a position in the TIMELINE, so 'The Keys Of Marinus' has been placed under ????.

Vasor says of the wolf packs: 'There are more than ever of them this winter'. Given that the map that Arbitan shows the travellers where the keys are hidden places all four locations on the same continent, the season applies to all the locations visited.

???? – 2000
???? – 700
???? – 20
???? – 5

Arbitan tells the Doctor that technology on Marinus 'reached its peak over two thousand years ago … All our knowledge culminated in the manufacture of this. At the time it was called the Conscience of Marinus … And then we added to it, improved on it, made it more and more sophisticated … Marinus was unique in the Universe … For seven centuries we prospered. And then a man named Yartek found a means of overcoming the power of the machine'.

It is noted that Arbitan himself made the keys. The natives of Marinus cannot possibly have life spans of over a thousand years, so we must assume that the keys themselves were one of the more recent 'improved' modifications made to the workings of the machine, presumably as a result of Yartek's initial threats. If we call the present year '0' we can ascertain that over 2000 ago (0-2000) their technology reached a point where a machine like the Conscience was possible. Over the next 1300 years the device was built, and then added to and 'improved', finally reaching its highest level of power in which the peoples of Marinus 'prospered'. For the next 700 years (0-700) the peoples of Marinus lived in peace. Then in more recent years, Yartek arrived on the scene …

Arbitan says it was 'many years' since the Voords' last assault on the island. It was as a result of this attack that the keys were hidden. Tarron says Arbitan invented the keys, and Sabetha says the keys were her father's 'life's work'. According to Kala the key in Millennius was brought by Arbitan 'years ago', say 20 years (0-20). It has only been recently that, 'through the years', Arbitan has sent his friends to recover the keys, now that the Voords 'have returned'; say five years (0-5).

327 BC ◦ ▓ ▓ ▓ ▓ ▓ ▓ ▓ ▓ ▓ ▓ ▓

In our history, Pyrrho lived around 360 BC to 272 BC. He travelled to India with Alexander the Great in 327, so it is likely the Doctor met both men at the same time.

DURATION

⇨ **Day One (Ep1-2)** ▓ ▓ ▓ ▓ ▓ ▓ ▓ ▓ ▓ ▓ ▓

It is day when the TARDIS lands on the island. The travellers arrive at Morphoton when 'it is late'. The somnor disks are placed while they sleep.

⇨ **Day Two (Ep2)** ▓ ▓ ▓ ▓ ▓ ▓ ▓ ▓ ▓ ▓ ▓

The travellers wake in the morning. 'Four hours' later the Doctor, Ian and Susan are subjected to the full force of Mesmeron. Barbara spends most of the day in hiding. At night the brains make plans for the humans 'as soon as it is light'.

⇨ **Day Three (Ep2-3)** ▓ ▓ ▓ ▓ ▓ ▓ ▓ ▓ ▓ ▓ ▓

The city of Morphoton is burned that morning. The travellers decide to split up. Barbara and Ian are in Darrius' hut when 'darkness' falls and the jungle moves in. They collapse in the snow mountains that night …

⇨ **Day Four (Ep4-5)** ▓ ▓ ▓ ▓ ▓ ▓ ▓ ▓ ▓ ▓ ▓

Ian and Barbara wake in Vasor's hut early the next day. They learn that the others had been there 'early last night'. It is 'getting dark' when Ian goes to search for Altos. It is later that same night when the travellers arrive in Millennius.

⇨ **Day Five (Ep5)** ▓ ▓ ▓ ▓ ▓ ▓ ▓ ▓ ▓ ▓ ▓

Ian awakens the following morning and is arrested for murder.

🕓 **Day Six – Seven (Ep5)** ▓ ▓ ▓ ▓ ▓ ▓ ▓ ▓ ▓ ▓

Two days pass off-screen …

⇨ **Day Eight (Ep5)** ▓ ▓ ▓ ▓ ▓ ▓ ▓ ▓ ▓ ▓ ▓

'Two days' later the Doctor shows up to help Ian. Ian is to be executed in 'three days'. The Doctor is given 'two days' to prove his innocence …

⇨ **Day Nine (Ep5)** ▨ ▨ ▨ ▨ ▨ ▨ ▨ ▨ ▨ ▨ ▨ ▨

Ian's trial continues, and the guilty parties are revealed. The travellers return to the island later that day.

THE AZTECS

+STORY LINK

The serial starts with a view of the TARDIS leaving Marinus, but there is a fade-to-black pause before the ship arrives in Yetaxa's tomb. There are no direct references to Marinus in 'The Aztecs', but in 'The Sensorites' the crew discuss their adventures since meeting in 1963, and they mention only the other previous television stories.

LANGUAGE

The only language spoken would be the language of the Aztecs.

TIMELINE DATES

1450 ▸ ▨ ▨ ▨ ▨ ▨ ▨ ▨ ▨ ▨ ▨ ▨ ▨ ▨

Barbara estimates that Yetaxa 'must have died around 1430 ... All these things belonged to the Aztecs' early period'. Susan recalls that 'Cortez landed in 1520', which gives an available spread of 90 years. (On a purely historical note, since the story features a full solar eclipse, the only recorded eclipses around that period were on 7 June 1415 and 16 March 1485, but both were visible only from the European continent.)

From the story narrative, Ixta's father, Chapal, built Yetaxa's temple. This suggests that the temple was completed before Yetaxa's death in 1430 (temples of that size would have taken decades to build, so it may have been built originally for a purpose other than solely as a burial chamber for Yetaxa, unless the priest knew he was dying very early on). Chapal would have been about 40 at the time, certainly younger than 52, as building a temple would be the honour of a man of advanced years in Aztec culture, and he was not yet due to retire to the Garden of Peace.

Chapal was subsequently sent to the Garden of Peace as was the custom for those 'who attain their fifty-second year', which would have been around 1442, some twelve years later. Chapal subsequently disappeared from the Garden 'a long time ago', according to Cameca.

Chapal's son Ixta, who knows that his father's secrets died with him, and who cannot be more than 25 himself, would presumably have been born before Chapal was sent to the Garden. Yetaxa's death would therefore have happened during Ixta's own lifetime. I would therefore place 'The Aztecs' twenty years after Yetaxa's death, in 1450.

1430

After studying the artefacts in the tomb Barbara estimates the time of Yetaxa's death to be 'around 1430, I should think … Aztec early period'.

1442

Chapal was sent to the Garden of Peace when he reached the age of 52 (see above).

1520 •

Susan knows about Aztec history, 'Cortez landed in 1520, didn't he?', to which Barbara concurs. This is not historically accurate; in our history Cortez landed in 1519. Presumably the Doctor and Susan were there; Susan certainly knows about the Aztecs' art of human sacrifice.

DURATION

⇨ **Day One (Ep1-2)**

The TARDIS arrives in daytime. The first sacrifice takes place 'when the sun's fire first touches the horizon to the west' (sunset).

⇨ **Day Two (Ep.2-3)**

The Doctor learns the secret of the temple from Cameca. The next sacrifice is 'three days from today' when there is to be a solar eclipse. Ian fights Ixta 'tonight, at sunset'. Ian is unconscious through the night.

⇨ **Day Three (Ep3-4)**

Ian wakes that morning, and that night he enters the secret tunnel.

⇨ **Day Four (Ep4)**

It is dawn when the travellers are reunited and try to enter the tomb. Autloc is attacked 'as the sun rises'. He leaves for the wilderness later that day.

⇨ **Day Five (Ep4)**

It is the day of the solar eclipse. The travellers escape in the TARDIS as the eclipse begins at 'noon'.

THE SENSORITES

+STORY LINK

There is a fade-to-black between the TARDIS's dematerialisation from the Aztec temple to the arrival on the spaceship, during which the crew have changed clothes. It is possible for an adventure to occur between 'The Aztecs' and 'The Sensorites', but shortly after landing on the Earth space vessel, the crew discuss their adventures to date: 'prehistoric times, the Daleks ... Marco Polo, Marinus ... and the Aztecs'. Although they do not mention the events of 'Inside The Spaceship', it is probable that the adventures from '100,000 BC' through to 'The Sensorites' are all consecutive.

OBSERVATIONS

- The Doctor is given a cloak by the First Elder after his jacket is ripped. This cloak will continue to appear on and off into the second Doctor's era. The Doctor must have quite a supply of black Edwardian jackets ('Of course I have others on my ship'), because he also leaves one behind in Paris in 'The Reign Of Terror' and another on Aridius in 'The Chase'.

LANGUAGE

The Sensorites understood the first human explorers when their minds opened, so they must understand English. The First Elder is able to read Carol's note. The Sensorite Scientist writes the word 'Negative' on the list of Districts. The test tubes are labelled in common numerals. The Sensorites use 'yards' and 'hours'. The Sensorites use a familiar English alphabet: 'XA2 ... XB3 ... XC4'. They also have written punctuation such as full stops.

TIMELINE DATES

2764 ◆ ■ ■ ■ ■ ■ ■ ■ ■ ■ ■ ■ ■ ■ ■

Maitland says 'we come from the twenty-eighth century'. This is not the same as saying that it is currently the twenty-eighth century. Maitland assumes the TARDIS travellers are from the twenty-first, which suggests that he thought they have been in some form of suspended animation to still be alive in this future time period. This could mean that he, Carol and John could also have been in suspended animation at some point during their space voyage, so it does not necessarily mean it still is the twenty-eighth century when the story takes place.

The fact that Maitland does not bat an eyelid on hearing what century Barbara is really from indicates that deep space-travel was possible in the twentieth century, as it is with the *Hydrax* in 1999 (see 'State Of Decay' and SPACE-FLIGHT).

In the absence of contrary evidence, using the Century Factor I have set 'The Sensorites' in 2764.

Carol hasn't seen John 'for months'.

1540 ·

King Henry VIII reigned 1509 – 1547. We could place the Doctor and Susan's visit towards the end of his reign, say 1540. This adventure took place 'long before [Ian and Barbara] appeared on the scene'.

1795 ·

Beau Brummell was born on 7 June 1778 and died 30 March 1840. He was a good friend of the prince King George IV (who reigned from 1820 to 1830). By 1816, Brummell was in debt due to excessive gambling and went into self-imposed exile, dying in poverty. The Doctor's meeting while Brummell would have been at the height of Brummell's popularity, between 1790 and 1799, say 1795.

2364

Maitland says that by the twenty-eighth century 'there hasn't been a London for 400 years'. This suggests that after the Dalek Invasion of 2164 – 2174 (see 'The Dalek Invasion Of Earth'), a new London was built over the ruins, which became Central City in 2364. It is still called Central City in the year 4000 (see 'The Daleks' Master Plan').

2734

Maitland says that John is '30'.

2754

The first five humans came to the Sense-Sphere '10 years ago'. The three stranded humans have been slowly poisoning the Sensorites 'in greater numbers every year'.

2760

John makes a mumbled reference to 'four years', which could be the number of years they have been trapped in orbit around the Sense-Sphere.

DURATION

⇨ **Day One (Ep1-6)**
The TARDIS lands on the Earth ship at some point after '3 o'clock', based on when Maitland's watch has stopped. The rest of the story appears to take place over just one day on the Sense-Sphere, as there are no apparent night scenes. But since the Sensorites are scared of the dark, it could be that there is no night on this planet.

THE REIGN OF TERROR

+STORY LINK

At the end of 'The Sensorites', Ian insults the Doctor, who threatens to throw him and Barbara out of the ship at their next point of landing. At the beginning of 'The Reign Of Terror' the Doctor is still prepared to carry out his threat. Also, they are still wearing their clothes from 'The Sensorites', signalling that 'The Sensorites' and 'The Reign Of Terror' are consecutive.

LANGUAGE

Everyone should be speaking French, although there is also a curious mix of French and English: 'The sign of The Chien Gris', 'Au revoir, mon capitaine' and 'Good night'. Ian and Barbara adopt strange accents when they are working at the Inn in Ep6.

TIMELINE DATES

1794, July 24 – 27 +
At the farmhouse, Barbara deduces that the clothes they find are 'Eighteenth century'. In Ep5 Robespierre declares that 'tomorrow, the twenty-seventh of July 1794, will be a date for history'. This is on the third day of the adventure, giving the date the TARDIS lands as 24 July.

HISTORICAL COMPARISON

While the exploits of James Stirling are fictitious, the events leading to the fall of Robespierre are fairly accurate, but with a few dramatic liberties taken.

1789, July 14
Leon Colbert talks to Ian about living in France 'six years ago before the Bastille',

which was on 14 July 1789 in our history.

1790 ▨ ▨ ▨ ▨ ▨ ▨ ▨ ▨ ▨ ▨ ▨ ▨ ▨ ▨
Stirling says he has been in France 'for several years', say since 1790.

1793 ⋆ ▨ ▨ ▨ ▨ ▨ ▨ ▨ ▨ ▨ ▨ ▨ ▨ ▨
Susan tells Barbara that the French Revolution is the Doctor's 'favourite period in the history of Earth'. In '100,000 BC', Susan borrows a book from Barbara about the French Revolution. After reading a brief passage she says, 'that isn't right', which indicates that Susan has also visited this time period before. The Doctor has Marie Antoinette's French lock-pick in 'Pyramids Of Mars' (he mentions her again in 'The Robots Of Death'), so it is likely that he obtains the lock-pick on one of his many visits to that period. Marie Antoinette was executed on 16 October 1793 in our history. Perhaps Marie Antoinette is the reason why this is his 'favourite period'? (See also LIFE ON GALLIFREY).

1794, May ▨ ▨ ▨ ▨ ▨ ▨ ▨ ▨ ▨ ▨ ▨ ▨ ▨ ▨
Jules Renan says he learned of the existence of James Stirling 'two months ago', being May.

DURATION

⇨ **Day One (24 July) (Ep1)** ▨ ▨ ▨ ▨ ▨ ▨ ▨ ▨
The TARDIS arrives at 'dusk' (Doctor: 'Are we going to stand here talking all night?' / Susan: 'Don't get lost in the dark'). It is night when the farmhouse burns. Ian, Barbara and Susan are marched to Paris.

⇨ **Day Two (25 July) (Ep2-4)** ▨ ▨ ▨ ▨ ▨ ▨ ▨ ▨ ▨
The others arrive in Paris and the Doctor awakens the next morning. It takes him 'hours' to walk the 12 kilometres to the city. It is early evening when he arrives (the Shopkeeper says 'Good evening, Citizen'). Susan and Barbara spend the night at Jules', the Doctor at the prison.

⇨ **Day Three (26 July) (Ep4-6)** ▨ ▨ ▨ ▨ ▨ ▨ ▨ ▨ ▨
Susan and Barbara go to the surgeon the next morning and are recaptured. That night Barrass meets with Napoleon at The Sinking Ship. There is a full moon.

⇨ **Day Four (27 July) (Ep6)** ▨ ▨ ▨ ▨ ▨ ▨ ▨ ▨ ▨ ▨
Ian and Barbara return to Jules' the following morning to report on what happened at the tavern. Susan is rescued later that day, and the travellers leave.

PLANET OF GIANTS

+STORY LINK

The travellers have had time to change clothes and clean up since 'The Reign Of Terror'. This serial appears to be consecutive with 'The Reign Of Terror': the Doctor says 'There we were in the late eighteenth century ...', the setting of 'The Reign Of Terror' (1794). It is possible, however, that he is referring to another adventure that takes place in the eighteenth century.

LANGUAGE

The Doctor can read and understand English chemical formulae, but cannot understand the giants' slurred speech. The fault locater in the TARDIS uses Earth alpha-numerics (QR18, A14D) and has GREEN NORMAL, YELLOW STANDBY and RED ALERT marked beneath the warning lights.

TIMELINE DATES

1964, March (Tuesday?) ∗ ▨ ▨ ▨ ▨ ▨ ▨ ▨ ▨ ▨ ▨
The Doctor says 'I tried another frequency to side-step the ship back into the middle of the twentieth century'. The laboratory is located in a rural area 10 miles from the south coast. It is connected to a local telephone exchange. The clothing styles suggest the early 1960s. Taking into account that Ian and Barbara have been with the Doctor for more than 150 days by this point in their journey, and assuming that the TARDIS has landed relative to the time they have been away since when they first left London, 'Planet Of Giants' could be set in March 1964.

The fact that Forrester's garden appears to be in full bloom and there is a bee with almost full honey sacs also supports the spring setting.

Farrow's holiday in France technically started 'yesterday'. Assuming he has taken at least a full week of leave starting on a Monday, then the current day would be Tuesday.

1917, October 17 ▪ ▪ ▪ ▪ ▪ ▪ ▪ ▪ ▪ ▪ ▪ ▪ ▪ ▪

The Doctor and Susan recall 'that air-raid … what infernal machines those Zeppelins were'. In our history London was bombed by German air-ships on 17 October 1917.

1960 ▪ ▪ ▪ ▪ ▪ ▪ ▪ ▪ ▪ ▪ ▪ ▪ ▪ ▪

Smithers refers to the destruction of 'the last year's work'. This indicates he has been working on the DN6 formula for quite some time. Indeed, Forrester, says he has been dealing with his contact Mr Whitmore at Whitehall 'for years', say since 1960.

DURATION

(TARDIS) (Ep1) ▪ ▪ ▪ ▪ ▪ ▪ ▪ ▪ ▪ ▪ ▪ ▪ ▪

The TARDIS is travelling in the Vortex when the doors open.

⇨ **Day One (Ep1-3)** ▪ ▪ ▪ ▪ ▪ ▪ ▪ ▪ ▪ ▪ ▪

The TARDIS lands in the daytime and leaves the same day.

(TARDIS) (Ep3) ▪ ▪ ▪ ▪ ▪ ▪ ▪ ▪ ▪ ▪ ▪ ▪ ▪

The TARDIS travels in the Vortex when the crew regain their size.

UNSEEN ADVENTURES

In 'Marco Polo' the Doctor says he has heard of Genghis Khan but has never met him. In 'The Dæmons' the third Doctor says he has seen the Khan, so we can assume that he has met the Khan at some point after his adventure with 'Marco Polo'. At the time of 'The Reign Of Terror' the Doctor had never met Napoleon, but in 'Day Of The Daleks', the third Doctor tells Jo he has met the General so this must have happened at some point between 'The Reign Of Terror' and 'The War Games'.

THE DALEK INVASION OF EARTH

STORY LINK

At the end of 'Planet Of Giants' the TARDIS scanner is not working properly when the ship lands. In the opening moments of 'The Dalek Invasion Of Earth' the Doctor, no longer wearing the cape he has on at the end of 'Planet Of Giants', is fussing over the console, bemoaning the fact that the scanner shows what looks to be water. After it is established that they are on Earth, Ian and Barbara hope they are home. This scene is a poor continuation of the closing scene of 'Planet Of Giants' so it is possible that the two stories are not consecutive. As covered under THE DOCTOR'S AGE, there must be at least a year between 'Planet Of Giants' and 'The Dalek Invasion Of Earth', in order to take into account that by 'The Chase' Ian and Barbara have been with the Doctor for 'two years'. This gap between 'Planet Of Giants' and 'The Dalek Invasion Of Earth' marks the start of their second year with the Doctor.

DALEK LINK

As covered under DALEK HISTORY, 'The Dalek Invasion Of Earth' is the fourth Dalek appearance. Despite the disappearance of one of their colony ships (it crashed in the mercury swamps of Vulcan – see 'The Power Of The Daleks'), the Daleks have continued to explore the galaxy in their spaceships. At some point they discover Earth …

OBSERVATIONS

- Craddock is confused by the travellers' ignorance of the invasion and asks: 'You been on moon station or something?' If he is referring to Earth's moon then one would expect that colonists there would know of the invasion. The old woman speaks of the Astronaut Fair. 'Nightmare Of Eden' is set in 2116, some 58 years earlier, when the galaxy has been explored. Humans have by then established bases on the moons of the outer planets as well as colonies in other parts of the galaxy, so that is probably what Craddock was referring to. David Campbell says 'I can't just run off and see what it's like on Venus', which suggests that that planet has been colonised. Indeed, in 'The Wheel In Space', set in 2080, plant life had been found on Venus.
- At the end of the story, the Doctor promises Susan that he would 'come back' to visit her. He never does. The fact that in 'The Five Doctors' the other Doctors seemingly ignore Susan when they meet up in the Dark Tower suggests that they are ashamed at having not kept this promise.

LANGUAGE

The Daleks speak English to the rebels and among themselves. One of the Daleks refers to having 'heard similar words [of resistance] from leaders of your different races', which suggests the Daleks have translator devices. They label their maps in English, but mark buildings, machinery and the robomen with alien symbols. The Daleks even refer to their spaceship as 'the saucer' – would they even know what a saucer was?

2174 ◆

When the Doctor and Ian search the warehouse, the Doctor finds a desktop calendar showing the year '2164' on the top page ('At least we know the century,' he says). The warehouse 'hasn't been used in years', which means the calendar does not show the current year.

According to Jack Craddock and David Campbell, the Daleks landed and invaded Earth 'about ten years ago'. The first part of the attack actually occurred 'about six months' prior to that, when the first of the meteorites fell. Taking the date on the calendar as the date of the invasion, the current year would be 2174. In 'Day Of The Daleks' and 'Remembrance Of The Daleks' the Doctor confirms that the Daleks invade Earth in 'the 22nd century'.

It should be noted however that there are references to the events of 'The Dalek Invasion Of Earth' in other stories, each of which gives a conflicting date for the invasion:

a) In 'The Space Museum', Vicki says the Daleks 'invaded Earth, about 300 years ago, wasn't it?' She left Earth in 2493, so that would place 'The Dalek Invasion Of Earth' around 2193.

b) In 'The Time Meddler', the Monk says he deposited money in a bank in 1968 and then withdrew it 200 years later, being 2168. It is doubtful that there would still be a functioning banking system in the years during or soon after the Dalek invasion.

c) In 'Mission To The Unknown', Lowery says the Daleks invaded Earth 'a thousand years ago'. 'Mission To The Unknown' is set in 4000, which puts the invasion at 3000.

d) In 'The Daleks' Master Plan', the Doctor tells Bret Vyon to 'tell Earth to look back in the history of the year two thousand one hundred and fifty seven and that the Daleks are attacking again', i.e. 2157.

e) In 'Genesis Of The Daleks' the Doctor states that the Dalek invasion of Earth was 'in the year 2000'.

If we use the Doctor's direct dating of the invasion as given in 'The Daleks' Master Plan', where did the calendar come from? It certainly was not printed during the years of the invasion, and it is highly unlikely that a calendar for 2164 would be printed seven years in advance.

It is best to accept the date of the calendar in 'The Dalek Invasion Of Earth' over the others, as it is the date that appears in the serial. The 'wrong' other dates can be explained by the speaker having their facts wrong, or that they are merely generalising. In the case of Lowery's comment in 'Mission To The Unknown' it is possible that he is referring to another invasion that took place in 3000 (see 'Mission To The Unknown', and DALEK HISTORY). The Doctor's reference to the year 2157 could also relate to another off-screen encounter involving the Daleks.

218 BC
Barbara mentions Hannibal, who crossed the Alps in our history in 218 BC (see also 'Marco Polo' and 'Robot').

1773, December 16
Barbara refers to the Boston Tea Party, which was on this date in our history. What would have been her reaction had she known that a future incarnation of the Doctor had been there? (see 'The Unquiet Dead').

1857, May 10
Barbara mentions the Indian Mutiny, which was on this date in our history.

1865, April?
Barbara mentions General Lee and the Fifth Cavalry. In April 1865 Lee surrendered to Grant.

2164
According to Jack Craddock and David Campbell it was 'about ten years ago' that the Daleks landed and invaded Earth; the date of the calendar found in the warehouse (see above).

I would also suggest that this was the date that the Monk collected his money from his bank.

2173
Jenny says the Daleks got her brother 'last year'.

DURATION

⇨ Day One (Ep1-3)
The TARDIS arrives in the day. It is night when the Dalek saucer is attacked.

⇨ **Day Two (Ep3-5)** ▨ ▨ ▨ ▨ ▨ ▨ ▨ ▨ ▨ ▨ ▨

It is 'getting light' when the rebels begin to evacuate London and the Daleks set their firebombs. That night Ian and Jack Craddock encounter the Slyther, and Barbara and Jenny are captured by Daleks. The last scene set at night is Craddock's death by his brother's hand.

⇨ **Day Three (Ep5-6)** ▨ ▨ ▨ ▨ ▨ ▨ ▨ ▨ ▨ ▨ ▨

Susan cooks breakfast in the next scene, as a new day begins. The capsule explodes 'one hour' after it is dropped down the shaft. The Daleks are defeated.

⇨ **Day Four? (Ep6)** ▨ ▨ ▨ ▨ ▨ ▨ ▨ ▨ ▨ ▨ ▨

Given that the travellers return to London on foot, it is probably the next day by the time they arrive and clear the TARDIS. Big Ben chimes twice – so it could be 2 o'clock.

THE RESCUE

+STORY LINK

Soon after landing on Dido, Ian and Barbara wonder what Susan is 'doing now', and Ian mentions the Daleks, so it is clear that 'The Dalek Invasion Of Earth' and 'The Rescue' are consecutive.

OBSERVATIONS

- When she hears that Ian and Barbara are from 1963 Vicki says: 'They didn't have time machines in 1963. They didn't know anything then', which implies that in Vicki's time such machines were in use – see 'The Space Museum' for more on this.

LANGUAGE

Presumably the Dido people and the crash survivors communicated during their brief encounter.

TIMELINE DATES

2494 ⋆ ▨ ▨ ▨ ▨ ▨ ▨ ▨ ▨ ▨ ▨ ▨

Vicki says she left Earth in '2493, of course'. This suggests that 2493 is a past year for her. She has been on Dido 'a long time' so I have placed 'The Rescue' in the following year, 2494.

The trip to Astra may have taken months, but the ship is too small to suggest a long trip, and there seems to be no provision for a large crew or passenger complement. The rescue ship is only '69 hours away', so we know the rescuers have a ship that can travel between planets (or a space station) quickly. Vicki works out that Barbara is 'about five hundred and fifty years old' when she learns that they come from 1963. To calculate this she must have guessed that Barbara was about 20 and therefore born around 1943. Barbara's actual age is never given in the series, however I would say that Vicki was way off the mark; Barbara is more likely to be over 30, and therefore born no later than 1933.

1933

As covered above, Barbara was born around this year.

2493

As mentioned above, this is the year Vicki left Earth. She was ill 'that night' of the feast when Bennett killed the crew and the Dido people. She was still ill 'for days' afterwards.

Before 2493 ·

The Doctor has been to Dido before, and is pleased to be back 'after all these years'. At the time of that previous visit the Dido people 'had just perfected' the construction ray device that Bennett uses as a weapon, so the Doctor's previous visit relative to Dido might not be all that long ago.

DURATION

⇨ Day One (Ep1-2)

The story takes place over a 17-hour period: when Vicki contacts the rescue ship at the beginning of the story it is still '69 flying hours away'. The Captain says they will contact her again in '17 hours from now'. Night falls when the Doctor goes to see Bennett (Vicki says 'It gets dark early'). The rescue ship calls again just after the TARDIS leaves, '17 hours' after their previous contact.

THE ROMANS

+STORY LINK

Vicki is disappointed with her first landing point after leaving Dido in 'The Rescue'; she was expecting adventure, so the two stories are clearly consecutive.

OBSERVATIONS

- The Doctor says he cannot play the lyre, and yet in 'The Five Doctors', he plays the Harp of Rassilon quite easily.

LANGUAGE

Presumably everyone is speaking Latin with the aid of the Time Lord 'gift', although the words on the maps and plans are seen in the original language: i.e. Nova Roma and Nero Fecit.

TIMELINE DATES

AD 64, June 15 – July 24

The Doctor says the date is '64 AD. July'. In our history, the great fire was reported to have started on July 18th or 19th, so these dates have been adopted here. The TARDIS crew have been at the villa for 'three or four weeks' according to Barbara, 'nearly a month' according to Vicki, and arrived 'about a month ago' according to the store-holder at the market. This would be about 25 days, placing their arrival around June 15.

HISTORICAL COMPARISON

If we refer to the work *Life Of Nero* by Suetonius, it is clear that the events of 'The Romans' are somewhat different than recorded history. Nero was much younger than depicted in 'The Romans', about 30 instead of in his 40s. Nero despised the sight of blood, and in fact banned gladiator contests in 57 AD – seven years prior to 'The Romans'. It is recorded that Nero was not even in Rome at the time of the fire, which is believed to have started at the circus on 18 July. He later punished a group of Christians for the inferno.

AD 64, pre-July

The Doctor has been to Rome more than once before ('You know, I think you'll like Rome. I remember once when I was there and I spoke to …') and later he says 'I shouldn't think there's a soul in this place that knows me'. Presumably this is also around the same year, but prior to the fire in July. (The Doctor mentions the fire and his visit to Rome in 'The Fires Of Pompeii' ('ages ago'), and notes that he didn't get the 'chance to look around properly'.)

1837 ·
The recorded year in which Anderson (1805 – 1875) published *The Emperor's New Clothes*.

???? ·
The Doctor says he 'used to teach the Mountain Mauler of Montana'. If he was a wrestler, then this could have been in the twentieth century, but I have placed this event in ???? due to the uncertainty.

DURATION

⇨ **Day (15 June) (Ep1)**
The TARDIS lands on the cliff in daytime. Birds are singing.

🕓 **Three or four weeks pass ...**

⇨ **Day One (11 July) (Ep1-2)**
The travellers have been at the villa for 'three or four weeks' and have been selling the produce from the villa in the market. It is morning in the opening scene. The Doctor says he has had 'breakfast'. It is night when Ian and Barbara are abducted (crickets are heard chirping). The same night Ascaris attacks the Doctor and Vicki at the road house.

🕓 **Day Two to Day Six (12 – 16 July) (Ep2)**
When Barbara is thrown in the cell, the other slave woman is ill from the '34 days' it took to get to Rome. I doubt that this applies to Barbara, as she is in no way 34 days worn out from her trek. Besides, Ian has been on the galley for only 'five whole days' (although he shows no sign of beard growth), so the passing of five days in total since they were abducted is a more likely duration. Barbara must have joined the rest of the slaves after their 29th day on foot. The storm hits the galley on the night of the sixth day.

⇨ **Day Seven (17 July) (Ep2)**
The Doctor and Vicki arrive in Rome in the morning and just miss seeing Barbara sold

as a slave. It is night (crickets chirping) when Ian and Delos are recaptured and thrown in jail (although the stock footage shots of the lions are in daytime, it is definitely night).

⇨ **Day Eight (18 July) (Ep3)** ▨ ▨ ▨ ▨ ▨ ▨ ▨ ▨ ▨
Nero meets Barbara and chases her 'around all morning'. The banquet is held that night, and Ian fights Delos.

⇨ **Day Nine (19 July) (Ep4)** ▨ ▨ ▨ ▨ ▨ ▨ ▨ ▨ ▨
The next morning the Doctor burns Nero's plans. It is night (crickets again) when the fires are lit and Rome burns.

⊙ **Day Ten to Day Thirteen (20 – 23 July) (Ep4)** ▨ ▨ ▨ ▨
If it took five days to get to Rome, it is more than likely that it takes a similar term to get back (but Ian still does not have five days' beard growth).

⇨ **Day Fourteen (24 July) (Ep4)** ▨ ▨ ▨ ▨ ▨ ▨ ▨
A cock can be heard crowing as Ian and Barbara arrive back at the villa, so it is early morning. Crickets are chirping when the Doctor and Vicki return, so the day has passed and it is now night.

THE WEB PLANET

+STORY LINK

'The Romans' and 'The Web Planet' are consecutive. At the end of 'The Romans' Vicki says the Doctor has been at the TARDIS controls 'for hours' after leaving Rome, and yet the crew are still wearing their Roman garb when the ship is dragged down towards Vortis. Barbara is still wearing Nero's gold bracelet, and tells Vicki how she got it. Vicki does not believe her because she wasn't aware that Ian and Barbara had been in Rome while she was there. By the time the ship lands, the crew have changed into new clothes. The Doctor wears a cravat similar to those later worn by his sixth persona.

OBSERVATIONS

- Much is made of the Doctor's ring in this story. Previously, the ring appeared to be nothing more than a piece of jewellery; he even used it to barter for some clothes in 'The Reign Of Terror'. In 'The Web Planet' he says 'this is not merely a decorative object' and that it is 'of untold value'. In 'The Daleks' Master Plan', he says the stone has 'certain properties', but he is reluctant to discuss it any further. Indeed, he even seems anxious and unwilling at first to even show Ian its capabilities. He uses it to open the TARDIS doors; with the power drained from the ship, he rigs up what appears to be a photoelectric cell in an annexe off the console room. The Doctor waves his ringed finger in front of the cell and the doors open (but why doesn't he just use the hand crank as in 'Death To The Daleks'?) Later, he uses the ring to manipulate the Zarbi, which is controlled by the gold necklet. He apprehensively entrusts the ring to Prapillus ('May I know its secret?' / 'You may not!'). In 'The Daleks' Master Plan' he uses it in conjunction with the 'unusual powers' of Tigus's sun to repair the broken TARDIS lock. In 'The War Machines' he uses it to dehypnotise Dodo. When he regenerates, the ring slips off his finger, and he discards it forever. This suggests that whatever power the ring has is no longer needed now that the Doctor had regenerated. Interestingly, the Monk in 'The Time Meddler' also wears a similar ring …

- The oldest inhabitant of the Isop Galaxy where Vortis is located is the Face of Boe (see 'Gridlock' for more about the Face of Boe).

LANGUAGE

The Menoptra and Optera speak the same language. The Animus understands the recording of the Menoptran invasion force.

TIMELINE DATES

4000 + ▓ ▓ ▓ ▓ ▓ ▓ ▓ ▓ ▓ ▓ ▓ ▓ ▓ ▓

In the scene linking 'The Romans' and 'The Web Planet', after leaving AD 64 the Doctor says 'somehow we've materialised for a split second of time' before being dragged down to Vortis (although the TARDIS does actually materialise on the planet's surface in its usual fashion), so it is possible that 'The Web Planet' is also set in AD 64. The Doctor does say 'we have strayed from our astral plane', which suggests a spatial journey only without temporal displacement.

Alternatively, with the following serial set in 1191, 'The Web Planet' could be set between AD 64 and 1191, the TARDIS having moved relative to both time zones.

Another date is suggested when the Doctor and Vicki are trapped in the Centre: the Animus says: 'What I take from you will enable me to reach beyond this galaxy, into the solar system, to pluck from Earth its myriad techniques and take from Man his mastery of space'. From this we can assume that the Animus is able to absorb their knowledge, and determine that Earth was an ideal next target. But what is 'mastery of space'? It could be a reference to intergalactic travel, the power to move across the Universe. This development was achieved around 2980 (see 'Terror Of The Vervoids' and 'The Ribos Operation'), and by 4000 (see 'The Daleks' Master Plan') humanity had developed strong political relationships with many of the outer galaxies (and possibly with the Isop galaxy, where Vortis is located). After 5005 Earth had been abandoned (see 'The Invisible Enemy', 'The Ark In Space' and 'The Sontaran Experiment'), so 'The Web Planet' would need to be set between 4000 and 5000. Of course the fact that the Doctor is a time traveller and Vicki from Earth's future means that the Animus might simply have absorbed their own relative future knowledge of 'Man's mastery of space', which does not necessarily apply to the current time period.

'The Web Planet' could be set in ????, however, based on the loosely tenuous idea that 'mastery of space' is the current state of affairs on Earth (as noted under 'The Daleks' Master Plan', in 4000 AD the 'solar system' is a term which describes Earth's galaxy and not just its own sun's system), I have set 'The Web Planet' in 4000 in light of the loose link to 'The Daleks' Master Plan'.

3800

It is not made clear how long the Animus has been on Vortis. The Doctor wonders 'how long it's taken to grow to that size, eh? A hundred or two hundred years?', while the Menoptra talk about waiting 'generations for this moment' to reclaim the planet, abandoned 'long ago' by 'our forebears'. I have used the Doctor's estimate of 200 years.

Before 3800 ⋆

The Doctor has been to Vortis before, but he does not know about the Zarbi. It was certainly prior to the arrival of the Animus.

DURATION

⇨ Day One (Ep1-6)

The stars and moons are visible in all scenes set on the planet surface. The Doctor and Ian see a light flashing in the distance in Ep1. All this suggests that it is night. However, in the final scene, the moons and stars are still visible but the Optera says 'light is good', which suggests daytime. The abundance of shadows cast also suggests day. The story certainly takes place over several hours.

THE CRUSADE

+STORY LINK

Ian is wearing the same shirt and parka he wears in 'The Web Planet'. Barbara tells Saladin and Saphadin that she comes 'from another world, a world ruled by insects. And before that we were in Rome at the time of Nero. Before that we were in England, far, far into the future', these being references to 'The Web Planet', 'The Romans' and 'The Dalek Invasion Of Earth' respectively. We can assume that 'The Web Planet' and 'The Crusade' are therefore consecutive. And later, when he is tied up in the desert, Ian displays a fear of ants, something that he may have developed as a result of his recent adventure on Vortis.

LANGUAGE

The Time Lord 'gift' allows the TARDIS crew to understand the people of Lydda and Ramlah who would speak a Muslim or Arabic language. In the twelfth century, French was the chief language of the ruling class and especially the royal court, so it is clear that Saladin and Saphadin can also speak French. The letter that Richard sends to them proclaiming the union between Saphadin and Joanna is, however, seen to be written in English.

TIMELINE DATES

1191, October, 20 – 21 +
In the next serial 'The Space Museum', Ian refers to their 'thirteenth century clothes', which would place the story somewhere between 1201 and 1300, but this is clearly a mistake. Of course, it is possible that in the N-Space Universe the Third Crusade took place a century later. We can set 'The Crusade' by comparing it to the Third Crusade in our own history, which lasted from 1189 to 1192.

HISTORICAL COMPARISON

The events in 'The Crusade', which take place over a period of two days, are in fact based on several isolated events that occurred over a period of several months from September to November 1191: mention is made of 'a victory like Arsuf', a battle which was fought on 7 September 1191; in our history, Joanna joined Richard on 20 October 1191, and Richard did command Joanna to marry Saphadin; William de Preaux's impersonation of the King following a surprise attack by Saracens occurred in November.

Given that Joanna's arrival in Jaffa occurs in Ep2, we can use the October 20 reference as the best date to set 'The Crusade'.

1190
Haroun tells Barbara how his family was killed 'last year'.

1191, September 7
The recorded date of the battle of Arsuf in our history.

1191 ✦
The Doctor seems to be familiar with Richard's jewelled belt ('Wait a minute, of course, yes, I remember … '), which suggests that he has been to this location and time period before.

DURATION

⇨ **Day One (20 October) (Ep1-3)**
The TARDIS arrives around mid-day, and the Doctor greets their attackers with a 'Good afternoon'. It is night when Barbara is recaptured in Haroun's house.

⇨ **Day Two (21 October) (Ep3-4)**
It is daybreak when Ian is attacked by Ibrahim's brother, and morning when Barbara is brought before El Akir. It is the night of this second day when the TARDIS leaves, evidenced by the sounds of hooting owls and chirping crickets.

THE SPACE MUSEUM

+STORY LINK

The story starts where 'The Crusade' leaves off, with the travellers frozen at the TARDIS console still dressed in their Crusade costumes.

OBSERVATIONS

- This is one of the few stories that deals with the paradoxes and complexities of time travel (see THE N-SPACE UNIVERSE). Vicki shows an incredible understanding of the mechanics of paradox in saying that 'time, like space, although a dimension in itself, also has dimensions of its own' (perhaps she was familiar with time travel – in 'The Rescue' she knew that they didn't have time travel in 1963). Curiously, for a Time Lord, the Doctor admits 'I've always found it extremely difficult to solve the fourth dimension. And here we are, face to face with the fourth dimension. You know, I think the TARDIS jumped a time-track and ended up here in this fourth dimension'. His lack of understanding in this field could explain why the Doctor failed in his initial attempt at a Triple First! (see 'The Ribos Operation'). Later, he finds the little circuit that has 'been giving us all this dimensional trouble ... We landed on a separate time-track', which confirms his theory.

- The Doctor says 'what we are doing now is taking a glimpse into the future – or what might be or could be the future'. They then spend quite some time trying to prevent the events that could lead to their deaths and subsequent placement in the museum. However, in Ep2 Ian unravels Barbara's cardigan to use as a trail of their movements through the corridors of the museum. Since the 'future' Barbara seen in the display cabinet is wearing a cardigan, they should have realised at that point that they have already changed the future.

LANGUAGE

The label on the Dalek display reads 'DALEK – PLANET SKARO'. The TARDIS food machine is labelled in English. The Moroks and Xerons must speak the same language. Vicki is able to speak English and still give the truth to the armoury computer, so clearly it must be able to understand her language. Does the 'gift' work on machines?

TIMELINE DATES

3065 *
<<3065>> *

The Doctor takes on board the 'Time and Space Visualiser' from the museum. In 'The Chase', Vicki says 'when I left Earth scientists were trying to invent a machine that would convert the energy from light neutrons into electrical impulses. That meant that you could just tune in and see any event in history'. The Doctor confirms that the Visualiser is precisely that. Vicki left Earth in 2493 (as given in 'The Rescue'). The fact that this Visualiser has the names of the planets in Earth's solar system on its face indicates that it is undoubtedly of Earth origin. We can therefore set 'The Space Museum' after 2493.

But where did the Moroks get the Visualiser from? Although they were once galactic conquerors it is clear that Earth is never one of their conquests; according to the Doctor the Roman Empire fell 'in many galaxies, far beyond [the Moroks'] reach'. We can therefore only assume that the Moroks obtained the Visualiser from an Earth colony in another galaxy, a galaxy that had fallen to the Moroks. On the basis that humans do not develop intergalactic travel until about 2980 (see 'The Ribos Operation', 'Terror Of The Vervoids' and SPACE-FLIGHT), then the Moroks could only have acquired the Visualiser at some time after the thirtieth century. Therefore, using a Century Factor of 1100, I have set 'The Space Museum' in the arbitrary date of 3065. Although the design was originally conceived around 2493, this particular model of Time and Space Visualiser is not necessarily over 570 years old.

1757 ▾

James Watt (1736 – 1819) first theorised his ideas for using steam as an energy force in 1757. In 1764 he studied the workings of steam engines, and in May 1765 invented the second condenser.

1884 ▾

One of the images the Doctor projects onto Lobos's scanner is a penny-farthing bicycle, and also of a period bathing costume. The penny-farthing was in common use around 1884.

2164

The Dalek on display in the museum is fitted with a power disc like those seen in 'The Dalek Invasion Of Earth'. Therefore, the Moroks would have captured this Dalek around 2164.

3055

The Moroks invaded Xeros when Tor and the others were 'children'. All the adult Xerons were shipped off 'to other planets' to work in slave labour camps when they reached puberty so Tor and his friends are some of the last of the Xerons on the planet. They appear to be in their teens, so we can assume that the Moroks have been on Xeros for no more than ten years.

DURATION

⇨ **Day One (Ep1-4)**

The story takes place over several hours during one single Xeron day: the TARDIS crew wander around the museum 'for hours' during Ep1-2, while in Ep3 the Zephron Gas is to be released 'in one hour'; it is still spreading through the museum at the beginning of Ep4.

THE CHASE

+STORY LINK

This story continues immediately after 'The Space Museum', with the Doctor starting to repair the Time and Space Visualiser. Barbara is making a new dress for Vicki (presumably using the material that they bought at the market in 'The Romans'). Ian and Barbara have now been with the Doctor for 'two years'.

DALEK LINK

As covered under DALEK HISTORY, 'The Chase' is the sixth Dalek appearance. There is a new Supreme Dalek, the last one having been destroyed on Earth in 'The Dalek Invasion Of Earth'. As noted in 'Day Of The Daleks' the Daleks 'have discovered the secret of time travel'. Their first use of this new ability results in the loss of their forces, which become 'trapped in a temporal paradox' (as seen in 'Day Of The Daleks'); so all historical aspects from a Dalek point of view covering 100 years in that story do not exist. Therefore, the events of 'The Chase' are in effect the Daleks' true sixth appearance once we cancel out 'Day Of The Daleks'. Despite this temporary setback, the Daleks continue to experiment with time, eventually developing a time machine more like the TARDIS. Their aim is to find and destroy the Doctor (not invade Earth again). Using their 'movement scanners' they locate the TARDIS leaving Xeros, and pursue it.

OBSERVATIONS

- The fact that the Doctor does not travel to 1965 with Ian and Barbara in the Dalek Time Machine, and then take it to 1963 to check up on the Hand of Omega ('Remembrance Of The Daleks'), suggests that the Doctor is not at all concerned about leaving the device unburied on Earth.
- This story could be said to be a turning point in the Doctor's character. In '100,000 BC', he is clearly scared of his secrets being discovered by Ian and Barbara; he was very much anti-human (for want of a better term). But with the departure of his first human travelling companions, the Doctor has clearly mellowed and become friendlier towards humans. From this story onwards he becomes a much lighter character.
- Of note, this story features the last appearance of the 'deckchair' beds, first seen in 'Inside The Spaceship', and also seen in 'The Web Planet'. Given that a TARDIS is designed to be essentially a temporary base used by Time Lords during exploration and observation missions, the fold-down 'deckchair' beds

were probably the only creature comfort needed by Time Lords for resting during those missions. (In 'The Deadly Assassin' the Doctor is connected to the Matrix via a couch-like terminal, so it is possible these beds in the TARDIS perform a similar function and can be linked to the Matrix, so in the case of the death of a Time Lord while away from Gallifrey his memories can be transferred into the Net.) These spartan but functional sleeping arrangements must therefore have suited the Doctor and Susan during their travels. But even when Ian and Barbara joined them, it appears nothing was done to change the sleeping amenities into facilities more comfortable for them during the two years they travelled in the TARDIS, possibly because that function of the ship was, like the time unit and chameleon circuit, not functioning correctly. The third Doctor probably wouldn't have slept inside the TARDIS when he was exiled on Earth, as no doubt he had his own quarters at UNIT HQ, however once the exile was lifted, and the TARDIS was once again fully functional, the ship must have been reconfigured back to a 'default' setting, as a couch-like bed, similar to the old 'deckchair' ones, makes an appearance in 'Planet Of The Daleks'. (Again, this bed might have a connection to the Matrix.) Although we do get a brief glimpse of a large room with a four-poster bed in an infrequently visited section of the TARDIS ('The Masque Of Mandragora'), the next time a bedroom is seen on-screen is Romana's in 'Full Circle'. It is not clear when – or even if – bedrooms were created for each of the Doctor's companions. Presumably Sarah had a room filled with her possessions such as the stuffed owl seen at the end of 'The Hand Of Fear'. But since she regularly returned to her own time on Earth it is unlikely she had a permanent bed in her room. Even when Leela joined the Doctor, in 'The Invasion Of Time' there is no sign of a bedroom near the console room, and in 'The Stones Of Blood' there is only a black void in the adjacent area. In 'Full Circle' Romana's room is fully furnished with bed, chairs and ornaments, no doubt items collected during her 11 years of travelling in the TARDIS. There are also old clothes draped over a chair (such as the one worn by the second Romana in 'City Of Death'), so we can assume that this room was 'created' by the second Romana after 'Destiny Of The Daleks', once her mission to locate the Key to Time was completed and she had decided to stay on with the Doctor. This room gets deleted in 'Logopolis', but Tegan and Nyssa's room, which is across the passage from the console room as seen in 'The Visitation', must have been 'added' to the architectural layout of the ship at some point after 'Castrovalva' – probably just prior to 'Kinda' so that Nyssa will have somewhere comfortable to sleep for 48 hours. Adric's room is seen in 'Earthshock' and 'Terminus', while Nyssa and Tegan's room appears again in 'Arc Of Infinity', 'Snakedance' and 'Terminus', but in those three instances, the room is quite different to the one seen in 'The Visitation', so presumably Nyssa did some redecorating following Tegan's departure at the end of 'Time-Flight'. The last time a bedroom is seen is in 'Planet Of Fire', when Turlough carries Peri following her near-drowning to what appears to be Tegan's old room.

LANGUAGE

The Daleks measure time and distance using a 'Dalekian scale', i.e. in Ep3, '7-7-3 Dalekian scale 9-1-5 degrees' equals '1-5 Earth minutes reducing'. The Daleks know the planet is called Mechanus, and call the robots 'the Mechons' not Mechanoids. Oddly enough, the controls in the Dalek ship are labelled in Earth numerals.

TIMELINE DATES

2215 ◆

From the Daleks' perspective, 'The Chase' takes place after 2174, because the Daleks mention their invasion of the Earth being delayed as if it were a recent event in terms of their own history. This places 'The Chase' some time prior to 2540 – the setting of 'Frontier In Space', a spread of some 366 years. These events are more likely to be closer to 2174 than to 2540. Therefore, I have taken a Century Factor of 250 years from 1965, being 2215 – which is also one year after the loss of the invasion force in 'Day Of The Daleks'.

The Doctor's new Time and Space Visualiser 'can only pick up things that happened in the past', so the events on Skaro should take place in the past relative to the events on Aridius, and it must be later than 2215 on Aridius. The Daleks use their 'movement scanners' to locate the TARDIS. The Daleks announce that the TARDIS is 'at present' on the planet Aridius. We can assume that 'at present' is subjective to the Daleks' time zone. In other words, their 'movement scanners' have been attuned to locate the Doctor's TARDIS as soon as it enters the current Dalek time zone, i.e. 'the present', therefore it is 2215 on Aridius too.

1966 (summer) ◆

Morton Dill says the time is 'three after twelve, ma'am', and the year is '1966, ma'am'. It would appear to be summer; there is no snow. Vicki says that 'ancient' New York 'was destroyed in the Dalek invasion' (see 'The Dalek Invasion Of Earth').

1872, November 24 ◆

In our recorded history the *Mary Celeste* left port on 5 November 1872. The abandoned ship was later discovered on 4 December 1872. The last entry in the Captain's log was dated 24 November 1872, some 10 days earlier.

1996 ·

The year appears on the sign on the box office at the exhibit: 'Festival of Ghana 1996', although this title is not necessarily reflective of the actual year. It is unlikely that this exhibition is taking place in Ghana itself, since that country's unit of currency is the cedi, and not the dollar, so the admission price of '$10' indicates that the Festival is taking place in a country that uses dollars (such as the United States, Canada, Singapore, Hong Kong, Australia or New Zealand?)

The fact that the Festival has been 'Cancelled by Peking' could be due to another World Peace Conference (see 'The Mind Of Evil' and 'Day Of The Daleks'), with the Chinese pulling out yet again.

3550 ·

The Mechanoids were sent to prepare the planet for colonisation 'about 50 years ago', so the sequences set on Mechanus are at a time when Earth was still colonising other planets. The planet was forgotten because 'Earth got involved in interplanetary wars', but there are no other stories in which Earth is involved in galactic wars.

In 'The Daleks' Master Plan' Sara Kingdom says that gravity force, which was being used in Steven's time, 'was abandoned centuries ago'. Steven says 'the technology of my age may be hundreds of years behind yours', so Steven comes from a time 'hundreds of years behind' Sara's time, which is 4000. Taking the 'centuries ago' quote from 'The Daleks' Master Plan' I have taken 3500 to be an approximate date for the wars, taking into account the Dalek wars of 3500 (see 'Death To The Daleks'). It is not clear if Steven already knows of the Daleks. He seems particularly familiar with them in 'The Daleks' Master Plan' despite seeing them only briefly in 'The Chase' so I assume that he does. Fifty years later would place this section in 3550.

1965, October

The tax-disc on the car at the end of the story reads 'DEC 65'. When Ian confirms that it is '1965', Barbara notes 'we're two years out'. The tax-disc expires in December 1965, so it could be anytime between December 1964 and December 1965. I have placed the month to be October, which is exactly two years since they left Earth. The Doctor does say 'I tried for two years to get you both home', so he probably set the controls of the Dalek time machine for this date to ensure they got home at the correct point in time relative to the length of time they spent with him.

1215 ▪ ▪ ▪ ▪ ▪ ▪ ▪ ▪ ▪ ▪ ▪ ▪ ▪ ▪ ▪

The Aridians say the two suns drew closer 'for a thousand years' and evaporated the oceans. However, given that the suns move quickly, making 'the days and nights [very] short', the years on Aridius are not necessarily the same length as on Earth. (It does seem odd that a water planet should be called Aridius, when that name applies more to the desert state of the planet after the waters had gone. Perhaps they changed its name..?)

1600, March 7 ▪ ▪ ▪ ▪ ▪ ▪ ▪ ▪ ▪ ▪ ▪ ▪

Henry IV (the play to which Queen Elizabeth I is referring in the scene) was first performed in our history on 6 March 1600, so we can assume that Shakespeare's audience with the Queen was the following day. Hamlet is believed to have been written by Shakespeare in late 1599 or early 1600, or possibly even 1601. The fact that the Doctor doesn't make any comment about the scene between Shakespeare and Francis Bacon suggests that the Doctor has not met Shakespeare yet (see 'Planet Of Evil' and 'City Of Death').

1863, November 19 ▪ ▪ ▪ ▪ ▪ ▪ ▪ ▪ ▪ ▪ ▪

The full date and event is asked for by Ian when he turns on the Time and Space Visualiser.

1965, April 15 ▪ ▪ ▪ ▪ ▪ ▪ ▪ ▪ ▪ ▪ ▪ ▪

Vicki says she has selected '1965' on the Time and Space Visualiser. 'Ticket To Ride' was released in April 1965 in our history (with 'Yes It Is' on the flip-side). The Beatles' performance was recorded on 10 April 1965, and broadcast on Top Of The Pops on 15 April 1965. To Vicki, the Beatles played 'classical' music.

3500 ▪ ▪ ▪ ▪ ▪ ▪ ▪ ▪ ▪ ▪ ▪ ▪ ▪ ▪

The Mechanoids came to the planet 'about 50 years ago'.

3548 ▪ ▪ ▪ ▪ ▪ ▪ ▪ ▪ ▪ ▪ ▪ ▪ ▪ ▪

Steven says he's been on Mechanus for 'about two years'. He says he crashed and 'wandered around for days' before being captured.

▪▪▪▪▪▪▪▪▪▪ **DURATION** ▪▪▪▪▪▪▪▪▪▪

In a slight departure from the usual format of Duration, the locations have been listed here in story order as opposed to date order.

(TARDIS) (Ep1) ▨ ▨ ▨ ▨ ▨ ▨ ▨ ▨ ▨ ▨ ▨ ▨ ▨

Since leaving Xeros the Doctor has been working on the Time and Space Visualiser, Ian reading a book, Barbara making a dress, while Vicki just gets in the way.

⇨ **Day One (Ep1-2)** ▨ ▨ ▨ ▨ ▨ ▨ ▨ ▨ ▨ ▨ ▨ ▨

The TARDIS arrives on Aridius at daytime. The days are very short. The sandstorm hits as night falls.

⇨ **Day Two (Ep1-2)** ▨ ▨ ▨ ▨ ▨ ▨ ▨ ▨ ▨ ▨ ▨ ▨

It is morning when the Dalek rises from the sand. It is night again by the time the TARDIS leaves Aridius.

(TARDIS) (Ep3) ▨ ▨ ▨ ▨ ▨ ▨ ▨ ▨ ▨ ▨ ▨ ▨

Back in the vortex the Doctor calculates the time differential between the TARDIS and the Dalek ship is 12 minutes ...

⇨ **Day One (1966) (Ep3)** ▨ ▨ ▨ ▨ ▨ ▨ ▨ ▨ ▨ ▨ ▨

It is 'three after twelve' (12.03 pm) when the TARDIS lands on the Empire State Building. The Dalek time ship lands 12 minutes later.

(TARDIS) (Ep3) ▨ ▨ ▨ ▨ ▨ ▨ ▨ ▨ ▨ ▨ ▨ ▨

The TARDIS returns to the time vortex for a few minutes.

⇨ **Day (1872) (Ep3)** ▨ ▨ ▨ ▨ ▨ ▨ ▨ ▨ ▨ ▨ ▨ ▨

The travellers spend about 10 minutes on the *Mary Celeste*.

(TARDIS) (Ep3) ▨ ▨ ▨ ▨ ▨ ▨ ▨ ▨ ▨ ▨ ▨ ▨

Once the TARDIS returns to the time vortex the time differential reduces 'to 8 minutes'.

⇨ **Day One (1996) (Ep4)** ▨ ▨ ▨ ▨ ▨ ▨ ▨ ▨ ▨ ▨ ▨

About 15 minutes is spent in Frankenstein's House of Horrors. Although Dracula greets them with 'Good evening', it is not necessarily the correct time – it is more likely to be a programmed line. The Daleks land '8 minutes' later.

(TARDIS) (Ep4) ▨ ▨ ▨ ▨ ▨ ▨ ▨ ▨ ▨ ▨ ▨ ▨

After leaving Earth the TARDIS travels for a while before landing on Mechanus.

⇨ **Day One (Ep4-5)** ▩ ▩ ▩ ▩ ▩ ▩ ▩ ▩ ▩ ▩ ▩

It is night when the TARDIS lands on Mechanus.

⇨ **Day Two (Ep5-6)** ▩ ▩ ▩ ▩ ▩ ▩ ▩ ▩ ▩ ▩ ▩

The travellers see the city in the morning. The TARDIS leaves Mechanus the same day.

⇨ **Day (1965) – (Ep6)** ▩ ▩ ▩ ▩ ▩ ▩ ▩ ▩ ▩ ▩ ▩

It is day when Ian and Barbara return to London.

THE TIME MEDDLER

+STORY LINK

'The Time Meddler' follows immediately on from 'The Chase'; after they leave Mechanus, the Doctor and Vicki find Steven in the TARDIS.

OBSERVATIONS

- The Monk is from Gallifrey (although the planet is not named). He has a jewelled ring like the Doctor's. The Doctor notes that the Monk has a Mark Four console, which does not necessarily mean that the whole ship is a Mark Four. It is a more modern model than the Doctor's, with a few improvements, such as a drift compensator; the Doctor is clearly jealous. When asked by the Monk what 'type' his is, the Doctor gets very defensive and says, 'Mind your own business!'

- The Monk has 'got something from every period and every place' in his TARDIS, including statues, paintings, antiques and weapons. The Doctor scolds him for disobeying 'the golden rule about space and time travelling. Never, never interfere with the course of history!' (see THE N-SPACE UNIVERSE). The Monk clearly does not fear being stopped by their Time Lord superiors because he simply replies with: 'And who says so? Doctor, it's more fun my way'. An interesting discussion is held between Vicki and Steven; they realise that if the Monk were to succeed in changing history then all the history books as well as their own memories would change to reflect the 'new' version of history. Steven says 'There's more to this time-travelling than meets the eye'.

LANGUAGE

The Saxons and the Vikings speak with the Monk. The Monk's battle plan scroll and checklist are both written in English, and Vicki reads from his diary. The letter the Doctor writes to the Monk is addressed 'To The Monk'. The Monk calculates distances from miles to kilometres with a slide-rule. He is clearly annoyed at having to use either form of measurement. The Monk has a first aid kit that is marked with the standard Red Cross symbol.

TIMELINE DATES

1066, September 15 – 17 *

After establishing that Edward died at 'the beginning of the year', the Doctor deduces that 'it must be 1066 … And judging by the appearance of these leaves, late summer!' Steven refers to it being 'the tenth century', but this is clearly a mistake.

The Monk is expecting the Viking fleet to arrive in 'two or three days'. In our history, the battle at Stamford Bridge, where King Harold fought the Vikings, was from 20 to 25 September 1066. The Doctor later says the Battle of Hastings will take place 'in a few weeks' time'. The battle was fought on 14 October 1066 in our history. All these clues point to setting 'The Time Meddler' in the second or third week of September, from about the 15th.

2000 BC

The outer rim trenches of what we know as Stonehenge were built circa 3100 BC. The inner stone monoliths, however, are believed to have been erected circa 2000 BC.

1050

Edith says the monastery has 'been deserted for years and years', say 16.

1066, January 5

Edith says Edward (who was King from 1042 – 1066) died at 'the beginning of the year'. In our history, Edward died on 5 January 1066.

1066, August

Edith tells the Doctor that the Monk came to the monastery 'a few weeks ago', which places his arrival as either late August or early September. I have selected the former to allow for a longer time for the Monk to set up his plan.

1066, October 14 ▨ ▨ ▨ ▨ ▨ ▨ ▨ ▨ ▨ ▨ ▨

The recorded date in our history of the Battle of Hastings.

1500 ▨ ▨ ▨ ▨ ▨ ▨ ▨ ▨ ▨ ▨ ▨ ▨

In 'The Seeds Of Death' the Doctor dates the da Vinci sketch seen in the space museum as being from 'about 1500'. This date has been used here for the Monk's visit with da Vinci.

1610 ✦ ▨ ▨ ▨ ▨ ▨ ▨ ▨ ▨ ▨ ▨ ▨

The Doctor states that he comes from Gallifrey '50 years earlier' than the Monk. This presumably refers to the number of years he has been away from Gallifrey, as opposed to there being 50 years between their respective GRTs; which is unlikely because of the TARDIS fail-safe (see GALLIFREY HISTORY). As covered under THE DOCTOR'S AGE, the Doctor left Gallifrey in GRT 1610.

1968
2168 ▨ ▨ ▨ ▨ ▨ ▨ ▨ ▨ ▨ ▨ ▨

The year and event are recorded in the Monk's diary. Two hundred years from 1968 is 2168 – which is actually during the Dalek Invasion of Earth (see 'The Dalek Invasion Of Earth'), so how did he manage to get his money? Perhaps after discovering that the Daleks destroyed London, he actually slipped back a few years prior to 2164 to collect his money then, and didn't change his diary entry.

DURATION

(TARDIS) (Ep1) ▨ ▨ ▨ ▨ ▨ ▨ ▨ ▨ ▨ ▨

The TARDIS clock in the opening scenes reads 9.44. The ship travels for a while before landing.

⇨ Day One (15 September) (Ep1) ▨ ▨ ▨ ▨ ▨ ▨ ▨

It is early evening ('It's going to get dark in a minute') when the TARDIS lands on the beach. The Monk's watch reads '11.50' when Steven finds it. The Doctor spends the night in the cell.

⇨ Day Two (16 September) (Ep2-3) ▨ ▨ ▨ ▨ ▨ ▨ ▨

The Monk serves the Doctor breakfast. It is 'twenty past five' when Steven and Vicki wake. It is night when the Vikings arrive at the monastery. The Vikings lock the Doctor in the cell overnight.

⇨ **Day Three (17 September) (Ep3-4)** ▬ ▬ ▬ ▬ ▬ ▬ ▬

Vicki says 'it all looks so different in daylight' when she and Steven and Vicki arrive at the tunnel leading into the monastery the following morning. It is later the same day that the travellers leave.

GALAXY FOUR

STORY LINK

There is nothing to suggest that 'Galaxy 4' follows directly on from 'The Time Meddler'. In 'The Time Meddler' Steven shaves off the beard he has in 'The Chase', while at the beginning of 'Galaxy 4' Vicki is giving him a haircut.

OBSERVATIONS

- It is not clear how the Doctor's astral map works so that it can indicate the correct number of days the doomed planet has left. The astral map is also used in 'The Web Planet', where it basically functions as a communications device. Perhaps it is also a portable time scanner like that used in 'The Macra Terror' and 'Doctor Who (The TV Movie)', or is more like the temporal scanners used on Gallifrey. The Doctor simply views ahead into the future as many days as is required until the planet no longer appears on the screen.

LANGUAGE

The Rills speak 'in thought' and therefore appear to speak English. 'Dawn' is a term for day in both the Drahvin and Rill language.

TIMELINE DATES

Beyond 4000 ▸ ▬ ▬ ▬ ▬ ▬ ▬ ▬ ▬ ▬ ▬

The planet on which this story takes place blows up. Why it should do so is not explained. Could it be one of the many planets destroyed by the entropy effect caused by the destruction of 'Logopolis' in February 1981? (see 'Logopolis').

At the end of the story, after the TARDIS has left the destroyed planet, the Doctor says they 'dematerialised from that galaxy a long time ago'. The TARDIS then passes Kembel in the year 4000 (see 'Mission To The Unknown', 'The Daleks' Master Plan'). On the assumption that the TARDIS has only travelled in space and not in time then 'Galaxy 4' could be set in 4000. However, the TARDIS subsequently lands on Earth in

1188 BC, so that date could now be applied to 'Galaxy 4'.

Maaga says she has 'heard of creatures' like humans. And even though the TARDIS crew do not mention their planet by name, she knows they are 'Earth creatures' and 'Earthmen'. Likewise, when Vicki says she is from Earth, the Rills recognise she is 'human'. And although the Rill says they don't know Earth, they do know 'you are from the solar system' (a term used in 'The Daleks' Master Plan' to describe the whole of Earth's galaxy). The fact that beings, from a galaxy different to Earth's, know of humans suggests placing 'Galaxy 4' in a future setting, when intergalactic travel had been developed, with humans having travelled to the fourth galaxy. This is a tenuous link to 'Mission To The Unknown' and 'The Daleks' Master Plan', in which Earth is said to hold great influence. On the basis that the TARDIS has travelled backwards in time from AD 4000 to 1188 BC between the end of 'Galaxy 4' and the start of 'The Myth Makers', we could assume that the TARDIS has been travelling backwards in time along the same temporal path ever since it left the fourth galaxy – so it has travelled from the future beyond 4000, stopping briefly in orbit around Kembel in the year 4000, then continuing on its backward flight, eventually materialising in 1188 BC. I have therefore placed 'Galaxy 4' in the non-specific period Beyond 4000.

Maaga says 'some 400 dawns ago we were investigating this particular sector of the galaxy', looking for a planet to colonise when they encountered the Rills. The two spaceships hung in space 'for four dawns' before they crashed. We see a 'flash-back' to the day of the crash. 'Dawn' is a term for day in both the Drahvin and Rill language, so they have been there for 400 days – but given that the days are very short on this world they have not been there for the equivalent of more than an Earth year.

DURATION

⇨ **Day One (Ep1-4)**

The days and nights on the planet are very short due to there being three suns (which explains how the Drahvins miscalculated the number of days the planet has left). The Doctor guesses 'the evenings last here for about four hours'. The TARDIS arrives when it is day. The Doctor and Vicki go to the Rill ship, as it gets dark.

⇨ **Day Two (Ep1-4)**

The Doctor and Vicki arrive at the Rill ship, as it gets lighter. It takes about '6 hours' to power up the Rill spaceship.

⇨ **Day Three (Ep4)**

The TARDIS leaves at 'dawn', as the planet begins to break up.

THE MYTH MAKERS

+STORY LINK

At the end of 'Galaxy 4' Vicki tells the Doctor she has hurt her ankle. At the beginning of 'The Myth Makers', she has a walking stick and the Doctor refers to her injury, indicating that the two stories are consecutive. In terms of story duration, Vicki has been with the Doctor for about 52 days.

OBSERVATIONS

- Vicki adopts the name Cressida, given to her by Priam, when she stays with Troilus. In 1602, William Shakespeare penned a tragedy about the two lovers. It could be that when the Doctor visited the Bard in 1600, when he was writing sonnets and *Hamlet* (see 'The Chase', 'Planet Of Evil' and 'City Of Death'), the Time Lord told Shakespeare about his adventure in Troy, and a few years later, the Bard based part of his play on that.

LANGUAGE

There are two languages here, Greek and that of the Trojans, although members from both camps are able to converse in both. At the end, Vicki stays with Trojans. Without the TARDIS or the Doctor present one would expect the power of the Time Lord 'gift' to cease, and yet Vicki is still able to converse with the Trojans, and presumably still able to do so for many years afterwards. Is the 'gift' permanent?

TIMELINE DATES

1188 BC ⭢

Recent academic research into the hidden meanings within Homer's *The Iliad*, particularly with regard to passing references to eclipses and full moons, has brought about new understandings as to when the battle of Troy may have taken place (although there is still some doubt that it ever took place). The new research theorises that the fall of Troy occurred close to 1188BC, with the war starting ten years earlier in 1198BC.

Diomedes died 'last week'.

HISTORICAL COMPARISON

The war between the Greeks and Trojans is known mainly due to Homer's epic poem, *The Iliad* (c.1000 BC – 800 BC) (in the TV serial, the Doctor says of the wooden horse: 'the whole story is obviously absurd. Probably invented by Homer as some good dramatic device'). Later, the Roman poet Vergil (70 BC – 19 BC) expanded upon the tale in *The Aeneid*. There is no historical basis for either version of the tale. What is believed to be the ruins of the city of Troy was found in 1870 by Heinrich Schliemann (the Doctor mentions this in 'The Stones Of Blood'), but there were no weapons or similar remains to suggest that a ten year war had even been waged near there. The romance between Vicki (as Cressida) and Troilus also conflicts with known 'facts'. Shakespeare and Chaucer wrote of the two lovers, but their fates are very different to that which occurs to Vicki and Troilus in 'The Myth Makers'.

1205 BC
Troilus says he is '17 next birthday', which makes his date of birth around 1205 BC.

1198 BC
The war between the Trojans and the Greeks lasted for 'ten long years'. The Rani was in Asia Minor during this time (see 'The Mark Of The Rani').

2478
Troilus says he is '17 next birthday' to which Vicki replies, 'That's hardly any older than me,' which makes her 15 or 16. She meets the Doctor in 2494 (see 'The Rescue'), so she was born no earlier than 2478.

DURATION

⇨ **Day One (Ep1)**
It is day when the TARDIS lands. Achilles and Hector have already been fighting for 'an hour or more'. The Doctor and Steven spend the night at the Greek camp.

⇨ **Day Two (Ep2-3)**
The TARDIS is discovered to be missing 'at sunrise in the morning'. The Doctor is given 'two days' to devise an attack plan. It is dark when Steven is brought into Troy. He and Vicki spend the night in the dungeons.

⇨ **Day Three (Ep3)**
The Doctor reveals his plans for a 'flying machine' the next morning. The Great Horse of Asia is built and left on the plains where it is found that night.

⇨ **Day Four (Ep3-4)**
The Horse is brought into the city that morning. The TARDIS leaves that same day.

Vicki remains with Troilus.

MISSION TO THE UNKNOWN
THE DALEKS' MASTER PLAN

CONTINUITY NOTE

Although in transmission terms 'Mission To The Unknown' falls between 'Galaxy 4' and 'The Myth Makers', I have placed it here because it acts as an introduction to 'The Daleks' Master Plan' and is part of that same story.

+STORY LINK

'The Daleks' Master Plan' follows directly on from 'Mission To The Unknown' in terms of the events taking place on Kembel, but from 'The Myth Makers' in terms of the TARDIS crew: Steven has been injured during the battle at Troy, and Katarina has joined the TARDIS crew and is still tending to his injuries, while the Doctor searches for a safe place to land.

DALEK LINK - 'MISSION TO THE UKNOWN'

As covered under DALEK HISTORY, 'Mission To The Unknown' is the tenth Dalek appearance. Since the end of the Dalek wars and the events of 'Death To The Daleks', the Daleks have left Earth's galaxy and turned their attention towards the Constellation of Miros and the ninth galactic system (where Spiridon is, see 'Planet Of The Daleks'). The Black Dalek on Kembel is presumably the same Dalek Supreme as seen in 'Planet Of The Daleks'.

DALEK LINK - 'THE DALEKS' MASTER PLAN'

As covered under DALEK HISTORY, this is the Daleks' eleventh appearance. Since the events of 'Mission To The Unknown', several months earlier, the Daleks have continued their alliance with the powers of the ten outer galaxies to destroy Earth's galaxy. The Time Destructor is nearly ready. Of note, the alien delegates who appear in this story look somewhat different from those in 'Mission To The Unknown'. This could be because the representatives are not actually the same. There is a gap of several months between the events of 'Mission To The Unknown' and 'The Daleks' Master Plan', and in that time the original representatives of the planets Gearon, Trantis, Malpha and Beaus (and possibly the others) have been replaced by their successors. Alternatively, the delegates who are now absent, Sentreal and Warrien, might have fallen out with the Daleks and elected not to return to Kembel for the second alliance meeting.

- Zephon says that Earth's solar system 'is nothing more than a part, however influential, of one galaxy'. He also says 'the solar system is exceptional. In its power lies influence far outside its own sphere'. The fact that the planet Desperus is known as 'the penal planet of the solar system' and that it is not a planet anywhere near to Earth (in fact it is closer to Kembel) supports that in the year 4000 AD the term 'the solar system' applies to a greater sector of the galaxy than just Earth's own solar system.

- The Monk has recently repaired his TARDIS and left 1066 where he was marooned at the end of 'The Time Meddler'. On regaining his freedom, the Monk's ultimate goal is revenge against the Doctor. The Monk knows of the Daleks 'by reputation'. The Doctor steals the Monk's guidance circuit, which causes the Monk to become stranded on an icy world. The Doctor has not encountered the Monk again (he is not the Master), so it is likely that he became trapped on the ice planet forever.

- The Doctor appears to age from the effects of the Time Destructor. Given that he appears normal again once the machine has been put into reverse mode, we can assume that the Doctor is returned to his previous age. Given that Sara's time stream is not reversed also, this is probably due to the fact that the Doctor is a Time Lord, and is therefore immune to massive time shifts (see THE DOCTOR'S AGE).

- In terms of the Doctor's apparent 'breaking of the fourth wall' when he looks to the camera and wishes 'a happy Christmas to all of you at home', this is not the only time the Doctor 'acknowledges' the TV viewers. He looks directly to camera in 'The Chase', 'The Smugglers', 'Inferno', 'Image Of The Fendahl', 'The Leisure Hive', 'Logopolis', 'Kinda', 'The Caves Of Androzani', and 'Revelation Of The Daleks'. He also speaks directly to the camera in: 'The Face Of Evil', 'Underworld', 'The Invasion Of Time' (three times), and 'Remembrance Of The Daleks', while in 'The Deadly Assassin' and 'Doctor Who (The TV Movie)' he actually narrates part of the story. Other characters also look or talk directly to camera: Tlotoxl ('The Aztecs'); Ian Chesterton ('The Crusade'); Ben and Polly ('The Smugglers'); a Cyberman ('The Tenth Planet'); Alex MacIntosh ('Day Of The Daleks'); the Master ('The Sea Devils'); Eldrad ('The Hand Of Fear'); the Graff Vynda K ('The Ribos Operation'); Vivien Fay ('The Stones Of Blood'); Count Scarlioni ('City Of Death'); Wrack ('Enlightenment'); Morgus ('The Caves Of Androzani'); a Cryon ('Attack Of The Cybermen');

the Valeyard ('The Trial Of A Time Lord'); Mags ('The Greatest Show In The Galaxy'); and Grace Holloway ('Doctor Who (The TV Movie)'). Even the unseen singer in 'The Gunfighters' narrates part of the story for the viewers. In all of these cases it is purely for dramatic reasons as opposed to any other reason. So, in terms of the Doctor's Christmas greeting, we could simply say that he is thinking of Ian and Barbara, who would be celebrating Christmas in London in 1965, as this would be their first since returning home in the October of that same year (see 'The Chase').

LANGUAGE

The Daleks and their alien allies must speak English because Marc Cory overhears their invasion plans.

The members of the Alliance Council are all able to converse in the same language. The Daleks know the names of the planets Desperus and Mira despite never having been there before. The Daleks are able to converse with Chen, the Doctor, the Monk, Sara and Steven. It is clear the Egyptians do not understand English, or else 'the Gods would speak words we understood', so when they speak with Steven and Sara the Time Lord 'gift' must be in application. The Daleks use an odd method of giving measurements, by actually 'translating' it into Earth terms when they speak, i.e. 'in four Earth minutes', 'one Earth hour', and 'seven Earth miles'.

TIMELINE DATES – 'MISSION TO THE UNKNOWN'

4000

Although the Daleks have been inactive in Earth's galaxy for '500 years', Lowery and Cory know of them, and that 'the Daleks invaded Earth a thousand years ago'. This appears to be a reference to the events of 'The Dalek Invasion Of Earth', which would set 'Mission To The Unknown' around 3164. However, 'Mission To The Unknown' is a direct prequel to 'The Daleks' Master Plan', which is set in 4000. 'Mission To The Unknown' must be set only a few months prior to 'The Daleks' Master Plan' (on the basis that Cory's relatively recently decomposed remains are found by the Doctor). Of course, it could be late 3999, but I have selected 4000 as the date.

Cory tells Lowery that the freighter that spotted the Dalek ship passed Kembel 'about a week ago'.

3000

Lowery says 'the Daleks invaded Earth a thousand years ago', which Cory confirms. This cannot be a reference to 'The Dalek Invasion Of Earth', because that was over

1800 years ago, in 2164. In that earlier story the Daleks actually occupied Earth for ten years. As covered under DALEK HISTORY, it would appear that the Daleks invaded Earth a second time, in 3000, presumably during the Dalek wars (see 'Death To The Daleks').

3500 ▨ ▨ ▨ ▨ ▨ ▨ ▨ ▨ ▨ ▨ ▨ ▨ ▨ ▨

Cory tells Lowery that the Daleks 'haven't been active in our galaxy for some time now … in the last 500 years they've gained control of over 70 planets in the ninth galactic system and over 40 more in the Constellation of Miros', both regions being 'millions of light years from our galaxy'. That Earth's galaxy is the target of the Daleks shows that Kembel could be in another galaxy (the galaxy where Mira is located is close to Kembel), however given that the aliens at the conference are from the 'outer galaxies', it seems more than likely that Earth, Skaro and Kembel are all in the same galaxy. (This is a good example of poor astrophysics appearing in *Doctor Who*.)

▨ TIMELINE DATES – 'THE DALEKS' MASTER PLAN' ▨

4000 ▸ ▨ ▨ ▨ ▨ ▨ ▨ ▨ ▨ ▨ ▨ ▨ ▨ ▨

Mavic Chen and Bret Vyon both mention that the year is 'four thousand'. This time zone covers all the sequences set on Kembel, Desperus, Earth and Mira. The Doctor has been to Mira before because he knows all about the Visians.

1965, December 25 ▸ ▨ ▨ ▨ ▨ ▨ ▨ ▨ ▨ ▨ ▨ ▨

One of the policemen says it is 'Christmas Day'. The full date apparently appears on a calendar at the police station, but this cannot be confirmed. What little visual reference that does still exist, however, clearly sets it contemporary to the mid-1960s.

1929 ▸ ▨ ▨ ▨ ▨ ▨ ▨ ▨ ▨ ▨ ▨ ▨ ▨ ▨

There is no date given for the Hollywood section of the adventure. The Arab film in production is a sound picture (a 'talkie'), so it must be after 1927 when, in our history, the first talking picture was released (Al Jolson's *The Jazz Singer* opened on 6 October 1927). There is still a mix of old and new, particularly with the appearances of silent stars such as Charlie Chaplin and a Keystone Cops-like chase. The clown appears to be Bing Crosby, who didn't rise to fame until after 1930 (when he made the film *King of Jazz*). Therefore, I have chosen 1929.

1965 (summer) ▸ ▨ ▨ ▨ ▨ ▨ ▨ ▨ ▨ ▨ ▨ ▨

The TARDIS's materialisation on the cricket pitch is difficult to place without the visual element from the missing episode. If the match were being played at the Oval in London [as suggested in the script], then it would be summer; cricket is a summer sport. We are told that the TARDIS is on the wicket for 'two and a half minutes'. There are only 'forty two and a half minutes' remaining in the match.

???? ∗ ▨ ▨ ▨ ▨ ▨ ▨ ▨ ▨ ▨ ▨ ▨ ▨ ▨
The Monk names the planet as Tigus, a planet that the Doctor describes as being 'a new planet … cooling down'. It is impossible to accurately set this segment. Tigus is in a galaxy known to the Doctor for having peculiar solar properties (see 'The Web Planet'), so it is not Earth's galaxy.

1965, December 31 – 1966, January 1 ∗ ▨ ▨ ▨ ▨ ▨ ▨ ▨
Before they dispatch their own time machine, the Daleks state the location of the TARDIS is 'Planet Earth; London; One-Nine-Six-Six' (i.e. 1966). Although we are lacking the visual elements from this segment to verify the time of the TARDIS's actual arrival, Big Ben is heard to chime, heralding the arrival of the New Year when the ship is parked in Trafalgar Square. From the Daleks' specification as to the year in which the TARDIS is currently located, it could be that the ship landed on Earth before midnight, which indicates that the reference to '1966' could equally refer to 31 December or 1 January, setting the New Year period as either 1965 / 1966 or 1966 /1967. On the basis that the previous Christmas sequence is set in 1965, I have also set this segment in 1965/1966.

2635 BC ∗ ▨ ▨ ▨ ▨ ▨ ▨ ▨ ▨ ▨ ▨ ▨ ▨ ▨
It is difficult to establish a precise date for the Egyptian segment. One of the Pharaohs has died and a tomb within a pyramid is being prepared (the tools for construction are still on site, so it is still under construction, or has at least been recently finished). In our history it was during the Fourth Dynasty that the largest pyramids at Giza were built, around 2680 BC to 2560 BC (different scholars and historians give varied ranges of dates, but the most common is that they are around 4600 years old). By applying a Century Factor from the year of production (1965), we get 2635, which is close to 2620 BC, being the half-way mark between 2680 BC and 2560 BC (see also 'City Of Death').

Oddly, the name of one of the Egyptians is historically inaccurate: Hyksos was in fact the name of a barbaric race that overran Egypt around 1680 BC to 1580 BC.

1900, May 17 ∗ ▨ ▨ ▨ ▨ ▨ ▨ ▨ ▨ ▨ ▨ ▨ ▨
The date in our history of the Relief of Mafeking, the siege of a town in Transvaal by

the Boers. The siege began on 13 October 1899. (See also 'The Invasion Of Time' and 'The Unicorn And The Wasp')

????, December 25 ⁺ ▨ ▨ ▨ ▨ ▨ ▨ ▨ ▨ ▨ ▨

In Episode 7 the Doctor gives a toast in order to celebrate Christmas. The Doctor is therefore clearly familiar with Christmas and the traditions associated with it, so he must have been on Earth during the festive season before. Given the Doctor's apparent disdain for the twentieth century in '100,000 BC' ('I tolerate this century, but I don't enjoy it'), it would appear that he experienced Christmas in an earlier century, possibly in eighteenth century France during his favourite period in the history of Earth? When the Doctor acknowledges the people 'at home' (see Observations), he is probably speaking of Ian and Barbara.

3950 ▨ ▨ ▨ ▨ ▨ ▨ ▨ ▨ ▨ ▨ ▨ ▨

Chen says 'it's taken 50 Earth years to acquire' the taranium from Uranus. He is the Daleks' 'most recent ally', but it is clear without doubt that Chen ordered the mining; he says 'why should I arrange that 50 years' be spent mining the taranium exclusively for the Daleks' Time Destructor. For this to be the case then, assuming Chen is human (his name and oriental features suggest he is Asian), he must be well over 70 years old (perhaps he is using spectrox? – see 'The Caves Of Androzani').

3975 ▨ ▨ ▨ ▨ ▨ ▨ ▨ ▨ ▨ ▨ ▨ ▨

Chen mentions the signing of the Non-Aggression Pact and the year during his TV speech.

3990
3995
3998 ▨ ▨ ▨ ▨ ▨ ▨ ▨ ▨ ▨ ▨ ▨

Lizan gives these dates as she briefs Karlton on Vyon's background.

▨▨▨ DURATION – 'MISSION TO THE UNKNOWN' ▨▨▨

⇨ **Day One (Ep1)** ▨ ▨ ▨ ▨ ▨ ▨ ▨ ▨ ▨ ▨ ▨

It is day on Kembel in the brief scene seen at the end of Galaxy 4. That sequence leads directly into the opening scene of 'Mission To The Unknown'. The first of the Dalek allies arrives after night has fallen. The conference itself 'will begin at first sun' the following day, although this is not seen on-screen.

DURATION – 'THE DALEKS' MASTER PLAN'

Episodes 1 to 6 all take place in the same time zone (4000 AD), but in different locations: Kembel, Earth, Desperus and the planet Mira. Three days pass on Kembel (in Eps1-2/ 6, 8 / 11, 12). Therefore the total duration of the adventure for the TARDIS crew is three days.

⇨ **Day One (Kembel) (Ep1-2)**
It is night on Kembel in the opening scenes.

⇨ **Day Two (Kembel) (Ep6/8)**
It is day when the Doctor, Steven and Sara return to Kembel in the stolen Dalek ship. Presumably the Dalek time machine is sent after the TARDIS the same day.

⇨ **Day Three? (Kembel) (Ep11-12)**
It is either the continuation of Day Two or now Day Three when the TARDIS returns to Kembel at the end of the adventure. The travellers are there for several hours.

⇨ **Day One (Desperus) (Ep3)**
It is dusk on Desperus. The Doctor and his friends are there for less than an hour.

⇨ **Day One (Earth, 4000) (Ep1)**
It appears to be day in the scenes set on Earth.

⇨ **Day Two? (Earth, 4000) (Ep4-5)**
This is either Day One or Day Two on Earth.

⇨ **Day One (Mira) (Ep5-6)**
It is night on Mira, which is located in a distant but 'strange galaxy'.

(TARDIS) (Ep6)
The TARDIS travels from Kembel to Earth …

⇨ **Day One (25 December 1965) (Ep6-7)**
It is early evening on Christmas Day. The TARDIS is there for about an hour.

(TARDIS) (Ep6)
The TARDIS travels from 1965 to 1929.

⇨ **Day One (1929) (Ep7)** ▨ ▨ ▨ ▨ ▨ ▨ ▨ ▨ ▨ ▨ ▨ ▨

The time travellers are in Hollywood for about half an hour.

(TARDIS) (Ep7) ▨ ▨ ▨ ▨ ▨ ▨ ▨ ▨ ▨ ▨ ▨ ▨

The travellers celebrate Christmas. The Doctor detects another time machine following them.

⇨ **Day One (Earth) (Ep8)** ▨ ▨ ▨ ▨ ▨ ▨ ▨ ▨ ▨ ▨ ▨

The TARDIS is on the cricket pitch for 'two and a half minutes'.

(TARDIS) (Ep8) ▨ ▨ ▨ ▨ ▨ ▨ ▨ ▨ ▨ ▨ ▨ ▨

The Doctor continues to monitor the other time machine.

⇨ **Day One (Tigus) (Ep8)** ▨ ▨ ▨ ▨ ▨ ▨ ▨ ▨ ▨ ▨ ▨

The TARDIS is on Tigus for about half an hour.

(TARDIS) (Ep8) ▨ ▨ ▨ ▨ ▨ ▨ ▨ ▨ ▨ ▨ ▨ ▨

The Doctor discusses the properties of his ring.

⇨ **Day One (1966/1967) (Ep8)** ▨ ▨ ▨ ▨ ▨ ▨ ▨ ▨ ▨ ▨ ▨

The TARDIS lands in Trafalgar Square as the New Year arrives.

⇨ **Day One (Egypt) (Ep9-10)** ▨ ▨ ▨ ▨ ▨ ▨ ▨ ▨ ▨ ▨

The TARDIS arrives in Egypt in the morning (the Monk uses the greeting 'Good morning, my son'). The Monk is given 'one Earth hour' to get the core from the Doctor. Hyksos arrives with his army 'when the sun is above us', which is noon. The TARDIS leaves shortly after.

THE MASSACRE OF ST. BARTHOLOMEW'S EVE

+STORY LINK

Steven does tell his new friends 'I've been in Egypt', possibly in reference to his recent time there with the Doctor and Sara while being pursued by the Daleks.

OBSERVATIONS

- A curious Production Factor is the coincidentally large number of Time Lords who bear an uncanny resemblance to inhabitants of France of the year 1572: in 'The Massacre Of St. Bartholomew's Eve', there are no less than five actors who would later appear in the programme as inhabitants of Gallifrey: Eric Chitty (Preslin, later Engin in 'The Deadly Assassin'); Leonard Sachs (de Coligny, later Borusa in 'Arc Of Infinity'); Chris Tranchell (Roger, is Andred in 'The Invasion Of Time'); Michael Bilton (Toligny, is a Time Lord in 'The Deadly Assassin'); Reginald Jessup (Servant, is Savar in 'The Invasion Of Time'). And there is, of course, William Hartnell (Abbot of Amboise, and the Doctor). The French Revolution is the Doctor's favourite period, and indeed actor Edward Brayshaw appears as Leon in 'The Reign Of Terror' and later as the renegade Time Lord, the War Chief, in 'The War Games'. Also, the robes and hairstyles worn by female Gallifreyan High Councillors (Thalia and Flavia) are very similar to the fashions of these two periods in French history. There is also the fact that the Doctor is attracted to Reinette ('The Girl in the Fireplace').

LANGUAGE

Everybody is speaking French. The Huguenots that Steven befriends recognise that he is English, despite the fact that he should be also speaking French with the aid of the Time Lord 'gift'.

TIMELINE DATES

1572, August 20 – 24 ⁕

Shortly after landing, the Doctor guesses it is 'the middle of the sixteenth century'. It is not until Ep4, when Anne reveals the current date to be 'August 23rd … 1572', that the actual date and year are given. The Doctor clearly knows the history and of the horrific events of the following day, the 24th.

HISTORICAL COMPARISON

The events of this story are based closely upon real events in our history, although the Abbot of Amboise is fictional.

1965, January ⁕

No date is given for Dodo's introduction; however, we do know that it is a weekday because Dodo is on her way home from school. In 'The War Machines', which is set in July 1966, Dodo is excited to see that the Post Office Tower is completed ('It's finished!'), which indicates that she must have joined the Doctor while it was still under construction, which would be from late 1964 (when construction started). In our history the Tower was officially opened on 7 October 1965, giving us an idea of the available period to set this section. In 'The Ark' Dodo has a cold, so we can put the month of her joining the TARDIS crew to be in the winter months over 1964 to 1965. The serial was recorded in January [of 1966], so this is the month I have selected, but with 1965 as the year.

1572, August 19
The royal wedding between Henri and Marguerite was held 'yesterday', being August 19. In our history this marriage actually took place on 18 August.

1572, September 17 – October 3
The Doctor tells Steven that the massacre continued for 'several days in Paris' before spreading to the provinces. The dates here are the dates of the event in our history.

1562, March
The events at Vassy were 'ten years ago'. In our history, the Vassy slaughter occurred in March of 1562.

DURATION

⇨ **Day One (20 August 1572) (Ep1)**
It is 'morning' when the TARDIS lands. Steven stays with Nicholas that night.

⇨ **Day Two (21 August 1572) (Ep2)**
Steven returns to the tavern in the morning. Plans are made to kill the Sea Beggar 'tomorrow'. Steven and Anne spend the night at Preslin's shop.

⇨ **Day Three (22 August 1572) (Ep3)**
Steven wakes at 'dawn'. De Coligny is shot around noon. The Abbot is killed that afternoon. Steven spends the whole of the night hiding from the soldiers.

⇨ **Day Four (23 August 1572) (Ep4)**
Steven returns to Preslin's shop later that afternoon having spent all 'morning' evading the guards. The evening curfew bell has rung when the Doctor returns.

⇨ **Day Five (24 August 1572) (Ep4)** ▨ ▨ ▨ ▨ ▨ ▨ ▨
'It's nearly dawn' when the Doctor and Steven return to the TARDIS and leave.

⇨ **Day One (1964) (Ep4)** ▨ ▨ ▨ ▨ ▨ ▨ ▨ ▨ ▨
The TARDIS stops for only a few minutes in London.

THE ARK

+STORY LINK

Dodo is still unfamiliar with the TARDIS and time travel, so it would seem that she has been on board for only a short while. Since leaving Earth (in 'The Massacre Of St. Bartholomew's Eve') she has had time to rummage in the Doctor's costume store and find a Crusader's outfit.

It is clear that the second landing on the Ark is consecutive to the first, because on their return Dodo says 'we've only been gone a few seconds'.

OBSERVATIONS

- In 'Frontios', the TARDIS issues the warning 'TIME PARAMETERS EXCEEDED' after the ship has drifted just over 10 million years into the future. There is no such warning on the TARDIS's arrival on the Ark for the second time, some 660 years beyond the time in which 'Frontios' is set. (There is also no warning in 'The End Of The World', set five billion years in the future, but since Gallifrey no longer exists in that time zone, the Time Parameter warning no longer applies.) Steven does say 'the TARDIS made the decision' to land on the Ark 700 years later. Later, the Doctor says 'the gravitational bearing must have rectified itself', so perhaps this circuit had failed, enabling the TARDIS to travel beyond its pre-programmed boundary limit. Another possibility is that the circuit is later repaired by the Doctor, or by other Time Lords on one of the Doctor's visits to Gallifrey prior to 'Frontios'.
- It's clear from the events of 'The End Of The World' that the Earth did not actually perish in the sun as seen in 'The Ark', and must have been saved from its fiery destruction. Of course this means that for some of the next several billion years the planet is uninhabited ... Which is not exactly all that impossible since the planet has been uninhabited for hundreds or thousands of years several times before ('The Ark In Space',

'The Sun Makers', 'The Mysterious Planet'). It's even possible that in the five billion years after 'The Ark' and 'Frontios' (while the original humans colonised and created new civilisations on other worlds such as Refusis II and 'Frontios') the planet was inhabited by other life forms that evolved such as Jabe's ancestors.

LANGUAGE

The Guardians still speak English, even ten million years in the future (and despite representing all races and cultures!). The signs on the doors, i.e. 'LAUNCHING BAY', and on the food containers, 'NEW POTATOES' and 'CHICKEN WINGS', are in English. The language is the same 700 years later. The Monoids speak English, presumably having been taught by the Guardians. Even the sole Refusian speaks the language. The Doctor criticises Dodo's use of slang, such as 'fab', and tells her, 'Once this crisis is over I am going to teach you English'.

TIMELINE DATES

10,000,000 • (Fifty-Seventh Segment)

It is Steven who first gives an indication of the time they are in. On learning that the Earth is about to be destroyed he says 'then we must have journeyed forward millions of years'. The Doctor also comments on the distance that the TARDIS has travelled: 'Good gracious! We must have jumped at least ten million years'. Later, Venussa refers to the TARDIS crew as having come from 'millions of years ago. They've travelled through time'. These references all place 'The Ark' as being millions of years in the future. It is not clear how the Doctor is able to calculate the period as ten million years on learning that they were in the Fifty-Seventh Segment of time (Rhos does refer to a past age as 'long ago as the twentieth century', so the Guardians are still familiar with the old form of dating), but the Doctor does recognise what the Ark is ('I know where I am now! This is a spaceship'), so it could be that he is already aware of the Earth's ultimate fate.

The Commander establishes that 'Nero, the Trojan wars, the Daleks … all that happened in the First Segment of Time'. Later, Zentos refers to the current segment as being 'the Fifty-Seventh Segment of Earth life'. The Commander comments that 'the Earth also is dying. We have left it for the last time'. This suggests that there have been many times when humanity has 'left' the Earth. In terms of later continuity, the first time could have been the solar flare crisis of 5001 (see 'The Ark In Space', 'The Sontaran Experiment'), and the second is probably the event in 20,000, when Earth is abandoned with the assistance of the Usurians (see 'The Sun Makers'). From this we can assume that Earth is abandoned a further 54 times in its future history, with 'the last time' being the 57th time, as seen in 'The Ark'.

Alternatively, the segments could refer to some other form of measurement. With the Fifty-Seventh Segment being some ten million years in the future, each segment would be roughly 175,438 years long.

It is not clear how far away from Earth the Ark is at the beginning of the story. The feet of the statue are complete, and yet the crew are close enough to view Earth plunging into the sun on their scanners. However, we can be certain that these Guardians were born on Earth, so probably no more than a year has passed since the Ark was launched. (See also 'The End Of The World', in which the Earth does finally succumb to destruction.)

10,000,700 ⟶ ▨ ▨ ▨ ▨ ▨ ▨ ▨ ▨ ▨ ▨ ▨ ▨ ▨
It is stated several times that the journey to Refusis II would take '700 years'. The Commander says 'in approximately 700 years time', and later to the Doctor, 'using your measurement of time, ah, 700 years'. And despite a difference of 700 years, it is curious to note that the descendants of the original Guardians wear the same clothes as their ancestors!

10,000,000 ⟶ ▨ ▨ ▨ ▨ ▨ ▨ ▨ ▨ ▨ ▨ ▨ ▨ ▨
As mentioned above, the Doctor may have been in this time zone before, probably when he encountered the Toymaker for the first time (see 'The Celestial Toymaker').

10,000,600 ▨ ▨ ▨ ▨ ▨ ▨ ▨ ▨ ▨ ▨ ▨ ▨ ▨
It is not clear when the Monoids took control of the Ark. Number One speaks of the 'recent revolution', but how recent is 'recent'? The best clue lies with the statue. It is said that it would take 700 years to complete the statue. Given that the bomb is in the Monoid head, we can establish that the Monoids took over before the head was made. The head is roughly 1/7th of the statue's height. It therefore took 600 years to build up to the neck, so we can set the revolution 100 years before planet-fall. As Number One himself planted the bomb in the head, it would seem that the Monoids have a longer life span than the humans, although the bomb could have been placed after the head was finished, and not necessarily during its construction.

Tenth Segment Of Time ▨ ▨ ▨ ▨ ▨ ▨ ▨ ▨ ▨ ▨
Rhos refers to 'the Primal Wars of the Tenth Segment'.

Twenty-Seventh Segment Of Time ▨ ▨ ▨ ▨ ▨ ▨ ▨ ▨

The Commander says 'experiments to pass through the fourth dimension were undertaken in the Twenty-Seventh Segment of time. They were unsuccessful'. As noted under THE N-SPACE UNIVERSE, the first humans to experiment with time are Maxtible and Waterfield ('The Evil Of The Daleks'). In terms of Earth history, Magnus Greel is one of the last, the Zygma Beam of the year 5000 proving to be unreliable ('The Talons Of Weng-Chiang'). It is clear from this comment in 'The Ark' that humans never successfully master time travel of any kind, even millions of years in the future.

9,999,950 ▨ ▨ ▨ ▨ ▨ ▨ ▨ ▨ ▨ ▨ ▨ ▨ ▨ ▨

The Commander says 'the origin of the Monoids is obscure. They came to Earth many years ago', say 50.

DURATION

⇨ **Day One (Ep1-2)** ▨ ▨ ▨ ▨ ▨ ▨ ▨ ▨ ▨ ▨
The travellers are on the Ark for at least one day.

⇨ **Day One (Ep2-4)** ▨ ▨ ▨ ▨ ▨ ▨ ▨ ▨ ▨ ▨
700 years later: The bomb is due to go off 'in 12 hours', so at least one day elapses while in this time zone.

THE CELESTIAL TOYMAKER

+STORY LINK

At the end of 'The Ark' the Doctor sneezes, and Dodo says, 'Oh, Doctor, don't say you're catching a cold now', and then he disappears. Dodo wonders if it is the work of the Refusians. Therefore, despite the fade-to-black between the TARDIS's departure from the Ark and its arrival in the Toyroom, 'The Ark' and 'The Celestial Toymaker' are clearly consecutive.

OBSERVATIONS

- It is clear that the seven other people within the Toyroom are poor unfortunate travellers who lost the Toymaker's games and have become trapped in his domain. Given the likely setting of the story, one wonders where these 'travellers' came from. Possibly one of Earth's colonies, of the many who fled from the destruction of Earth (as in 'The Ark' and 'Frontios').

- The Doctor says, 'The Toymaker is immortal. He's lasted for thousands of years'. It is unlikely that the Toymaker is an Eternal, because in 'Enlightenment' the Doctor claims not to know of those beings.

LANGUAGE

All the signs and markers seen during the various Earth games are in English. The ingredients in Mrs Wiggs's kitchen are all labelled in English.

TIMELINE DATES

<<10,000,700>>

The TARDIS travels from 10,000,700 ('The Ark') to 1881 ('The Gunfighters'), so it is possible that the Toyroom is located at some time between these two dates.

Of the Toymaker's victims the Hearts, the clowns, the dolls, and Cyril are all from the Victorian era so the Toyroom could be located in this period: Cyril is akin to Frank Richards' literary character Billy Bunter, whose adventures first appeared in 1908.

In the case of Sgt Rugg, his period would be around 1815; Rugg mentions 'the Iron Duke', being the Duke of Wellington who defeated Napoleon at Waterloo. However, the presence of a tub of margarine in Mrs Wiggs' kitchen, where Rugg is located, indicates the time frame is no earlier than 1873 (when margarine was officially patented). However, the robot in the Toyroom suggests a 'future' time period.

It is entirely possible that the Toyroom exists in the far distant future, around the same time period as 'The Ark': the Toymaker tells the Doctor that since their last meeting he hoped that the Doctor's dabbling in his 'researches round the Universe had not dulled' him. This suggests that their previous meeting was soon after the Doctor left Gallifrey. The Toymaker then says he brought the Doctor to the Toyroom because he needs him; the Toymaker is bored and he wants someone on the same intellectual level to become his 'perpetual opponent' with whom to play his games. The Doctor deduces that the Toymaker draws his opponents into his domain 'like a spider does to flies'. However, in the case of the Doctor, the Toymaker deliberately sought him out ('You know, I think I was meant to come here,' says the Doctor on arriving). Given the extent of the Toymaker's powers, one is given to wonder why he hadn't done this to the Doctor earlier. Therefore we can conclude that the Toymaker can only draw in the TARDIS when it is in the time zone that the Toyroom is located. Given that the time period of 'The Ark' is in the far distant future, which is not a time period that the Doctor has visited (on-screen) before or since (bar 'Frontios'), then it is likely that the Toyroom exists in the region of the 57th Segment of Time. As covered under 'The Ark', it would seem that the Doctor certainly has been to that time zone before, which was when he learned of the fate of the Earth, and when he most likely encountered the Toymaker for the first time. And this might also explain why after leaving the Ark the Doctor fears they are under some form of attack – he might have suspected that on returning to this segment of time he would once again be in the domain of the Toymaker …

On these grounds I have set 'The Celestial Toymaker' in the same period as 'The Ark', but at the end of the Ark's journey to Refusis. This means that for the Toymaker, around 700 years have passed since his previous encounter with the Doctor.

1964

Dodo sees an image of herself on the Toymaker's memory window: 'That's me, the day my mother died'. She met the Doctor in January 1965 (see 'The Massacre Of St. Bartholomew's Eve'), and she lives with her Great Aunt, so on the basis that Dodo appears to be no younger in the flashback than she is now, her mother probably died the previous year.

<<10,000,000>> ›

The Doctor has encountered the Toymaker previously, who says 'I've been waiting for you a long time' (to return). Given that the Toymaker recognises the Doctor (he refers to him as 'elderly') and is familiar with the TARDIS and how it works (he mentions how he was able to make the scanner go blank) we can assume that the previous meeting is recent in terms of the Doctor's life stream, so it was probably soon after he left Gallifrey. As noted above, the Toyroom seems to be located in the 57th Segment of Time, so the Doctor's first meeting with the Toymaker was probably around 10,000,000. The Doctor did not 'stay long enough for a game' (the Doctor recognises the Trilogic Game), so the Toyroom, which the Doctor also recognises, was not destroyed. Therefore it is the same domain the Toymaker had before. The Doctor was able to leave unscathed, presumably before the Toymaker made him intangible thus rendering him unable to operate the TARDIS controls.

DURATION

(TARDIS) (Ep1)

The TARDIS travels for a while before arriving at the Toyroom.

⇨ **Day One (Ep1-4)** ▨ ▨ ▨ ▨ ▨ ▨ ▨ ▨ ▨ ▨ ▨ ▨

There are no breaks during this story, with the effect that the entire adventure has the duration of the actual serial, no more than 90 minutes (screen-time).

THE GUNFIGHTERS

+STORY LINK

'The Gunfighters' follows directly on from 'The Celestial Toymaker': the cause of the Doctor's sudden collapse at the end of 'The Celestial Toymaker' is revealed to be acute toothache caused by the Doctor biting into one of Cyril's sweets. Also, both Steven and Dodo are wearing the same outfits from 'The Celestial Toymaker' at the beginning of the new serial.

LANGUAGE

Despite the Time Lord 'gift', Steven and Dodo still adopt corny Hollywood American accents, whereas the Doctor doesn't.

TIMELINE DATES

1881, October 24 – 26 • ▨ ▨ ▨ ▨ ▨ ▨ ▨ ▨ ▨ ▨

The famous shootout at the OK Corral is recorded in our history as being on 26 October 1881 so; taking into account the three days duration, the historical date has been applied. Holliday arrived only just 'this mornin'' on the first day.

HISTORICAL COMPARISON

The events seen in 'The Gunfighters' do not correlate with any of the recorded facts in our history. Wyatt Earp was not Marshal of Tombstone, but a local gambler. Bat Masterson and Doc Holliday were both dealers at his casino. The Sheriff of Tombstone was one John Behan, who disliked the Earps. Behan does not feature in 'The Gunfighters'. There were only three Clanton boys: Ike, Billy and Phineas. Reuben Clanton did not exist, and as such, there was no feud between the Clantons and Holliday, who had killed poor Reuben in 'The Gunfighters'. Likewise, Wyatt's brother Warren Earp is a figment of writer Donald Cotton's imagination. The McLaury brothers, Frank and Tom, neither of whom are even mentioned in this serial, assisted the Clantons. After the shootout, one of the McLaurys was dead, the other and Billy Clanton only injured. John Ringo did exist, but was not in Tombstone until he was sent to drive out the Earps and Holliday under Behan's orders months later. As for Tombstone itself, records show it was a populous and prosperous town, not a small backwater place with only a few inhabitants as shown in this serial.

1879 ■ ■ ■ ■ ■ ■ ■ ■ ■ ■ ■ ■ ■
Johnny Ringo says he followed Kate and Holliday 'for nigh on two years'.

1881, October ■ ■ ■ ■ ■ ■ ■ ■ ■ ■ ■ ■
The pianist at the Last Chance Saloon was 'shot last week'.

c1933 ᛜ ■ ■ ■ ■ ■ ■ ■ ■ ■ ■ ■ ■
When he sees Steven in his new Western garb, the Doctor comments: 'And why you'd want to dress up like Tom Mix, I'll never know'. Thomas Mix (6 January 1880 to 12 October 1940) started acting in silent films in 1910, and became famous for rodeo stunts and fancy-dress cowboy costumes during the late 1920s / early 1930s. He gave up acting when sound films became popular, and started Tom Mix's Circus and Wild West Show in 1933. The Doctor could have heard of Mix at any time during his stay in 1963, or possibly when he visited Hollywood in 'The Daleks' Master Plan'. It is even possible that he has met the man.

DURATION

⇨ **Day One (24 October) (Ep1-3)** ■ ■ ■ ■ ■ ■ ■ ■
It is late afternoon when the TARDIS lands (Doc Holliday bids Wyatt Earp a 'Good afternoon'). Ringo shoots Charlie that night.

⇨ **Day Two (25 October) (Ep3-4)** ■ ■ ■ ■ ■ ■ ■ ■
The next morning Dodo goes to see Holliday about 'taking me back to my friends today'. Steven and the Doctor find Charlie's body as they come down for 'breakfast'. The rest of this day passes quickly on-screen. It is night when Warren is shot.

⇨ **Day Three (26 October) (Ep4)** ■ ■ ■ ■ ■ ■ ■ ■
The Doctor goes to see the Clantons when there is still 'only about two hours to sun-up' which is when the shootout is due to take place. After the gunfight the travellers leave, presumably later the same day.

THE SAVAGES

There is a fade-to-black after the TARDIS leaves Tombstone, before its landing on the savage planet at the end of 'The Gunfighters', so 'The Savages' does not necessarily follow 'The Gunfighters' consecutively. As covered in 'The War Machines', Dodo has been with the Doctor for many months. Most of this time would have passed between 'The Gunfighters' and 'The Savages'. (In terms of story duration, Steven has been with the Doctor for only 25 days, but given the gap noted above, this total could be more like several months.)

OBSERVATIONS

- After he has survived the transference the Doctor says 'it was as though all my powers were being sapped'. Given his weakened state, this experience may have prematurely triggered the Doctor's regenerative cycle, which took a few days to take effect as seen in 'The Tenth Planet'.
- The Elders obviously have had no difficulty plotting the Doctor's journeys through time and space, so one must ask why is it that the Time Lords were never able to track the Doctor down? (But as is noted under 'The War Games', it is clear that the Time Lords were tracking the Doctor; they just didn't act upon it.)

LANGUAGE

The Elders and the Savages speak the same language. Jano takes on the Doctor's mannerisms and speech patterns following the in-transference, but he still speaks in his own language and not in Gallifreyan.

TIMELINE DATES

The Future ◆ ▨ ▨ ▨ ▨ ▨ ▨ ▨ ▨ ▨ ▨ ▨ ▨ ▨

At the end of 'The Gunfighters', the Doctor announces that they are 'in the future. Very much in the future. We've now reached the distant horizon of an age … an age of peace and prosperity'.

The Doctor refers to the Savages as being 'human beings' on several occasions. In fact, on one occasion he says 'They are men. Human beings. Like you and me'. This suggests that the planet is an Earth colony (Jano even speaks of 'Mankind' when referring to his people). However, as covered under THE N-SPACE UNIVERSE, the term 'human' is simply a reference to humanoids.

Edal tells the Doctor that the Elders 'have been plotting the course of your space time ship for many light years. They estimated your arrival some time ago'. Later, Jano says 'We have all known about you for a long time. Look, we have charted your voyages from galaxy to galaxy and from age to age' / 'Doctor, for many light years we looked forward to your arrival on this planet'. Jano shows the Doctor a circular chart that appears to represent the Universe. The chart is covered in a series of lines, which probably represent the Doctor's journeys. It is not clear if the Elders have been plotting the journeys of just the first Doctor, or whether they have in fact been charting the travels of the TARDIS throughout of all the Doctor's incarnations.

On the basis that there is no specific date to use, instead of setting 'The Savages' in ????, I have placed it in the inconclusive date of 'The Future'.

DURATION

⇨ **Day One (Ep1-4)**

Edal refers to the arrival of the strangers as being 'this morning'. Jano announces that 'It is getting dark' in Ep4, which indicates that the story takes place over one day.

THE WAR MACHINES

+STORY LINK

Dodo is wearing the same dress she has on in 'The Savages', and she says that Steven 'would have liked it here [in London]', so it is more than likely that 'The Savages' and 'The War Machines' are consecutive.

Dodo is happy to be back in London: 'It seems ages ago since I left'. The Doctor, however, says he doesn't think it's been 'all that long.' In terms of direct story durations, Dodo has been with the Doctor for only about 10 days, but given that she left in January 1965 (see 'The Massacre Of St. Bartholomew's Eve'), on the basis that the passage of time could be relative for her, then she would have to have been with the Doctor for 18 months, however this is more likely to be only several months (see THE DOCTOR'S AGE).

The Doctor comments that he has taken her 'all the way around the world, through space and time'. The only other place on Earth she visits on-screen is America ('The

Gunfighters'), so it would appear that there are many more untelevised adventures on Earth. Most of this time would have passed between 'The Gunfighters' and 'The Savages'. Dodo has never encountered the Daleks.

On the second day of the story the Doctor is looking forward to Dodo showing him around London. Despite his having spent five months in the Shoreditch area (see '100,000 BC'), the Doctor can't have seen much of the city, although he does know about the Post Office Tower ('So that's it'), so he must have been in London at some other point when the Tower was still under construction, or he simply never ventured far from Shoreditch and into central London.

OBSERVATIONS

- Brett says that WOTAN is 'ten years ahead of its time'. WOTAN is probably a precursor to BOSS (see 'The Green Death'), and the K1 robot ('Robot').
- Soon after arriving in London, the Doctor experiences the strange feeling he gets whenever the Daleks are around. As it so happens, there are Daleks in London at the time that this story takes place – see 'The Evil Of The Daleks'.

TIMELINE DATES

1966, July 14 – 20

Sir Charles says 'C-Day – that's Computer Day – will be next Monday, July 16th. That is in four days' time.' No year is given in the serial but with 16 July falling on a Monday, the year is 1962, 1973 or 1979. This would suggest that the intention was to set the serial in the near-future.

However, the year which Ben and Polly come from is given as '1966' in the following story, 'The Smugglers', as well as in 'The Tenth Planet', 'The Power Of The Daleks', 'The Underwater Menace' and 'The Moonbase', while in 'The Faceless Ones' Ben says 'July the Twentieth, 1966 is when it all began. We're back to when it all started.' This date could be either the date on which Ben and Polly first met the Doctor, or the date on which they left in the TARDIS. The latter is the most likely.

In order to reconcile 'The Faceless Ones' with 'The War Machines', it is necessary to re-interpret Sir Charles' comment. It is more likely that he got the date wrong than the day of the week, so we can accept that 'Monday' is correct, but that 'July the Sixteenth' is wrong. On the basis that 1966 is the correct year, we can make C-Day to be 'next Monday', July the Eighteenth. The story therefore starts four days prior to C-Day, 14 July. The duration is three consecutive days plus the day when the TARDIS leaves London. As given in 'The Faceless Ones', that day is 20 July, so a further four days passes between WOTAN's destruction and the Doctor's departure.

The Doctor's abductions in 'The Three Doctors' and 'The Five Doctors' most likely take place during this four-day period. Also, the Doctor probably visited the Shoreditch area to check up on the Hand of Omega (see 'Remembrance Of The Daleks'), and possibly to see Ian and Barbara. Following the adventures in 'The Three Doctors' and 'The Five Doctors', the Doctor goes back to the TARDIS to wait for Dodo.

1966, January
The tramp has been in prison 'for the last six months'.

1966, July 7
Polly first met Ben 'last week' at the 'Inferno' nightclub.

DURATION

⇨ **Day One (14 July) (Ep1-2)**
The TARDIS lands during the day. The press meeting takes place that 'evening'. Polly takes Dodo to the hottest 'night spot' in town.

⇨ **Day Two (15 July) (Ep2-3)**
The tramp is killed shortly after 3.00 am. Ben and Polly make a date for lunch but she fails to show. 'Four hours' after he leaves for the warehouse Ben escapes with the news that the War Machines will attack at 'noon tomorrow'.

⇨ **Day Three (16 July) (Ep3-4)**
After a Cabinet meeting 'this morning' the army attacks the warehouse. The re-programmed War Machine attacks WOTAN at 11.49 am, 11 minutes before WOTAN is due to give the 'noon' attack order.

🕐 **Day Four (17 July) to Day Six (19 July) (Ep4)**
These three days pass off-screen. It is during the 'missing' three days between Day Three and Day Seven that I believe the Doctor is taken out of his time stream by the Time Lords in 'The Three Doctors', and then later time scooped by Borusa in 'The Five Doctors' (see 'The Three Doctors' below).

⇨ **Day Seven (20 July) (Ep4)**
Four days later the Doctor leaves with Ben and Polly.

THE THREE DOCTORS

+STORY LINK

As covered above, I believe the Time Lords abducted the Doctor during the events of 'The War Machines'.

The first Doctor is seen in a garden. The Time Lords either obtain this image from the TARDIS memory banks in 'The War Games', or as noted in that story, the Time Lords have in fact been observing the Doctor's travels ever since he left Gallifrey.

Given his manner of dress we can assume that the first Doctor is time scooped by the Time Lords during his TV adventures, however the possibility does exist that he comes from a point in his time stream after he had left Gallifrey but before the events in '100,000 BC'. Indeed, the fact that the first Doctor looks different could be taken as a pointer that the Doctor is from a different point in his life than the TV adventures.

If we select a point from within his TV adventures, then there are only a few points in which it would be possible for the Doctor to be scooped without 'interrupting' on-screen events: it could have been during the Doctor's 'absence' in 'The Keys Of Marinus', during the weeks in Italy in 'The Romans' (prior to the Doctor changing into period costume), or during the non-consecutive gaps between 'Planet Of Giants' and 'The Dalek Invasion Of Earth', and 'The Gunfighters' and 'The Savages'.

As covered under GALLIFREY HISTORY it is most likely that the Time Lords remove the Doctor from a point in his time stream closest to his regeneration, because to send a transportation unit further back in time to an earlier point in the Doctor's time stream would be a needless waste of a 'temporal energy' when they could just grab him from a later time. The most likely point is during the four days he spends in London at the end of 'The War Machines', being 17 – 20 July 1966. We see him in a garden (possibly the one at Sir Charles Summers' country house?), and no doubt he is returned to this point again by the Time Lords. Because he remembers the second Doctor in 'The Five Doctors' ('the little fellow'), it would appear that the future Time Lords forgot to erase his memory of 'The Three Doctors' adventure.

- Refer to 'The Three Doctors' under the third Doctor's stories for more details on this adventure.

TIMELINE DATES

1966, July (17 – 19) ∗

The Doctor is taken from the garden by the Time Lords (of GRT 1666) while he is in

London, during 'The War Machines' adventure.

DURATION

⇨ **Day One (Ep1)** ▪ ▪ ▪ ▪ ▪ ▪ ▪ ▪ ▪ ▪ ▪
The Doctor is taken from the garden during the day. (He spends a few hours trapped in the time eddy.)

THE FIVE DOCTORS

+STORY LINK

The first Doctor is seen walking in a large garden, but he looks different to that in the other first Doctor stories. However, since he recognises the Police Box form of the TARDIS and the Dalek, this means that he comes from some point after 'The Dalek Invasion Of Earth', when Susan has left.

Due to the close consecutiveness between stories there are only a few places during which the Doctor could be time scooped. As covered under 'The Three Doctors' above, the most likely place where he would be in a garden alone would be during the four days spent in London at the end of the WOTAN affair, from 17 – 20 July 1966 (see 'The War Machines'). The first Doctor wonders 'what happened to the little fellow' (the second Doctor), which means that this first incarnation remembers the Omega affair (so this is after 'The Three Doctors'). Since the first Doctor is in a garden when he is snatched for that adventure, it is possible that the garden seen in 'The Five Doctors' is the very same one from 'The Three Doctors'. Borusa therefore probably snatches the Doctor only moments after being returned by the Time Lords in 'The Three Doctors'.

After 'The Five Doctors' the Doctor is returned to the garden. His memory is probably altered by the remaining members of the High Council of the Time Lords to remove all recollection of both 'The Three Doctors' and 'The Five Doctors' adventures.

In terms of 'The War Machines' continuity, after being returned to the garden, the Doctor goes back to the TARDIS in London to wait for Dodo, as seen in the closing scene in 'The War Machines'.

- Refer to 'The Five Doctors' under the fifth Doctor's stories for more details on this adventure.

TIMELINE DATES

1966, July (17 – 19) +

The Doctor is time scooped by Borusa (in GRT 1983) while he is in London, during 'The War Machines' adventure; see above.

DURATION

⇨ **Day One**

The Doctor is time scooped by Borusa from the garden during day. (He spends a few hours on Gallifrey.)

THE SMUGGLERS

+STORY LINK

This story takes place immediately after Day Seven of 'The War Machines', with Ben and Polly entering the TARDIS for the first time.

TIMELINE DATES

1672 +

The Doctor establishes the time period to be the 'seventeenth century', based on the period clothes worn by the people in the village. When Ben finds a tombstone marked 1592, Polly reminds him 'this is sixteen hundred and something'. A more accurate date is provided by Pike, who says that in comparison to Avery 'Morgan was a woman'. In our history, Sir Henry Morgan (1635-1688), who became a pirate in 1660, rose to fame for his ravage of Cuba and the Central American coastline, and the eventual sacking of Panama in January 1671. He was arrested in April 1672, but was released and knighted in 1674 by King Charles II (who reigned 1660 – 1685; Blake is a King's Revenue officer). I would say that it is the attack on Panama to which Pike is referring. This places the events of 'The Smugglers' between 1671 and 1688. I would say it was around 1672.

1671, January 18

The date of Morgan's attack on Panama (see above).

DURATION

⇨ **Day One (Ep1)**
It is late afternoon when the TARDIS arrives on Earth. It is getting darker when the travellers arrive at the inn. According to Kewper, they are the only people who have been to the church 'this night'.

⇨ **Day Two (Ep1-4)**
Although there is no break from night to day, the Squire greets Pike and Cherub with 'A good morning, gentlemen … have you breakfasted?' (The break would appear to be in Ep1 between Ben and Polly's arrest by the Squire for Longfoot's murder, and the Doctor's arrival on Pike's ship).

⇨ **Day Three (Ep4)**
Although the sequences are in daylight, the pirates were expected to come ashore 'at two o'clock' the following morning.

THE TENTH PLANET

+STORY LINK

At the end of 'The Smugglers' the Doctor announces that they had arrived at 'the coldest place in the world'. In 'The Tenth Planet' Polly says 'the Doctor was right about this being the coldest place on Earth', which shows that 'The Smugglers' and 'The Tenth Planet' are most probably consecutive.

CYBERMAN LINK

As covered under CYBERMAN HISTORY, this is the Cybermen's second appearance (but chronologically their third visit, when taking into account the Cybermen who time travelled from Telos in 'Attack Of The Cybermen'). The Cybermen in 'The Tenth Planet' are the original versions, without modifications required for different functions (see CYBERMAN DESIGNS). The Cybermen know of the Z Bombs, which is why they have attacked the Snowcap Base; the Cybermen presumably obtained their information about the weapon during the 1970 invasion ('The Invasion'). Ironically, it is possible the bombs are made with International Electromatics components!

OBSERVATIONS

- The Doctor knows all about the Cybermen. As seen in 'The Tomb Of The Cybermen', he has details about them in his 500 Year Diary, and in 'The Five Doctors' he knows that the Cybermen are mentioned in the legends of the Death Zone on Gallifrey.
- In 'Attack Of The Cybermen' it is revealed that Mondas has a propulsion unit, which is rather different than simply drifting through space. It is more than likely that the controlled propulsion system is a later development, built well after Mondas began to drift away, and designed as a means by which to aid the planet's return to its original location. After all, it does seem rather coincidental that Mondas happens to return to its place of origin just as its power is running out.
- When the Doctor regenerates the TARDIS seems to come alive; the controls on the console move of their own accord, the lights dim and flash, and the column rises and falls. As the new Doctor says in 'The Power Of The Daleks', 'It's part of the TARDIS. Without it I couldn't survive'. As demonstrated in 'Robot' and 'Castrovalva' (and presumably in 'Spearhead From Space'), the reason for the Doctor's homing-pigeon-like instinct for the TARDIS following a regeneration would appear to be an attempt to get to the Zero Room in which to recuperate. In this case, the Doctor collapses before he can get to the Zero Room, so presumably the TARDIS takes over and reconfigures the console room to become a temporary form of Zero Room to ensure the Doctor survives his first metamorphosis.
- Ben wonders 'if they've got to the moon yet', to which the American Sergeant replies that 'an expedition just returned'. Ben left Earth in July 1966 (see 'The War Machines'). Richard Lazarus ('The Lazarus Experiment') names Neil Armstrong, and in 'Blink' Martha mentions the 1969 moon landing (which in our history was on 21 July 1969).

LANGUAGE

The Cybermen speak English. Wigner speaks French.

TIMELINE DATES

1986, December ◆

The year and month are given on a calendar at the polar base. The date structure is correct for December 1986 of our own history.

15,000,000 BC ⁕

The Doctor says that 'millions of years ago there was a twin planet to Earth'. Later, the lead Cyberman says that 'Aeons ago our planets were twins. Then we drifted away from you on a journey to the edge of space. Now we have returned'. It is not clear what the planets being 'twins' mean. Were the two planets in orbit around each other or were they in orbits on opposite sides of the sun and always hidden from each other? It is clear that they underwent a similar process of continental drift given the duplication of the landmasses on Earth and Mondas, so I favour the opposite side of the sun idea.

There is nothing to suggest that the Earth reptiles (see 'Doctor Who And The Silurians' and 'The Sea Devils') knew of the existence of a twin planet before they went into hibernation in 70,000,000 BC, which supports the view that the planets were hidden from each other, or that Mondas had already drifted away long before the reptile civilisation rose to domination. By supporting the opposite side of the sun theory, the reptiles would not have been aware of the planet anyway.

In 'Image Of The Fendahl' we discover that the Time Lords destroyed the planet of the Fendahl in 12,000,000 BC. In Time Lord legend this was 'the fifth planet' of the Sol 3 solar system. If Mondas were still in orbit 12 million years ago, then the Fendahl planet would be more accurately the sixth planet. Therefore, the latest time period in which Mondas went on its journey into space was well before the Gallifreyans put the Fendahl planet in a time loop. The fact that millions of years have passed on Earth means that millions must have passed on Mondas too, but this seems unlikely given the seemingly quick evolution of the Cybermen from their humanoid origins. Therefore we can accept that a time dilation effect caused by Mondas' voyage through space means that only a few thousand years have elapsed on Mondas.

Using the link with dates to the Fendahl planet I have accepted that Mondas drifted away before the Fendahl came to Earth, say no more than 15 million years ago. For the Doctor to know 'what this planet is and what it means to Earth' means either that he was there when Mondas drifted away, or that he read about the event while studying at the Time Lord Academy.

DURATION

⇨ **Day One (Ep1-4)**

It is 'morning' at the start of the story (General Cutler says 'Good morning, gentlemen' to the two astronauts). Terry Cutler's capsule is launched at '1459 hours' (i.e. 2.59 pm). The TARDIS leaves later the same day.

THE POWER OF THE DALEKS

+STORY LINK

This story takes place immediately after 'The Tenth Planet', continuing with the Doctor undergoing his first regeneration.

DALEK LINK

As covered under DALEK HISTORY, this is the Daleks' third appearance, however this story is out of place with the other Dalek stories because the Dalek ship has been buried in the mercury swamp for 200 years. In terms of when the Dalek ship crashed, in the centuries since the events of 'The Daleks', the Daleks have developed space travel, in capsules that appear to be dimensionally transcendental, which contain incubator units. The Daleks are still reliant on static electricity as a power source. The ships are constructed from a special corrosion-proof metal.

The first activated Dalek seems to recognise the newly-regenerated Doctor, which suggests that the Dalek has encountered the second Doctor in a previous (but off-screen) adventure in terms of its own time stream (prior to 'The Power Of The Daleks').

OBSERVATIONS

- When the Doctor regenerates, his clothes also change (this also happens during the Doctor's fourth regeneration). He says he has been 'renewed' (he does not use the term 'regenerated', but there is no doubt that he has indeed undergone a full regeneration). He says of his transformation: 'It's part of the TARDIS. Without it I couldn't survive'. It is not clear if the 'it' refers to the transformation itself, or to the TARDIS. As seen in 'Castrovalva' and 'Mawdryn Undead', it is clear that a TARDIS can be instrumental in aiding a Time Lord's regeneration process.

- This story sees the introduction of the Doctor's 500 Year Diary. It appears again in 'The Underwater Menace' and 'The Tomb Of The Cybermen', and is mentioned in 'The Sontaran Experiment' and 'The Caves Of Androzani'. The diary is found in the TARDIS trunk. It is not known when the first Doctor put it there, but Polly knows that the Doctor kept it. (Susan refers to the Doctor's 'notebook' in '100,000 BC', and in 'The Keeper Of Traken' the Doctor produces some of his 'old time logs'.) In 'The Tomb Of The Cybermen' the Doctor finds an entry in the diary about Cybermats. Since the Doctor knows about Mondas and the Cybermen in 'The Tenth Planet', we can establish that this entry was at least made before 'The Tenth Planet'.

LANGUAGE

The Daleks speak English with the colonists and each other. The Doctor's diary has the words '500 Year Diary' on the cover.

TIMELINE DATES

2120

The Vulcan colonists are unfamiliar with the Daleks and are still in radio contact with Earth, so 'The Power Of The Daleks' must be set prior to the Dalek invasion of 2164 (see 'The Dalek Invasion Of Earth'). Lesterson believes the Daleks' technology 'could revolutionise space travel'. This suggests that in this time period space technology is still limited in terms of the distances that can be travelled, perhaps only as far as those regions of space still relatively close to Earth.

Vulcan is a mining colony that is still associated with Earth; it is not an independent colony established simply for habitation. An Earth Examiner is sent every so often (the next is not due 'for another two years'). Lesterson does wonder why the Examiner has come 'all the way from Earth', implying that Earth is some distance away, but then the rocket trip to Vulcan cannot be lengthy considering that Quinn only recently sent for the Examiner, who responds and arrives fairly quickly.

As covered under 'Nightmare Of Eden', warp drive is discovered around 2106. This new technology leads to the eventual exploration of the galaxy. I would suggest that the Vulcan colony is one of the first off-world colonies, which is why an Examiner is still considered necessary. It is possible that Vulcan is one of the colonies being serviced by the space wheels in 2068 (see 'The Wheel In Space'), but I prefer to think of it as being further out than Earth's solar system, and therefore post-warp drive. Therefore, 'The Power Of The Daleks' must be set between 2106 and 2164. Taking into account 'The Space Pirates', which is set in 2146, we can narrow the date down even further. I would bring this down to 2120, a full century after Zoe's time. [Note: The year 2020 has sometimes been applied to 'The Power Of The Daleks', a date that originates in the *Radio Times*, but there is nothing on-screen to support this.]

1900

As noted under 'The Daleks', the Daleks must have developed interplanetary space-flight around the year 1900.

1920

The Daleks have been buried for 200 years 'at least'.

1986, December › ■ ■ ■ ■ ■ ■ ■ ■ ■ ■ ■

The Doctor regenerates at the end of 'The Tenth Planet', and the TARDIS is still parked near the Snow Cap station.

2110 ■ ■ ■ ■ ■ ■ ■ ■ ■ ■ ■ ■

It is not stated how long the colony has been on Vulcan. Janley says 'the colony is running down'. The fact that there is a rebel element shows that the colony has been there for several years. Given that warp drive is not developed until 2106, the colony can only be, say, no more than 10 years old.

DURATION

⇨ **Day (1986) (Ep1)** ■ ■ ■ ■ ■ ■ ■ ■ ■ ■

The TARDIS is still on Earth in the opening moments of the story.

(TARDIS) (Ep1) ■ ■ ■ ■ ■ ■ ■ ■ ■ ■ ■

The TARDIS is in flight between Earth and Vulcan for a few minutes.

⇨ **Day One (Ep1-2)** ■ ■ ■ ■ ■ ■ ■ ■ ■ ■

The TARDIS lands on Vulcan in the late afternoon. It is night when the Doctor enters the Dalek capsule for the first time. Resno is killed in the last scene set at night.

⇨ **Day Two (Ep2-6)** ■ ■ ■ ■ ■ ■ ■ ■ ■ ■

The Dalek is shown to the Governor the following morning. In Ep4 the rebel meeting in the rocket room is held at '20:00 hours' (8 pm). The rest of the story takes place during the night.

⇨ **Day Three (Ep6)** ■ ■ ■ ■ ■ ■ ■ ■ ■ ■

The final conflict against the Daleks continues into the small hours of the morning. It is day when the TARDIS leaves Vulcan.

UNSEEN ADVENTURES

In 'The Abominable Snowmen', Padmasambhava says to the Doctor 'it's good to look upon your face again', indicating the Doctor was in his second incarnation when they first meet in 1630. This can only have happened between 'The Power

Of The Daleks' and 'The Highlanders'. The Doctor appears to have visited Det Sen more than twice; the first visit was probably by the first Doctor ('The Abominable Snowmen').

THE HIGHLANDERS

STORY LINK

There is no indication that 'The Highlanders' follows directly on from 'The Power Of The Daleks'. In 'The Abominable Snowmen', it is stated that it is the second Doctor that visited Det Sen monastery in 1630. Since Jamie has not been to Tibet before, that unscreened adventure can only have taken place between 'The Power Of The Daleks' and 'The Highlanders'. However, in 'The Highlanders' Polly says, 'the last time we went to the past I had to wear boys' clothes all the time' which appears to be a direct reference to 'The Smugglers', and in 'The Underwater Menace', when the TARDIS lands on the beach, Polly thinks it's Cornwall, to which Ben says 'You said that last time', and Polly replies, 'And I was right!', which is again clearly a direct reference to 'The Smugglers'. From this it appears Ben and Polly have not travelled into the past since 'The Smugglers'. Of course, it is possible that only the Doctor went to Det Sen monastery in 1630, and Ben and Polly remained (asleep?) in the TARDIS. This is the most likely explanation. It is clear however that many months have passed since the adventure on Vulcan.

LANGUAGE

The Highlanders all appear to speak English even when together, and not Gaelic.

TIMELINE DATES

1746, April 16 – 17 ·
The year is not stated, but it is several months prior to October because Grey expects to see Trask back in London 'at the end of October'. There are non-date references to real historical events, such as 'Culloden Moor', 'Jacobites', 'King George the Second' (George II ruled from 1727 – 1760), 'Prince Charles' and 'the Duke of Cumberland', all of which place the date to be 16 April 1746, when the battle of Culloden, which is coming to an end in the opening moments of the story, took place in our history. It is not until 'The Underwater Menace' that the year is confirmed by the Doctor as '1746'.

However, in 'The Faceless Ones' Jamie gives his date of origin as '1750' and in 'The War Games' the date for the battle against the Redcoats is given no fewer than three times as '1745', once even by Jamie himself. From a purely historical viewpoint, 1746 is the best date.

HISTORICAL COMPARISON

In our history the battle of Culloden was fought on 16 April 1746. The story told in 'The Highlanders', while being purely fictional, is set against a background of factual events.

DURATION

⇨ **Day One (16 April) (Ep1-3)**

It is day when the TARDIS lands. 'It'll be dark soon', according to Kirsty, just before Polly falls in the pit. The *Annabelle* is to be loaded up by 'tonight'. Ben and Jamie are taken aboard.

⇨ **Day Two (17 April) (Ep3-4)**

It is morning when Kirsty and Polly arrive in town dressed as orange sellers. It is 'night' when Ben is dunked in the sea and escapes. It is later that same night (or possibly very early the next morning) when the TARDIS leaves.

THE UNDERWATER MENACE

+STORY LINK

This story follows directly on from 'The Highlanders', with the TARDIS still in 1746, and with Jamie entering the TARDIS for the first time. When they explore the volcanic island, Ben, Polly and Jamie are still wearing the same clothes they had on when they left Scotland, but before venturing out of the TARDIS the Doctor does have time (off-screen) to change into a different pair of checked trousers.

Soon after landing on the volcanic island, Ben wonders if they will encounter the Daleks, an inference that 'The Power Of The Daleks' is relatively recent.

OBSERVATIONS

- In 'The Underwater Menace' Atlantis is located south of the Azores on the Atlantic ridge. In 'The Time Monster' Atlantis is established as being south of Greece in the Mediterranean Sea. Zaroff says the Atlanteans have been living in the extinct volcano ever since 'Atlantis was submerged at the time of the flood'. King Thous says they have held the sea 'at bay for so many centuries', suggesting that after the Mediterranean Atlantis sank, the survivors travelled to this new island in the Atlantic and have been living there since 1527 BC (the date of 'The Time Monster'). Centuries later there was a 'flood' and their new city was submerged beneath the sea: Zaroff says 'some life continued in air-pockets in the mountain caves thanks to the natural air-shafts provided by the extinct volcano'. In other words the civilisation seen in 'The Underwater Menace' is not the Atlantis seen in 'The Time Monster', but a temporary refuge later established by the survivors. In terms of Zaroff's plan, the island is simply where the drilling is taking place, and when the sea drains away the original Atlantis in the Mediterranean (the one in 'The Time Monster') will no longer be under water, and the Atlanteans would leave the island and return to their once great city.
- The Atlanteans of 'The Underwater Menace' worship the goddess Amdo, whereas in 'The Time Monster' they worship Poseidon. It would seem that after the Mediterranean Atlantis is destroyed, the Atlanteans decided to worship a new deity.

LANGUAGE

Polly knows some basic 'Do you speak …?' phrases in French, German and Spanish, but this is not translated. Jamie speaks to the Atlanteans in Gaelic, but the Doctor doesn't understand and has to ask him what language that was. The Atlanteans all speak English (Polly is surprised by this: 'He speaks English!'). All the signs in Zaroff's lab are marked in English: 'DANGER', 'KEEP OUT LIVE CABLES' and so on, but considering Zaroff's Eastern European accent, it is odd he does not use his native tongue.

TIMELINE DATES

2070, March 20 ▪ ■ ■ ■ ■ ■ ■ ■ ■ ■ ■ ■ ■ ■
Polly finds a souvenir ('Aztec. Fake, of course') stamped with 'Mexico Olympiad'. She guesses the year was 'about, um, 1970'. Ben adds that the Mexico Olympic Games

weren't due 'until 1968' (he and Polly are from 1966). They both deduce from this that it is 'any time later than that'. Sean recognises that the TARDIS is 'a flaming English police box', so he might come from prior to the 1980s, a time when police boxes were still around (such as 1981, as seen in 'Logopolis'). The story could therefore be set at any time from 1968 to 1981.

Another possible year is 2070 – at the end of 'The Underwater Menace', after dematerialising from the island, the TARDIS is caught in the gravity-pull of the Gravitron on the moon. Since this happens immediately as the TARDIS dematerialises from the island, it suggests that the ship must have materialised in space in order for the Gravitron to affect the TARDIS, as it's highly unlikely the Gravitron could affect the TARDIS in the time vortex. Therefore, the TARDIS either moved 100 years or so in time from Atlantis to 2070, or it was already in the same time zone as 'The Moonbase'.

Professor Zaroff's drilling equipment was obviously of advanced design, plus it was he who taught Damon the technique to turn humans into fish-people, which again suggests it is not the 1970s but a much later time period.

I think these links are much stronger than an ambiguous date of a piece of broken pottery, and therefore I have set 'The Underwater Menace' in 2070, at the same time as 'The Moonbase'. Sean's knowledge of old police boxes is obviously from an historical perspective rather than from any personal experience. Indeed, in 'The Seeds Of Death', which is set in 2096, Daniel Eldred recognises that the TARDIS is 'a twentieth century police box', so it is therefore not unlikely that Sean would know what one was. As for the Mexico Olympiad souvenir, maybe Mexico hosted the Olympic Games in the twenty-first century.

The month and day are derived from Lolem's comment that the TARDIS crew were prophesied to 'fall from the sky in time for our Festival of the Vernal Equinox'. Atlantis is located 'south of the Azores. The Atlantic ridge', so it is in the northern hemisphere; the Vernal Equinox in that hemisphere falls on March 20.

25,000,000 BC

The Doctor dates the rock on the island to be 'Miocene. Twenty five million years old'.

1527 BC

King Thous says they have held the sea 'at bay for so many centuries'. As seen in 'The Time Monster', Atlantis is destroyed in 1527 BC. See also Observations.

1759, January 25

The Doctor gives '1759' as the year in which Robert Burns was born. In our history, Burns was born on 25 January 1759, and died 21 July 1796.

2050 •

The main story is set in 2070. The Doctor knows 'a great deal' about Zaroff and his experiments on food production, and is pleased to see him: 'Let me say how glad I am to see the reports of your death of twenty years previous were, ah, premature', being 2050. In 'The Moonbase', it is clear that from the Doctor's knowledge of the Gravitron that he has been to 2050 before, so it is likely that he knew about Zaroff's disappearance at the same time. It is not clear if Zaroff has been in Atlantis for the full 20 years, or when the drilling was first started, but he does state that 'we have been working on it for many years'.

1968, October 12 – 27

These are the dates of the Mexico Olympic Games in our history (see also Invasion of The Dinosaurs).

DURATION

(TARDIS) (Ep1)

After leaving 1746 Scotland the TARDIS travels for a while before landing on the island.

⇨ **Day One (Ep1-3)**

It is day when the TARDIS lands on the island and when it departs. The story takes place underground, so it is hard to ascertain the passage of time. In Ep2 Thous greets Lolem with a 'good evening'. Ep3 Zaroff announces that 'everything will be ready in two days from now', but by Ep4 he has brought the countdown forwards.

🕑 **Day Two (Ep3)**

A day passes off-screen, during which time the Doctor prepares his plan to kidnap Zaroff; he need time to get disguises, guards uniforms, and find out Zaroff's movements, etc …

⇨ **Day Three (Ep3-4)**

The attempted kidnapping of Zaroff takes place later the next day. Sean notes that the world is going to blow up 'in a couple of hours', although Zaroff does bring forward the countdown to 'zero'.

THE MOONBASE

+STORY LINK

'The Moonbase' follows directly on from 'The Underwater Menace', with the TARDIS caught in the Gravitron's gravitational pull. (The travellers were supposed to be going to Mars.) In the opening TARDIS scene Polly, Ben and Jamie are still wearing the clothes they had on at the end of 'The Underwater Menace', but they all change before venturing out onto the surface of the moon. Of note, Jamie had left his original highlander clothes in Atlantis, but has clearly found a new kilt in the TARDIS wardrobe.

CYBERMAN LINK

As covered under CYBERMAN HISTORY, this is the Cybermen's fifth appearance. These Cybermen are the few survivors of the Cyber-War, which ended in 2025 (see 'Revenge Of The Cybermen'), so when Hobson says 'There were Cybermen once. Every child knows that. They were all destroyed ages ago', he is referring to the war, and not to Mondas's destruction in 1986. The fact that Hobson says 'every child knows that' clearly indicates that the Cybermen were all destroyed before he was born. If he is referring to the Cyber-War, with 'The Moonbase' set in 2070, and Hobson being aged about 45-50, the war could only have been in the 2020s. The Cybermen are now dying out, their machinery has stopped because of the war, hence their attack on the Moonbase. They have probably come from their base on Planet 14 (see 'The Invasion').

OBSERVATIONS

- When the TARDIS crew first arrive on the Moonbase, Hobson asks 'You are from Earth aren't you?' This indicates that Hobson thinks they might also have come from another planet, which shows clearly that as early as 2050 humans have colonised other worlds, presumably all in the solar system: i.e. Mars, or perhaps even Cassius (see 'The Sun Makers').
- The Doctor uses the TARDIS time scanner: 'instead of the normal picture

showing where we are it gives you a glimpse of the future ... I haven't used it very much. It's not very reliable as you can see'. This device would appear to be similar to the roof-mounted screen the eighth Doctor uses in 'Doctor Who (The TV Movie)' to see into the future 'one minute after midnight'.

LANGUAGE

The Cybermen appear to speak in English; the multinational personnel in the base all understand them.

TIMELINE DATES

2070, March 20 •

Hobson gives the year as '2070'. Benoit says Evans 'could flood half of Europe if he keeps the Gravitron aligned with spring tides'. Spring in the European northern hemisphere is about March 21 to June 20. Considering that the previous serial, 'The Underwater Menace', is set on 20 March, this supports further the idea that the TARDIS moved spatially only.

Three men came down with the disease in 'the past few hours' prior to the Doctor's arrival.

1888 •

The Doctor tells Polly 'I think I took a degree once. In Glasgow. 1888, I think. Lister'. In our history, Joseph Lister never visited Glasgow in 1888!

2050 •

According to Hobson the Gravitron has been in operation 'for the last twenty years'. The Doctor knows about the device, and assumes the date is '2050', so it is clear that he has been in that time period before – this was presumably the first Doctor. 2050 is also the year in which Professor Zaroff disappeared (see 'The Underwater Menace'), so it is possible the Doctor learned of that incident during the same visit to this time period.

2070, March 6

There are 19 crewmembers in the base. The disease first broke out sometime 'in the past two weeks', giving the approximate time that the Cybermen first landed on the moon.

DURATION

⇨ **Day One (Ep1-4)**

The TARDIS lands at 'the end of Period Eleven this present lunar day' (12 noon?). The Gravitron begins to play up for the first time 'about the beginning of Period Twelve'. The Moonbase lights are dimmed during Ep1 for the 'night' cycle. 'Six hours' pass after the first few Cybermen in the base are destroyed with Polly Cocktail because Benson has been in the control room for 'six hours' by the end of Ep4.

THE MACRA TERROR

+STORY LINK

'The Moonbase' ends with the Doctor operating the time scanner; a Macra's claw appears on the screen signifying their future. In 'The Macra Terror' Ben and Polly are wearing the same clothes they have on in 'The Moonbase' and Jamie makes a reference to 'what we saw on that time scanner', which strongly suggests that 'The Moonbase' and 'The Macra Terror' are consecutive. The night they spend at the colony is the first time Ben, Polly and Jamie have had a chance to sleep since Jamie joined the TARDIS crew.

LANGUAGE

The Macra communicates with the colonists in English.

TIMELINE DATES

3567

The Doctor says 'according to my calculations we're certainly in the future'. The colony itself is several centuries old: the Pilot says 'this colony was founded many centuries ago by our ancestors who came from the Earth planet', say about 500 years ago. As noted in 'Gridlock', the Macra are native to galaxy M87, so this colony may have been one of the first established soon after intergalactic travel was developed in 2980 (see 'Terror Of The Vervoids'). A Production Factor of say 1600 years gives us the arbitrary date 3567.

Medok has been getting worse 'day by day'.

3000

An estimated date; the colony 'was founded many centuries ago', soon after the development of warp drive in 2980 (see 'Terror Of The Vervoids').

3557 ▨ ▨ ▨ ▨ ▨ ▨ ▨ ▨ ▨ ▨ ▨ ▨ ▨
The Pilot says 'it has taken our combined computers years to perfect' the chemical formula for the gas, say ten years?

DURATION

⇨ **Day One (Ep1-2)** ▨ ▨ ▨ ▨ ▨ ▨ ▨ ▨ ▨ ▨
The TARDIS arrives late in the day. The crew retire to their rooms that night and are subjected to voice control. The Doctor wakes his friends during the night.

⇨ **Day Two (Ep.2-4)** ▨ ▨ ▨ ▨ ▨ ▨ ▨ ▨ ▨
It is 'morning' when Jamie emerges from the pit shaft. The travellers leave later that day.

THE FACELESS ONES

STORY LINK

There is no indication that this story follows directly on from 'The Macra Terror'. Although Jamie is still wearing his roll neck sweater (which he began wearing in 'The Moonbase'), it would appear that a considerable amount of time has elapsed for Jamie since he joined the Doctor. Jamie is now less 'primitive' than he was from 'The Highlanders' to 'The Macra Terror', so it seems that the Doctor has spent a lot of time educating the young Scot (although, Jamie doesn't know what aircraft or photographs are). And this is supported in 'The Dominators', when Rago, the Dominator, notes that Jamie shows 'signs of recent rapid learning'. Jamie can now read (as seen in the airport concourse), and from 'The Tomb Of The Cybermen' onwards he wears a wristwatch. As noted under THE DOCTOR'S AGE, at least a year has passed between 'The Macra Terror' and 'The Faceless Ones'. Ben and Polly have therefore been with the Doctor for about two years in total [although in terms of direct story duration it is really only about 15 days].

OBSERVATIONS

- The Chameleonised Polly uses the name Michelle Leuppi, but this is not necessarily Polly's surname, while the Chameleonised Jamie does not have a Scots accent.

LANGUAGE

The Chameleons speak English, presumably as a result of taking over the bodies and minds of their human victims.

TIMELINE DATES

1966, July 19 - 20 ·
In the final scene at the hangar in 'The Faceless Ones', the date 'July the 20th, 1966' is given by the Doctor (presumably his '12 hours' airport pass has the date on it). In 'The Evil Of The Daleks' it is stated that the TARDIS was stolen from the hangar at '3 o'clock' (the time appears on Bob Hall's time sheet: 'Police Tel Box. Collection: 3 o'clock'). In Ep4 of 'The Faceless Ones' the Chameleon Tours flight to Rome is at '15:30 hours', i.e. 3.30 pm. Therefore these two events are on two separate days: the final scene of 'The Faceless Ones' and the start of 'The Evil Of The Daleks' are set on 20 July 1966, with the bulk of 'The Faceless Ones' therefore taking place on 19 July 1966. Ben and Polly realise that 20 July 1966 is the very same day in which they first entered the TARDIS (see 'The War Machines').

Ben and Polly have spent at least two years with the Doctor (see THE DOCTOR'S AGE), so they are now out of sync with Earth. The same 'out of sync' effect happens to Jamie and Zoe in 'The War Games', Jo in 'Colony In Space' and 'The Time Monster', Tegan in 'Time-Flight' and 'Resurrection Of The Daleks', Turlough in 'Planet Of Fire' and Rose Tyler in 'Aliens Of London'.

1966, March 17
Jean Rock says the Chameleons operate '7 or 8' flights a day, each with about 50 passengers (based on the fact that Samantha finds 50 postcards, one per passenger). That would mean about 400 passengers are abducted each day. With a target of 50,000 humans to collect this would take no less than 125 consecutive days to achieve. The Chameleons have just about completed their set target when the story takes place. The Doctor goes on 'the last flight of the season' to their space station at about 6.30 pm on 19 July. 125 days earlier is 17 March 1966.

1966, July
Brian Briggs disappeared 'about a week ago', and Meadows moved house 'last week'.

DURATION

⇨ **Day One (19 July) (Ep1-6)**
Jenkins says 'There was a bit of bother this morning', referring to the Doctor and Jamie at passport control. In Ep4 the '15:30' (3.30 pm) CT flight to Rome leaves. Meadows then goes off duty for 'a couple of hours', returning to his post in Ep5, making it about 5.30 pm. The 'last [CT] flight of the season goes in an hour' at that point, being 6.30 pm. This is the flight the Doctor takes to the satellite.

⇨ **Day Two (20 July) (Ep6)**
It is '3 o'clock' when the TARDIS is stolen. It has therefore taken all night and up until mid-afternoon to get all the missing humans down from the satellite.

THE EVIL OF THE DALEKS

+STORY LINK

This story follows directly on from 'The Faceless Ones', with the Doctor and Jamie chasing the stolen TARDIS from Gatwick Airport at '3 o'clock'.

DALEK LINK

As covered under DALEK HISTORY, this is the Daleks' twelfth appearance. Since the events of 'The Daleks' Master Plan', the Daleks on Skaro have concentrated on determining why humans have always defeated them (referring also to off-screen encounters with humans). The Daleks' experiments into time travel have resulted in a time corridor, which is clearly more advanced than their time machines used in 'The Chase' and 'The Daleks' Master Plan'. We can assume that the Daleks' time corridor extends only between 4066 and 1866. The Daleks are unable to reach 1966 with their own tunnel – there is no sequence in which the Daleks are seen to travel between 1966 and 4066 – and instead use the corridor established by Maxtible and Waterfield, which presumably only operates between 1866 and 1966.

The Daleks give Waterfield photos of the Doctor and 'Mr James McCrimmon' but it is never explained how the Daleks know who Jamie is nor how they got the photos. It is possible that human Dalek agents based at Gatwick Airport take the photos and learn Jamie's name when the TARDIS lands in 'The Faceless Ones'. Another solution is that the Daleks have encountered the second Doctor and Jamie before during an adventure in the Doctor and Jamie's own relative future, some time prior to 'The War Games' (and presumably featuring some of the Daleks from 'The Power of the Daleks'). Since Jamie doesn't recognise the Daleks, it is possible that during this unseen adventure, the Daleks see Jamie but he doesn't actually meet them. Another idea is that the Daleks give Waterfield photographs of all the known Doctors and companions (including Ben and Polly, who are also seen at the airport), with instructions that should any of these people be seen in London they are to be lured to the shop.

As noted under 'The War Machines', the first Doctor detects the presence of the Daleks soon after landing in London.

OBSERVATIONS

- The trap to bring the Doctor from 1966 to 1866 is fairly elaborate, even by Dalek standards. It does appear to be an overly extreme step for them to go to all the trouble of buying a shop and stocking it just to trap the Doctor (the Daleks could just as easily have grabbed the Doctor while he was in the airport hangar). I would suggest that the shop is actually Maxtible and Waterfield's idea. We can assume that their time travel experiments are the first step towards their plans to make a lot of money. Maxtible wants the secret of transmuting lead into gold, so we can guess that he wants lots of it. Their plan, we can assume, is to set up the shop where they sell authentic Victoriana brought from 1866, make a nice tidy profit from the venture, convert the money into gold, return to 1866, convert the gold back to cash and use the money to fund further time experiments. However, before the two scientists could set in motion their plan the Daleks appear in the time cabinet when Maxtible and Waterfield test their device for the first time. We can assume that the Daleks force the two men to adopt their intended plan in order to maintain their co-operation (as well as by holding Victoria prisoner), and use the shop as part of the plan to trap the Doctor. The antique shop is probably utilised by Waterfield for several months while waiting for the Doctor to show up. We know from 'The Chase' that the Daleks can trace the TARDIS, so it appears that the Daleks simply expected that the Doctor would show up in this time zone as some point soon.
- The Doctor announces that he is 'a professor of a far wider academy of which human nature is merely a part. All forms of life interest me.' If we capitalise the word 'academy' the Doctor could be referring to the Academy on Gallifrey.
- The Doctor names one of his test Daleks 'Omega'. Given that the Gallifreyan called Omega was a childhood hero of the Doctor's (see 'The Three Doctors'), might we assume that Alpha and Beta were also the names of high-ranking Time Lords from the Doctor's youth?

- To gain access to the Dalek city the Doctor opens a covered tunnel on the mountainside. Jamie wonders how the Doctor knows that was there. This entrance could be the same one used by the Thals, Ian and Barbara to enter the Dalek city in 'The Daleks', which was 5 years ago (see THE DOCTOR'S AGE).

LANGUAGE

The Daleks use Earth numerals on the weighing machine in Victoria's cell. It is clear that they can speak English, because they communicate with the humans before the Doctor arrives on the scene.

TIMELINE DATES

1966, July 20 ·

The story continues directly on from 'The Faceless Ones', the last day of that adventure being 20 July 1966. The TARDIS is stolen at '3 o'clock', as given on Bob Hall's clipboard.

1866, June 2 – 3 ·

Theodore Maxtible says 'The date is June second, eighteen hundred and sixty six'.

4066 ·

Maxtible says they have undertaken 'a journey through space' to Skaro, which suggests that the events on Skaro are also set in 1866. However, this does not tie in with Dalek history in terms of when they develop time travel (see 'Day Of The Daleks').

As covered under DALEK HISTORY, the Doctor knows that the Daleks are still active in 4000 AD ('The Daleks' Master Plan'), so when he declares this to be 'the final end' of the Daleks he is speaking in terms of Dalek history. Therefore these Daleks are from a time period after 'The Daleks' Master Plan'. Since Maxtible's time corridor operates between 1866 and 1966, using a Century Factor Skaro could be set in a year ending with '66, say 4066, 4166, 4266, 4366, etc. Given that in 'Destiny Of The Daleks', which has been set in 4500, the Daleks return to Skaro centuries after it has been abandoned we can assume that the survivors of this civil war abandon the planet. On this basis 4066 is an ideal date for this sequence.

All Daleks are ordered back to Skaro. It is not clear if this order relates just to the Daleks on Earth or to all Daleks everywhere. Given that during the battle scenes there are only a few Daleks in the City, I think the former applies; there are still other Daleks in other parts of the Universe (and as covered under 'Destiny Of The Daleks', some are in fact currently engaged in a 'war' with the Movellans).

1854

Maxtible says that J Clerk Maxwell studied electromagnetism 'twelve years ago', which is 1854. He also speaks of 'all my years of labour', which suggests that he started his experimentation around this same year. In our history, James Clerk Maxwell lived 13 June 1831 to 5 November 1879.

1854, October 25 *

This is the recorded date of the Charge of the Light Brigade in our history. The Doctor says it was a 'magnificent folly'. The Doctor was at another famous battle on 25 October, Agincourt in 1415 (see 'The Masque Of Mandragora', 'The Talons Of Weng-Chiang').

1854, November 5

This is date of the battle of Inkerman in our history.

DURATION

⇨ **Day One (20 July 1966) (Ep1-2)**
The story starts at '3 o'clock' in the afternoon. The Doctor and Jamie go to the Tricolour cafe later that afternoon. The clocks at the antique shop all show different times when the Doctor and Jamie arrive for their 'ten o'clock' meeting. Jamie notes that it is 'half past the nine o'clock' (9.30 pm). The Doctor confirms that they are early. It is about 9.50 pm when they are taken to 1866.

⇨ **Day One (2 June 1866) (Ep2-5)**
It is morning when the Doctor and Jamie awaken. Night falls at the end of Ep3 as Jamie begins his search for Victoria.

⇨ **Day Two (3 June 1866) (Ep5-6)**
It is morning when the three test Daleks are activated. The Doctor says 'I've been up all night' working on the test to extract the Human Factor. The Doctor says the three test Daleks will 'grow up very fast within a matter of hours'. The house is destroyed later this day, after the Daleks withdraw.

⇨ **Day One (Skaro) (Ep6-7)**
It appears to be night when the Doctor arrives on Skaro.

THE TOMB OF THE CYBERMEN

+STORY LINK

This story directly follows on from 'The Evil Of The Daleks', with the TARDIS still on Skaro and Victoria entering the ship for the first time. There is a fade-to-black pause before their arrival on Telos, however, given the Doctor and Jamie's reference to Victoria's new dress, and the Doctor's later conversation with Victoria about missing her father, it is unlikely that there is another adventure between 'The Evil Of The Daleks' and 'The Tomb Of The Cybermen'.

CYBERMAN LINK

As covered under CYBERMAN HISTORY, this is the Cybermen's sixth appearance. After the failed attack on the Moonbase in 2070, the Cybermen probably abandoned their base (on Planet 14?) and returned to Telos, where a base had already been prepared and to where the Cyber-Controller moved when the Cyber-War started in 2020. The 'city' discovered by Parry is only the gateway to the other tombs that are presumably scattered all over the planet, which is why the tombs seen in 'Attack Of The Cybermen' are so different. And each of these different tombs houses the different types of Cybermen (see the discussion about Cyber Designs under CYBERMAN HISTORY).

LANGUAGE

Hardin recognises the Doctor's accent as 'English'. The symbols on the control panels include Earth numerals. The Cybermen speak English.

TIMELINE DATES

2526 +

As covered under CYBERMAN HISTORY, 'The Tomb Of The Cybermen' is best set in 2526, shortly before the events of 'Earthshock'. The Cyber-Controller reveals that the Cybermen 'were becoming extinct', which was why they attacked the Moonbase to get replacement 'parts' from the humans. The Controller refers to the defeat on 'the lunar surface' as if it were a recent event for the Cybermen. This implies that they went into hibernation soon after the events of 'The Moonbase', which is set in 2070. This would set 'The Tomb Of The Cybermen' around 2570. But a 2570 setting conflicts with 'Earthshock', in which the Cybermen refer to the second Doctor confining 'the Cybermen to their ice tomb on Telos'; so 'The Tomb Of The Cybermen' must be set

'500 years' earlier than 2526. It should be noted that the Cybermen themselves don't actually state how long they have been in hibernation, so Parry's reference to '500 years' is only an estimate in terms of how long it had been since the Cybermen were officially last seen in Earth's system according to Parry's records.

[In a BBC production document, a memo to the wardrobe department gives the date for this story as 2067, which is a Century Factor of 100 years. This would certainly explain the seemingly 'modern' appearance of the clothing worn and equipment used by the expedition members. But this date can't be applied since the expedition members refer to the Cybermen having died out 500 years earlier; on what basis have they obtained this information? Also, the spaceship they use – not to mention the distance they have travelled – rules out this being the twenty-first century.]

To satisfy the '500 years' reference and the date in 'Earthshock', we can set the year in which Parry believes the Cybermen 'died out' to be before 2026, which means there was at least one 'off-screen event' in Cybermen history in which they 'died out'. As covered under 'Revenge Of The Cybermen', there is a Cyber-War after which it is also said the Cybermen were believed to have been wiped out. This is too attractive a coincidence to not take as a direct association: the Cybermen died out following the Cyber-War, but Parry did not know of the glitter-gun (possibly due to his research records being incomplete because of the Dalek invasion in 2164).

We can speculate that upon returning to Earth, Parry reveals to the authorities that the Cybermen still exist on Telos, and are still a potential threat to Earth. With this news, confirming what Earth authorities had already been told by Commander Stevenson (from 'Revenge Of The Cybermen'), the conference in 'Earthshock' is organised. Therefore, I have set 'The Tomb Of The Cybermen' earlier in the same year as 'Earthshock'.

The Earth expedition has already been on Telos for at least one night, as it is aware of how cold it gets at night.

1213

The Doctor says 'in Earth terms' he is '450' years old. The Earth year of the Doctor's birth is calculated as 1213 (see THE DOCTOR'S AGE).

2070

As noted under Cyberman Link above, the Cybermen retreat to Telos soon after the failed attack on the Moonbase in this year.

DURATION

⇨ **Day (Skaro) (Ep1)**
The TARDIS is still on Skaro in the opening moments of the story.

⇨ **Day One (Telos) (Ep1-3)**
It is day when the tombs are opened. The expedition plans to leave 'an hour' after '16.30' but the ship is sabotaged. They spend the night in the tombs.

⇨ **Day Two (Telos) (Ep3-4)**
It is daylight when Hopper returns with news that the ship is repaired. It was going to take '72 hours' although it is certain that three days have not passed.

THE ABOMINABLE SNOWMEN

+STORY LINK

This adventure is probably consecutive with 'The Tomb Of The Cybermen', because Jamie and Victoria are wearing the same outfits from that story. Jamie also compares the cold of the Himalayas to that of 'the Cybermen's tomb'.

OBSERVATIONS

- The Doctor says 'Every time I visit Det Sen, the monastery seems to be in some sort of trouble or another', which means that he has been there more than once prior to 'The Abominable Snowmen'. He took the Ghanta in 1630, his previous visit there in terms of the monastery's history. Padmasambhava recognises the second Doctor: 'It's good to look upon your face again. So many years.' This means that the Doctor's previous visit in 1630 was also during his second incarnation. (An alternative thought is that Padmasambhava is a Time Lord – see below.) Jamie has not been there before, so it was before he met the Doctor, which can only mean the visit in 1630 took place between 'The Power Of The Daleks' and 'The Highlanders' when the Doctor was with Ben and Polly. However, in 'The Highlanders' Polly complains that the last time she was in the past she had to wear boys' clothes, a direct reference to 'The Smugglers', which means she hasn't been to Earth's past since 'The Smugglers'. Also, the Doctor's statement that his return to the monastery 'after all this time' is a subjective statement which suggests it was years ago, and yet it is only recently that he has regenerated. Either Padmasambhava can see the Doctor's Time Lord 'aura' (which means the meeting in 1630 was with the first Doctor), or there is indeed a period of at least a year between 'The Power Of The Daleks' and 'The Abominable Snowmen'. Polly's comment could be explained as being a reference to a different, off-screen, adventure set in the past in which she had to wear boys' clothes. As noted under THE DOCTOR'S AGE, I think it is best to take it that there is a period of no more than one year between 'The Power Of The Daleks' and 'The Highlanders'.

- Is Padmasambhava a Time Lord? If he were, that would explain why he could be over 300 years old, and how he seems to recognise the second Doctor ('It's good to look upon your face again, Doctor'; is he reading the Doctor's Time Lord 'aura'?) And the fact that his lengthy name is very similar to Romanadvoratrelundar… And indeed, Time Lords do seem to possess an affinity for Tibetan meditation, and evidenced by K'Anpo / Cho Je in 'Planet Of The Spiders'.
- The Doctor finds a strange plastic gizmo with bells on it in his trunk, which he hasn't seen 'for years'.

LANGUAGE

Presumably the Monks all speak Tibetan. Travers converses with them, so we can assume that he too speaks that language (the Doctor speaks Tibetan with K'Anpo in 'Planet Of The Spiders', but in 'The Creature From The Pit' he needs a Tibetan dictionary to read the language). The label on the bag containing the Ghanta is in English.

TIMELINE DATES

1935 ◆
The Doctor mentions the 'attack in 1630' when the Holy Ghanta was taken from the monastery which, as is mentioned several times, was 'three hundred years ago', setting 'The Abominable Snowmen' in 1930. However, in 'The Web Of Fear', Victoria tells Anne Travers that they met her father in Tibet in '1935'. I have taken 'The Web Of Fear' reference as being correct.

1630 ◆
The Doctor refers to this year as being when he last visited the monastery and took the Ghanta (see Observations).

1635
1735
Songsten says Padmasambhava 'laboured for nearly two hundred years. With the help of the Intelligence he built the creatures and the other wonderful machines'. Padmasambhava was alive in 1630, so his encounter with the Great Intelligence must have been soon after that, say 5 years, and it wasn't until a hundred years after that that the Great Intelligence first instructed the master to begin construction. The reason it takes Padmasambhava so long to build the equipment is that the materials (metal, glass, fur, and so on) are not readily available in Tibet.

1915
When the Doctor meets Travers the explorer says for 'Twenty years I've been searching' for the Yeti.

DURATION

⇨ **Day One (Ep1)**
It is night when John is killed (Travers tells the monks 'it was dark' when they were attacked).

⇨ **Day Two (Ep1-4)**
The TARDIS arrives the next day. It is getting dark when the Yeti is captured; shortly after this Travers bids everyone 'Goodnight all'. It is still dark when the Doctor and Jamie head back to the TARDIS.

⇨ **Day Three (Ep4-6)**
It is daylight by the time the Doctor and Jamie reach the TARDIS. The Intelligence wants the monastery to be cleared by 'nightfall'. The Intelligence is defeated later that day.

THE ICE WARRIORS

+STORY LINK

The TARDIS crew are all wearing the same outfits they had on in 'The Abominable Snowmen'. On seeing snow again Jamie says 'Tibet was bad enough. I think you've put us down just further up the mountain'. Later the Doctor tells Clent they have 'been in retreat in Tibet', so 'The Abominable Snowmen' and 'The Ice Warriors' are consecutive.

- Brittanicus Base is the European Ioniser operation. It is located within a Victorian house (which Victoria says is like 'my home'), which has been preserved within a protective plastic dome due to its historical significance. Other Ioniser bases are located in America, Australasia, Asia and South Africa (Clent says 'all the major continents are threatened with destruction under the glaciers of the second Ice Age'). Africa is designated an evacuation point, so it cannot be threatened by the glaciers as much as Europe. Storr, who is Scottish, says he knows the countryside because he has 'lived here all my life'. Miss Garrett fears an explosion would 'wipe us off this island', so it seems that the Brittanicus Base is on one of the islands off the coast of Scotland.
- One of the (incorrect) causes of the Second Ice Age suggested by the Doctor is 'sun spot activity'. It is ironic therefore that the time of the Great Break Out ('The Invisible Enemy') and the deployment of the Nerva station ('The Ark In Space'), both the following year, are due to solar flare activity.
- The crew of Brittanicus Base do not know of the Martian warriors, which suggests that 'The Ice Warriors' has to be set before 'The Curse Of Peladon' and 'The Monster Of Peladon', in which the Martians are allied with Earth in the Galactic Federation. But with 'The Ice Warriors' set in 5000, some 1725 years after 'The Monster Of Peladon', it could simply be that historical records from the Federation years had been long-since forgotten, and no one can remember the warriors. Alternatively, the only Federation representatives of the Martians seen on Earth could have been the 'Lord' faction like Slaar ('The Seeds Of Death'), Izlyr ('The Curse Of Peladon') and Azaxyr ('The Monster Of Peladon'), and not the soldier class to which Varga and his crew belong. (Incidentally, Varga refers to 'my warriors'.) So, when Walters first sees the buried 'Viking' he says, 'Proper ice warrior, isn't he, sir'; Walters may therefore have been familiar with the Martian race, and jokingly referred to the frozen 'Viking' in this way without actually realising it was indeed a Martian 'Ice Warrior'!
- When the Doctor is given Penley's notes on the Omega Factor, he displays some concern: 'Omega? What does he mean? Omega?' It could be that he initially thought it was a reference to his Gallifreyan hero (see 'The Three Doctors').

Varga is able to speak to Victoria, and later with the Ioniser scientists.

TIMELINE DATES

5000 +

This is a future Earth, in which the Great World Computer directs human civilisation. Clent knows about 'reactor turbine', 'ion jet' and 'anti-gravity' all being forms of energy used to power spacecraft, so clearly space travel is common in this time period. Humans still live on the surface of the planet, but there is little plant life. Given that in 'The Mutants', set in the thirtieth century, it is stated that 'no one lives on the ground; the air is too poisonous', 'The Ice Warriors' is therefore unlikely to be set in the late-thirtieth century or early-thirty-first century. [A date of 3000 for 'The Ice Warriors' appears in the script and publicity material only, but there is absolutely no evidence on-screen to support this date.]

The only on-screen reference to a date is Clent's comment that the glaciers of 'the second Ice Age' will destroy 'five thousand years of history', which is a meaningless remark without knowing from which millennium Clent believes human history began, unless he is merely stating it is the year 5000.

In 'The Talons Of Weng-Chiang', the Doctor refers to 'the Ice Age about the year five thousand'. It is therefore more than likely that the Ice Ages in 'The Ice Warriors' and 'The Talons Of Weng-Chiang' are one and the same. The only other story set in this time period is 'The Invisible Enemy', which is set 'about five thousand AD'. Of note, the collars of the uniforms worn by the staff at the Brittanicus base are very similar to those as worn by the hospital staff at the Bi-Al Foundation; possibly this is the fashion in this time period.

In 'The Daleks' Master Plan', which is set in 4000, the Earth does not appear to be in the middle of an Ice Age, so it is doubtful that there would be two Ice Ages within the space of 2,000 years: one in 3000 and then one in 5000 (from 'The Talons Of Weng-Chiang'). Also, Miss Garrett knows that Mars does not have a breathable atmosphere (she describes is as being 'chiefly nitrogen. With virtually no oxygen or hydrogen'), and yet in 'The Daleks' Master Plan' (set in 4000) Mars is an Earth colony. Obviously by setting 'The Ice Warriors' in 5000 we can say that Mars has become uninhabitable to humans in the 1,000 years after 'The Daleks' Master Plan'.

Of course, the crew of Brittanicus Base do not recognise the Martians, and given that in 'The Curse Of Peladon' and 'The Monster Of Peladon' the Martian race was an ally of Earth, 'The Ice Warriors' should be set prior to the two Peladon stories, which are set in 3225 and 3275. However, I feel that the link to the two Ice Ages is a stronger dating tool. The year 5000 is the best date for this story.

Penley helped develop the Ioniser and worked with Clent before becoming a scavenger some 'six weeks ago'. At the start of the story Clent has been on a 'ten hour' shift.

10,000 BC ▨ ▨ ▨ ▨ ▨ ▨ ▨ ▨ ▨ ▨ ▨ ▨ ▨ ▨

Walters says that the Martian looks 'pre-Viking', to which Arden replies 'But no civilisation existed in prehistoric times before the first Ice Age'. Later the Doctor says the creature has been 'frozen for centuries in the ice', and later 'when this man was frozen to death only primitive cavemen existed'. Victoria later tells Varga that he has been frozen 'since the First Ice Age, thousands of years ago'. The most recent Ice Age in our history lasted for 2,500,000 years, ending some 12,000 years ago. On the basis that the Martian spaceship and the frozen crew are near the surface of the glacier, we can assume they crashed towards the end of the First Ice Age, around 10,000 BC.

1066 + ▨ ▨ ▨ ▨ ▨ ▨ ▨ ▨ ▨ ▨ ▨ + ▨ ▨

Jamie recognises a Viking helmet, so presumably he has seen one during his travels with the Doctor.

4900 ▨ ▨ ▨ ▨ ▨ ▨ ▨ ▨ ▨ ▨ ▨ ▨ ▨ ▨

Clent says 'we conquered the problem of world famine a century ago'.

4990 ▨ ▨ ▨ ▨ ▨ ▨ ▨ ▨ ▨ ▨ ▨ ▨ ▨ ▨

It is not stated when the Second Ice Age started. Clent asks the Doctor 'where have you been all these years?' which suggests that it was some time ago. We learn that because of over population and the lack of plants, the oxygen levels dropped causing the planet to lose heat. 'Then suddenly one year there was no spring'. The ice began to move at that point. It took the community of world scientists 'years' to calculate the advances. The fact that people are still being evacuated to Africa suggests that it is only a few years since the Ice Age started, but I favour a longer period of, say, 10 years.

▨▨▨▨▨▨▨▨▨ DURATION ▨▨▨▨▨▨▨▨

⇨ Day One (Ep1-2) ▨ ▨ ▨ ▨ ▨ ▨ ▨ ▨ ▨ ▨

It is day when the TARDIS lands. Varga takes Victoria to the ice mountain to free the other Martians that 'night'.

⇨ Day Two (Ep3-6) ▨ ▨ ▨ ▨ ▨ ▨ ▨ ▨ ▨ ▨

The search for Victoria begins at dawn (Clent later greets the Doctor with 'Good morning'). The story ends later that day, within the deadline of 'six hours' before the worldwide concerted operation of all Ionisers takes effect.

THE ENEMY OF THE WORLD

+STORY LINK

'The Ice Warriors' and 'The Enemy Of The World' are probably consecutive: the Doctor tells Kent and Astrid 'my friends and I have been out of touch … On ice, shall we say', referring to 'The Ice Warriors'. Also, Jamie notes that the purpose of Salamander's Suncatcher satellite is like 'the Ioniser', but the Doctor says that the Suncatcher works on 'a rather different principle, I think'.

OBSERVATIONS

- In this time period, the Earth is controlled by the United World Zones organisation. Only four zones are named on-screen: the Australasian Zone (where the Kanowa research station was located); the Central European Zone (Salamander's headquarters were in Hungary), the South African Zone and the Eastern European Zone. It is not clear what zone the Americas fall under. The Suncatcher Mark 7 had made soil in Canada fertile; and Salamander refers to Alaska, so it is clear that the United States of America still exists (see 'Dalek', which is set in 2012).
- On 5 February 1993 in our own history, the Russians put a large reflector mirror into orbit to focus sunlight onto the European continent in an experiment to extend day-light hours and provide light for crops during the night – precisely the function of the Suncatcher.

TIMELINE DATES

2017 ▸ ■ ■ ■ ■ ■ ■ ■ ■ ■ ■ ■ ■ ■

From the original telesnap photographs it is possible to see a date on the metal plate affixed to the rear wall of the helicopter cockpit behind Astrid. The plate says 'Valid Until 31 Dec 2013' or '2018' – it is not clear which year it is. This therefore places the story prior to one of these dates.

[The blurb on the back of the novelisation sets the year as 2030, but this date is never given in the text of the book. In his notes for his proposed 1980 novelisation of the story, author David Whitaker had planned to set the novel 50 years in the future, which is probably where the 2030 blurb originated. Given that Whitaker may also have set his original 1967 script 50 years in the future, then the story could be set in 2017.]

A second date appears on the newspaper found by Swann – it apparently says

'Friday August 2041' [the day of week cannot be read clearly from the Telesnaps]. Obviously this year does not match the licence plate details.

From a technological point of view it is either the late twentieth or very early twenty-first century: vidi-links and radiotelephones are commonplace. Although the characters travel from Europe to Australia by 'rocket' in only two hours, mention is made of hovercars and hover-truck, and yet there are still modern-looking hovercraft and helicopters (Astrid's helicopter is the same make and model as the one used by UNIT in various stories and in 'Fury From The Deep'). There are also holiday liners. However, the technology needed to produce the 'natural' disasters is apparently highly advanced, as is the Mark VII Suncatcher satellite.

The Doctor clearly knows nothing about Salamander, which suggests he has not been to this time period before. Salamander has already been in power for at least five years. That would set 'The Enemy Of The World' some time in the first quarter of the twenty-first century.

In 'Doctor Who (The TV Movie)' there is no indication of the World Zones Organisation in 1999, so clearly the WZO is established at some time in the early twenty-first century. The space wheels of 2080 (see 'The Wheel In Space') are manned by a mixture of nationalities, suggesting there is still the same unified Earth under the United Zones concept seen in 'The Enemy Of The World'. Bruce appears sceptical when Victoria describes the TARDIS as a sort of spaceship, which suggests that there is no advanced space technology to the level as seen in 'The Wheel In Space' in this time period, so on that basis 'The Enemy Of The World' would need to be set prior to 2020.

The Suncatcher Mark VII satellite operates as a weather control system. In 2050, the Gravitron is set up on the moon to perform a similar function (see 'The Moonbase'). The Suncatcher would not be needed if the Gravitron were in operation, so I am certain that 'The Enemy Of The World' is set before 2050. (Perhaps the Gravitron is based in principle on the Suncatcher?)

From the available 'evidence' of the telesnap dates, I would tend to go with the licence plate in the helicopter; the 2018 year of expiry is probably correct, so I have selected 2017.

[Should the new series of Doctor Who remain in production beyond 2015, it is unlikely there will be any acknowledgement of the events of this story, in which case the dating of 'The Enemy Of The World' might need to be extended beyond 2017.]

1550 ▬ ▬ ▬ ▬ ▬ ▬ ▬ ▬ ▬ ▬ ▬ ▬ ▬

Denes says the Eperjest Tokyar ranges in Hungary have been extinct since the 'sixteenth century'.

2012

Salamander says that 'in a few short weeks we, the survivors, will have been down in this shelter for exactly five years'. Both Colin and Mary were 'teenagers' then.

Interestingly, the student called Gareth in 'Doctor Who (The TV Movie)' discovers a way to predict earthquakes in 2009. Perhaps it was based upon his research that Salamander was able to invent a means by which to create earthquakes only three years later.

2013

Kent says he and Salamander 'planned this for years!', and Kent says to the Doctor: 'Four years ago, Doctor, when one country wanted to invade another it set about attacking the confidence of that country', suggesting that world-wide peace was reached once Salamander took power. Therefore, given that the people in the bunker have been there for 'five years', Salamander most likely started taking control of the Zones four years earlier, in 2013, when the first 'artificial' earthquake hit.

2015

Bucharest was 'devastated by the elements two short years ago'.

2016

According to the bunker survivors, 'it's nearly a year' since anyone accompanied Salamander out onto the surface. The newspaper with the headline about the holiday liner sinking has 'last year's date'.

DURATION

There are two locations in this story, one in the northern hemisphere, and the other in the southern hemisphere. The action takes place simultaneously.

⇨ Day One (Ep1-2)

It is day when the TARDIS lands in Australia.

⇨ Day Two (Ep.2-4)

When the action shifts to Budapest, on the other side of the planet, it must be the next day, since it is daylight there (it takes them 'only two hours by rocket' to fly from Australia to Hungary; during that time Bruce drives the 200 miles to the Kanowa centre). Denes is killed shortly after '11 o'clock' that night. At least two hours pass between Ep3 and Ep4, during which Astrid makes the return rocket flight to Australia.

⇨ **Day Three (Ep4-6)** ▦ ▦ ▦ ▦ ▦ ▦ ▦ ▦ ▦ ▦

It is day in Australia when Salamander kills Swann. It is night when the TARDIS crew return to the ship at the end of the story.

THE WEB OF FEAR

+STORY LINK

The start of 'The Web Of Fear' follows on directly from 'The Enemy Of The World': the TARDIS is still out of control following Salamander's expulsion into the vortex ('He's not in a very enviable position, you know, at the moment, floating about time and space'). Before the fade-to-black in the TARDIS, the Doctor is wearing a band-aid on his cheek, from his injury sustained when Salamander's headquarters explodes in 'The Enemy Of The World'. After the fade-to-black the band-aid is gone, but the wound is still visible on the Doctor's face, so it is doubtful that there are off-screen adventures during the fade-to-black.

In this scene the Doctor is seen eating a sandwich. Previously the TARDIS travellers have only ever been seen eating tablets from the TARDIS food dispenser (in 'The Daleks' and 'The Space Museum'). Presumably the Doctor has replaced the dispenser with a more conventional food preparation system since Ian and Barbara left.

TIMELINE DATES

1967, September 4
1967, September 5
1967, September 6
1967, September 7
1967, September 9
1967, September 30 ⊹ ▦ ▦ ▦ ▦ ▦ ▦ ▦ ▦ ▦

In terms of on-screen evidence, according to Victoria 'The Abominable Snowmen' was 'in 1935', an event which Travers says was 'over … forty years ago'. This sets 'The Web Of Fear' no earlier than 1975. 'The Abominable Snowmen' is also said to have been 300 years after 1630, which is 1930, so 40 years after that is only 1970.

Harold Chorley works for 'London Television', a television channel that does not exist, which supports a non-contemporary setting (I doubt he is referring to London Weekend Television, which came into existence in August 1968, some eight months after 'The Web Of Fear' was recorded).

Weams says the Post Office Tower is one of the tallest buildings around. (It was the tallest building on London's skyline until losing that status in 1981 to the NatWest Tower.) As noted under 'The Massacre Of St. Bartholomew's Eve' the Tower was opened on 7 October 1965. This would mean that 'The Web Of Fear' is set after October 1965.

There are also pointers that suggest a contemporary setting. In Ep6 the Doctor passes a poster in one of the Underground stations, the artwork of which is clearly identifiable as that for the film *In The Heat Of The Night* [Rod Steiger, Sidney Poitier; directed by Norman Jewison, released in the US on 2 August 1967], but the actual name of the film has been covered over by a flash that reads 'BLOCK-BUSTERS'. Also, the Underground stations are adorned with other posters and notices of a 1967/1968 contemporary nature, and the maps of the Underground show the routes as they were in early 1968 when the story was made [which was January 1968; additional lines that were added to the system in the 1970s do not, of course, appear on the maps.] Actor Jack Watling was 44 when he made 'The Abominable Snowmen'. If we apply this age to Travers, then he would have to be around 84 in 'The Web Of Fear', however I feel that Travers does not look or act like someone of that age.

Despite some clues to a future setting, 'The Web Of Fear' is best set no later than 1967, the same year that the film *In The Heat of the Night* was released (see also THE UNIT YEARS). It is possible that Victoria is mistaken about the year in which 'The Abominable Snowmen' was set. Alternatively, due to his age, Travers could be wrong and the earlier adventure in Tibet was only 32 years ago, based on Silverstein's comment that the Yeti stood in his museum 'for thirty years'. Travers would therefore be over 75 years old. (In 'The Sound Of Drums', reference is made to the United Nation's 1968 First Contact policy; presumably this was drawn up soon after the Yeti invasion.) 1967 is therefore my preference for the year.

In Ep2, when the web starts to move, Weams says it 'hasn't moved at all the last three weeks'. Dates are given during the slide show in Ep3: the web first appeared on 'the fifth' and 'by the sixth' it had moved to include South Kensington. On 'the seventh' the web was first reported in the Underground. The Yeti 'weren't sighted until the ninth'. Assuming that the month is no later than September, and assuming that the web first appeared over London soon after the Yeti was reactivated, the opening scenes at the museum would be 4 September. The Yeti were sighted on 9 September. The web then became dormant for a while, then 'three weeks' later it started moving again, the same day the Doctor arrived, which is around the 30th.

DURATION

(TARDIS) (Ep1)
The ship is out of control in the Vortex before stabilising. The TARDIS travels a while before being forced to materialise in space.

⇨ **Day (4 September) (Ep1)**
It is night in the museum when the Yeti reactivates.

🕒 **Three weeks or so pass...**

⇨ **Day One (over 'three weeks' later) (30 September) (Ep1-6)**
'It's broad daylight' on the surface when the TARDIS arrives. Captain Knight greets Lethbridge-Stewart in Ep3 with 'Good afternoon, Colonel'. There are no night scenes, so the rest of the story appears to take place that same day.

THE TWO DOCTORS

PLACEMENT

Unlike 'The Three Doctors' and 'The Five Doctors', in which the Doctors are deliberately removed from their time streams and brought together with the aid of Time Lord technology, the meeting between Doctors in this story is purely accidental. As the sixth Doctor explains to Peri: 'when you travel around as much as I do, it's almost inevitable that you'll run into yourself at some point'. Indeed, given that the second Doctor's TARDIS is not on Earth when the sixth Doctor lands, the TARDIS fail-safes do not activate (see MEETING OTHER TIME LORDS). Therefore, I have split the story in two. Details concerning the sixth Doctor's segments are covered under his stories in STORYFILE.

The fact that the sixth Doctor collapses in the TARDIS, similar to the fifth Doctor in 'The Five Doctors' (when his other selves are time scooped), might suggest that a time scoop is involved. But as is pointed out in both 'The Three Doctors' and 'The Five Doctors', to use a time scoop drains too much energy, so it is clear that the second Doctor is not being manipulated by Time Lords from a time period outside of his own GRT, i.e. 1984, the time zone in which that the story takes place, or 2113, which is the sixth Doctor's GRT.

Placing this adventure within the second Doctor's time stream is difficult, given that the story includes several continuity errors. The main ones are: the second Doctor is knowingly acting for the Time Lords when he is still a 'pariah, exiled from Time Lord society'; he has complete control of the TARDIS; and he also looks older [Troughton is 15 years older]. Jamie, also visibly older, displays a previously undisclosed knowledge of the Time Lords, whom he doesn't encounter until 'The War Games'.

There are two placements available for 'The Two Doctors'. One has been named as Season 6B in *Doctor Who – The Discontinuity Guide*. My reasons why this placement does not work are below. The best placement therefore is prior to 'Fury From The Deep', during the time when Victoria travelled with the Doctor. The stories of this period [Season Five] are predominantly consecutive (see the individual Story Link headings for each). The best gap to place 'The Two Doctors' is between 'The Web Of Fear' and 'Fury From The Deep'. Victoria has been delivered somewhere so she can 'learn graphology' (the study of handwriting), although Jamie is doubtful that the Doctor will actually get them back to her!

Of course this placement does not explain or take into account the obvious ageing of the Doctor and Jamie or the other points noted above. But we can ignore the actors' ages, as the first Doctor is noticeably older in 'The Three Doctors' and yet he must come from a point in his time stream prior to 'The Tenth Planet', while the first Doctor looks completely different in 'The Five Doctors' without any explanation for this. The third Doctor is considerably older in the same story, and yet we must accept that he is from a point prior to 'Planet Of The Spiders'. These illustrate that using the age of the actor is not always a recommended method, so I think we can safely ignore the actors' ages. As for the TARDIS console and console room being of a later design, it should be noted that the design and layout of the TARDIS console room did in fact change from story to story during the second Doctor's era, so its different appearance in 'The Two Doctors' is not altogether unusual.

As for the Doctor agreeing to work as an agent for the Time Lords, it is well-documented that this was a scripting error: writer Robert Holmes was under the mistaken belief that it was the second – rather than the third – Doctor who acted as an agent for the Time Lords. [For what it is worth, I think the story would have worked better if it had been the sixth Doctor who was sent to space station Camera by the Time Lords to act under his authority as President of the Time Lords, and it was the second Doctor, who crossed time streams due to the disruptions in the time vortex caused by Kartz and Reimer's time experiments, who comes to his rescue!] My ideas about this are covered below under Gallifrey Link.

SEASON 6B

In the book *Doctor Who – The Discontinuity Guide*, the authors created a mid-season period they called Season 6B, which was an attempt to solve the continuity problems noted above. They theorised that the Doctor was 'hijacked' while on his way to Earth to begin his exile, and allowed to go free so long as he worked for the Celestial Intervention Agency. Jamie and Victoria were taken out of their time streams to be with the Doctor, and the three of them travelled for many more years, which explains why the Doctor and Jamie have aged. Once the Time Lords had finished with the Doctor, he was sent to Earth to begin his exile, and his companions returned to their own time periods. While this idea works in theory, it actually creates just as many continuity problems as it tries to solve!

One of the main flaws is that we are expected to accept the rather unlikely concept that Jamie and Victoria are forcibly removed from their new homes and lives to be reunited with the Doctor because the Time Lords decide he needs to have companions. It is not clear if Jamie has been with the Doctor for 15 more years, or whether he joined the Doctor when he was 15 years older. If the latter, he was removed from Scotland in 1761, and in all likelihood, he would have a wife and family by then. Why would he leave them to go travelling with the Doctor? His memory of his time spent with the Doctor was 'erased' permanently – this is confirmed by the Doctor in 'The Five Doctors'. We assume the events of 'The Highlanders' were not erased. Jamie did not have a temporary block on his memory. As far as Jamie is concerned, he knew the Doctor over a two-day period in April 1746, and he last saw him by the TARDIS, and moments later he 'woke' to find himself being attacked by a lone redcoat (as is glimpsed in 'The War Games'; of note in that scene Jamie is wearing period clothes (the clothes he had on in 'The Highlanders' were left in Atlantis in 'The Underwater Menace') and has been equipped with a sword (which he didn't have at the end 'The Highlanders'!)). An alternative is that the Time Lords reinstated Jamie's memory. But how is that possible when the Doctor makes a point of saying Jamie's memory was erased?

If the Time Lords had to select companions to secure the Doctor's cooperation, it is understandable that they would choose Jamie, but why Victoria, when the Time Lords know of Zoe and that she was with the Doctor at the time of his trial? After all, Victoria left the TARDIS because she was tired of the constant danger she faced (in 'Fury From The Deep' she says, 'Everytime we go anywhere something awful happens … Why can't we go anywhere pleasant? Where there's no fighting. Just peace and happiness?'). It is unlikely she would want to resume that nomadic lifestyle, even 15 years later. In 'Pyramids Of Mars', the Doctor says Victoria 'travelled with me for a time' (in the singular), which precludes any notion that there was a second time.

Other reasons why Season 6B does not work are:

- In 'Frontier In Space', the Doctor tells Jo about his trial and reasons for his exile to Earth. Although this account is slightly modified from the events we see in 'The War Games', he doesn't mention any subsequent missions for the Time Lords, so unless the Doctor's memory of this period was erased at the same time that the other memory blocks were effected prior to his enforced regeneration but not restored along with his other memories at the end of 'The Three Doctors', it is somewhat out of character for the third Doctor to not boast about this period in his life.

- If the second Doctor is working for the CIA, then surely the Time Lord Tribunal who exiled him in the first place would notice he was 'missing'? As is seen in 'Terror Of The Autons' and 'Colony In Space', the Time Lords have been keeping close tabs on the Doctor, and would therefore presumably have been monitoring his journey from Gallifrey to Earth to ensure he arrived in the time and place they had intended, and also to check that his regeneration occurred without any major trauma. They would certainly have been alerted by the fact that he had disappeared *en route* to Earth …

Once you boil it down a bit, the Season 6B theory creates far more continuity issues than it attempts to solve, and it requires much contortion of other established continuity elements to make it work.

I think ignoring the actors' ages and placing 'The Two Doctors' within its intended position – prior to 'Fury From The Deep' – and having the TARDIS crew's memories altered before and after the mission, is a less-contorted and much cleaner explanation than an artificial placement post-trial, pre-exile, with Jamie and Victoria returning through contrived means as is suggested by the Season 6B scenario.

STORY LINK

In 'The Invasion' Jamie says that it 'seems like a couple of weeks ago' that he met Lethbridge-Stewart in 'The Web Of Fear', although four years have passed for the Brigadier. Taking into account that Jamie is alone on space station Camera for 'ten or twelve days', which is only a few days shy of two weeks, we can accept that 'The Two Doctors' takes place a few days after 'The Web Of Fear'. We also have to accept there are no other Time Lord missions for the second Doctor after 'The Two Doctors'. Jamie says he hasn't eaten since 'yesterday'.

GALLIFREY LINK

As a back-story to this adventure, we can assume that the Time Lords who have been monitoring the temporal experiments being conducted by scientists Kartz and Reimer in 1984 are from the second Doctor's 'present' (his GRT is 1663 at this point in the Doctor's time stream). They detect the 'hiccups in the time continuum' caused by the experiments some 321 years in the future in 1984, and presumably discover the dead bodies of the unfortunate Androgums who were sent into time but who never returned. Any time experiments are of grave concern to the Time Lords. Since the Doctor knew Dastari (he attended the inauguration of the space station) he was the only one suited to go to Camera and investigate. (The idea of the Time Lords sending the current Doctor into what is technically Gallifrey's future has also been seen in 'Colony In Space', 'The Curse Of Peladon', 'The Mutants', 'The Brain Of Morbius', and 'Attack Of The Cybermen', so it is not as if this sort of interference in future history was unusual.)

The chief Tribunal official at the Doctor's trial in 'The War Games' says 'we have noted your particular interest in the planet Earth. The frequency of your visits must have given you special knowledge of that world and its problems', which clearly suggests that the Time Lords have always been aware of where the Doctor has been ever since he left Gallifrey, and have been observing (or even manipulating?) his landings on Earth (see LEAVING GALLIFREY).

Although the Doctor is still 'a pariah', the Time Lords know where he is and are able to contact him. In 'The Deadly Assassin' it is hinted that the Doctor once worked for the Celestial Intervention Agency (CIA) (see LIFE ON GALLIFREY), so it would seem that the Doctor is more responsive to enter a dialogue with them rather than with the High Council. Of course there is the possibility that the Doctor is being blackmailed into working for the CIA. Although the Doctor tells Jamie that Victoria is away learning graphology it is possible that she is actually being held hostage by the CIA to ensure the Doctor's cooperation (see Observations).

OBSERVATIONS

- It is clear from the events of 'The War Games' that the Doctor and Jamie have no recollection of their adventure in Spain, as Jamie does not demonstrate any prior knowledge of the Time Lords in 'The War Games'. In fact the Doctor goes to great lengths to explain who they are to Jamie and Zoe. Therefore, we must assume that following the completion of 'Mission Camera' the Time Lords for whom the Doctor is working as an agent erase or alter their memories. We know the Time Lords can do this, as Jamie has his memory erased again in 'The War Games' (the poor lad!) and the Doctor has a block placed on his prior to his exile. (A mind erase and a mind block are two completely different things: a block implies the memory can be restored, as it is in the case of the Doctor in 'The Three Doctors'. But for Jamie his is a permanent erasure, with 'erased' being the term used by the second Doctor in 'The Five Doctors'.)

In 'The Two Doctors' the second Doctor is given the drug siralanomode, which he knows 'affects the memory'. [This is clearly a plot device included in the script to explain why the sixth Doctor doesn't recall this adventure either.] However, it is not clear how this drug works in erasing selective memory. The second Doctor certainly does not appear to be suffering from any memory loss at the end of 'The Two Doctors'. And it is clear from 'Fury From The Deep' that the Doctor still recalls some of his more recent adventures, as he mentions Astrid Ferrier ('The Enemy Of The World') and the Yeti ('The Abominable Snowmen' and 'The Web Of Fear'), and the Doctor later has little trouble projecting thought patterns of 'The Evil Of The Daleks' for Zoe's benefit in 'The Wheel In Space'. Therefore the drug must affect only those memories obtained a few hours after the drug has been administered.

We know that Dastari intended to frame the Time Lords, leaving 'clues' that they were responsible for the massacre on the space station. The Time Lords for whom the second Doctor is working would no doubt want to ensure there was no evidence or record of this. Altering the Doctor and Jamie's (and Victoria's?) memories would be an obvious step for them to take. I would suggest therefore that the manipulating Time Lords erase the TARDIS crew's memories of this entire adventure. Indeed it is even possible that the Time Lords also implanted false memories at the onset of the mission, which is why the Doctor and Jamie knowingly act for the Time Lords. And as for Victoria, it is not clear why she wants 'to learn graphology'. A more likely scenario is that she is being held 'hostage' (on Gallifrey?) to ensure the Doctor's cooperation. On this basis, much of the conversation between Jamie and Doctor in the TARDIS in the opening sequences is false!

And at the end of the adventure, the Doctor and Jamie are reunited with Victoria, all have their memories altered to block certain aspects of their recent exploits (particularly the involvement of the sixth Doctor) and they continue on their way, eventually arriving on the south coast of England, as seen in 'Fury From The Deep'. The second Doctor is totally oblivious of all that has happened to him, and the CIA have protected their secrets. In Spain, the bodies of Dastari, Chessene, Stike, Varl, Shockeye, and an unidentified truck driver, plus the wreckage of the Sontaran spacecraft would be removed. All the bodies in the space station would be removed as well.

1984, August
This date is justified under the sixth Doctor's stories.

1663
The Doctor's GRT is 1663 (see THE DOCTOR'S AGE).

DURATION

⇨ **Day One (Ep1)**
The Doctor and Jamie arrive on the space station before lunch or dinnertime; Jamie hasn't eaten since 'yesterday'.

🕐
'Ten or twelve days' pass – Jamie is alone on the station … while the second Doctor arrives on Earth …

⇨ **Day Thirteen (Ep1-3)**
The sixth Doctor and Peri arrive on the station '10 or 12 days later' and they find Jamie.

⇨ **Day One (Ep1-3)**
Several hours pass on Earth. The augmented second Doctor and Shockeye go to town for lunch.

FURY FROM THE DEEP

STORY LINK

The Doctor mentions Astrid Ferrier – as if 'The Enemy Of The World' was a recent adventure – and the Yeti, so 'The Web Of Fear' is a fairly recent event for him. Jamie and Victoria have been travelling together 'a long time now'. Taking into account Jamie's comment in 'The Invasion' that his meeting with Lethbridge-Stewart between 'The Web Of Fear' and 'The Invasion' 'only seems like a couple of weeks ago', the passage of time between 'The Web Of Fear' and 'Fury From The Deep' can only be a matter of days. When factoring in Jamie's participation in 'The Two Doctors', which takes place between 'The Web Of Fear' and 'Fury From The Deep', and in which he spends 'ten or twelve' days alone on the space station, then the amount of time that can have passed between 'The Web Of Fear' and 'Fury From The Deep' cannot be any more than twelve days.

Victoria comments that they 'always seem to land [on Earth]', to which Jamie notes 'Aye, and it's always England'. Victoria's comment is accurate; the only alien planet she has visited in the TARDIS (on-screen) is Telos (in 'The Tomb Of The Cybermen'), but Jamie's comment is somewhat inaccurate: the only previous (on-screen) occasions when the TARDIS lands in England (during his journeys with the Doctor) are in 'The Faceless Ones' and 'The Web Of Fear'. The other Earth landing sites are an island in the Atlantic Ocean ('The Underwater Menace'), Tibet ('The Abominable Snowmen'), Scotland? ('The Ice Warriors'), Australia ('The Enemy Of The World'), and Spain ('The Two Doctors'). If we take Jamie's comment at face value, then there have been many off-screen adventures since 'The Web Of Fear', all of which are set in England. One of these adventures must have been set during a war, because Victoria mentions that it would take 'a bomb dropping' to wake Jamie; the concept of bombs being dropped from aircraft is an innovation from well after her own time of 1866. (It is an historical fact that fuse-burning explosives were dropped from hot-air balloons onto the city of Venice on 21 August 1849, some 17 years earlier, but I feel Victoria's reference to bombs is more to those released from airplanes.) In another of these off-screen adventures, Victoria must have worn the dress that Sarah finds in the TARDIS wardrobe in 'Pyramids Of Mars'. From a story duration perspective, Victoria has been with the Doctor for about 28 days in total.

Victoria's desire to leave the Doctor and Jamie could have been brought about in part by her recent solo 'adventure' learning graphology (see 'The Two Doctors').

The Doctor says his sonic screwdriver 'never fails' so although it makes its first on-screen appearance in this story, this is not the first time he has used the device.

TIMELINE DATES

1995, February ·

The story was recorded in February [of 1968], which can be the month selected to match seasonal conditions.

The technology of the period, such as video-links, stun weapons, and the refinery itself, could indicate the near future, but the hairstyles and psychedelic wallpaper in the Harrises' quarters suggest the late-1960s. At one point Robson speaks of Harris's 'tuppence ha'penny tin pot ideas', however this is a figure of speech used even today (meaning that something is out of date), so it is not necessarily an indication of the setting being a pre-decimal Britain (Britain went decimal on 15 February 1971).

According to the Doctor in 'The Wheel In Space', Victoria now lives in 'a good historical period; very few wars, great prosperity'. The reference to 'very few wars' is odd, considering that there are mentions of an 'air defence', 'national defences' and 'armed forces' in 'Fury From The Deep'.

The ESG refinery 'supplies all the gas for the whole of the south of England ... and the whole of Wales'. In terms of an historical context, at the time of production [1968], North Sea gas was a relatively new concept, the first major British gas fields being exploited in the mid-1960s (the first strike was in late 1965). Robson says 'I've been drilling for gas in the North Sea for most of my life'; he appears to be in his early 40s, so he could have commenced his career with ESG when in his late teens. Robson also says he is not prepared to 'ruin the reputation of 30 years', but he must be speaking of ESG's reputation, rather than his own. Assuming that ESG began drilling in 1965, then 'Fury From The Deep' is set no more than 30 years after that, say 1995. (Interestingly, by setting the story in the mid-1990s, in some 22 years' time, Victoria will experience Salamander's rise to power as dictator of the world all over again!)

There have been disturbances in the pipes 'for three weeks now'.

1750

The Doctor shows Jamie and Victoria a picture of the weed creature in a book he has in the TARDIS. The picture is based on descriptions 'supplied by ancient mariners in the North Sea in the middle of the eighteenth century'. Jamie remarks that 'that's my time' (1746), so I have chosen 1750.

1965
1970 – 1974

Robson says 'I've been drilling for gas in the North Sea for most of my life', and that he is not prepared to 'ruin the reputation of 30 years'. As noted above, he was probably on one of the first rigs after the discovery of North Sea gas in 1965 (as in our history). Robson appears to be in his early 40s; so he probably started his career with ESG when he was around 18 years of age, say 1970. He once spent 'four years' on one of the early rigs without ever going ashore, so we could say this was his first four years working for ESG.

Greg Sutton mentions North Sea gas in 'Inferno' (set in 1970) so we know that gas was being exploited at the time of that story. In 'Doctor Who And The Silurians' the cyclotron at the Research Centre is 'not the only atomic research centre in the country', and the Nuton Power Complex in 'The Claws Of Axos' and 'The Dæmons' provides 'power for the whole of Britain' (1972 – 1973).

DURATION

⇨ **Day One (Ep1-6)**

It is 'morning' when the TARDIS arrives. Megan Jones is called in that afternoon. She arrives 'three hours' later. The Doctor spends over 'an hour' on the rig and it takes 'one half hour' to rig up the sound amplifiers. A celebratory meal is held that night. Victoria tells Jamie she wants to stay on Earth.

⇨ **Day Two (Ep6)**

The Doctor and Jamie leave early the next morning.

THE WHEEL IN SPACE

+STORY LINK

The serial opens with the closing moments of 'Fury From The Deep' as the Doctor and Jamie say good-bye to Victoria. There is a fade-to-black after the TARDIS dematerialises and before it lands on the *Silver Carrier*, so it is possible for another adventure to take place here, but since Jamie talks about Victoria while they examine the *Silver Carrier*, it seems likely that the two stories are consecutive. Jamie slept at the Harrises' the night before leaving in the TARDIS, and yet he falls asleep on the *Silver Carrier*, which suggests that some time may have passed since they left Earth, in which Jamie his fallen tired.

CYBERMAN LINK

As covered under CYBERMAN HISTORY, this is the Cybermen's fourth appearance near Earth. After the Cybermen fail to obtain control of the validium in 1988 (in 'Silver Nemesis'), they retreat to their base (on Planet 14?), where they make preparations to attack humans in ways other than direct attacks on Earth. They therefore turn their sights on Earth's outposts, space stations and transporter ships. The first phase of the attack is to gain control of space Wheel 3, and spearhead an invasion of Earth through that means. First they need to set in motion a series of events that will result in the detonation of a sun and planets in the Hercules cluster, sending a stream of meteors towards the (soon to be defenceless) station …

OBSERVATIONS

- Gemma Corwyn gives Jamie and the Doctor a thorough medical examination ('you and your friend are healthy specimens'). This includes listening to the Doctor's chest. She later comments that the Doctor's x-rays show an 'extraordinary' result. Oddly she makes no comment about the Doctor having two hearts.
- Gemma Corwyn refers to Zoe's training 'at the city'. Zoe refers to 'the city' being her home in 'The Mind Robber'. The image of the city in that story appears to be that of Brasilia, the capital of Brazil.

LANGUAGE

The Cybermen appear to speak English, since all the Wheel's crew understand them, even when the Doctor is not present, and the TARDIS is not on the station. The two members who first encounter the Cybermen on the *Silver Carrier* understand them (however the TARDIS is on board and could be acting as a translator).

TIMELINE DATES

2080 ◆

This is a difficult story to date. The Doctor does not know what time zone they are in. He says: 'If I knew when "Now" was, I might be able to hazard a guess'.

Zoe says 'pre-century history isn't really my field' (although she does show a surprisingly good knowledge of Earth wars in 'The War Games'). In 'The War Games', she states twice that she was born 'in the twenty-first century'. While dreaming in 'The Mind Robber' she says she used to read the Karkus comic strip 'in the year 2000'. In 'The Invasion' the Brigadier estimates Zoe to be 'about 19 or so', which suggests that Zoe may have been born in the early 2000s.

Bill Duggan says the laser on the Wheel is there for 'self-defence. We can blot out any attacker up to ten thousand miles in any one direction'. Given that in 2084 Earth is in a state of war, it could be that he was referring to attack by the Sentinel Seven satellites as seen in 'Warriors Of The Deep'. This would suggest setting 'The Wheel In Space' in the 2080s. Another dating clue is that Wheel 3 issues 'advanced weather information' to Earth. This suggests setting 'The Wheel In Space' before 2050, when the Gravitron was in use ('The Moonbase'), otherwise why would Earth need weather information if the Gravitron already controlled the weather?

The Cyber-Planner does not recognise the second Doctor's face, but on hearing the name 'Doctor' says: 'The Doctor is known and recorded. An enemy'; so it is clear that they know of the Doctor by name only: the Cybermen probably know of the first Doctor from 'The Tenth Planet' and the seventh from 'Silver Nemesis'; and the Cybermen in 'The Moonbase' recognise the second Doctor, either from Planet 14 ('The Invasion'), or from 'The Wheel In Space', which would support setting 'The Wheel In Space' before 2070. It is odd therefore that the crew on the Wheel, including Zoe, have never heard of the Cybermen ('Cybermen? Where did you dream up a name like that?'), considering Hobson's comment in 'The Moonbase' that 'there were Cybermen. Every child knows that'. Of course Zoe does confess that pre-century history is not her field, so we can at least understand her ignorance of the attack of Mondas in 1986 ('The Tenth Planet') and when five million Cybermen appeared on Earth for one day in 2007 ('Army Of Ghosts'). Of course, the people of the world affected by the Cybermen incursion probably did not know these 'metal men' (as Harold Saxon described them on television in 'The Sound Of Drums') were called Cybermen. And as Rhys and Beth in *Torchwood* say, it was probably a mass-hallucination brought about by 'psychotropic drugs' in the public water supplies. On this basis we can take it that the crew were simply not overly familiar with either invasion.

As also covered under CYBERMAN HISTORY, the best placement for 'The Wheel In Space' is after 'The Moonbase' (2070) and before 'The Seeds Of Death' (in which Zoe has never heard of the T-Mat system). I have therefore set 'The Wheel In Space' in 2080.

The Perseus Cluster exploded 'a week ago' / 'within seven days'. The *Silver Carrier* is 'nine weeks overdue'.

2050 – 2080

Earth now has an advanced space technology. There is a 'space fleet' with 'deep spaceships'. There are several references to 'the space programme'. There is the 'Voyager Five', a manned space vessel, which could simply be an ordinary orbital craft like our own Shuttle. There are at least five space Wheels, each serviced by freighters like the *Silver Carrier*. The third Wheel appears to be situated between Earth and Venus; it gives weather reports to Earth, and the fact that Wheel 5 is only 87 million miles away shows clearly that Wheel 3 is near to Earth.

The Wheel acts as 'a half-way house for deep spaceships', which suggests that Venus has been colonised: Bill Duggan has a flower from that planet, and he refers to 'interstellar' flora, which by definition seems to mean space travel to other solar systems. (But 'deep space' is not necessarily exclusive to meaning other parts of the galaxy. Rather it could simply be a reference to the other planets in Earth's own solar system: after all, Gemma Corwyn's husband died in the asteroid belt.)

2077 ▨ ▨ ▨ ▨ ▨ ▨ ▨ ▨ ▨ ▨ ▨ ▨ ▨ ▨
Gemma tells that Doctor that her husband 'died in the asteroid belt three years ago'.

DURATION

(TARDIS) (Ep1) ▨ ▨ ▨ ▨ ▨ ▨ ▨ ▨ ▨ ▨ ▨ ▨ ▨
The Doctor and Jamie are in the TARDIS for a while before landing on the freighter.

⇨ **Day One (Ep1-4)** ▨ ▨ ▨ ▨ ▨ ▨ ▨ ▨ ▨ ▨ ▨ ▨
The Doctor and Jamie spend a few hours on the *Silver Carrier*. They are brought to the space Wheel and are there for several hours.

⇨ **Day Two (Ep4-6)** ▨ ▨ ▨ ▨ ▨ ▨ ▨ ▨ ▨ ▨ ▨ ▨
Duggan destroys the radio equipment in Ep4 at 'approximately 12.52 hours'. (The events of 'The Evil Of The Daleks' (Redux) take place while the TARDIS is still onboard *Silver Carrier* ...)

THE EVIL OF THE DALEKS (REDUX)

+STORY LINK

At the end of 'The Wheel In Space' the Doctor shows Zoe a thought-projection of the sort of dangers she is likely to face if she chooses to travel in the TARDIS. He projects a mental image of 'The Evil Of The Daleks'. [This leads directly into a repeat screening of that story. Over the opening moments of Ep1, there is a specially recorded conversation between the Doctor and Zoe as he narrates the complete story of 'The Evil Of The Daleks' for her.] Presumably the TARDIS is still on board the *Silver Carrier* during the entire narrative ...

OBSERVATIONS

- In 'The Trial Of A Time Lord' the Doctor asks how is it possible for the Matrix to show events at which he is not present. It is then explained to him that the TARDIS has been 'bugged' with 'the new surveillance system'. However, it is clear that the TARDIS already has this system in place, otherwise how could the Doctor show Zoe parts of 'The Evil Of The Daleks' at which he was not present? And more to the point, the TARDIS is stuck in 1966 for most of the story before being transported to Skaro, and yet the Doctor is able to project images of scenes in 1866 at which he isn't even present ...

Other *Doctor Who* stories were repeated during the series' run, with some even scheduled during breaks between stories, and in two instances actually between episodes of a new story. While 'The Evil Of The Daleks' (Redux) is the only instance in which a repeat is incorporated into the narrative, we could assume the Doctor (and/or his companions) has at other times reviewed past adventures using the thought projection equipment, thus incorporating other 'repeats' into the series' narrative.

DURATION

(TARDIS (Ep1-7)

With the TARDIS still on board the *Silver Carrier* it must take the Doctor several hours to project the entire 'adventure' for Zoe.

THE DOMINATORS

+STORY LINK

Zoe is still wearing her space Wheel uniform, and the Doctor says he is exhausted after 'projecting all those mental images', a reference to his having shown Zoe a projection of his recent encounter with the Daleks (see 'The Evil Of The Daleks' (Redux) above), so 'The Dominators' directly follows on from the 'repeat' of the adventure with the Daleks. Despite seeing the potential dangers of time travel Zoe has obviously decided anyway to join the Doctor and Jamie on their travels.

The Dominators note that Jamie has undergone 'recent rapid learning', being the education that the Scots lad has gained during his years with the Doctor (See THE DOCTOR'S AGE).

OBSERVATIONS

- Toba says the Dominators are 'masters of the ten galaxies'. Clearly Earth's galaxy is not one of these. Rago, however, says they rule just one galaxy but are spreading their forces to others. If they are indeed the masters of ten galaxies, it is surprising that we have never seen or heard of them before or since. With 'The Dominators' set in 1970, by 1987 perhaps the Dominators had been overthrown, which is why the 12 galaxies in 'Dragonfire' are not under Dominator control. Certainly by 4000 AD the major galaxies are controlled by individual powers – some of which are represented at the Daleks' alliance on Kembel ('The Daleks' Master Plan').

LANGUAGE

The Dominators and Quarks are able to converse with the Dulcians when the Doctor is not present, so presumably they all speak the same language. The signs on the radiation meter at the research station are in English: e.g. RADIATION / NORMAL / DANGER. Balan refers to tremors on Dulkis as 'earthquakes'.

TIMELINE DATES

1970, July +

The Doctor says 'We are from a different world, a different time' (in terms of the Doctor's GRT he is from 1663). At the end of the adventure the TARDIS is trapped in the lava flow of a volcano. In the next adventure, 'The Mind Robber', the Doctor uses the emergency unit, which 'moves the TARDIS out of the time space dimension. Out of reality … We're nowhere'. As Zoe then points out, 'we're not actually in flight', so the ship has simply been shifted sideways, not forwards or backwards in time. Returning to the TARDIS from the white void, the Doctor activates the TARDIS, the time rotor moves, and there is the familiar dematerialisation sound. However, the rotor stops and the vibration begins, leading to the TARDIS disintegrating, so it seems that the ship returns to the white void. At the beginning of 'The Invasion' the TARDIS emerges from 'nowhere' on the dark side of Earth's moon in July 1970. It is therefore logical that if the TARDIS emerges from 'nowhere' in 1970 then it must also have entered in 1970. Accordingly, I have set 'The Dominators' in the same time zone as 'The Invasion'.

Pre-1798

The Doctor was previously on Dulkis 'some time ago', presumably during his first incarnation, because Jamie has never been there before. The Doctor remembers the Dulcians as being friendly and peaceful, and yet he does not recall the Island of Death, so clearly his visit was at a time before the atomic test on the island in 1798 (see below).

1798

Balan says that the island was used as an atomic test site 'a hundred and seventy two years' ago. Toba later confirms that it was 'seventeen point two decades ago'. Senex says 'for centuries we have lived in peace', ever since Director Olim banned all weapons.

⇨ **Day One (Ep1-5)**

It is day on the island and at the capital (which is '8 minutes' from the island by capsule). There are no night breaks, so the story takes place over one Dulcian day. The island and the capital are both in the southern hemisphere of Dulkis.

THE MIND ROBBER

+STORY LINK

This story directly follows on from 'The Dominators', with the TARDIS still on Dulkis and in the path of the lava flow.

OBSERVATIONS

- Trapped in the void, Zoe sees images of her home, the city she lived in. This appears to be Brasilia, the capital of Brazil.
- If we accept that the story is a collective dream, we can theorise as to how the dream state is created. It is possible that it is all part of the TARDIS's defence mechanism, a way of telling its crew of the danger outside in the white void. In 'The Wheel In Space' the TARDIS projects images of more pleasant places to be as a warning of the danger. Similarly, in 'Inside The Spaceship', the ship projects images of Time being taken away as a warning to the crew of the danger outside the ship. In 'The Mind Robber' the mercury leak could have triggered the same defence system; although it is odd that the Doctor does not recognise it as such considering how relatively recent 'The Wheel In Space' is for the Doctor and Jamie. Alternatively, the white void has 'infected' the crew so they see images of their homes, and this leads to the nightmare. The fact that we hear a mocking laughter suggests that there is an intelligence living in the void and that it is that which 'infects' their minds. That Jamie and Zoe encounter the white robots in the void indicates that they are real and therefore not part of the dreamscape.

  The high-pitched sound the TARDIS crew hear just before the TARDIS appears to break up is the trigger for the dream, and it works on the imagination centres of the brain, much like the mind parasite in 'The Mind Of Evil' and the hypno-sound device the Master uses in 'Frontier In Space' affect the fear centres of the mind (did the Master get the parasite from the white void?). Whatever the actual cause of the nightmare, the effect is the same. We could even interpret the fictional characters that the time travellers encounter as having been 'robbed' from the TARDIS crew's minds, and given physicality by whichever of the crew encounters them first: the unicorn, the redcoat, Rapunzel, the image of the Highlands, and the white robots all came from Jamie's mind. In fact, Jamie is having a dream about the unicorn shortly before the TARDIS 'breaks' up. The city, Medusa, the Minotaur and the Karkus are all from Zoe's mind. As stated, Zoe knows the Karkus from the comic strip pages of her local newspaper, the *Hourly Telepress*. Gulliver (who 'set sail from Bristol on May 4th 1699'), the clockwork soldiers and the five children are all from the Doctor's mind (he has read E Nesbit's novels?) We could even interpret these characters as being specific to their memories: the white robots are Jamie and Zoe's collective impression of the Cybermen. Gulliver could be the Doctor's recollection of a fellow Time Lord (see 'The War Games') or of himself, while the Master could be based on the Doctor's enemy, the Master. But more curiously, who could the children be based on? Does the Doctor have more than one grandchild? The fact that the Doctor rearranges Jamie's face could be an oblique allusion to regeneration, and perhaps specifically to being able to select future regenerations (as he is later offered in 'The War Games'). Indeed, the whole weird landscape into which the Doctor is cast could also be a reflection of the Matrix on Gallifrey ...

- The writer is controlled by the Master Brain computer, which considers humans to have the greatest imagination. The Master is getting old, and wants the Doctor to take over because 'you, Doctor are ageless. You exist outside the barriers of time and space'. It is never revealed who built the Master Computer. Considering that the characters encountered and the titles of the books seen in the citadel are all of Earth origin ('this vast library [has] all the known works of fiction. All the masterpieces written by Earthmen since the beginning of time'), it is apparent that other people have been snatched from Earth over time to serve as the Master. As this is part of the dream-state, the computer could be the intelligence in the white void.
- When they enter the old house, Zoe comments 'there must be somebody here. These candles are alight'. However, in 'The Space Pirates' Jamie takes great delight in explaining to Zoe what candles are: she has never seen them before. Also, Zoe says she read the adventures of the Karkus 'in the strip section of the *Hourly Telepress*', which was published 'in the year 2000', implying that this is the time that she comes from. However in 'The War Games', while under a lie detector, she says she was born in the 21st century (her first adventure, 'The

Wheel In Space', is set in 2080). If she wasn't born until long after 2000, then how can she read the newspapers from that time? She may be referring to having read old copies of the paper, or maybe even a later reprint of the strip, which was first published in 2000. These anomalies could simply be part of Zoe's 'dream-state'.

- Although *The Adventures of Captain Jack Harkaway* was created for this serial, a fictional character called Jack Harkaway did exist. In July 1871, author Bracebridge Hemyng introduced readers of *Boys Of England* magazine to Jack Harkaway. His adventures continued until June 1899, when the magazine (which debuted in November 1866) ceased publication.

TIMELINE DATES

<<1970, July>>
The TARDIS is trapped in the white void (which is 'nowhere') after leaving Dulkis. Both 'The Dominators' and 'The Invasion' are set in July 1970. The TARDIS has only moved its spatial location, not its temporal location, between these stories, so 'The Mind Robber' must also be set in July 1970. At the beginning of 'The Invasion' the TARDIS crew are still in the same positions they are in when the TARDIS appears to break up in 'The Mind Robber', and the writer who is the Master of the Land of Fiction is nowhere to be seen, nor is he referred to. It is hinted at that 'The Mind Robber' adventure is nothing more than a shared nightmare brought about by the mysterious force which assaults the TARDIS in the white void. Given the strange things that happen to the characters in the Land Of Fiction – such as Jamie's face changing – the adventure cannot be real, so the idea of it all being a dream is therefore highly likely, and the option I prefer.

I like to think that all the scenes in the TARDIS up to the shot of the ship breaking up are real, but from that point on, up to the closing moments of 'The Mind Robber' and opening scenes from 'The Invasion', everything is a 'dream'. In fact, at the beginning of 'The Invasion', Jamie says 'Hey, Doctor, it's all right, it worked', which could merely be a reference to the Doctor succeeding in pulling the TARDIS free from the void, just as he is trying to do in 'The Mind Robber', rather than their escape from the Land of Fiction. Therefore, I have not included any of the details – such as the dates given by the writer ('I left England in the summer of 1926' / 'for 25 years I delivered 5,000 words every day'), or those from Gulliver – in the TIMELINE.

DURATION

⇨ **Day One (Ep1–5)**
After leaving Dulkis, the TARDIS is trapped in the white void for several hours, while the TARDIS crew experience a shared nightmare (in which there are still breaks for night and day: it is night in the forest of words – until the lights are turned on – and it is dark again when the unicorn appears. It is day when Jamie meets Rapunzel, but it is night during the final scenes on the rooftop).

THE INVASION

+STORY LINK

'The Invasion' follows directly on from 'The Mind Robber', with the TARDIS reassembling itself. The TARDIS crew are in the same positions they are in when the TARDIS appears to break up.

Jamie says it 'seems like a couple of weeks ago' that he met Lethbridge-Stewart in 'The Web Of Fear'. Taking into account the duration of the stories between 'The Web Of Fear' and 'The Invasion', as well as 'The Two Doctors' (with a duration of 12 days for the second Doctor), it can be determined that indeed about 14 days have passed for Jamie since 'The Web Of Fear'.

CYBERMAN LINK

As covered under CYBERMAN HISTORY, 'The Invasion' is the Cybermen's first appearance on Earth. The Cyber-Planner confirms that they have not been on Earth before. These Cybermen are an advance party sent out from Mondas, who set up a base somewhere close to Earth (on Planet 14?), from which to prepare the way for the return of Mondas in 1986. Tobias Vaughn detected their communications, and they began an alliance that lasts for five years. Troops of Cybermen are brought to Earth (via ships that are reported as UFOs), and they are cocooned at one of the International Electromatics buildings until they are revived. A Cyber-Planner device, representing the Cyber-Controller, is set up in each of Vaughn's IE offices.

OBSERVATIONS

- It is not made very clear, but it seems that International Electromatics, which achieved its monopoly 'suddenly', only reached its position with the aid of Cyber-technology. With Vaughn having worked with the Cybermen for five years planning the invasion, it seems likely that the micro-monolithic circuit inside the electronic devices is of Cyber-design, and over these five years IE has grown to dominate world markets as part of the invasion plans. (In a strange twist of fate, it is possible the Z Bombs from 'The Tenth Planet' are made with IE components, and that the Cybermen on Earth informed their counterparts approaching Earth on Mondas of these bombs, and where they were located, which is why the Cybermen specifically attacked the remote Snowcap base in 1986.)

- Only the Americans and the Russians have missiles ready to fire. At the time of the invasion the Russians are planning to launch a manned orbital lunar survey rocket. A man walked on the moon in 1969 ('Blink'), and by the end of 1970, Mars was being explored (see 'The Ambassadors Of Death').

LANGUAGE

Only a few Cybermen are seen to speak. The Cyber-Planner device speaks with Vaughn in English.

TIMELINE DATES

1970, July ＊

When the Doctor and Jamie meet Lethbridge-Stewart, the Brigadier says the Yeti invasion 'must be four years ago now' from his perspective. (From the Doctor and Jamie's perspective 'it only seems like a couple of weeks ago, doesn't it?'). The production team intended to set 'The Web Of Fear' in 1975, and therefore 'The Invasion' in 1979, but as covered under THE UNIT YEARS, this dating is impossible given later on-screen details, such as the Global Factor and Mawdryn Factor. By reinterpreting some of the clues in 'The Web Of Fear' I have set that story in 1967. 'The Invasion' can now be set in 1970, if we take the four years referred to by the Brigadier as being 1967, 1968, 1969 and 1970 rather than 1967-68, 68-69, 69-70, which is only three. [In 'Dalek', Van Statten has the head of a Cyberman in his museum. A detail not on-screen, but visible in production photos of the casing, is the location and year in which the head was recovered: 'London Underground Sewer Date 1975'. However this year is not necessarily the date of the invasion itself, but is merely the year in which the head was found. But since the text on the label is not visible on-screen, I have discounted it as a dating reference.]

The Doctor deduces that it is 'twentieth century. England, in summer time, I should say. See the rain clouds'. He could be joking, but I will accept his observation as being correct. This would be mid-June to mid-September. Although the serial was recorded in September (of 1968), I have selected July, in order that 'Spearhead From Space' can be set 'months' later in October (see below).

The day of the invasion is a weekday; two of the victims are dressed in business clothes.

Professor Watkins 'left about a week ago'; at the same time that Isobel was kicked out of her studio.

Pre-1965

The Cyber-Planner recalls encountering the Doctor and Jamie on 'Planet 14'. During that adventure the Cybermen discover the Doctor 'has a machine', the TARDIS, which they subsequently recognise and fire a missile at in 'The Invasion'. This off-screen adventure takes place in Earth history terms prior to 1965, before Vaughn contacts the Cybermen, when the invasion plans began in terms of the Cybermen's chronological history. But for the Doctor and Jamie the adventure on Planet 14 would have to have taken place some time after 'The Invasion', but before 'The War Games'.

1965

It was Vaughn who first made contact with the Cybermen and 'provided the means by which they could travel to Earth'. He says 'I have worked with the Cybermen for five years preparing this invasion', which would be since 1965. The invasion is brought forward by 24 hours because of the threat posed by the Doctor.

1967

Lethbridge-Stewart says he was put in charge of the British division of UNIT soon after the Yeti invasion (see 'The Web Of Fear'). In 'Terror Of The Zygons' he recalls being sceptical 'before I joined UNIT', which clearly indicates that UNIT was not set up as a result of the Yeti invasion, and had existed prior to then, but for some reason was not called in to service during that incident.

1969 early

UFO sightings had been reported for 'well over a year now', being about early 1969 when the Cybermen first started to arrive at the IE compound.

1970, June

According to Isobel the Traverses left for America 'about a month ago'. They have gone 'for a year'.

⇨ **Day One (Ep1-6)**

The TARDIS lands very early in the morning. It is still before noon when Vaughn contacts Routledge in Ep4 (he greets the Major with 'Good morning'). In Ep5 Vaughn declares that the invasion will take place 'in 15 hours' time … at dawn tomorrow'; assuming that dawn is at 6.00 am, this scene takes place at 3.00 pm. Red Sector reports in to UNIT HQ at '20:30 hours' (8.30 pm) just before Watkins is rescued (it is dark outside Vaughn's office when Gregory reports back to IE). The Doctor and Zoe spend all night making the polarisers.

⇨ **Day Two (Ep6-8)**

The Cybermen emerge from the sewers 'at dawn' the next morning. It is a business day, based on the clothing worn by some of the collapsing pedestrians. It takes Turner '2 hours 7 minutes' to fly to Russia. He gets there shortly before 10 am. The Russian rocket is launched, and four hours later, 'approximately six hours' short of its reaching the Cyber-ship, it is diverted (the clock at Henlow Downs Base reads '2.20' pm). The Cyber-ship is destroyed '12 minutes' later, at '2.32' pm. Isobel is wearing the same dress she had on the last two days, so we can assume the TARDIS leaves later on Day Two.

UNSEEN ADVENTURES

In 'The Invasion', the Cyber-Planner recalls an encounter with the Doctor and Jamie (but not Zoe?) on 'Planet 14', and even knows about the TARDIS (see CYBERMAN HISTORY), but the Doctor does not know this adventure, so clearly it must come later in the second Doctor's time stream.

THE KROTONS

STORY LINK

At the end of 'The Invasion', Jamie's right leg is bandaged and he is limping (having been shot and wounded on Day Two of 'The Invasion'). But in 'The Krotons' there is no sign of a wound, bandage or limp, so some time must have passed since the

Cyberman adventure, during which time Jamie's leg has fully healed.

OBSERVATIONS

- A variety of periods are given for the length of time the Krotons have been on the planet: from 'thousands of years' to 'a thousand years'. Vana and Abu are announced as 'Class 3196'. Zoe is announced as 'Class 3197' and the Doctor 'Class 3198'. This would imply that this is the number of Gonds that have so far been processed. Selris says the two best Gond students are selected 'every so often'. Abu and Vana are 'alone of [their] generation' to be selected, so it is possible that, with perhaps no more than two Gonds taken every 20 or so years, the Krotons have been on the planet for 3196 x 20 years. I have not included this date in the TIMELINE due to its uncertain nature.

LANGUAGE

The Gonds presumably speak the same language as their teachers, the Krotons. The dials on the learning machines and in the Dynatrope are labelled with Earth numerals. The Gallifreyan acronym HADS also stands for the same words in English. The Doctor writes down instructions for Beta to follow.

TIMELINE DATES

????

No relative dates are given, so I have placed 'The Krotons' under ????

DURATION

⇨ Day One (Ep1-2)

It is day (there are two suns) when the TARDIS lands. It is night when the Gonds attack the learning machines (the custodian carries a torch).

⇨ Day Two (Ep2-4)

It is morning when the Doctor re-examines Vana, and he and Zoe enter the Dynatrope. Jamie enters 'about an hour after' them. 'The Dynatrope will exhaust in three hours' from a point half-way into Ep3, and reserve power will last 'for 27 more minutes' at a point into Ep4, so the duration from Ep3 and for all of Ep4 is no more than three hours 27 minutes.

THE SEEDS OF DEATH

+STORY LINK

Zoe is wearing the same plastic dress she is wearing in 'The Krotons', so it would appear that 'The Seeds Of Death' immediately follows that story.

OBSERVATIONS

- In terms of Martian history, this is their first true encounter with the people of Earth – and the Doctor. The Doctor says that 'Mars is a dying planet'. In 'The Wheel In Space' it is established that our solar system has been explored fully, so this would include Mars. Obviously these Martians have either been in hibernation on Mars, or have come from a colony planet.

LANGUAGE

The warriors speak to the humans on the moon, so it is clear that the Martians all speak English.

TIMELINE DATES

2096, February ▪ ▪ ▪ ▪ ▪ ▪ ▪ ▪ ▪ ▪ ▪

Like 'The Wheel In Space', this story is difficult to date. The Doctor places the ion jet rocket as being a product of the 'twenty-first century'. Eldrad recognises the TARDIS as a 'twentieth century police box', so it is clearly the twenty-first century, somewhere between 2001 and 2100.

There are many references to the fact that there is no longer a space programme ('Nobody cares any more about exploring space' / 'Except by out of date rocket' / 'We gave up training astronauts years ago' / 'But surely that equipment hasn't been used for years' / 'rockets haven't been used for years' / 'It's been years since we sent up a satellite'). Given that Zoe is unaware of the T-Mat, 'The Seeds Of Death' should be set after her time, 2080 (see 'The Wheel In Space'). However, the fact that Eldrad's ion jet was originally designed to go 'beyond the moon' suggests that in this time period the moon was as far as space exploration has reached and there is not yet a space fleet or space programme as there is in Zoe's time, so 'The Seeds Of Death' could therefore be set before 'The Wheel In Space'.

From the fact that England's weather is controlled from the Weather Control Bureau in London, and that there are other Weather Control Bureau around the world, it is clear that 'The Seeds Of Death' should be set after 'The Moonbase', after

2070. In that story, the Gravitron on the moon controls the world's weather. It is a logical progression that direct control of a country's own weather would supersede the Gravitron. Therefore, 'The Seeds Of Death' must be set after 2070. In addition, in 'The Seeds Of Death' there is a video-link between Earth and the T-Mat base, but in 'The Moonbase' there is no such communications link, which again suggests that 'The Moonbase' is set in a time before 'The Seeds Of Death'.

In 2084 the world is in a state of potential war between two power blocs ('Warriors Of The Deep'). In 'The Seeds Of Death' the T-Mat is connected to most European capital cities. If the 2084 war is between Western and Eastern Europe then it would appear that the political situation in 'The Seeds Of Death' has long since eased. Brett says that Moscow will 'think we're deliberately sabotaging their stuff if this goes on', which suggests that the political relationship with Russia (or at least its twenty-first century equivalent) is still unstable (following the end of the war crisis?). There is still a United Nations (presumably reinstated following the Salamander affair of 'The Enemy Of The World', in which the world is divided into Zones, each governed by a single representative of the World Zone Organisation).

The T-Mat 'system is still in its early stages', but it has been around for several years: Eldrad and Radnor haven't spoken 'for a good many years' since Radnor left Eldrad's laboratory and went to work for the Government Administration for T-Mat. Given that Eldrad has 'been in rocketry all my life', and he appears to be in his late 60s, we can assume that there was a flourishing space programme for at least 40 of those years. There are still rockets in use in 2070 (in 'The Moonbase'), so this supports setting 'The Seeds Of Death' after 2070. The T-Mat itself is probably no more than 10 years old.

As mentioned in 'Nightmare Of Eden', the Galactic Salvage and Insurance, formed in 2068, went into liquidation in 2096. We could assume that this was because T-Mat superseded rockets as the primary form of travel, meaning there was no longer any space junk to salvage. On this basis we should set 'The Seeds Of Death' around 2096.

Eldrad states that the seedpods have been sent only to capital cities in 'cold climates. All northern hemisphere. In all those cities it's winter, as it is here'. Winter for England would set the period mid-December to mid-March. We can use February as a halfway point.

1500
The Doctor dates da Vinci's drawing as being 'about 1500' (see also 'The Time Meddler').

1961, April 12 (+?)
The Doctor dates the Russian space helmet as being 'certainly not later than 1960'.

He then realises the figure is 'Gagarin, the first Earth man in space'. In our history, Gagarin made his historic journey into space on 12 April 1961. (Gagarin blasted off in Vostock I at 9.07 am Moscow Time, and orbited for 1 hour 29 minutes. He landed at 10.55 am Moscow time). The fact that the Doctor is a year out could be simply explained that he means the helmet itself was developed 'not later than 1960'; he is not necessarily dating the actual space-walk. The Doctor was not necessarily on Earth at the time, hence the (*?) notation.

2056
2086
2096

Eldrad says his ion jet rocket 'was to have been the vehicle to take Man beyond the moon. T-Mat put an end to all that'. He designed the rocket: 'I have been in rocketry all my life. My father engineered the first lunar passenger module, and I travelled on the last trip back to Earth before it all finished … space travel … no more money, no more facilities. My life's work abandoned just like that. All because of T-Mat'. Eldrad is about 60, so he has been in rocketry since 2056. It has been 'a long time past' that he built the rocket with which he had planned 'an unauthorised journey into space', but his poor health and age meant he could no longer see his dream realised. In Zoe's time Earth has a highly advanced space programme; there is a space fleet, Venus and the asteroid belt had been explored, all of which are 'beyond the moon'.

We can speculate that when Eldrad was born, there was still a strong space programme. However, exploration of the outer planets soon became expensive, and eventually only the moon was the extent to which space travel went, hence the lunar passenger module. Eldrad designed and built the first ion jet rocket, which had a cheaper and more efficient power source, to once again take Man beyond the moon. Around this time the Gravitron on the moon was closed down and weather control was given to each individual country. Then, around 2084, the world's political situation changed and the Earth was placed in a state of near-war (see 'Warriors Of The Deep'). The last of the lunar modules returned to Earth as a result. T-Mat was then developed around 2086, which put an end to the war. Space exploration was no longer a priority.

2096 – 2164

Given that the next Earth-bound story in the TIMELINE is 'The Dalek Invasion Of Earth', there is no reason to assume that the T-Mat was not still in use by the time of the Dalek Invasion.

DURATION

⇨ **Day One (Ep1-6)**

Fewsham has been on duty on the moonbase 'all night' relative to the crew T-Mat control in England. It is 'morning' when Radnor arrives at T-Mat control. There are no night scenes during the rest of the story, but sufficient time needs to be taken into account for preparing the rocket launch. Looking at the Duration from the point of the moonbase crew, clearly the equivalent of only one day has passed for them. It appears to be night in England when it rains at the end.

THE SPACE PIRATES

STORY LINK

There is nothing to suggest that 'The Space Pirates' takes place immediately after 'The Seeds Of Death'. At the end of 'The Seeds Of Death', Jamie and Zoe get wet because of the rain. In 'The Space Pirates' they are both wearing new outfits. When they arrive on the beacon, the Doctor says: 'I don't think we're quite where I expected', which suggests that he had a specific destination in mind.

TIMELINE DATES

2146 ✦

When Hermack requests Milo Clancey's registration details, the registration record for the *LIZ 79* appears on the monitor. The actual text cannot be read clearly [but according to BBC documentation the text says the year in which the ship had its registration cancelled was '1992']. Given that Hermack later says the *LIZ 79* has 'been afloat for about 40 years', this suggests a setting of not earlier than 2032. This date fits in quite well with the period when Earth was staring space exploration. If the *LIZ 79* had been registered initially prior to 1992, this would mean that space exploration was quite advanced by the late 1980s (as is definitely the case in 'The Android Invasion', and in 'State Of Decay', in which the *Hydrax* was shown to have been launched around 1999 (see 'State Of Decay'), in that deep space explorer ships were being launched in the 1990s (see also SPACE-FLIGHT). However, on the basis that the date cannot actually be seen clearly, I prefer not to use 1992 as a valid dating tool.

It is stated on several occasions that the mineral argonite is 'the most valuable mineral known to Man'. Zoe is not at all familiar with argonite, which suggests that 'The Space Pirates' is set well after her time of 2080. Given that the Daleks invade Earth in 2164 (see 'The Dalek Invasion Of Earth'), and that the V-Ship is in regular contact with Central Flight Information on Earth, it is clear that 'The Space Pirates' should be set before 2164.

As covered under 'Nightmare Of Eden', warp drive was not developed until around 2106. Given that Ta is 'the most productive planet in the entire galaxy', it would appear that by this time period the whole galaxy has been explored, which would set 'The Space Pirates' many years after 'Nightmare Of Eden'. Taking into account the Dalek invasion there is now an available spread of 58 years.

According to Hermack and Warne, Clancey was 'the last' of the 'old mining prospectors [who] were the first men to go out into deep space. For a time they had the place to themselves, roaming the space-ways, looking for planets, jumping each other's claims ... And then the Space Corps came along and started to enforce law and order'. The Space Corps is also mentioned in 'Nightmare Of Eden', which supports setting 'The Space Pirates' in the same century.

If Clancey is indeed one of the very first pioneers to go 'into deep space', then the LIZ 79 (a C-Class freighter) is probably one of the first ships fitted with warp drive, so 'The Space Pirates' would therefore be set no more than 40 years after that was discovered, around 2146. This date fits in with the events of 'The Dalek Invasion Of Earth'.

2116
Milo lost his registration papers for the LIZ 79 'about 30 years ago'.

2121
Milo and Issigri were partners for '15 years' before going their own ways, say from 2121 to 2136.

2121
2131
It took Milo and Dom 'about 10 years' to drill the mine on Ta clean.

2136
Milo has been alone on the LIZ without a transponder for about '10 years', from 2136 to 2146.

2142
2143 ▓ ▪ ▪ ▪ ▪ ▪ ▪ ▪ ▪ ▪ ▪ ▪ ▪ ▪ ▪

Dom Issigri disappeared 'years ago now'; being a prisoner of Caven's 'for years', say 2142 to 2146. He tried to escape during 'the first year', 2143.

2144 ▓ ▪ ▪ ▪ ▪ ▪ ▪ ▪ ▪ ▪ ▪ ▪ ▪ ▪ ▪

Milo had been sending the Space Corps reports on the pirates' activities for 'the last 2 years', which was around the time that Madeleine Issigri tried to buy Milo out, '2 years ago'.

DURATION

Although there are a number of different locations – the space beacons, the V-Ship, the planets Lobos and Ta – the story takes place in the same time zone; Duration is therefore based from the perspective of the Space Corps.

⇨ Day One (Ep1) ▓ ▪ ▪ ▪ ▪ ▪ ▪ ▪ ▪ ▪ ▪ ▪

In Ep1 Hermack calls a staff meeting for '20:00 hours Sector Four solar time'. We never see the meeting take place, but this shows that the story begins prior to 8.00 pm, say 7.30 pm. It takes the V-Ship '2 hours 20 minutes' to reach Alpha 4, being 9.50 pm. The ship is still some '90 minutes' away when the beacon explodes, say 10.40 pm.

⇨ Day Two (Ep2-5?) ▓ ▪ ▪ ▪ ▪ ▪ ▪ ▪ ▪ ▪ ▪

'3 hours' after Beacon Alpha 4 explodes (1.40 am, which makes Ep2 the next day 'solar time'), Milo Clancey is brought on board (after he has tried to cook his 'breakfast'). Later, Warne spends 'a few hours' following Clancey. When Warne calls Hermack, who is on Ta, in Ep2 and Ep3, he opens with what appears to be the time of his call: '13:00', '13:10', '13:30', which places his calls after 1 pm. It is at '13:30' when Warne reports that Clancey has docked with Beacon Alpha 4, where he meets the Doctor and his friends. In Ep4, when the Doctor and his friends are imprisoned on Ta, Milo takes an 'hour' to find them, which places these sequences earlier that evening.

⇨ Day Three (Ep5?-6) ▓ ▪ ▪ ▪ ▪ ▪ ▪ ▪ ▪ ▪ ▪

In Ep6, the V-Ship will be in position to attack the pirates in '55 minutes'. Caven's bomb is set to go off at '12:00', presumably noon, so the V-Ship sets off around 11.55 am. Given that the time is '13:30' in Ep3, for it to be noon in Ep6, it must be 23 hours or so later. The story ends at some point after noon.

THE THREE DOCTORS

STORY LINK

The Time Lords observe the second Doctor running across a smoky wasteland so we can assume that this is where they remove him from his time stream. (They either obtained this image from the Doctor's TARDIS memory banks in 'The War Games', or as noted in that story, the Time Lords have in fact been observing the Doctor's travels ever since he left Gallifrey.)

If this relates to an on-screen adventure, it can only be at a point in his own time stream after 'The Invasion', because the Doctor knows Benton and the Brigadier from the Cybermen invasion (however he does not instantly recognise Benton, so it is not immediately after 'The Invasion'). The Doctor says he has been brought 'into my own future, so to speak'. The wasteland could be the 1917 war zone from 'The War Games', the smoke being the time barrier mist. The Doctor tears his right trouser knee early in that story, but the Doctor's trousers are undamaged in 'The Three Doctors', so the Doctor would have to have been pulled from time during Ep1 of 'The War Games'. However, the scarf in the Doctor's coat pocket is different, so it is more likely that the Doctor is taken from before instead of during 'The War Games'.

As covered under GALLIFREY HISTORY, because removing the Doctor from his time stream is such a drain of 'temporal energy', the Time Lords would have needed to cast the transportation unit only as far back as to a point just before the Doctor's regeneration, because it would otherwise have been a needless waste of energy to go back and take the Doctor from an earlier point. Besides, by taking the second Doctor towards the end of his time stream, they also get a Doctor with more experience. On this basis, I have set 'The Three Doctors' between 'The Space Pirates' and 'The War Games'.

OBSERVATIONS

- The Doctor has a memory cube in his pocket with which to contact the Time Lords in 'The War Games'. It is possible that the Time Lords from 'The Three Doctors' put it there when they return him to the planet. When the second Doctor is returned to his own time stream, these Time Lords do not erase his memory of the Omega adventure. This would explain why the Doctor rejects the faces offered to him at his trial (because he knows what his new appearance is), and why in 'The Five Doctors' he is able to recall 'The Three Doctors' adventure.
- Omega is the Doctor's boyhood hero. Of note, the second Doctor names one

of his Daleks in 'The Evil Of The Daleks' Omega, and shows some distress then confusion on hearing of Penley's Omega Factor in 'The Ice Warriors'.

TIMELINE DATES

????
The time zone of the planet from which the second Doctor is scooped is not known.

- Refer to 'The Three Doctors' under the third Doctor's stories for more details on this adventure.

DURATION

⇨ **Day One (Ep1)**
The second Doctor is on a planet when he is abducted by the Time Lords. (He is on Earth and Omega's domain over a period of a few hours.)

THE WAR GAMES

TIMELINE NOTE

At the end of the story, the Time Lords 'dematerialise' the War Lord. The effect of this is that the war games never actually take place, except within an 'alternative' timeline. Only the Doctor and the other Time Lords are aware that this 'alternative' reality even occurred (see THE N-SPACE UNIVERSE). This could be one of the reasons why the Time Lords wiped Jamie and Zoe's memories.

STORY LINK

When the Doctor attempts to open the safe in Smythe's room, Jamie jokingly wonders if he will use 'a tuning fork'; the Doctor used one to open a locked door in 'The Space Pirates'.

As noted above, I believe that the point from which the second Doctor is removed by the Time Lords in 'The Three Doctors' is between 'The Space Pirates' and 'The War Games'. From a story duration perspective, Zoe has been with the Doctor for only about 17 days, but this term is probably longer once gaps between non-consecutive stories are factored in. Likewise, Jamie has been with the Doctor for no more than two years.

GALLIFREY LINK

This is the first time the Doctor has returned to his planet since he left in GRT 1610. He has been away for 53 years (see THE DOCTOR'S AGE). The three Time Lords who try the Doctor are members of the Tribunal (they are not named as such until 'Terror Of The Autons'). The Tribunal is an independent department that answers to the High Council (in a similar way to how our own Ministry of Justice answers to the Government). And while some members of the High Council are apparently secretly part of the Celestial Intervention Agency, some members of the Tribunal are no doubt also involved with the CIA, and it is probably with the approval of both factions that the Doctor is given only the minor sentence of exile (see 'The Deadly Assassin'). The fact that he is allowed to keep the TARDIS (he did after all steal it) also indicates that his exile is not solely a punishment for the Doctor, but is for their own benefit, since they can use the Doctor as an agent ...

OBSERVATIONS

- The map of the war zones found by the Doctor in Smythe's safe is split into 12 sections: 1917 War Zone; American Civil War Zone; Crimean War Zone; Roman War Zone; Mexican Civil War Zone; English Civil War Zone; 30 Years War Zone; Boer War Zone; Peninsular War Zone; Russo-Japanese War Zone; and Greek Zone; with the Alien HQ in the centre. There are three other war zones which are referred to but not positioned on the map: 1745, from where the Redcoat was abducted; 1871, where Private Moor is from; and one of the Resistance leaders appears to be from the French Revolution of 1794 (see 'The Reign Of Terror').

- The SIDRATs are similar to TARDISes, but have 'dimensional flexibility' and a 'remote control'. The Doctor says that 'in my day these things were impossible to achieve without shortening the life of the time control units'. The War Chief has in fact not solved that problem, meaning that the machines are nearing the end of their natural life span. Indeed, the War Chief later reveals that only two machines have enough power remaining. In 'The Two Doctors' the second Doctor is given a Stattenheim remote control by the Time Lords (the sixth Doctor says he's always wanted one of those), which means that the problem of subsequent power loss when using a remote control had been solved while the Doctor was absent from Gallifrey. The Rani has a remote in 'The Mark Of The Rani', and by 'The Trial Of A Time Lord', the Master also possesses one, so remote controlled TARDISes must have become commonplace during the 53 years that the Doctor is away from Gallifrey.

- If the Doctor was on the run from his own people, why did he carry the components for the memory cube in his pocket? It could be that he was given the box by the Time Lords (the CIA?) when they returned him to his own time stream at the end of 'The Three Doctors', knowing that he would use it in the near future, to ensure that he would be captured to stand trial in due course.

- While the Doctor is on trial, we see two technicians examining his TARDIS. As this point in the story the Doctor has not yet been sentenced, so it is unlikely that they are preparing the ship for the Doctor's impending exile to Earth. It is more likely that they are installing the Mark Three Emergency Transceiver, which the Doctor later disconnects (see 'The Creature From The Pit'), and downloading the TARDIS's flight computer and memory banks into the Matrix, so the Time Lords can find out where the Doctor has been. At his trial the head Time Lord says 'we have noted your particular interest in the planet Earth. The frequency of your visits must have given you special knowledge of that world and its problems'. This indicates they have either been fully aware of where he has been ever since he left Gallifrey, or they have simply read the Doctor's time logs from the TARDIS during the recess.

- Although the Doctor 'borrowed' the TARDIS, the Time Lords let him keep it when they exile him to Earth. They could have quite easily delivered him to Earth by other means (Time Ring, for instance). As is revealed in 'The Deadly Assassin', the Type 40 capsule was by that time obsolete, so obviously they had no further use for the ship. But one reason for letting him keep the ship was because he would need some means by which to communicate with the Time Lords (through the telepathic circuits – see 'The Three Doctors' and 'Frontier In Space'), and also in the case of a regeneration crisis he would need the Zero Room. The Time Lords wouldn't be so cruel as to deny him that. The fact that they give him a homing device indicates that they wholly intended for him to have access to the TARDIS at all times. And besides, he would need the ship if he were to act as their agent from time to time …

- Jamie spends at least one full year with the Doctor, and Zoe less than a month, but both are returned 'to a moment in time just before they went away' with the Doctor, so they are now out of sync with Earth. The same 'out of sync' effect happens to Ben and Polly in 'The Faceless Ones', Jo in 'Colony In Space' and 'The Time Monster', Tegan in 'Time-Flight' and 'Resurrection Of The Daleks', Turlough in 'Planet Of Fire' and Rose Tyler in 'Aliens Of London', and Martha Jones ('Smith And Jones' to 'The Sound Of Drums').

- The Doctor leaves Gallifrey to begin his exile in 1970 (see 'Spearhead From Space') but, as covered under 'The Five Doctors' below, the Doctor manages to gain control of the TARDIS and lands instead in 1984 …

LANGUAGE

The Doctor cannot understand the soldier Du Pont, who speaks in French. The Germans who capture the ambulance believe the Doctor is an English spy, presumably because of his accent. The Time Lords call Earth 'Earth', and not one of the names in other languages for it, i.e. Erde, Terre. The Aliens must speak the languages of the various soldiers they have abducted – German, French, Spanish, etc – unless, with their ability to hypnotise their victims, they give the appearance of speaking their languages.

TIMELINE DATES

<<1917>> +

The War Chief is tried by the Time Lords and found guilty. His sentence is to be dematerialised: 'It will be as though you had never existed'. The result of this is that the war games never take place. With the kidnapped soldiers plus Jamie and Zoe's memories adjusted, the only people who will ever remember the events that take place in 'The War Games' will be the Doctor and the tribunal Time Lords. They are immune to the 'cancellation' effect (see also 'Carnival Of Monsters'). Of course, this means that the War Chief could still be alive. But if the Time Lords are immune to the changes in the time lines, then logically the War Chief would still have to be dead ...

Despite the fact that the War Games never actually take place, it is still necessary to determine a time zone for the alternative timeline.

The War Chief says of humans: 'For a half a million years they have been systematically killing each other'. This statement is quite ambiguous, and could mean:

a) The Aliens visited many different time zones in Earth history in order to select from which of several time periods they would take soldiers. To account for the War Chief's comment, they probably covered a total spread of 500,000 years, spanning from the Stone Age in 100,000 BC (see '100,000 BC') to the far distant future of AD 400,000.

b) The Aliens themselves have come from the far future, around 400,000, and they have been observing human history for 500,000 years, taking into account that human history began about 100,000 BC (see '100,000 BC').
This option is highly unlikely, however, on the grounds that if the Aliens are from the future and came to the past to invade the galaxy, they would know if they failed or succeeded by the simple fact that in their own future time, they should already be the rulers of the galaxy.

c) The War Chief is speaking in terms of his being a Time Lord, and as such he would know about Earth's past and future.

The purpose of the war games is for the Aliens to build an army from the survivors with which 'to conquer the entire galaxy. A thousand inhabited worlds'. One wonders if Gallifrey is included here. The War Chief says the Aliens intend to invade 'our galaxy', so this suggests that Gallifrey's location is in Earth's galaxy, as also established in 'Terror Of The Autons' and 'Pyramids Of Mars' (but contradicted in 'Doctor Who (The TV Movie)'; see THE N-SPACE UNIVERSE).

It is expected that Earth would also be included in the invasion plans. In fact, the Security Chief asks, 'Have we taken humans from later than the Earth year 1917?' The Alien Scientist replies, 'Of course not. Greater technological knowledge would be dangerous'. From this it should be taken that if Earth's technology post-1917 is considered too advanced for their own army then the Aliens would not be attempting to conquer the galaxy in a time period in which they could be defeated by superior technology from Earth. Therefore it is logical that the Aliens are planning to invade Earth's galaxy in a time period prior to 1917.

The War Chief reveals that he brought the space/time machines, the SIDRATs, to the planet (the Aliens only know how to operate them but not 'how to construct them'). On this basis alone only (c) above can be considered, and this I have selected.

Lady Jennifer recalls how she was 'driving through a forest, and all of a sudden there was this strange sort of mist. Fog'. After passing through it, she found herself on the war planet. This seems to suggest that the SIDRATs themselves were not used for the initial abductions. The SIDRATs appear to be used merely to travel between the time zones on the war planet. Perhaps they are no longer capable of time travel. The War Chief reveals to the Doctor that there are only two functioning machines left operational (but out of how many originally?). This is a strange development considering the ultimate goal of the Aliens. To me this suggests that once the human army was fully ready, the Aliens would invade the galaxy using conventional spaceships, which again supports the pre-1917 dating for the war games. Considering the number of planets there are to invade ('a thousand inhabited worlds'), the Aliens would have to attack several planets at once to make the invasion effective. This would be a difficult task to achieve with only a few time-capable ships.

It seems logical also that the war games are taking place in the same time zone from which that the Aliens themselves come (the Aliens travel to and from their 'home planet' with considerable ease, presumably by conventional spaceship and not by SIDRAT), which would also be the time zone in which the invasion was intended to take place: 1917.

On the other hand, the Aliens also pilot one of the SIDRATs from the war planet to

Gallifrey. On the assumption that the ship is no longer capable of time travel, then the war planet and Gallifrey are contemporaneous. However, based on the Doctor's GRT, the year on Gallifrey is 1663.

I have selected 1917 as the most likely date on the basis that Earth post-1917 would be too advanced enough to be able to withstand the Aliens' invasion, and that the army would be amassing on the planet in the same time zone they intend to invade.

???? ▾
The TARDIS makes three brief landings before arriving on Gallifrey: the Doctor sets the coordinates 'to take us to a planet on the outer-most fringes of the galaxy', and the ship lands on the surface of an ocean (which could actually be Earth relative to the location of the Aliens' planet); then to a 'place where we will be safe', which is 'in outer space'; then a 'quick transference jump' to an alligator-infested swamp. None of these landings can be dated accurately.

1663 ▾
When the Doctor calls in the Time Lords, he does so by sending a telepathic signal to Gallifrey. The Time Lords who respond would have to be those in the Doctor's 'present', his GRT. As covered in THE DOCTOR'S AGE, the Doctor's GRT at this point in his time stream is 1663.

83 BC
Returning to the 1917 war zone, the Doctor says 'where we were attacked by the Romans it is two thousand years ago', which is 83 BC.

1618 – 48
The War Chief mentions this war, and it is also seen on the war zone map. These are the years of the Thirty Years War in our history.

1642 – 48
The name is seen on the war zone map. These are the dates of the English Civil War in our history (see 'The Awakening').

1745
The Redcoat says he comes from '1745'. Both the Doctor and Jamie state incorrectly that Jamie is also from '1745', when they should be saying 1746 (see 'The Highlanders'). Of note, the war zone map seen in Ep8 does not have a 1745 or 1746 war zone.

1746, April 17

Jamie is 'returned to a moment in time just before [he] went away' with the Doctor, which was on 17 April 1746, as seen in 'The Highlanders'. The Time Lords have been able to replicate his original period clothes, which were left on Atlantis ('The Underwater Menace').

1794

One of the resistance soldiers is dressed in the uniform of a French soldier from this period (see 'The Reign Of Terror'), although there is no 1794 war zone on the zone map seen in Ep8.

1807 – 14

The name is seen on the war zone map. The Peninsular War in Spain was fought during these years in our history.

1821

'Greek Zone' is seen on the war zone map. It is not clear which war this is, probably the Greek war of independence, which was in 1821 in our history.

1854, March 24 – 1855, September 8

The 'Crimean War' is seen on the war zone map. These are the years of this war in our history.

1862

Zoe gives the date as 'America. 1862. That was the American Civil War, wasn't it?' In our history the American Civil War began on 12 April 1861 and came to an end on 26 April 1865 (but see 'The Chase'). The 1862 date is, however, historically inaccurate given that Harper should not be there on the grounds that black men did not enlist in the Northern army until 1863!

1871

When trying to hypnotise Moor, Von Weich says, 'The year is 1871. You're in the British Army'. The War Chief says the soldiers have been taken 'from most of the major wars in the Earth', but there was not a (historically recorded) major war in 1871. Of note, there is no 1871 war zone on the map seen in Ep8.

1899 – 1902

The name is seen on the war zone map, but there are no dates. In our history, the Boer

War began on 11 October 1899 and came to a conclusion on 31 May 1902. Russell was taken during the war, say 1900 (perhaps from Mafeking? – see 'The Daleks' Master Plan', 'The Invasion Of Time', 'The Unicorn And The Wasp').

1905, May 27 – 28

The War Chief mentions 'the war between Russia and Japan of Nineteen Hundred and Five', and the name 'Russo-Japanese War' is seen on the war zone map. In our history, this was a sea battle that was triggered by events in October 1904 when the Russian naval fleet moved into Japanese waters.

1910, November 20

'Mexican Civil War Zone' appears on the war zone map. The Mexican Civil War in our history was fought in this year. It was a revolution against the dictator Porfirio Diaz, who was eventually deposed on 25 May 1911.

1917

There are many references to the '1917 War Zone'; the Doctor refers to it as 'the 1914/18 war' at one point.

2080

Zoe is 'returned to a moment in time just before [she] went away' with the Doctor, which is 2080 (see 'The Wheel In Space'). She is wearing her space Wheel uniform that she left behind on Dulkis (see 'The Dominators'). The Time Lords must have replicated the uniform.

DURATION

The war games take place on an Earth-like planet. In order to maintain the illusion that the soldiers think they are still on Earth, the planet selected for the games would have to be identical to Earth in almost every way, including the days being exactly 24 hours long. The days and nights are in sync across all the war zones, despite them being different 'time zones'. I think that the term 'time zone' does not mean that each war exists within a different temporal location on the planet but rather the term is used to describe the different periods of Earth history. This is evidenced by the fact that the Redcoat in Ep2 manages to walk from his own zone (1745) and into the 1917 zone; he has not actually travelled in time by changing his location. However, the 'mist' between the war zones must be capable of allowing movement between different zones even if they are not adjacent. This is evidenced by the fact that the ambulance moves from the 1917 zone to the Roman Zone even when, as can be seen by the war zone map in Ep8, these two zones are not adjacent. This suggests that the SIDRAT devices act simply as transporter units between non-adjacent zones rather than as time machines.

⇨ **Day One (Ep1-2)**

It is day in the '1917 Zone' when the TARDIS arrives. The Doctor is to be executed 'at dawn tomorrow'.

⇨ **Day Two (Ep.2-3)**

Zoe wakes at dawn to rescue the Doctor. The clock at the prison appears to read 9.15 am when Jamie is rescued. It is night when the travellers return to the Chateau to get the war zone map.

⇨ **Day Three (Ep3-4)**

It is day when the travellers are captured by the Germans. They stop 'for the night' at the barn in the 'America, 1862' zone. The Doctor and Zoe travel to the Alien HQ.

⇨ **Day Four (Ep4-8)**

A cock is heard crowing at the 1862 barn signalling it is the next day. As everyone is sleeping, it is presumably night when Villar arrives at the Chateau.

⇨ **Day Five (Ep8-9)**

By morning Russell has returned to the Chateau with the Resistance leaders. The TARDIS leaves later the same day.

(TARDIS) (Ep10)

The TARDIS makes three quick landings at three different locations before arriving on Gallifrey.

⇨ **Day One (Ep10)**

A few hours are spent on Gallifrey.

THE FIVE DOCTORS

+STORY LINK

For the second Doctor to know that Jamie and Zoe had their memories erased by the

Time Lords, his visit to the UNIT reunion in 1984 would have to be at a time after his trial in 'The War Games'. It is of note that during his trial, the right knee of the Doctor's trousers is ripped. When the third Doctor falls from the TARDIS in 'Spearhead From Space' we can see that the right knee of his trousers is still torn, which shows a direct line between 'The War Games' and 'Spearhead From Space'. The second Doctor's trousers are not torn in 'The Five Doctors', so by placing that story between 'The War Games' and 'Spearhead From Space' we lose this nice piece of continuity. I would suggest that prior to 'The Five Doctors' the Doctor changed clothes, and then prior to 'Spearhead From Space' he put the old pair back on, or he also tore the knee of his new trousers.

Given that he is seen spinning off on his way to begin his exile on Earth at the end of 'The War Games', we can only theorise that he was somehow able to break free of the Time Lords' control of the TARDIS and take the ship on a wild journey across time to evade recapture. He says 'For once I was able to steer the TARDIS. And here I am! ... I really shouldn't be here at all. I'm not exactly breaking the laws of time, but I am bending them a little', which could refer to the fact that he has jumped forwards in time from his intended arrival in 1970, which seems to indicate that he is surprised at how easy it was!

Now, having evaded the Time Lords and postponed his exile, he still ends up on Earth, but in 1984, 14 years in the future to the time zone to which he was being sent. He finds out the year he is in by reading a copy of *The Times*. Knowing what time zone he is in, he probably makes the decision to track down his only friends on Earth, such as Travers and the Brigadier, whom he expects will still be alive in this time zone. Reading of the UNIT reunion, he takes the TARDIS back in time by one day. He knows where UNIT HQ is because he has been there before (in 'The Three Doctors'), but given that UNIT has several HQs all over England, he was rather lucky that the reunion was held at the same location of his previous visit 13 years earlier (relative to the Brigadier).

Later, when the black obelisk chases him and the Brigadier, the Doctor says 'I think our past is catching up with us – or maybe it's our future?' This could mean that he fears that the Time Lords have finally discovered that he is 'missing' and have sent the obelisk to recapture him in order to ensure that his 'future' of an exile on Earth is delivered.

The Doctor's comment about the Brigadier's office being redecorated and about the quality of his replacement (the third Doctor) is quite humorous given that he was in the UNIT offices only just recently within his own time stream (in 'The Three Doctors', which is set between 'The Space Pirates' and 'The War Games'). Also, it is interesting that he makes no comment about Colonel Crichton's resemblance to Lt

Jeremy Carstairs, the British soldier whom he met on the Alien war planet only days earlier [both characters having been played by the same actor, David Savile].

At the end of 'The Five Doctors', the Doctor and the Brigadier are presumably returned to UNIT HQ on Earth. On the journey back to Earth the Doctor's memory is most likely altered by the High Council to remove all recollection of 'The Three Doctors' and 'The Five Doctors' adventures, just as they had done with Jamie and Zoe in 'The War Games'. The Doctor is guided back to his own TARDIS (which is somewhere near UNIT HQ). Still hoping to evade the Time Lords, he is unsuccessful. The Time Lords presumably regain control of the TARDIS, the ship is sent to 1970, and the Doctor's second regeneration triggered … (see 'Spearhead From Space').

- Refer to 'The Five Doctors' under the fifth Doctor's stories for more details on this adventure.

OBSERVATIONS

- While reminiscing with the Brigadier, the Doctor mentions 'the terrible Zodin' who 'happened in the future'. In 'Attack Of The Cybermen' we discover that Zodin is a woman. It is possible that she is a Time Lord. I have not included the Doctor's encounter with her in the TIMELINE.

TIMELINE DATES

1984, March ▸ ▨ ▨ ▨ ▨ ▨ ▨ ▨ ▨ ▨ ▨ ▨
This is the date of the Brigadier's reunion: refer to 'The Five Doctors' for details.

DURATION

⇨ **Day One** ▨ ▨ ▨ ▨ ▨ ▨ ▨ ▨ ▨ ▨ ▨
It is day when the Doctor and the Brigadier are abducted. They are on Gallifrey for several hours. Both are eventually returned to the same point in time and space. (He is on Gallifrey for a few hours.)

SPEARHEAD FROM SPACE

+STORY LINK

The Doctor leaves Gallifrey at the end of 'The War Games' to begin his exile on Earth.

As covered under 'The Five Doctors' entry above, the second Doctor manages to break free from the Time Lords' control of the TARDIS and travel to 1984. After the Brigadier is safely returned to his own time at the end of 'The Five Doctors', the second Doctor is unsuccessful in evading the Time Lords again, and they regain control of the TARDIS. His mind is wiped of the secret of the TARDIS – and presumably of his encounter with his future selves (in 'Spearhead From Space' he says he has lost his memory) – and his forced regeneration occurs shortly before his landing in Oxley woods. The newly-regenerated Doctor, still wearing his previous persona's clothes, including torn trousers (but different shoes and now wearing a ring on the little finger of his left hand), stumbles out of the TARDIS ...

UNIT HQ – LONDON # 1

UNIT HQ is no longer in a Hercules transporter plane (as in 'The Invasion'). The actual location used in 'Spearhead From Space' is a central London railroad depot and Lethbridge-Stewart confirms that this is the 'London HQ'.

We see the Brigadier's office and a couple of corridors. The UNIT lab is situated in a large open area with partitions. It only has one level, and apparently no windows. The walls have the standard whitewashed brick finish.

UNIT also has its own radar tracking station but it is unlikely to be part of the London-based buildings. It could be the same one seen in 'The Claws Of Axos'.

There have been a few changes of personnel since the events of 'The Invasion'. Captain Turner is no longer with UNIT, having been replaced by Captain Munro. Sergeant Walters and Corporal Tracy are also absent, the latter being replaced by Corporal Forbes, perhaps? Corporal Benton is, however, still with UNIT (although he does not appear in this story). Captain Mike Yates, although not seen in 'Spearhead From Space', was put in charge of the clean-up following the Auton attack, as is mentioned in 'Terror Of The Autons'.

OBSERVATIONS

- In 'The War Games' the Time Lords inform the Doctor that they have noted his interest in the planet Earth and that he is to be exiled to the twentieth century. A century covers a long time so there must have been a reason why they selected the latter quarter as opposed to the early or the middle part of the century in which to exile him. They probably noted his association with Travers and Lethbridge-Stewart in 1970 and therefore determined that this time period was appropriate, and could also be considered technologically primitive by Gallifreyan standards to ensure that the Doctor is unable to reactivate the TARDIS. It is also possible that the CIA has a hand in selecting this period having noted that Earth is particularly vulnerable to alien attacks at this point in its history. As noted under GALLIFREY HISTORY and THE DOCTOR'S AGE, the Doctor's exile to Earth is in their relative future (relative to GRT 1663), by some 307 years.

- It is a common but mistaken belief that UNIT was set up as a result of the Yeti invasion (see 'The Web Of Fear'). But in 'Spearhead From Space' the Brigadier tells Liz Shaw that 'since UNIT was formed there have been two attempts to invade this planet', and that the Doctor helped 'on both occasions'. He is clearly referring to the Yeti and Cybermen invasions ('The Web Of Fear' and 'The Invasion'), which shows clearly that UNIT was already in existence at the time of the Yeti invasion but for some reason was not directly involved. In 'Terror Of The Zygons' the Brigadier states that 'before I joined UNIT I was highly sceptical', which supports that he was not involved in the setting up of UNIT. It is possible that the Dalek invasion in 1963 (see 'Remembrance Of The Daleks') was but one major turning point that leads to UNIT being established. In that story, it is the 'Counter Intrusion Measures, United Kingdom' forces which battle the Daleks. In 'The Sound Of Drums', reference is made to the 1968 First Contact policy. Presumably this was drawn up soon after the Yeti incursion. In 'The Lost Boy', Sarah's UNIT file contains a note that UNIT was formed in response to something relating to the Underground, but most of the text is obscured.
- During the shower scene in Ep2, it is revealed that the Doctor has a tattoo on his lower right arm. No other Doctor has this marking, so what could it signify? The markings could be a Time Lord brand, placed on the Doctor's arm as part of his sentence and subsequently removed when his exile is lifted, since it cannot be seen on the fourth Doctor's uncovered arm in 'Robot' and 'The Hand Of Fear' or the fifth's in 'Planet Of Fire' or the ninth's in 'Dalek'.

LANGUAGE

Channing speaks English, but this could be from Hibbert's mind. When the Doctor is unconscious at the hospital he mumbles not in Gallifreyan but in English.

TIMELINE DATES

1970, October •

In 'Planet Of The Spiders', the Brigadier says that 'one time I didn't see [the Doctor] for months and what's more, when he did turn up again he had a new face'. This is clearly a reference to the relative time that has passed for the Brigadier between 'The

Invasion' and 'Spearhead From Space'. In 'The Sontaran Stratagem', the Doctor says he used to work for UNIT a 'long time ago. Back in the Seventies. Or was it the Eighties?' Therefore, 'Spearhead From Space' can't be set prior to 1970 (if it was 1969 or earlier, the Doctor would also have said he'd worked with UNIT 'in the Sixties'.) The story can't be set any earlier than October 1969 due to the fact that the song 'Oh Well – Part One' by Fleetwood Mac which is heard on the plastics factory radio had not been released before October of that year. 'The Invasion' has been set in July 1970, so 'Spearhead From Space' can be set 'months' later, say October, to match seasonal conditions ['Spearhead From Space' was filmed in October of 1969].

It appears to be a workday when the Autons attack in Ep4; the victims are dressed for work or shopping.

1,000,000,000 BC

Channing says that the Nestenes 'have been colonising other planets for a thousand million years'. This means that these worlds must have been highly advanced civilisations that had at least mastered the principle of manufacturing plastics.

1961 – 1970

Lethbridge-Stewart tells Liz Shaw that 'in the last decade we've been sending probes deeper and deeper into space'. One of the first satellites is launched in 1959 (see 'Delta And The Bannermen'). In 'A Day In The Death', Owen refers to NASA sending out messages into space 'in the Seventies'. The Institute of Space Studies in Baltimore has established that there are 'over 500 planets in [Earth's] section of the galaxy capable of supporting life'. Once Mankind develops warp-drive and deep space travel (in 2106, see 'Nightmare Of Eden' and SPACE-FLIGHT), many of these planets will be colonised.

1970, April

The Brigadier tells Liz the first swarm of energy units landed 'six months ago'. 'Six months' is also the length of time that Ransome spent in the States.

DURATION

⇨ Day One (Ep1-4)

At first it is stated that the Doctor arrives 'early this morning', but later it is twice given as 'last night'. It is daylight when the TARDIS lands so the former is more correct. General Scobie spends a 'most interesting afternoon' at Auto Plastics. His facsimile replaces Scobie later that day.

⇨ **Day Two (Ep4)** ▨ ▨ ▨ ▨ ▨ ▨ ▨ ▨ ▨ ▨ ▨ ▨

Most of this day passes off-screen. The Doctor and Liz arrive at the wax museum just before 'closing time'. The attendant says that General Scobie's body was delivered to Madame Tussaud's 'just this morning'. Liz says Scobie had been at the factory 'yesterday afternoon' (as seen in Day One). The Brigadier spends all this day at the Home Secretary's. The replicas at the wax museum are activated 'tonight'.

⇨ **Day Three (Ep4)** ▨ ▨ ▨ ▨ ▨ ▨ ▨ ▨ ▨ ▨ ▨ ▨

The Doctor and Liz spend until 'half past five' in the morning working on the ECT device just as the attacks begin (in Day Two Channing says 'at dawn we will activate the Autons'). The Autons are destroyed later that same day.

DOCTOR WHO AND THE SILURIANS

STORY LINK

No more than one month has passed between 'Spearhead From Space' and 'Doctor Who And The Silurians' (see Timeline Dates). The Doctor now has his new car, 'Bessie' (named after Liz, perhaps?), as promised by the Brigadier ('I was very lucky to get her'). Bessie has a plate with the registration WHO 1. I like to think that the Brigadier chose that car for the Doctor for the simple fact that it already had an appropriate registration number, rather than WHO 1 being something the Doctor later selected. Although Captain Mike Yates does not appear (on-screen) until 'Terror Of The Autons', in that later story the Doctor says that Yates 'had the job of cleaning up the last time' the Nestenes had visited Earth (in 'Spearhead From Space'). This task probably happened concurrently with 'Doctor Who And The Silurians', which explains Yates' absence from the Research Centre. Captain Munro has been replaced by Captain Hawkins – which suggests Yates was not a Captain at that time, as UNIT would not have had more than one Captain in the ranks. The new Corporal is Nutting, while the new Sergeant is named Hart.

UNIT HQ – LONDON #1

All we see of UNIT HQ is the inside of the garage where the Doctor is working on Bessie. Given that the Doctor and Liz drive through busy London streets from UNIT to Wenley Moor, we can assume that this is the same depot location seen in 'Spearhead From Space'.

LANGUAGE

The Reptiles speak with Quinn before the Doctor arrives so they must speak English. When the Doctor meets the Reptile in Quinn's cottage he asks 'Do you understand me?', and the creature nods.

TIMELINE DATES

1970, November •

As covered under THE UNIT YEARS, this story is best placed in 1969 or 1970, prior to the introduction of decimal currency in February 1971: it is clearly approaching winter, as the characters are wearing warm clothing and hats outside; Quinn has a fire burning in his cottage (although this could be solely for the benefit of the 'Silurian' he has hidden there); and it gets dark early during the story, so these months have been retained. ['Doctor Who And The Silurians' was filmed in October and November of 1969.] With 'Spearhead From Space' set in October 1970, 'Doctor Who And The Silurians' can be set the following month. The events of Day Three (see Duration) appear to take place on a weekday, based on the fact that most of the commuters seen at the train station are workers.

200,000,000 BC
70,000,000 BC

Applying known Earth history and evolution to the 'facts' presented in 'Doctor Who And The Silurians' is impossible. The Old Reptile says 'we ruled this planet millions of years ago'. The Doctor says the globe found in Quinn's office (presumably given to Quinn by the Reptiles) 'is the world as it was before the great continental drift, two hundred million years ago. And these notes, well, they're calculations of the age of the Earth with particular reference to the Silurian era'. In our history the Silurian Period was some 420 million years ago. In 'The Sea Devils' the Doctor tells Jo that Quinn 'got the period wrong. Properly speaking they should have been called the Eocenes'. The Eocene Epoch was 55 to 38 million years ago, and followed the period that saw the mass extinction of the dinosaurs and the emergence of mammals, particularly the apes. The Reptiles saw apes as pests which 'used to raid our crops', and in 'The Sea Devils' the Sea Devil Leader says 'my people ruled the Earth when Man was only an ape'. Apes and mammals didn't evolve until millions of years after the dinosaurs died out. And the fact that the Reptiles have what looks like an allosaurus places their time before the dinosaurs became extinct around 65 million years ago (see 'Earthshock'). As for the moon, it is estimated as being just as old as the Earth, and evidence of prehistoric tidal activity supports that it has been in orbit around Earth for several billions of years, not just millions as suggested in 'Doctor Who And The Silurians'.

I have decided to act upon my Rule that what appears on-screen is more correct that actual facts, so I have placed the time of the emergence of the Reptile civilisation as 200 million years ago, as is suggested by Quinn's globe, and the time of their hibernation as 70 million years ago (which also takes into account that the dinosaurs died out 65 million years ago, as given in 'Earthshock').

Pre-65,000,000 BC ›

The Doctor says he has seen live dinosaurs, so this must have been prior to 65,000,000 BC when they were wiped out (see 'Earthshock'). He recognises a plesiosaurus in 'Carnival Of Monsters'.

1965

The Brigadier says Baker 'slipped up badly some years ago', say five, being 1965.

1970, May

Quinn says he has not had his cottage for long and that he bought it 'a few months after I got the job here'. This suggests that he has been there for less than a year. The Research Centre itself is relatively new, and so can't have been in operation for more than, say, six months, being May (see August below).

1970, August

Major Baker says the first disturbances started 'three months' ago, which would be in August. This was when the 'Silurians' began to draw power from the 'new' energy source at the Centre, which supports that the Centre has only been in operation a few months by that time (see May above).

2020 ›

The Reptile scientist says he has 'set the controls to revive us in fifty years from now', which is 2020. The scientist is instructed by the young leader to 'see that the Apes are destroyed'. Assuming that the Brigadier does not totally destroy all the creatures when he blows up the caves, the Reptile scientist nearly succeeds with his orders in 2084. It is possible that the Doctor was there when the shelter was reactivated (see 'Warriors Of The Deep').

DURATION

⇨ **Day (Ep1)** ▨ ▨ ▨ ▨ ▨ ▨ ▨ ▨ ▨ ▨ ▨ ▨

Davis and Spencer are attacked in the cave. Spencer wanders 'around [the] caves for hours' before being found.

🕓 **Several days later?** ▨ ▨ ▨ ▨ ▨ ▨ ▨ ▨ ▨ ▨ ▨

⇨ **Day One (Ep1-2)** ▨ ▨ ▨ ▨ ▨ ▨ ▨ ▨ ▨ ▨ ▨

An undetermined number of days later the Doctor and Liz arrive at the Centre. The wounded Reptile hides in Squire's barn after night has fallen. The Doctor spends 'most of the night examining the equipment' at the Centre.

⇨ **Day Two (Ep.2-4)** ▨ ▨ ▨ ▨ ▨ ▨ ▨ ▨ ▨ ▨ ▨

Squire is killed the following morning. It is dark when the Doctor finds Quinn dead. Masters arrives, having 'been travelling most of the night'. The Brigadier plans an assault in the caves 'first thing in the morning'.

⇨ **Day Three (Ep5-7)** ▨ ▨ ▨ ▨ ▨ ▨ ▨ ▨ ▨ ▨ ▨

The Doctor returns to the caves ahead of the Brigadier. Baker is released later that morning. The clock at the station reads 4.07 pm when people start collapsing from the plague. The Doctor and Liz spend 'hours' working on the antidote. The Reptiles return to their base later that day.

⇨ **Day Four? (Ep7)** ▨ ▨ ▨ ▨ ▨ ▨ ▨ ▨ ▨ ▨ ▨

It is the next or maybe even a later day when the Doctor and Liz leave the Centre; the Doctor promises to return 'tomorrow' with more equipment and scientists.

THE AMBASSADORS OF DEATH

STORY LINK

No more than one month has passed since 'Doctor Who And The Silurians'; it is winter (see Timeline Dates). Liz has had her hair cut shorter. The Doctor has removed the TARDIS console from the TARDIS and has been trying to repair the Time Vector Generator. UNIT is now involved with security at the Space Centre. The Doctor's lab is different to the one in 'Spearhead From Space', so presumably UNIT has a new HQ.

Benton is now a Sergeant, which suggests he was promoted following the death of Sergeant Hart in 'Doctor Who And The Silurians'.

UNIT HQ – COUNTRY #1

UNIT HQ is not far from the Space Centre, which is located inside a hillside. This suggests that this HQ is out in the country.

The Doctor's lab features a barred semi-circular window. The walls are wooden, and there are paintings on the walls. This looks like it could be a manor house.

OBSERVATIONS

- Mars Probe 7 is so named presumably because it is the seventh probe to Mars. Mars Probe 6 was crewed by Carrington and Jack Daniels. Carrington believes the aliens are hostile: 'Why else should they invade the galaxy? They were on Mars before we were'. This last comment is ambiguous: 'we' could refer to either the Mars Probe 6 crew, or to the human race. If the latter is the case, then that means that Mars Probe 6 was the first manned probe – the previous five being unmanned. These could be the deep space probes the Brigadier referred to in 'Spearhead From Space'.
- At the end of 'The Ambassadors Of Death' the aliens are returned to their mother-ship. One wonders if something significant happened in getting them back to their ship. Given that the aliens wanted to make peaceful contact with humans, it seems to have been a wasted trip for them if they didn't exchange some knowledge. It is possible the aliens were able to give humans advanced sciences and knowledge to improve space hardware (see 'The Time Warrior'). It was probably from this that the XK rocket series was developed, enabling humans to travel further into space as seen in 1973 ('The Android Invasion'), followed by the *Hydrax* in 1999 (see 'State Of Decay').

LANGUAGE

The Doctor says the aliens have 'some kind of translation machine'. He is unable to decipher the aliens' pictographic writing. The Doctor has a sign that reads 'Anti Thief Device' on Bessie's dashboard. The Doctor refers to 'our human speech'. The Doctor has heard the sound made by the aliens before, but cannot remember where ('It's all here in my mind. The information's here but I can't reach it').

TIMELINE DATES

1970, December *

As covered under THE UNIT YEARS, this story is best placed in 1970: 'The Ambassadors Of Death' was recorded in January / February [of 1970] so the serial should be set in the same month to match winter seasonal conditions, for example there are deciduous trees without leaves. The Doctor comments that the Brigadier is at Space Centre 'to occupy his mind now that he's blown up the Silurians', which indicates that the gap between 'Doctor Who And The Silurians' and 'The Ambassadors Of Death' is not as long as the three months that a February setting would suggest (otherwise the Brigadier and UNIT have been inactive all that time). I prefer to take the Doctor's reference to the Silurians over the seasonal conditions and place 'The Ambassadors Of Death' in the month following 'Doctor Who And The Silurians', being December. The seasonal conditions can still apply, but to the beginning of the season as opposed to the end.

The Brigadier says he has known the Doctor for 'several years, on and off'. In terms of the Brigadier's relative time it has been nearly four years since he first met the Doctor in 'The Web Of Fear', in 1967.

1965

The Doctor sends an SOS message, a signal that Benton says 'they did away with years ago', say five, 1965?

1969, September
1970, April

The length of time it takes for Mars Probe 7 to return to Earth is given as several different lengths, usually by Ralph Cornish and John Wakefield: 'seven months' twice / 'seven months space time' / 'nearly eight months ago' / 'seven and a half months' which is an average of 7.2 months. The journey to Mars is described by Wakefield as being a 'long outward journey to the red planet', so we can safely assume that the outward journey was also 7.2 months, making it a 14 and a half month round trip. The Probe was on Mars 'for a full twelve hours' before it took off again. With 'The Ambassadors Of Death' set in December 1970, this means that Mars Probe 7 left Earth at least 15 months earlier, around September 1969, and arrived on Mars around late April 1970. The Doctor does not already know about the mission, so clearly it happened before he arrived on Earth in October 1970.

1969, January
1969, September
1970, April ▨ ▨ ▨ ▨ ▨ ▨ ▨ ▨ ▨ ▨ ▨ ▨

Given that Carrington first encountered the aliens when he was an astronaut on Mars Probe 6 (which must have also taken 7.2 months to get back to Earth), the plan to kidnap the aliens seems to have been in operation at least 14 months before 'The Ambassadors Of Death' takes place. This seems odd considering the urgency of Carrington's plan as well as the high expectation that the aliens would even still be on Mars by the time Mars Probe 7 got there. To explain this, we can speculate about the events that took place after Carrington encountered the aliens on Mars:

Immediately after leaving Mars, Carrington contacts Earth and tells them of the alien 'threat'. Mars Probe 7 is launched soon after. By the time Carrington gets back to Earth, Mars Probe 7 has already reached Mars (the two ships pass each other in space). This means that Mars Probe 6 originally left Earth around January 1969, and reached Mars 7.2 months later, in September 1969 (which is the same month in which Mars Probe 7 is launched, as above). Dobson says he has been Taltalian's 'chief assistant for two years', so presumably they were both on hand during Carrington's mission. Once back on Earth, Carrington is put in charge of 'the newly-formed Space Security Department' (as in newly formed following his warning about the alien threat). From this point on, all Carrington has to do is wait for Mars Probe 7 to return in seven months' time. The isotopes that were sold 'some months ago' are readied for the aliens.

So in summary, the Mars Probe voyages went as follows:

1969, January	MP6 launched
1969, September	MP6 reaches Mars
1969, September	MP6 leaves Mars
1969, September	MP7 launched
1970, January	MP6 and MP7 pass each other
1970, April	MP6 reaches Earth
1970, April	MP7 arrives on Mars
1970, December	MP7 returns to Earth

DURATION

The duration is difficult to establish, as there are no night scenes. Ralph Cornish wears a cream coloured tie from Ep1 to Ep2, changing it for a brown one before going to the wasteland to retrieve Recovery 7. He keeps that tie until his first scene in Ep4, in which he has gone back to wearing the cream one, which he retains until the end of the serial. This suggests a duration of three days, but the narrative does not support this. In another clothing-related clue, Liz Shaw wears a pink dress and boots from Ep1 to the beginning of Ep3, and wears a blue skirt, hat and boots when she visits Quinlan in Ep3. She retains this outfit right to the end of the serial. This suggests two days. In Ep4 Reegan refers to 'paying two visits tonight' with the aliens, one visit being to kill Quinlan, but it is broad daylight when this happens, and also in all the subsequent scenes. I believe that Liz's change of clothes represents the passage of one day, with Quinlan's death occurring on the second night. The Doctor spends several hours in space, so that would most likely bridge the gap between that night and the third day.

⇨ **Day One (Ep1-3)**
Late in Ep2 Dobson mentions checking the computer 'this morning', so the story starts in the morning. 'Some hours' pass between signals from the capsule. It is later that day when the aliens are taken to Heldorf's laboratory.

⇨ **Day Two (Ep3-6)**
The next morning the Doctor, the Brigadier and Liz visit Quinlan (Liz wears her new outfit). This appears to be a weekday; the gravel quarry is manned and in operation. Reegan takes one of the aliens to attack the Centre and to kill Quinlan 'tonight' (the sun is low on the horizon when Reegan arrives at the Centre). Once the Doctor has been cleared, it takes 'two hours' until the actual launch of Recovery 7. The Doctor spends several hours in space.

⇨ **Day Three (Ep6-7)**
It is possible that this is a weekend, because the 'missing' Earth astronauts believe they are 'watching' a football match when the Doctor finds them in the alien mother-ship. In Ep6, while the Doctor begins his return to Earth, the Americans announce their plan to launch an unmanned satellite. It will take 'six hours' to prepare the launch. The Doctor returns to Earth and is in decontamination for about 'an hour'. Later, in Ep7, the American satellite finally reaches the alien ship before disintegrating, so six hours pass during Ep6 and Ep7. The story ends towards the end of this third day.

INFERNO

STORY LINK
It is now seven months since 'The Ambassadors Of Death' (see Timeline Dates). There

is no mention of the radioactive aliens, or of UNIT's involvement in returning them to their ship. The Doctor has been continuing his experiments on the TARDIS console.

It is also a year ago now since Edward and Anne Travers left for the United States, as is mentioned in 'The Invasion'. If they were now back in England as they had intended after spending one year abroad, it is possible that the Doctor has taken the time to visit them. (On that note, I wonder if the Doctor has also visited Ian, Barbara, Dodo, Ben or Polly during his exile on Earth … ?)

The Doctor twice refers to the length of his association with the Brigadier: 'You ask me my name after all the years you and I have – ?', and 'We don't want to bear a grudge … Not after all the years that we've worked together'. Since the Doctor has only been in exile on Earth for nine months, the Doctor must be speaking from the Brigadier's perspective, it now being five years since Lethbridge-Stewart first met the Doctor in 1967 (see 'The Web Of Fear').

OBSERVATIONS

- The Doctor uses 'Venusian Karate' for the first time in this story.
- The Doctor says 'it's a matter of great scientific interest … First penetration of the Earth's crust. Well, naturally I'm interested'. The Doctor has in fact previously witnessed an attempt at penetration of the Earth's crust: on the Atlantic Ridge in 2070 (see 'The Underwater Menace'), which in terms of THE DOCTOR'S AGE was only two years earlier.

LANGUAGE

The Doctor speaks English, even when talking to himself! The mutants cannot speak.

TIMELINE DATES

1971, July 20 – 24 ٭
<<1971, July 23 – 24>> ٭ ■ ■ ■ ■ ■ ■ ■ ■

Liz's hair is the same length as it was in 'The Ambassadors Of Death', but it would appear that quite some time has passed since 'The Ambassadors Of Death'. The calendar on the Brigade-Leader's desk shows '23 July'. This does not necessarily mean the same date as in the Doctor's Earth, but considering almost everything else is mirrored in the parallel world, this date could apply too. With 'The Ambassadors Of Death' set in December 1970, 'Inferno' would be July of the following year, 1971 (see THE UNIT YEARS). Liz has therefore known the Doctor for nine months.

23 July is the day the Doctor spends in the parallel world, which is an amalgamation of the third and fourth days in the Doctor's 'real' world. The fourth day would most

likely be the 23rd, as that is the day in which the Doctor's Earth would have been destroyed had the Doctor not interfered in time (see Duration).

4,600,000,000 BC

The Doctor says the world (in the parallel dimension) would 'dissolve in a fury of expanding gases just as it was billions of years ago'. In 'The Runaway Bride', the Earth is formed 4.6 billion years ago. (The planet is destroyed 9.6 billion years later – in 5 billion (see 'The End Of The World').)

1883, August 26 ›

The Doctor says he heard the screaming sound before on 'Krakatoa, the Sundra Straits, during the volcanic eruption of 1883'. In our history, the island erupted on 26 August 1883. The ninth Doctor was on Sumatra at the time (see 'Rose' and 'The Lost Boy').

1904 ›

The Doctor says he knew the Queen's great-grandfather in Paris. In our history, Edward VII (9 November 1841 to 6 May 1910) reigned from 1901 (he was crowned on 9 August 1902). The King visited Paris in 1904 for Entente-Cordiale with the UK, so the Doctor probably met him there.

<<1943>>

The Brigade-Leader says he has full authority under the 'Defence of the Republic Act 1943'. We can assume that the Republic was established as a result of the outcome of the Second World War in this parallel dimension (see THE N-SPACE UNIVERSE).

1960

Stahlman says 'I've been concerned with this operation for eleven years', which is 1960. Petra Williams has been his assistant 'for some years now'.

1971, July 17

Sir Keith Gold says he noted a malfunction on Number 2 pipe 'several days ago', say 3 days.

1971, July 26

On July 25 the Brigadier says the reactor is to be dismantled 'tomorrow'.

⇨ **Day One (20 July) (Ep1)**
The Doctor sets himself up at the project, and 'within a few hours of [his] arrival' Slocum kills the technician in the 'late afternoon' (as the Brigadier states when he arrives the following day).

⇨ **Day Two (21 July) (Ep1-4)**
The Brigadier arrives this morning (he is greeted 'Morning, sir' by Benton). Penetration Zero is in 59:28:48 hours when Greg Sutton arrives. The Doctor vanishes 10 hours later when Penetration Zero is in 49:18:33 hours. Sir Keith heads for London for an appointment with the Minister 'later on today'; Penetration Zero is in 48:49:51 hours. Sir Keith crashes on his way back from London that night, after 'a day's hard talking to convince the Minister' to close the project down.

⇨ **Day Three (22 July) (Ep5-6)**
Sir Keith's disappearance is noted by the Brigadier: 'He left the Minister yesterday evening. He should have been back here by last night'.

⇨ **<<Day One (22 July) to Day Two (24 July)>> (Ep3-6)**
Given that the Doctor is absent from his own dimension for 46 hours, it is logical that 46 hours also pass in the parallel dimension, otherwise the TARDIS console has indeed moved him back and forwards in time; the Doctor is adamant that he has only moved 'sideways'. Although there are no night scenes, the effect of the volcanic rupture could have turned night into day and two days have passed during the emergency after Penetration Zero is reached. I have therefore been unable to determine where the bridge between days is located. The day the Doctor arrives in the parallel universe is an odd mixture of Day Two and Day Four in his own universe: the Doctor is attacked by Wyatt on his arrival in the parallel dimension, followed shortly by Bromley but he is not attacked by Bromley until after his return to his own continuum on Day Four. The calendar in the Brigade-Leader's office says '23 July'. Penetration Zero is 'three hours, twenty two minutes' (3:22) away when the Doctor is captured; in this world Sir Keith died '24 hours ago' (on 22 July); and Director Stahlmann's mutation takes place over a much shorter period of time, whereas Professor Stahlman's takes a full three days.

⇨ **Day Four (24 July) (Ep7)**
The Doctor returns after being missing for 46 hours: Penetration Zero is now in 3:22:38

(unless of course Stahlman has advanced Penetration Zero due to faster drilling, but this is unlikely). The Doctor is able to prevent the disaster when Penetration Zero reaches 'minus thirty five seconds'.

⇨ **Day Five (25 July) (Ep7)**

The Doctor and Liz have spent all this day working on the TARDIS console. It is now afternoon, because the Brigadier says 'word came through this morning, this project is being officially abandoned'. The reactor is to be dismantled 'tomorrow'.

UNSEEN ADVENTURES

While exiled on Earth ('Spearhead From Space' to 'The Three Doctors'), the Doctor spends his time trying to fix the TARDIS. But he also has time to join a gentlemen's club ('Terror Of The Autons'), as well as catch up on scientific journals and books such as Professor Clifford Jones' paper on DNA synthesis ('The Green Death'); Lavinia Smith's paper on the teleological response of the virus ('The Time Warrior'); and Sir Charles Grover's book *Last Chance For Man* ('Invasion Of The Dinosaurs'). The Doctor is a keen cricketer, as seen in 'The Ark In Space', 'The Hand Of Fear', 'The Ribos Operation' (he's a keen leg-spinner), 'The Horns Of Nimon', 'Castrovalva', 'Four To Doomsday' (the Doctor once took five wickets for New South Wales; he can bowl a good chinaman), and 'Black Orchid', and yet in 'The Daleks' Master Plan' he claimed to not know the game. Therefore, it is likely that he developed an interest in the game during his exile.

TERROR OF THE AUTONS

STORY LINK

There is no direct link to 'Inferno'. The Brigadier says the Doctor's 'been agitating for a new assistant ever since Miss Shaw went back to Cambridge'. The Doctor appears to have joined a gentlemen's club while on Earth. He mentions speaking with Tubby Rowlands at 'the club only the other day', however this could simply be a joke to offend Brownrose.

Jo Grant has recently completed her training to be a UNIT agent. She got the job with the help of her Uncle, who worked with the United Nations. The Brigadier assigned her to be the Doctor's assistant only because he didn't know what else to do with her.

UNIT HQ – COASTAL #1

A stretch of water can be seen through the window of the Doctor's lab. This is a canal, the coast, or a river – perhaps even the Thames in London. However, the sound of ships' horns is clearly audible, and when the Doctor throws the Master's bomb out the lab window, seagulls can be heard squawking, which indicates that the HQ is more likely to be on the south or east coast. From the angle of the coastline through the window, this building appears to be up high, perhaps on a hillside.

The Doctor's lab has two storeys – there is a spiral staircase leading to an upper level. The lab itself appears to be on an upper floor as there is a downwards stairway visible outside the lab door.

GALLIFREY LINK

The Time Lord who visits the Doctor is the first (on-screen) direct contact he has had with his people since his exile began. The Doctor seems to know the messenger personally ('sarcasm always was a weak point with you, wasn't it'). The Time Lord says 'the Tribunal thought that you ought to be made aware of your danger', concerning the arrival of the Master (so it is clear that the Time Lord is not Borusa, since in 'The Deadly Assassin' Borusa says he does not know the Master). The Doctor has been in exile for a whole year now, so it would seem that the Tribunal has been keeping a watchful eye on him, and the Master too for that matter …

The sound of a TARDIS materialising accompanies the arrival of the Time Lord; it is possible that he is using one of the same types of transportation units used in 'The Three Doctors'.

MASTER LINK

When the evil Time Lord phones the UNIT lab, the Master does not recognise the Doctor's voice, and vice versa ('Hello. Doctor, is that you?' / 'Who is this?'), which suggests that the Doctor has never met the Master in this current [Delgado] persona before. Given that the Doctor and the Master are the same age, we can safely take it that this [Delgado] incarnation is not the Master's first (which would logically be an elderly man like the first Doctor). In fact, chances are that this is his second incarnation.

We can assume that the Master left Gallifrey before the Doctor did. In 'The Deadly Assassin' the Doctor says the Master was a Time Lord 'a long time ago'. The Time Lord messenger tells the Doctor that the Master 'has learnt a great deal since you last met him'. In 'The Mind Of Evil', when attacked by the Keller Machine, the Master 'sees' the Doctor as his greatest fear, so it is clear that the two have been enemies for a very long time. Curiously, the Doctor doesn't 'see' the Master as one of his greatest enemies when he is attacked by the Machine. In fact, the Doctor says the Master is 'an unimaginative plodder', and that 'all he ever does is cause trouble', so it is clear that the Doctor does not consider the Master to be a great threat.

When we see the Master arriving at the circus this is clearly not his first visit to Earth; as Farrell says to 'Masters': 'You have done your homework': indeed the Master knows the Doctor is on Earth, and he knows of UNIT, plus the whereabouts of the Nestene sphere. The Master has examined several plastics factories before selecting Farrel's (on the basis that it has been producing 'less than half volume for over a year'). The Master also knows Luigi Rossini's real name, so he has certainly had a lot of time to set this plan in motion before the story begins.

AUTON LINK

Since the events of 'Spearhead From Space', the Nestene Consciousness has been banished from Earth. Captain Mike Yates was put in charge of the clean-up operation. One surviving energy unit has been placed in the care of the National Space Museum under the Brigadier's authority. The Master orchestrates another bridgehead to be established with which to bring the entity back to Earth. None of the Nestenes' previous Autons is reactivated during the new invasion, so presumably Autons are activated and controlled only by the swarm leader that initially energised them.

OBSERVATIONS

- Ironically, part of the final confrontation between the Doctor and the Master takes place in the control room of a radio telescope, which is also the location of the Doctor and Master's final confrontation at the end of 'Logopolis', and the precursor to the fourth Doctor's regeneration.

LANGUAGE

One Auton speaks in English when talking to Farrel.

TIMELINE DATES

1971, October •

As covered under THE UNIT YEARS, this story is best placed in 1971: when Jo Grant puts out the fire in the Doctor's lab, he tells her she has just ruined 'three months' delicate work' on the dematerialisation circuit. Later he says he's been 'trying to repair [the circuit] for months'. Given that in 'The Ambassadors Of Death' and 'Inferno', the

Doctor is working on the TARDIS console, and not the circuit, we can assume that these three months do not include the period prior to 'Inferno'. That story has been set in July 1971, so 'Terror Of The Autons' can be set three months later – in October, which also matches seasonal conditions of filming in that month [the serial was filmed in September / October 1970]. Of course, there is the possibility that the Doctor has been working on the circuit prior to 'Inferno'.

1664

The Time Lord messenger has travelled 'twenty nine thousand light years' – presumably direct from Gallifrey – to Earth (see THE N-SPACE UNIVERSE). In terms of the Doctor's GRT, the year on Gallifrey is 1664, meaning that the messenger has travelled forward 307 years in time to 1971.

1970

The Master says that Farrel's factory has been producing 'less than half volume for over a year'.

DURATION

Jo wears two outfits during this story: at first a green blouse, dark dress with waistcoat, and neck band (#1); the other a pink jumper, leather jacket and trousers (#2). The Duration of this story has been based in part on the cycle of changes of these clothes:

⇨ Day One (Ep1)

It is day when the Master arrives at the circus, presumably a Saturday or a Sunday, the traditional days for day-time circuses. The National Space Museum appears to be closed when the Master breaks in, so this is either the night of this first day, or the Museum is closed on weekends.

⇨ Day Two (Ep1)

Goodge is eating his breakfast when he is killed by the Master, because in a later scene at UNIT Jo greets the Brigadier with 'Good morning, sir'. Jo wears dress #1.

⇨ Day Three (Ep1-3)

The Master goes to Farrel's factory for the first time. Jo visits the factory in outfit #2. Later, McDermott accuses 'Masters' of having 'ruined a whole day's production'. John Farrel is killed soon 'after lunch'. The attack by the Autons in the quarry occurs later that day. Farrel reports the failure to the Master.

⇨ **Day Four? (Ep3)** ▦ ▦ ▦ ▦ ▦ ▦ ▦ ▦ ▦ ▦ ▦ ▦

Jo is in outfit #1 in the next UNIT scene, so it is either the next day or she has simply changed clothes, the other suit having got dirty in the quarry. The Autons begin to hand out the plastic daffodils. The coach has been hired for a 'week'.

🕐 **Several days ((four?) pass ...** ▦ ▦ ▦ ▦ ▦ ▦ ▦ ▦ ▦ ▦

⇨ **Day Eight? (Ep3-4)** ▦ ▦ ▦ ▦ ▦ ▦ ▦ ▦ ▦ ▦ ▦ ▦

After 'days of exhaustive investigation' UNIT has failed to locate the Autons. There has been 'a wave of sudden deaths all over the home counties'. The Doctor and Brigadier visit the now-abandoned plastics factory (according to the desk calendar they left 'today'). The killer phone cord attacks the Doctor later that day.

⇨ **Day Nine? (Ep4)** ▦ ▦ ▦ ▦ ▦ ▦ ▦ ▦ ▦ ▦ ▦ ▦

Jo is back in outfit #2 when the Doctor begins experimenting on the daffodils, so it is likely to be the next day. He has 'an hour and a half' to solve the mystery before the RAF begins its attack on the coach. When the Doctor and Master finally come face to face the Master greets his foe with a 'Good afternoon, Doctor'. The Doctor and Jo arrive at the quarry with only seconds away from the RAF strike. The story ends later that day.

THE MIND OF EVIL

+STORY LINK

As noted under THE UNIT YEARS, at least a full year has passed since 'Terror Of The Autons'. The Doctor says 'something's been worrying me about this Keller Process ever since I first heard of it'. The Doctor refers to the events of 'Inferno' as being 'some time ago'; it was over 14 months ago.

It was on 4 June 1972, during this twelve month period, that UNIT seizes from a personal collector the Tunguska Scroll, which had crashed into Siberian Russia in 1908. It is admitted to the UNIT tech team for study. It is later sealed within the Black Archive (see 'Enemy Of The Bane').

UNIT HQ – LONDON #2

This HQ is in central London (although it could actually be temporary quarters set up in central London while UNIT is concerned with security at the nearby

Peace Conference). It is in a white multi-levelled terraced house, numbered '24', in Kensington Gardens. We do not see the Doctor's lab. The Brigadier's office has a window that overlooks the outside streets. There have been yet more staff changes at UNIT: Corporal Bell has presumably replaced Corporals Tracy ('The Invasion') and Champion ('The Ambassadors Of Death'). But it could simply be that each UNIT HQ is staffed by different personnel.

MASTER LINK

With his TARDIS no longer functioning, the Master is stranded on Earth at the end of 'Terror Of The Autons'. He must have already had the mind parasite creature in the TARDIS when he came to Earth, perhaps intending to use it against the Nestene Consciousness? (As noted under 'The Mind Robber', it is possible that the parasite creature comes from the white void.)

During the long months since 'Terror Of The Autons', the Master had adopted the guise of Emil Keller and based himself in Switzerland. At some point he also met Chin Lee at an Embassy reception and hypnotised her. (He wants to involve the Chinese in his plans, as they are suspicious of Western ideals.) With her assistance, they install the machine at Stangmoor prison, but presumably due to beaurocratic red-tape, the machine could not be used. The parasite was removed and a second machine built, with which 112 prisoners in Europe are processed successfully with Professor Kettering's assistance. During this time Keller's reputation continues to grow. As the months pass, the Master is delighted when Chin Lee is selected to accompany the Chinese delegation to the next World Peace Conference to be held in London. For his plan to work, it was imperative that the machine at Stangmoor be given approval, which ultimately it is, 'nearly a year' after it was first installed. The mind parasite is transferred to the Stangmoor machine. When the Master learns of the Thunderbolt missile that is to be disposed of during the Conference, a third factor to his plan falls into place...

OBSERVATIONS

- The courtyard where Chin Lee attacks Benton is coincidentally the very same courtyard in which the Doctor captured a War Machine in 'The War Machines' in 1966.

LANGUAGE

The Doctor speaks both Hokkien and Cantonese. Although Emil Keller is apparently Swiss (and would therefore speak French, German, Italian or Romansch), the controls on the Keller Machine are in English.

TIMELINE DATES

1972, November *

There is evidence of fallen leaves, which indicates autumn [the serial was recorded in October 1970]. At the end of 'Terror Of The Autons' the Master is stranded on Earth, his TARDIS immobilised by the Doctor. In 'The Mind Of Evil' the Master has assumed the guise of Emil Keller. With Chin Lee's help he set up the Machine in Stangmoor Prison, which according to the Governor, was 'nearly a year ago', which indicates there is a gap of over eleven months between 'Terror Of The Autons' and 'The Mind Of Evil'. Presumably the machine at Stangmoor was set up months after the Master had become Keller, maybe two to three? We also need to allow time for his meeting Chin Lee, so I would say that 13 months have passed since 'Terror Of The Autons', and it is now November 1972.

1250

The Doctor says that Stangmoor Prison 'used to be a fortress in the Middle Ages'. 1250 is an arbitrary date.

1592 *

The Doctor tells Jo of this meeting with Sir Walter Raleigh. In our history, Raleigh (c.1554 – 1618) was imprisoned by Elizabeth I at about this time.

1935 *

Mao Zedong (aka Mao Tse-Tung) was born in China on 26 December 1898. He was leader of the Chinese Communist Party from 1931, Chairman (chief of state) of the People's Republic of China from 1949 until his retirement in 1959, and chairman of the Party till his death on 9 September 1976. No dates are given for when the Doctor met Zedong (nor in which incarnation). In the novelisation, the Doctor met Mao during the Long March, which ended on 20 October 1935. I have selected this same year.

1971, December

The Prison Governor tells the Doctor that the Keller machine was installed 'nearly a year' ago by Chin Lee and Keller. See Master Link above.

DURATION

⇨ Day One (Ep1-3)

It is morning when the Doctor and Jo arrive at Stangmoor Prison (the Warden greets the witnesses with a 'good morning'). The Chinese delegate is killed at midday (Chin Lee says she remembers hearing the clock 'striking twelve'). She telephones the Brigadier 'at exactly 12.24' (12.24 pm). Chin Lee tries to kill Alcott that evening after dinner. Mailer has Jo locked up in a cell: 'Good night'.

⇨ Day Two (Ep3-4) ▨ ▨ ▨ ▨ ▨ ▨ ▨ ▨ ▨ ▨ ▨

The missile convoy meets at UNIT HQ at '0700 hours' and they collect the missile at '0815 hours'. Chin Lee is brought to UNIT HQ later that morning; the Brigadier is asleep at his desk. Mike phones ('Oh, morning, Yates') to advise they are having trouble with the crane, which delays their departure. That night (just 'before it gets light') the Master shows Mailer his plans to steal the missile. The Doctor is in a coma all the night.

⇨ Day Three (Ep4-5) ▨ ▨ ▨ ▨ ▨ ▨ ▨ ▨ ▨ ▨

The Doctor and Jo are brought some breakfast. The missile convoy is attacked as it passes the prison. The Doctor and Jo are kept in the cell 'all day'. He tells her his story about Sir Walter Raleigh.

⇨ Day Four (Ep5-6) ▨ ▨ ▨ ▨ ▨ ▨ ▨ ▨ ▨ ▨

UNIT storms the prison this morning ('Morning, mate'). It is 'afternoon' when the story ends.

THE CLAWS OF AXOS

+STORY LINK

A meeting is being held at UNIT HQ to discuss the Master. The Doctor says, 'I keep telling you, he's left Earth by now', in reference to 'The Mind Of Evil'. As covered below, Bill Filer's involvement is probably related to the events at the World Peace Conference. The two stories are most likely consecutive, with only a few days separating them.

UNIT HQ – COASTAL #1

It is possible that this is the same HQ from 'Terror Of The Autons'. This HQ has a radar tracking station. The UNIT convoy manages to get to the South Coast where Axos has landed fairly quickly, so it is unlikely to be the HQ in central London seen in 'The Mind Of Evil'.

All we see of the interior is the radar station and rooms leading off it, the Brigadier's office, and some corridors. One of the corridors is marked with a large '6', which suggests that this is the sixth floor. There is a balcony outside the window. The style of construction of the rooms indicates that like the house in 'The Ambassadors Of Death', this HQ could be a converted manor. Corporal Bell is still with UNIT.

MASTER LINK

After regaining control of his TARDIS at the end of 'The Mind Of Evil', the Master leaves Earth. He encounters Axos by accident and becomes their prisoner. The mind of Axos says 'The bargain, you remember, was that if we spared you and your TARDIS you would lead us to this planet in return for the death of the Doctor … And the destruction of all life on Earth'.

LANGUAGE

Axos's mayday ('Axos calling Earth') is in English, although with the Master on board, his use of the Time Lord 'gift' could apply. While a prisoner of Axos, the Doctor is forced to 'think' of time travel formulae so Axos can obtain the secret of time travel. The formula is shown as a series of mathematical symbols, which also includes Greek and English terms, as well as some alien symbols.

TIMELINE DATES

1972, November •

As covered under THE UNIT YEARS, this story is best placed in 1972: all the trees are bare, so it is winter [The story was filmed in January 1971]. It is likely that Bill Filer has been sent by UNIT's Washington HQ to investigate the Master because of what happened to the American Senator at the Peace Conference in 'The Mind Of Evil'. Therefore, I have set 'The Claws Of Axos' the same month as 'The Mind Of Evil'.

DURATION

⇨ Day One (Ep1-3)

In the opening scene we see the sun rising on the horizon. The conference at UNIT HQ starts that morning ('Good morning'), although the clock in the radar room reads 12 o'clock.

⇨ Day Two (Ep3-4)

There are no night scenes but in Ep3 a transporter to Washington is 'due for take off 1100 hours GMT' (Greenwich Mean Time), and one to Baikonur 'ETA 1230 GMT', so

I suspect this represents the next day; this means the Doctor spends the whole night a prisoner inside Axos. In Ep4 the nutrition cycle is activated. This could mean that the intended 72-hour period has passed, but I feel sure that distribution was achieved well before the 72-hour deadline, given that there is no bridge to a third day.

COLONY IN SPACE

STORY LINK

At the end of 'The Claws Of Axos' the Doctor is unsure if the Master has escaped from Axos ('Well, I can't be absolutely sure, but I'm ninety percent certain ... Well, I suppose he could have got away – Just!'), however in 'Colony In Space' the Brigadier has field agents out looking for the Master. These agents are always reporting sightings of the Master ('Look at what happened last time. The man they arrested turned out to be the Spanish Ambassador!') The Doctor says the Master's TARDIS 'is working again now. He could be anywhere in space and time', which contradicts his uncertainty at the end of 'The Claws Of Axos'. This suggests that UNIT has had an off-screen encounter with the Master between 'The Claws Of Axos' and 'Colony In Space'.

Jo remarks that the Doctor has been working on his new dematerialisation circuit 'for simply ages'. The new circuit is an attempt to 'bypass the Time Lords' homing control' first mentioned in 'The Claws Of Axos'. His knowledge with which to build the new circuit may have been possible due to his encounter with Axos, which broke through the mental block on his mind to obtain the secret of time travel.

The TARDIS console room is significantly different from its appearance in 'The Claws Of Axos', so the Doctor has obviously spent some time altering the ship's internal configuration.

The Doctor refers to the length of his exile by asking Jo, 'Do you realise how long I've been confined to one planet?' By 'Colony In Space' he has been on Earth for 17 months.

UNIT HQ – LONDON #3

The exterior is not seen, but the sound of traffic outside can be heard during the lab scenes. Only the UNIT lab is seen. It has the same barred semi-circular windows as seen in 'The Ambassadors Of Death' and 'Terror Of The Autons', but I doubt that they are the same building, because in the corridor outside the lab doors can be seen red bricks. I would say that this is yet another London-based HQ. The words 'AUTHORISED PERSONNEL ONLY' are stencilled on the single glass door on the left. A second, arched green door is on the right. (Incidentally, when the TARDIS returns to the lab in Ep6, the room layout is quite different.)

MASTER LINK

The Master's TARDIS has several cabinets containing numerous paper files. Before he first left Gallifrey, or during a subsequent revisit, the Master stole the (paper-based?) file and maps on the Doomsday Weapon. Given that in his next three appearances on Earth he attempts to control an ancient power from Earth's past, he probably also stole files on Azal, the Sea Devils (he says he had done so in 'The Sea Devils'), and Kronos at the same time. The Doomsday Weapon provided the best option for Universal domination, so certainly he would go for that first. The Doctor notes from the files that the Master had 'visited a lot of planets recently. Must be looking for something', which suggests that the Time Lord files do not specify what planet the Doomsday Weapon is on, which is odd considering the Time Lords manage to send the Doctor to the correct planet before the Master arrives. While on his way to Uxarieus the Master intercepts the colonists' request for an Adjudicator. He ambushes Martin Jurgens and assumes his identity. He configures his TARDIS to take on the form of the Adjudicator's spaceship.

GALLIFREY LINK

The Time Lords have a file on the Doomsday Weapon. They are probably concerned because it has the power to destroy a sun – just as the Hand Of Omega was once capable of doing. On discovering the theft of the file, the Time Lords immediately think of the Doctor (no doubt because of his previous experiences with dealing with the Master). This shows clearly that the Time Lords have been monitoring the events that have recently taken place on Earth. I do not believe the three Time Lords who are discussing the Doctor at the beginning of the story are the High Council, because there are only the three of them, and none appears to be the President. They could be part of the Tribunal, but their conspiratorial ambience suggests otherwise. On the basis that they have a file on the Doomsday Weapon I would say that they are members of the Celestial Intervention Agency, and it is they who dispatch the Doctor to Uxarieus, a function that only the CIA would consider doing ('as long as it serves our purpose').

LANGUAGE

What appears to be the Doctor's Gallifreyan name appears on the screen behind the CIA members; the text is made up of Greek-like symbols. The Primitives are telepathic, and the colonists are able to communicate with them by thought. The Guardian of the weapon seemingly speaks in English.

TIMELINE DATES

1665 ·
The Time Lords who contact the Doctor are from his GRT, which, as covered under THE DOCTOR'S AGE, is 1665.

1972, December ·
In 'Day Of The Daleks' Jo says their adventure in 'Colony In Space' took place '500 years in the future' (in 2472), which suggests that the year was 1972, while Jo's conversation with Mary Ashe in 'Colony In Space' indicates that 1971 is a past year for Jo ('You left in 1971?'): Jo realises at this point that she has not only travelled in space to an alien world but also in time. Since Mars has been explored in 1969 and 1970 (see 'The Ambassadors Of Death'), it is clear from this that Jo accepts that interplanetary colonisation is possible even in her own time. And as covered under THE UNIT YEARS, this part of the story is best placed in 1972. On the basis that 'The Claws Of Axos' has been set in November 1972, we can set 'Colony In Space' a month later.

The Time Lords return the TARDIS to UNIT HQ (which looks noticeably different in Ep6 than its appearance in Ep1) 'just a few seconds after it left', although the Doctor and Jo have been gone for four days (see Duration). This contradicts the Blinovitch Limitation Effect law. The TARDIS should have returned to Earth four days later. One side-effect of this is that Jo is now out of sync with her relative time on Earth. When they first activate the TARDIS the Time Lords probably did not take into account that the Doctor would be travelling with someone else, and therefore did not allow for the Limitation Effect. (It happens to Jo again in 'The Time Monster'.)

Of note, these are not the only times that one of the Doctor's companions has been 'out of sync' with their own Earth Mean Time: Ben and Polly are returned to Earth the same day they left with the Doctor, but they have both aged many months in the interim (see 'The War Machines', and 'The Faceless Ones'). Jamie spends at least a whole year with the Doctor, and Zoe several months, but both are returned 'to a moment in time just before they went away' with the Doctor in 'The War Games'. Sarah becomes out of sync by a few weeks between 'The Time Warrior' and 'Invasion Of The Dinosaurs'. Tegan meets the Doctor in 1981 in 'Logopolis', and is returned to 1981 in 'Time-Flight', despite quite some time passing between 'Logopolis' and 'Time-Flight'. And Turlough is out of sync with his brother and the other Trions in 'Planet Of Fire'. Rose Tyler is a whole year out of sync with her mother ('Rose' and 'Aliens Of London').

2472, March 2 – 5 ·
Jane Leeson changes the calendar in their dome from 'MON 2 MARCH 2472' to

'TUES 3 MARCH 2472'. These dates are in fact wrong; in 2472 March 3 would be a Thursday. The calendar is, however, correct for 2471. Of course, it's not impossible for the world calendar to have been changed at some point prior to 2472.

1054, July 4

This is the recorded date in our history on which the explosion in the Crab Nebula was seen from Earth. Some scientists have placed the explosion later, in 1140, but the 1054 dating is the more popular.

2471, January

Ashe tells the Doctor that he made a preliminary survey of the planet before sending for the others. If the others arrived in February 2471, then Ashe must have made his survey around January.

2471, February

The colonists have been on Uxarieus for 'just over a year', which would be since around February 2471.

2472, March 1

The giant lizards were first sighted on this day, when the IMC ship first landed.

10,000,000,000 (+?)

The Doctor seems very sure when he says that Earth's sun will explode in 'ten thousand million years time'. Presumably he was there to see it happen. (In 'The End Of The World' the Earth's sun expands five billion years in the future, destroying the Earth, so the sun has another five billion years before it finally explodes and dies.)

DURATION

⇨ **Day One (Ep1/6)**
It is around late afternoon on Earth. The TARDIS returns 'a few seconds after it left'.

⇨ **Day One (2 March 2472) (Ep1)**
The TARDIS lands 'this morning'. It is about noon when the Doctor and Jo arrive at the dome; a meal (lunch?) is being set up. The Leesons are attacked 'late' that night.

⇨ **Day Two (3 March) (Ep1-3)**
Norton arrives at the colony this morning. The Doctor examines the Leesons' dome.

Holden is killed around 'dinner' (lunch) time. The colonists plan to attack the IMC ship 'tomorrow morning'.

⇨ **Day Three (4 March) (Ep3-5)** ▨ ▨ ▨ ▨ ▨ ▨ ▨ ▨
Jo is captured by the Primitives and taken to their city at dawn. The Master arrives. The IMC attack the dome when night falls. The Doctor and Jo spend the night trapped in the Master's TARDIS.

⇨ **Day Four (5 March) (Ep5-6)** ▨ ▨ ▨ ▨ ▨ ▨ ▨ ▨
The Doctor and the Master go to the Primitive City in the morning. The TARDIS leaves later that day.

THE DÆMONS

STORY LINK

There is no mention of the events of 'Colony In Space'. The Doctor has been working on a remote control unit for Bessie. He has also been trying to turn Jo into a scientist. Reference is made to the Nuton Power Complex, which is still operating, so it is not totally destroyed at the end of 'The Claws Of Axos', or it has been totally rebuilt in five months.

UNIT HQ – COUNTRY #1

When the Doctor 'drives' Bessie out of the garage we see a large wooded area and a flat field, which indicates that this HQ is in the country. We see the duty room with a TV and bunk. There are no brick walls, so this could be the same HQ seen in 'The Ambassadors Of Death'. The fact that UNIT has its own helicopter indicates that it also has its own heliport or airfield – so this certainly is not one of the central London bases.

MASTER LINK

There is no reference to 'Colony In Space'. Presumably the Master learned of Azal and how to resurrect him from files he stole from the Time Lords (see 'Colony In Space'). Clearly, the Master goes to Devil's End only to take advantage of Horner's dig. Horner is acting alone; he is not under the Master's control. It is only after reading (?) about the proposed dig that the Master sets in motion his plans, as there is no way that he could have summoned Azal without Horner's assistance. (See 'The Time Monster' to see how the events of 'The Dæmons' could be directly linked with those in 'The Time Monster'.)

It is clear that Squire Winstanley is not part of the coven when he says 'there have been a lot of queer goings-on the last few weeks', which is probably when the Master first arrived in Devil's End, replacing Canon Smallwood, 'who left in such mysterious circumstances … suddenly, in the middle of the night'. Professor Horner says of Miss Hawthorne: 'That daft woman's been pestering me for weeks', presumably in response to her suspicions about Canon Smallwood's disappearance.

The Master tells the Doctor: 'You always were an optimist, weren't you'.

OBSERVATIONS

- The Doctor knows of the Dæmons. Their planet, Damos, is 60,000 light years away, on the other side of the galaxy, and they have visited Earth on and off for nearly 100,000 years, their visits influencing various moments in history. Their appearances have entered into different cultures in many forms, always associated with horns.

LANGUAGE

The words used by the Master to summon Azal are a curious mix of English and an alien language, presumably one used by the Dæmons. The Doctor knows that Magister is Latin for Master; but the 'gift' does not translate the name and reveal the fact to him earlier! Also, the Doctor has to verbally translate the Venusian lullaby 'Klokleda partha menin klatch' for Jo, even though she is with him when he speaks the lullaby.

TIMELINE DATES

1973, April 29 – May 1

The barrow is opened at 'midnight' on 'April 30th. Beltane'. The story ends the next day, 'May Day', which is 1 May.

No year is given but Alistair Fergus states that the controversy over what lies within Devil's Hump has raged 'for some two hundred years', and that the first attempt to open the barrow was in '1793'. This sets 'The Dæmons' no later than 1993, which is well beyond the range of dates usually assigned to UNIT stories.

On the night the barrow is opened, Benton and Yates watch highlights of a rugby match from Twickenham on BBC3TV, and the Brigadier goes out for (a regimental?) dinner, which suggests April 30 is either a Friday night, making the year 1971, 1976 or 1982; a Saturday night, being 1977; or Sunday, 1972 or 1978.

Horner says his new book 'comes out tomorrow' (on 1 May). Books are rarely published on a weekend, so this would appear to coincide with the day being a Sunday (1972 and 1978).

Many of the villagers are able to attend the Master's meeting in Ep3, and during the Morris Dancing and later during the Master's capture there are many children, so it certainly does seem to be a weekend day as opposed to a school day.

The baker's man is delivering bread when he encounters the heat barrier around Devil's End. It is unlikely that he would be doing his deliveries on a weekend.

As covered by THE UNIT YEARS, 1973 is still the best date for 'The Dæmons'. This places the events of the story on Monday, 30 April and Tuesday, 1 May. (Horner's book therefore is published on Tuesday.)

98,000 BC

The Doctor tells Jo how the Dæmons first came to Earth 'nearly one hundred thousand years ago', to 'help Homo sapiens take out Neanderthal man'. This would be around 98,000 BC. In our history, Neanderthal man existed from about 110,000 BC to 35,000 BC (see '100,000 BC'), which is at odds with the dates here. Therefore we can gather that evolution in the N-Space Universe is at a different rate to ours (see also 'Ghost Light', in which Nimrod is said to be the last surviving specimen of the Neanderthal race).

2925 BC

The Doctor refers to the Egyptian god Khnum, who was indeed a god from the New Kingdom, worshipped around the time of the First Dynasty, which existed from 2925 to 2775 BC, and continued until the early centuries AD.

2029 BC

Azal tells the Master that 'my race destroys its failures – remember Atlantis'. The Doctor has visited Atlantis before (see 'The Underwater Menace') and will visit it later, as will the Master (see 'The Time Monster'), so I have placed the destruction of Atlantis at the same time of Kronos's capture. A possible link between the Dæmons and Kronos is explained in more detail under 'The Time Monster'.

800 BC

Professor Horner claims the barrow contains the grave of a Bronze Age warrior, from '800 BC'. This must be when Azal went into hibernation.

750 BC – 550 BC

The Greek civilisation flourished from about 750 BC to 550 BC in our history.

1223 ∗ 🔲 🔲 🔲 🔲 🔲 🔲 🔲 🔲 🔲 🔲 🔲 🔲 🔲 🔲
The year in our history in which Genghis Khan proclaimed himself as lord of Asia, so it is appropriate that this should be the time when the Doctor would have visited the period (see also 'Doctor Who (The TV Movie)').

1560 🔲 🔲 🔲 🔲 🔲 🔲 🔲 🔲 🔲 🔲 🔲 🔲 🔲 🔲 🔲
The age when the Renaissance started in our history.

1644 – 1647 🔲 🔲 🔲 🔲 🔲 🔲 🔲 🔲 🔲 🔲 🔲 🔲
Matthew Hopkins existed in our history, his famous witch-hunts lasting from 1644 to 1647, which ties in with Fergus's placing Hopkins as being 'seventeenth century'.

1750 🔲 🔲 🔲 🔲 🔲 🔲 🔲 🔲 🔲 🔲 🔲 🔲 🔲 🔲 🔲
Alistair Fergus mentions that the third Lord of Aldbourne practised his black arts in the 'eighteenth century'.

1793 🔲 🔲 🔲 🔲 🔲 🔲 🔲 🔲 🔲 🔲 🔲 🔲 🔲 🔲 🔲
Fergus mentions Flint and the date during his broadcast rehearsal.

1760-1830 🔲 🔲 🔲 🔲 🔲 🔲 🔲 🔲 🔲 🔲 🔲 🔲 🔲 🔲
There were two Industrial Revolutions; the first from 1760 to 1830, and second in the late nineteenth century. The Dæmons would most likely have influenced the first.

1939 ∗ 🔲 🔲 🔲 🔲 🔲 🔲 🔲 🔲 🔲 🔲 🔲 🔲 🔲 🔲
The Doctor thinks he may have witnessed one of ('that bounder') Hitler's speeches, so 1939 would be a most likely date for this, a time before World War Two when Hitler rose to power.

1939, May 🔲 🔲 🔲 🔲 🔲 🔲 🔲 🔲 🔲 🔲 🔲 🔲 🔲 🔲
Fergus and Horner mention Sutton Hoo, which is located near Woodbridge, Suffolk. In our history this was the site of the grave of an early Anglo-Saxon king, which was excavated in May of 1939. The grave contained a ship filled with treasure. The tomb is believed to be that of Raewald (who died in 625) or Aethelhere (died 654), based on the coinage found in the tomb.

1951 🔲 🔲 🔲 🔲 🔲 🔲 🔲 🔲 🔲 🔲 🔲 🔲 🔲 🔲 🔲
Miss Hawthorne mentions the repeal of the Witchcraft Act and the date.

1973, April ▨ ▨ ▨ ▨ ▨ ▨ ▨ ▨ ▨ ▨ ▨ ▨

As covered under Master Link above, the Master must have arrived in Devil's End in this month. In terms of his GRT, four months have passed since he encountered the Doctor on Uxarieus.

DURATION

There is a clock in the hall of the vicarage that is always fixed at 12.00. The clock in the pub is always fixed at 9.00.

⇨ **Day One (29 April) (Ep1)** ▨ ▨ ▨ ▨ ▨ ▨ ▨ ▨ ▨

Jim is killed during the storm this night.

⇨ **Day Two (30 April) (Ep1)** ▨ ▨ ▨ ▨ ▨ ▨ ▨ ▨ ▨

Alastair Fergus pre-records parts of his interview 'this afternoon'. The live telecast starts at '11.45 pm'. The barrow is opened on the first stroke of midnight. PC Groom is on guard over the barrow all night.

⇨ **Day Three (1 May) (Ep.2-5)** ▨ ▨ ▨ ▨ ▨ ▨ ▨ ▨

PC Groom is killed this morning. Mike and Benton arrive by helicopter; they have not had any breakfast. Azal is destroyed later that afternoon.

DAY OF THE DALEKS

STORY LINK

Since 'The Dæmons' the Doctor has continued to work on the TARDIS console ('If I could only cut out their override on the dematerialisation circuit … '). This is the third and final story in which the Doctor removes the console from the TARDIS (also seen in 'The Ambassadors Of Death' and 'Inferno'). It is possible that each of these consoles is from a different console room, the Doctor testing them all individually in the hope of finding one that has not been affected by the block put on by the Time Lords.

In 'The Android Invasion' it is clear that the Doctor has no knowledge of the launch of the XK5, the first deep space freighter, which vanished near Jupiter in July 1973. The best explanation for his ignorance of the disaster was that he was away from Earth at the time. Although the TARDIS was not functioning for him, the Time Lords may have sent him away on another of their missions in July 1973, a couple of months after 'The Dæmons'.

UNIT HQ – COASTAL #1

Auderly House is 'about 50 miles north of London' – some distance from UNIT HQ, so the base is clearly not in the central London area. The Brigadier's office looks like the one from 'The Claws Of Axos', so it is possible that this is that coastal HQ again. It has a canteen.

The Doctor's lab has large green doors like those seen in 'Colony In Space', but this is clearly a different set of rooms.

DALEK LINK

As covered under DALEK HISTORY, this is the Daleks' fifth appearance. Since 'The Dalek Invasion Of Earth' in 2164, the Daleks have discovered the secret of time travel; the Daleks' machines have dematerialisation circuits like those used in a TARDIS, and their very first use of this new discovery is to have another go at conquering Earth. However, a flaw in their time machines delivers them into a Continuous Dual Time Line and they become 'trapped in a temporal paradox'.

The Doctor says the 'Daleks have been my bitterest enemies for many years'. He first encountered them in 'The Daleks', which was eight years ago in terms of his own GRT.

LANGUAGE

The Daleks and the Ogrons clearly speak English with their human prisoners.

TIMELINE DATES

1973, September 11 – 14 ∗

The month is given as 'September'. Jo refers to her adventure with the colonists and the IMC in the year 2472 (see 'Colony In Space') as being '500 years in the future', which suggests that 'Day Of The Daleks' takes place in September 1972. However, as covered under THE UNIT YEARS, the UNIT sections of the story are best placed in 1973. With 'The Dæmons' set in April / May 1973, 'Day Of The Daleks' can be set in September 1973. Jo tells the Controller that the exact date she left her own time was 'September the 13th' (which is Day Three). (See CALENDAR SEPTEMBER 1973.)

<<2173>> ∗

The Doctor dates the weapon technology as being from 'about two hundred years ahead of its time', i.e. 2173. Reference to these events being '200 years' in the future is given on several occasions.

1815, June 15 ⋅ ▨ ▨ ▨ ▨ ▨ ▨ ▨ ▨ ▨ ▨ ▨ ▨ ▨

Although the first Doctor has visited the time of the French Revolution many times, he missed seeing Napoleon in 1794 (in 'The Reign Of Terror'). For the Doctor to have finally met Napoleon by 'Day Of The Daleks' he must have done so at a point in his time stream after 'The Reign Of Terror' and before his trial in 'The War Games'. The quote 'An army marches on its stomach' was attributed to Napoleon in November 1816. We can therefore place the meeting between the Doctor and Napoleon to have occurred on the eve of the Battle of Waterloo, which, according to 'Human Nature', began on '16th June 1815'.

<<2073>> ▨ ▨ ▨ ▨ ▨ ▨ ▨ ▨ ▨ ▨ ▨ ▨ ▨

The Controller says 'towards the end of the twentieth century a series of wars broke out. There was a hundred years of nothing but killing, destruction'. Given that the conference took place in 1973 then the war lasted until 2073, which is when the Daleks invaded. The Daleks ruled for another 100 years, till 2173, the time period visited by the Doctor and Jo.

2214 ▨ ▨ ▨ ▨ ▨ ▨ ▨ ▨ ▨ ▨ ▨ ▨ ▨

The Daleks have 'discovered the secret of time travel' and have invaded Earth 'again', no doubt in reference to the invasion of 2164, so the Daleks from 'Day Of The Daleks' must come from a time after 'The Dalek Invasion Of Earth' of 2164 – 2174.

One date we could use would be one close to 2540, the setting of 'Frontier In Space', to tie in with the Daleks using Ogrons in both stories. However, it would seem odd that even after developing time travel, the Daleks would then invade the galaxy without using this new technology. It is clear from the way the Daleks gloat to the Doctor about their achievements in this field that these Daleks pre-date those from 'The Chase'. The time machine in 'The Chase' is a new development, which means that the time machines sent by the Daleks to invade Earth were much less advanced. It is stated by Anat that the Daleks developed the Time Transference Modules while they were already on Earth, so in my mind, the Daleks' time travel technology has progressed from the machines they used to get to Earth to the TARDIS-like machines seen in 'The Chase' and 'The Daleks' Master Plan'. It should be noted, of course, that the Daleks' new time technology and history seen in 'Day Of The Daleks' never happens, due to the fact that that particular branch of Time is erased.

I have therefore taken the arbitrary date of origin of these Daleks as being 50 years after the invasion of Earth began, in 2214.

DURATION

⇨ **Day One (11 September) (Ep1)** ▤ ▤ ▤ ▤ ▤ ▤ ▤ ▤
Styles is attacked while 'working late' at night.

⇨ **Day Two (12 September) (Ep1)** ▤ ▤ ▤ ▤ ▤ ▤ ▤ ▤
UNIT is called in the next morning to investigate. Styles flies to Peking. The Doctor and Jo spend the night at Auderly House. A clock chimes 8 times when the Doctor has his one-man wine and cheese party (Jo gives the date as 'September the Twelfth').

⇨ **Day Three (13 September) (Ep1-2)** ▤ ▤ ▤ ▤ ▤ ▤ ▤
The guerrillas arrive but wait 'till it's light' before going to the House. The conference is set for 'tomorrow night'. The Doctor and Jo are transported to the 22nd Century ... (Jo gives the date as 'September the Thirteenth').

⇨ **Day Four (14 September) (Ep4)** ▤ ▤ ▤ ▤ ▤ ▤ ▤ ▤
Styles returns to England 'at 1800 hours' in time for the conference that evening. However, when the Doctor and Jo return to Auderly, the clock in the hallway reads 10.55 (which is wrong because it is daylight).

⇨ **Day One (2173) (Ep1/2-4)** ▤ ▤ ▤ ▤ ▤ ▤ ▤ ▤
There are no night scenes in the future. The Doctor and Jo arrive on the equivalent of 'September 13' and return to their own time the following day, so in terms of the Blinovitch Limitation Effect, they must have spent the equivalent time away in the twenty-second century.

CALENDAR SEPTEMBER 1973						
SUN	MON	TUES	WED	THUR	FRI	SAT
2	3	4	5	6	7	8
9	10	11 Day Of The Daleks	12 Day Of The Daleks	13 Day Of The Daleks	14 Day Of The Daleks	15 The Curse Of Peladon
16	17 The Sea Devils	18 The Sea Devils	19 The Sea Devils	20 The Sea Devils	21	22
23	24	25	26	27 The Mutants	28	29 The Time Monster
30						

As given on-screen, 'Day Of The Daleks' is set from 11 to 14 September, and 'The Time Monster' on 29 September. In terms of THE UNIT YEARS, the year is 1973 for both stories. Since there is no allowance for a 12-month period between 'Day Of The Daleks' and 'The Time Monster' [as was probably intended], all the stories of Season Nine take place during the same month. Jo has a date with Mike Yates in 'The Curse Of Peladon', which we can assume is on a Friday or Saturday night, which would be the 17th or the 18th. In 'The Sea Devils' Trenchard is planning a forthcoming 'weekend' golf tournament. This places the four-day duration of 'The Sea Devils' around the beginning of a week; say the 17th to the 20th. The brief UNIT scene in 'The Mutants' is therefore set on the 24th, 25th, 26th, or 27th. Given the fact that the Doctor is not concerned about the Master's whereabouts in 'The Mutants', and is working on the minimum-inertia super-drive for Bessie, which he uses in 'The Time Monster', chances are it is around the 27th.

THE CURSE OF PELADON

+STORY LINK

With 'Day Of The Daleks' set from 11 – 14 September and 'The Time Monster' on 29 September 1973, the Doctor and Jo's departure from Earth in 'The Curse Of Peladon' must take place a few days after 'Day Of The Daleks'. Jo is 'all dolled up for a night out on the town with Mike Yates', which suggests it is a Friday or Saturday night. The best date is 15 September. (See CALENDAR SEPTEMBER 1973.)   The Doctor told her 'we'd only be a few minutes', but Jo scolds him because 'we've been simply ages'.

GALLIFREY LINK

The Time Lords who control the TARDIS are from the Doctor's GRT, which is 1666 at this point in his life. In order for the Doctor to succeed in his mission it is quite possible that the Time Lords deliberately cause the real Earth delegate to be late to enable the Doctor to assume her role. It is not clear why the Time Lords would even be concerned with the events on Peladon, considering they are not of major universal significance in comparison to other tasks they have given or later give to the Doctor. Of course Peladon does play a vital role fifty years later, during the war with Galaxy Five (see 'The Monster Of Peladon'). It's therefore possible the Time Lords needed to ensure that Peladon joined the Federation so its mineral wealth could be used for the war effort. (And if Galaxy Five was indeed later allied with the Daleks in the year 4000 ('The Daleks' Master Plan'), the Time Lords might have foreseen this and manipulated events on Peladon to ensure a 'favourable' outcome of the war.)

LANGUAGE

The delegates of the Federation are all from different races, and yet they converse with each other and the 'Pels' in English. The letter 'H' has the same meaning on Peladon as it does on Earth (Grun writes 'H' to indicate 'Hepesh' to the Doctor).

TIMELINE DATES

3225 ◆ ▨ ▨ ▨ ▨ ▨ ▨ ▨ ▨ ▨ ▨ ▨ ▨ ▨

Establishing the setting for 'The Curse Of Peladon' and its sequel 'The Monster Of Peladon' is difficult, because in this future period Earth is a member of a larger Galactic Federation, which includes an 'Ice Warrior'-ruled Mars, a situation which does not appear in any other story.

In 2096 Earth had its first true encounter with the Martian 'Ice Warriors' ('The Seeds Of Death'), although only a few of the human survivors actually saw them. 'The Curse Of Peladon' and 'The Monster Of Peladon' both need to be set well after 2096. In 'The Ice Warriors', set in 5000, the humans at Britannicus Base do not know of the 'Ice Warriors', so 'The Curse Of Peladon' and 'The Monster Of Peladon' should be set after 5000. One major problem with this date is that in the years after 5000 Earth has been abandoned because of solar flare activity, a condition that lasts for 10,000 years (see 'The Ark In Space', and 'The Sontaran Experiment'). On this basis 'The Ice Warriors' cannot be used as a dating tool; the reason the staff of Britannicus do not identify the creatures they encounter as being Martians is because the events of 'The Ice Warriors' and 'The Monster Of Peladon' are centuries apart, and the base staff had little knowledge of that far back in Earth's past. Very few of the crew even see the Martians in 'The Ice Warriors', and so they don't immediately identify the creatures as having once been Earth's allies. Besides, they had more important things to worry about at the time.

In 'The Monster Of Peladon' the Federation is at war with Galaxy Five. In 'The Daleks' Master Plan', set in 4000, the Fifth Galaxy is allied to the Daleks. Assuming that Galaxy Five and the Fifth Galaxy are one and the same, we could set 'The Monster Of Peladon' before the events of 'The Daleks' Master Plan' (as a result of losing the war with the Federation, despite signing a peace treaty, Galaxy Five make a secret alliance with the Daleks to invade Earth); or after 'The Daleks' Master Plan' (following the defeat of the Daleks on Kembel and the death of their representative Zephon, Galaxy Five troops, allied with 'a breakaway group' of Martians, mount their revenge on Earth with a 'vicious and unprovoked attack' on the Federation). In 'The Daleks' Master Plan' Mavic Chen mentions the Non-Aggression Pact of 3975, which has joined the planets in the Solar System (which is understood to mean the whole galaxy – not just Earth's system) in a peaceful unity, which could very well also be part of the treaty signed between the Federation and Galaxy Five. In the 25 years since the Pact was signed, there has been peace in the Solar System that would hopefully 'spread throughout the Universe'. On the assumption that the Non-Aggression Pact of 3975 is linked to the Galaxy Five surrender, then 'The Monster Of Peladon' could be set in 3975, with 'The Curse Of Peladon' '50 years' earlier, in 3925. This is a tenuous link, but one that I feel could be significant in terms of a dating tool. Certainly, in 'The Daleks' Master Plan' Mars is still an Earth colony, and there is no indication that the 'Ice Warriors' have any influence. And there is no evidence of the Federation in 'The Daleks' Master Plan', so it could be that by the year 4000 Earth was not yet a member; or it had long since pulled out of the Federation.

An alternative is to ignore the tenuous link to 'The Daleks' Master Plan' and look at the Federation itself as a dating tool. Previously Earth was the centre of a vast Empire that stretched across the galaxy. This Empire was declining towards the end of the 30th century (in 2971, see 'The Mutants'). We can assume that Earth joined the Federation at some point soon after its Empire is officially dissolved. This would probably have taken centuries to complete, to enable all its colonies to achieve independence or dominion status. Earth is therefore probably in a strong position for membership of the Federation by 3200. We do not know which planets initially formed the Federation. It is highly unlikely that Earth is a founding member. However, of the four representatives of the Preliminary Assessment Commission on Peladon, the Earth delegate is the chairperson, whose experience and wisdom are highly respected by the other delegates, so certainly by this time Earth holds a significant position within the Federation. There is also the fact that Peladon's mother is from Earth, so the planet is not unknown to the 'Pels'. It is also very clear that the Federation consists of more than just the four planets represented by the Commission (since the Federation is on a Galactic level, is Draconia a member?)

At the time of the Federation, Mars is ruled independently by the 'Ice Warriors' who had returned to reclaim their planet. We know from 'The Daleks' Master Plan' that humans had colonised Mars by the 40th century. When the new regime of 'Ice Warriors' return to their old world, they accept that humanity is now the ruler of Mars. A treaty of sorts is signed; the 'Warriors' will live at the polar regions of the planet and have places on the governing councils on the planet. Much later, under mutual agreement, total control of Mars is eventually returned to the 'Warriors'. A few of the human colonies are allowed to remain. SSS agent Bret Vyon is therefore born on Mars while it is under 'Ice Warrior' rule, but is still considered by some to be an Earth colony. I prefer it that Earth joins the Federation relatively soon after its Empire collapses, which places 'The Curse Of Peladon' and 'The Monster Of Peladon' around the first quarter of the 4th millennium, as opposed to the last quarter. The quarter point would be 3250. Bridging 'The Curse Of Peladon' and 'The Monster Of Peladon' around that date, we can use the years 3225 and 3275. The fact that the Federation neither appears nor is mentioned in any other stories later than these dates can be put down to either the Federation having only a low profile during the latter decades of the 40th century, considering Mavic Chen's position of Guardian of the Solar System; or the Federation has by then simply disbanded. With 'The Curse Of Peladon' and 'The Monster Of Peladon' we are, after all, dealing with events that in effect take place over a few days within a span of 1000 years, so the political environment within the galaxy would certainly have changed several times during that period of time, and the collapse of the Federation is not implausible.

This is a bit of a mess, but given the contradictions, one of the above ideas is likely to be correct. I have therefore decided to take the dates 3225 / 3275.

1559, January 13 *
The date of Elizabeth I's coronation in our history.

1838, June 28 *
This is the date of Victoria's coronation in our history. Surprisingly, the Doctor is not concerned about seeing Victoria's coronation again, even if it could mean that he would meet his earlier self there. It is likely that the Time Lords (or the TARDIS safeguard device) would prevent this from happening.

1973, September 15 *
The Doctor and Jo leave Earth in this year and month (see Link above, and CALENDAR SEPTEMBER 1973).

c3215
Peladon was only 'a boy' when his father died. If he is about 25 in 'The Curse Of Peladon', then he became King about 20 years earlier.

DURATION

⇨ **Day One (Ep1-3)**
Torbis is killed early that evening. The Doctor is held prisoner 'until dawn'.

⇨ **Day Two (Ep3-4)**
The Doctor fights Grun that morning at 'dawn'. Alpha Centauri finds its communicator

broken 'this morning'. Hepesh is defeated later that day.

⇨ **Day Three? (Ep4) – A day (?) passes ...** ▓ ▓ ▓ ▓ ▓ ▓

⇨ **Day Four? (Ep4)** ▓ ▓ ▓ ▓ ▓ ▓ ▓ ▓ ▓ ▓
It appears to be days later when Peladon is crowned, to allow time for the preparations for his coronation

THE SEA DEVILS

+STORY LINK

At the end of 'The Curse Of Peladon' the Doctor and Jo decide to attend Queen Victoria's coronation, but with the TARDIS still under Time Lord control, they might not have got there (if only to prevent the Doctor from accidentally encountering his earlier self who was already there). It is likely that the ship is returned to Earth within seconds of leaving, as it did in 'Colony In Space'. Jo probably still makes it in time for her 'night out on the town with Mike Yates'. The Doctor probably begins his repairs on the Interstitial Beam Synthesiser.

MASTER LINK

The Master has been in prison since 'The Dæmons' for about five months (the Doctor says the authorities wanted to execute the Master). The Master says he wished this had happened to him earlier, which means he has never been in prison before. He learned about the marine reptiles 'from the Time Lords' files', presumably stolen at the same time he took the file about the Doomsday Weapon (see 'Colony In Space'). Given that the first ship only disappeared a 'few weeks' ago, we can assume that the Master begins his control over Trenchard only just before the events of the story. He refuses to tell the Doctor where his TARDIS is. It's unlikely to have been at Devil's End otherwise the Doctor would have found it.

OBSERVATIONS

- This story sees the Doctor's first use of the phrase 'reverse the polarity of the neutron flow'.

LANGUAGE

The marine reptiles speak English with the Doctor and the Master, but not to any other humans, so we can assume that the 'gift' is responsible.

TIMELINE DATES

1973, September 17 – 20 ✦

As covered under THE UNIT YEARS, this story is best placed in 1973: the Master watches part of 'The Rock Collector' episode of *Clangers*, which first screened on 24 April 1971, a Sunday. However, later, in Ep2, Trenchard talks to Hart about the golf tournament at 'the weekend', which means the story takes place during the week, so the episode being viewed by the Master must therefore have been a repeat (or possibly even a video recording). 'Day Of The Daleks' is set from 11 – 14 September and 'The Time Monster' on 29 September. The UNIT YEARS does not allow for a twelve month period between those two stories (as was probably intended), so 'The Sea Devils' must be set during the same month (possibly the 17th to 20th – see CALENDAR SEPTEMBER 1973). Also, 'Johnny Reggae' by The Piglets, heard on the sea fort radio, didn't reach the charts until November 1971, so 'The Sea Devils' can't be set earlier than that year.

Hart says that three ships had vanished 'in the same area in the last few weeks'.

200,000,000 BC
70,000,000 BC

See 'Doctor Who And The Silurians' for the dates given for the time of the 'Sea Devils'.

1797 ✦

Nelson (born 1758, died on 21 October 1805) became an admiral in 1797 in our history, so this is the most likely year that the Doctor met him and became 'a personal friend'.

1854, October 25 ✦

The Doctor (jokingly?) tells Robbins he was wounded in the Crimean War. In 'The Evil Of The Daleks' the Doctor says he saw the Charge of the Light Brigade, so these two incidents were probably around the same time.

1915, April 25 ✦

The Doctor (jokingly?) tells Robbins that he was wounded at Gallipoli. The date of the main battle was 25 April 1915 in our history.

1942, October 23 ▪
This is the date in our history on which the battle at El Alamein started, in Egypt. The Doctor (jokingly?) tells Robbins he was there.

1963 – 1973
Seventy ships have been lost in the 'last 10 years', according to Hart.

DURATION

⇨ **Day One (17 September?) (Ep1)**
It is night when the SS *Pevensey Castle* is attacked.

⇨ **Day Two (18 September?) (Ep1-2)**
The clock in the Master's room reads '11.00' when he meets with the Doctor and Jo. It is after noon when the Doctor visits the Naval Base (he greets the guards: 'Good afternoon'). Later, when the Master watches *Clangers* the clock reads '12.15'. Later that 'afternoon', the Doctor and Jo go to the Fort (Jo notes that 'it's getting dark'). They spend the night on the fort.

⇨ **Day Three (19 September?) (Ep2-4)**
The Doctor and Jo are rescued in the morning. The Doctor returns to the prison and is locked up; the clock in the Master's cell reads '1.00'. It is '2.07' on the clock when Jo returns, and '2.20' when they escape to the beach. The sub is attacked around '4.00'. The marine reptiles attack the prison base around '8.45' that night.

⇨ **Day Four (20 September?) (Ep4-6)**
It is morning when Trenchard's body is found, and when Walker arrives ('Good morning, my dear'). The Special Taskforce is due to be in position to bomb the marine reptile base 'at 1350'. The story ends later that afternoon.

THE MUTANTS

+STORY LINK

There is no direct link to 'The Sea Devils'. The Master has escaped but this does not concern the Doctor and Jo. The Doctor is 'making a minimum inertia drive for Bessie', which he later installs, prior to 'The Time Monster'. On the blackboard in the London

UNIT lab we can see a series of formulas and calculations. This is possibly an attempt by the Doctor to break the block on his memory.

UNIT HQ – LONDON #3

Jo tells Ky that she lives 'in London', so this could be the same HQ from 'Colony In Space' (unless she commutes to UNIT HQ from her home in London). It is not the house from 'The Mind Of Evil'. We see only the Doctor's workshop, which has the usual green / white brick walls. We do not see any doors, so the angle used in this scene could simply be one taken from the other side of the same laboratory from 'Colony In Space'.

GALLIFREY LINK

It is not explained how the Time Lords came to be in possession of the stone tablets, or how they obtained Ky's palm print for the sphere (curiously, the Earth Investigator and his entourage appear to be dressed rather like Time Lords!). We can assume that an exploration team from Gallifrey time-travels into the future and discovers that the life cycle on Solos is 'unique in the history of the Universe'. They spend some time observing the four stages of metamorphosis. Then the humans come, and the Time Lords become aware of this new threat posed to the Solonian life form. They subsequently observe the Marshal's and Jaeger's atmospheric tests on the surface of the planet 500 years later, and see that this causes a premature mutation. Realising they cannot help without jeopardising their mission, they establish who the strongest Solonian warrior is – Ky – then one of them returns to Gallifrey with the tablets they had found and translated, and Ky's body print. With the assistance of the CIA the tablets are sent to the Doctor …

OBSERVATIONS

- Solos orbits its sun elliptically every '2000 years', making each of its four seasons '500 years long'. When Solos is first colonised, it has just entered spring, and so the natives had already mutated into their humanoid 'warrior' form. The insectoid mutant is simply the 'chrysalis' stage between the spring and summer forms. The summer form is that of a rainbow-coloured being that possesses thought-transference and teleportation. Ky speaks of 'the Old Ones', who were probably the summer form of 2000 years earlier. It is never revealed what the winter or autumn Solonians looked like, however based on the designs on the four stone tablets, we see stick-like figures on the spring tablet (the warriors), sun-like figures on the summer tablet (the Old Ones), star-like figures on autumn and spiral designs on winter. We can assume that the insectoid stage occurs with all four of the metamorphic periods. The

Solonian mutants are not in any way related to the Mutt insectoid species seen in 'The Brain Of Morbius'. The Mutts come from the Nebula of Cyclops and have space technology. They also have body hair and their head, eyes and mandibles are vastly different to the Solonian variety.

LANGUAGE

The Doctor tells Jo '*Au revoir*'. The Solonians speak English, most likely taught to them by the Over-Lords. The Doctor is unable to read 'the language of the Old Ones'. On the blackboard in the Doctor's laboratory at UNIT HQ we can see a series of formulas, using familiar numerals and letters. These are probably an attempt by the Doctor to crack the Time Lords' block on the TARDIS. It is very similar to the formulas seen in 'The Claws Of Axos'.

TIMELINE DATES

1973, September 27 •

As covered under THE UNIT YEARS, this part of the story is best placed in 1973. With 'Day Of The Daleks' set from 11 – 14 September and 'The Time Monster' from 29 September, 'The Mutants' must take place between these dates, most likely one of the days from the 21st to the 27th. The Doctor is occupied with building the new drive for Bessie and not chasing after the Master, so I think the 27th is the more likely date (see CALENDAR SEPTEMBER 1973).

The TARDIS is under control of the Time Lords, as in 'Colony In Space' and 'The Curse Of Peladon', so we can assume that the ship returns to Earth again only seconds after leaving.

2973 •

The Doctor says 'according to the TARDIS's instrument readings we are now in the thirtieth century Empire'. The description of Earth ('politically, economically and biologically finished' / 'grey' / 'slag, ash, clinker' / 'No one lives on the ground. The air is too poisonous') contradicts 'Terror Of The Vervoids', in which Earth still has farms in 2986, so it is possible that 'The Mutants' could be set earlier in the century. Since the Doctor and Jo leave Earth in 1973, we can set the story in 2973, a Century Factor of 1000.

Coincidentally, in 'Terror Of The Vervoids', there is an intergalactic ship called *Hyperion III*. In 'The Mutants' the Earth Investigator's shuttle is called *Hyperion*. It could be that the ship in 'Terror Of The Vervoids' is a later model of the same type of vessel. This tenuous link supports setting 'The Mutants' before 2986.

The first mutations occurred 'in recent months'.

1666 ■ ■ ■ ■ ■ ■ ■ ■ ■ ■ ■ ■ ■ ■

The Time Lords who contact the Doctor are from his GRT, which is 1666 at this point in his time stream (see THE DOCTOR'S AGE).

2473 ■ ■ ■ ■ ■ ■ ■ ■ ■ ■ ■ ■ ■ ■

Earthmen came to Solos 'some 500 years ago', during the Solonian 'spring', because of the thaesium needed to power spaceships and 'everything'. 2473 is also near the time period of 'Colony In Space', so the situation on Earth over the next 500 years is of a steady decline towards decay.

2958 ■ ■ ■ ■ ■ ■ ■ ■ ■ ■ ■ ■ ■ ■

The Marshal says he has 'put years of my life in this planet', say 15 years.

2963 ■ ■ ■ ■ ■ ■ ■ ■ ■ ■ ■ ■ ■ ■

Sondergaard has been living on Solos 'for many years' and was 'given up for dead years ago', say 10.

DURATION

⇨ **Day (Earth) (September 1973) (Ep1)** ■ ■ ■ ■ ■ ■ ■

It is 'well past lunch time' on Earth, meaning mid-afternoon, in the London UNIT lab.

⇨ **Day One (Solos) (Ep1)** ■ ■ ■ ■ ■ ■ ■ ■ ■

The old Mutt is killed prior to '42 06' (Solos time). The TARDIS lands at night on 'the eve of the independence conference'. The Doctor and Jo spend the night locked up.

⇨ **Day Two (Solos) (Ep1-3)** ■ ■ ■ ■ ■ ■ ■ ■

Jo observes the dawn through the Skybase window. The Administrator arrives in the morning. It is night when the Doctor and Varan go to Solos.

⇨ **Day Three (Solos) (Ep3-6)** ■ ■ ■ ■ ■ ■ ■ ■

The Over-Lord guards attack the caves this morning. The *Hyperion* is due 'ETA 22:20:29 Solos time'. It is night when Sondergaard returns to the Skybase. The Doctor and Jo leave later that evening.

THE TIME MONSTER

+STORY LINK

Since 'The Sea Devils', UNIT has placed an 'A1 priority' on the Master, now that he is 'an escaped prisoner'. In 'The Mutants' the Doctor is working on a minimum-inertia super-drive for Bessie. In 'The Time Monster' it is fully installed and working. The Doctor says his work on the dematerialisation circuit will 'have to wait'; he has abandoned that to make a 'time sensor' to track down the Master. Jo notes that the TARDIS control room 'looks different'. The Doctor replies: 'Oh, just a spot of redecoration, that's all'. This change has been made since Jo last travelled in the TARDIS, which was in 'The Mutants'.

UNIT HQ – LONDON #2

The Doctor's lab is very much like the one in 'Terror Of The Autons' and has a spiral staircase going to an upper floor, but out the window of the Doctor's lab we can see a row of terraced houses, so it appears that this HQ is in London. It could be the one first seen in 'The Mind Of Evil'. We catch a brief glimpse of the Brigadier's office, which does look similar to the one from 'The Mind Of Evil'. In fact, when he sees the TARDIS dematerialise, the farmer says 'Londoners!'

The Doctor wants the Brigadier to 'put out a world-wide alert. Alert all your UNIT HQs', and the Brigadier mentions 'every section of UNIT'. In 'The Claws Of Axos', Bill Filer comes from 'Washington HQ', the first intimation of UNIT being truly an international organisation.

MASTER LINK

Having escaped from prison at the end of 'The Sea Devils', the Master sets about the release of Kronos. He has a map of Atlantis and the smaller Kronos crystal, but it is not explained how he came to possess them. It is likely that he stole them from the Time Lords' files (see 'Colony In Space'). The small shard from the larger crystal is in the temple, and vanishes with Krasis when the Master pulls him to 1973, but it is not with the priest when he materialises in the TOMTIT lab. The Doctor explains that the crystal made 'the jump through interstitial time'; therefore it probably emerged from the vortex into real time and was later found there by the Time Lords.

With Kronos under his control, the Master's plan is to dominate the Universe. The fact that Azal claims to have been responsible for Atlantis' destruction in 'The Dæmons' (see also Observations below) could in part be related directly to the events of 'The Time Monster'. What if the Master had the Kronos crystal in his possession before the events of 'The Dæmons'? He may have first posed as Thascales as early as April, soon after failing to obtain the Doomsday Weapon (see 'Colony In Space'). He needed to release Kronos from the Crystal, but to do so he needed to open a break in interstitial time. And then once Kronos had been freed, the Master needed the power of the Dæmons with which to control the Chronovore. The Master has been to Athens University – possibly to obtain further information about Atlantis – and it is probably while there that he discovers that Ruth Ingram is already working on the concept of opening interstitial time at Cambridge (she says she has been working on the concept 'for months'), and offers his assistance (using hypnotism and faked credentials from Athens University). Once everything is ready at Cambridge, the Master goes to Devil's End. The events of The Dæmons take place, and the Master is arrested. Meanwhile in Cambridge, Ruth continues with the TOMTIT project alone. The Master is imprisoned from May to September ('The Dæmons' to 'The Sea Devils'). After escaping at the end of 'The Sea Devils', he retrieves his TARDIS, and goes to Cambridge to re-establish contact with Ruth, who has by now gained outside interest in the project.

OBSERVATIONS

- In 'The Underwater Menace', Atlantis is established as being located south of the Azores in the Atlantic Ocean, and yet in 'The Time Monster' it is now in the Thera group of islands south of Greece in the Mediterranean. Jo and Mike discuss the location of Atlantis in Ep1; Jo says that the Atlantic Ocean theory is 'a bit out of date'. Azal claims that the Dæmons were responsible for the destruction of Atlantis (see 'The Dæmons'). So how can all three versions work? The Dæmons reference is probably chronologically the first in terms of Atlantean history. In 'The Time Monster' Dalios remembers seeing Kronos released and nearly destroying Atlantis 500 years earlier. It could have been the Dæmons who assisted the priests in releasing Kronos in the first instance, creating the chaos spoken of by Dalios ('If Kronos came again, Atlantis would be doomed, destroyed, never to rise again'). Azal assumed that Atlantis had been destroyed, but he was wrong: the Atlanteans had trapped Kronos in the crystal before total destruction was completed. After the Master releases Kronos for the second time, Atlantis is indeed ultimately destroyed and, as covered in 'The Underwater Menace', the few survivors leave (in boats?) and find a new home inside a volcanic island near the Azores, where they live for several centuries. In 2070 their dream of seeing Atlantis raised again from beneath the sea again is nearly fulfilled by Professor Zaroff.
- The ancient Atlantean priests tried to destroy the crystal but only managed to break off a small shard. The larger crystal was kept in the labyrinth guarded

by the Minotaur, and the shard put in the Temple of Poseidon. As outlined earlier, the smaller crystal came into the Time Lords' possession (and was subsequently stolen by the Master). When connected to the TOMTIT machine, the crystal is able to link with itself in the Temple through interstitial time. The Doctor says the crystal 'isn't really here at all. It's made the jump through interstitial time. Must be linked to that other crystal all those thousands of years ago. Or rather it is the other crystal' still in Atlantis in 1527 BC.

- When asked by Jo what happens if the Master wins, the Doctor replies: 'the whole of creation is very delicately balanced in cosmic terms, Jo. If the Master opens the floodgates of Kronos's power, all order and all structure will be swept away and nothing will be left but chaos'. Although he fails this time, the Master partially succeeds in destroying the whole of creation again in 'Logopolis'. And interestingly, the Doctor's speech also almost mirrors the White Guardian's in 'The Ribos Operation', when he explains to the Doctor what would happen if the Key To Time is not assembled in time. It is also similar to what would happen when Davros used the Reality Bomb in 'The Stolen Earth'.

LANGUAGE

When Jo hears the Doctor's unconscious thoughts they do not seem to be in English. The Doctor knows that Thascales is Greek for Master (although the Time Lord 'gift' doesn't translate the name for him and reveal the Master's alias earlier!). The Doctor shouts in (cod) Spanish when he fights the Minotaur. Krasis speaks English with the Master. The Doctor's TARDIS has a '6' on the console, while on the Master's TARDIS console a dial is marked with 'DANGER' and 'ZERO'. The Doctor and the Master speak English when they communicate via their TARDIS communications circuits. The Master feeds the Doctor's words back to him and they come out backwards.

TIMELINE DATES

1973, September 29 ⊹

The farmer recalls the fall of the doodlebug of 1944. The farmer cannot be much older than 40. For him to recall the doodlebug he would have to be at least no younger than 7 or 8 during the war. That places the date of 'The Time Monster' no later than 1976. As covered under THE UNIT YEARS, the twentieth century segment of the story is best placed in 1973 (making the farmer 11 in 1944).

Jo wishes Sergeant Benton a 'Merry Michaelmas', which is the Feast of St Michael the Archangel, celebrated on 29 September. With 'Day Of The Daleks' set from 11 – 14 September 1973, 'The Time Monster' is set later in the same month (see CALENDAR

SEPTEMBER 1973).
Jo is returned to her own time (but to the TOMTIT lab) only moments after she left it, despite spending two days in Atlantis. As noted under 'Colony In Space', she is once again out of sync with her Earth Mean Time.

1527 BC (autumn) ⋆
The Doctor says their adventure in Atlantis happened 'three thousand five hundred years ago', which from 1973 is 1527 BC.
Hippias asks Dalios if his people's love will fill their bellies when the granaries are empty 'in the winter', so it is probably late autumn.

2064 BC
Dalios says the temple was built '537 years ago', which is 2064 BC from 1527 BC.

2027 BC
The Doctor says the crystal 'was used four thousand years ago to capture the Chronovore', which from 1973 is 2027 BC. And Krasis says the secret to Kronos's power has been lost 'for five centuries', from 2027 BC to 1527 BC.

1200
The knight is dressed in jousting garb, suggesting that he comes from the late twelfth / early-thirteenth century.

1642 -1648
The Master refers to the Roundheads as 'seventeenth century poltroons'. The English Civil War occurred during the years 1642 and 1648 (see also 'The War Games' and 'The Awakening').

1944 ⋆
The farmer says 'It was just about here where that doodlebug fell. Back in 1944, that were'. But if the doodlebug explodes in the very same field back in 1944, how can it also explode there in 1973? The Doctor appears familiar with doodlebugs, so he was probably on Earth during the Second World War at some point.

1947, November
1973, November
Stuart Hyde is 25; his 26th birthday is in 'seven weeks' time'. He was therefore born in November 1947.

1973, April
Ruth says she has lived with the concept of stepping outside space/time 'for months'; say since April (see Master Link above).

1973, September 28
Jo mentions the eruption on Thera.

DURATION

⇨ **Day One (29 September) (Ep1-4 / 6)**
The Doctor falls asleep after working 'all night'. The TOMTIT demo is set for 'two' (i.e. 2.00 pm), but Ruth and Stuart have the test run at '11.00' am (as seen by the clock tower). The Doctor and Jo leave in the TARDIS later that afternoon. When the Doctor and Jo return from Atlantis, Stu is feeding the baby Benton the remains of Stu's 'lunchtime sandwiches'. At least 12 hours have passed (bridged across two days) for the Doctor and Jo since they left in the TARDIS, but no more than an hour or so seems to have passed between the Ruth and Stu scene in Ep4 and the follow-on scene at the end of Ep6. It would seem that the Blinovitch Limitation Effect has not worked here, and Jo is once again out of sync in time as she was in 'Colony In Space', and possibly 'The Mutants'.

(TARDIS) (Ep4-6)
The Doctor and Jo spend quite some time travelling in the TARDIS and later when caught in the vortex after the Time Ram.

⇨ **Day One (1527 BC) (Ep2-3)**
It is a stormy night when Krasis and the Crystal vanish, and later the same night when Hippias and Dalios talk of Kronos.

⇨ **Day Two (1527 BC) (Ep5-6)**
It is afternoon when the Doctor and Jo arrive in Atlantis (the Doctor greets the Master with a 'Good afternoon'). They spend the night in the cell.

⇨ **Day Three (1527 BC) (Ep6)**
Dalios dies 'this morning'. Atlantis is destroyed later this day.

(Vortex) (Ep6)
The Doctor, Jo and the Master spend a few minutes in the vortex.

THE THREE DOCTORS

STORY LINK

There are no references to the events of 'The Time Monster', although the Doctor is wearing the same red jacket. But as stated in Timeline Dates below, 'The Three Doctors' is a few months later. The Doctor has once again reconfigured the TARDIS console room since 'The Time Monster'.

Benton refers to the events of 'The Invasion' as being 'all those years ago' (which was in July 1970). The Doctor has been exiled to Earth for just over three years now (since October 1970). Despite the negative attitude towards Earth displayed by the Doctor during his first and second incarnations, the Doctor has by now accepted Earth as his 'home'. Indeed, from this story on (and specifically the stories of the fourth Doctor) he often states that humans are his 'favourite species' and Earth his 'favourite planet'. (In 'The Stones Of Blood', Romana states that 'everybody knows that'.)

UNIT HQ – COUNTRY #2

When they arrive on Omega's homeworld, the Brigadier says 'we're probably miles from London'. The building appears to be out in the country, but it is not the same house seen in 'The Ambassadors Of Death'. It has a large sign on the driveway, which reads:

MINISTRY OF DEFENCE
U.N.I.T.
HEADQUARTERS
Brigadier Lethbridge Stewart
NO UNAUTHORISED ENTRY

So much for keeping UNIT a secret organisation! The HQ has a garage. This same building is still being used 11 years later in 1984 – as seen in 'The Five Doctors'. Although the HQ is not in central London, like the one from 'The Mind Of Evil', it clearly lies in the outer regions of the city.

The Doctor's lab is on the ground level. The window on the right looks out across the grounds. The lab has two sets of double blue doors, on opposite sides of the room, both leading out onto the usual brick-lined corridors.

UNIT has not had a Corporal in the ranks for some time, but Corporal Palmer is now on duty at UNIT HQ. (Captain Mike Yates is not on duty during this story; presumably he is on leave.)

GALLIFREY LINK

The Chancellor in 'The Three Doctors' looks like one of the Tribunal present at the Doctor's trial [Clyde Pollitt plays both], while the Time Lord technician looks like one of the conspiring Time Lords from the CIA in 'Colony In Space' [Graham Leaman plays both], although he now has a beard so he might not actually be the same Time Lord. If he is the same, then even 'junior' Time Lords such as technicians can still be members of the 'secret' CIA.

The Doctor's exile is lifted and he is given back his freedom at the end of 'The Three Doctors'. It is said by Engin in 'The Deadly Assassin' that the Doctor's 'sentence was subsequently remitted at the intercession of the CIA', no doubt due in part to the Time Lord technician's report to his co-agents following the Omega affair, who in turn put the motion to the Tribunal and the High Council.

As covered under GALLIFREY HISTORY it is impossible for the first and second Doctors to have entered the transportation units sent to collect them without them being 'rejected' because they do not conform to the GRT of the third Doctor's Time Lord contemporaries. The reference to 'temporal energy' could explain the process needed to break the time stream barrier to enable the Doctors to travel into their future.

It is significant that the first Doctor is moved in time from GRT 1661 (during 'The War Machines') to GRT 1666, which is only five years into his future, and the second Doctor by only three years (from GRT 1663, prior to 'The War Games'). This shows clearly that even over relatively short distances in time there is still a severe drain of temporal energy.

That the first Doctor is trapped in a 'time eddy' inside his transport unit suggests that the second Doctor is also picked up by a similar device from his time stream (the transport unit is possibly a mini-TARDIS, and it is clearly a different method of time stream crossing than that seen in 'The Five Doctors', 'The Two Doctors' and 'The Trial Of A Time Lord'). The second Doctor was probably briefed by the Time Lords while still inside the transportation unit.

- Refer to the *Timelink* entries under the first and second Doctors for details of where they were removed from their own time streams …

OBSERVATIONS

- It has been theorised by some fans that after the Doctor's departure from Gallifrey, the Time Lords had been unable to track him down and bring him back, otherwise they would have done so prior to 'The War Games'. However, in 'The War Games', the head Time Lord says 'we have noted your particular interest in the planet Earth. The frequency of your visits must have given you special knowledge of that world and its problems', which indicates that they have indeed been monitoring his movements. Then in 'The Three Doctors', the Time Lords are able to lock onto the time traces of both the first and second Doctors with relative ease. So why didn't they locate and bring the Doctor back to Gallifrey earlier? (And on that same note, they were able to bring the Master to Gallifrey with relative ease in 'The Five Doctors', so why not the Doctor?) My guess is that the Doctor deactivated both the Mark Three Emergency Transceiver (see 'The Creature From The Pit') and the TARDIS recall circuit (mentioned in 'Arc Of Infinity'). And because he had also lost his reflex link (see 'The Invisible Enemy'), the Time Lords were unable to trace him accurately through the telepathic circuits. They could watch him but not contact him. Then, when the Doctor contacts the Time Lords at the end of 'The War Games', they are able to lock onto his signal and as a result bring him back to Gallifrey. With the TARDIS back on Gallifrey in 'The War Games' the Time Lords probably downloaded into the Matrix the flight-records of all its journeys since it left Gallifrey. They also reactivated the recall device and fitted the TARDIS with the most up-to-date in surveillance devices (The Trial Of Time Lord). With the information obtained from the TARDIS, the Time Lords are now able to access from the Matrix all details of where the Doctor has been at any point in his past, and thus they are able to locate the first and second Doctors in order to bring them into the 'future' in 'The Three Doctors'.

- As also noted under GALLIFREY HISTORY, Omega was once a member of the High Council on Gallifrey. This shows that the Gallifreyans already had this form of government long before they became Time Lords. He is fully aware of what is currently happening on Gallifrey, of who the Doctor is, and that he as in exile on Earth. He also has some knowledge of Time Lord history, including the discovery of time travel, of the nature of the First Law of Time and of the High Council's position regarding non-interference in the affairs of other planets. Omega is also fully aware of regeneration and deduces correctly that the second and third Doctors are in fact aspects of the same person. We can only assume that he is able to monitor Gallifrey and has been doing so for the millions of years he has been trapped, which has ultimately led to his quest for revenge, knowing that he has been forgotten. (Of course, he lives in a singularity, where time is meaningless, and as such he has probably only been trapped in his world for a few thousand years.)
- Much comment is made about the tackiness of Omega's domain from a

design point of view [citing the lack of budget as a major factor]. However, this is probably deliberate; after all, Omega is from a pre-time travel period of Gallifrey's history, and would therefore have little if any off-world experience. Therefore, when he gets trapped within the singularity and uses his will to create a world, he would of course base this upon the only environment with which he was familiar. The bland walls of the 'castle' are therefore like the corridors of the Gallifreyan Capitol, while the desert landscape of the exterior reflects areas like the Outside from 'The Invasion Of Time' and the Death Zone of 'The Five Doctors'.

- When the first Doctor signals to make contact with them, the second Doctor mistakenly thinks someone else is trying to get through to them; he points upwards and says: 'You don't think..?' The third Doctor scolds him, 'I hardly think so!' Who is the second Doctor pointing to? The Guardians perhaps … or someone or something else..?

- The Doctor activates the Extreme Emergency lever on the TARDIS console to contact the Time Lords. It is the very same lever that Jo pulled in 'The Time Monster' to pull the Doctor out of the time vortex.

- When Omega's world disintegrates, the black hole becomes a new energy source for the Time Lords. But Omega himself is not destroyed – he reappears for a second attempt at revenge 318 years later in 1983 (see 'Arc Of Infinity'). The Eye of Harmony, which is still hidden beneath the Panopticon (until it is released in 'The Deadly Assassin'), probably draws part of its power from the new black hole.

LANGUAGE

Omega speaks with the humans, so we can assume that the 'gift' of languages existed long before the Gallifreyans became Time Lords. Omega compares himself to Atlas, so he knows of Greek mythology, which is hardly surprising given his Greek-like name.

TIMELINE DATES

1666

In terms of THE DOCTOR'S AGE and GALLIFREY HISTORY the events on Gallifrey take place in GRT 1666. The fact that Omega's actions directly threaten the Time Lords of Modern Gallifrey indicates that the events on Omega's world must take place contemporaneously to the events on Gallifrey.

The fact that the first Doctor correctly deduces that the 'space lightning' is a '*time bridge*' (my emphasis) implies that the Gell guards have been projected in time as well

THE THREE DOCTORS

as in space in order to seek out the Doctor, meaning that Omega's world (and therefore Gallifrey) is not in the same time zone as Earth. This idea is further supported by the fact that when UNIT HQ is transported through the black hole, it dematerialises first, and is not just lifted into space.

1973, November ◆ ▨ ▨ ▨ ▨ ▨ ▨ ▨ ▨ ▨ ▨ ▨

As covered under THE UNIT YEARS, this part of the story is best placed in 1973. Dr Tyler refers to Cape Kennedy, which was named as such until 1973 when it reverted to Cape Canaveral. It's possible Tyler refers to Canaveral by its old name out of habit. The previous two Earth-bound stories are set during September 1973, so 'The Three Doctors' would take place later in the same year or early 1974. Some of the trees at the bird sanctuary are bare of leaves, which suggests autumn [the story was recorded in November 1972]. I have used the same month to match these seasonal conditions. The Doctor has been exiled to Earth for just over three years now (since October 1970).

Dr Tyler first detected the appearance of the space lightning after his seeing the results from 'last week's test'. This suggests that the organism has been searching for the Doctor for some time.

10,000,000 BC ▨ ▨ ▨ ▨ ▨ ▨ ▨ ▨ ▨ ▨ ▨

Omega tells the Doctor that 'many thousands of years ago when I left our planet all this was then a star. Until I arranged its detonation' (we can assume that this is a direct reference to his using the Hand of Omega, see 'Remembrance Of The Daleks'). He was trapped in the explosion that turned the star supernova, which provided Gallifrey with a power source, which eventually led to them becoming Time Lords. The second Doctor later says 'long, long ago we learned the secret of time travel' and the third Doctor says 'all my life I've known of you and honoured you as our greatest hero', both of which indicate that this happened well before the Doctor was born. (Omega does not know the Doctor, so it is clear they have never met before, putting lie to the possibility that they had met, as is hinted at in 'Remembrance Of The Daleks' and 'Silver Nemesis'). In 'The Deadly Assassin' the narration at the beginning says that 'through the millennia the Time Lords of Gallifrey led a life of ordered calm' which supports the facts from 'The Three Doctors'. However, in 'The Trial Of A Time Lord' it is implied that the Time Lords have been around for '10 million years', clearly contradicting the time frame given in 'The Three Doctors' and 'The Deadly Assassin'. As analysed under GALLIFREY HISTORY, the time of Omega's death has been set at 10,000,000 years ago.

DURATION

⇨ **Day One (Ep1-4)**
It is day on Omega's world. The scenes on Gallifrey are contemporaneous to the events on Omega's world.

⇨ **Day One (1973) (Ep1-2/4)**
Hollis vanishes early 'this morning', and returns later the same day in time for 'supper'.

CARNIVAL OF MONSTERS

STORY LINK

When the TARDIS lands, Jo says 'we're still on Earth', and later remarks that 'we've slipped back about forty years in time' to 1926, which suggests that their point of departure was around 1966. With 'The Three Doctors' set in November 1973 and 'The Green Death' set in May 1974, they must have originally left Earth at some point between those dates. At the end of 'The Three Doctors' the Doctor had to build a new force field generator, so some time has passed since then, say no more than two months, making their initial point of departure around January 1973. There is however no reason to assume that this is the TARDIS's first trip since 'The Three Doctors'; they could quite have easily taken an unplanned detour to 1966 (which is 40 years later than 1926), while trying to get to Metebelis Three.

OBSERVATIONS

- According to the Doctor, the disappearance of the *SS Bernice* 'was as famous a sea mystery as the *Mary Celeste*' (see 'The Chase'). However, the Doctor returns the ship to its 'original space/time coordinates' of 4 June 1926 – so in effect it never actually disappeared. Therefore the Doctor has changed history. The fact that Jo is unfamiliar with the disappearance of the ship suggests that in terms of her history the *SS Bernice* never did vanish. As the Doctor is a Time Lord, his sense of time is different and as such his own memory is not affected. Being a Time Lord, the Doctor is immune to changes in the time lines. Although history has been changed, his memory does not change; he will still remember the 'original' time line. So, while the *SS Bernice* did vanish in the time line that the Doctor knows, it didn't vanish in the one that Jo recalls. Everyone else – Jo, the passengers and crew on the ship – will only ever know the new time line (see THE N-SPACE UNIVERSE).

- The Mini-Scope mainly contains creatures from Earth's galaxy, but Inter Minor and Lurma are in the distant Acteon Galaxy, so it is clear that the Mini-Scope is a technology that originates from Earth's galaxy, which is why the Time Lords were able to ban them. As noted above, Vorg has been to Earth, so it would appear that he obtained the Scope during one of his trips to that galaxy.

LANGUAGE

The Lurmans have 'translator diodes' which enable them to speak with the Inter Minorans. The Doctor doesn't understand Vorg when he uses carnival palare.

TIMELINE DATES

1974, January ·

There are many possibilities for dating this story:

a) Jo says she has never heard of the anti-magnetic cohesion process which holds in place the metal plate in the *SS Bernice*'s deck because, as the Doctor says, she 'was born about a thousand years too early for that'. Jo is about 21 and is from 1974, suggesting the date the *SS Bernice* was placed in the Scope to be about 2953. Vorg has had the Scope for a few years, so it is now some point after 2953. Of course, the Doctor's comment does not necessarily mean that that was when the Scope was built or when the *SS Bernice* was installed; he could simply be meaning that anti-magnetic cohesion won't be discovered on Earth for another thousand years, which is why Jo hasn't heard of it.

b) One of the specimens in the Scope is an Ogron, which Vorg knows to be 'used as servants by some race, called, um, Daleks, I believe'. The Ogrons are used by the Daleks from 2273 to 2373 (see 'Day Of The Daleks') and later in 2540 (see 'Frontier In Space'), so 'Carnival Of Monsters' could be set around those dates or after 2540. The ship and the plesiosaur are both from the past, so it is possible that the Scope can only take items from the past, which places the story at any time after 2540.

c) The journey from Inter Minor into hyperspace in 'Frontier In Space' could be spatial and not temporal, setting 'Carnival Of Monsters' in 2540, which ties in with the reference above to the Ogrons and the Daleks.

d) It is possible that the planned journey from Earth to Metebelis Three was spatial only. This is supported by Jo's comment that 'instead of swanning around some distant galaxy we've slipped back about 40 years in time', which indicates that as far as Jo was aware the journey to Metebelis Three was not supposed to have involved temporal displacement. Thus the TARDIS has over-shot Metebelis Three in spatial terms only and arrived on another planet in the Acteon Galaxy (it is clear that Lurma, Inter Minor, Demos, and Grundle are in the same galaxy. Earth is in 'a distant galaxy', so it is logical that these planets are in the Acteon Group also). Therefore, the events of 'Carnival Of Monsters' are still relative to the 'current' date on Earth, 1974.

e) Vorg says he has 'worked many a Tellurian fairground', and he knows 'Tellurian carnival lingo' (Tellurian is a term meaning Earth human), so Vorg has clearly been to Earth at a time that that kind of lingo was common on Earth.

f) The Doctor tells Jo how he got the Time Lords to ban Mini-Scopes, presumably when he was still on Gallifrey (see LIFE ON GALLIFREY). Vorg's Scope was missed from being called in and destroyed. The Doctor says it is 'absolutely vintage stuff'. The Doctor clearly accepts that they are in a time zone after the recall; he does not say they must be in a time period before the recall when Jo asks why this particular Scope was missed, so Inter Minor must be set in a time zone relative to when the Doctor subsequently left Gallifrey (this is probably because Vorg took the Scope to the Acteon galaxy and away from Gallifrey's influence in Earth's galaxy, which is why it missed the recall). According to THE DOCTOR'S AGE, the banning of the Scopes would be prior to GRT 1610. 'Carnival Of Monsters' would therefore be set relative to the Doctor's GRT, which is 1666 at this point in his time stream.

Given that four of the six possibilities conform to a contemporary setting, I have set 'Carnival Of Monsters' in January 1974, which is relative to the time between 'The Three Doctors' and 'The Green Death' (see Story Link): therefore the journey from Earth to Inter Minor involves spatial movement with no temporal displacement (see also details surrounding the Doctor's subsequent journey to Metebelis Three covered under 'The Green Death').

The Doctor's reference to anti-magnetic cohesion now means he was speaking of the discovery of the procedure on Earth in Jo's relative future.

130,000,000 BC
The Doctor says 'the plesiosaur has been extinct for a hundred and thirty million years'.

1026 BC ▦ ▦ ▦ ▦ ▦ ▦ ▦ ▦ ▦ ▦ ▦ ▦ ▦ ▦

Kalik says 'for thousands of years, ever since the great space plague, our world has stood alone'. Inter Minor has only recently opened itself to allow alien visitors. The Lurmans Vorg and Shirna are among the first. We can place the time that Inter Minor became closed at, say, 3000 years ago.

1887 ⁕ ▦ ▦ ▦ ▦ ▦ ▦ ▦ ▦ ▦ ▦ ▦ ▦ ▦

The Doctor says he 'took lessons from John L Sullivan himself'. American-born John Lawrence Sullivan (15 October 1858 to 2 February 1918) won the world boxing championship in 1887, holding on to that title until 7 September 1892. (He won 31 of 35 bouts between 1878 and 1905). It is recorded that Sullivan visited England in 1887, so this is the most likely year in which the Doctor met him.

1926, May (first week) ▦ ▦ ▦ ▦ ▦ ▦ ▦ ▦ ▦ ▦ ▦

Claire says the *SS Bernice* has been away from England 'nearly four weeks' which, from June 4 when the ship vanished, places the departure date to be in the first week of May, which was the 2nd to the 8th.

<<1926, June 4 >> ⁕ ▦ ▦ ▦ ▦ ▦ ▦ ▦ ▦ ▦ ▦

The Doctor says the *SS Bernice* vanished 'two days out from Bombay on June 4th, 1926'. There is a calendar on the Major's cabin wall showing June 1926, with the 4th a Tuesday. However this is wrong, June 4th was actually a Friday in 1926. The copy of *The London Illustrated Times* on the ship is however correctly dated for 'Saturday, April 3 1926'. The anomaly cannot be passed off as being part of the Scope mechanism, because after the *SS Bernice* is returned to 1926 the Major crosses out the 4th on the same calendar.

One explanation for this 'error' is that the ship upon which the trapped humans are living inside the Mini-Scope is only a copy of the real SS Bernice which is itself located elsewhere in the machine. In order to release the passengers and crew from their imprisonment the Doctor first sent the real ship back to 1926 then transferred the humans from the duplicate to the original. But he not only transferred the people he also transferred some of the fittings from the fake ship, the calendar being one of the items that was switched.

The sequences on the *SS Bernice* are locked into a repeating cycle running from 6.40 pm to 7.35 pm, based on the clock on the cabin wall. The cycle is repeated five times, either completely or in part.

1954 ▦ ▦ ▦ ▦ ▦ ▦ ▦ ▦ ▦ ▦ ▦ ▦ ▦ ▦
Vorg says this incident was 'many years ago'; say 20.

2953 ▦ ▦ ▦ ▦ ▦ ▦ ▦ ▦ ▦ ▦ ▦ ▦ ▦
The Doctor tells Jo that she 'was born about a thousand years too early' for anti-magnetic cohesion.

DURATION

⇨ **Day One (Ep1-4)** ▦ ▦ ▦ ▦ ▦ ▦ ▦ ▦ ▦ ▦ ▦
It is day on Inter Minor. Night falls when Kalik and Orum begin to scheme.

⇨ **Day Two (Ep4)** ▦ ▦ ▦ ▦ ▦ ▦ ▦ ▦ ▦ ▦ ▦
It is getting lighter through the portals of the spaceport so it must be dawn when the Drashigs break from the Scope.

FRONTIER IN SPACE

+STORY LINK

Both Jo and the Doctor are wearing the same outfits they have on in 'Carnival Of Monsters'. Jo says: 'we keep landing in one terrible situation after another'. The trip to Inter Minor in 'Carnival Of Monsters' could be Jo's first trip in the TARDIS following the events of 'The Three Doctors', so this could be a reference to other (untelevised) adventures that took place after 'Carnival Of Monsters'. However, when subjected to the Master's hypno-device, Jo twice 'sees' a Drashig (as well as a Solonian Mutant and a Sea Devil), which indicates her encounter with the Drashigs was fairly recent.

The TARDIS console room is different yet again, having been modified by the Doctor once he got the TARDIS operating again following 'The Three Doctors'.

DALEK LINK

As covered under DALEK HISTORY, 'Frontier In Space' is the Daleks' seventh appearance. Since the events of 'The Chase', the Daleks have abandoned further time travel experiments, concentrating instead on their plans for galactic conquest. Realising that the forces of Earth and Draconia are likely to prove effective against an attack, the Daleks realise it would be easier to set the two Empires against one another, so the Daleks could concentrate their efforts on other planets and then move in after the war had weakened both Empires. A Dalek task force travels to Spiridon to prepare the Dalek army and to experiment with invisibility, while another smaller group allies itself with a renegade Time Lord called the Master to settle the Earth / Draconia problem.

MASTER LINK

Having been released from the vortex by Kronos at the end of 'The Time Monster', the Master has since allied himself with the Daleks. Given that the attack on Earth Cargo Ship C-982 is the 'third attack this month', we know that the Master has been working with the Daleks for at least a month. From the Doctor's point of view at least four months have passed since 'The Time Monster'; so taking into account their common GRT, then the passage of time since 'The Time Monster' would be the same for both Time Lords. The Master is aware that the Daleks are 'old friends' of the Doctor's. The Master's fear-inducing device appears to be an improved version of the Keller machine from 'The Mind Of Evil'.

OBSERVATIONS

- The Master poses as a Police Commissioner from Sirius 4, an ex-colony that had recently achieved dominion status. Sirius 4 also has control over Sirius 3. Sirius is the second-nearest star to our own sun, which suggests that it was one of the first planetary systems colonised in the early twenty-second century (see 'Nightmare Of Eden'). Sirius 5 is the location of the Academius Stolaris ('City Of Death'). The Daleks attacked a Sirian settlement in 'Destiny Of The Daleks'. The Androzani planets are two of the five planets in the Sirian system (see 'The Caves Of Androzani').

LANGUAGE

The Draconians speak English to the Earthmen. Presumably they all speak Draconian on Draconia. The Ogrons converse with the Master and the Daleks. The Master reads *War Of The Worlds*.

TIMELINE DATES

2540, December ꞏ ▮ ▮ ▮ ▮ ▮ ▮ ▮ ▮ ▮ ▮ ▮ ▮
From his calculations the Doctor reckons the time period they are in is 'somewhere in the twenty-sixth century … Interstellar travel's pretty routine by now … spreading their Empires throughout the galaxy … colonising one planet after another'.

Hardy gives the time the Earth Cargo Ship C-982 enters hyperspace as 'twenty-two-oh-nine seventy-two two thousand five hundred and forty psg.' (e.g.: 22:09 72 2540 psg). The time is confirmed by the same figures appearing on the ship's digital clock. '72' is unlikely to be 7 February or the 72nd day of the year, being 5 March, because later the Earth President gets invited to make an address at the Historical Monuments Preservation Society's 'annual meeting on the tenth of January'. This suggests that the current month is December. '2540' could be the year, however, Stewart gives the time the ship comes out of hyper-space as 'twenty-two thirteen seventy two seven-two-four-zero' (e.g. 22.13 72 7240). The time has correctly advanced four minutes but the 'year' has now changed. [This appears to be a fluff; the actor should have said 2540]. We could apply a Century Factor of 600 and set the story in 2572, but I prefer to use 2540 as the year. [The novelisation is also set in 2540.]

The attack on ECS C-982 is the 'third attack this month', so from this we know that the Master has been working with the Daleks for longer than a month.

There were anti-Draconian riots in Peking 'last week', and there was a report of further attacks on cargo vessels 'last night'.

1666

The Time Lords that the Doctor contacts are those from his own GRT, which is still 1666. The Time Lords are presumably the same High Council that is in office during 'The Three Doctors'.

2040 *

The Fifteenth Emperor of Draconia 'reigned 500 years ago', which would be in 2040. The Doctor says he 'spent quite some time there' on his previous visit to Draconia. When he says this was 'many years ago' / 'a long time ago' he is referring either to the 500 years that have passed relative to the time zone he is now in, or relative to his own time stream. The Doctor clearly made that journey in the same TARDIS (the Draconian Emperor is aware of the name), so it was probably soon after his departure from Gallifrey.

2526

The Draconian Prince says that General Williams started the war '20 years ago' when he 'destroyed a Draconian ship'. With 'Frontier In Space' set in 2540, this would place the incident in 2520. 'Earthshock' is set in 2526, and there is no evidence of a war against Draconia being fought at the time, so we can assume that the war was over by 2526. Another possibility is that '20 years ago' is a merely a general rounding up from 2526; the Draconians were in fact going to Earth to attend the Conference to sign the pact against the Cybermen when they were 'attacked' by Williams.

2530

It can be assumed that the Earth / Draconia war lasted a couple of years; it is stated that after the war there were 'many years of peace' between Earth and Draconia (i.e. there were more years of peace than years of war). I have picked 4 years as an arbitrary duration for the war.

2539

Patel reminds Professor Dale that they met 'last year, just before your arrest'.

2540, November

Professor Dale says 'there was an attempt last month' to escape from the lunar penal colony.

2541, January 10

As mentioned above, the Earth President is invited to make an address at the Historical Monuments Preservation Society's 'annual meeting on the tenth of January'.

???? ·

The Doctor tells Jo of how he was once captured by the Medusoids and subjected to their mind probes while on his way to attend the Third Intergalactic Peace Conference. This has been placed in ????.

DURATION

There are several different locations in this story, but all are relative to the passage of time on Earth. Accordingly, Duration here is based on the number of days on Earth.

⇨ Day One (Ep1-2)

The story starts in space at '22:09' as given by Hardy, presumably 10.09 pm. Although the intercutting scenes set on Earth are in the daytime, this is probably due to the International Date Lines, making it probably 10.09 am there. (There are, however, a few anomalies with regard to the cargo ship's clock: in Ep1 the clock reads '22:09' in the opening scenes. But when the 'dragon' ship locks on, the clock reads '22:01'. It then reads '22:40' when the Doctor and Jo are locked in the brig. It is '22:27' when the Earth Battle Cruiser locks on.) Presumably the trip to Earth takes several hours. Finally reaching Earth where it is still the same day (the President is wearing a peach robe with high collar in all the Earth scenes of Ep1 and Ep2), the Doctor and Jo spend '12 minutes to be exact' waiting on board the ship after it lands, and presumably several hours in prison before being interviewed.

⇨ **Day Two (Ep.2-3)** ▨ ▨ ▨ ▨ ▨ ▨ ▨ ▨ ▨ ▨ ▨ ▨

The President wears a blue dress in the opening scenes of Ep3 and for all subsequent Earth scenes until Ep6, so this is presumably the next day. Although there is no pause between scenes with the President in which night has passed, we can only assume that it takes all night for the Draconians to get the Doctor to the Draconian Embassy. It is morning when he is interrogated. Jo is given a new black outfit. Some time must then pass for the Doctor to get to the moon, and it is hours later when he tries to escape with Professor Dale.

⇨ **Day Three (Ep3-5)** ▨ ▨ ▨ ▨ ▨ ▨ ▨ ▨ ▨ ▨ ▨

The clock in the Master's stolen police ship reads '04:35' when they leave the moon. It is '04:49' when the Doctor tells his story to Jo. It is '05:35' when the Doctor goes space-walking. The clock reads '21:36' when they land on Draconia, giving a flight-time of 16 hours spent in the spaceship's holding cell.

⇨ **Day Four (Ep5-6)** ▨ ▨ ▨ ▨ ▨ ▨ ▨ ▨ ▨ ▨ ▨

It is daytime back on Earth (the President is still wearing her blue dress). The journey to the Ogron planet probably took several hours to prepare, and with the delay caused by the electrical fire, quite some time to reach given that it was located at the remote edge of the galaxy. It took '20 minutes' to orbit.

PLANET OF THE DALEKS

+STORY LINK

'Frontier In Space' and 'Planet Of The Daleks' are consecutive; the injured Doctor contacts the Time Lords and asks them to send the TARDIS after the Dalek ship.

In 'Frontier In Space', the Doctor has his sonic screwdriver confiscated from him when he is sent to the moon penal colony, but he uses a sonic screwdriver while on Skaro, so it is clear that he has built several and has a supply of them in the TARDIS.

Jo refers to the Doctor having been frozen once before, presumably from 'The Dæmons'.

DALEK LINK

In their eighth appearance (following on from 'Frontier In Space'), the Daleks are ruled by Dalek Command and the Dalek Supreme. Latep tells Jo that the Dalek Supreme is one of the Supreme Council. Dalek Command identifies the Doctor as being 'the greatest enemy of the Daleks'. Presumably it was the Gold Dalek who encountered the Doctor on the Ogron planet in 'Frontier In Space' that passed this information to Dalek Command. (The Gold Dalek says 'we shall now return to our base and prepare the army of the Daleks'. This base cannot have been Spiridon, since the Gold Dalek does not appear in 'Planet Of The Daleks', so the Daleks must have a central command base on another planet.)

The Thals and the Doctor refer to the events of 'The Daleks': for the Doctor this was 'many years ago' (in terms of the Doctor's age it was eight years ago, in GRT 1658). For the Thals it was 'generations ago'. The Thals know the legend of the Doctor, Earth, the TARDIS, Barbara, Ian and Susan.

OBSERVATIONS

- The Doctor tells Taron that 'throughout history you Thals have always been known as one of the most peace-loving peoples in the galaxy'. As this is only the Doctor's second encounter with the Thals, we can only assume that he had heard further of them during his travels since 'The Daleks'.

LANGUAGE

Jo is able to speak with Wester and the Thals without the Doctor being present, so presumably they all speak English. The text on the TARDIS scanner is in English.

TIMELINE DATES

2540, December +

At the end of 'Frontier In Space' the Doctor sends a message to the Time Lords: 'I told them about the Dalek spaceship leaving the Ogron planet and told them to send the TARDIS after it'. Therefore, 'Planet Of The Daleks' is set in the same time period as 'Frontier In Space', which is December 2540. Curiously, that spaceship, which carries the Gold Dalek, is not seen to arrive on Spiridon. However, there is mention of a rescue ship coming to Spiridon; perhaps that is the Dalek ship from 'Frontier In Space'.

3000

The Doctor says 'it would take centuries' to melt out the frozen Dalek army, say 500 years, being 3040. To make a link with the Daleks Wars mentioned in 'Death To The Daleks', I have set the time of the Daleks' release to be in 3000.

DURATION

(TARDIS) (Ep1)
The Doctor and Jo are in the TARDIS for a short time before they land ...

⇨ **Day One (Ep1-5)**
It is 'daybreak' when the TARDIS lands on Spiridon. The survivors spend the night at the Plain of Stones.

⇨ **Day Two (Ep5-6)**
Vaber is captured and killed at dawn. Two Daleks are pushed into the ice pool 'this morning'. The story ends later that day.

UNSEEN ADVENTURES

After returning to Earth following the events of 'Planet Of The Daleks' the Doctor and Jo visit Karfel, where the Doctor reports Magellan to the presidium (as reported in 'Timelash').

THE GREEN DEATH

STORY LINK

The Doctor and Jo have been back on Earth for some time since their long trip in the TARDIS ('Carnival Of Monsters', 'Frontier In Space', and 'Planet Of The Daleks'). (In 'Planet Of The Daleks' Jo is infected with the spray. After Wester cures her, he says her arm will be sore 'for a few days'; there is no sign of an injury to her arm in 'The Green Death', so more than a few days have passed since the adventure on Spiridon.) The Doctor and Jo's trip to Karfel (with someone else: Mike, the Brigadier or Benton?) as mentioned in 'Timelash' has to have taken place between 'Planet Of The Daleks' and 'The Green Death'. Since 'The Three Doctors' the Doctor has made further adjustments to Bessie, including major engine modifications that have resulted in a larger bonnet.

The Doctor is still trying to get to Metebelis Three at the beginning of 'The Green Death', so we know that he and Jo never got there during their recent travels in the TARDIS. The Doctor has not had any more trouble with the dematerialisation circuit.

He says 'I can now take the TARDIS wherever and whenever I like. I've got absolute control over her'. This would be the first time he has had total control of the ship since he first left Gallifrey. As noted under TRAVELS IN THE TARDIS, the TARDIS has by this time been removed from the list of Type 40s due to be de-registered (see 'The Deadly Assassin'). The Doctor notes that the 'space / time co-ordinate programmer' has 'nearly worn out'. The TARDIS 'is getting on a bit', which supports the reason why the Type 40 is deemed obsolete.

The Doctor has wanted to meet Professor Jones 'for a long time', having read his paper on DNA synthesis.

UNIT HQ – COUNTRY #2?

We don't see the exterior of this building. The Doctor's lab is different from that seen in 'The Three Doctors'; the double blue doors, windows and bricks are similar, however they are not exactly the same as in the previous story, so it is not the same set of rooms. It is possible that on returning after their recent journey, the TARDIS materialised in a different room in the same building, and the Doctor didn't bother shifting it back to his previous lab, instead he just moved some of his lab equipment to this new room.

OBSERVATIONS

- Although BOSS ('Bimorphic Organisational Systems Supervisor') is the first computer to be directly connected with a human brain (Stevens'), he is really only a more sophisticated version of WOTAN, which went on line in 1966 ('The War Machines'). BOSS plans to connect with the computers at Global Chemicals' other international offices (which are in New York, Zurich and Moscow). BOSS has read the Doctor's 'computer record at UNIT'.
- The Prime Minister in this story is called 'Jeremy'. The identity of this man is discussed in POLITICALLY INCORRECT.

TIMELINE DATES

1974, May •

Four different calendars are seen in the story: the first appears in the pit office: a circular wall plate reads 'THURSDAY 5 APRIL', the likely years being 1973 and 1979. The second appears in the guardhouse at Global Chemicals and shows a 29-day month with the 29th falling on a Tuesday. This leap year structure applies only to 1944, 1972 and 2000. The third is seen only briefly in Episode 4, and is an art deco calendar on the wall of the visitor's suite at Global Chemicals. The nodule and ring format of the calendar gives the date as 'MON 28 APRIL'. The relevant years that this date applies to are 1969, 1975, 1980 and 1986. A fourth calendar is in Elgin's office, and is another of the art deco calendars; all that can be seen of the date is the month 'MAY'. Taking into account the setting for 'The Time Warrior' and 'Invasion Of The Dinosaurs', the year cannot be later than 1974.

All four calendars are deliberately placed props, and therefore have to be considered as being correct. Dave says the mine's 'been out of action a year' ('the National Coal Board were forced to close the pit last year'). Although there are regular 'monthly' inspections of the pit, it's likely that no one has bothered to change the calendar from when the pit office was closed. So while the calendar suggests it is April 1973, it could now be sometime around April 1974. Presumably Elgin would keep his office wall calendar (which reads 'MAY') up to date, whereas the one in the visitor's suite might have been untouched for some time, so the date could be May 1974. As for the calendar in the guard house, although it represents a leap year February, the year cannot be 1972, as that would mean in order to satisfy the 1974 setting for 'Invasion Of The Dinosaurs' Mike Yates would have to be on leave for over two years! So, for some reason, the calendar would have to be a couple of years old.

In terms of THE UNIT YEARS, with 'Invasion Of The Dinosaurs' set in 1974, 'The Green Death' is best set earlier in that same year. Mike Yates is on extended leave for no more than a few months (say three) between these two stories. Given the available options, a date of May 1974 works best. Jo Grant has therefore known the Doctor for 19 months (since October 1971).

It would appear to be a weekday, as Global Chemicals is fully operational and there is a Government cabinet meeting in session.

The Wholeweal community tried to borrow cutting equipment from Global 'a few weeks back'.

Rock- and spear-throwing creatures inhabit Metebelis Three. There are other life-forms: snakes and flying animals with large feet. In 'Planet Of The Spiders' the Doctor says this visit to the planet was at a time before the arrival of the Earth colonists, which would be before 2985 (see 'Planet Of The Spiders'). As with the intended trip in 'Carnival Of Monsters', we can assume that the Doctor's journey from Earth to Metebelis Three is only spatial with no temporal displacement, so it is also May 1974 on Metebelis Three.

1884
The year Professor Jones says the book *Up The Amazon With Rifle And Camera* was published.

1954
Dai Evans says 'I spent 20 years of my life' working down in the pit.

1973, April 5
The date the mine was closed is based on the calendar seen in the mine office (see above).

1974, June
Cliff proposes to go up the Amazon 'in about a month's time'.

DURATION

⇨ **Day One (Ep1-4)**
The demonstrators have been at the gates 'since early this morning'. Jo has an apple for 'breakfast'. The clock reads '3.06' when Jo meets Cliff (however it should be noted that that clock seems to be stuck on 3.06 throughout the whole story. In fact, there are about five clocks in the Wholeweal house, all of which appear to be broken!). The Brigadier speaks with the Prime Minister that 'afternoon'. The maggot attacks Jo that night.

⇨ **Day Two (Ep4-6)**
UNIT troops arrive 'this morning'. BOSS intends to go on line at '4 o'clock this afternoon'. The Doctor arrives at Global at about 3.45 and stops BOSS with only a few minutes to spare. It is sunset when the Doctor drives away. This means that Jo gets engaged to a man she only met the day before!

⇨ **Day (Metebelis Three) (Ep1)**
It is either sunrise or sunset on Metebelis Three (the sun is on the horizon).

THE TIME WARRIOR

STORY LINK

There is no mention of Jo's departure. Just as the Doctor is about to leave in the TARDIS, the Brigadier says: 'Remember what happened to you on Metebelis Three', which shows clearly that the Doctor has not travelled in the TARDIS since that brief trip in 'The Green Death', which can only have been a short time ago (see below). The

Doctor has at some point before 'The Time Warrior' completed the construction of his new car (seen for the first time in 'Invasion Of The Dinosaurs' and again in 'Planet Of The Spiders'), and he has also made a new TARDIS key, which is now a flat ankh-shaped pendant.

Sarah Jane Smith is the only child of the late Barbara (neé Wilson) and Eddie Smith, and was born in the small village of Foxgrove in May 1951. Following the death of her parents in a car crash on 18 August 1951 (when she was only three months old), Sarah was raised by her Aunt Lavinia, her father's older sister, the 'family genius'. 13 years later, Sarah's best friend Andrea Yates is killed during a school trip on 13 July 1964 (in 'Whatever Happened To Sarah Jane?'). It was partly due to the circumstances of Andrea's death and meeting Maria Jackson that Sarah became a journalist. Exactly ten years later, when Sarah is a qualified journalist working for *Metropolitan* magazine, she uses her Aunt's name to infiltrate a top-secret UNIT base, where she meets the Doctor... Although she meets the Doctor for the first time at the Research Centre and her world is inexorably changed forever, it is by no means the first time that Sarah's life has been influenced by the actions of the Doctor. In fact, the only reason why Sarah meets the Doctor is because she meets the Doctor! This can be illustrated by this course of circular logic:

- In 'The Temptation Of Sarah Jane Smith', Sarah goes back in time to 1951...
- Sarah's presence in 1951 results in her parents' deaths when she is only three months old
- The young Sarah is raised by her Aunt Lavinia
- When she is 23, Sarah uses her Aunt's name to infiltrate the Research Centre
- Sarah meets the third Doctor
- In 1978 the fourth Doctor delivers K9 Mark Three to Sarah's flat ('K9 And Company')
- Sarah meets the tenth Doctor. He gives her K9 Mark Four ('School Reunion')
- With a renewed allure into the thrilling world of the Doctor, Sarah begins to investigate aliens and mysterious phenomena
- Using alien technology she has acquired, Sarah goes back in time to 1951...

SONTARAN LINK

This is the first of the stories featuring the 'perpetual war between the Sontarans and the Rutans'. Linx is a 'lowly commander' in the 'Fifth Sontaran Space Fleet' of the Sontaran Empire. He reveals that 'in the Sontaran Military Academy we have hatchings of a million cadets at each muster parade'.

Sontaran Military Intelligence has done a report on Gallifrey, and concludes the Time Lords lack 'the morale to withstand a determined assault'. Despite this the Sontarans initially succeed in invading Gallifrey in GRT 1963 (see 'The Invasion Of Time').

Linx says he 'was on a reconnaissance mission when I was attacked by a squadron of Rutan fighters' and forced to crash on Earth. He says 'My race has been at war for millennia. There is not a galaxy in the Universe which our space fleets have not subjugated'. (The Doctor confirms that the Sontarans and Rutans have been at war for 50,000 years in 'The Sontaran Stratagem'.) In 'The Sontaran Experiment', Styre's robot is made of the metal tellurian which the Doctor knows is not found in Earth's galaxy, which suggests that the Sontaran home world (named as Sontar in 'The Sontaran Stratagem') is in another galaxy. Indeed, in 'The Last Sontaran', we learn that Sontar is in the Metasaran Galaxy. Clearly they are now moving into Earth's galaxy for the first time, although Earth itself 'has no military value. No strategic significance'. This position will change in 1984 ('The Two Doctors'), 2009 ('The Sontaran Stratagem') and 15,000 ('The Sontaran Experiment').

The Sontarans have the limited ability to travel in time, using 'a matter transmitter' on an osmic projector. And by adapting his ship's frequency modulator Linx was able to project himself forward as far as he could – to the twentieth century.

The Doctor has met the Sontarans before ('unfortunately') and is aware of their war with the Rutans. The second Doctor encounters the Sontarans in 'The Two Doctors', however it is clear in that story that he already knows of them from a prior encounter.

LANGUAGE

Linx uses a translator device, so his conversations with the humans are aided. There is an 'S' on Linx's flag – presumably this stands for Sontaran. Irongron cannot read Edward's 'Norman scribbles' in his letter to Lord Salisbury. The letter would most likely be written in French, as this was the language used by nobles in this time period. Edward and Eleanor comment on the strange 'manner' of Sarah's speech; they do not understand her words, but do understand the meaning. Clearly the Time Lord 'gift' is not working to its full capacity in this instance, but of course the Doctor does not make contact with Sarah until much later in the story, in order for him to have been able to properly 'share' the 'gift' with her.

TIMELINE DATES

1274 *

The Doctor explains that the 'matter transmitter' has a 'time transference' which is 'being worked from several centuries ago'. He later tells Rubeish they 'have been brought to the early years of the Middle Ages'. In 'The Sontaran Experiment', Sarah tells Styre that Linx was 'destroyed in the thirteenth century'.

On a less direct method of dating, Edward says the King has taken all his troops 'to fight in these interminable wars'. Bloodaxe mentions 'Saracens', the name given to the peoples of Arabia (see 'The Crusade'). Irongron also mentions that all the King's troops 'are at the wars'. The 'wars' would be the Crusades: the Fourth Crusade was 1201 – 1204, when John was King; the Fifth was 1217 – 1221, with Henry III on the throne (he reigned 1216 – 1272). Henry III was still King during the Sixth (1228 – 1229), and Seventh Crusades (1248 – 1254). The 'wars' could also refer to the Barons' War of 1264 – 68, when Henry III was King (1216 – 1272). Edward I was the next King (1272 – 1307). Edward I himself had in 1270 been at the Eighth and last crusade (1270 – 1291), returning to England in 1274.

If we use the Century Factor from when the UNIT section of the story is set (see below), we can place 'The Time Warrior' in 1274, 700 years earlier. This also satisfies the dates of the Eighth Crusade.

1974, July *

As covered under THE UNIT YEARS, the UNIT part of the story is best placed in 1974: when asked by Linx what century she is from, Sarah relies: 'twentieth', which is the only reference to her time period. 'Invasion Of The Dinosaurs' has been set in July 1974. In that story the Doctor estimates they have been away from the Research Centre 'give or take a few weeks'. Therefore, 'The Time Warrior' can be set in the same month.

Rubeish says he hasn't seen his family 'for three days', which gives the time he has been at the Centre.

Later, when in the past, Rubeish says the other scientists haven't eaten or slept 'for days', so they have been 'missing' for a week at least.

1956

In 'Invasion Of The Dinosaurs' Sarah says she is '23', which means she was born in 1951, which is confirmed in 'The Temptation Of Sarah Jane Smith' [Elisabeth Sladen was born in February 1948]. The Doctor reasons that Sarah must have been 'five years old' when she 'wrote' her aunt's paper.

DURATION

In terms of the story narrative, night falls at the same time in both temporal locations.

⇨ **Day (Ep1)**

It is 'but an hour till dawn' when Linx lands on Earth. Irongron brings Linx to his castle.

🕐

Linx spends the next few weeks kidnapping scientists from the future ...

⇨ **Day One (Ep1)**

Lady Eleanor instructs Hal to shoot Irongron when he walks the battlements 'at dawn'. Linx travels to 1974 and kidnaps Rubeish that night.

⇨ **Day Two (Ep1-3)**

The TARDIS arrives this morning. It is 'about four in the afternoon' when the Doctor finds Rubeish. It is later that afternoon when the Doctor is rescued by Sarah and Hal (he says 'Good evening' to the guards before he knocks them out). That night the folk at Edward's castle make the dummies for the battle 'tomorrow morning'.

⇨ **Day Three (Ep3-4)**

Irongron attacks Edward's castle 'at dawn' (Hal earlier tells Edward that Irongron 'marches here before noon'). It is late afternoon when Irongron's men fall asleep (when he meets them at the castle, the Doctor greets Sarah and Hal with 'Good evening' but it is still daylight). The TARDIS leaves later the same day.

⇨ **Day One (1974) (Ep1)**

On the night of Rubeish's third day at the Research Centre the Doctor arrives.

⇨ **Day Two (1974) (Ep1)**

Linx travels to 1974 that night and abducts Rubeish. It is 2.00 am on the clock in the corridor when the Doctor sees Linx's image.

INVASION OF THE DINOSAURS

+STORY LINK

'Invasion Of The Dinosaurs' takes place soon after 'The Time Warrior' for the Brigadier (he mentions the Doctor and Sarah leaving on their 'last little jaunt'), and for the Doctor and Sarah (she is wearing the same clothes as in 'The Time Warrior', but her hair is much shorter). She refers to their adventure in the Middle Ages ('Alien monsters, robber barons') so 'The Time Warrior' and 'Invasion Of The Dinosaurs' are probably conseccutive for them. Interestingly, the Doctor says they have been away 'give or take a few weeks' relative to 1974, but they only spent two days in 1274. Sarah is therefore now out of sync with Earth (unless they spend two weeks travelling without leaving the TARDIS).

UNIT HQ – COUNTRY #2?

Although UNIT's HQ does not feature in this story, the fact that the Doctor sets the TARDIS for UNIT HQ but that it lands in central London suggests that the UNIT base that they were using at the time of 'The Time Warrior' was one of the London sites. The Doctor says the HQ 'can't be far away' from the TARDIS's landing site. However, the fact that UNIT sets up a temporary HQ in a school within central London shows clearly that their current HQ must be located outside the central London area. The 'current' HQ could therefore be the one from 'The Three Doctors'; the TARDIS has overshot its programmed destination by several hundred miles! (Indeed the Doctor does say 'the space / time coordinates were a bit out, that's all'.)

OBSERVATIONS

- The spaceship hoax offers some interesting observations about space travel in the 1970s in the N-Space Universe: there are seven ships in all, bound for another planet – a journey which is to take three months. Apart from Mark, Adam and Ruth, all the other passengers are in suspended animation; the three leaders have been awake for three months. The journey is said to be nearly over when Sarah awakens. Sarah correctly points out that 'the nearest possible solar system to us is four light years away. With the most advanced spaceships developed it would take hundreds of years to reach there'. Mark replies that 'One of our members invented a new space drive'. Although the ship is a hoax, the passengers obviously believed and accepted without question that it would be possible to make the trip, which suggests that (apparent) space technology has reached even newer levels since the Mars

Probes of 1970 (see 'The Ambassadors Of Death') and the XK5 launched in 1973 ('The Android Invasion') (See also A HISTORY OF SPACE-FLIGHT.)

- The Doctor refers to a Chinese scientist, Chun Sen, who experimented into time travel, but he isn't born until well after 1974.
- The Doctor speaks of the Earth becoming a garbage dump inhabited with rats, caused by pollution and waste; which echoes a similar speech made by the seventh Doctor in 'The Curse Of Fenric'. We might therefore assume that it was the first or second Doctor that had visited the Earth at the time of the Haemovores, possibly even soon after he imprisoned Fenric in the shadow dimensions.

TIMELINE DATES

1974, July

Sarah she says she is '23' years old. In 'The Temptation Of Sarah Jane Smith', we learn that Sarah was born in May 1951, and in 'Whatever Happened To Sarah Jane?', Sarah was 13 in July 1964. This makes the current year 1974.

Sarah refers to 'the last Olympics'. The Games relative to Sarah's time would be Mexico (1968) and Munich (1972) (with Montreal in 1976 and Moscow in 1980). 'Invasion Of The Dinosaurs' was recorded in October [of 1972], but apart from the greenery in the common, there is nothing else that matches seasonal conditions.

Given that Mike Yates has only just returned from 'a spot of leave' after 'all that business in Wales with the giant maggots', only a few months can have passed since 'The Green Death'. The Doctor says 'Mike my dear fellow, how are you? Good to see you again'; which means he hasn't seen Mike since Wales. No more than, say, two months can have passed since 'The Green Death'.

I would therefore set 'Invasion Of The Dinosaurs' two months after 'The Green Death', which is July 1974. The Olympics Sarah is referring to are therefore the 1972 Munich Games.

Mike says he saw a fox in Piccadilly 'yesterday'.

170,000,000 BC

The estimated time in our history when flying reptiles appeared. The Doctor confirms that the dinosaurs died out '65 million years ago, to be precise' (see also 'Earthshock').

455 ▪ ▮ ▮ ▮ ▮ ▮ ▮ ▮ ▮ ▮ ▮ ▮ ▮ ▮ ▮
The Vandals sacked Rome around this time in our history.

1204 ▮ ▮ ▮ ▮ ▮ ▮ ▮ ▮ ▮ ▮ ▮ ▮ ▮ ▮
The peasant says Richard's 'in the Holy Land; John rules now'. John was King from 1199 – 1216, having taken over from Richard I (see 'The Crusade' and 'The King's Demons').

1951 ▮ ▮ ▮ ▮ ▮ ▮ ▮ ▮ ▮ ▮ ▮ ▮ ▮ ▮
Sarah says she is '23'; with the current year being 1974, she was born in 1951.

1954 ▮ ▮ ▮ ▮ ▮ ▮ ▮ ▮ ▮ ▮ ▮ ▮ ▮ ▮
The bunker was built 'twenty years ago' during the Cold War, but the plan was 'shelved when the situation ceased', being 1954. (In our history, the Cold War lasted much longer, from 1947 – 1990.)

1972, August 26 – September 11 ▮ ▮ ▮ ▮ ▮ ▮ ▮ ▮
The Munich Olympiad was held on these dates in our history.

1974, January ▮ ▮ ▮ ▮ ▮ ▮ ▮ ▮ ▮ ▮ ▮ ▮
With 'Invasion Of The Dinosaurs' set in July 1974, Whitaker disappeared 'about six months ago' and Grover 'has only been Minister for six months', which is January 1974.

There is a back-story surrounding the setting up of the bunker. We can speculate that following refusal for a grant to experiment with time, Whitaker went into seclusion. For many years Grover had a desire to rid the world of pollution (he even wrote a book, *Last Chance For Man*, which the Doctor says he has read). Grover, who was on the grants-board and who, as a newly-positioned Minister, also knew of the existence of the nuclear bunker, was able to contact Whitaker and put to him the notion to put his time travel theories into practice; that way both would achieve their goals. In the following four months they built the 'spaceship', which was then 'launched'. Two months later the dinosaurs first began to appear in order to clear London …

1974, April ▮ ▮ ▮ ▮ ▮ ▮ ▮ ▮ ▮ ▮ ▮ ▮ ▮
With 'Invasion Of The Dinosaurs' set in July 1974, the Chosen have been on the fake ship for 'three months', which is since April.

DURATION

⇨ **Day One (Ep1-5)**
It is probably morning when the TARDIS lands. Sarah spends the night unconscious in the spaceship; her bruise has not healed. It is that same night when the Doctor is arrested.

⇨ **Day Two (Ep5-6)**
Sarah escapes and returns to UNIT HQ 'early this morning' (she says she was on the spaceship 'a matter of hours'). It is night at the end of the story.

DEATH TO THE DALEKS

+STORY LINK

At the end of 'Invasion Of The Dinosaurs' the Doctor tempts Sarah into going with him to the planet Florana. At the beginning of 'Death To The Daleks' they are on their way.

The TARDIS control room is different from its previous appearance ('Planet Of The Daleks').

DALEK LINK

As covered under DALEK HISTORY, this is the Daleks' ninth appearance. Since the events of 'Planet Of The Daleks', in which the Dalek army was frozen under the icecano, the Daleks have abandoned their original plans for galactic conquest and set into motion a new plan, which results in the Dalek War. At the end of the final war, the Daleks leave Earth's galaxy, but a few small forces remain to continue fighting human colonies.

LANGUAGE

The surface Exxilons speak an alien language, as well as English. The Exxilons and humans understand the Daleks.

TIMELINE DATES

3500 +
Jill Tarrant mentions 'the colonists' on 'the outer worlds', which suggests that in this time zone Earth still has an Empire, setting 'Death To The Daleks' prior to 2973 (see 'The Mutants').

It is not made very clear if the Daleks themselves were responsible for the disease that is ravaging the outer worlds. In 'Planet Of The Daleks' the Daleks work on a bacterium, so it is possible that the virus in 'Death To The Daleks' is the same germ from 'Planet Of The Daleks', which is set in 2540. This supports the idea that after the Dalek army is thawed out on Spiridon they continue with their orders to conquer the galaxy, but this time they do it with bacteriological weapons. They refine the Spiridon virus so it is no longer effective against Daleks. The Daleks in 'Death To The Daleks' are therefore the 'clean-up' force, left behind in Earth's galaxy to get rid of the survivors of the war using further biological agents, while the main Dalek fleet leaves to invade other galaxies.

Alternatively, the Marine Space Corps is the Military and Science division of the Galactic Federation of 'The Curse Of Peladon' and 'The Monster Of Peladon' (around 3250).

As mentioned in 'Mission To The Unknown', the Daleks have been absent from Earth's galaxy in the 500 years prior to 4000. In 'Death To The Daleks' reference is made to 'the last Dalek war'. This could mean either 'last' as in final or as in the most recent. We can assume that this war sees the Daleks' final appearance in Earth's galaxy before leaving to attack other galaxies. Therefore 'Death To The Daleks' would be set around 3500. This date seems to me to be the most likely of the three given above.

Before 400,000,000 BC

Bellal says 'Exxilon had grown old before life had even begun on other planets. Our ancestors solved the mysteries of science, built craft that travelled through space. They were the supreme beings of the Universe'. Since life began on Earth 400 million years ago (see 'City Of Death'), we can place the history of the Exxilons prior to that date.

The City is believed to be 'thousands of years' old. The Doctor examines the soil on Exxilon and says 'I doubt if anything's grown here for centuries' (which makes one wonder what the Exxilons eat). The Doctor and Bellal find skeletons of dead Exxilons, some of which 'must have been here for centuries'.

1150 *

The Doctor says he has been to Peru and saw a temple covered in the same markings as the Exxilon City. From this he believes it was the Exxilons who had been to Earth and built – or at the very least influenced the building of – the temple. The Incas lived in Peru from the twelfth to sixteenth centuries before being wiped out by the Spanish. Therefore, we can place the time of the Exxilons' (and the Doctor's?) visit at around the mid-twelfth century.

3000

Given that the Daleks' plan to invade the galaxy in 'Frontier In Space' and 'Planet Of

The Daleks' is delayed by 'centuries' after their army is frozen on Spiridon, we can set the first Dalek war 500 years after 2540, soon after the army is totally thawed out. Given that the Daleks invade Earth in 3000 (see 'Mission To The Unknown'), they probably thaw out at some point prior to 3000.

3480

Peter Hamilton's 'father was killed in the last Dalek war'. Peter is not much older than 30, so the last war was sometime during the last 30 years at least.

DURATION

⇨ **Day One (Ep1)**

Jack is killed the night the TARDIS lands. The fact that the TARDIS loses power while in flight *en route* to Florana means that the ship is travelling spatially, not temporally – it is unlikely that the City is able to drain power from the vortex – which means that Florana is in the same time zone as Exxilon.

⇨ **Day Two (Ep1-4)**

It is dawn when the Doctor meets the MSC personnel. It is night when the Doctor enters the City.

⇨ **Day Three (Ep4)**

It is dawn when the Doctor emerges from the City and it is destroyed.

THE MONSTER OF PELADON

+STORY LINK

Sarah wants to get home, so it is clear that they have not come from Earth; the landing on Peladon must therefore be part of the same trip to Florana that began in 'Death To The Daleks'. Sarah criticises the Doctor for landing them in 'another rotten, gloomy old tunnel'. The TARDIS 'scanner is still on the blink'; it had broken down on Exxilon, which indeed has gloomy tunnels. From this it seems that 'The Monster Of Peladon' follows directly on from 'Death To The Daleks'. Of course, they might have actually been to Florana after 'Death To The Daleks', since that was their original destination. The Doctor says 'I've been meaning to pay a return visit to Peladon for ages', so it is clear that this landing is deliberate.

OBSERVATIONS

- The 'Pels' seem to have a longer life span than humans; Ortron says 'right from the day Chancellor Hepesh died I served your father loyally'. This was 50 years ago, and yet Ortron does not appear to be much older than 60, which would have made him about 10 in 'The Curse Of Peladon'. Also, he does not recognise the Doctor, so he cannot have been a direct member of Peladon's royal court in 'The Curse Of Peladon'.
- Azaxyr refers to his troops as 'Ice Warriors', whereas in 'The Ice Warriors' this term is coined by one of the humans who find Varga in the snow. They are more correctly named Martians, so it would seem that even in their own history they have adopted the name 'Ice Warriors' for themselves.

LANGUAGE

Eckersley is from Earth (from England?) and converses with the 'Pels', Ice Warriors and Vega Nexos.

TIMELINE DATES

3275 ⁕

'The Monster Of Peladon' is set '50 years' after 'The Curse Of Peladon', which is set in 3225.

3255

Peladon died when Thalira was 'a child'. She is about 20 now.

DURATION

⇨ Day One (Ep1-6)

There are no night scenes, so the story appears to take place over just the one day.

UNSEEN ADVENTURES

It was the first, second or third Doctor who previously encounters Raston warrior robots ('The Five Doctors').

THE FIVE DOCTORS

STORY LINK

For the third Doctor to know who Sarah Jane is, he must have been time scooped at some point after he and Sarah are back on Earth following their attempt to visit Florana (see 'Invasion Of The Dinosaurs' and 'Death To The Daleks'). Since 'The Time Warrior' to 'The Monster Of Peladon' are consecutive, the gap between 'The Monster Of Peladon' and 'Planet Of The Spiders' is the best position. With 'Planet Of The Spiders' set in March 1975, the sequence from 'The Five Doctors' can be set around February 1975.

The Doctor is surprised to see Mike, whom he hasn't seen since 'The Green Death'. The Doctor looks older than he does in 'The Monster Of Peladon'. This is either a Production Factor, or we could accept that this is related to the Doctor's ageing by 196 years during the gap between 'The Monster Of Peladon' and 'Planet Of The Spiders' (refer to THE DOCTOR'S AGE for more on this). It is during this off-screen gap, when the Doctor is 603 years old, that he encounters Lady Peinforte and launches the Nemesis statue into space (see the back story under 'Silver Nemesis').

We can assume that the Doctor has recently returned to Earth following his long absence and is taking Bessie for a spin when he is time scooped by Borusa.

- Refer to 'The Five Doctors' under the fifth Doctor's stories for more details on this adventure.

TIMELINE DATES

1975, February ⋆
The Doctor is time scooped at some point shortly before the events of 'Planet Of The Spiders'. See above.

DURATION

⇨ **Day One**
It is day when the Doctor is abducted. He is on Gallifrey for several hours. He and Bessie are returned to the same point in time and space.

PLANET OF THE SPIDERS

STORY LINK

After 'The Five Doctors', both the Doctor and Bessie are returned to the country road. His memory is probably altered by the remaining members of the High Council of the Time Lords to remove all recollection of 'The Five Doctors' adventure ...

There is no indication as to the length of time that has passed between 'The Monster Of Peladon' and 'Planet Of The Spiders'. In 'Robot', which is consecutive to 'Planet Of The Spiders', Sarah comments on Benton's recent promotion to Warrant Office One by saying 'Congratulations. About time too', which shows a sign of familiarity between Benton and Sarah. Given that she only meets him for the first time in 'Invasion Of The Dinosaurs', it appears that quite a considerable amount of time has passed between 'The Monster Of Peladon' and 'Planet Of The Spiders', during which they become friends.

On the assumption that Sarah and the Doctor return to Earth only a week or so after their departure at the beginning of 'Death To The Daleks', then as much as up to ten months have elapsed for Sarah since their return to Earth. Given that Sarah is not a member of UNIT, and only renews her association with them in 'Planet Of The Spiders' when she is contacted by Mike, in all likelihood she might have had only minimal contact with the Doctor since then. In 'The Five Doctors' the Doctor is surprised to see Mike, whom he hasn't seen since the Operation Golden Age affair in 'Invasion Of The Dinosaurs' nearly a year previously. [Although this year-long gap since 'Invasion Of The Dinosaurs' might not have been the intention of the programme makers, this is the period that results when applying on-screen dates.]

As covered under THE DOCTOR'S AGE, the Doctor has (probably) aged 196 years between 'The Monster Of Peladon' and 'Planet Of The Spiders'. It is shortly before 'Planet Of The Spiders' that the Doctor is time scooped to Gallifrey (see 'The Five Doctors' above). In that story, when the 'older' Doctor meets an older Sarah, he seems pleased to see her, as if he hadn't seen 'his' Sarah for some time, therefore his ageing 196 years happens away from Earth.

Since 'Invasion Of The Dinosaurs' the Doctor has made a few improvements to his new car, including a new roof and windscreen (and possibly adding the ability to fly), and is now 'doing a little research into ESP' (possibly as a result of an adventure he had during his 196 years away from Earth). He has been to the music hall before (probably several times in fact) to see Professor Clegg perform. Sarah is still working for *Metropolitan*. Mike says he went to the meditation centre 'to sort myself out, I suppose, after that Golden Age mess'. He also says he hasn't seen the Doctor or the Brigadier since 'I pulled a gun on them', in 'Invasion Of The Dinosaurs'. The Doctor tells Sarah he brought the blue crystal back from Metebelis Three 'some time ago'. From Earth terms this was only last year, but from his own perspective it was 196 years ago.

Ten months have passed since 'The Green Death'. It would appear that the parcel from Jo is the first contact they have had with her since she left with Cliff Jones in June 1974. The couple has visited 29 villages in that time.

UNIT HQ – COASTAL #2

In 'The Ark In Space', Harry says they are 'from London'. However, this doesn't necessarily mean that UNIT HQ is located there, but that they live there. The exterior buildings seen in this story are vastly different to those in 'The Three Doctors'. And given that the chase in Ep2 takes place on country roads and then across the sea this HQ would appear to be another coastal HQ. It is not the one in 'Terror Of The Autons', because in that the Doctor's lab has a second level connected by a spiral staircase, whereas in 'Planet Of The Spiders' there is no staircase. In 'Robot' we can see what looks like a radar dish out the lab window, which is probably another radar tracking station like the one seen in 'The Claws Of Axos'.

We see the Doctor's lab, which has the same basic layout as the one from 'The Three Doctors' (glass wall partition, Venetian blinds and computer console standing in one corner, but the large blue double doors are very different). This suggests that the Coastal #2 and the Country #2 HQs were selected because they have the same basic interior layout. So despite Harry saying he is from London in 'The Ark In Space', this HQ is clearly not that same as ones seen previously.

OBSERVATIONS

- The Doctor returns the blue stone to Metebelis Three in 3418, which means that while the other blue stones in the Great One's web are relatively 1444 years older (from 1974 when the Doctor visited Metebelis Three in 'The Green Death'), the Doctor's stone had not aged by that much in relative terms. He says in 'Planet Of The Spiders' that he has 'wired' the coordinates for Metebelis Three into the TARDIS. The fact that the Doctor materialises the TARDIS in the middle of the Two-Legs' village suggests that the site where the village is located is the same site where the TARDIS had landed in 'The Green Death', or is near the cliff from where he took the crystal. A cliff can be seen by the village, which supports this idea.
- The Spiders were able to detect the location of the blue crystal 'by its vibrations through space and time'. The Great One had 'searched all time and space for it'. The fact that the Spiders can travel from Metebelis Three in the distant

future to Earth in 1975, as well as communicate between the two time zones, shows that the Eight-Legs have a form of time-travel at their disposal, a power possibly inherent actually in the blue crystals themselves. This could have been one of the reasons why the Doctor originally wanted one of the crystals.

- K'Anpo Rimpoche is the Doctor's guru, apparently the hermit he mentions in 'The Time Monster' (and later in 'State Of Decay'). It is unlikely that K'Anpo is his Gallifreyan name, and is more likely to be an adopted Tibetan name. (Although it is not stated so on-screen, it would appear that K'Anpo might actually be Azmael – see 'The Twin Dilemma'.) K'Anpo knows that the Doctor borrowed the TARDIS and left Gallifrey. K'Anpo himself regenerated and came to Earth some time later. It is even possible that K'Anpo went to Earth specifically to keep an eye on the Doctor when he was exiled to Earth. He did not need a TARDIS to travel to Earth, because as the Doctor says, 'I hadn't your powers', which suggests that K'Anpo has a special ability. Indeed it is demonstrated that K'Anpo does have the ability to project and give corporeality to his own future-self, to materialise and dematerialise his own body across space, and to supply energy needed to trigger another Time Lord's regeneration. In fact, it is possible that K'Anpo passes some of this power to the Doctor in order to help him regenerate. This would explain how the Doctor is later able to project an image of his own future-self in 'Logopolis'. This power is subsequently lost, which is why the Doctor has not projected future-selves since.
- When K'Anpo gives the Doctor the energy boost to trigger his regeneration, it could be significant – or it could be merely coincidental – that the energy beam is similar to the energy cloud that issues from the Eye Of Harmony in 'Doctor Who (The TV Movie)' which brings Grace and Chang Lee back to life. This suggests that some Time Lords and some TARDISes, such as the Doctor's, possess this ability.
- This is the first story in which the concept of regeneration is discussed. In previous stories ('The War Games', 'Day Of The Daleks', 'The Three Doctors', 'Frontier In Space') the Doctor's metamorphosis had simply been referred to as a 'change of appearance', which seemingly only the Doctor was capable of undertaking.

LANGUAGE

The Spiders speak English through Lupton. They call their planet Metebelis Three, as do the human colonists; but the Doctor already knew it by that name before the colonists got there. The spiders are able to communicate through time as well as across space.

1975, March 10 – 13 •
1975, April 3 •

As covered under THE UNIT YEARS, this part of the story is best placed in 1975: Day One of 'Robot' is 3 April, so the final Earth scene of 'Planet Of The Spiders' is the same day. The Doctor is missing 'over three weeks' after leaving Metebelis Three, so the majority of 'Planet Of The Spiders' takes place in March. Since 'Invasion Of The Dinosaurs' is set in August 1974 and 'The Android Invasion' in July 1975, 'Planet Of The Spiders' must be March 1975.

The Doctor regenerates on 3 April (see also 'Robot'), which is 'three weeks' after he was last seen; on Day Four, which would be 13 March.

Although the Doctor has been missing for 'over three weeks' from Sarah's perspective, it is not clear if this same period of time applies to the Doctor. When he returns to Earth he says 'I got lost in the time vortex. The TARDIS brought me home', but was he lost in the vortex for three whole weeks? Given that K'Anpo / Cho Je appears in the UNIT lab, in order for his GRT to remain the same as the Doctor's, K'Anpo is either three weeks older too, or he has used his powers to time travel three weeks – or however long the Doctor was lost for – into the future to help the Doctor? I prefer to think that the Doctor was indeed 'lost' in the vortex for the same three weeks.

3418 •

The humans on Metebelis Three are the descendants of Earth 'Colonists. Explorers. Four hundred and thirty-three Earth years ago their starship came out of its time-jump with no power left and crashed on Metebelis Three'. (It is odd that the spiders and the colonists both call the planet Metebelis Three, the name by which the Doctor already knew the planet, centuries before the spiders and colonists had even been there.) The reference to 'time-jump' suggests time travel, however it is clear from 'The Ark' that humans never develop time travel. Time-jump is therefore probably just a generic term for the new form of faster than light travel that was available at the time ('time-jump' could be the same as Jethryk-drive, see 'The Ribos Operation'). The fact that Metebelis Three is in the Acteon Galaxy shows that the original colonists came from a time period in which intergalactic travel was possible. As covered under 'Terror Of The Vervoids', this was around 2980. That the humans were also 'explorers' suggests they left Earth soon after the development of intergalactic travel, say 2985; 433 years later would be 3418.

1662 ▸ ▨ ▨ ▨ ▨ ▨ ▨ ▨ ▨ ▨ ▨ ▨ ▨ ▨

Samuel Pepys (23 February 1633 to 26 May 1703) married on 10 October 1655, and his wife, Elizabeth Marchand de Saint-Michel (who was only 15 years old when they wed), died on 10 November 1669. In order for the Doctor to taste Mrs Pepys's coffee, it would have had to be at some point between those dates. 1662 is an arbitrary mid-way date.

c1915 ▸ ▨ ▨ ▨ ▨ ▨ ▨ ▨ ▨ ▨ ▨ ▨ ▨

Houdini lived from 24 March 1874 to 31 October 1926. He moved from America to England in 1900. He made his name as an escapologist during the early 1900s in our history, continuing to perform the act until 1923. I have selected 1915 as being a most likely date.

1949
1974 ▨ ▨ ▨ ▨ ▨ ▨ ▨ ▨ ▨ ▨ ▨ ▨ ▨

Lupton worked for a company for 'twenty five years' until he was no longer needed after a big take-over. He tried to make it on his own, but the bigger company forced him into closure. We can allow one year for him to try on his own, and 25 years earlier being 1949.

1964 ▨ ▨ ▨ ▨ ▨ ▨ ▨ ▨ ▨ ▨ ▨ ▨ ▨

The Brigadier was given his watch by Doris 'eleven years ago', being 1964. He will eventually marry her in the early 1990s (see 'Battlefield').

2985 ▨ ▨ ▨ ▨ ▨ ▨ ▨ ▨ ▨ ▨ ▨ ▨ ▨

As covered above, this is a likely date for when the original Earth colonists and explorers left Earth for the Acteon Galaxy.

▨▨▨▨▨▨▨▨▨▨▨ **DURATION** ▨▨▨▨▨▨▨

⇨ **Day One (10 March) (Ep1)** ▨ ▨ ▨ ▨ ▨ ▨ ▨ ▨

It is daylight in the opening scenes (but it is later referred to as being 'last night') when Mike sees the group in the cellar and when the Doctor and Brigadier go to the music hall.

⇨ **Day Two (11 March) (Ep1-2)** ▨ ▨ ▨ ▨ ▨ ▨ ▨

Clegg visits UNIT the next day. It is 'afternoon' when Sarah goes to the meditation centre. That night she and Mike see the spider arrive.

⇨ **Day Three (12 March) (Ep.2-3)** ▨ ▨ ▨ ▨ ▨ ▨ ▨ ▨ ▨

The following morning Sarah tells the Doctor about what she saw in the cellar. The chase passes the policeman at '10.15 hours'. It is 'about half past ten' (10.30 am) when Lupton vanishes during the chase. The Doctor and Sarah travel to Metebelis Three later that day. It is night when Lupton's group knocks out Mike. Tommy spends the night reading.

⇨ **Day Four (13 March) (Ep5-6)** ▨ ▨ ▨ ▨ ▨ ▨ ▨ ▨ ▨

Mike awakens the following morning (it is daylight out the window). The hall clock reads 2.57 (pm) when Lupton's group attacks Tommy. The Doctor returns to Metebelis Three.

🕐 **(Ep6) 'Three weeks' pass ...** ▨ ▨ ▨ ▨ ▨ ▨ ▨ ▨ ▨

⇨ **Day Twenty Seven (?) (3 April) (Ep6)** ▨ ▨ ▨ ▨ ▨ ▨ ▨ ▨

'Over three weeks' later the TARDIS returns to UNIT HQ. The Doctor regenerates.

⇨ **Day One (3418) (Ep4)** ▨ ▨ ▨ ▨ ▨ ▨ ▨ ▨ ▨

Sarah arrives on Metebelis Three in the afternoon. 'It will soon be dark' when the Doctor arrives. The Doctor spends the night in a coma, and Sarah in the spiders' larder.

⇨ **Day Two (3418) (Ep4-6)** ▨ ▨ ▨ ▨ ▨ ▨ ▨ ▨ ▨

The Doctor awakens from his coma as the morning curfew bell tolls. The Doctor and Sarah leave Metebelis Three later that day. When the Doctor returns alone to Metebelis Three, it is presumably later the same day, which indicates that the relative passage of time on Earth in 1975 and Metebelis Three is the same.

ROBOT

+STORY LINK

'Robot' follows immediately on from 'Planet Of The Spiders', with the Doctor regenerating on the floor of his lab at UNIT HQ.

UNIT HQ – COASTAL #2

See entry under 'Planet Of The Spiders'.

OBSERVATIONS

- After his regeneration the Doctor loses his desire to stay on Earth. Although he has his freedom back at the end of 'The Three Doctors', the third Doctor still continues his association with UNIT and Sarah. He says in 'Planet Of The Spiders', after becoming lost in the vortex for three weeks, 'the TARDIS brought me home'. This shows he considered Earth to be his home; when he is originally tried in 'The War Games', he is rather displeased about being forced to live on Earth. However, following his third regeneration, the first thing the Doctor does is try to sneak away in the TARDIS. And once fully recovered he takes off again, but this time with Sarah and Harry. The fact that the new Doctor has regained the desire to wander the Universe is reinforced in 'Pyramids Of Mars': 'The Earth isn't my home, Sarah', and he states he has better things to do than run around following the Brigadier's orders.
- Also of note is that while the third Doctor was researching into ESP, the fourth Doctor does not continue with this work.
- When preparing the metal virus the Doctor rolls up his sleeves. The tattoo seen in 'Spearhead From Space' is not there, indicating that the mark has been removed, either by the Time Lords when they lifted his exile, or when the Doctor regenerated.
- The Doctor is invited to Buckingham Palace, but does the Queen know that he was the same Doctor named as an enemy of the crown in the Torchwood Charter of 1879? ('Tooth And Claw').

TIMELINE DATES

1975, April 3 – 6 ＊
As covered under THE UNIT YEARS, this story is best placed in 1975: when Sarah goes to Think Tank on the second day, her pass shows the date to be '4 April'. With 'Invasion Of The Dinosaurs' set in August 1974 and 'The Android Invasion' in July 1975, 'Robot' must be April of 1975. In Ep2, Sarah heads off home, with the remark that she's a 'working girl', which suggests the following day is also a week day. The story takes place over four days (see Duration), being Thursday through Sunday.

327 BC ＊
The Doctor thinks Lethbridge-Stewart is Alexander the Great. See dating under 'Marco Polo'.

218 BC ▪

The Doctor mistakes the Brigadier for Hannibal (who is also mentioned in 'Marco Polo'). If the Doctor has met Hannibal, it was probably in 218 BC, when he began his historic march across the Alps (see also 'The Dalek Invasion Of Earth' and 'Aliens Of London').

1954

The bunker was built 'back in the Cold War days', which began in our history in 1947 soon after World War Two, and ended in 1990. But in this Universe, the Cold War ended in the 1950s. The bunker in 'Invasion Of The Dinosaurs' was built in 1954, so I have taken that date.

1970

Kettlewell says he left Think Tank 'some time ago'. Winters says the SRS has been working and planning for 'many years' to control the world. Assuming that Kettlewell's departure and the SRS's objectives began at the same time, we can set this say five years earlier, in 1970.

1975, January

The destructor codes were given to Britain 'a few months ago', say January.

1975, March (late)

In Ep1 Benton is called 'Mr Benton' by the Brigadier (and he shows Sarah his new rank patch in Ep2). He is still called Sergeant Benton in 'Planet Of The Spiders', so his promotion must have been granted during the three weeks the Doctor was missing following his departure from Metebelis Three; this was between 13 March and 3 April 1975.

DURATION

⇨ **Day One (3 April) (Ep1)**

There is no indication as to the number of days the Doctor is unconscious. The robot steals the disintegrator gun plans at night, so it could be the evening of the same day the Doctor regenerates.

⇨ **Day Two (4 April) (Ep1-2)**

UNIT is called in to investigate the theft. The Doctor awakens. Sarah returns to Think Tank at 3.50 pm (her visitors pass, which expires at '4 pm', is still valid 'for another ten minutes'). The Robot goes to Kettlewell that night.

⇨ **Day Three (5 April) (Ep 2-3)**
Sarah goes to the SRS HQ the next day (it is a week day). The Doctor calls in on Kettlewell and meets the Robot. The SRS meeting is held 'TONIGHT'. The SRS members move to the bunker.

⇨ **Day Four (6 April) (Ep 3-4)**
UNIT arrives at the bunker. (It is not clear if this is still 5 April or the next day; all the scenes at the bunker follow on from the last scene at the SRS meeting, which is held at night, and yet it is still daylight outside the meeting hall and for the scenes set at the bunker. I have decided that the scenes at the bunker are the next day.) The TARDIS leaves later in the day (Sarah is wearing the same floral dress).

THE ARK IN SPACE

+STORY LINK
This serial takes place immediately after 'Robot' – this is Harry's first journey in the TARDIS. Both he and Sarah are wearing the same clothes from the end of 'Robot'. They are supposed to be taking 'a little trip to the moon'.

LANGUAGE
Vira finds it hard to understand Harry's 1970s' slang, and the Doctor says 'we do seem to have a small communications problem', but it would still appear that English is the language of the survivors, given that the pallets are marked with standard lettering and numerals.

TIMELINE DATES

15,000 +
Clearly it was intended that the time of the solar flares was to be in the early thirtieth century. This is evidenced by three clues: firstly there is the Doctor's comment that 'judging by the macro-slave drive and that modified version of the Bennett Oscillator I'd say this was built in the early thirtieth century ... Late twenty-ninth, early thirtieth, I feel sure' (he later says 'by the thirtieth century human society was highly compartmentalised'); secondly, Vira's comment that 'our scientists calculated it

would be five thousand years before the bio-sphere became viable again'; and thirdly, the High Minister's statement that the Nerva personnel 'have slept longer than the recorded history of Mankind' indicates that at the time her speech was made the 'recorded history of Mankind' was less than 5000 years. These three points mean the solar flare crisis was around the year 3000 and the station was to become reactivated 5000 years later, around 8000. However, the year 3000 contradicts suggested dates for 'The Chase' (3550), 'The Daleks' Master Plan' (4000), 'The Ice Warriors' (5000), 'Death To The Daleks' (3500), 'The Talons Of Weng-Chiang' (5000), 'The Invisible Enemy' (5000) and 'Destiny Of The Daleks' (4500), in which Earth is still inhabited.

Given that Nerva is a survival ship built from the old Nerva Beacon of 2525 (see 'Revenge Of The Cybermen'), we can solve this problem by simply saying that only the Bennett Oscillator is from the thirtieth century, but the rest of the Nerva's fittings are from a much later time period. (The Doctor's added comment 'I feel sure' could be on account of his making a guess as to the date, as his memory might still be somewhat unstable following his recent regeneration.) It is clear that the complete interior of the old beacon has been stripped in order to make it into the Nerva. About the only parts of the station that appear the same in both 'The Ark In Space' and 'Revenge Of The Cybermen' are the outer circular corridor and the transmat platform. Everything else is different; even the doors open differently (in 'The Ark In Space' they slide upwards, whereas in 'Revenge Of The Cybermen' they open sideways). The control panel where the Doctor sees the Bennett Oscillator is not there in 'Revenge Of The Cybermen', nor is there a shuttle platform. We can therefore speculate that Nerva beacon was decommissioned after its 30-year assignment in orbit around Voga and converted into a space buoy or something similar. Then, at some point in the late twenty-ninth / early thirtieth century, the ex-beacon was fitted with the new Bennett Oscillator and the other controls that the Doctor recognises. Then in 5000, some two thousand years later, it is completely refitted and converted into the survival ark, but with many of the old components retained, such as the Bennett Oscillator.

The Doctor is only guessing as to how long the humans have been asleep: 'Ten thousand years? … Fifteen thousand, a hundred thousand? Time is immaterial'. Later he says to Vira 'you've overslept by several thousand years'. Harry later tells Sarah it is was 'ten thousand'. In 'The Sontaran Experiment' the Doctor says 'no one's set foot here [on Earth] for thousands of years'. (Although see 'The End Of The World'.) He later tells the Galsecs that the sleepers have been asleep for 'oooh, ten thousand years?' Assuming that he is right in his assumption, 'The Ark In Space' can be set in 15,000, which is at least 10,000 years after the solar flares, which were around 5001 (see below).

Vira says it would take '72 hours for complete revivification, another 24 to evacuate the Ark', but with the subsequent loss of the shuttle, it would probably take longer using only the three-person transmat system.

1555 ◆ ▨ ▨ ▨ ▨ ▨ ▨ ▨ ▨ ▨ ▨ ▨ ▨
Between 1547 and 1566 in our history Nostradamus rose to fame with his prophecies and foretelling. He published his prophecies in 1556. We might assume that these prophecies are based in part on the Doctor's own knowledge of the future, as related by him to Nostradamus.

5001 ▨ ▨ ▨ ▨ ▨ ▨ ▨ ▨ ▨ ▨ ▨ ▨ ▨
As covered under 'The Invisible Enemy', the time of the solar flares was most likely around the year 5001, the Great Break Out of 5000 being the mass evacuation of the planet due to that same crisis. Some groups elect to stay in 'thermic shelters' on Earth, some leave in ships, while a chosen few are placed in the Nerva.

5001 – 6000 ▨ ▨ ▨ ▨ ▨ ▨ ▨ ▨ ▨ ▨ ▨
The Noah-Wirrn says that 'long ago humans came to the old lands. For a thousand years the Wirrn fought them but you humans destroyed the breeding colonies. The Wirrn were driven from Andromeda'. Vira's surprise at this ('Andromeda? So, our star pioneers succeeded') is odd considering that in 'The Daleks' Master Plan' Earth already has a political relationship with that galaxy in 4000. We can assume that these star pioneers were part of the Great Break Out of 5000.

10,000 ▨ ▨ ▨ ▨ ▨ ▨ ▨ ▨ ▨ ▨ ▨ ▨ ▨
The Doctor tells Vira 'a long time ago, when you were dormant, you had a visitor'. We see the arrival of the Wirrn Queen from her point of view. Nerva is already in orbit around Earth, so it would seem that the 5000 years predicted for Earth to become viable again has passed. Nerva has engines and can be piloted, as seen in 'Revenge Of The Cybermen'. We can presume that Nerva was originally sent out on a curved orbit to take it out of the path of the solar flares, which would extend across half the solar system, and then Nerva slowly curved back to Earth over 5000 years.

DURATION

⇨ **Day One (Ep1-4)** ▨ ▨ ▨ ▨ ▨ ▨ ▨ ▨ ▨ ▨
The TARDIS crew are on the Ark for no 'more than an hour' before the first of the humans is revived. The rest of the story takes place over a few hours.

THE SONTARAN EXPERIMENT

+STORY LINK

This serial follows directly on from 'The Ark In Space' with the Doctor, Sarah and Harry travelling via transmat from Nerva to Earth.

SONTARAN LINK

This is, in their timeline, the final story in the Rutan / Sontaran war saga. The Sontarans are still at war with the Rutans even 15,000 years in the future; they had already 'been at war for millennia' by the time of 'The Time Warrior' in 1274. In 'The Time Warrior' Linx says Earth is of 'no military value. No strategic significance'. But by the year 15,000 the on-going war with the Rutans has reached a point where Earth is of strategic importance in the Sontarans' planned invasion of 'the galaxy'. Also by this time, the Sontarans have five fingers on each hand, as opposed to only three as seen in 'The Time Warrior', 'The Invasion Of Time', 'The Two Doctors' and 'The Sontaran Stratagem'. So either the Sontaran race has evolved, or Styre's battalion has undergone some genetic modification. Styre is a Field-Major in the G-3 Military Assessment Survey. He was acting under the orders of the Grand Strategic Council, and answered to the Marshal.

OBSERVATIONS

- The Galsec men know the 10,000 year-old legend of Nerva, but do not know of Atlantis when the Doctor mentions it. Vural says that while the people in Nerva slept 'our people kept going and they made it. We got bases all across the galaxy now. You do nothing for ten thousand years while we made an empire'. In 'The End Of The World', the Doctor says 'the New Roman Empire' existed in the year 12,005, which suggests (one of?) the Galsec empires was based upon the empire of ancient Rome. As noted under 'The Ark', this Empire could signify the Second or even a later Segment of Time.
- The Doctor refers to his 500 Year Diary, and says 'I remember jotting some notes on the Sontarans'. Given that the second Doctor is already familiar with the Sontarans in 'The Two Doctors', the Doctor's initial encounter with them was probably during his first incarnation.

LANGUAGE

Styre speaks the same language as the accented Galsec colonists. Although it is not referred to, Styre is probably using a translator device like the one used by Linx in 'The Time Warrior'. The fact that Sarah adopts the Galsec survivors' vernacular 'yunnerstand' indicates that their language is derivative of English.

TIMELINE DATES

15,000 +

'The Sontaran Experiment' is set on the same day as 'The Ark In Space'. Styre has been on Earth for not less than nine days, as Experiment Number 4 died as a result of water deprivation after 'nine days, seven hours'. Vural encountered Styre on their 'first night', when Vural 'was gone for hours'.

DURATION

⇨ **Day One (Ep1-2)**

It is day. This story appears to take place over the actual duration of the story, about 48 minutes.

GENESIS OF THE DALEKS

+STORY LINK

After transmatting from Earth at the end of 'The Sontaran Experiment', the Doctor, Sarah and Harry expect to be back on Nerva (although Sarah prophetically refers to it as a 'beacon'; it is not until 'Revenge Of The Cybermen' that she learns Nerva was once a space beacon), meaning 'Genesis Of The Daleks' follows directly from 'The Sontaran Experiment'.

DALEK LINK

As covered under DALEK HISTORY, this is the Daleks' first appearance in their timeline. Davros has been working on his project for 50 years (see Timeline Dates).

GALLIFREY LINK

The Doctor's GRT is now 1862; he is 649 years old (see THE DOCTOR'S AGE). The Doctor says 'I will not tolerate this continual interference in my life'. The Time Lord messenger replies: 'Continual? ... We seldom interfere in the affairs of others ... You are our special case. You enjoy the freedom we allow you. In return, occasionally, not continually, we ask you to do something for us'. Given that by this time the Time Lords have used the Doctor directly on only a few occasions (on-screen) – in 'Colony In Space', 'The Curse Of Peladon', and 'The Mutants' – these few occasions hardly equate to 'continual'. Therefore, it would appear that there have been other (untelevised) Time Lord 'interferences' that took place during the 'missing' 196 years between 'The Monster Of Peladon' and 'Planet Of The Spiders'.

OBSERVATIONS

- When speaking of the ethics and moral responsibilities of his experiments, Davros says 'that power would set me up amongst the gods'. In 'The Impossible Planet', the Doctor refers to the Kaled God of War.
- It is clear from 'The Five Doctors' that the Time Lords have always known about the existence of the Daleks. The Time Lord tells the Doctor that 'we foresee a time when [the Daleks] will have destroyed all other life-forms and become the dominant creature in the Universe'. As noted under THE N-SPACE UNIVERSE, the future time that the Time Lords observed was probably one of several possible future timelines, predicted by the Matrix. I would suggest that the reason the Time Lords were even looking at Dalek history was because of the events of 'Frontier In Space', in which the Doctor sent a message to the Time Lords asking for their help in sending the TARDIS after the Daleks. This mention of the Daleks prompted the Time Lords to examine the Dalek time line, which they spent part of the last 197 years doing.

  By 1862, which is the GRT of the Time Lords, there are only two Dalek stories, 'Genesis Of The Daleks' and 'The Daleks', available from 'real time history' for them to see. They are however able to view 'future' history from recordings from the Doctor's TARDIS obtained during his trial in 'The War Games': these records include 'The Chase', 'The Daleks' Master Plan', 'The Power Of The Daleks', 'The Evil Of The Daleks', 'Day Of The Daleks', 'Frontier In Space', 'Planet Of The Daleks', and 'Death To The Daleks'. From this we can assume that the Time Lords used the temporal projectors to view the far future ('throughout all eternity'), witness the destruction of Gallifrey in the 'last Great Time War' ('Dalek', 'Bad Wolf', etc), and maybe even beyond to see a time in which the Daleks have taken over the Universe. To ensure that this future does not happen, the Time Lords send the Doctor to Skaro. In other words, the Doctor actually creates the future timeline of which his past selves have already been a part. Of note, the Time Lords only want the Doctor to 'affect [the Daleks'] genetic development so they evolve into less aggressive creatures' – not to affect their technical or scientific (i.e. space and time travel) development. This suggests that they are unable to alter this future outcome.

LANGUAGE

Presumably the Time Lord 'gift' works on the Skaro language. The Kaleds and Thals converse with one another so we can assume they speak the same language. All signs are seen in English (i.e. 'SAFE / TOXIC LEVEL') in both Kaled and Thal buildings. After nearly being eaten by a giant clam Harry speaks Latin, but the Doctor claims not to understand him.

TIMELINE DATES

300 +

In 'The Daleks' Master Plan', the Doctor sees an embryo Dalek and comments: 'Millions of years of progress reversed back'. Although he does not know it at the time, he is actually seeing the Dalek creatures de-evolving back through the enforced genetic process introduced by Davros that pushed millions of years of evolution into a 50 year period (see Timeline Dates below) and beyond to the life form that the people of Skaro naturally evolved from, so this reference to millions of years cannot be taken literally.

In 'Genesis Of The Daleks' the Doctor says 'I know that although the Daleks will create havoc and destruction for millions of years I know also that out of their evil must come something good'. This reference to 'millions of years' also suggests that the events of 'Genesis Of The Daleks' take place millions of years in the past. But the Doctor already knows that the Daleks of the future have time travel, so it is possible that he is simply referring to the fact that the Daleks will use their time technology to 'create havoc and destruction for millions of years' throughout future history. On that basis I don't think we can set 'Genesis Of The Daleks' that far back in the past. In fact in 'Destiny Of The Daleks', set in 4500, the Doctor says that the Daleks 'were created thousands of years ago', and that Davros has been 'dead for centuries', which does not equate to millions of years. I have already established that 'The Daleks' is set in 900 AD. In that, a war with the Thals took place '500 years' before. That war cannot be the same one as the war in 'Genesis Of The Daleks'. The Dalek city does not exist in 'Genesis Of The Daleks'; in 'The Daleks' the Thals say the Daleks retreated into the city after the war, so it is clear to me that there were two major Thal / Kaled wars in the history of Skaro, the one in 'Genesis Of The Daleks', and another one that took place 500 years prior to 'The Daleks'. The Daleks therefore built their city after the events of 'Genesis Of The Daleks', and then 500 years later there was another war with the Thals, a neutronic one that lasted only one day. It would probably have taken them over 100 years to build a city of that size, so there is at least 600 years between 'Genesis Of The Daleks' and 'The Daleks', which places 'Genesis Of The Daleks' no later than 300 AD.

700 BC
The war between the Kaleds and Thals has lasted 'a thousand years', which from 300 AD is 700 BC.

700 BC - 600 BC
The chemical weapons that created the mutos 'were used in the first century of this war'.

250
Davros says the Kaled Government has tried 'many times in the last 50 years' to interfere in his research, giving the approximate time when he started the original Dalek travel machine project.

1862
<<The Far Future>>
The Time Lord messenger is from the Doctor's GRT, which, in terms of THE DOCTOR'S AGE, is now 1862. Coincidentally, this date is only some 38 years before the Daleks leave Skaro for the first time, in 1900 (see 'The Power Of The Daleks'). The Time Lords must have become aware of this, which is why they had cast a future projection (see Observations). It is possible the far future they view is the Time War, in which Gallifrey is destroyed in the final war against the Daleks, and it is this future they wish to prevent (see 'Bad Wolf').

4590 *
17,000 *
The Doctor is forced to give details about future Dalek defeats: 'The Dalek invasion of the Earth in the year 2000 was foiled because of an attempt by the Daleks to mine the core of the planet. The magnetic properties of the Earth were ... On Mars the Daleks were defeated by a virus that attacked the insulation on the cables in their electrical systems ... ... Venusians in the Space Year Seventeen Thousand was halted by the intervention of a fleet of war rockets from the planet Hyperon. The rockets were made from a metal that was completely resistant to Dalek firepower. The Dalek task force was completely destroyed'.

The first event appears to be the Dalek invasion seen in 'The Dalek Invasion Of Earth', but that was in the year 2164, not 2000. Either the Doctor is lying or he has forgotten the true date – or, he could be deliberately misleading Davros. The second report may refer to the Movellan virus which saw an end to the Movellan / Dalek war around the year 4590, as seen in 'Resurrection Of The Daleks'. It is not clear what a 'Space Year' is. It could be the 17,000th year after the Big Bang. As it is ambiguous, I have taken it to mean the 'Earth' year 17,000. The fact that it is imperative that the Doctor destroys the tape containing this information means that it is truthful in most respects.

DURATION

⇨ **Day One (Ep1-3)**

It is day when the Doctor arrives on Skaro. Sarah sees the first Dalek being tested by Davros at night. She leads the rebelling prisoners up the rocket tower that night.

⇨ **Day Two (Ep3-6)**

The Doctor is with the Kaled leaders all night. It is day when the meeting ends. The travellers leave Skaro later the same day.

REVENGE OF THE CYBERMEN

+STORY LINK

The Doctor, Sarah and Harry return to the beacon from Skaro via the Time Ring. Harry and Sarah are wearing the same clothes they had from 'Genesis Of The Daleks' – but the Doctor is no longer wearing his hat and long overcoat that he had on when they left Skaro. It is possible that another adventure, in which the Doctor loses these garments, occurs between 'Genesis Of The Daleks' and 'Revenge Of The Cybermen'.

Sarah confesses she has no faith in the Doctor, considering what has happened to her 'in these past few weeks'; a time that presumably encompasses all the adventures from 'Planet of the Spiders' (during which there was a gap of three weeks) through to 'Genesis of the Daleks'.

CYBERMAN LINK

As covered under CYBERMAN HISTORY, 'Revenge Of The Cybermen' is the seventh appearance of the silver giants. These particular Cybermen are survivors from the Cyber-War, which occurred around 2020 – 2025.

OBSERVATIONS

- The walls and floors of the Vogan chambers, as well as the Vogans' robes, are adorned with the spiral symbol that is also Rassilon's seal. Given that the TARDIS does not arrive on the beacon until the precise moment the Cybermen are destroyed and the beacon is saved, we can assume that the Time Lords have been controlling the Doctor's journey ever since he left Skaro. The similarity between the seals suggests that there is a relationship of some sort between the Time Lords and the Vogans. Perhaps they were regular customers for Vogan gold; it is stated that the Vogans once traded gold 'with other planets in the galaxy' because there was 'more gold here on Voga than in the rest of the known galaxy'. Is that why the Time Lords sent the Doctor to that time zone; to protect Gallifrey's supply of gold? Perhaps the Doctor should ask Gold Usher ...

LANGUAGE

Kellman communicates with both the Vogans and the Cybermen, so it is clear that both alien races speak English. The Doctor even criticises the Cyber-Leader for not speaking 'decent English'. The Cybermen read English off the beacon's screens. The Doctor speaks Latin again: '*Cogito ergo sum*' ('I think, therefore it missed'), but the phrase is not translated automatically into its correct meaning of 'I think, therefore I am'.

TIMELINE DATES

2525, November, 3rd week, 3rd day ▪

When Warner logs the signal he detects coming from Voga the readout says: '18.57Hrs DAY 3 WEEK 47'. On a standard calendar, the 47th week is traditionally the third week of November. 'Day 3' would either be Tuesday or Wednesday depending on whether the calendar week starts with a Sunday or a Monday.

In 'Earthshock', the Cybermen refer to the events of 'Revenge Of The Cybermen' as part of their past history, which shows clearly that 'Revenge Of The Cybermen' is set prior to 2526. Some fan chronologists insist on setting 'Revenge Of The Cybermen' after 'Earthshock', on the assumption that the Cyber-War the Cybermen lose is the same war the Cybermen are trying to prevent in 'Earthshock'. But there is no indication in 'Earthshock' that a war ever takes place. In fact, it is stated in 'Time-Flight' that the Cyber-fleet that was gathering in 'Earthshock' has dispersed. The date usually assigned to 'Revenge Of The Cybermen' is 2875, taking into account the Doctor's line in 'The Ark In Space' that the Nerva beacon was built in 'the late twentieth, early thirtieth century'. Another chronologist theory is that the Cybermen of 'Earthshock' have time-travelled into the past from the far future. However, in 'Attack Of The Cybermen' the Doctor clearly states that the Cybermen never develop time-travel. Also, the 'Earthshock' Cyber-Leader clearly shows surprise when the Cyber-computer causes the freighter to go into time warp. It is my firm belief that the 'Earthshock' Cybermen do not possess time-travel. Besides, if they did, then surely there are more important events in Earth history that they would travel to in order to destroy the planet – such as going back to 1985 as they do in 'Attack Of The Cybermen', or even back 65 million years! – than simply destroying a conference on Earth?

After careful consideration, I have set 'Revenge Of The Cybermen' one year before 'Earthshock' (see 2020 below for further details).

c1915 ▸

The Doctor met Houdini around this time – refer 'Planet Of The Spiders'.

2020 – 2025 ▸

To establish the date of the Cyber-War, we need to take into account factors from another Cyberman story, 'The Tomb Of The Cybermen', and its relationship to 'Revenge Of The Cybermen' and 'Earthshock'. I suggest that in 2020, the Cybermen abandon further attacks on Earth and set their sights on the new colonies that Earth is establishing on the other planets in the solar system, as well as attacking Earth's space fleet ships.

The war itself probably lasted only five or so years. It is clear that the Doctor was there at the time (probably the third Doctor, during the 'missing' years after 'The Monster Of Peladon': in 'The Five Doctors' he talks to Sarah Jane about one of his encounters with the Cybermen).

Five years into the war, humans discovered the Cybermen's weakness to gold. They needed vast quantities, which Earth just did not have. Voga traded its gold with other planets, so Voga and Earth both already had a trade agreement or humans found the planet during a search of their sector of the galaxy, travelling as far as their spaceships could at the time (this was before the discovery of warp drive). The Cybermen attempt to destroy Voga but fail. All but a handful of the silver giants are destroyed. The remaining Cybermen probably split their forces: one group would return to and remain hidden on Planet 14, while the majority of the surviving Cybermen go to Telos to set up the hibernation hives for the other Cybermen to join them at a later time ('The Tomb Of The Cybermen'). A single spaceship, containing 'enough spare parts' to build a whole army, follows Voga as it drifts through space. The Cybermen on Planet 14 are the ones who later travel to Earth's moon to obtain replacement parts from the

Gravitron moonbase in 2070 ('The Moonbase').

The Doctor knows the Cybermen disappeared after their attack on Voga 'at the end of a Cyber-war'. Voga has been 'drifting in the vacuum between star systems' for 'centuries', its people living underground 'for generations'. Given that 'Revenge Of The Cybermen' takes place 500 years after the Cyber-War, Voga's system of origin is probably fairly close, on a galactic scale, to Earth's.

And as far as Earth is concerned, the Cybermen have completely died out (the crew of the Gravitron moonbase know that the Cybermen 'were all destroyed ages ago' – a reference to the Cyber-War, and not the destruction of Mondas). The attack on the moonbase in 2070, 45 years after the war, is an isolated event that is probably hushed up, given that there are no further sightings of the Cybermen near Earth after that year.

450 years after the war, Voga drifts into Earth's system. Because of Commander Stevenson's report about the Cybermen's return to Earth's solar system, Klieg and Kaftan of the Brotherhood of Logicians, finance Professor Parry's scientific team to find the lost origins of the Cybermen. The expedition eventually discovers the buried city on Telos ('The Tomb Of The Cybermen'). On his return to Earth, Parry informs Earth authorities that the Cybermen still exist in force on Telos, and could still pose a new threat. On that warning, Earth goes to red alert and organises a conference with the governments of many powerful planets to join in an alliance against the new Cybermen threat (as seen in 'Earthshock') ...

2475

Voga 'was first detected in our system 50 years ago and it was captured by Jupiter', in 2475. Voga has probably only been in Jupiter's actual orbit for about six months or so, which is how long Kellman has been surveying the asteroid.

2523

Vorus says he has 'planned this moment for years', but 'Magrik and his team have been working on it [the rocket] for two years'.

2525, May

Kellman has 'spent the last six months studying rock samples' from Voga, which would be since May. It was probably when he first landed on Voga that Kellman encountered the Vogans. He agreed to locate the Cybermen and lure them to Voga (he says to the Cybermen 'You might never have found Voga if it hadn't been for me').

2525, August 16

The crew began to die 'in these last months'. Lester says that 'this is the 79th day' since the plague broke out, which places the first death on 16 August.

2525, November, 2nd week

The four survivors have 'managed for one week' without the other crew. Kellman has remained in his cabin 'these last few days'. The man Harry examines soon after they arrive has been dead 'a week or two'.

2525 – 2555

Nerva Beacon is on a '30 year assignment' to guide spaceships around the new asteroid.

DURATION

⇨ **Day One (Ep1-4)**

Pluto-Earth One-Five radios in at '18.00.36' (6pm). It is '18.57' (6.57pm) when the signal from Voga is logged. In Ep2 Vorus says it will take 'four hours' to get the rocket launched. It is launched in Ep4 so at least four hours pass between Ep2 and Ep4.

TERROR OF THE ZYGONS

+STORY LINK

This story takes place immediately after 'Revenge Of The Cybermen', the Brigadier having summoned the Doctor back to Earth with the 'space time telegraph system' at the end of that story. The Doctor comments that they have travelled '270 million miles' to Earth from Jupiter – the location of Nerva Beacon. The Doctor lost his hat at some point between 'Genesis Of The Daleks' and 'Revenge Of The Cybermen', but by 'Terror Of The Zygons' he has obtained a new one.

In 'Revenge Of The Cybermen' Sarah remarks that 'in these past few weeks' she has come to doubt the Doctor's judgement. This suggests that the time relative for the Doctor, Sarah and Harry since 'Robot' is only a matter of a few weeks (indeed, in terms of individual story duration, the equivalent of about only four days have passed since 'Robot'). Harry has therefore been with the Doctor for only a brief period of time.

UNIT HQ – COUNTRY #2?

In Ep4 the UNIT personnel return 'to London HQ', and at the end of the story, the Doctor and Sarah set off in the TARDIS, which is still in Scotland, *en route* to 'London', which suggests that this is one of the HQs within central London. However, in 'Pyramids Of Mars', the TARDIS lands in the Scarman priory in 1911, the old site on which UNIT HQ now stands. But the priory is clearly way out in the country, so the HQ seen in 'Terror Of The Zygons' must be one of the country HQs. The walls of the communications room have the familiar green / white brick walls, so it is possible that this is the same house from 'The Three Doctors'.

OBSERVATIONS

- The Doctor left the psionic beam with the Brigadier and it was 'only to be used in an emergency'. We can assume that the Doctor gave the Brigadier the device at some point before he left in the TARDIS in 'Robot'. It certainly can't have been before 'Planet Of The Spiders', otherwise the Brigadier could have used it to locate the Doctor when he vanished after leaving Metebelis Three. We can assume that the Doctor takes the machine away from the Brigadier (for misusing it?) prior to returning to Scotland to retrieve the TARDIS, given that the Brigadier does not use the device during the Doctor's absence between 'Terror Of The Zygons' and 'The Android Invasion', or any time since.

- The Skarasen is the Loch Ness Monster. In 'Timelash' it is implied that the Borad is the creature. It is therefore likely that, given the number of sightings over the years, there is in fact more than one monster in the Loch.

LANGUAGE

The Zygons speak English when talking among themselves, and use 'Earth miles' for distances. Sarah thinks she might have trouble reading 'Medieval Latin'.

TIMELINE DATES

1975, April 25 – 27 ▪

In 'Pyramids Of Mars', Sarah tells Scarman she's 'really from 1980'. This would suggest that this was the year she left Earth at the end of 'Terror Of The Zygons', but this cannot be correct in terms of the Mawdryn Factor. One of the solutions given under THE UNIT YEARS is that Sarah spends several months in 1980 prior to landing in 1911 (see also Link under 'Pyramids Of Mars').

In terms of THE UNIT YEARS, with 'Robot' set in April 1975 and 'The Android

Invasion' in July 1975, 'Terror Of The Zygons' is best set in either April, May or June of that same year. The Brigadier does not appear to show concern over Harry's absence from his UNIT duties, so only a short time can have passed since 'Robot' (Sarah says 'It's nice to see you again, Brigadier'.) The story was recorded in April [of 1975], so this month can be used to match seasonal conditions. In this way the events of 'Terror Of The Zygons' take place for UNIT only a few weeks after 'Robot'. Indeed, the stag's head was given to the Inn by Broton, posing as the Duke, 'just this last week', which must have been when UNIT set up base in the Inn, so that the Zygons could keep an eye on them.

The rig is destroyed at night during a full moon. The April 1975 full moon was on the 25th. There have been 'three rigs destroyed in a month'.

565

The Zygons have been on Earth for 'centuries by your time-scale'. The monster has been sighted on and off 'since the Middle Ages'. In our history the first official recorded sighting of the monster was in 565, by the Irish saint Columba. The Zygons say the Skarasen was only an embryo when they came to Earth, so depending on how quickly the Skarasen grew, the Zygons may have arrived on Earth some time before 565. It is only recently that they have set about their plans to restructure Earth into a new home planet.

1050

The Duke says 'there has been a monastery on this site from the eleventh century onwards', say from 1050.

1275

The Duke says 'my family have served this country for seven centuries', which would be 700 years before 1975, being 1275.

1870

Angus mentions the Jamieson brothers, and gives us the year of their disappearance.

1922

The year and event are given by Fergus ('Nineteen hundred and twenty two').

1941, May 27

The Doctor mentions the Bismarck ('and we all know that story'), which sank on this date in our history.

1975, March ▨ ▨ ▨ ▨ ▨ ▨ ▨ ▨ ▨ ▨ ▨ ▨ ▨
Huckle says there have been 'three rigs destroyed in a month'.

2475 ▨ ▨ ▨ ▨ ▨ ▨ ▨ ▨ ▨ ▨ ▨ ▨ ▨
Broton says it will be 'many centuries' before the Zygon fleet arrives, say 500 from 1973, being 2473, however it is not known if they actually arrive ...

DURATION

⇨ **Day One (25 April) (Ep1)** ▨ ▨ ▨ ▨ ▨ ▨ ▨ ▨ ▨
The rig is attacked at night. There is a full moon.

⇨ **Day Two (26 April) (Ep1-4)** ▨ ▨ ▨ ▨ ▨ ▨ ▨ ▨
The TARDIS lands in the morning (the Doctor greets the Duke with 'Good morning'). They visit the Hiberian Oil Company offices 'this afternoon'. After the Zygon ship lands in Brentford, Broton announces that 'Tomorrow I will demonstrate my ultimate power'.

⇨ **Day Three (27 April) (Ep4)** ▨ ▨ ▨ ▨ ▨ ▨ ▨ ▨
The first scene of Day Three is at UNIT HQ: Sarah says 'it's been hours now', and they've had no word on the Zygon ship. The Brigadier speaks with the PM (who is about to leave for the Conference). The clock at Westminster (Big Ben) gives the time as '10.55' when the conference starts. Then, taking into account the travelling time from London to Tullock by train and car, the last scene at the TARDIS is later that same afternoon, or possibly even the next day.

PLANET OF EVIL

+STORY LINK

At the end of 'Terror Of The Zygons' the Doctor promises to return Sarah to London 'five minutes before leaving Loch Ness', so 'Terror Of The Zygons' and 'Planet Of Evil' are consecutive. The TARDIS control room is slightly different to the way it appears in 'Death To The Daleks', gaining a doorway leading into the ship's interior. Intriguingly, there does not appear to be a scanner.

LANGUAGE

The signs on the Morestran probe ship are in English, although there are also odd symbols, being a mix of alphanumeric and Greek symbols, on some of the doors.

TIMELINE DATES

37,166 (7y2) ∗

The Doctor says they have overshot London (of 1975, see 'Terror Of The Zygons') by 'thirty thousand years', which would put the date for them at 31,975.

A date appears on Egard Lumb's grave-mast:

DIED HERE 7 γ 2
IN THE YEAR 37,166

This could simply be a Morestran method of dating. Other symbols like '7 γ 2' appear on the doors of the Morestran probe ship. Given that the symbol 'γ' is similar to a lower case 'gamma' or 'zeta', which given the name of the planet is appropriate, the symbols on the grave marker could instead refer to the location – to go with the word 'HERE', i.e. Egard Lumb dies here on Zeta Minor in the year 37,166 – as opposed to the month and day.

The Morestrans appear to be of human descent based on the diversity of the races of the crew. Salamar even appears to be familiar with Earth ('An oxygen-type. Could be an Earthling' / 'To Earth? You said you came from Earth'). I would say that they could be from an Earth colony, and thus have retained the old Earth dating method, so therefore I have set 'Planet Of Evil' in 37,166.

Sorenson's party have 'been on the surface for months'. They had only been working 'a few weeks' before the first death.

13,000,000,000 BC ∗

The Doctor is familiar with the concept of a world of anti-matter, saying that 'from the beginning of time it has existed side-by-side with the known Universe. Each is the antithesis of the other. You call it "nothing"; a word to cover ignorance. And centuries ago scientists invented another word for it: anti-matter, they called it' (see 1930 below). The fact that the Doctor is aware of the other universe and its relationship with the known N-Space Universe suggests that he has had first-hand experience with it (perhaps his adventure with Omega in 'The Three Doctors'?) As covered under 'The Curse Of Fenric' and 'Secrets Of The Stars' the Universe was created around 13 billion years ago.

1600 ⏺

The Doctor tells Sarah, 'I met him once, you know … Shakespeare. Charming fellow. Dreadful actor'. I assume that the word 'once' can't be taken literally, as it's clear the Doctor has had several encounters with the Bard. We know from 'City Of Death' that the Doctor had a hand in the writing of *Hamlet* when Shakespeare had sprained his wrist writing sonnets, so this must be the same meeting referred to in 'Planet Of Evil'. The sonnets are believed to have been written between 1592 and 1598, while the dating of *Hamlet* is just as imprecise, believed to have been written between 1599 and 1601. In 'The Chase', the Doctor sees, via the Time and Space Visualiser, Francis Bacon giving Shakespeare the suggestion to write about Prince Hamlet in March 1600. We could therefore date the Doctor's subsequent meeting with the Bard in 1600, regardless of whether or not it is historically accurate. In 'The Chase', the Doctor does not make any comment about the exchange between Bacon and Shakespeare, so we can assume that the Doctor met Shakespeare at some point after 'The Chase' (see also 'The Myth Makers'). The tenth Doctor meets Shakespeare in 1599 ('The Shakespeare Code'), which in terms of the Bard's timeline, is his own first encounter with the Doctor. He does recognise the fact that the Doctor is from out of time, so when Shakespeare met the (fourth?) Doctor, he knew who the Time Lord was; Shakespeare may have deduced that this Doctor was the same man he had met earlier, but carefully avoided making direct reference to that previous encounter.

1930

The year in our history in which P A M Dirac first predicted the existence of anti-matter.

37,156

Sorenson fears the other Morestrans will 'destroy years of my life's work', say 10 years.

DURATION

⇨ **Day One (Ep1)**

It is nearly 'full night' when Braun activates the distress signal before dying.

⇨ **Day Two (Ep1-4)**

It is 'nearly dawn' when the Morestrans find Sorenson, which is shortly after the Doctor and Sarah's arrival. The oculoid tracker is sent out 'at first light'. The Morestran probe ship takes off when 'it is nearly night' again. The Doctor has '30 minutes' to get all the anti-matter, including Sorenson, back to the planet.

UNSEEN ADVENTURES

Prior to 'The Face Of Evil', the Doctor helps the Mordee Expedition when it becomes stranded on a planet (in the year 5000) and the Doctor fixes their computer, Xoanon. (See THE DOCTOR'S AGE and Story Link under 'Pyramids Of Mars' for more on this event.)

And at some point prior to 'The Hand Of Fear', Sarah obtains a large stuffed toy owl.

PYRAMIDS OF MARS

STORY LINK

There is very poor continuity between 'Terror Of The Zygons', 'Planet of Evil' and 'Pyramids Of Mars'. At the end of 'Terror Of The Zygons' the Doctor promises to take Sarah back to London in the TARDIS. At the beginning of 'Planet Of Evil' they are still on their way, and at the end of the same story, the Doctor reminds her that they are late and should be getting back to UNIT HQ. However, in the opening TARDIS scene of 'Pyramids Of Mars', the Doctor is very moody and distant, not looking forward to returning to UNIT HQ, which is the total opposite of his attitude in 'Terror Of The Zygons' and 'Planet Of Evil'. So why the sudden change?

The Doctor says he has 'lived for something like 750 years'. As covered under THE DOCTOR'S AGE, it is possible that as much as 100 years has passed for the Doctor between 'Planet Of Evil' and 'Pyramids Of Mars', and as covered under THE UNIT YEARS, Sarah could have spent up to three months stranded in the year 1980 (which explains her claim to be from 1980 when in fact she comes from 1975).

It is likely that during this 'gap' between 'Planet Of Evil' and 'Pyramids Of Mars' the Doctor encounters the Mordee expedition and fixes their 'damaged' computer Xoanon ('The Face Of Evil'). The Doctor has now changed into a new coat, having worn the same short red jacket with leather elbow patches since 'Robot'.

After 100 years without Sarah, the Doctor eventually returns to 1980 and is reunited with her. The opening TARDIS scene of 'Pyramids Of Mars' picks up following their reunion. The Doctor, now 100 years older, is not looking forward to going back to Earth, having had plenty of time over the 100 years to reflect that it is time to break his ties with UNIT.

OBSERVATIONS

- The Doctor tells Sutekh that the TARDIS controls are 'isomorphic', and is therefore spared from being killed because Sutekh needs the TARDIS to escape from his prison. The Doctor cannot possibly have been lying because Sutekh is able to read the Doctor's mind. The existence of isomorphic controls is contradicted on many occasions in which others have operated the TARDIS controls: Leela in 'The Invisible Enemy', Steven in 'The Daleks' Master Plan', Adric in 'The Visitation', and Tegan in 'Castrovalva' and 'Four To Doomsday', to name but a few. We can explain this by saying the TARDIS 'let' them operate the controls because they are friends of the Doctor's, but what of the Outlers in 'Full Circle'? They are able to pilot the ship. I would tend to think that the TARDIS does have isomorphic controls, but the pilot is able to switch the circuit off; the Doctor has always left the circuit permanently switched off. But after returning to 1911 from the jaunt to the alternative '1980' the Doctor probably switches the isomorphic control circuit back on because he has a feeling that Sutekh might try to steal the TARDIS. The Doctor turns the control off again after leaving 1911.
- The Doctor tells Laurence Scarman the Doctor has 'the advantage of being slightly ahead of you. Sometimes behind you but normally ahead of you'. This could be a reference to the fact that the Doctor's GRT is now 1962, which is 51 years 'ahead' of his present location in 1911.

LANGUAGE

The Egyptians assisting Scarman speak English. Even Sutekh speaks English when speaking with Scarman. The warning that has been transmitting from Mars for 7000 years ('Beware Of Sutekh') is in English. The Doctor notes that 'E' is the most common letter in the English language.

TIMELINE DATES

1911, April

Lawrence Scarman gives the year as 'Nineteen hundred and eleven' ('Ah! Splendid! An excellent year, one of my favourites', says the Doctor – see also 'The Ribos Operation'). According to Dr Warlock, Marcus Scarman 'hasn't been seen for weeks'. Therefore, I have placed the opening of the tomb in the month prior to May (see below).

1911, May *

The month has been selected to match the seasonal conditions of when the story was recorded [May of 1975]. Namin has, according to Collins, 'only been here a few days', having recently brought the treasures from Egypt.

<<1980>> ∗ ▆ ▆ ▆ ▆ ▆ ▆ ▆ ▆ ▆ ▆ ▆ ▆
The year is given several times by Sarah and the Doctor (see THE UNIT YEARS for several explanations as to why Sarah says she comes from this year).

5089 BC ▆ ▆ ▆ ▆ ▆ ▆ ▆ ▆ ▆ ▆ ▆ ▆ ▆
Marcus says 'This tomb must date back to the First Dynasty of the Pharaohs', which in our history was from 3100 BC (see also 'The Daleks' Master Plan'). The Doctor, however, says Sutekh was imprisoned by Horus 'seven thousand years ago', which from 1911 would be 5089 BC, some 1989 years too early. I have taken the Doctor's date, as Scarman is probably only guessing the date; Sutekh may have been in Egypt longer than the First Dynasty.

1666, September 1 ∗ ▆ ▆ ▆ ▆ ▆ ▆ ▆ ▆ ▆ ▆
The Doctor says he doesn't want 'to be blamed for starting a fire ... We had enough of that in 1666'. The date given here is when the fire started in our history (see also 'The Visitation'). It is not clear who the 'we' is; it certainly is not Sarah.

1793, October ∗ ▆ ▆ ▆ ▆ ▆ ▆ ▆ ▆ ▆ ▆ ▆
To have been given her pick-lock, the Doctor would have had to have met Marie Antoinette before her death on 16 October 1793 ('charming lady. Lost her head, poor thing'). The French Revolution is the Doctor's favourite period of Earth history (see 'The Reign Of Terror'), so perhaps she was the reason why?

1911 ∗ ▆ ▆ ▆ ▆ ▆ ▆ ▆ ▆ ▆ ▆ ▆ ▆
The Doctor says that 1911 is 'one of my favourites'. Either he is joking, or he has been to this time period before. Certainly the Doctor's predilection for clothing fashions from around this period would indicate that he has been there often (see also 'The Ribos Operation'). The Doctor meets Marie Curie around this time (see 'Doctor Who (The TV Movie)'), which could be another reason why it is a favourite period!

1951 ▆ ▆ ▆ ▆ ▆ ▆ ▆ ▆ ▆ ▆ ▆ ▆ ▆
The Doctor congratulates Laurence Scarman 'for inventing the radio-telescope forty years early', which would be circa 1951. However the first radio-telescopes were built as early as 1937. I have taken the Doctor's date as being correct.

8911

The Doctor projects Sutekh 'a thousand years beyond the twentieth century', then intends to send him 'on for another ten thousand', but Sutekh only 'lived about seven thousand years'.

DURATION

(TARDIS) (Ep1)

The Doctor and Sarah spend time travelling in the TARDIS. Sarah has been exploring the wardrobe.

⇨ **Day (Ep1)**

Scarman opens the tomb at day.

🕐 **Weeks pass ...**

⇨ **Day One (Ep1-2)**

'Weeks' later the TARDIS lands in the Priory; it is day. The Doctor, Sarah and Laurence spend the night in the priest-hole (owls are heard hooting).

⇨ **Day Two (Ep2-4)**

It is morning when Ernie checks his traps and runs into the force field barrier. The clock at the lodge seems to be stuck on the same time throughout Ep3 (either 11.30 or 5.55), a possible side-effect of the barrier around the estate. It is night when the Priory burns.

⇨ **Day One (Ep2)**

The Doctor takes Sarah and Lawrence Scarman into an alternative time stream in 1980.

THE ANDROID INVASION

STORY LINK

There is nothing to suggest that 'The Android Invasion' follows on immediately from 'Pyramids Of Mars', other than that the Doctor and Sarah are still trying to get back to UNIT HQ, as intended at the end of 'Terror Of The Zygons' (but taking several detours on the way (see 'Planet Of Evil' and 'Pyramids Of Mars')). On the basis that it was April 1975 when they left at the end of 'Terror Of The Zygons', and it is now July, the relative passage of time for Sarah could be three months, which she spent most of in 1980 (see THE UNIT YEARS).

OBSERVATIONS

- The XK5 is a space freighter. It is clear that this is only a test flight, so it is not carrying any cargo. It is more likely to have been the prototype freighter vessel to service a space station or colony on one of the outer planets or moons (see A HISTORY OF SPACE-FLIGHT). On its test flight, the XK5 experiences stabiliser failure that sends it into orbit around Jupiter. Colonel Faraday confirms that Crayford has 'been further into space than any other human being'. Given that Jupiter is the fifth planet, this could explain the XK5 designation. If there were earlier ships of that class it could be that XK1 was for exploring Mercury, XK2 for Venus, and so on. The ship is a conventional rocket; it does not possess warp-drive. The fact that the XK5 travels from Oseidon to Earth 'through the space/time warp' is due purely to Kraal technology.

LANGUAGE

The Kraals speak English with Crayford.

TIMELINE DATES

1975, July 5 – 6 ⋆

When the TARDIS lands Sarah asks the Doctor, 'Has the TARDIS brought us home or not?' ('home' being her own time period). The Doctor replies that 'the coordinates were set for your time', to which she facetiously replies, 'so we could be anytime, anywhere'. Given that Crayford has been missing for 'two years' from both Sarah's and UNIT's point of view, 'The Android Invasion' it is not later than Sarah's relative time; she is not in her own future, it is definitely her present. (Sarah tells the Doctor that she was in Devesham 'about two years ago'. Harry confirms that Crayford has spent 'two years in space'.) The Brigadier is still with UNIT so 'The Android Invasion' has to be set prior to 1976, in terms of the Mawdryn Factor.

The coins in the 'dead' UNIT soldier's wallet and in the till at the Fleur de Lys tavern are all minted with 'the same year'. In the same pub, the Doctor sees a calendar dated 'JULY 6 FRIDAY' on every page. No year is shown but July 6 falls on a Friday in 1973, 1979 and 1984. We are told by Styggron that the images of the pub, the surrounding countryside and the villagers have all been copied from Crayford's 'memory cells'. Therefore the date could reflect when Crayford was last in the pub before leaving Earth. Crayford says 'I have recently re-established radio contact with Earth', which explains how he knows that the Brigadier is in Geneva, and how the Kraals are able to make androids of Colonel Faraday, Benton (in his recently promoted rank of Warrant Officer), and Harry (who doesn't appear to have been a member of UNIT in 1973).

Taking the available evidence, the best date for 'The Android Invasion' is two years after July 1973, say July 1975, some three months after 'Robot'. The Doctor comments that oak trees 'don't grow anywhere else in the galaxy'. Oaks are deciduous, and since the oaks seen in the story are in full leaf, it must be summer [the story was filmed in August of 1975], so that could also apply with July being the current month.

On the day that Crayford returns to Earth Benton makes a dance date with his 'kid sister' for '8 o'clock'.

Taking into account the long journey from Oseidon to Earth and that Crayford arrives 'in time for a late breakfast', the sequences on the Kraal planet would be the day before.

1712 – 1722 ♦
The years in our history that the Duke of Marlborough held this title.

1876, February 12 ♦
This is the recorded date in our history that Bell (1847 – 1922) officially patented the telephone. The patent was eventually granted on 7 March the same year. The first telephone call was made a few days later on 10 March – see 'Father's Day'.

1973, July 6
Assuming that the date on the calendar in the pub is from shortly prior to when Crayford left Earth, this was Friday, 6 July 1973. Crayford says he has only heard of the Doctor, and never met him, so the XK5 was apparently launched during the third Doctor's time with UNIT. The Doctor, on the other hand, does not appear to be familiar with the XK5, so he must have been away from Earth at the time. As I've noted under 'Day Of The Daleks', the Time Lords had probably sent the Doctor away on a mission in July 1973 which is why he was not on Earth when the XK5 was launched.

DURATION

⇨ **Day One (Ep1-3)**
It is before noon when the TARDIS lands; the clock at the Inn chimes '12' as the

signal for the androids to activate. After the village is dispersed, the XK5 launches '90 minutes' later.

🕐 ▬ ▬ ▬ ▬ ▬ ▬ ▬ ▬ ▬ ▬ ▬ ▬ ▬

It takes some time (but likely to be no more than one day) to travel from Oseidon to Earth 'through the space/time warp'. The Doctor and Sarah are unconscious for most of the journey …

⇨ **Day One (Ep4)** ▬ ▬ ▬ ▬ ▬ ▬ ▬ ▬ ▬ ▬ ▬ ▬

Crayford lands 'in time for a late breakfast' indicating it is mid-morning (Benton makes a date with his kid sister for '8 o'clock' that night). The Doctor and Sarah leave later the same day.

THE BRAIN OF MORBIUS

STORY LINK

There is nothing to suggest this story follows on directly from 'The Android Invasion'. The Doctor is wearing a leaf in his hat at the end of 'The Android Invasion' but it is no longer there in 'The Brain Of Morbius', and he told Sarah he would take her home (presumably directly to her flat in South Croydon). The Doctor abuses the Time Lords for dragging them 'a thousand parsecs off course', which means they were headed for a specific (but unnamed) destination.

The Doctor is still 'only 749' (see THE DOCTOR'S AGE).

GALLIFREY LINK

The Time Lords send the Doctor to Karn to deal with Morbius – and not the crisis facing the Sisterhood. This is his first contact (on-screen) with his own people since 'Genesis Of The Daleks'. As usual, the Doctor knows they have diverted the TARDIS.

OBSERVATIONS

- During the mind-bending contest with Morbius, we see eight faces that appear to be previous incarnations of the Doctor. The identity of these faces is examined under MORE THAN A TIME LORD, which concludes that the faces are probably not the Doctor's.

LANGUAGE

If Solon is from Earth, presumably he speaks his native tongue (his first name is Mehendri, so is he perhaps Indian?). Condo would pidgin-speak the same language, having been taught how to speak by the scientist. Solon converses with the Sisters, even writing a letter to them. Presumably Solon is able to converse with Morbius due to the latter's Time Lord 'gift', which still works even in his disembodied state or without the aid of a TARDIS. Ohica is unable to read the text on the Doctor's firecracker.

TIMELINE DATES

2975 •

This story is a difficult one to date. The only reference to a date is when the Doctor tells Sarah that Solon comes from a period 'considerably after your time' (which in terms of 'The Android Invasion' is 1975). We could take 'considerable' to its extreme definition and set 'The Brain Of Morbius' a thousand years after Sarah's time, say 2975, a Century Factor of 1000.

One of Solon's victims is a 'Mutt ... a mutant insect species; widely established in the Nebulae of Cyclops'. The Mutt is the not same creature as the Solonian mutant from 'The Mutants', set in 2973, despite the similarity in appearance and name. The Doctor specifically says the Mutt is from Cyclops, not Solos. Solon describes the Mutt as 'an oxygen breather', which contradicts the poisonous atmosphere breathed by the Mutts on Solos. Also, the Mutt has hair, and its eyes are very different to the Solonian mutants. Besides, the Solonian mutants are only the transitional stage during the Solonian life cycle, so it is highly unlikely that they would develop space cruisers and travel to other worlds. A noted under THE N-SPACE UNIVERSE, there are many different races that look like Earthlings, so there is no reason why there can't be more than one insectoid race. Therefore, I feel sure that the dates of 'The Mutants' cannot apply to 'The Brain Of Morbius'. [This is simply one of several examples in which an old costume is re-used; in 'Mindwarp', the delegate from Posicar is a Terileptil ('The Visitation') painted pink!]

Solon's tissue transplant methods appear to be similar to those used by Crozier to transplant Kiv's brain in 'Mindwarp', set in 2379, so Solon and Crozier could be contemporaries. However, the year 2379 is only some 404 years after Sarah's time, which is not exactly 'considerable' in that context.

Another possibility is that 'The Brain Of Morbius' is set in the Doctor's GRT. This is based on it being the Time Lords from the Doctor's GRT who have presumably sent him to Karn (see Timeline Dates below). It is stated that the Time Lords and the Sisterhood have shared the elixir 'for years' ... 'since the time of the stones' (the

Time of Chaos?) This and the fact that Karn and Gallifrey are in the same region of space ('within a couple of billion miles') suggests that when the Time Lords need the elixir they travel across space to Karn, without temporal displacement. The Sisters are hundreds of years old, so the elixir has been available for quite some time. It is certainly available in the Doctor's time because he knows of its uses for assisting a failed regeneration. Given that Solon is from Sarah's future, this would mean that the Doctor's GRT is in the far future. As analysed under GALLIFREY HISTORY and THE DOCTOR'S AGE, this is unlikely, given that the Doctor's GRT at this point in his life is only 1962.

Of course, if we set 'The Brain Of Morbius' in the future, why would the Time Lords of the Doctor's 'present' be concerned about supplies of the elixir running low in the future when there would still be sufficient supplies in their present? Surely the threat to the elixir supplies would be more of a concern to the Time Lords that lived contemporary to Karn in this time zone? This shows clearly that the Time Lords from the Doctor's GRT send the Doctor to Karn to deal with Morbius and not the elixir crisis.

Given the choices available, I feel comfortable with setting 'The Brain Of Morbius' in 2975 (but without any links to Solos, despite this date being two years after 'The Mutants'). The Time Lords from Gallifrey in GRT 1962 have sent the Doctor to Karn to deal with Morbius, and his arrival on Karn just happens to coincide with the crisis facing the Sisterhood. The Doctor corrects the problem with the elixir, ensuring that further supplies are available for the Sisterhood and the Time Lords on Gallifrey in this future time zone.

As for Solon, he joined the Cult of Morbius when Morbius travelled into his time zone, a thousand years in the future. In fact, Solon might have already been on Karn when Morbius first visited this time period.

AD 79, August 24-25
The Doctor refers to Mount Vesuvius, which erupted on this day in our history, totally destroying the city of Pompeii. (See also 'The Empty Child' and 'The Fires Of Pompeii'.)

1957
Morbius was a Time Lord 'of the first rank' who 'once led the High Council of the Time Lords' and 'offered them greatness once but he was betrayed and rejected', which suggests that he was President, or at the very least a prominent Chancellor or Cardinal. He left Gallifrey to amass an army, the Cult of Morbius, which destroyed civilisations on many planets including Karn, after they were denied the elixir of life. The Doctor

knows of Morbius (he recognises Morbius's mind, presumably from a time before he left Gallifrey, when he was still connected to the Time Lord Intelligentsia (see 'The Invisible Enemy', and LIFE ON GALLIFREY)), but Morbius does not know the Doctor ('a mere nobody'), which means Morbius cannot be one of the senior Time Lords seen in 'The War Games', 'Terror Of The Autons', 'Colony In Space', and 'The Three Doctors', so we can assume that Morbius's rise to power within the Council was at a time after 'The Three Doctors'. Taking into account that five years have passed since Morbius's execution and his eventual death (see 2970 below), and applying this to the Doctor's GRT, Morbius is executed in GRT 1957, which puts this during the off-screen period between 'Planet Of Fire' and 'Pyramids Of Mars'. We can assume that it took only a year for Morbius to amass his cult of followers.

1962

The Doctor believes it is the Time Lords who send him to Karn, but there is a remote possibility that he is mistaken; it could simply be – as usual – a random landing made by the TARDIS. As covered under THE DOCTOR'S AGE, his GRT is now 1962.

2475

Maren says she has 'served the flame for centuries', say 500 years.

2970

Solon has been on Karn for 'many years'. He amputated Condo's arm 'many years ago' when the Dravidian starship crashed. Solon was probably in the early stages of building the hybrid creature at the time and needed Condo's arm, so we can assume from this that 2970 is when Morbius is executed, five years or so earlier. Solon abandoned using the glass brain case 'a long time ago'.

2974

Maren says there has been no elixir 'for over a year'.

DURATION

⇨ Day One (Ep1-2)

It is very late at night when the TARDIS lands. (In Ep3, when it is light, Solon says 'the Doctor and the girl have only been here a few hours'.) The Doctor is a prisoner of the Sisters overnight.

⇨ **Day Two (Ep.2-4)** ▓ ▒ ▒ ▒ ▒ ▒ ▒ ▒ ▒ ▒ ▒
The Doctor is to be sacrificed at 'sunrise'. It is night again when Morbius is destroyed.

THE SEEDS OF DOOM

STORY LINK

The Doctor is contacted by the World Ecology Bureau (WEB) through UNIT, which means that he and Sarah have both been back on Earth for some time since their excursion to Karn (see 'The Brain Of Morbius'). The Doctor is still aged 'only 749' (see THE DOCTOR'S AGE).

TIMELINE DATES

1975, October (early) ⁎ ▒ ▒ ▒ ▒ ▒ ▒ ▒ ▒ ▒ ▒
As covered under THE UNIT YEARS, this story is best placed in 1975. The Brigadier is still with UNIT, so in terms of the Mawdryn Factor, 'The Seeds Of Doom' must be set before 1976. (The Brigadier is in Geneva, perhaps negotiating the terms of his retirement from UNIT? See 'Mawdryn Undead'.)

Chase says to Amelia Ducat: 'what a shame you should come in the autumn'. The season is supported by an abundance of fallen leaves at Chase's estate. But on the wall of Sir Colin's office is a calendar which, although out of focus, appears to be for 'February', which is winter! But given that it is background dressing [a Production Factor] and readable only when using a freeze-frame, it can be dismissed from being a valid dating tool. In Keeler's laboratory there is a board with twenty two rows of numbers, presumably representing dates, arranged vertically starting at '27/4' and ending at '30/7' – e.g. 27 April to 30 July.

Taking the 'autumn' reference as being the more direct, with 'The Android Invasion' set in July 1975, 'The Seeds Of Doom' can be mid-autumn, say October, of the same year, 1975. At the end of the story, Sir Colin invites the Doctor to attend a meeting on the 'fifteenth', suggesting the story is set early in the month.

23,000 BC ▓ ▒ ▒ ▒ ▒ ▒ ▒ ▒ ▒ ▒ ▒ ▒
Moberley says the first pod has been in the ice for 'twenty thousand years' and is from 'the late Pleistocene period', which was 1,000,000 to 25,000 years ago. Later, Dunbar says the pod has spent 'twenty, thirty thousand years under the ice'. 25,000 years is mid-way to both given periods. From 1975 this can be rounded down to 23,000 BC.

1455 – 1485
Harrison Chase mentions that most of the manor 'was built during the Wars of the Roses', which was 1455 – 1485 in our history.

1587
Harrison Chase gives the date of his ancestor's execution.

1881, November 5
1960, March 23
The Doctor says American humorist, Franklin Adams, lived '1881 to 1960'. These are the dates of Adams' life in our history.

1975, October 15
The date of the Floral Society's meeting is given by Sir Colin as being on the 'fifteenth'.

DURATION

With two locations at opposite ends of the world for the first three episodes, the Duration needs to be split to represent this. The different days in England are easily recognised by the different patterns of Chase's ties. The scenes set in England are in normal text, the scenes at the Antarctic Base are in *italics*:

⇨ **Day One (Ep1)**
The first pod is found after 'lunch'. The pictures are transmitted to London. The Doctor is called in by WEB and he leaves for the South Pole 'immediately'. Chase sends Scorby and Keeler. (Chase's tie: criss-cross).

⇨ **Day Two (Ep1)**
The pod has grown 5cm 'since this morning'. Winlett is infected that night. The Doctor is 'due in tomorrow'.

⇨ **Day Three (Ep1-2)**
The Doctor and Sarah arrive. The medical team is expected 'tomorrow'. Dunbar visits Chase that night (Chase's tie: black with white spots). *It is night when the Base is blown up.*

⇨ **Day Four (Ep3)**
It is morning when the rescue team arrives (the Doctor says 'Good morning'). Presumably it takes the rest of this day to travel back to England.

⇨ **Day Five (Ep3-5)**

Everyone has returned from the South Pole by Day Five. Scorby and Keeler return to Chase 'two hours' before the Doctor reports in to WEB (Chase's tie: blue and grey stripes). Amelia Ducat visits Chase that evening ('Good evening, Miss Ducat'). Sarah and the others are trapped in the cottage overnight.

⇨ **Day Six (Ep5-6)**

UNIT arrives in the morning (Chase's tie: floral pattern; dark suit) and the Krynoid is destroyed.

⇨ **Day Seven? (Ep6)**

It is presumably the next day: both Sarah and Sir Colin are wearing clothes different to those in Day Six. Thackeray says he is expected 'home for tea'. *The Doctor and Sarah arrive in Antarctica.*

THE MASQUE OF MANDRAGORA

STORY LINK

At the end of 'The Seeds Of Doom' the TARDIS lands at the South Pole while *en route* to Cassiopeia. Sarah is not wearing the swimsuit she has on at the end of 'The Seeds Of Doom' in 'The Masque Of Mandragora', so it appears that the two stories are not consecutive. When the TARDIS enters the Mandragora Helix, the Doctor says 'I thought we'd avoided it', which indicates that their flight path passed by the Helix's location in space. The TARDIS is therefore not time-travelling. Given that the old wooden control room first appears in this story, and is in use until 'The Invisible Enemy', the Doctor has only just closed the number two control room for redecoration. The Doctor is surprised to see the old control room, so he was not specifically seeking it while wandering the TARDIS corridors with Sarah. Since 'The Seeds Of Doom' the Doctor once again has a new TARDIS key, a standard-looking 'Yale' type like the one used previously from '100,000 BC' to 'The Green Death'.

OBSERVATIONS

- The Doctor says he is looking forward to meeting Leonardo da Vinci, but he never gets the chance to meet the man in San Martino. In 'City Of Death' and 'Doctor Who (The TV Movie)' the Doctor says he is a good friend of the scientist, which indicates that at some point between 'The Masque Of

Mandragora' and 'City Of Death' the Doctor meets da Vinci.

- The dust-covered jacket and shirt the Doctor finds in the wooden console room are similar to those the third Doctor wears in 'The Curse Of Peladon', 'The Time Monster', 'The Three Doctors' and 'Planet Of The Spiders', suggesting that this is probably the console room the third Doctor used during the 196 years between 'The Monster Of Peladon' and 'The Five Doctors' / 'Planet Of The Spiders'. The presence of a wooden recorder suggests that the first or second Doctor also used the control room at one time.

LANGUAGE

The Doctor explains to Sarah about the 'Time Lord gift' that enables her to understand alien and foreign languages. They would be speaking a form of Latinate in this story.

TIMELINE DATES

1492, April •

The Doctor dates a glass bottle he finds to be 'late fifteenth century'. He later wishes he had Galileo's telescope, but says that won't be available for 'another fifty years'. In our history Galileo invented the astrological telescope in 1609, which would place 'The Masque Of Mandragora' in 1559, but that is the sixteenth century, and is inconsistent with the other clues given.

The Doctor tells Sarah that the Helix's 'constellation will be in position to try again in about … five hundred years', which Sarah calculates will be 'just about the end of the twentieth century'. From that the story would be set in the 1490s.

It is mentioned that Leonardo da Vinci's patron is the Duke of Milan, which would set the date somewhere between 1482 and 1493 when da Vinci was indeed living in Milan. (He would live in Florence between 1503 and 1505, as seen in 'City Of Death'.) Also, Giuliano tells Sarah of his belief that the Earth is a sphere. This theory is not proven until Columbus discovers America on 12 October 1492 and after his return many months later. On this basis I would set 'The Masque Of Mandragora' prior to October 1492.

Hieronymous calls upon the 'house of the Ram' as part of his prophecy of the Duke's death. This is Aries, placing the date at some point between March 21 and April 20. He later confesses his anxieties during 'these last few weeks as the summer solstice approaches'. The summer solstice is 21 June. As the Ram reference is given in the present tense I prefer to accept April as the month. The approaching solstice is still relevant in this context as it is only two months away.

The Helix portion of the story must also be set in 1492. Hieronymous declares to the Doctor that 'had it not been you there would have been other travellers drawn into Mandragora Helix. Earth had to be possessed. Unchecked, Man's curiosity might lead him away from this planet until, ultimately, the galaxy itself might not contain him. We of Mandragora will not allow a rival power within our domain'. Mandragora is speaking in the present tense, which shows clearly that the Helix enters the TARDIS at a time before Man has space travel, which would be the late twentieth century (ironically the time period in which the Helix would next be in orbit near Earth – see below). On this basis I would say that when the Helix possesses the TARDIS it simply takes the ship to Earth across space but not in time. This is supported by the later fact that the Helix's constellation has to be in position to attack Earth again in the twentieth century; so its current orbit is in line with the Earth of 1492.

508 BC

The High Priest says it's 'a dream of two thousand years come true' for the Cult to achieve power, which from 1492 is around 508 BC, giving the approximate year in which the Cult was formed.

30 BC *

Cleopatra ruled Egypt from 51 BC to 30 BC in our history. The Doctor was probably there towards the end of her life.

350 *

According to the Doctor, the Cult 'died out in the third century', say 350. He may have been there at the time.

1342

The Doctor says 'it must be at least one hundred and fifty years since wire drawing machines were invented', being 1342.

1415, October 25 *

This is the date of the battle of Agincourt in our history (see also 'The Talons Of Weng-Chiang').

1482

Hieronymous says he came to San Martino 'many years ago' when a voice told him to come. He also speaks of being scoffed at 'for years', say 10?

1854, November 5 ⁑
The Doctor mentions Florence Nightingale, so it is possible that he met the nurse when he was in the Crimea during the war (see 'The Evil Of The Daleks' and 'The Sea Devils').

2000, December 25 ⁑
The Doctor tells Sarah that Mandragora's constellation will be in position to attack Earth again 'in about five hundred years'. Sarah guesses that would be 'just about the end of the twentieth century'. With 'The Masque Of Mandragora' set in 1492, that would make Mandragora's return to be around 1992.

In 'Doctor Who (The TV Movie)', the Doctor tells Chang Lee not to be in San Francisco on 25 December 2000. It could be that the Doctor knew that that was the date on which Mandragora returns – turning its sights this time on the similarly-named San Francisco as opposed to San Martino. The eighth Doctor does find a scarf very much like the fourth Doctor's in the hospital, so it is possible that the fourth Doctor has been to San Francisco twice before – prior to December 1999 and later in 2000. This makes his comment to Sarah in 'The Masque Of Mandragora': 'Now, that was an interesting century', to which Sarah cries, 'What do you mean "was"?' all the more intriguing, given that 25 December 2000 is indeed near the end of the century. His adventure in San Francisco probably took place during the 'missing' 100 years between 'Planet Of Evil' and 'Pyramids Of Mars'.

DURATION

(TARDIS) (Ep1)
The Doctor and Sarah spend some time in the TARDIS before arriving at the Helix …

⇨ **Day One (Ep1)**
The Duke dies shortly before the curfew bell rings. Federico declares that Giuliano must die 'in two days' time'.

⇨ **Day Two (Ep1-2)**
Hieronymous casts Giuliano's horoscope 'this morning'. Soon after leaving the Helix, the TARDIS lands on Earth 'at the noon hour'. It is night when the Doctor meets Marco and Giuliano, and Hieronymous speaks with Mandragora.

⇨ **Day Three (Ep2-4)**
Sarah has breakfast with Giuliano. It is three o'clock (a bell chimes three times) when

Marco is captured. Federico dies that night. Blockades are built around the palace through the night.

⇨ **Day Four (Ep4)** ▦ ▦ ▦ ▦ ▦ ▦ ▦ ▦ ▦ ▦ ▦
The Doctor has been in Hieronymous's lab 'since this morning' working on his calculations. The eclipse occurs at '9.43.08' that night.

⇨ **Day Five (Ep4)** ▦ ▦ ▦ ▦ ▦ ▦ ▦ ▦ ▦ ▦ ▦
The previous night, the Doctor asks for a salami sandwich. The Doctor is carrying a stick of salami when he and Sarah leave in the TARDIS, so it most likely the next day.

THE HAND OF FEAR

STORY LINK

There is no indication that 'The Hand Of Fear' follows directly on from 'The Masque Of Mandragora'. Just before leaving the TARDIS for the last time, Sarah complains about being chased by 'bug-eyed monsters'. Very few of the alien creatures she encounters on-screen fit this description (the Eight-Legs, 'Planet Of The Spiders'; the Wirrn, 'The Ark In Space'; the Morbius hybrid, 'The Brain of Morbius'; and possibly the Daleks, 'Genesis Of The Daleks'), so it is possible she encounters monsters of the bug-eyed variety in off-screen adventures. Sarah has known the Doctor for just over two years (since 'The Time Warrior', set in May 1974).

LANGUAGE

The Kastrians speak English in the opening scene. The figures seen on the TARDIS screen are Earth characters.

TIMELINE DATES

150,000,000 BC ▦ ▦ ▦ ▦ ▦ ▦ ▦ ▦ ▦ ▦ ▦ ▦
The Doctor estimates the age of the fossil as being '150 million years' when he finds it imbedded in 'Jurassic limestone'. Our Jurassic period was some 170 to 140 million years ago.

1976, June + ▦ ▦ ▦ ▦ ▦ ▦ ▦ ▦ ▦ ▦ ▦ ▦
As covered under THE UNIT YEARS, 'The Hand Of Fear' needs to be set before

December 1981 (see 'K9 And Company'). The stock footage of the Harrier and Buccaneer jets is from a 15 July 1976 edition of the technology programme *Tomorrow's World*, so the year of 1976 or at least a few years prior to 1976 could be applied to 'The Hand Of Fear'.

When Eldrad asks what the expansion factor to reach Kastria is, the Doctor says 'Oh, just punch up 7-4-3-8-Oh-Oh-Oh-1-2-1-2-7-2-7-2-9-Double-1-E-8-E-E-X-4-1-1-1-3-Zero-9-11-5, and then see what happens'. After the ship dematerialises, the following text appears on the TARDIS scanner:

78b REF. 66735
144328X 66e 8
0257634 RD = 77
144092R 31751
246X56

Although none of these numbers corresponds with the coordinates the Doctor has given, the term 'RD' could stand for 'Relative Date'. On the basis that the Doctor insists that the journey from Earth to Kastria is in space only, without any temporal displacement ('I'll take you back, but it must be in the present time') the '77' could mean the Relative Earth Date was 1977. Of course, it could be argued that if this is the Earth date, why doesn't it show the full date as 1977. Accordingly, I do not consider this figure to be the date.

With 'The Seeds Of Doom' set in October 1975 we could set 'The Hand Of Fear' any time after that date in order to stay relative to Sarah's time. The story was filmed in June [of 1976], so we could use that month to match seasonal conditions. In that case it would be the year following 'The Seeds Of Doom', 1976.

Susie Watson tells her father about her day at school when he rings home ('Your headmistress must have been very pleased'). This tells us it is a weekday and still during the school term before summer break in early July. It is possible that Susie received the results of an end of term exam, hence the pleasure shown by her headmistress.

When the Doctor returns Sarah home (it's not South Croydon, but Aberdeen, as revealed in 'School Reunion') we can assume it's still relative to 1976.

DURATION

⇒ **Day One (150m BC) (Ep1)**
A few minutes are seen on Kastria before Eldrad's death.

⇨ **Day One (Ep1-4)** ▓ ▓ ▓ ▓ ▓ ▓ ▓ ▓ ▓ ▓ ▓ ▓

The sequences on Earth appear to take place over one day. Carter is unconscious for 'an hour'. Susie is home from school when Dr Watson telephones, so it is late afternoon at the time of the crisis at Nunton. The Doctor and Sarah spend a few hours at the most on Kastria. (It is dark on the planet – there is no sun.)

⇨ **Day Two? (Ep4)** ▓ ▓ ▓ ▓ ▓ ▓ ▓ ▓ ▓ ▓ ▓ ▓

It is day when Sarah is returned to Earth (in Aberdeen). This could be later in Day One, or else it is possibly the next day.

THE DEADLY ASSASSIN

+STORY LINK

'The Deadly Assassin' follows directly from 'The Hand Of Fear' with the Doctor still on his way to Gallifrey.

GALLIFREY LINK

This is the Doctor's first visit to Gallifrey since his trial, some 299 years earlier ('The War Games'). Since the events of 'The Three Doctors', all Type 40s – bar the Doctor's TARDIS – have been de-registered because the model has been considered 'obsolete'. It is not clear if the summons to Gallifrey is that all Time Lords have been recalled because of the Presidential resignation ceremony, or whether it is the Master's doing.

When the Doctor is put on trial following the assassination there is no mention of his participation in saving Gallifrey during the Omega crisis ('The Three Doctors') or of his help in the Morbius affair ('The Brain Of Morbius'), so it would seem that the High Council has carefully covered up the Doctor's involvement in these. (But the Doctor doesn't bring either of them up as part of his defence. Why?) It would seem that the CIA was responsible for sending the Doctor to Karn; a secret unknown to Goth and the other High Councillors.

The Council probably kept the Omega affair a secret because they wanted to hide the fact that they had broken the First Law of Time to achieve their ends. Also, there was the more important fact that one of their greatest heroic figures from millions of years in their past had still been alive, one who could have offered them a considerable amount of information about their past history that was missing from their records, but who was destroyed before they could take advantage of his knowledge.

The President who is resigning could be the same President who was in office in 'The Three Doctors', some 297 years ago, but he has since regenerated. The Doctor says he never met the current President. This could be because the President was elected after the Doctor left Gallifrey 352 years earlier, in GRT 1610. However, just because the Doctor never met him doesn't mean that that President wasn't in office when the Doctor was still on Gallifrey. The Doctor was by no means a high-ranking Time Lord, so he simply never had the opportunity to meet the President before his departure from Gallifrey. A previous President who lived in the life-time of one of the Time Lords attending the ceremony was Pandak the Third, who ruled for 'nine hundred years', which was considered a long time for a President, mainly because more recent Presidents had the habit of 'chopping and changing every couple of centuries'.

Borusa does not know of the Master, so it is unlikely that Borusa is the Time Lord who visits the Doctor in 'Terror Of The Autons'.

Considering that Goth, as well as many of the other high-ranking Time Lords, knows nothing about the Doctor, we cannot automatically assume that Goth is one of the Time Lords at the Doctor's trial, despite the fact that they look alike. [Actor Bernard Horsfall, who plays Goth, played one of the Time Lords at the Doctor's trial in 'The War Games'.]

MASTER LINK

The Master was last seen on-screen escaping from the Ogrons' planet ('Frontier In Space'). Goth says he found the dying Master on the planet Tersurus. We can assume that the Master's emaciated appearance is due to an injury sustained on Tersurus (he looks burned, so perhaps it was a fire or acid?), or the dying Master had actually transferred his essence (as he does in 'The Keeper Of Traken' and 'Doctor Who (The TV Movie)' into the already-emaciated body of his latest victim. Whatever the cause of the severe injuries, the Master was no longer able to regenerate because, as Goth states 'he was dying. No more regeneration possible ... He had come to the end of his regeneration cycle'. (As noted under 'Doctor Who (The TV Movie)', the Master in 'The Deadly Assassin' is not the post-San Francisco 1999 Master.)

Given that the Doctor is 749 years old and that they were at school together (see LIFE ON GALLIFREY), the Master must also be around 749 years old. (As noted under 'Terror Of The Autons', the [Delgado] Master is likely to be his second incarnation.) The Doctor is 454 in 'Frontier In Space', so in the subsequent 295 years the Master has used up all his regenerations (he states in 'Doctor Who (The TV Movie)' that 'I wasted all my lives because of you, Doctor'), so it is clear that the Doctor has encountered later incarnations of the Master off-screen between 'Frontier In Space' and 'The Deadly Assassin'. As pointed out in THE DOCTOR'S AGE, the third Doctor comments on the

Master's new appearance in 'The Five Doctors', which indicates that he has indeed encountered other post-Delgado incarnations ('another regeneration?') And there is the fact that the fourth Doctor has no trouble recognising the Master, despite his emaciated appearance, which again suggests a familiarity with the Master prior to this near-dead body.

It is odd that none of the Time Lords, including Borusa, have heard of the Master, considering it was a representative of the Tribunal who warned the Doctor about the Master in 'Terror Of The Autons'. As the Doctor points out, the Master has removed all record of his existence from the data extract files, so we can only assume that the Tribunal has special knowledge of the Master, as does the CIA, which clearly knows of the renegade, as seen in 'Colony In Space'.

OBSERVATIONS

- The history of the Time Lords in this story is at odds with that given in 'The Three Doctors'. In 'The Three Doctors', it is Omega who was credited with creating the means by which time travel was possible – when he detonated a star turning it supernova. In 'The Deadly Assassin' it is Rassilon who is given all the credit – having entered a black hole and trapping its nucleus in the Eye of Harmony, which he brought back to Gallifrey. There is no reason to suspect that Rassilon's black hole is the same as Omega's supernova, or that the two were even contemporaries. The only time they are said to have worked together is in 'Silver Nemesis' when they are both credited with creating validium. I prefer to think that their relationship is one of circumstance: Omega's supernova was the energy source used initially to power the early time machines. Once that power source had exhausted, possibly centuries later, Rassilon entered a black hole and created the Eye of Harmony as a replacement source of temporal energy. As for creating validium, Omega probably started the initial research into its development. Centuries or so later Rassilon continued Omega's work. (This is examined further in GALLIFREY HISTORY.)

- The Time Lords in 'The Deadly Assassin' – including the Doctor – are all ignorant of certain aspects of their past. The only official record is 'The Book Of The Old Time' of which a modern transgram is kept in the Archives. The Time Lords only know of the Eye of Harmony as a myth ('It no longer exists'); they have no idea it is hidden beneath the Panopticon. They also have no idea of the significance of the Sash and the Rod. In fact, 'The Deadly Assassin' is a turning point in the history of the Time Lords. With the discovery of the Eye Of Harmony on Gallifrey, they now have knowledge about their past they never had before. This explains why, in 'The Invasion Of Time', 'Arc Of Infinity' and 'The Five Doctors', the Time Lords all know about Rassilon and the Eye of Harmony. Presumably it is in the Master's hidden chamber beneath the Capitol that Borusa later finds the Black Scrolls of Rassilon that enable him to locate the sealed Games Room (see 'The Five Doctors').

- The dreamscape inside the Matrix is a projection from Goth's mind. Given the nature of the images (an alligator, a samurai, a bi-plane, spider, clown, surgeon, trains, war ground, and so on) it would appear that Goth has visited assorted time periods on Earth.

LANGUAGE

Everyone should be speaking Gallifreyan. Curiously, Spandrell has a strong almost East European accent. The letter to the guards the Doctor writes is in a form of Gallifreyan script, which is not translated into English text. The Doctor signs his name over the Prydon Seal.

TIMELINE DATES

1962 +

As covered under THE DOCTOR'S AGE and GALLIFREY HISTORY, this adventure takes place in the Doctor's GRT, which is now 1962.

10,000,000 BC

The Doctor (in the voice-over narration at the beginning of the story) says 'through the millennia, the Time Lords of Gallifrey led a life of ordered calm'. As given in 'The Trial Of Time Lord' the Time Lords have existed for 'ten million years', so this would be the date of the capture of the Eye of Harmony (see GALLIFREY HISTORY).

DURATION

(TARDIS) (Ep1)

The Doctor travels alone in the TARDIS for a while before arriving on Gallifrey ...

⇨ Day One (Ep1-4)

The story takes place over one day, starting in the equivalent of late afternoon. In Ep2, Spandrell says there have been 'four cold-blooded killings in one day', the first being a guard soon after the Doctor's arrival. Spandrell requests the Panopticon to be opened late that night ('at this hour?') The Doctor is within the Matrix for 'over four minutes'.

Later Borusa wants the Doctor to leave 'Gallifrey tonight'. Presumably it is later that same night that he does.

UNSEEN ADVENTURES

At some point between 'The Masque Of Mandragora' and 'City Of Death' the fourth Doctor meets Leonardo da Vinci in 1503 when the Mona Lisa is being painted ('City Of Death').

THE FACE OF EVIL

STORY LINK

There is nothing to indicate that the Doctor has just left Gallifrey. At the end of 'The Deadly Assassin' he is wearing his floppy white shirt, having left the rest of his usual costume – his long coat, vest and scarf – in the Panopticon museum. In 'The Face Of Evil' he is wearing a new coat, hat and scarf. Given that he is 749 years old in 'The Seeds Of Doom' and is 750 in 'The Robots Of Death', no more than one year has elapsed since 'The Deadly Assassin' (it is now GRT 1963).

He is bound for Hyde Park when he lands on Leela's planet, so there is sufficient room for several adventures to take place between 'The Deadly Assassin' and 'The Face Of Evil'. He has placed a knot in his handkerchief.

OBSERVATIONS

- The barrier between the jungle and 'the place of land' is a time barrier using displacement, pushing everything on one side a few seconds into the future. No doubt this is Xoanon's achievement taken from the Doctor's mind because as covered in 'The Ark', humans never develop time travel.

LANGUAGE

All the text and numerals on the relics in the Sevateem village and on the spaceship are in English. Xoanon has its own emerging personality that was presumably based on English. The Doctor probably gave it half a Gallifreyan consciousness.

TIMELINE DATES

6000 ✦
When Jabel meets the Doctor, he says 'I do you honour, Lord of Time. We've waited a long time for your return'. It is hard to establish how long it would have taken the Survey Team to de-evolve into the savage Sevateem. The crew of the *Hydrax* in 'State Of Decay' regressed from scientists and explorers into farmers and peasants over a period of a thousand years, so the same could be applied to the Mordee descendants. The relics in the Sevateem village are all in good condition and some of the equipment, such as the bio-analyser, still works, so it is reasonable to deduce that no more than a thousand years has passed. As covered below, the Mordee Expedition probably left Earth around the time of the Great Break Out in 5000, which sets 'The Face Of Evil' around 6000.

1307, November ✦
The legend of William Tell places his time to be between the twelfth and early fourteenth centuries; some accounts of his deeds even narrow the date down to November 1307, although there is no evidence that he even existed!

4900
The Doctor says 'for generations teams of technicians had worked on the computer trying to extend its power'. By the time the computer was installed on the Mordee Expedition ship it had evolved into a new life form. It was 'born' soon after the ship 'was stranded' on the planet, which was when the Doctor arrived. There is no specific time given, so I would say the work on the computer began about one hundred years prior to the ship's launch. This means that the computer was not built specifically for the Mordee spaceship. Rather, it was a standard flight computer designed for use in other ships.

5000 ✦
In 'The Invisible Enemy', the Doctor says the time of Leela's ancestors was 'about 5000 AD'. This was probably when the Mordee Expedition set out, presumably from Earth (is Mordee the name of the ship or the destination planet, or perhaps the name of the ship's captain?) Given that 5000 was the time of Leela's ancestors, we can assume they left Earth because of the solar flares (see 'The Ark In Space').

Considering that the idol on the mountain has a scarf, the Doctor's earlier encounter with Xoanon can't have been in the period [as suggested in the novelisation] when the Doctor is still recovering from his post-regenerative coma during 'Robot', because the Doctor doesn't begin wearing his scarf until after he has fully recovered and changed out of his hospital gown. There is no actual point during 'Robot' in which the Doctor could have slipped away in the TARDIS. Also, in 'The Face Of Evil', the Sevateem are aware that the Evil One 'eats babies' i.e. jelly babies. In 'Robot', the Doctor produces his (first on-screen) bag of the sweets in the last scene in an attempt to cheer up Sarah. Indeed, the way he produces the sweets from his pocket even suggests he had just bought them for her as a peace offering.

In 'The Face Of Evil' the Doctor does not immediately recognise where he is, so it is clearly a long time ago from his perspective. The best position is during the 100-year gap between 'Planet Of Evil' and 'Pyramids Of Mars', when the Doctor travels without Sarah (see THE UNIT YEARS and THE DOCTOR'S AGE).

DURATION

⇨ **Day One (Ep1)**
Days and nights appear to be short on this planet: it is night when Leela is banished. She has 'until sunrise' to reach the boundary ...

⇨ **Day Two (Ep1-2)**
Leela meets the Doctor near dawn. The Doctor is taken to the village as night falls again ('Good evening. I think you're going to be very happy I came here tonight').

⇨ **Day Three (Ep2-4)**
It is dawn when Leela rescues the Doctor and shows him the idol on the mountain. He and Leela reach the spaceship later that day. The Doctor is knocked unconscious ...

⇨ **Day Four (Ep4)**
The Doctor is unconscious during the fourth day ...

⇨ **Day Five (Ep4)**
The Doctor wakes after being unconscious for 'two days'. He and Leela leave later that day.

THE ROBOTS OF DEATH

+STORY LINK

'The Face Of Evil' and 'The Robots Of Death' are clearly consecutive; Leela is unfamiliar with the TARDIS, and she still has the gun she has when she enters the TARDIS at the end of 'The Face Of Evil'. The Doctor has now 'lived 750 years' (see THE DOCTOR'S AGE).

OBSERVATIONS

- The Doctor demonstrates to Leela how the TARDIS is bigger on the inside than it is on the outside by using two differently-sized boxes. He says the 'insides and outsides are not in the same dimension'. This is 'trans-dimensional engineering. The key Time Lord discovery'. Leela thinks this is 'silly'. Indeed, the demonstration that the Doctor gives Leela has more to do with the nature of optics than spatial mechanics.

LANGUAGE

The text on the scanners in the Storm Mine is in English, as is the panel holding the Laserson probes. The labels on the robots use Earth letters and numerals: D84, SV7, V3. The Doctor and Leela converse with the robots – but does the Time Lord 'gift' work on automatons?

TIMELINE DATES

2777 •

In order to date 'The Robots Of Death', it needs to be determined whether or not the Storm Mine 4 crew are of Earth descent. The Doctor refers to this as a 'robot-dependent civilisation', not colony, which is quite a difference in terms of definition. Chubb is 'from one of the founding families ... One of the twenty', which could at least mean that the crew are descended from a colony, but not necessarily one from Earth.

The pointers to this being an Earth colony are: the crew play chess; the mix of races and accents; the crew and the robots use the term 'human'. However, aliens with different races and accents are seen in other stories such as 'Planet Of Evil', 'The Deadly Assassin', 'Meglos' and 'Mindwarp'. Also, the term 'human' is used more often than not to describe 'humanoids' as opposed to someone who is from Earth (see THE N-SPACE UNIVERSE).

The pointers that indicate that this is not an Earth colony are: Dask is unfamiliar with the Doctor's allusion to the sinking of the *Titanic*; Uvanov does not know who Marie Antoinette was; Poul does not know what bumblebees are; the crew have odd names (in the majority of stories which feature an Earth colony, the characters still have modern Earth names). Granted, one of the reasons why they do not know the historical references could be put down to the fact that both events happened centuries ago relative to this future period.

Another clue against this being an Earth colony is the robot technology. In no other story set in Earth's future have we seen a level of development where robots can think and operate independently of human operators. Only the K1 robot (in 'Robot') possesses comparative independent control. The pre-programmed robots of Dracula and Frankenstein's monster from 1996 (in 'The Chase') are primitive by comparison, while the robots seen in 'The Chase', 'The Wheel In Space', 'Colony In Space', and 'Paradise Towers' are cumbersome service robots, possessing little or no independent control. The Kandy Man ('The Happiness Patrol'), in 2788, and Bellboy's robot clowns ('The Greatest Show In The Galaxy'), in 3000, are really the only true examples of advanced human robot technology. In 'Terror Of The Vervoids', set in 2986, it is said that the scientists bred the Vervoids in order to replace the robots working in factories and on farms on Earth, but we can only guess at the level of robot technology that exists in that time period. (Since the Vervoids are humanoid creatures we could assume that the robots are also humanoid.) Finally, there are life-like androids and robots in 'The Caves Of Androzani', set in 3983; so if the Storm Mine 4 crew are humans, we could set 'The Robots Of Death' relative to any one of those dates.

One of the Dalek prisoners in 'Destiny Of The Daleks' is wearing a uniform similar to those worn by the Storm Mine 4 crew, so 'The Robots Of Death' could be set relative to 'Destiny Of The Daleks', in 4500.

Given the uncertainty, 'The Robots Of Death' should be set in ????, however I will work on the assumption that the crew are of Earth descent, and on the basis that the Storm Mine 4 robots are comparable only to the Kandy Man in terms of their being able to speak and operate independently, I have used the Century Factor to set 'The Robots Of Death' relative to 'The Happiness Patrol', in 2777.

Poul tells Leela the Storm Mine has been 'out from base eight months now'. It is on a 'two year tour'.

1793, October 16 ◆

The date in our history on which Marie Antoinette was executed (see also 'The Reign Of Terror' and 'Pyramids Of Mars').

2767

Zilda's brother was killed '10 years ago', during Uvanov's first command.

DURATION

(TARDIS) (Ep1)

The Doctor and Leela travel in the TARDIS before landing in Storm Mine 4.

⇨ **Day One (Ep1-4)** ▦ ▦ ▦ ▦ ▦ ▦ ▦ ▦ ▦ ▦ ▦
The story takes place over several hours in Storm Mine 4.

THE TALONS OF WENG-CHIANG

STORY LINK

There is nothing to suggest that this serial follows directly on from 'The Robots Of Death'. The Doctor wants to educate Leela about her early ancestors by taking her to the theatre. It is clear from the fact that they are already wearing period clothing when the TARDIS lands that the Doctor had 'Victorian London' in mind. In fact, he was hoping to catch one of Little Titch's performances. This is the first time Leela has worn clothing other than her skins.

OBSERVATIONS

- Greel thinks the Doctor might be a 'Time Agent'. Greel is from the fifty-first century, and so has had dealings with the Time Agents in that time period. Captain Jack Harkness (introduced in 'The Empty Child') is an ex-Time Agent, now a freelance and a con-man.

LANGUAGE

The Doctor says he can 'speak Mandarin, Cantonese, all the dialects', and then proceeds to do so. The British policemen in the room at the time are unable to understand the conversation.

TIMELINE DATES

1892, February ▸ ▦ ▦ ▦ ▦ ▦ ▦ ▦ ▦ ▦ ▦ ▦
The Doctor says it is 'Victorian London' and Greel refers to it being the 'nineteenth century', so it is before Queen Victoria's death in 1901. Jago mentions 'the Electric Lighting Company', so this is after Edison developed the electric light bulb around 1887. Casey mentions 'Jolly Jack … The Ripper', who terrorised London in 1888 in our history (see below); the Doctor mentions 'Little Titch', who lived from 1868 to 1928 in our history, giving a vague spread of some 13 years from 1887 to 1900 within which to set 'The Talons Of Weng-Chiang'.

Litefoot can be see reading the 'FEBRUARY MDCCCXCII' (i.e. February 1892) edition of Blackwood's Edinburgh Magazine. It is apparently still winter because

'Litefoot lights a good fire' and always has one blazing in his dining room hearth. Therefore February 1892 appears to be the current year and month.

We can confirm the year by examining Litefoot's past: his father went to China in '1860' and Litefoot himself 'was brought up in China'. That means either he was born there or he was very young at the time, say no older than 10. That makes his birth year no earlier than 1850. The Litefoots brought the Time Cabinet to England when they 'came home in 'seventy three', being 1873. Litefoot would have been about 23 by then and would be of a suitable age to have then gone on to medical school. In 'The Talons Of Weng-Chiang' I would say Litefoot was about 45, certainly no older than 50, making the year no later than 1895. I have selected the 1892 date on the magazine as the best date.

Jago tells the Doctor that auditions are 'on Saturday ... at ten o'clock'; therefore, 'The Talons Of Weng-Chiang' takes place over three weekdays (see Duration).

Emma Buller disappeared at the theatre 'last night'. She was first hypnotised by Chang 'last week'.

c730 ◆

Famous historian and theologian, the Venerable Bede, was born in 673 and died 25 May 735, so 730 is a likely year for when the Doctor met him.

1415, October 25 ◆

This is the date on which the Agincourt battle was fought in our history. The Doctor must have been there to know that Leela would enjoy it (see also 'The Masque Of Mandragora'). Of note, the Doctor was also at another famous battle on the same day but different year: on 25 October 1854, the Doctor witnessed the Charge of the Light Brigade ('The Evil Of The Daleks').

1492 ◆

The Doctor can't remember where he has seen Chang's face before (it was actually on the poster at the music hall) and thinks he may have met Chang in China, but then goes on to say, 'No, I haven't been in China for four hundred years'. In this context the Doctor is referring to the fact he cannot have met Chang during his last visit to China, which was in 1492 (being 400 years before 1892) and not when he was 400 years younger (which, given that he was 750 in the previous story, would have been when he was 350). The Doctor has been to China twice before: in 'Marco Polo', which was set in 1289, and in 'The Mind Of Evil' the third Doctor mentions having met Mao Zedong (Tse-Tung). The visit to 1492 is therefore a reference to an untelevised adventure. (See 1892 below.)

1842
Litefoot's gun hasn't 'been fired for 50 years'.

1860
Litefoot gives the year of the expedition.

1865
Jago has spent 'thirty years in the halls'.

1870
1873
The Litefoots were given the Cabinet by the Chinese Emperor before they returned to England in "seventy three' (1873). Chang says Greel 'came like a god ... I saw him, and helped him ... He was ill for many months'. They have been searching for the Time Cabinet 'ever since'. He has served Weng-Chiang 'for many years'. Presumably Greel arrived in China a few years before the Litefoots returned to London, so we can say around 1870. Therefore, Chang and Greel have been searching for the Cabinet for just on 25 years.

1888, August 31
1888, September 8
1888, September 30
1888, November 9
These are the recorded dates of five of the murders attributed to 'Jolly Jack' – otherwise known as Jack the Ripper. (He killed two women on 30 September.) An earlier murder on 7 August 1888 is believed to have been Jack's first victim, although there is still some doubt as to who was responsible.

1891, August
The Bullers were married 'six months ago'.

1891, October
We are told by Chang that the House Of The Dragon was 'prepared over many months' for Greel, which at least gives us an indication as to how long the Tong has been in London, say five months, which is June.

1892+
The Doctor knows of the Tong of the Black Scorpion (no doubt in their native China;

he is surprised to see them in London), as well as the legends of Weng-Chiang, so he has been in China at the time they existed (see also 1492 above). This contradicts his earlier comment that he hasn't been in China for 400 years.

5000 *
5001 ▨ ▨ ▨ ▨ ▨ ▨ ▨ ▨ ▨ ▨ ▨ ▨ ▨ ▨

The Doctor says that Greel is from 'the Ice Age, about the year five thousand', while Greel himself says he is from 'the fifty-first' century. Strictly speaking, the year 5000 is the final year of the fiftieth century, so the time that Greel comes from would be a few years after 5000. Given that the Earth was threatened by solar flares around the same period (see 'The Ark In Space' / 'The Sontaran Experiment'), we would have to accept that Greel left shortly before the solar flare crisis began, say in 5001. It could even be that he fled from his own time partly because of the solar flare threat to Earth. The Filipino army's attack on Reykjavik, in which the Doctor took part, therefore took place in 5000.

DURATION

⇨ **Day One (Ep1-3)** ▨ ▨ ▨ ▨ ▨ ▨ ▨ ▨ ▨ ▨ ▨ ▨
It is early evening when the TARDIS lands. The Doctor spends the night at Litefoot's house.

⇨ **Day Two (Ep3-6)** ▨ ▨ ▨ ▨ ▨ ▨ ▨ ▨ ▨ ▨ ▨ ▨
Leela arrives at the theatre as dawn breaks. When Chang abducts Teresa he greets her with 'Pleasant are the dreams of morning … ' The rest of the story takes place this day and into the night.

⇨ **Day Three (Ep6)** ▨ ▨ ▨ ▨ ▨ ▨ ▨ ▨ ▨ ▨ ▨ ▨
It is dawn when the muffin man is heard calling. The Doctor and Leela leave later this same morning.

HORROR OF FANG ROCK

STORY LINK

The Doctor reminds Leela that she saw boats 'on the Thames' which is a direct reference to 'The Talons Of Weng-Chiang', but there is nothing else that directly indicates that

'The Talons Of Weng-Chiang' and 'Horror Of Fang Rock' are actually consecutive. Beginning with this story the Doctor wears his new 20 foot-long scarf.

SONTARAN LINK

This is the second of the series of stories in the Rutan / Sontaran war saga. Further to what we learn about the Rutan / Sontaran war in 'The Time Warrior', the Rutans now consider Earth to be of strategic importance, something it wasn't back in 1274 when it was dismissed by Linx as being of no military value. Therefore it is clear that by 1902 the war has advanced to Earth's sector of the galaxy (the Doctor knows the Rutans 'used to control the whole of the Mutter's Spiral once'), making Earth attractive as a staging ground. Earth will once again become of strategic importance in 1984 (see 'The Two Doctors'). The Rutans are from Ruta Three, 'an icy planet'.

OBSERVATIONS

- The Doctor is interrupted before he can continue with his story about lighthouses on Gallifrey. From this we might assume that Gallifrey has oceans. Indeed, Morbius ('The Brain Of Morbius') refers to his imprisonment as being like 'a sponge beneath the sea', so it appears that he is at least familiar with some of the marine life on Gallifrey, unless he is referring to an off-world encounter with a sponge.

LANGUAGE

Everyone speaks English, including the Rutan, however it probably inherited this ability when it duplicated Reuben's body.

TIMELINE DATES

1902, January? ✦

Vince mentions 'King Edward'. Given that electricity is fairly new, this must be King Edward VII, who reigned from 22 January 1901 to 6 May 1910.

A line of dialogue spoken softly by Skinsale in Ep3 actually provides a very accurate marker for dating this story. He says 'Some men make me nervous when I'm with them. Salisbury. Bonar Law ...'. Lord Robert, the Marques of Salisbury, who died on 22 August 1903 in our history, was Prime Minister of Britain from 25 June 1895, and retired from that office on 11 July 1902. Andrew Bonar Law entered Parliament in 1900, and became Parliamentary Secretary to the Board of Trade in 1902. Since Skinsale refers to being with both men in the present tense, they must be current Members of Parliament. Therefore, 'Horror Of Fang Rock' can't be set any later than July 1902. Given the weather conditions, winter 1902 would be the best date, say January?

It is probably a Sunday: Lord Palmerdale is anxious to get back to London 'before the 'change opens', i.e. the Stock Exchange.

Vince is on a 'three month' tour.

280 BC ▸

This is the most recent estimated date in our history for the erection of the Pharos tower. Previously it had been thought to have been built around 48 BC, but more modern evidence has provided the earlier date.

1822

The beast was last sighted 'back in the 'twenties' – see above.

1861

The Doctor says 'The Malicious Damage Act 1861 covers lighthouses'.

1872

Reuben has 'been thirty year' in the lighthouse service. He once 'served twenty year' in an oil-powered lighthouse.

DURATION

⇨ **Day One (Ep1-3)**

The story takes place over one night. The Rutan crashes when it is 'just getting dusk'. The TARDIS lands 'a couple of hours' later. Reuben is killed at the end of Ep2. His body is found at the end of Ep3: 'He's been dead for hours'.

⇨ **Day Two (Ep3-4)**

The clock above the door in the crew room appears to read 3.15 in Ep3, so it is early in the morning when the TARDIS leaves.

THE INVISIBLE ENEMY

STORY LINK

There is nothing to suggest that 'The Invisible Enemy' follows directly on from 'Horror Of Fang Rock'; however, the Doctor reminds Leela of their visit to London (in 'The

Talons Of Weng-Chiang') as if that were a recent event. The Doctor tells Leela 'we're still in the time of your ancestors', i.e. the people of the Mordee Expedition (as seen in 'The Face Of Evil'). Give that the previous television story is set in 1902, the fact that the Doctor uses the word 'still' suggests that their actual previous (but untelevised) adventure was also around 5000 AD.

The Doctor returns to the newly-modified 'number two control room' for the first time since he stopped using it at the beginning of 'The Masque Of Mandragora', the room having been 'closed for redecoration'. The time rotor is rising and falling when they enter, so it would appear that the Doctor has already been to the control room, and activated the console (unless all consoles within the TARDIS move in unison during flight).

As noted under THE DOCTOR'S AGE, only a matter of months (as opposed to years) has passed between 'The Masque Of Mandragora' and 'The Invisible Enemy'. Given that the Doctor is 749 in 'The Seeds Of Doom' and is 750 in 'The Robots Of Death', he must have had his 'birthday' at some point during this period, but certainly a whole year has not passed between 'The Masque Of Mandragora' and 'The Invisible Enemy'.

It appears that the Doctor has been teaching Leela how to read and write (she is left-handed) (see Language below).

OBSERVATIONS

- K9 is a product of late fiftieth century technology with a memory covering at least the last 5000 years: he knows everything that Professor Marius does 'and more'. Given that the Doctor's GRT at the time of 'The Invisible Enemy' is 1963, he now has at his disposal another vast storehouse containing information and knowledge about the future!
- The Doctor tells Leela (or to be more accurate the clone of the Doctor tells the clone of Leela) that his connection to the Time Lord Intelligentsia was lost when he was kicked out. He notes that the reflex link connects 'a thousand super brains in one'. This suggests that there are only (and can only ever be) one thousand Time Lords living on Gallifrey (this idea is covered in more detail under GALLIFREY HISTORY). This implies that once a Time Lord dies, a new candidate is selected from the new graduates from the Academies. The fact that Runcible ('The Deadly Assassin'), and Rodan and Andred ('The Invasion of Time') are not Time Lords but all went to one of the Academies supports this view. This could also make sense of the fact that the Doctor was considered such a disappointment to his teachers (as mentioned in 'The Deadly Assassin', 'The Invasion Of Time' and 'The Ribos Operation'); he was

not true Time Lord material, but he was only selected to fill the required numbers.

The virus of the Nucleus of the Swarm speaks English ('Contact has been made'), but this is probably only due to the virus being attached to its victim's brain. However the Doctor also says it when he is infected. The signs at the Bi-Al Foundation are in a form of literal writing; for example: EMERGENCEE EGSIT, SHUTLE AIRLOK, KRYOGENICS SEXSHUN, ISOLAYSHUN WARD. The Doctor has been teaching Leela how to write her name – but how does he know it was spelt 'Leela', and not 'Lela', 'Leila' or 'Leala'? She can't have told him. (Perhaps he just came up with the simplest spelling …)

TIMELINE DATES

5000 ⁕

The Doctor tells Leela the year is 'about 5000 AD … 5000 AD! We're still in the time of your ancestors … That was the year of the Great Break Out … When your forefathers went leap-frogging across the solar system on their way to the stars. Asteroid belt's probably teaming with them now. New frontiersmen, pioneers, waiting to spread across the galaxy like a tidal wave – or a disease'. The fact that the Doctor says 'about 5000' could mean that 'The Invisible Enemy' is probably set a year or so before 5000 (not after because of the solar flares – see below), however I have taken 5000 to be the year.

The Doctor's description of the Great Break Out is inconsistent with many other stories where it is clear that Mankind has already colonised most of the galaxy by the thirtieth century (see 'The Mutants'). In fact, 'The Invisible Enemy' could quite comfortably be placed circa 2106 when warp-drive is discovered (see 'Nightmare Of Eden').

Given that there are four significant – but unrelated – historical events all happening 'around the year five thousand', it is necessary to place them into a logical sequence: the Solar Flare crisis ('The Ark In Space') needs to be placed last in sequence – the mass evacuation of Earth means that the others must occur earlier. The Great Break Out is logically the abandonment of Earth due to the solar flares, more so than the evacuation of the planet due to the threat of the second Ice Age ('The Ice Warriors') or World War Six ('The Talons Of Weng-Chiang'). Of note, the collars of the uniforms worn by the hospital staff at the Foundation are similar to those as worn by the Brittanicus Base personnel in 'The Ice Warriors', which suggests the two stories are set in the same period.

The Doctor is familiar with the Great Break Out, and he knows the co-ordinates for the Bi-Al Foundation, so he has been to this time period before (as in 'The Ice Warriors'?, see also 'The Talons Of Weng-Chiang').

2000

The Nucleus says 'for millennia we have hung dormant in space' waiting for a host, say 3000 years.

3922

K9 mentions that cloning experiments took place in this year.

4992

Meeker says 'I qualified for exploration eight years ago'.

DURATION

(TARDIS) (Ep1)

The Doctor and Leela explore the TARDIS before it arrives in 5000 AD ...

⇨ Day One (Ep1-4)

It takes 'half an hour' for the SOS from Titan to reach the TARDIS. When Marius analyses the Doctor he says it is 'night', and then wishes the Doctor a 'Good evening'. The clones survive for about 'ten minutes fifty five seconds' (the real-time Duration of Ep3 is therefore only about 12 minutes). The TARDIS leaves with K9 a matter of hours later.

IMAGE OF THE FENDAHL

STORY LINK

The Doctor is examining K9's inner workings. K9 is in perfect working order at the end of 'The Invisible Enemy'. It is possible that an untelevised adventure takes place between 'The Invisible Enemy' and 'Image Of The Fendahl' in which K9 is damaged and gets a touch of corrosion. Leela has had her hair cut shorter.

OBSERVATIONS

- It is stated that Dr Fendelman was 'one of the richest men in the world', and a leader in electronics. But what of Tobias Vaughn and International Electromatics, which had the monopoly during the late 1960s? (see 'The Invasion')? It is possible that Fendelman once worked for IE, and on Vaughn's death (in 1970) took over. Alternatively, he was one of Vaughn's rivals. His European accent suggests that his business empire was not in England. His work on missile guidance systems 'about ten years ago' suggests that he was previously involved in his country's defence during the latter years of the Cold War (see 'Invasion Of The Dinosaurs' and 'Robot').

- Before leaving for the fifth planet the Doctor promises to return by sundown of the next day, some 20 hours later. He must have known that the round journey to and from 12 million years would take at least 20 hours in terms of the Blinovitch Limitation Effect. The TARDIS makes similar trips in time in 'Inside The Spaceship', 'The Ark', 'Castrovalva', and 'Frontios', so it is clear that to travel back millions of years takes a long time even in a TARDIS.

TIMELINE DATES

1978, July 29 – 31 ⁎
On Day Three Granny Tyler says 'It's Lammas Eve', which is July 31. On the morning of Day Two, when Adam Colby finds the hiker's body, church bells can be heard ringing. This suggests that it is a Sunday. July 30 is a Sunday in 1972, 1978 and 1989. 'Image Of The Fendahl' can't be set earlier than 1973 because the hiker is whistling 'The Entertainer', the theme tune from the film, *The Sting*, which was released in 1973. Given the hair lengths and clothing fashions, 1978 is preferable over 1989.

12,000,000 BC ⁎
The volcanic sediment in which the skull was found 'is 12 million years old'. 12 million is also the same number of years since the fifth planet broke up according to Time Lord legends. This shows that a Gallifreyan year and an Earth year can be close equivalents (see GALLIFREY HISTORY).

The Fendahl is a creature from Time Lord mythology. As discussed under GALLIFREY HISTORY, the early Time Lords from after 10 million BC probably travelled to the fifth planet two million years in their own past. The Doctor theorises that the Fendahl affected Man's evolution, which has also been accredited to the Dæmons ('The Dæmons') and Scaroth ('City Of Death'). In terms of chronological proportions, Scaroth's splinters are responsible for later influences, as are the Dæmons, while the Fendahl is responsible for the initial evolutionary triggers.

The Doctor theorises that the Fendahl went past Mars on its way to Earth. Although he doesn't actually state it, the implication is that the Fendahl was responsible for destroying life on the planet. Given that the 'Ice Warriors' evolved on Mars, the Doctor is either wrong or the damage caused by the Fendahl was only minor.

4,000,000 BC
According to Colby, the skull got buried 'at least eight million years before he could have possibly existed', which, if the skull is 12 million years old, places the birth of 'Mankind' to be around 4 million BC. In 'The Ark In Space' the Doctor says that 'it's only a few million years since [Man] crawled up out of the mud and learned to walk'.

1968
Fendelman says it was 'about ten years ago' that he first got the impulse to build the Time Scanner.

1978, July 9
The read-out on the Time Scanner shows '98:56:43.7' on Day Two. Fendelman and Stael work with the Scanner for all of the first night, say eight hours. If we assume that the scanner has been running for similar periods, in order for 100 hours to have been recorded, the Scanner must have first been used about twenty days earlier, on 9 July. The skull was found as a result of the Scanner tests, so the scientists have been at the priory for less than a month. Indeed, Granny Tyler says the basement hasn't been used 'for years'.

DURATION

(TARDIS) (Ep1)
The Doctor and Leela spend some time in the TARDIS; the Doctor works on K9.

⇨ **Day One (29 July) (Ep1)**
The hiker is killed while Fendelman and Stael work 'all night'.

⇨ **Day Two (30 July) (Ep1-3)**
Thea has breakfast. The security guards are due to arrive 'in two hours'. The Doctor does wish the cows a 'Good morning', but given that it is dark when he and Leela arrive at the priory, which is only one mile away, it is more likely to be late afternoon. The Doctor promises the Tylers he will be 'back tomorrow sundown'. Adam Corby

and Dr Fendelman spend all night, and all of the next day tied up in the basement.

⇨ **Day Three (31 July)** ▨ ▨ ▨ ▨ ▨ ▨ ▨ ▨ ▨ ▨
The coven members arrive during the day. The TARDIS returns after sundown. The priory burns down that night.

(TARDIS) (Ep4) ▨ ▨ ▨ ▨ ▨ ▨ ▨ ▨ ▨ ▨ ▨
The TARDIS takes about 20 hours to travel to and from the fifth planet.

THE SUN MAKERS

STORY LINK

At the end of 'Image Of The Fendahl' Leela changes into her old brown skins ('this is the old one'), which she is still wearing at the beginning of 'The Sun Makers'. When the TARDIS lands on Pluto the Doctor says 'We're still in the solar system', which suggests that 'The Sun Makers' directly follows on from 'Image Of The Fendahl'. However the Doctor was intending to drop the Fendahl skull into a supernova located in the distant constellation of Canthares. It is possible that between 'Image Of The Fendahl' and 'The Sun Makers' the Doctor has been to Canthares and disposed of the skull, and that the TARDIS has since returned to Earth's solar system for a series of untelevised adventures. Alternatively, the TARDIS stops on Pluto *en route* to Canthares. This would explain the Doctor's surprise that the TARDIS has landed, blaming it on 'that confounded paint' (in reference to the new console room in 'The Invisible Enemy'). If he still has the skull in 'The Sun Makers', the Doctor probably disposes of it before 'Underworld'. The Doctor and K9 play chess while the TARDIS passes through 'the time spiral'.

Given the reference to the new paint, which was applied when the console room was closed for redecoration between 'The Masque Of Mandragora' and 'The Invisible Enemy', this shows clearly that a relatively short period of time has passed for the Doctor and Leela between 'The Invisible Enemy' and 'The Sun Makers'. The Doctor is still only aged 750 (see 'The Robots Of Death' and THE DOCTOR'S AGE).

The Doctor and K9 have been playing chess, with Leela assisting K9 by moving his pieces for him. Since Leela makes the correct moves, e.g. 'Queen to Knight six', 'Bishop to Queen six', this demonstrates she has been taught some basics of the game.

OBSERVATIONS

- The Usurians have information on the Doctor and Gallifrey in their records. The Doctor 'has a long history of violence and of economic subversion'. With 'The Sun Makers' set in 25,000, either the Usurians are a long-lived race, or the Doctor has encountered them in this time period before. The fact that the Usurians have recently undertaken a 'market survey' on Gallifrey shows that the Time Lords are still the oligarchic rulers of Gallifrey in the year 25,000. However, as noted under 'Bad Wolf', Gallifrey was destroyed by the Daleks during the Time War, around the year 2349 (see THE DOCTOR'S AGE). So how is it possible for the planet to be surveyed by the Usurians recently by 25,000? It is possible the Time War itself created a paradox in that although Gallifrey was destroyed in 2349, from between 4663 and 5000, the destruction of the planet hadn't happened yet. Refer to Observations under 'Bad Wolf' for more on this concept.

LANGUAGE

The Collector's computer ascertains correctly that the word 'Sevateem' is a 'linguistic corruption' (of Survey Team). This indicates that translation of the words in the Collector's language is the same as in English. There are, however, alien symbols on the keyboard on the Collector's desk.

TIMELINE DATES

25,000 ▸

On discovering that Pluto has an atmosphere, the Doctor says 'It's all wrong. It shouldn't be like Earth. Unless, of course, the Sun's turned nova', which clearly means that he has never been in this time zone before.

Around 5001 Earth is abandoned because of the solar flare crisis (see 'The Ark In Space'). The planet is colonised again around 15,000 (after 'The Sontaran Experiment'). 'The Sun Makers' needs to be set at a reasonable point after the events of 'The Sontaran Experiment' and probably before 'The Mysterious Planet', when Earth is again nearly destroyed, this time by a fireball (caused by the Time Lords), or perhaps even set after the events of 'The Mysterious Planet', but certainly before Earth plunges into the sun in 'The Ark'.

Gatherer Hade refers on several occasions to 'old Earth'. The Collector says 'Earth was running down, its people dying. We made a deal ... Yes. We moved them all to Mars ... Then, when the resources of Mars were exhausted in their turn, we created a new environment for them here on Pluto'. Coincidentally, in 'The Sontaran

Experiment' Vural says 'Earth's been junked … It's worn out, useless, and too far from the freight routes', which almost matches the Collector's description. However, Styre says 'there has been no intelligent life on this planet since the time of the solar flares', so it is unlikely that the humans that are moved from Earth to Mars are colonists who returned to Earth once it had become viable again between 10,000 and 15,000 while the Nerva sleepers were still in suspension.

The 'running down' of Earth could even have been a result of the poison from 'half a million years of industrial progress', as mentioned by the Doctor in 'The Curse Of Fenric'.

I prefer to assume that Earth is colonised again by the Nerva sleepers following the events of 'The Ark In Space' and 'The Sontaran Experiment'. In 'The Ark In Space' it is stated that it would take 5000 years for Earth to become habitable again. We can assume that the Nerva colonists rebuild the planet over the subsequent centuries, the planet eventually becoming exhausted again, say 5000 years later (in the year 20,000). Mars is a smaller planet so it probably didn't take as long to use that planet's resources, say 3000 years, making it 23,000 when Humanity is moved to Pluto.

The Doctor reckons 'it must have taken them centuries to build a city like that'. There are six Megropolises on Pluto, so it probably took 1500 years to build all six. Gatherer Hade says 'many people nowadays are not even aware that our species originated on old Earth' because it isn't taught in the schools. We need to take this loss of identity into account, setting 'The Sun Makers' say 2000 years after Pluto was colonised, making the time of the Doctor's visit around 25,000.

The Doctor later says 'the Earth will have regenerated itself since you left', some 10,000 years earlier. We learn that Kandor served 'three years' in the correction centre, but we don't know when this was.

2106

The solar system is fully explored by the early twenty-first century (see 'The Wheel In Space'). Warp-drive is discovered in 2106 (see 'Nightmare Of Eden'), so it is likely that Cassius is discovered around this time.

20,000
23,000

See 25,000 above.

24,960

Cordo's father was 'a municipal servant for 40 years'.

24,995 ▪ ▪ ▪ ▪ ▪ ▪ ▪ ▪ ▪ ▪ ▪ ▪ ▪ ▪
Cordo says 'it has taken me years to save' the taxes used for his father's funeral, say five.

DURATION

It should be noted that, while it takes Pluto some 250 Earth years to orbit the sun, the colonists still use 'years' and 'hours' in terms of old Earth time scales. The Gatherer even has a 'monthly budget', and there hasn't been a public steaming 'for months'; Pluto doesn't have any natural moons, so a month must be based on the old Earth calendar.

(TARDIS) (Ep1) ▪ ▪ ▪ ▪ ▪ ▪ ▪ ▪ ▪ ▪ ▪ ▪ ▪
The Doctor and K9 have been playing chess …

⇨ Day One (Ep1-4) ▪ ▪ ▪ ▪ ▪ ▪ ▪ ▪ ▪ ▪ ▪ ▪
There is no night on Pluto because of the six suns. Cordo's father 'ceased at one ten' (1.10 pm?). The TARDIS lands 'hours' later. The Doctor is unconscious in the rehab centre for 'about an hour'. The Others eat a meal during Ep2. The rest of the story takes place over several more hours during the same day.

UNDERWORLD

STORY LINK

There is nothing to suggest that 'Underworld' takes place immediately after 'The Sun Makers'. Leela is wearing a different costume to the one she had on in 'The Sun Makers'. The Doctor is painting something in the inner room – perhaps the outer casing of the new K9 Mark Two? (If he is redecorating the inner room because of the recent redecoration of the console room (see 'The Invisible Enemy', 'The Sun Makers'), then only a short passage of time has passed for the Doctor and Leela since 'The Sun Makers'.) The TARDIS is travelling through space only, not in time, when it is pulled towards the spiral nebula, so it is possible that the Doctor has just has dropped the Fendahl skull in the Canthares constellation supernova as he said he would do at the end of 'Image Of The Fendahl', and has set the ship drifting in space while he paints.

OBSERVATIONS
• The Doctor says he has 'often wanted to know' who the Flying Dutchman was.

- In order to get inside the P7E, the Doctor uses the Trojan Horse-style subterfuge of sneaking into the ship inside mining carts: 'It's not my plan exactly but it has worked before. Fellow called Ulysses pulled it off a little while ago,' he says. The Doctor is very modest considering that it was actually his plan, as seen in 'The Myth Makers' (where Ulysses is called by his other name, Odysseus, in that tale). The fact that Leela knows who Ulysses is suggests that the Doctor has told her the story, or that she has met him; perhaps she and Doctor encounter the Greek during his famous exploits in a time after the Trojan War?

LANGUAGE

If the Time Lords gave the Minyans their technology it is more than likely they gave the Minyans their language as well, so it is possible that the Minyans speak Gallifreyan; but the deck panels on both ships are marked with Earth letters and numerals: YU1, GC3, ZY9, YC1, IC1, and so on. The R1C Minyans use 'miles'.

TIMELINE DATES

1963

The Doctor says 'perhaps those myths are not just old stories of the past, you see, but prophecies of the future'. If the legend of Jason and his quest for the Golden Fleece is directly linked to the Minyans in terms of what the Doctor means, then 'Underworld' could be set at a time after the Greek legend, about 2000 BC.

When examining the Minyan artefact K9 says the 'isotope decay indicates One Hundred K range'. The Doctor confirms 'that's a hundred thousand years old. The Minyan civilisation was destroyed a hundred thousand years ago, on the other side of the galaxy'. The crew of the R1C and the Seers on the P7E also state independently of the Doctor's comment the same time scale. From this it is clear that an Earth year, a Gallifreyan year and a Minyan year are the same length. Minyos was destroyed 100,000 years ago in terms of the Doctor's personal GRT history, so 'Underworld' must be set in the Doctor's present, being GRT 1963.

In the new planet 'there were two more births yesterday'.

98,037 BC

100,000 years before 1963 is 98,037 BC. In terms of the Time Lord history, the Time Lords encountered the Minyans when the Gallifreyans were 'still new to space / time exploration'. The Time Lords became lords of time 10,000,000 years ago (see 'The Trial Of Time Lord') so to influence the Minyans the Time Lords must have travelled forwards in time.

2333
The journey to Minyos II will take '370 years' which, from 1963, is 2333.

DURATION

(TARDIS) (Ep1)
The Doctor spends some time in the TARDIS painting …

⇨ **Day One (Ep1-4)**
The story takes place over several hours on the R1C and then inside the planet.

THE INVASION OF TIME

STORY LINK

The Doctor says he met the Vardans 'a long time ago'. But he may be instead referring to a much earlier encounter rather than his more recent contact with them. The Vardans don't possess time travel, so this previous encounter must have been within the same time zone (c1962). With 'The Invasion Of Time' set only a year after 'The Deadly Assassin' (see GALLIFREY LINK below), Leela has been travelling with the Doctor for less than a year.

The Doctor has had time to build the components for the new K9, something he must have done between adventures, probably beginning soon after 'Image Of The Fendahl' when he first detects corrosion in the original K9's circuits; he probably thought he could make a new one that is corrosion-proof.

GALLIFREY LINK

The Doctor is back on Gallifrey for the first time since 'The Deadly Assassin'. In terms of THE DOCTOR'S AGE, the Doctor is now 750, so no more than a year has passed since 'The Deadly Assassin'. The Citadel and the Panopticon have been completely rebuilt. Borusa has regenerated and has assumed the office of Chancellor following ratification of the position by 'the Supreme Council'. In 'The Deadly Assassin' it is stated that a new President had to be elected 'within 48 hours'. Clearly 'The Invasion Of Time' is set more than 48 hours after 'The Deadly Assassin'. At the Doctor's induction into the Presidency Gomer says 'normally it takes years to consider an induction, let alone assemble one', which supports the idea that the gap between 'The Deadly Assassin' and 'The Invasion Of Time' is fairly minimal. Other changes since 'The Deadly

Assassin' include Kelner being the new Castellan (Spandrell having died or retired), and Andred is the new Commander following the death of Hilred. Andred informs Kelner that 'only two Time Lords are absent from their duties here on authorised research missions'. Kelner obviously isn't aware of the Master, the Rani, the Monk, or the Doctor when he wonders 'who is in that capsule?' approaching Gallifrey.

In the same year that this story takes place, the Hand of Omega is sent back to Gallifrey (see 'Remembrance Of The Daleks'). Its journey from Earth to Gallifrey is either instantaneous or, given the distance between Earth and Gallifrey, it is possible that the Hand doesn't return for centuries …

SONTARAN LINK

This is the third in the stories about the Rutan / Sontaran war saga. Stor is a commander of the Sontaran Special Space Service. The Sontaran fleet flew in the standard arrowhead formation. Somehow they knew of the Great Key. The Sontarans already had (albeit limited) time travel capabilities back in 1274 ('The Time Warrior'). By invading Gallifrey they plan to attain mastery over all Time and swarm throughout 'all Universes'. By 1984 they will still be seeking this ability (see 'The Two Doctors'). The Sontarans used the Vardans to break down the barriers to invade Gallifrey.

OBSERVATIONS

- When the Doctor signs the Vardan contract his signature has a definite '?' shape. This symbol later becomes synonymous with the Doctor in this and in subsequent incarnations (in 'Remembrance Of The Daleks' the Doctor's calling card has a question mark on it).

LANGUAGE

All the Time Lords speak Gallifreyan (a form of written Gallifreyan appears as computer text in Ep1). Rodan is familiar with the French term 'déjà vu' and uses the Greek word 'Beta' as part of a code sign. Borusa can read an English newspaper. The Sontarans probably speak Gallifreyan with the aid of translators (see 'The Time Warrior'). The Vardans also converse with the Time Lords. The Sontarans obviously speak English, since the Doctor comments upon the alliterative nature of 'Sontaran Special Space Service'.

TIMELINE DATES

1963 ◆ ▨ ▨ ▨ ▨ ▨ ▨ ▨ ▨ ▨ ▨ ▨ ▨ ▨ ▨ ▨ ▨
'The Invasion Of Time' is set a year after 'The Deadly Assassin', in 1962. See also

GALLIFREY HISTORY and Gallifrey Link. (Coincidentally, the first Doctor and Susan are living on Earth in '100,000 BC' around this time.)

1900, May 17

The Doctor mentions the relief of Mafeking – see 'The Daleks Master Plan' (and 'The Unicorn And The Wasp').

1912, April 16*

In our history, the *Titanic* hit the iceberg around 11.40 pm on 14 April 1912, and some two hours later had sunk completely – by 2.20am on 15 April. Borusa is seen reading the *Daily Mirror* newspaper head-lining the tragedy. The date appears to be 'Tuesday April 16 1912'. Although the Doctor claims not to be responsible for the tragedy ('I had nothing to do with this, I promise you'), he was probably in that time zone to have obtained the paper. Given that the fourth Doctor mentions the sinking of the *Titanic* in 'Robot' (and 'The Robots Of Death') we can assume that his visit to 1912 was during his first, second or third incarnation. (The ninth Doctor was in Southampton on 9 April, the day before the ship was launched (see 'Rose'), and was on board it when it struck the iceberg – see Observations under 'The End Of The World' for a commentary on the *Titanic* in *Doctor Who*.)

DURATION

⇨ **Day One (Ep1-6)**

There are no night scenes, so the story appears takes place across one full day. In Ep3 the Doctor says 'Well, that's a good morning's work'. It is daylight when Leela and Rodan venture outside.

UNSEEN ADVENTURES

The fourth Doctor helps Theseus to find his way through the labyrinth (the young Athenian wanted to unravel the Doctor's scarf!) prior to 'The Creature From The Pit'. It was the fourth Doctor who visited Tigella and helped Zastor ('a long time ago') ('Meglos'). The fourth Doctor meets the Monitor ('Logopolis'). It is also the fourth Doctor who gets drunk with Azmael ('The Twin Dilemma'). The fourth Doctor delivers K9 Mark Three to Sarah Jane's flat in South Croydon in 1978 ('K9 And Company'). Presumably all these happen between 'The Invasion Of Time' and 'The Ribos Operation'.

THE RIBOS OPERATION

STORY LINK

The Doctor is aged '750' in 'The Robots Of Death'. In 'The Ribos Operation' he is '759' (we have no reason not to believe Romana's claim), so nine years have passed since 'The Robots Of Death', most of which elapses between 'The Invasion Of Time' and 'The Ribos Operation'. In the years since he left Gallifrey the Doctor has already built the new K9, and is testing out a new dog whistle in the opening moments of 'The Ribos Operation'. The Doctor's character has also undergone a complete change, from a darker brooding persona, to more of a clown. He also looks older physically; clearly spending nine years travelling with a computer-dog would drive anyone to that condition!

In 'K9 And Company', we learn that K9 Mark Three was delivered to Sarah's flat in South Croydon in 1978. The Doctor most likely did this during the gap between 'The Invasion Of Time' and 'The Ribos Operation'.

He tells K9 they are going on a holiday, so we can assume that they have just completed a tiring adventure. When the Guardian summons the Doctor, the TARDIS doors open and he steps out onto a rocky plateau. Since the TARDIS rotor hasn't been moving, we can assume that the TARDIS is still parked on the planet of the Doctor and K9's most recent adventure.

GALLIFREY LINK

In the nine years since the Doctor's visit to Gallifrey in 'The Invasion Of Time', a new President has been elected, probably Borusa, given that he is President when the Doctor returns to Gallifrey 11 years later in GRT 1983 (see 'Arc Of Infinity'). The Guardian, who sends Romana to the Doctor's TARDIS, impersonates the new President.

Since his last two visits to Gallifrey, the Doctor has become something of a known figure. Romana knows that Earth is his favourite planet ('How did you know that?' / 'Oh, everybody knows that!'), and she even says 'I was even willing to be impressed' to meet him. Romana knows of the Doctor by reputation and has either studied his academic record ('That information is confidential!' shouts the Doctor) or spoken with K9 and Leela about him. She plans to write her thesis about the Doctor when she gets back to Gallifrey, however in terms of the subsequent events in 'Warriors' Gate', she never does.

OBSERVATIONS

- Professor Marius' original K9 was a product of late fiftieth century technology (see 'The Invisible Enemy'). K9 Mark Two, on the other hand, seems to have an information databank that is a combination of the old K9's memory, the TARDIS computer, and the Doctor's own memory. The Doctor has recently manufactured a silent dog whistle for this new K9.

LANGUAGE

It is not clear if Unstoffe is from Earth or not, but he has mastered a variety of Earth accents. For Garron, the Graff and the Ribosians to communicate it is clear that they all speak the same language. The Graff Vynda K uses the phrase 'the dreams of avarice', which is a common saying on Earth.

THE GUARDIANS

Can the Guardians time travel? This is a question that bugs me whenever I view the Key To Time season or the Guardian trilogy in Season Twenty. Even after repeated viewing I am still unsure.

With names like 'the Guardian of Light and Time' and the 'Guardian of Darkness' one would expect that these two powerful beings are capable of time travel – what is the point of their purpose if they can't? – but in the six stories in which they appear or are heard there is actually no indication on-screen that they can time travel. (The Marshal of Atrios begs to the Shadow 'once you have the secrets of Time, please give me my victory'. Since the Shadow is an agent of the Black Guardian, then we can only assume that it is the Guardian who wants the 'secret of Time'.) And of course it depends on when one dates 'Terminus' and 'Enlightenment', but as seen under the entries for those two stories I have set them both in 1983.

And what of the Randomiser? This device (which uses 'a very complex scientific principle called pot luck') is installed into the TARDIS's navigational systems by the Doctor so the Black Guardian can't track him down. But in 'The Ribos Operation' the Doctor thinks Garron or the Graff might be agents of the Black Guardian. From this it is clear that the Doctor knows how the Guardians operate – by using others, i.e. Drax, Wrack, and the Doctor himself. If the Guardians simply rely on and use other time travellers for their purposes, why then would they need to time travel themselves? Therefore, I would conclude that the Randomiser is there to prevent not the Guardian from tracking the TARDIS, but one of his time-travelling agents.

True, the Guardians are immensely powerful. They have the ability to project their bodies across space; they can materialise someone into a green limbo ('Mawdryn Undead'); they can change their 'form or shape at will' (but why do they only ever appear as old men?); they can control, enter and appear on the scanner screen of a TARDIS (although as demonstrated in 'Enlightenment' even doing this drains much energy). But what exactly is their purpose? In 'The Ribos Operation' the Guardian tells the Doctor that the two Guardians maintain the balance of the Universe, but where do they come from? In 'Mawdryn Undead' the Black Guardian confesses to Turlough that he 'may not be seen to act in this. I must not be involved' – but seen by whom? The White Guardian perhaps? And then in 'Enlightenment', the White Guardian says they will both continue to exist 'until we are no longer needed' – but by whom? This suggests that there is yet a higher force that controls the Guardians. But can they time travel?

I think the answer to this has to be no. It is clear from the events at the end of 'The Armageddon Factor' and later in 'Mawdryn Undead' that the Black Guardian has a linear life stream. In support of this view is the fact that the Guardians need the Key To Time – although the Doctor says the Key is made from 'Guardian technology' there is the already noted fact that they only use other beings who do have the ability to travel in time to do their bidding; and the fact that it takes the Black Guardian 11 years to act on his revenge against the Doctor ('Doctor, you shall die for this'), when one would expect that he would just pop ahead in time to destroy the Doctor, further supports this view.

So, no, I do not believe that the Guardians can time travel. But they are probably both immortal, and certainly very long-lived. Therefore, the Randomiser (which is removed in 'The Leisure Hive'), probably only prevents the TARDIS from landing in the Doctor's GRT. This is why none of the subsequent adventures are set in a year that is that same as the Doctor's GRT. It is not until 1983 ('Mawdryn Undead') that the TARDIS lands in the Doctor's GRT again – which is also when the Guardian reappears …

TIMELINE DATES

1972 ◆ ■ ■ ■ ■ ■ ■ ■ ■ ■ ■ ■ ■ ■ ■
To me it is significant that the White Guardian never appears at the end of 'The Armageddon Factor' to collect the Key To Time. With this and after careful examination of the opening scene in 'The Ribos Operation', where the Doctor meets with the White Guardian, and the final scene with the Black Guardian in 'The Armageddon Factor', I have come to the conclusion that the Doctor's mission is false; it is the Black Guardian in disguise ('I can change my form or shape at will') who meets the Doctor in 'The Ribos Operation'. In other words, it is not the White Guardian who sends the Doctor to collect the Key To Time in order to prevent 'rapidly approaching' Universal chaos, but the Black Guardian who sends the Doctor to collect the Key To Time in order to cause 'rapidly approaching' Universal chaos. The meeting is simply a deception by the Black Guardian to obtain the Key so he can set 'the two halves of the entire cosmos at

THE RIBOS OPERATION

war'. My analyses of 'The Ribos Operation' and 'The Armageddon Factor' are therefore based on this viewpoint.

The opening moments of 'The Ribos Operation' are set on the rocky plateau where the Doctor receives his orders from the (Black) Guardian. The Guardian tells him 'there are times, Doctor, when the forces within the Universe upset the balance to such an extent that it becomes necessary to stop everything ... For a brief moment only ... Until the balance is restored. Such a moment is rapidly approaching. These segments must be traced and returned to me before it is too late. Before the Universe is plunged into eternal chaos'. Although this is a lie, in order to obtain the Doctor's confidence, the Guardian has to select his words carefully. As covered under GALLIFREY HISTORY, the Doctor can only encounter Time Lords from his own GRT. The same is most likely true of the Guardians.

On this basis, the meeting on the plateau must be in the Doctor's present GRT as well as the Guardian's equivalent present (Guardian Mean Time?). Therefore the 'bogus' approaching chaos has to be approaching the Doctor's own GRT for the deception to work, which was why this incarnation of the Doctor in this specific point in this time stream is selected for the mission. The Doctor is intelligent enough to know this. This is also stressed by the Guardian's carefully noted point that if the Doctor chooses not to take on the quest for the Key 'nothing' would happen to him, 'ever'. This clearly means that the supposed chaos is approaching the Doctor's relative current GRT – if the Doctor fails there won't be a GRT beyond this moment in time.

As covered under THE DOCTOR'S AGE, his GRT at this point in his time stream is 1972. As covered under my analysis of 'The Armageddon Factor', the Key itself apparently needs to be assembled in the very same time zone for which it is required, which is 1972.

Of course, I could be wrong, and the mission for the White Guardian could be *bona fide*; there is an 'approaching' chaos. If we accept that the being the Doctor encounters is the White Guardian, then what exactly is the Universal chaos? And what of the fact that the White Guardian never collects the assembled Key at the end of 'The Armageddon Factor'? Is the chaos in fact prevented? Perhaps not. Perhaps it was the entropy field that destroys much of the Universe in 1981. Although the Doctor appears to be the one who stops the entropy field in 'Logopolis', the White Guardian may be manipulating him from behind the scenes, using the Key's power while the Universe was stopped in 1972 to stop the entropy in 1981. Perhaps the white Watcher in 'Logopolis' is the White Guardian's agent: in the same way the White Guardian uses the Doctor to assemble the Key, the White Guardian is using a future projection of the Doctor to help the Doctor stop the Master (see Observations under 'Logopolis' for more on this idea).

3010 ▸ ▮ ▮ ▮ ▮ ▮ ▮ ▮ ▮ ▮ ▮ ▮ ▮ ▮

Ribos is clearly in Earth's future, because Garron has a vehicle capable of moving between Cyrhennis Minima and Ribos. Garron explains to Romana that Jethryk is 'only the rarest and most powerful element in the Universe. Without Jethryk-drive there'd be no space-warping and I'd still be safely at home on Earth'. The warp-drive that enables travel within Earth's galaxy is developed around 2106 (see 'Nightmare Of Eden'), but Jethryk-drive is a much more advanced power source, as even a small piece has enough energy to move ships 'across the Universe'. This sets 'The Ribos Operation' at a time after Mankind has reached the technological development of having intergalactic travel. In 'Terror Of The Vervoids' the *Hyperion III* is 'an intergalactic liner' in 2986. The Mogarians say that humans 'are going through the Universe like a plague of interplanetary locusts'. I offer that it is Humanity's discovery of the uses of Jethryk when exploring the planets within the Cyrhennic Alliance that puts in motion the steps towards Humanity's achieving intergalactic travel. In 'Planet Of The Spiders' the Metebelis Three colonists speak of 'time-jump', which is probably just another name for Jethryk-drive.

Ribos is situated beyond the Megallanic Clouds. Garron left Earth (after he tried to sell Sydney Harbour to an Arab) 'a long time ago. I was an ambitious boy in those days, taking my first steps in life'. Garron would be aged about 45 to 50, so we can assume that he left Earth a few years after intergalactic flight is discovered; having earned himself a reputation in Earth's galaxy, it was time to set his sights on other galaxies. Garron was probably about 20 when he left. This suggests that the events in 'The Ribos Operation' are therefore at least 30 years after humans developed intergalactic flight in 2980, say 3010.

1449 ▸ ▮ ▮ ▮ ▮ ▮ ▮ ▮ ▮ ▮ ▮ ▮ ▮ ▮

As noted under THE DOCTOR'S AGE and LIFE ON GALLIFREY / ACADEMY DAYS, the Doctor was 236 when he graduated and first piloted the TARDIS, in GRT 1449.

1833 ▮ ▮ ▮ ▮ ▮ ▮ ▮ ▮ ▮ ▮ ▮ ▮ ▮ ▮

Romana says 'I'm nearly 140, you know'. Given that the Doctor is 759, and their GRT is 1972, she was born in 1833 (see THE DOCTOR'S AGE).

1911 ▸ ▮ ▮ ▮ ▮ ▮ ▮ ▮ ▮ ▮ ▮ ▮ ▮ ▮

When he uses sleight-of-hand to pick Garron's pocket, the Doctor says 'I was trained by Maskelyne'. British magician John Nevil Maskelyne was born on 22 December 1839 and died on 18 May 1917. His techniques greatly influenced the development of sleight-of-hand. Maskelyne's book on the theory of magic, *Our Magic*, co-written with David Devant, was published in 1911. This is the date I have selected for his meeting with the Doctor. Interestingly, in 'Pyramids Of Mars', the Doctor notes that 1911 is one of his favourite years, perhaps also because of the magician?

2978
Binro was hailed a heretic 'many years ago now'. Ribos is currently in its Ice Time (winter), one of two seasons which last '32' Livithian years, which are probably similar to one Ribos year. If we assume that this was before the current Ice Time, then it was at least 32 years previously, say 2978.

2980
As covered above, intergalactic flight was discovered around 2980 (see also 'Terror Of The Vervoids' and A HISTORY OF SPACE-FLIGHT). Garron was a 'boy' of about 20.

2992
Garron says the Graff's ship is 'stuffed with 18 years of loot'. This was when the Graff went to the Frontier Wars and was deposed. It is possible that the Frontier Wars were fought against Earth humans who were moving slowly out across the Universe from Earth's galaxy, having recently discovered the secret of Jethryk, and who were beginning to intrude and colonise worlds within the Cyrhennic Alliance.

3003
Unstoffe says he and Garron have 'worked together for a long time'. Garron says he acquired the lump of Jethryk 'some years ago', probably no more than ten, say seven, being 3003.

DURATION

⇨ **Day One (Ep1)**
The Doctor meets the Guardian on a rocky plateau. The TARDIS remains stationery there while the Doctor and Romana check on the location of the first segment ...

⇨ **Day One (Ep1)**
Unstoffe enters the Treasure Room after the night curfew is sounded. Garron chants, '4 of the clock and all is well', as the Doctor and Romana arrive.

⇨ **Day Two (Ep1-4)** ▨ ▨ ▨ ▨ ▨ ▨ ▨ ▨ ▨ ▨ ▨ ▨

It will be 'daylight soon' when the Doctor and Romana arrive at the Treasure Room. It is night again when Unstoffe steals the gold from the Treasure Room.

⇨ **Day Three (Ep4)** ▨ ▨ ▨ ▨ ▨ ▨ ▨ ▨ ▨ ▨ ▨ ▨

If we can believe the Doctor, it is just after '4 o'clock' in the morning when the TARDIS leaves Ribos.

THE PIRATE PLANET

+STORY LINK

The Doctor is seen placing the first segment of the Key To Time in the stasis safe in the opening TARDIS scene. He then enters the control room and wishes Romana a 'Good morning'. This implies that at least the equivalent of night has passed in the TARDIS since 'The Ribos Operation'. Romana is already up, and has been spending time familiarising herself with the TARDIS' operational procedures.

LANGUAGE

Romana guesses correctly that a circuit from the time-jump engines is a macromat field integrator – and that is precisely the same name the Captain has for the circuit, even though Romana would not have known this beforehand. Also, the citizen the Doctor speaks with in the street names the scattered gems as diamonds and emeralds, before the Doctor shows them to him. The 'gift' could not possibly have anticipated this to be able to translate it, so they must all be speaking English. The Captain uses the phrase 'beyond the dreams of avarice' which is an Earth proverb. More importantly, he says it before the TARDIS lands, so it must be a saying common to either Zanak or his home planet (see also 'The Ribos Operation'). Both the Doctor and the Captain give the galactic coordinates for Earth as '5-8-0-4-4-6-8-4-8-8-4', which means that they share a common astronomical principle of mapping the galaxy. The planets destroyed by the Captain are known by the same names that the Doctor knows them by. The labels in the trophy room are in English.

TIMELINE DATES

1872 ⁺ ▨ ▨ ▨ ▨ ▨ ▨ ▨ ▨ ▨ ▨ ▨ ▨ ▨

On arriving on Zanak the Doctor says, 'According to these space-time coordinates we have arrived at precisely the right point in space at precisely the right time', so he at least knows the time zone they are in. Later he speaks of Earth being inhabited by 'billions and billions of people'. The population on Earth reached the one billion mark around 1850, two billion around 1930 and reached the three billion circa 1970, which at least suggests a twentieth century setting. (In 'Image Of The Fendahl', the Doctor says the population of Earth is 'four thousand million', and in 'Aliens Of London' (set in 2006) the Doctor refers to 'five billion lives').

However, the Doctor says Bandraginus 5 'disappeared without trace about a hundred years ago' (it was mined by Zanak). I would say that the Doctor is speaking of a hundred years ago relative not to Zanak's history but to his own history, his own 'present', which is 1972 at this point in his time-stream (see 'The Ribos Operation'). This would place Bandraginus 5's disappearance around 1872.

The fact that minerals from Bandraginus 5 are lying about in the street, and that its husk is in the Captain's trophy room shows that Bandraginus 5 is one of the planets mined before Calufrax. It may even be the planet that Zanak is mining when the story opens, before Zanak jumps to Calufrax.

I would therefore set 'The Pirate Planet' in 1872, the year in which Bandraginus 5 vanished. Although the Doctor's comment about the Earth's population being 'billions' no longer applies in 1872, the Doctor is probably speaking subjectively about the Earth that he knows well, that is in his GRT, the 1970s.

1449 ▸

Romana reveals that the Doctor has operated the TARDIS for '523 years'. He is 759, and the GRT is 1972, so he got the TARDIS in 1449 when he was 236 years old (see THE DOCTOR'S AGE).

1666 ▸

This is the year in our history in which Newton is supposed to have formulated his principles of gravity. Romana doesn't know who Newton is, and yet in 'The Five Doctors' she not only understands Newton's principle of 'action/reaction' and that he is attributed for it, but that he also went to university at Cambridge; so at some point after 'The Pirate Planet' she must have either studied up on the man or, given the Doctor's friendship with the scientist, she may even have ended up meeting him.

1802

Balaton remembers how bad life was 'when I was a lad ... under old Queen Xanxia'. From other comments it is clear that this was before the arrival of the Captain. It is said 'she had some kind of evil power. The legend says she lived for hundreds of years'.

This means that Xanxia had used an evil power to prolong her own life to a great age even before she used the Captain's time dams to prolong her life even further. Xanxia (the Nurse) herself says her new body contains 'all the memory patterns and the brilliance built up over the centuries', which confirms this. From Balaton's point of view, Xanxia was already very old when he was young. Balaton appears to be about 70 (he is Mula's grandfather), so 'old Queen Xanxia' ruled at least as early as 1802, around the time when Balaton was born.

1812

After each planet is mined, more psychic energy is produced, which leads to the 'birth' of another Mentiad. Mula says that for 'all my life I've been taught to hate and loathe them'. Since the Mentiads came into being once Zanak started planet-jumping and Mula seems not much older than 25, then Zanak has already been jumping for at least 25 years. The Captain says he 'should have obliterated the Mentiads years ago'. No more than ten Mentiads are ever seen together. But is this all of them? The chief Mentiad says that 'for generation upon generation our planet has been assailed by a nameless evil' (the Captain). His arrival is also part of a 'legend' (he arrived 'one night'). This most certainly was during Balaton's lifetime, because he can remember life before they were slaves to the Captain ('things were different then'), so the Captain must have arrived no more than 60 years before, when Balaton was a 'lad' (say about 10, being 1812).

1903

Romana says she got an air-car as 'a present for my 70th birthday'. She was born in 1833 (see 'The Ribos Operation'), so she was aged 70 in 1903. The fact that an air-car would be used outside suggests that Romana's family lived outside the Capitol, as did the Doctor's family when he was a child (see FAMILY).

DURATION

(TARDIS) (Ep1)

The Doctor and Romana spend time in the TARDIS before they land on Zanak.

⇨ Day One (Ep1-4)

Events take place over one day on Zanak. The Doctor does greet the Captain with a 'Good morning' in Ep4, but as there are clearly no night scenes I would say he was merely being his usual flippant self.

THE STONES OF BLOOD

+STORY LINK

As the story opens, Romana is wearing the same clothes she had on in 'The Pirate Planet'. The second segment has just been retrieved and converted, so 'The Pirate Planet' and 'The Stones Of Blood' are consecutive.

OBSERVATIONS

- When asked by Emelia if he is from Outer Space, the Doctor replies 'No. I'm more from what you'd call Inner Time'.
- As noted under 'The Ribos Operation' and 'The Armageddon Factor', it is more than likely that it's the Black Guardian posing as the White who sends the Doctor and Romana on their quest. Therefore, the voice of the White Guardian heard by the Doctor and Romana in the TARDIS probably belongs to the real White Guardian, who has discovered what his opposite is planning to do with the Key. With the TARDIS travelling in the vortex from 1872 to 1978, the Guardian is only able to contact the Doctor as the TARDIS passes the Doctor's and his own GRT, in 1972.

LANGUAGE

Despite the Time Lord 'gift', the Doctor cannot read the script on the Megara's cell door. Cessair of Diplos speaks English while in her guise of Vivien Fay, but this is probably only due to her having lived in England for 4000 years.

TIMELINE DATES

1978, June 21 – 23 + ▨ ▨ ▨ ▨ ▨ ▨ ▨ ▨ ▨ ▨ ▨

Emelia Rumford places the date of the stone circle as being 'about 2000 BC. Nearly four thousand years'. The clothes and telephones seen in the story reflect a contemporary setting, i.e. the late 1970s. Unlike the TARDIS's previous couple of landings on 1970s Earth, the tracer now controls the ship, so 'The Stones Of Blood' does not necessarily have to be sequential to 'The Hand Of Fear' or 'Image Of The Fendahl'. Coincidentally, Romana changes into contemporary Earth clothes before she discovers she is even going to Earth (Romana says 'everybody knows' that Earth is the Doctor's 'favourite planet'). The Doctor, however, judges that they are in the 'present' when he sees the stone circle ('No, not now! Thousands of years ago when these were built'). The story was recorded in June [of 1978], so I have selected the month to match seasonal conditions, and the year to match other contemporary visual factors.

There is a full moon in the opening scenes of the story; the full moon appeared on 21 June 1978.

2000 BC

Emelia Rumford estimates the stone circle to have been built 'about 2000 BC'.

28 BC

The Doctor says they gave up teaching hyperspace theory on Gallifrey 'two thousand years ago' which, given that the Doctor's GRT is 1972, would be 28 BC.

1178

Vivien Fay says the convent was founded in the 'twelfth century' going back 'seven hundred odd years'. Using a Century Factor, the date I have selected is 1178.

1536

In our history this was the year Henry VIII began the dissolution of the monasteries.

1572

Emelia says this was the year the Hall was built.

1650

The Doctor says 'I always thought that Druidism was founded by John Aubrey in the Seventeenth Century as a joke'. Aubrey (12 March 1626 to June 1697) was awarded a fellowship to the Royal Society in 1663 following his studies of the Avebury stone circle. 1650 is an arbitrary date.

1700

Emelia finds there are no records in the Hall dated 'prior to 1700'.

1701
1754

The dates appear on the painting of Dr Thomas Borlase at the Hall. 1754 was the year that Borlase surveyed the stones, and was crushed by one of them.

1820
1874
1911 ▨ ▨ ▨ ▨ ▨ ▨ ▨ ▨ ▨ ▨ ▨ ▨ ▨ ▨
Emelia Rumford gives all of these dates for surveys of the stones. Reverend Bright surveyed the stones in 1820.

1750
1840
1900 ▨ ▨ ▨ ▨ ▨ ▨ ▨ ▨ ▨ ▨ ▨ ▨ ▨ ▨
Emelia says that the paintings found in the priest hole cover a period of 'one hundred and fifty years'. Allan Ramsay (born 13 October 1713, died 10 August 1784) painted Lady Montcalm, which would place her time at about 1750. The last painting is of Senhora Camara, which would have been painted 150 years later, around 1900. The second painting was of Mrs Trefusis, who was a recluse for 'sixty years', so her painting was probably done 60 years before Senhora Camara's, in 1840.

1873 ▨ ▨ ▨ ▨ ▨ ▨ ▨ ▨ ▨ ▨ ▨ ▨ ▨ ▨
The Doctor mentions Schliemann digging up Troy. This is the year in our history in which Schliemann believed he found the remains of the city. He published his findings in 1874. (See 'The Myth Makers').

1945 + ▨ ▨ ▨ ▨ ▨ ▨ ▨ ▨ ▨ ▨ ▨ ▨ ▨ ▨
Einstein had retired by this time, making it more likely to be when he met with the Doctor. Interestingly enough, in 'Time And The Rani' the seventh Doctor rescues Einstein from the Rani, but the scientist does not recognise that Doctor, of course.

DURATION

(TARDIS) (Ep1) ▨ ▨ ▨ ▨ ▨ ▨ ▨ ▨ ▨ ▨ ▨ ▨ ▨
The Doctor and Romana spend time in the TARDIS before landing on Earth.

⇨ **Day One (21 June) (Ep1)** ▨ ▨ ▨ ▨ ▨ ▨ ▨ ▨ ▨
The meeting of Druids is held on the night of a full moon.

⇨ **Day Two (22 June) (Ep1-3)** ▨ ▨ ▨ ▨ ▨ ▨ ▨ ▨ ▨
The TARDIS lands in the late 'afternoon'. Romana is transported to the hyperspaceship that night. The Doctor and Romana spend all night on the prison ship.

⇨ **Day Three (23 June) (Ep4)** ▨ ▨ ▨ ▨ ▨ ▨ ▨ ▨ ▨

It is in the early hours of the next morning that the two campers are killed. Cessair is turned to stone at dawn.

THE ANDROIDS OF TARA

+STORY LINK

There is nothing to suggest that 'The Androids Of Tara' takes place immediately after 'The Stones Of Blood'. Romana is wearing her white robe from 'The Ribos Operation'. The Doctor has found time to play chess with K9 between 'The Stones Of Blood' and 'The Androids Of Tara', despite the Guardian stressing 'the need for urgency'. Romana is familiar with the moves, and quickly deduces mate in eleven moves; perhaps the Doctor has been teaching her the game between TARDIS landings?

LANGUAGE

There are Earth numerals and words in Madame Lamia's laboratory. The clock in the throne room is illustrated with the 12 signs of the Earth zodiac, with four additional symbols. Given the similarity in the names of the astrological signs that are used on the planet Chloris ('Aquatrian' / 'Capris' / 'Ariel') (see 'The Creature From The Pit'), it is clear that the Tarans also have a similar view of the same constellations as seen from Earth.

TIMELINE DATES

2378 ⋆ ▨ ▨ ▨ ▨ ▨ ▨ ▨ ▨ ▨ ▨ ▨ ▨ ▨

The Doctor tricks Romana into believing that he is entitled to a rest 'of 50 years' after 'a journey of 400 years and 12 parsecs'. From this, we can assume that he means 400 years from their last landing, which was 1978 in 'The Stones Of Blood'. This could be either 400 years backwards to 1578 or 400 years forwards to 2378. A journey of 12 parsecs would keep them still within Earth's galaxy, which indicates that Tara might be an Earth colony, suggesting a future setting at a time after warp-drive was available; after 2106 (see 'Nightmare Of Eden').

However there are in fact very few pointers that even suggest an Earth origin for the Tarans: the Doctor calls the Tarans 'humans'; there is a chart labelled 'THE HUMAN EYE' in Lamia's laboratory; after examining Romana, Lamia unquestioningly accepts that Romana 'is not Taran'; Tara has 'Earth-type gravity'; and the twelve signs of the zodiac adorn the 'clock' in the throne room.

Despite these clues I find it highly unlikely that Tara is an Earth colony given the medieval history of the planet: there is a long-established tradition in the royal court, such as Strella being a descendant of various courts, something which I doubt would be possible in a colony that could at the most be only 300 years old; if 'The Androids Of Tara' is set in 2378, Tara would have had to have been colonised in the twenty-first century. The statue that forms part of the fourth segment of the Key To Time is clearly more than 200 years old and has a superstition attached to it, something that a technologically-advanced colony from Earth would hardly maintain, let alone begin. Advanced android technology has never existed on Earth in any other story, so the ability is clearly a Taran talent; and if nine-tenths of the population was wiped out '200 years ago', why did they go to the trouble of 'building androids to replace the people' when all they needed to do was contact Earth to send new colonists? Of course, the threat of plague may have been a deterrent to others to go to Tara, but this is a minor point.

I think we can accept that the Doctor is actually telling the truth about having travelled 400 years because Romana selects a modern outfit: 'According to our records it's what everyone on Tara is wearing this year. Isn't that right, K9?' (K9 replies: 'Affirmative'). This shows that all three of them know what the current year on Tara is. A journey of 400 years more than likely refers to a journey forwards in time. Although I do not think that Tara is an Earth colony, I have placed the story in the future date.

1653 *

Of his antique fishing rod, the Doctor says: 'Gosh, that takes me back. Or forward. That's the trouble with time travel. You can never remember ... . The last time I used this I was with Izaak Walton'. Izaak Walton (9 August 1593 to 15 December 1683) wrote his famous books *Angling* in 1644 and *The Compleet Angler* in 1653, the latter of which is a likely date for when Walton went fishing with the Doctor.

1917, October 17 *

One of the objects in the TARDIS cupboard is a World War One gas-mask. The Doctor probably obtained this during the air-raid mentioned by Susan in 'Planet Of Giants'.

1927, September? *

The Doctor mentions both the year and event. The Cuban Jose Raul Capablanca (19 November 1888 to 8 March 1942), chess world champion since 1921, lost to Russian Alexander Alekhine (1 November 1892 to 24 March 1946) in Buenos Aires. The chess match started in September 1927 and lasted several months, ending on 29 November

1927. The Doctor comments that he must have left before the game finished!

K9 states that he is programmed for all championship chess tournaments 'since 1866'. It is not known whether this is part of Professor Marius' original program, or a later addition of the Doctor's.

2178
Zadek informs the Doctor that the plague tunnels were 'built 200 years ago'.

DURATION

(TARDIS) Ep1
The Doctor and K9 have been playing chess for some time in the TARDIS before Romana plugs in the tracer and they land on Tara ...

⇨ Day One (Ep1)
The TARDIS arrives in the day. Both the Doctor and Romana are drugged and sleep all night.

⇨ Day Two (Ep.2-4)
Romana wakes after being unconscious for '12 hours'. The clock in Castle Gracht is divided into 16 segments. Since the arms of the clock pass between each segment in a short space of time, the arm movements clearly do not represent the passing of hours. However, the King must be crowned at 'the appointed hour', which is at the 12 o'clock position, so this could still be midday. It is night when the Doctor duels with Grendel.

THE POWER OF KROLL

+STORY LINK

There are no references to 'The Androids Of Tara'. However, in the next story, 'The Armageddon Factor', the Doctor assures K9 that there is 'no water or swamps' on Atrios, which suggests that Tara and the moon of Delta Three are the previous two landing points for the TARDIS, which indicates that 'The Androids Of Tara' and 'The Power Of Kroll' are probably consecutive. We might even assume that after rescuing the stranded K9, the Doctor and Romana stayed on Tara to attend the wedding between Reynart and Strella, and maybe also to ensure that Count Grendel was apprehended ...

OBSERVATIONS

- The symbol of Kroll's power was a holy relic (in actual fact the fifth segment of the Key To Time), which was brought to the moon by the Swampies' ancestors at the time of the resettlement. The relic gave the holder of the relic the power to see into the future.

LANGUAGE

The Swampies have a written language (an alien script), and yet they do not understand the concept of a signature. The Swampies also speak English: they are able to communicate with Rohm-Dutt, and Mensch takes orders from the refinery crew.

TIMELINE DATES

2978 ♦

Kroll, then 'just your average giant squid', was brought to the third moon of Delta Magna along with the Swampies 'centuries ago'. After swallowing the holy symbol of his power and the high priest, the giant squid disappeared into the swamp, where it mutated into an even bigger giant squid. Kroll would appear again 'every couple of centuries', say every 200 years. Kroll's fourth manifestation is at dawn of Day Two in 'The Power Of Kroll', which suggests that his first manifestation was some 600 years earlier. If Delta Magna was colonised in the period soon after warp-drive is discovered around 2106 (see 'Nightmare Of Eden'), then 'The Power Of Kroll' would be set at least 800 years later, say 2906. Using the Century Factor, 'The Power Of Kroll' can be set in 2978. This places 'The Power Of Kroll' at a time when Earth's empire is already starting to decline (see 'The Mutants'), which is supported by the fact that some of the Delta Magna colonists, the Sons Of Earth, wanted the colony to return to Earth.

The refinery has been on the moon for 'months'. Rohm-Dutt left Delta Magna 'a couple of days ago'.

1920 ♦

It would appear that the Doctor has met Australian-born singer Nellie Melba, who was born on 19 May 1861 and died on 23 February 1931. Melba made her operatic debut in Brussels in 1887 after studying singing for five years. She was made a Dame of the British Empire in 1918 (due to her charitable work in World War One), so the Doctor might have met her after that date, say 1920. She returned to Australia in 1926.

.2178
.2378
.2578
.2778 ▨ ▨ ▨ ▨ ▨ ▨ ▨ ▨ ▨ ▨ ▨ ▨ ▨ ▨

It is stated that Kroll reappears 'every couple of centuries'. His fourth manifestation is in 2978 in 'The Power Of Kroll'. The colony would have been established soon after warp-drive was developed in 2106.

.2968 ▨ ▨ ▨ ▨ ▨ ▨ ▨ ▨ ▨ ▨ ▨ ▨ ▨ ▨

Thawn says 'I spent many years persuading the Company to back this project', say ten years.

DURATION

⇨ **Day One (Ep1-2)** ▨ ▨ ▨ ▨ ▨ ▨ ▨ ▨ ▨ ▨
The TARDIS lands at day. It gets dark early.

⇨ **Day Two (Ep2-4)** ▨ ▨ ▨ ▨ ▨ ▨ ▨ ▨ ▨ ▨
Romana is about to be sacrificed shortly after the night orbit shot is fired, at least 'one hour' before dawn. Kroll rises for the first time 'at dawn'. The second orbit shot is programmed to fire '12 hours' later, which occurs at the end of the story. The total duration of the adventure is a little over 12 hours, bridged over two days.

THE ARMAGEDDON FACTOR

+STORY LINK

The Doctor assures K9 that there are 'no water or swamps' on Atrios, in reference to K9's stranding in the castle moat in 'The Androids Of Tara', and to the swampy moon of Delta Magna in 'The Power Of Kroll'. This would certainly point to 'The Power Of Kroll' and 'The Armageddon Factor' as being consecutive. When they first materialise, the Doctor comments on their location being 'another underground passage', presumably in reference to the catacombs on Ribos, or the escape tunnels on Tara, rather than to another adventure after 'The Power Of Kroll'.

OBSERVATIONS

- After the Doctor denies the Black Guardian the Key, the Guardian swears revenge ('Doctor, you shall die for this'). The Randomiser built into the TARDIS at the end of 'The Armageddon Factor' enables the Doctor to evade the Black Guardian – or, on the basis that the Guardian cannot time-travel and therefore follow the TARDIS himself, his agents – for 11 years (see THE DOCTOR'S AGE) until it is deactivated on Argolis (see 'The Leisure Hive'). Then, in 1983, before the Black Guardian is able to track down the TARDIS and kill the Doctor, the TARDIS falls into E-Space where even the Guardians probably have no dominion. The TARDIS emerges from E-Space in 1981 – two years before it entered (see 'Full Circle') so the Black Guardian is still unable to locate the ship. Besides, the Keeper takes it to Traken. The Doctor states in 'The Keeper Of Traken' that only a being with great powers could control the TARDIS, which implies that the Keeper is more powerful than the Black Guardian. In order to destroy the Doctor, the Black Guardian seeks a new agent, and finds one in 1983 (which is the Doctor's GRT, and therefore his own, in that story) called Vislor Turlough … . (see 'Mawdryn Undead').
- Romana deduces that Astra is the sixth segment of the Key To Time when she learns that the Princess is 'the sixth child of the sixth generation of the sixth Dynasty of Atrios'. But what if the TARDIS had landed on Atrios before the other planets upon which segments were to be found? The Doctor and Romana would be looking for their first segment. I think that since the tracer sends the TARDIS to each destination it is programmed to search out each segment in a specific order. Therefore the sixth segment is the indeed the sixth segment (the Shadow seems to be under this impression too, which is why he went on ahead to wait for the Doctor to arrive). Interestingly, in terms of the Doctor's GRT and given the dates I have used, the first and fifth segments are in the future, the third in the near future, the sixth in the present, and the second and fourth in the past. Only the sixth is located in another galaxy.
- The Doctor scatters the Key again ('round through space and time'), so presumably the segments take on new forms. With Astra returned to life at the end of the story, we can only assume that she is no longer the sixth segment, which has now taken on another form.

LANGUAGE

Despite being Gallifreyan, Drax has a cockney accent, due to his time in Brixton prison ('I had to learn the lingo'). The Shadow has been communicating with the Marshal for at least five years (in the Atrion language?) The language on the screens is in Earth text and numerals. The Doctor's Academy nickname 'Theta Sigma' is, like Omega, Greek in origin.

1972 ⋆ ▆ ▆ ▆ ▆ ▆ ▆ ▆ ▆ ▆ ▆ ▆ ▆ ▆ ▆

Atrios and Zeos are both located in the Helical Galaxy. According to Romana this fact is taught at the Time Lord Academy. But what is significant enough about the twin planets for inclusion in the Academy curriculum? If it is the fact that the two planets are at war, this suggests that the twin planets are contemporaneous with modern Gallifrey, which in terms of the Doctor's age is still GRT 1972. On the other hand, the Doctor says Astra was 'a human being', which suggests the Atrions are from Earth, but there is no actual indication that the Atrions are Earth colonists. Indeed, the fact that the Royal House of Atrios extends back some six generations and six dynasties indicates that the Atrion civilisation has been ruled by a monarchy for perhaps millennia, which would set 'The Armageddon Factor' far in Earth's future. Astra's biological destiny must have been created from the very beginning, so the genetic factor that makes her the sixth segment would need to have been introduced at a time when Atrios was inhabited. On all these grounds, I do not think the Atrions are descended from Earth colonists.

The Shadow has 'waited since eternity began' to obtain the Key To Time. He says 'I have waited so long even another thousand years would mean nothing for me … I have watched you and your jackdaw meanderings'. And later: 'Whereas you have been scavenging across space and time I have located the sixth piece here'. If we take it that the Shadow was 'created' by the Black Guardian for the sole purpose of obtaining the Key To Time, then that could indicate also that Atrios is thousands of years in the future.

The Marshal says to the Doctor 'Your coming here had been foretold', which suggests that every event seen in 'The Armageddon Factor' (and, to a point, the events of all the stories spanning 'The Ribos Operation' to 'The Armageddon Factor' too) is leading ultimately towards Astra's metamorphosis. Astra herself knows what is going to happen ('My destiny no longer lies on Atrios … This is the time of my becoming. My transcendence … Metamorphosis'). It would otherwise be all too coincidental that everything happens on Atrios when it does. Astra's transformation into the sixth segment is her biological destiny. The fact that she changes at the specific moment that she does change shows clearly that that precise moment in time on that specific day is the moment that she is destined to change. In other words, she couldn't have transformed any sooner or later than she does. It is coming into contact with the semi-completed Key that triggers the transformation. But she doesn't change in the TARDIS when she reaches out to the Key earlier, which shows that her metamorphosis is not intended to occur then.

The Black Guardian knows the exact moment that Astra will change, which is why the Shadow already knows that Astra is the sixth segment. All he needs is for the Doctor to bring to him the other five segments.

Once the Doctor has the entire Key, he does not move the TARDIS out of the time zone they are in. He just waits for the White Guardian to arrive. The Doctor still believes that the White Guardian wants the Key to prevent an approaching catastrophe. On the basis that the Doctor knows that the Guardians cannot themselves time-travel, he must have been under the impression that the Guardian could only prevent the 'chaos' in the time zone in which the Key is fully assembled ('You said once it was assembled it would stop the entire Universe and enable you to restore the natural balances of good and evil throughout the whole of the Universe' – significantly he doesn't say 'throughout the whole of time'; he is actually referring to one small specific point in the 'now'), so therefore Atrios and Zeos exist in the epicentre of the 'chaos', and the events of 'The Armageddon Factor' take place in the 'now' of the 'chaos', again the time zone in which the Key is needed. We can therefore assume that all the events in 'The Armageddon Factor' take place in the same time zone as the Doctor's initial encounter with the 'White' Guardian, being 1972.

1549

Drax refers to the Class of '92, '450 years' ago. The Doctor is 759 and their GRT is 1972, which would place this event in 1522. However, as noted under THE DOCTOR'S AGE, in order that the true Gallifrey Date ends in '92, Drax could be generalising and is referring to only 423 years ago.

1967

Drax has been on the Shadow's planet of evil 'about five years. After the war started', which would have been in 1967. K Block had been 'closed down years ago' due to radiation. No one has been on Zeos 'for years'.

We also learn that Drax got 'ten years' in Brixton prison. Since we do not know when exactly this was in Drax's personal time stream, I have not included it in the TIMELINE.

DURATION

(TARDIS) (Ep1)

The TARDIS is travelling *en route* to Atrios in the opening moments.

⇨ **Day One (Ep1-6)**

The story takes place during one Atrion day in three different but contemporaneous locations. In Ep4, when the localised time loop is established around the Marshal's ship, the Doctor calculates that they have 'about an hour in real time' before the loop decays totally. The loop is broken towards the end of Ep6.

DESTINY OF THE DALEKS

+STORY LINK

The Randomiser is still in place and the Doctor has been making some repairs to K9. Romana is in the inner room regenerating and tries on several bodies before selecting a facsimile of Princess Astra (see 'The Armageddon Factor'), so it is likely that 'The Armageddon Factor' and 'Destiny Of The Daleks' are consecutive.

The Doctor refers to his previous adventure on Skaro (in 'Genesis Of The Daleks'), which was 'a long time ago'. In terms of the Doctor's age, 'Genesis Of The Daleks' was at least 109 years ago.

DALEK LINK

As outlined in DALEK HISTORY, this is the Daleks' thirteenth appearance. Since the events of 'The Evil Of The Daleks', the Daleks have abandoned Skaro ('They ravaged the place and left it for dead as you can see') and headed into deep space where they joined up with other Daleks who have engaged the Movellans, their battle computers locking the two races in an impasse of logic. Reference is made to the Dalek Supreme, who is most likely the replacement for the one destroyed in 'The Daleks' Master Plan'. Davros has been 'dead' 'for centuries'.

During the impasse, these Daleks have evolved, shedding most of the organic and becoming more robotic.

OBSERVATIONS

- Romana's apparent regeneration is different to those experienced by the Doctor. We do not witness the cause of her metamorphosis. Given the

Doctor's surprise it must have been a sudden regeneration; she may have had an accident in one of the TARDIS inner corridors. However, the three bodies that walk into the console room and parade before the Doctor probably aren't stable regenerations. Given that one of the forms is a small blue-skinned 'alien', it is doubtful that this is a proper regeneration. Also, due to the fact that the three 'bodies' all wear different clothes, and there is no time for Romana to change so quickly between reappearances, these are probably only holographic images of potential new incarnations. After all, the Doctor is offered a choice of new faces at his trial in 'The War Games'; K'Anpo (see 'Planet Of The Spiders') was able to project his next incarnation; and the Watcher in 'Logopolis' is a projection of the Doctor's near future-self, so it is not impossible that these are only projections too; Romana has already fully regenerated into a body like Princess Astra's, but has decided to 'tease' the Doctor by showing him other forms.

LANGUAGE

Tyssan is able to understand both Daleks and Movellans, so it is clear that all three speak English. Romanadvoratrelundar is the full spelling of her Gallifreyan name, but abbreviated to Romana by the Doctor only. However, the other prisoners scratch 'ROMANA' on her gravestone, which shows clearly that her name is spelt the same in both English and Gallifreyan. The words and symbols on the Movellan scanner screen are Earth letters and numerals: the Movellans use Greek words in the coordinates – D5 Gamma 2 Alpha is their name for Skaro. Romana knows the home galaxy of the Movellans as Star System 4X Alpha 4. The Daleks use 'hours' as a measurement of time.

THE HITCHHIKER'S CONNECTION

Oolon Colluphid, author of the book *The Origins Of The Universe* which the Doctor reads while trapped beneath a fallen beam, originates from Douglas Adams' cult radio serial (and other media spin-offs) *The Hitchhiker's Guide To The Galaxy*. And in 'The Christmas Invasion', the Doctor refers to Arthur Dent as being 'a nice man', which might be interpreted to mean that he has met him. This could mean that the continuity of that series must also belong to the *Doctor Who* canon. However, I have elected not to do so given that in *Hitchhiker's*, the Earth is destroyed by the Vogon Constructor Fleet in the late 1970s, an event that does not also occur in *Doctor Who*. (See also 'Mindwarp' with regard to the *Alien* film series and 'Remembrance Of The Daleks' to *Quatermass*.)

TIMELINE DATES

4500 ∗
'Destiny Of The Daleks' takes place after the Daleks have been at war with the Movellans for 'centuries'. In terms of Dalek history, 'Destiny Of The Daleks' is set after 'The Evil Of The Daleks': the Doctor explores the Dalek City after it had been all but destroyed in the Civil War of 'The Evil Of The Daleks'. We can assume that after the war of 4066 the few surviving Daleks ravaged what was left of the planet and abandoned it, going out into deep space, where they become locked in an 'impasse of logic' for, say 500 years. That would set 'Destiny Of The Daleks' around 4500.

Tyssan says he has 'been on the run for days'.

13,000,000,000 BC ∗
The Universe is estimated to be 15 billion years old (see 'Secrets Of The Stars'). The Doctor wonders why Oolon Colluphid didn't 'ask someone who saw it happen?', which suggests that the Doctor was there.

4066
The year in which the war with the Movellans started. See 'The Evil Of The Daleks', Dalek Link above and DALEK HISTORY.

4498
Tyssan says 'by my time-scale I was taken captive two years ago'.

DURATION

(TARDIS) (Ep1)
The Doctor repairs K9, while Romana regenerates.

⇨ **Day One (Ep1-4)**
The story is set over one day on Skaro. A Dalek deep space cruiser was due to land in 'six hours' in Ep4. It doesn't arrive.

CITY OF DEATH

CITY OF DEATH

+STORY LINK

The Doctor refers to the Randomiser: '[it's] a useful device but it lacks true discrimination'. The Doctor says his sonic screwdriver proved 'very useful against the Daleks on Skaro', so it is likely that 'Destiny Of The Daleks' and 'City Of Death' are consecutive.

OBSERVATIONS

- Scarlioni and the Countess have been married for 'years' but did she not once ever suspect the truth about him? (Didn't they ever have sex?)
- Scaroth says he was 'flung into the time vortex and split into twelve different parts which lead – or have led – independent but connected lives in times in this planet's history'. The twelve splinters include the one who 1) introduced fire, 2) introduced the wheel, 3) built the pyramids (we see Scaroth as an Egyptian, and in a painting of an Egyptian god), 4) mapped the Heavens, 5) was a Greek, 6) was a Roman, 7) was a Crusader, 8) was named Tancredi, 9) obtained the first draft of Hamlet, 10) is called Scarlioni. The unidentified remaining two were probably involved in assembling the Guttenberg Bibles, and other antiquities such as the Ming Vase and Louis XV chair.
- It has been suggested that perhaps King Richard ('The Crusade') is also one of Scaroth's splinters [actor Julian Glover played both roles], but this theory really doesn't work. Richard has a sister, Joanna, and a brother, John (see 'The King's Demons'), and they would have all grown up together as children. Unless of course Scaroth has killed the real king and assumed his place – but that would mean that it is a coincidence that Scaroth's human face is the same as Richard's. But could that be why he chose to impersonate the king – they shared the same face? The Scarlioni/Tancredi faces are a masks, a visage shared also by the other Scaroth splinters we glimpse briefly during one of the mind-slips; some have beards and long hair, so the mask must be made of some sort of biological matter that can grow hair. We don't understand fully how the face masks work, but it is obvious that the design is modelled on a particular adult face. Some of these earlier faces pre-date Richard's time period, so Richard is unlikely to be the model for the face. We also don't know how the time 'splintering' occurred. One possible suggestion is that when Scaroth got splintered into twelve he was duplicated – rather like cc-ing an email to twelve different people – and so each of the twelve versions

is a perfect copy of the original with the same memories and instincts. In other words, Scaroth just 'appears' in his Jagaroth form in each of the twelve splintered time zones, and takes on the identity of the same 'human' that the first splinter adopted.

LANGUAGE

With the story set in France, there are several oddities: all the signs are in French but the television news item is read out in English; the Louvre guide uses a mixture of English and French; the Doctor speaks English to Duggan and then to the cafe patron without changing languages. The note the Doctor writes for the Italian Leonardo in mirror-writing is in English. The Doctor speed-reads a French book while Romana does a crossword. The Doctor writes 'THIS IS A FAKE' in felt pen on all the canvas boards to be used by da Vinci for the six copies of the Mona Lisa, so it will show up on an x-ray – but he writes it in English, and not in or Italian or French.

TIMELINE DATES

400,000,000 BC *

The time factor 'four hundred million years' is stated several times. In our history, life is believed to have started 2,700 million years ago, with basic single-celled bacteria and algae. By 400 million years ago, the first marine vertebrates were in existence. This tells us that life on the planet Earth in the N-Space Universe is not as old as our own. (All the various extraterrestrial influences seen during the series would explain how this Earth reached different evolutionary levels in a much shorter time than our own; note 'The Dæmons' and 'Image Of The Fendahl').

1979, May *

The Doctor says 'It's 1979, actually'. The billboard at the French Natural History Museum advertises that the Evolution exhibit on display there runs from '26 Janvier – 31 Mai 1979', which not only confirms the year, it also gives a spread of five months in which to set the story. There are blossoms on the trees, indicating spring, so the month can be determined from when the story was recorded, May [of 1979].

1505 *

Tancredi gives the year. In our history, the Borgias – for whom the soldier is working – lived and ruled from c.1480 – 1520.

700,000 BC
Based upon fossilized remains of ash found with their skeletons, it is believed that fire was first used by Peking Man, who existed some 700,000 years ago.

3500 BC
In our history, it is believed that the Sumerians were the first humans to use the wheel. The Sumerians lived around this time.

2680 BC
The Great Pyramids at Cheops in Cairo, Egypt, are estimated to have been built between 2680 and 2345 BC (see 'The Daleks' Master Plan').

300 BC
One of Scaroth's splinters is dressed as a Roman senator. The Roman civilisation flourished from around 300 BC to AD 410 in our history.

1452
1519, May 2
The Louvre guide gives '1452' and '1519' as the years of da Vinci's birth and death. His date of death is recorded as 2 May 1519 in our history.

1503 ◆
This is the stated on-screen [and factual] year that the Mona Lisa was painted. When the Doctor writes the note to Leonardo, he ends it with 'See You Earlier, Love The Doctor', which shows that their first meeting was before 1505 (but after 1492, see 'The Masque Of Mandragora'). The Doctor first meets Leonardo at the time when the artist is painting the Mona Lisa, because the Doctor recalls that the woman wouldn't sit still (see also 'Doctor Who (The TV Movie)', the Doctor was with Leonardo at a time when the painter had a cold).

1529
The Doctor comments that the Chateau had been restored 'four or five hundred years ago'. It is stated that the six extra Mona Lisas have been walled up for '474 years', so it is therefore logical that the paintings were placed in the Chateau in 1505, before the restoration work began some 14 years later.

1600 ◆
This is estimated to be the year in which Shakespeare wrote *Hamlet* – see also 'Planet

Of Evil' for further discussion about this date. In 'The Chase', the Doctor and his friends actually view (on the time/space visualiser) Shakespeare getting the inspiration to write that very play in March 1600. The Doctor also refers to the Bard in 'The Two Doctors' and 'Time And The Rani'.

1911, August 22

During the television news item about the theft of the Mona Lisa from the Louvre, the announcer gives the dates of the other times that the painting had been stolen. All we can catch of the bulletin is 'August the Twenty Second Nineteen...', and ' ... on January ... ', but unfortunately the rest cannot be heard clearly. In our own history, the painting was stolen on 21 August 1911 (and recovered in December 1913). I have used a mix of both dates.

DURATION

⇨ Day One (400mBC) (Ep1/Ep4)

The Jagaroth ship has been on the planet for a short while. Romana rigs the device to return Scaroth to 1979 after only 'two minutes', so the travellers spend only a short amount of time in this time zone.

⇨ Day One (1505) (Ep 2-3)

It is day in 1505. The Doctor stays no more than a few hours, relative to the time he is away from 1979.

⇨ Day One (1979) (Ep1-3)

The Doctor and Romana go to the cafe for 'lunch'. The hands on the clock in the sketch of Romana read '1.50'. It is '4.10 pm' on the clock in the Chateau when the Doctor, Romana and Duggan are brought in. The Doctor leaves for 1505 after night has fallen. The Louvre is robbed that evening. Hermann returns with the stolen Mona Lisa shortly before '11.25 pm'. Romana and Duggan spend the night at the cafe.

⇨ Day Two (1979) (Ep4)

The Doctor returns from 1505 in the morning of the second day. He and Romana leave Paris later that afternoon.

THE CREATURE FROM THE PIT

STORY LINK

There is no reference to the Paris adventure (see 'City Of Death'), so any length of time can have passed between stories. As covered under THE DOCTOR'S AGE, it is highly likely that 11 years pass between 'The Armageddon Factor' and 'The Leisure Hive', so 'The Creature From The Pit' falls somewhere within that extended off-screen period. The cloak and hat worn by the Doctor in 'The Talons Of Weng-Chiang' hang on the coat rack in the console room.

The Doctor has by now long completed his repairs to K9, and the robot dog now has a different voice, possibly due to the laryngitis he has in 'Destiny Of The Daleks'. The Doctor and K9 are reading Peter Rabbit, which Romana also knows all about (she also knows of Beatrix Potter's other books and characters).

Romana has been cleaning out Number 4 hold which contains 'the most awful lot of junk', including the hyper-space cannon from 'The Stones Of Blood', the jawbone of an ass, a brass diving helmet, a ball of string (given to the Doctor by Theseus and Ariadne), and the Mark Three Emergency Transceiver.

OBSERVATIONS

- The Mark Three Emergency Transceiver's function is 'to receive and send distress signals'. The Doctor disconnected it mainly because he 'was never in distress', but also because he 'kept getting calls from Gallifrey all the time – would you do this, would you do that', which he found 'such a bore'. This cannot refer to the control the Time Lords put on his TARDIS during his exile on Earth because technically these were not distress calls. Rather, I would say that the device was disconnected at the time when the Doctor left Gallifrey so the Time Lords could not contact him to summon him back home. (Although it appears that they have been monitoring his journeys; see 'The War Games'.)
- Also in the Number 4 hold is a ball of string given to the Doctor by Theseus and Ariadne. Since they wanted to unravel his scarf to aid them through the labyrinth to defeat the Minotaur, we can assume it was the fourth Doctor but at a time before he is joined by Romana. The most likely would be when he was with Sarah or Leela, or in the years between 'The Invasion Of Time' and 'The Ribos Operation'.
- Tythonians 'live for up to 40,000 years'.

LANGUAGE

The Doctor is unable to read a book written in Tibetan despite his ability to speak the language fluently, as demonstrated in 'Planet Of The Spiders'. Erato uses 'ninods' (26 ninods is one hour, seven seconds). The trade agreement between Chloris and Tythonus appears to be written in English. Erato uses a device with which to communicate, using the larynx of another being.

TIMELINE DATES

2116 +

In 'Nightmare Of Eden' the Doctor responds to the *Empress*'s mayday. This could be because the Mark Three Emergency Transceiver, which responds to Erato's distress signal in 'The Creature From The Pit', might still be connected to the TARDIS. Of course, with the TARDIS still being controlled by the Randomiser, we can assume that the Mark Three Emergency Transceiver overrides the Randomiser's control, and that the Transceiver is still in this mode when the TARDIS picks up the *Empress*'s mayday. Therefore, with 'Nightmare Of Eden' set in 2116, this is also the date I have applied to 'The Creature From The Pit', the TARDIS simply moving spatially from Chloris to the *Empress*, without temporal displacement.

Organon says he has been in the pit for 'many moonflows'. On the wall of the cavern that he has made his home we can see numerous crescent shapes, which is probably Organon marking off the days he has been in the pit. It is not possible to see how many there are, but certainly it is over 20.

1150 BC +

When Romana cleans out the TARDIS Number 4 hold, she finds the jawbone of an ass. In our history, in the 12th century BC, Samson supposedly defeated the invading Philistine army by crushing their skulls with the jawbone of an ass. Presumably Samson gave the jawbone to the Doctor when they met. The date used here is arbitrary.

2096

Torvin says he hasn't 'seen a piece of zinc as big as that for, oh, 20 years or more'.

2101

According to Adrasta, Erato was cast in the pit 'fifteen years' ago.

2111

Erato says the neutron star has been on its way 'for several years'. He has been trapped in the pit for 15, so we could say the star was diverted towards Chloris around ten years later.

DURATION

(TARDIS) (Ep1) ▨ ▨ ▨ ▨ ▨ ▨ ▨ ▨ ▨ ▨ ▨
Some time is spent in the TARDIS before it lands on Chloris …

⇨ **Day One (Ep1)** ▨ ▨ ▨ ▨ ▨ ▨ ▨ ▨ ▨ ▨ ▨
It is night in the opening scenes at the pit.

⇨ **Day Two (Ep1-4)** ▨ ▨ ▨ ▨ ▨ ▨ ▨ ▨ ▨ ▨
The TARDIS lands at daytime. The bandits attack the palace that night.

⇨ **Day Three (Ep4)** ▨ ▨ ▨ ▨ ▨ ▨ ▨ ▨ ▨ ▨
It is day when Erato's ship leaves Chloris. (It took him one hour, seven seconds to weave a new shell for his spaceship). Presumably it took all night to pull him out of the pit.

NIGHTMARE OF EDEN

+STORY LINK

There is nothing to indicate that 'Nightmare Of Eden' is consecutive to 'The Creature From The Pit'. As noted under 'The Creature From The Pit', there is an 11-year off-screen gap between 'The Armageddon Factor' and 'The Leisure Hive'. However, it is likely that there is a degree of consecutiveness to the previous story, in which the TARDIS answers Erato's distress call when the Mark Three Emergency Transceiver is connected to the console. In 'Nightmare Of Eden' the TARDIS answers the *Empress*'s mayday, so it is possible that the Mark Three Emergency Transceiver is still connected and picks up the signal. The Transceiver probably overrides the Randomiser.

OBSERVATIONS

- The CET works on a similar principle to the Mini-scopes of 'Carnival Of Monsters'. Also, the dimensional field of the machine is like the TARDIS – bigger on the inside. There are eight planets named on the dial on the CET machine – Eden, Vij, Zil, Darp, Lvan, Brus, Gidi and Ranx, but there are twelve crystals in Tryst's collection. It is said that the projections have left bald patches on the surface of the planets. But some of the projections seen also feature sky, so are there bald patches in the air as well?

- Romana wonders if the people who make Russian dolls 'realised they were making a model of the Universe ... As a primitive concept.' This would explain the relationship that N-Space has with E-Space (see 'Full Circle', 'State Of Decay', 'Warriors' Gate'). In 'Army Of Ghosts', the Doctor describes there being 'billions of Universes all stacked up against each other'.

LANGUAGE

Although Fisk and Costa are from Azure, it is likely that they are colonists from Earth, as opposed to being native to Azure.

TIMELINE DATES

2116 ◆
When Rigg checks Galactic Salvage & Insurance on his computer, it says the company was:

FORMED LONDON * EARTH 2068
LIQUIDATED 2096

Rigg then tells the Doctor that the company 'went out of business 20 years ago'. This places 'Nightmare Of Eden' in 2116. (The reason the company went out of business may have been due to T-Mat, which puts an end to space travel in the last decade of the twenty-first century. See 'The Seeds Of Death'.)

2020 ◆
We learn that the only previously known source of vrax was 'stamped out long ago'. With 'Nightmare Of Eden' set in 2116, we can assume that the source was destroyed in the early 21st century, when there were early colonies on other planets. Romana seems to possess first-hand knowledge about vraxoin. Given that she had never been away from Gallifrey prior to 'The Ribos Operation', she must have learned of this from the Time Lord files or during her 11 years with the Doctor.

2068
2080 ⋆
2096 ▨ ▨ ▨ ▨ ▨ ▨ ▨ ▨ ▨ ▨ ▨ ▨ ▨ ▨

The years of Galactic Salvage & Insurance's operation, as seen on the *Empress*'s computer. The Doctor knows of them, so he must have visited the time period when they were still in operation, say 2080.

2106 ▨ ▨ ▨ ▨ ▨ ▨ ▨ ▨ ▨ ▨ ▨ ▨ ▨ ▨

Space travel ceased by 2084 (see 'The Seeds Of Death', 'Warriors Of The Deep' and A HISTORY OF SPACE-FLIGHT). With rockets back in service at the end of 'The Seeds Of Death' we can assume that warp-drive was discovered soon afterwards. With 'The Seeds Of Death' set in 2096 and 'Nightmare Of Eden' in 2116, we can assume that warp was discovered mid-way through the intervening 20 years, say 2106, which provides sufficient time for Tryst's many expeditions to other planets. Even by 2116 warp was still relatively new because the *Empress* passengers wear 'protective coveralls'.

Warp enables travel across the galaxy. Azure is in the West Galaxy, the *Empress* travelling there from Station Nine (presumably one of the space wheels as seen in 'The Wheel In Space').

Tryst says his objective is to 'qualify and quantify every species in our galaxy. One more trip and I may achieve it'. This indicates that he has spent many years undertaking his research.

2111 ⋆ ▨ ▨ ▨ ▨ ▨ ▨ ▨ ▨ ▨ ▨ ▨ ▨ ▨

Tryst's expeditions must have taken several years, so the CET was built, based on Professor Stein's research, say five years prior to 'Nightmare Of Eden', around 2111. For the Doctor to know Stein by reputation he must have visited this time period before.

2115 ▨ ▨ ▨ ▨ ▨ ▨ ▨ ▨ ▨ ▨ ▨ ▨ ▨ ▨

Stott has been living inside the Eden projection for '183 days', after disappearing for 'two hours on Eden the day before he was 'killed''. Depending on the month in which 'Nightmare Of Eden' is set (this is unknown) this was either 2115 or 2116. I have chosen 2115. Stott is a Major in the Intelligence section of Space Corps, which could be the same as the Interstellar Space Corps in 'The Space Pirates'.

DURATION

⇨ **Day One (Ep1-4)**

The female passenger is annoyed by the long delay: 'We should have been on Azure hours ago'. In Ep3 the Doctor starts to separate the ships at '20:01' ship's time, and finishes at '20:25'. This gives the Duration as being over several hours.

THE HORNS OF NIMON

+STORY LINK

As noted under 'Nightmare Of Eden', there is an 11-year off-screen period between 'The Armageddon Factor' and 'The Leisure Hive', during which 'The Horns Of Nimon' takes place.

At the end of 'Nightmare Of Eden' the Doctor and Romana leave to return the projections contained in Tryst's CET machine to the planets from whence they came. There are twelve crystals in total, so it is likely that it would have taken quite some time (possibly even years?) to travel to each of the planets, given the TARDIS' navigation problems and the Randomiser connection.

OBSERVATIONS

- The Doctor points out he was glad 'this time I reminded them to paint their ship white. The last time anything like this happened I completely forgot. Caused quite a hoohah'. This statement implies that he was there when Theseus defeated the Minotaur in the old Greek legends. As the legend goes, Theseus was supposed to hoist a white sail on his journey home from killing the Minotaur to show his father the King that he was still alive. However, in his haste to return home, Theseus forgot to change the sail, and when the King saw the black sail on the horizon he threw himself into the sea. In fact, in 'The Creature From The Pit' the Doctor mentions how Theseus wanted to unravel his scarf in order to make his way through the labyrinth, so the two events are probably part of the same untelevised adventure, which must have been long before the Doctor met Romana.

LANGUAGE

The TARDIS manual is labelled 'TARDIS HANDBOOK TYPE 40'. The Nimon on Skonnos speaks the Skonnon language, as must do the Anethans. The labels on the computers and other machines in the Nimon's power complex use Earth symbols.

TIMELINE DATES

2116 ♦

The fact that K9 has information in his memory banks about the Skonnon Empire, which 'extended over one hundred star systems', suggests that the Skonnon Empire is part of Earth's galaxy, but located in a region that does not include Earth itself nor any of its colonies. The original K9 was built around 5000 AD, which would set 'The Horns Of Nimon' prior to that date. It is stated in 'The Invisible Enemy' that K9 knows everything Professor Marius knows ('and more'), which could include files on Skonnos. Although the Doctor built K9 Mark Two, the robot would still contain the same memory as Mark One, enhanced by the Doctor's own memories and recordings from the TARDIS computer banks. It is clear that the Doctor knows nothing of Skonnos so unless the information had been extracted from the TARDIS, this K9 already knew of the Empire.

To take this further, 'The Horns Of Nimon' could be set at the same time period as 'Nightmare Of Eden', in 2116. To ensure that the TARDIS is able to travel to each of the twelve planets so they can return the twelve projections from the CET crystals to the correct planets in the same time zone, the Doctor may have had to disconnect not only the Randomiser but also a specific circuit of the TARDIS. After they have completed returning the projections the Doctor reconnects the circuit but then decides to do some further maintenance while parts of the TARDIS systems are still shut down, as he is seen doing in the opening scenes of 'The Horns Of Nimon'.

Given that the year 2116 satisfies both of the above scenarios, that is the date I have selected.

2096
2101

The Skonnon Empire fell no more than two generations earlier: Teka says 'our grandparents' saw the Skonnon warships 'in the days of the first conquest' of Aneth. Soldeed was the only surviving scientist from the civil war days, so the fall of Skonnos was within his own lifetime. The Doctor deduces (incorrectly?) that the Skonnon ship is 'centuries' old; it had dated from the time of the first Skonnos Empire. We can place the fall of the Empire around 20 years earlier, in 2096, and the arrival of the Nimon a few years, say 5, later, in 2101. Tributes from Aneth have been made 'every year'.

2111 ▪ ▪ ▪ ▪ ▪ ▪ ▪ ▪ ▪ ▪ ▪ ▪ ▪ ▪ ▪ ▪

Sezom tells Romana he had been experimenting with jasonite 'for years', as an aid to ridding the Nimon from his planet, say 5 years.

DURATION

⇨ **Day One (Ep1-4)** ▪ ▪ ▪ ▪ ▪ ▪ ▪ ▪ ▪ ▪ ▪

The spaceship is '12 hours out from Aneth' and 'only another 12 to Skonnos', but is delayed due to the accident. The sky is light outside the window in all the scenes on Skonnos, so the story takes place over one Skonnon day. Romana is on Crinoth for a short while.

UNSEEN ADVENTURES

In 'The Pirate Planet', Romana says she doesn't know who Newton was but by the time of her abduction by Borusa in 'The Five Doctors' she knows the scientist studied at Cambridge and of his discoveries about action/reaction forces, so it is possible that the Doctor told her about Newton, or she has met the scientist in the intervening period.

THE FIVE DOCTORS

STORY LINK

Given the manner of the Doctor's clothes (he is not wearing his burgundy coat), the Cambridge 'adventure' is set prior to his change of clothes, which is prior to 'The Leisure Hive'.

All the previous Doctors are time scooped from a point very close to their regeneration; this may be one reason why the fourth Doctor is trapped in the vortex – his regeneration is, relatively speaking, still some time away.

As noted under 'The Horns Of Nimon', 'The Five Doctors' segment takes place during the 11-year off-screen gap. Romana knows all about Newton having studied in Cambridge, and yet in 'The Pirate Planet' she didn't know who he was. Clearly she has had some education about the Earth scientist since 'The Pirate Planet'.

OBSERVATIONS

- The Doctor and Romana are time scooped when they are punting on the river Cam. When they are eventually released from the vortex, they are no longer in the punt: Romana is in the TARDIS and the Doctor is trapped under a wire fence. It is possible that these views are simply from a later point during the same day following their return to the punt.
- Refer to 'The Five Doctors' under the fifth Doctor's stories for more details on this adventure.

TIMELINE DATES

1979, October ·
The fourth Doctor says 'it's October' (they were actually supposed to arrive 'for May Week' which is 'in June'). I have set the scene in the same period of the fourth Doctor's time stream as his visit to France in 1979 ('City Of Death').

DURATION

⇨ **Day One**
It is day when the Doctor and Romana are time scooped, and they are eventually released the same day.

UNSEEN ADVENTURES

During the time Romana spends with the Doctor, she experiences numerous adventures, of which only a handful are seen on-screen. Many of the adventures and experiences that are noted in the section on Romanadvoratrelundar under NAME-DROPPING occur at this point.

THE LEISURE HIVE

STORY LINK

There is nothing to suggest that this story follows directly on from 'The Horns Of Nimon' or from the Doctor and Romana's visit to Cambridge ('The Five Doctors'). The only link to the previous season is the mention of the Randomiser, which the Doctor has disconnected temporarily in order to get to Brighton. He says 'I can't spend the rest of my life running away from the Black Guardian', which reinforces the idea that several years have passed since 'The Armageddon Factor'. Romana is now 150 years old (she was 'nearly 140' in 'The Ribos Operation'), which means she has been with the Doctor for some 11 years.

At some point after 'The Horns Of Nimon' K9 has regained his original voice, and since 'The Five Doctors' the Doctor has selected a new colour-coordinated wardrobe.

LANGUAGE

The Doctor is unable to understand the Foamasi language, although they seem to understand English. Given that the majority of visitors to the Hive appear to be from Earth, it would appear that the Argolins speak English. The generator computer also speaks English.

TIMELINE DATES

1980, April •

The Doctor says he has twice missed the opening of the Brighton Pavilion, which was in 1825 (he is also trying to get to Brighton in 'Horror Of Fang Rock'). The Palace Pier, which opened in 1899, is visible in the opening shot. Romana points out to the Doctor that 'you've got the century wrong, you've got the season wrong'. This indicates that they are not in the nineteenth century.

There is a brief glimpse of modern traffic signals arching across the road behind the TARDIS, just before K9 is damaged, so it must be no later than the twentieth century. In addition to this, the West Pier, which is situated further up the beach, is also visible. The West Pier was severely damaged in the hurricane that hit Southern England in 1987 to the extent that the pedestrian walkway collapsed into the sea. The West Pier is intact in the shots that are visible.

From these clues I would tend to place this portion of the story in the same month and year that it was made, April 1980. The anachronistic beach huts could be from a festival or some such.

2290 •

Romana gives the year of the Foamasi / Argolin war as being 'in relative Earth date 2250', which 'was 40 years ago' according to 'Brock'. This dates 'The Leisure Hive' as 2290.

1825
This is the year in our history in which the Brighton Pavilion was opened.

2250
Romana gives the year of the war as 'relative Earth date two thousand two hundred and fifty'.

2260
2270
Pangol says 'for 20 years a moratorium was declared on the technique [of cloning] until I came of age'. He is about 30. The Argolins probably experimented for 10 years after the war, until about 2260, when Pangol was born. After say 10 years of failed experimentation, the moratorium is declared in 2270.

2285
The fake Brock says 'after all our years of dealings over the telecommunicator, here I am at last'. We can assume that he and the Argolins have been negotiating for about five years at the most.

2289
Morix says 'bookings for last year were bad'.

2386
Romana says 'this part of the galaxy doesn't discover unreal transfer until two thousand three hundred and eighty six'.

2550
Mena says the surface of Argolis 'won't be habitable for three centuries'. From the year of the war, that would be 2550.

DURATION

⇨ **Day One (Earth) (Ep1)**
The Doctor and Romana are at Brighton for at least a few hours.

⇨ **Day One (Ep1)**
The first scenes set on Argolis would appear to be one day, with Brock's arrival being the next day, given the time factor required for the journey from Earth to Argolis.

⇨ **Day Two (Ep1-4)** ▨ ▨ ▨ ▨ ▨ ▨ ▨ ▨ ▨ ▨ ▨ ▨

Brock arrives this day. Pangol's demonstration of the generator in the 'morning' is an 'hour and a half' in duration. The Doctor and Romana arrive at the beginning of the speech. The Doctor is 'tried' by the generator that night.

⇨ **Day Three (Ep4)** ▨ ▨ ▨ ▨ ▨ ▨ ▨ ▨ ▨ ▨ ▨ ▨

'Dawn' breaks on Argolis soon after the fake Brock's unmasking. The Doctor and Romana leave that morning.

MEGLOS

+STORY LINK

'Meglos' follows on directly from 'The Leisure Hive': Romana is still wearing her bathing suit, and she and the Doctor are fixing K9 following his 'swim' at Brighton beach. The rotor is moving, but the ship is only travelling in space. The TARDIS control room has been modified yet again.

OBSERVATIONS

- Romana knows of the screens of Zolfa-Thura from 'in the history books'. Since she came direct from Gallifrey, we can presume she means history books on Gallifrey. This means that the period in which 'Meglos' destroyed his home world is in the Time Lords' own past (see GALLIFREY HISTORY).
- For Meglos to be able to put the TARDIS into a chronic hysteresis, the Zolfa-Thurans must have had rudimentary knowledge of time travel, one of the few races in the Universe to achieve this.

LANGUAGE

The Gaztaks speak English with the Earthling. Meglos later speaks through the Earthling to the Tigellans. Even the writing on the computer screens on Zolfa-Thura is in English.

TIMELINE DATES

1983 ⚹ ▨ ▨ ▨ ▨ ▨ ▨ ▨ ▨ ▨ ▨ ▨ ▨ ▨

The clothes worn by the Earthling suggest the early 1980s [the story was made in mid-1980]. The Gaztaks do not have time travel capabilities so the events on Tigella are contemporaneous to the time period from which the Earthling is taken.

The Doctor and Romana are summoned back to Gallifrey at the end of the story. Given that in 'Full Circle', after returning the human to his own time on Earth, the TARDIS then travels spatially to Gallifrey (K9 says 'Spatial drive initiated' / 'Flight path clear'), the scenes on Earth and Tigella must be in the same year as on Gallifrey. As covered under THE DOCTOR'S AGE, the Doctor and Romana's GRT is now 1983.

8000 BC

Twice Meglos says 'Ten thousand years'. It is not clear to what he is referring, but we can assume that this was when the Dodecahedron was taken to Tigella. Deedrix says 'for thousands of years our lives have been dominated by a mystery' – the artefact. On the assumption that a Tigellan year is similar to an Earth year, the Dodecahedron fell to Tigella around 8000 BC.

1933 •

The Doctor says it 'must be 50 of your years since I was last' on Tigella. There is no indication as to how long a Tigellan year is, but the Doctor is probably making the comparison between a Tigellan year and a Gallifreyan year. Given that planetary orbits are similar (see THE N-SPACE UNIVERSE), we can assume that it was around 1933.

Zastor says 'You haven't changed much, Doctor. A little older, a little wiser,' which means that the Doctor was in his fourth incarnation when he visited. It is not established when this was in the Doctor's time-stream, but the Doctor says it was 'a long time ago' – so his visit was probably during the 'missing' 100 years between 'Planet Of Evil' and 'Pyramids Of Mars'.

DURATION

(TARDIS) (Ep1)

The Doctor and Romana spend time in the TARDIS repairing K9, as the ship drifts into the Prion system.

⇨ Day One (Ep1-4)

The full duration of the story appears to be only a few Tigellan hours, based upon the fact that the city's power is cut off at the beginning of the story and cannot be resumed for 'three hours'. Meglos only needs 'one hour' to obtain the Dodecahedron. It is day in all the scenes on the surface of Tigella. It is day in the early Zolfa-Thura scenes but night in Ep4 when the TARDIS lands.

⇨ **Day Two (Ep4)** ▦ ▦ ▦ ▦ ▦ ▦ ▦ ▦ ▦

It is day on Tigella when the TARDIS leaves (unless the planet's orbit around its sun is different to Zolfa-Thura's orbit in which case it could still be Day One).

FULL CIRCLE

+STORY LINK

'Full Circle' takes place immediately after 'Meglos'. The TARDIS is on Earth in the opening moments, the Doctor having just dropped the Earthling back home as promised.

OBSERVATIONS

- Alzarius and Gallifrey share the same coordinates from Galactic Zero Centre, however Alzarius has negative coordinates. Interestingly, Nefred on Alzarius resembles a native of Gallifrey: the Keeper of the Matrix (The Trial Of A Time Lord) [actor James Bree played both roles].
- The TARDIS falls through a Charged Vacuum Emboitement (CVE). With 'Full Circle' set in 1983, it could be that the CVE is in fact the very same one the Doctor stabilised in Cassiopeia two years earlier in 1981! (See 'Logopolis'). In other words, the TARDIS enters E-Space two years after it exits.

LANGUAGE

The instruction panels on the Starliner hatches are written in English.

TIMELINE DATES

<<1983>> ▦ ▦ ▦ ▦ ▦ ▦ ▦ ▦ ▦ ▦

The TARDIS is on 1983 Earth in the opening moments of the story, 1983 now being the Doctor and Romana's GRT (see THE DOCTOR'S AGE). K9 then announces 'spatial drive initiated'. The ETA to Gallifrey is '32 minutes'. The fact that K9 also announces 'flight path clear' shows clearly that this is a journey only in space, and not also in time. Although the Doctor does say they have landed in the 'wrong place, at the wrong time', and that a CVE is 'one of the rarest space / *time* events in the Universe' (my emphasis), it is clear that the journey from Earth 1983 to modern Gallifrey is in the same time zone. With the image of Gallifrey appearing on the scanner, but the ship being on Alzarius, the relative date for 'Full Circle' must still be 1983.

<<98,017 BC>>

Romana estimates that the ship crashed 'four thousand generations ago'. Assuming that a generation is 25 years (as the Doctor states in 'Four To Doomsday'), that puts the crash 100,000 years ago, around 98,017 BC.

<<1933>>

Login tells the Doctor that Mistfall occurs 'every 50 years or so'. Dexeter comments that it was '50 years ago' that Corellis and Dell made their initial discoveries.

DURATION

(TARDIS) (Ep1)

The TARDIS is in flight for '32 minutes' prior to landing on Alzarius.

⇨ Day One (Ep1-4)

When Mistfall first appears the Alzarians have 'two hours' before the Starliner is sealed. Dexeter has to wait 'an hour' before he can begin his examination of the small Marsh creature. Reference is made in Ep4 to Adric's injury, sustained in Ep1, which was 'hours ago', so the story takes place over several hours of just one day.

STATE OF DECAY

+STORY LINK

'State Of Decay' is consecutive with 'Full Circle'; Adric is revealed to have stowed away on board the TARDIS.

OBSERVATIONS

- The *Hydrax* was heading for Beta Two in the Perugellis Sector. By 1973 the furthest that a man had travelled in space was past Jupiter (see 'The Android Invasion', and A HISTORY OF SPACE-FLIGHT), so it is only expected that over 20 years later space technology would have reached a point where even further distances are possible. In 'Logopolis' the CVE that the Doctor and the Master stabilise is in line with the constellation of Cassiopeia. Therefore it is possible that Beta Two is located in this constellation (creating a nice irony that the Doctor creates the CVE through which the vampire and the *Hydrax* fall, making him ultimately responsible for the events that unfold in this adventure).

LANGUAGE

Since the villagers are descendants from the crew of the *Hydrax*, they speak English. The map of their island is labelled in English, and Kalmar understands the text on the computer screen.

TIMELINE DATES

<<2929>>*

K9 describes the planet as having a 'day equivalent of 23.3 Earth hours; year to 350 Earth days'. It is stated on many occasions that The Three Who Rule have reigned for 'a thousand years', but since the planet has a shorter day and year than Earth's, we cannot place the story 1,000 years from when the *Hydrax* was launched (2999). However, it is possible to calculate the relative date on Earth from the data given:

Planet: 23.3 x 350 = 8155 hours in a year
Earth: 24 x 365.25 = 8766 hours in a year

8155 / 8766 = .93 x 1,000 = 930 + 1999 = 2929

The relative date on Earth is therefore 2929.

Before 10,000,000 BC
1999, January

According to the Doctor the Vampires 'swarmed all over the Universe ... [in] the misty dawn of history, when even Rassilon was young'. The vampires 'came from nowhere' (which suggests that they could have in fact originated from E-space). The Time Lords 'hunted them down across the Universe in a war so long and so bloody that we were sickened of violence for ever'. When he hears the Doctor use the term 'Time Lords', Aukon knows them to be 'the ancient enemies of the Great One', so it is clear that the Gallifreyans had mastered time travel at the time of the war. As covered under GALLIFREY HISTORY the Time Lords came into being some 10,000,000 years ago, so the war was presumably less than 10,000,000 years ago. Aukon says 'thanks to the blood and souls we have fed to him for so long his body is healed of wounds, regenerated and whole once more'. Since the *Hydrax* has only been on the planet for a thousand years, one wonders how the vampire survived for the tens of millions of years after the war. And indeed, given that there are many planets in E-Space, why did the creature not summon other life forms on which to feed, rather than wait millions of years for humans to come?

Given that the *Hydrax* is launched around 1999, I think it safe to assume that the war with the vampires actually took place in the Time Lords' own future; the fact that 'certain time vehicles' such as Type 40s are installed with the Record of Rassilon supports that the war with the vampires took place in a time zone different to Rassilon's GRT. The Time Lords therefore travelled into the late twentieth century where they encountered the vampires. The CVE the King Vampire fell through is probably the one in Cassiopeia, stabilised by the Doctor in 1981 in 'Logopolis', as this is the only CVE that still existed after 'Logopolis' was destroyed in 1981. So, at the end of the war in 1999, the vampire falls through the Cassiopeia CVE and is dormant on the planet for a short time before the arrival of the *Hydrax*.

1998, December 12
<<1999, January>>*
The date the *Hydrax*'s data file was written appears as '12/12/1998' on the computer record of the ship's manifest. It would be expected that the ship was launched at some date after this, say January 1999 (see A HISTORY OF SPACE-FLIGHT). The Doctor recognises the Arrow Class spaceship, so he has seen one before.

<<2429>>
Aukon says the vampires have bred dullness, conformity and obedience into the peasants 'for 20 generations'. If a generation is 25 years, this makes it 500 years, since 2429. It is clear from the ship's computer log that the villagers are the descendants of the ship's scientific crew rather than being native to the planet; the computer shows files on the three senior officers, and a cross-reference to 'Tech Grades'.

DURATION

⇨ Day One (Ep1-2)
It is dawn when the selection is made. The Doctor and Romana head for the Tower that 'night'.

⇨ Day Two (Ep2-4)
It is morning when the Doctor and Romana reach the Tower. The vampire is killed soon after 'midnight' (which on this world is at '23.3' hours).

WARRIORS' GATE

At the end of 'State Of Decay' the Doctor tells Adric he is being taken back to the Starliner, but in the opening moments of 'Warriors' Gate' there is no further discussion of this. Also, in 'State Of Decay' Adric wears a patch on the right knee of his pants (from when he wounded his knee in 'Full Circle'). In 'Warriors' Gate' the patch is no longer there. It is likely that they have been trying to return to the Starliner for some time, but keep getting caught in a time-Rift.

Romana confirms that she doesn't want to go back to Gallifrey. The Doctor and Adric are still Gallifrey-bound at the beginning of 'Logopolis', so it appears that only a very short time has passed between 'State Of Decay' and 'Warriors' Gate' – a matter of weeks or months as opposed to years. This is supported by the fact that in terms of their personal GRT, the Doctor and Romana entered E-Space *en route* to Gallifrey (see 'Full Circle') in 1983. 'Arc Of Infinity', in which the Doctor finally gets to Gallifrey, is set in May 1983. Therefore, the Doctor is stuck in E-Space for several months only. As noted under 'The Armageddon Factor', the Black Guardian probably loses trace of the Doctor when the TARDIS falls into E-Space.

As is covered under 'Logopolis', the Doctor probably teaches Adric how to read Earth numbering at this point.

OBSERVATIONS

- The time when the Gundans overran the Tharil palace in the void appears to have been decades previously based on the state of the cobwebs in the banqueting hall. I have not included this period in the TIMELINE because it is impossible to establish a firm date.

LANGUAGE

The slavers speak English, as do the Tharils. The slavers' currency is written as '100 Imperials'.

TIMELINE DATES

<<1981, February 26>>
The story is set in a white void where time-rifts flow between the negative E-Space Universe and the positive N-Space Universe, so true dates cannot apply. In fact, after another failed attempt to escape the void, Sagan says 'Home readings show no space,

no time, just like before'.

As the slavers have sophisticated warp-drive engines, and supralight-speed with dampers, the story could be placed in the future after warp-drive is discovered (after 2106, see 'Nightmare Of Eden'), although there is no reason to suspect that the slavers are from Earth. The Doctor and Romana both know that dwarf star alloy can be used against time-sensitives. Since they are from N-Space, then it is possible that the slavers are also from N-Space. The slavers have Earth-type names, and there is even graffiti saying 'Kilroy Was Here' on the spaceship walls, but since one of the crew is called Kilroy it is not necessarily suggesting a link to the popular graffiti slogan used on Earth. Another pointer to a possible Earth origin is the mention of 'sardines' and 'custard', while the food eaten by the crew resembles recognisable items such as pickles. However, the slavers use a coin currency called Imperials, which does not match any future-time Earth period. Given that the Tharils only travel within E-Space, and that humans do not need time-sensitives to warp-travel in N-Space, plus the fact that the slavers have Tharils 'enslaved on many planets' it is pretty clear that the slavers are native to E-Space.

At the end of 'Warriors' Gate' the TARDIS is blown back into N-Space and lands on Traken on 26 February 1981, so it is logical that this is also the relative date for 'Warriors' Gate'. (A similar thing happens to the TARDIS in 'The Mind Robber' and 'The Invasion'.)

<<1980, November>>

The slavers have been 'stuck in this nothing for months and months'. I have selected November for this – being three months prior to when 'Warriors' Gate' is set.

DURATION

⇨ Day One (Ep1-4)

The story takes place over the space of several hours in the void. At one point Aldo and Royce are ordered to bring out 'lunch'.

THE KEEPER OF TRAKEN

+STORY LINK

'The Keeper Of Traken' follows on directly from 'Warriors' Gate' (Adric comments that they are 'supposed to be on our way back to Gallifrey'). In fact, the closing TARDIS scene of 'Warriors' Gate' flows into the opening TARDIS scene of 'The Keeper Of Traken' so smoothly that it almost appears to be a direct continuation of the very same conversation.

MASTER LINK

The Master appears to be in the same decayed state he was in at the end of 'The Deadly Assassin', although he has achieved some stability, so we can assume that he went to Traken soon after the events of 'The Deadly Assassin'. In terms of his and the Doctor's GRT it was 1962 in 'The Deadly Assassin'; it is now 1983 in 'The Keeper Of Traken', which means the Master has been on Traken for 21 years. If we assume that the Master went to Traken specifically to take over the Keepership, it seems odd that, with a fully functioning TARDIS, he would arrive 21 years before the changeover of Keepers was due. To explain this he probably went to Traken with the original intention of arriving to see how long he would need to wait before jumping ahead in time to the changeover point. But he failed to anticipate the influence of the planet, which freezes his 'new ship', effectively stranding him in the wrong time zone. All he had to do is wait. He does say 'You will find immobility endurable, Doctor. I speak from experience', which supports the idea that he has been trapped for a very long time.

The Master has a proper TARDIS (disguised as a grandfather clock, as it was in 'The Deadly Assassin'), inside his 'Melkur' ship, which he says is 'my new ship'. This vessel has the usual roundels and TARDIS hum, but it might not necessarily be a TARDIS, but some other kind of time machine that the Master has acquired, and modified to resemble a TARDIS.

OBSERVATIONS

- The Master takes over Tremas' form, and as such is no longer a pure Time Lord. In 'The Mark Of The Rani' it is clear that he still has two hearts ('Next to my hearts. Both of them'). It is also clear from 'Earthshock' that the Doctor is the only alien in the caves with two hearts, as detected on Walters' scanner; Nyssa – and therefore other Trakenites – does not have two hearts, so the Master must have retained this aspect of his Gallifreyan physiology during the transference.

LANGUAGE

Adric is able to read the Doctor's time logs (but has trouble with the handwriting!). These are presumably written in Gallifreyan, so the Time Lord 'gift' must be assisting Adric. The numeral symbols 3 and 7 are the same on Traken as they are on Earth.

TIMELINE DATES

1981, February 25 – 27 ·

Nyssa contacts the Doctor in 'Logopolis' while the TARDIS is on Earth, on 28 February 1981. On the assumption that the message has been sent without going through a time warp (the Trakenites do not have this level of technology), then the events in 'The Keeper Of Traken' take place prior to 28 February 1981. Assuming that Nyssa contacts the Doctor soon after discovering that her father has vanished, we can place the three days of 'The Keeper Of Traken' as being 25 – 27 February 1981 (see Duration). (See also CALENDAR FEBRUARY / MARCH 1981.)

981

The Doctor says 'it's a pity about that poor chap having to sit for thousands of years in a chair', while Kassia says that the current Keeper has only been in power 'for a thousand years'. We could say that Kassia was correct, and the Doctor is just generalising.

Tremas remarks that the Source has been 'expanded over the years'.

1962

The arrival of the Melkur 'was many years ago'. Kassia has been tending Melkur 'all those years', ever since she 'was a child'. In the 'flashback' shown to the Doctor and Adric by the Keeper, Kassia looks to be a teenager, possibly younger. As covered in Master Link above, the Master arrives in 1962. Kassia looks to be about 35 in 1981, making her around 14 in 1962. [It is a Production Factor that Kassia does not actually look only 14.]

DURATION

⇨ Day One (25 February 1981) (Ep1)

Tremas and Kassia's wedding is that night.

⇨ Day Two (26 February 1981) (Ep1-2)

A body is found the next day. It is getting dark when the TARDIS lands. The Doctor and Adric are placed under Tremas' custody as dawn breaks.

⇨ Day Three (27 February 1981) (Ep2-4)

The Doctor has breakfast with Tremas. At the end of the tale, the hands of the clock-TARDIS read '11.56', so it is probably that night if the clock-TARDIS shows a true reflection of the time.

LOGOPOLIS

The Doctor and Adric both refer to leaving Traken, after having dealt with the Master, and they are now once again heading for Gallifrey, just as the ship is at the end of 'Meglos'. (The Doctor's GRT is still 1983; see THE DOCTOR'S AGE.) At the end of 'The Keeper Of Traken' the Doctor speaks of giving the TARDIS an overhaul. This implies that 'Logopolis' follows directly on from 'The Keeper Of Traken'. Adric refers to the Doctor having taught him how to read Earth numbering and he knows about Earth being 'the planet with all the oceans'. This instruction about Earth probably takes place between 'State Of Decay' and 'Warriors' Gate', as there seems to be insufficient time between 'The Keeper Of Traken' and 'Logopolis' for such a detailed lesson. Also, in 'Earthshock' the Doctor refers to the times he and Adric have had discussions on a variety of topics. Given that most of the stories from 'Logopolis' to 'Earthshock' are consecutive, Adric must have had considerable time between 'State Of Decay' and 'Logopolis' to learn these things.

The Doctor refers to his hurried departure from Gallifrey, which 'was ages ago'; and to fixing the chameleon circuit, which broke in '100,000 BC': 'I've been meaning to do this for centuries'. In terms of THE DOCTOR'S AGE, the latter happened 325 years ago.

Having stolen Tremas' body, the Master leaves Traken in his second TARDIS and follows the Doctor. Using his new powers of the Keepership the Master is able to read the Doctor's mind and anticipate his plan to measure a police box, and arrives on Earth before the Doctor. On discovering the Doctor's plan to then go to Logopolis, the Master sees this as a perfect opportunity to hold the Universe to ransom. Since 'Logopolis' and 'Castrovalva' are consecutive, the Master must have anticipated that the Doctor might in fact stop him, and so the Master sets in motion a series of contingency plans should they be needed: such as kidnapping Adric and using the boy to send the Doctor's TARDIS back in time to 'Event One', and then setting up a space / time trap at Castrovalva should the Doctor escape. The Master probably devised these plans while stuck on Traken for over 20 years.

- At the beginning of 'Logopolis' the Doctor decides to go to Logopolis to fix the chameleon circuit. But first he needs to go to Earth to measure a real police box. He tells Adric that police boxes are 'more or less obsolete by the time we'll be arriving'. It is curious therefore that he doesn't set the TARDIS for, say 1963, when police boxes would be commonplace, making the job easier for him.

- The Monitor recognises the fourth Doctor ('Time has changed little for either of us, Doctor'), indicating that the Doctor's previous visit was during this same incarnation. The Pharos dish was not there then (it is a 'recent addition'), so it was long before 1981 (I have not placed this meeting in the TIMELINE). It is during this previous visit that the Logopolitans offer to fix the chameleon circuit, but for reasons unknown the Doctor never takes them up on it.

- The concept of CVEs first appears in 'Full Circle'. As noted under 'State Of Decay' and 'Logopolis' above, the CVE that features in these stories is probably the very same one. To recap chronologically, the Logopolitans create CVEs thousands of years ago. By 1981 they establish a means by which to keep a CVE open of its own accord (the research team's final project, as revealed in 'Logopolis'). In 1981 the Doctor and the Master stabilise the CVE in Cassiopeia ('Logopolis'). In 1983, the TARDIS falls through this CVE into E-Space ('Full Circle'). Then in 1999, the Great Vampire and the spaceship *Hydrax* fall through the same CVE into E-Space ('State Of Decay').

- There is no explanation as to where the white Watcher comes from, other than 'he was the Doctor all the time'. As covered under 'Planet Of The Spiders', it is possible that the Watcher is a projection of the Doctor's future regeneration, an ability passed to the Doctor by K'Anpo when the Time Lord provides the energy required to trigger the third Doctor's regeneration. The projection is an involuntary side-effect, and the Doctor is untrained in controlling it, which is why the Watcher appears as a shapeless figure and does not look like the fifth Doctor. There is one aspect of the Watcher that could be significant regarding the Doctor's apparently mysterious past: the Watcher is able to unset the coordinates and disconnect 'the entire coordinate sub-system' to take the TARDIS 'right out of time and space', which the TARDIS isn't supposed to do. Perhaps the Watcher is drawing on knowledge from K'Anpo, or perhaps from knowledge hidden deep within the Doctor's subconscious. Alternatively, if the Doctor has indeed been to the Old Time, as is implied under MORE THAN A TIME LORD? and AN ENIGMA CALLED SUSAN, perhaps it is by using this method to take the ship out of time and space that overrides the TARDIS fail-safe (GALLIFREY HISTORY) which enables it to travel into Gallifrey's past.

- When the Watcher takes the TARDIS 'outside space and time', on the scanner,

Adric and Nyssa see 'the whole Universe', a huge white cloud-like mass. The Universe is described as being a closed system. In 'Nightmare Of Eden' Romana reveals that the Universe is just like a Russian doll with smaller Universes inside it.

LANGUAGE

The Master records his 'blackmail' speech into an ordinary dictaphone tape recorder, which he then broadcasts to the 'Peoples of the Universe'. The Time Lord 'gift' must somehow be able to translate this message into every language that exists; either that or every being in this Universe understands Gallifreyan or English. The Logopolitans use Earth numbering, but only so they can operate the Pharos computer.

Adric says the Doctor has taught him how to read 'Earth symbols'. But why would this be necessary if the Time Lord 'gift' translates languages?

TIMELINE DATES

1981, February 28 – March 1

Tegan remarks to her Aunt Vanessa that 'it's the 1980s'. In 'Four To Doomsday', the date of Tegan's flight is given as 'A778 17.30 hours … February the 28th, 1981'. Vanessa says she has been having problems with her car 'this morning' and the police detective greets the Doctor with 'Good morning', so Tegan is therefore on her way to Heathrow, for her first flight, on the morning of February 28. Since the flight is not until 5.30 pm, she probably has a few hours of preparation time before departure.

The sequences set on Logopolis and the subsequent scenes set at the Pharos Project on Earth are clearly contemporaneous (on the grounds that the Logopolitans have a copy of the Pharos computer room – they don't have time travel abilities – and the entropy field is eroding the Universe in the same time zone for both planets), but there is no reason to suggest that these sequences also take place on 28 February 1981. Certainly, the Watcher travels from 1981 Earth to Traken to collect Nyssa and take her to Logopolis without the readily apparent aid of a spaceship, which suggests that the three planets are contemporaneous, but then we don't fully understand the nature of the Watcher, so it is possible that the being is capable of independent time travel as well as movement through space.

The reason for my uncertainty about the date lies in Tegan's motives: Tegan travels to the Pharos Project in the Master's TARDIS because she wants to get home ('the Doctor is my return ticket back to London airport'). After the Doctor regenerates, she leaves in the TARDIS with Adric and Nyssa (in 'Castrovalva'). But there would seem to be no logical reason for her to do so. Considering that in the subsequent four stories

('Castrovalva', 'Four To Doomsday', 'Kinda', 'The Visitation') Tegan still wants to get home ('or he'll lose me my job'), it is odd she doesn't stay behind at the Pharos Project. Yes, it is true the Doctor is weak following his regeneration, but Tegan has known the Doctor for what is only a matter of a few hours. She has been accidentally 'abducted' by him and getting home is top priority as far as she is concerned, so it is highly unlikely she would stay with the TARDIS due to loyalty to the Doctor, who is still a stranger to her. She could have stayed on Earth after the Doctor was safely on board the TARDIS in 'Castrovalva', because the Pharos security guards got 'zapped' by the Master, so she was in no danger of being arrested by them. Common sense therefore rules that Tegan stays with the TARDIS because the events at the Pharos Project (and at Logopolis) do not take place on 28 February 1981. Tegan simply does not realise at the time that the Doctor is unable to get her back to her own time (as demonstrated in 'Four To Doomsday' and 'The Visitation', she is annoyed at the Doctor's inability to do just that).

The Doctor receives Nyssa's message while still on Earth on 28 February 1981. On the assumption that the signal has come direct from Traken, this shows that Traken still exists on 28 February 1981. Given that Nyssa's home is destroyed by the entropy field we know for sure that the destruction of the Universe begins in a time period after 28 February 1981, which means that Logopolis and Pharos would be in Tegan's future, any time from 28 February 1981 onwards, which was why she did not stay on Earth in 'Castrovalva' when she had the opportunity to do so. Of course, this does not explain how the Logopolitans are able to make a copy of the Pharos computer room and dish.

In the absence of clues to point to other dates, I am willing to set the whole story in 1981, with it being the night of 28 February 1981 when the Doctor arrives at the Pharos Project, and the dawn of 1 March 1981 when he regenerates. Tegan's decision to help the Doctor and not stay on Earth is based in part on the fact that it is now 1 March – the day after her flight – and she is under the (mistaken!) belief that the Doctor can return her to Earth in time to catch her flight on 28 February 1981.

(See CALENDAR FEBRUARY / MARCH 1981.)

Before 10,000,000 BC ▨ ▨ ▨ ▨ ▨ ▨ ▨ ▨ ▨ ▨

The Monitor reveals that the Universe 'long ago passed the point of total collapse ... we opened the [closed] system by creating voids [CVEs] into other Universes'. After the Master's meddling the Universe begins to slowly collapse 'after aeons of constraint'. Given that 'aeons' is an indeterminable amount of time it is difficult to place this event accurately. As noted under 'State Of Decay', the Great Vampire fell through the CVE in 1999, after the battle with the Time Lords, so this was probably the same CVE in

Cassiopeia that the Doctor stabilises 18 years earlier in 1981.

The Logopolitans have therefore been working on the problem of keeping the CVEs open on their own accord for thousands of years. It is only recently that they have reached the point of success in finding a way to keep the CVE open of its own accord, which is why they created the duplicate of the Pharos Project.

Given that the Time Lords came into being in 10,000,000 BC, it seems odd that they were not aware of the situation. This suggests that the start of the Universe's collapse happened long before the time of the Time Lords. Therefore, I have set the events at 'before' 10,000,000 BC.

1883 ✦
In our history, the renowned biologist Thomas Huxley (4 May 1825 to 29 June 1895) was President of the Royal Society from 1883 to 1885, so the Doctor probably met him around this time.

1981, January? ✦
The Doctor recognises that the computer room and dish at Logopolis are an exact duplicate of the Pharos Project on Earth, so clearly he has been to the Project site before, presumably at a time months or so earlier.

DURATION

(TARDIS) (Ep1)
The TARDIS is on its way to Gallifrey. The Doctor has spent some time brooding within the cloisters …

⇨ **Day One (28 February 1981) (Ep1-4)**
It is 'morning' when Tegan is on her way to the airport for her flight at 5.30 pm, still some seven or so hours away. After the failed attempt to flush out the Master, the Doctor heads for Logopolis. The Master, the Doctor and Tegan arrive at Pharos later that night. They spend all night working on the computer link.

⇨ **Day One (Ep2-4)**
Several hours are spent on Logopolis …

⇨ **Day Two (1 March 1981) (Ep4)**
It is 'dawn' when they make their way to the tower. The Doctor regenerates …

CASTROVALVA

+STORY LINK

'Castrovalva' follows on immediately from 'Logopolis', with the Doctor regenerating (although visual (e.g. production) continuity between these two stories is very poor).

MASTER LINK

The Master has obviously had both the Event One trap and Castrovalva in mind prior to his attempt to destroy Logopolis, because he implements the Event One trap using Adric only moments after the Doctor falls from the Pharos tower. The Master must have planned all this during the 20 years he was stuck on Traken in the hope that he would encounter the Doctor again.

OBSERVATIONS

- It takes the duration of Ep1 and part of Ep2 for the TARDIS to travel from 1981 to the in-Rush. In 'Inside The Spaceship', the TARDIS makes a similar journey back in time, which takes the duration of two episodes to achieve. Lengthy journeys of several million years in time also occur in 'Image Of The Fendahl', 'City Of Death' and 'Frontios'. These examples all indicate that it takes several hours even for the TARDIS to travel millions of years in time.

- The Doctor jettisons a full quarter of the TARDIS interior into the Event One maelstrom. A quarter of an infinitely vast time ship is a significantly large mass. Is it possible that this mass, when introduced into Event One, was instrumental in the formation of Earth's galaxy? (See THE N-SPACE UNIVERSE.)

- As mentioned above, after the TARDIS has apparently been destroyed in the in-rush, the Master tells Adric he 'had in store a trap behind that trap that would have been a joy to spring', this other trap being Castrovalva. In the very next TARDIS scene Nyssa and Tegan read about Castrovalva on the computer and head for it. From this we have to accept that the Master had the Block Transfer projection of Adric program the TARDIS for both destinations (as the Doctor says, 'The Master leaves nothing to chance'). This suggests that as soon as the Master sees that the Doctor is on his way to Castrovalva, he takes his TARDIS to the Andromedan planet and with Adric's mathematical skills and Block Transfer Computations creates the city and populates it. Then the Master sets himself up as the Portreeve to await the Doctor's eventual arrival ...

- It does seem odd that the Master plans to go to such lengths to kill the Doctor, particularly when we take into account his efforts to seize the Doctor's body in "The Keeper Of Traken". Surely he has a better reason to keep the Doctor alive and to try and take his body again? It would seem that having taken Tremas's body, the Master has taken his one and only chance at taking a new body; the power of the Keepership only affords one transference. The Master's subsequent transfer in 'Doctor Who (The TV Movie)' is his last attempt to take a new body once the Tremas hybrid body begins to decay.

LANGUAGE

The countdown on the TARDIS console is in Earth numerals. There is a box marked 'Handle With Care' in one of the storerooms on board the TARDIS. Both Tegan and Nyssa read the flight computer, programmed by the duplicate of Adric. The initials 'I.F.' stand for Index File in English as well as Gallifreyan. The Doctor, Tegan and Nyssa read the Condensed Chronicles of Castrovalva. The Doctor understands Shardovan's handwritten notations found in one of the volumes. (Considering that Castrovalva is created by Adric one would think the language would be Terradonian or Alzarian-based.)

TIMELINE DATES

5,000,000,000 BC ⋆
There are two possible settings for the hydrogen in-rush sequence:

a) 5,000,000,000 BC: In the TARDIS computer file (which is programmed by the bogus Adric, as instructed by the Master), 'Event One' is noted as being 'the creation of the galaxy'. Our own galaxy is estimated as being about 5 billion years old (see 'Inside The Spaceship').

b) 13,000,000,000 BC: Despite the references to it merely being 'the creation of the galaxy', Event One could in fact the Big Bang – the creation of the Universe. The term 'Big Bang' is used to describe the origin of the Universe in 'Four To Doomsday'. In 'Terminus' both 'Event One' and 'the Big Bang' are used to describe the same cosmic event. In 'Secrets Of The Stars', the Big Bang was said to be thirteen billion years ago. (More recent research has theorised that the Universe may only be 8 billion years old.) In 'Terminus' it is explained that the Big Bang was an outward explosion of energy from the exploding fuel pod, and not the in-rush of hydrogen as seen in 'Castrovalva'. However, it could be that following the initial explosion caused by the Terminus, as with any explosion, there followed an in-rush of energy. There is also the fact that the TARDIS is travelling backwards in time, so the In-Rush could simply be an illusion caused by the temporal direction of the time ship; it is actually a hydrogen out-rush, but it is in reverse because the TARDIS is travelling in reverse.

I interpret Event One in this case to refer to the creation of the galaxy, as is stated on-screen. The in-rush is therefore dated to 5 billion BC.

140,000,000 BC ✦ ▨ ▨ ▨ ▨ ▨ ▨ ▨ ▨ ▨ ▨ ▨

The Master appears to have been at Castrovalva for 500 years waiting for the Doctor to arrive. This is based on the fact that after he believes the forces of Event One have destroyed the TARDIS, the Master gloats to Adric about a second trap he had planned for the Doctor, the trap being Castrovalva itself. He describes it as 'a journey back in time ... a long waiting'. The *Condensed Chronicles Of Castrovalva* are themselves 'about five hundred years old', and the history they purport to contain covers 'twelve hundred years'. This suggests that the Master, with Adric, travelled to the planet, set up the Dwellings of Simplicity, and then waited there in the guise of the Portreeve for some 500 years for the Doctor to show up. One flaw with this idea is how does Adric live 500 years trapped in the Hadron web? Another problem is that it places the Master's GRT 500 years out of sync with the Doctor's.

There are four main options available for setting the Castrovalva sections of 'Castrovalva':

a) In escaping the hydrogen in-rush, the TARDIS moves spatially to the galaxy of Andromeda (which is older than the new galaxy the TARDIS has just witnessed forming). The date is still 5,000,000,000 BC.

b) In 'Time-Flight' it is stated that the Master 'came [to Earth] seeking [the] power' of the Xeraphin, which means he went there deliberately. He has been there for some time, setting up the induction loop and creating the exponential time contour. The fact that the time contour extends to 1980s' Earth suggests that he is trying to reach his own GRT, which is 1983 (see GALLIFREY HISTORY and THE DOCTOR'S AGE). Alternatively, the time contour is configured to reach the time period in which the Master's TARDIS was last in the twentieth century – which was at the Pharos tower on 28 February / 1 March 1981, as in 'Logopolis' and 'Castrovalva'. However, the Doctor deduces that the Master's dynomorphic generator has been exhausted, which was why he went to Earth in the first place. He needs the power of the Xeraphin as a replacement. This, to me, suggests that the Master's TARDIS was damaged in his attempt to escape from Castrovalva. He knew of the Xeraphin being on Earth, so he limped across space without temporal displacement to (prehistoric) Earth. This means that Castrovalva is located in the same time zone as 'Time-Flight', 140 million years BC. Another clue to this idea is that the Master steals some components from the Doctor's TARDIS, without which 'we can only travel in this time zone'. If the Master's TARDIS is lacking these components, that suggests his own ship is also trapped in the same time zone, presumably a condition that has existed since he escaped from Castrovalva.

c) The TARDIS leaves Earth in 1981. After escaping the in-Rush the ship moves forward in time back to the year of its departure. This idea is supported by the fact that the following story, 'Four To Doomsday', is also set in 1981.

d) 'Castrovalva' could be set at any point in time after the creation of the Andromedan galaxy, but based on the fact that there is extensive plant- and animal-life on the planet, several billions years of evolution would need to be factored in.

I have chosen option (b), 140 Million BC, in view of the link with 'Time-Flight', and the comments about the missing relative circuit components.

1981, March 1 ▸ ▨ ▨ ▨ ▨ ▨ ▨ ▨ ▨ ▨ ▨ ▨
This is the same date as at the end of 'Logopolis', the Doctor having just regenerated.

DURATION

(TARDIS) (Ep1-2) ▨ ▨ ▨ ▨ ▨ ▨ ▨ ▨ ▨ ▨ ▨
Several hours are spent in the TARDIS travelling back in time to Event One, and then before making planet-fall.

⇨ **Day One (Ep2-3)** ▨ ▨ ▨ ▨ ▨ ▨ ▨ ▨ ▨ ▨
It is late 'afternoon' when the TARDIS lands. The girls climb the rocks at night. They all sleep in the city that night.

⇨ **Day Two (Ep3-4)** ▨ ▨ ▨ ▨ ▨ ▨ ▨ ▨ ▨ ▨
The travellers have breakfast with the Portreeve. They leave the planet later that day.

CALENDAR FEBRUARY / MARCH 1981						
SUN	MON	TUE	WED	THUR	FRI	SAT
22	23	24	25 The Keeper Of Traken	26 Time-Flight / Warriors' Gate / The Keeper Of Traken	27 The Keeper Of Traken / Time-Flight	28 Logopolis / Time-Flight / Four To Doomsday / Kinda / Logopolis
1 Logopolis / Castrovalva / Kinda	2 Kinda	3	4	5	6	7

FOUR TO DOOMSDAY

STORY LINK

There is nothing to suggest that 'Four To Doomsday' follows on directly from 'Castrovalva'. The crew are all wearing the same clothes, just as they do for the next few stories. The Doctor is trying to return Tegan to Earth ('he promised to get me back to Heathrow or he'll lose me my job'), just as he is still trying to do in later stories. Since 'Four To Doomsday' through to 'Time-Flight' are consecutive, there is plenty of time between 'Castrovalva' and 'Four To Doomsday' for several adventures to have occurred (as well as for the Doctor to have his hair cut), but in total duration I would say it is only a matter of weeks between TV adventures, certainly not months, and definitely not years.

OBSERVATIONS

- Enlightenment knows of 'a galactic legend about a Rassilon; he who found the Eye of Harmony', which suggests that the Urbankan civilisation itself must be well over 10,000,000 years old (see GALLIFREY HISTORY). Monarch is credited with bringing the Urbankan people out of the slime and on to the land, which suggests that Monarch himself is millions of years old.
- The Doctor mentions having once taken 'five wickets for New South Wales'. When the TARDIS lands in the middle of a cricket match in 'The Daleks' Master Plan', the Doctor shows complete ignorance of the game, but by the time of his fourth incarnation, he is familiar with the game and has even

developed a particular bowling style (the fourth Doctor demonstrates his bowling techniques in 'The Ark In Space', 'The Hand Of Fear', 'The Ribos Operation' and 'The Horns Of Nimon'; and the fifth in 'Four To Doomsday' and 'Black Orchid'). It is likely that the Doctor developed his liking for the game during his exile on Earth. The fact that the Doctor finds a recorder and a cricket bat by the same coat-stand / mirror in the corridor outside the TARDIS's cricket pavilion might even suggest that it was during his second incarnation that the Doctor took an active interest in the sport.

LANGUAGE

One would expect the androids to all speak Urbankan, or at least their own 'native' tongues. It is odd that both Bigon and Lin Futu speak English, a language that did not exist in their own times (of course, given that Monarch has received messages from Earth for 50 years, the androids could have been programmed to speak other languages – although why would they need to, given that the humans were all to be killed?) The Urbankans understand the Doctor when he speaks through the monopticons; would the Time Lord 'gift' function through a machine? The Doctor is unable to understand Kurkutji, whereas Tegan can converse with him in his ancient Aboriginal language. The Doctor says '*Au revoir*' to Enlightenment, who understands what the French phrase means. Tegan regards the instructions in the TARDIS handbook – which has the words 'TARDIS HANDBOOK TYPE 40' stencilled on its black cover – as 'mumbo jumbo'. Nyssa reads a book on mathematics by Bertrand Russell, which is written in English. The dragon-dance costume has the words 'Kung Fu Club' embroidered on it.

TIMELINE DATES

1981, February 28 ·

The Doctor reads the date and time from the TARDIS console: 'February the 28th, 1981 … It's only 16:15 hours'. Since the TARDIS has been drawn off course by Monarch's ship's magnetic field, it is possible that the TARDIS is also moved temporally, but I accept the above date as being correct. This therefore sets the events in 'Four To Doomsday' happening simultaneously with the events in 'Logopolis'.

Monarch's ship is 'four days' from Earth, making the intended arrival date to be March 4.

55,000 BC
35,000 BC
6019 BC
2019 BC
519 BC
731 ■ ■ ■ ■ ■ ■ ■ ■ ■ ■ ■ ■ ■ ■

We learn from Bigon about Monarch's previous visits to Earth: 'The first visit was over 35,000 years ago, when Kurkutji was taken. It took 20,000 years for the Urbankans to reach Earth. Monarch has doubled the speed of the ship on every subsequent visit'. Monarch departed from Urbanka for the first time in 55,000 BC. Bigon himself was taken on Monarch's last visit, his third, '2,500 years ago' (being around 519 BC). For the current journey to Earth, Monarch left Urbanka '1,250 years ago' (around AD 731). The Doctor estimates that the Futu Dynasty in China was '4,000 years ago' (being 2019 BC), and that the Mayans flourished '8,000 years ago' (6019 BC). But the Doctor is wrong with his estimate of when Kurkutji was taken, saying it was only '12,000 years' (i.e. around 10,000 BC), when according to Bigon it was 35,000 BC. Some of these dates are historically inaccurate: the Mayans didn't flourish in 6000 BC.

It is impossible to take the ship's doubling its speed literally in order to factor in the Doctor's estimations. Bigon could have been generalising, simply meaning that the ship had significantly increased its speed with every journey to and from Earth.

574 BC ■ ■ ■ ■ ■ ■ ■ ■ ■ ■ ■ ■ ■ ■

Bigon says his silicon chips hold 'my memory of 2555 years'. Bigon was taken '2500 years ago', and given that he must be 55 years old, thus puts Bigon's date of birth at 574 BC.

Bigon says his microchips were once placed in the cabinet 'for over a hundred years' following his first and only attempt at revolt. I have not placed this event in the TIMELINE.

1588, August 8 + ■ ■ ■ ■ ■ ■ ■ ■ ■ ■ ■ ■ ■

It was on this date in our history that the English forces under Sir Francis Drake destroyed the Spanish Armada in battle off the coast of France. Given the use of the term 'Armada' in 'Four To Doomsday', we could say that this was the event during which the Doctor met Drake.

1931 ■ ■ ■ ■ ■ ■ ■ ■ ■ ■ ■ ■ ■ ■

Monarch says 'We have been receiving messages from Earth for 50 years', which would be since 1931.

1978 ⊹ ▨ ▨ ▨ ▨ ▨ ▨ ▨ ▨ ▨ ▨ ▨ ▨

The Doctor tells Monarch that some humans use safety-pins as earrings, so the Time Lord has obviously been to Earth during the punk rock era, which was from about 1976 to 1980.

DURATION

⇨ **Day One (28 February 1981) (Ep1-4)** ▨ ▨ ▨ ▨ ▨ ▨

It is 4.15 pm when the TARDIS lands on Monarch's ship. The story takes place over the space of a few hours.

KINDA

+STORY LINK

At the end of 'Four To Doomsday' Nyssa faints. It is mentioned in 'Kinda' that she fainted 'twice', so we can assume that the TARDIS crew arrived on Deva Loka almost immediately after leaving Monarch's ship. The Doctor deleted Romana's bedroom in 'Logopolis', but by 'The Visitation' a new set of living quarters located across from the console room has been 'created' for Tegan and Nyssa. Presumably this room was created prior to 'Kinda', and is where Nyssa spends 48 hours asleep (see also Observations under 'The Chase').

OBSERVATIONS

- It is never revealed what happened to Roberts and the other two missing survey team members. Dukkha says 'they always ask that' when Tegan questions him, so it is possible that they too fell asleep by the chimes and were possessed. Perhaps Dukkha is Roberts and the strange couple playing chess are the other two missing members, all three now possessed by the Mara.
- It is worth noting that the Kinda have a prophecy about the arrival of the Not-We and the return of the Mara through an unshared mind. In the sequel, 'Snakedance', the people of Manussa also have a legend of the return.
- According to Panna and Karuna, it is impossible for a man to look into the Box of Jhana without being driven mad. The Box does not affect the Doctor; his Time Lord attributes notwithstanding, could it be that the Doctor is not a man?

LANGUAGE

Sanders appears to understand Karuna when he meets her in the forest. The dome panels are printed with numbers ('34', '00830', 'G3'), and the colonists have their names printed in English on the backs of their chairs.

TIMELINE DATES

1981, February 28 – 1981, March 2 ·

Dating 'Kinda' is difficult given the number of dating clues available.

The explorers have English surnames: Sanders, Hindle, Todd, and Roberts, but apart from that there is little else which suggests they come from Earth or an Earth colony. In fact, there are other examples where aliens have Earth-like names; Jackson in 'Underworld' and Stratton and Bates in 'Attack Of The Cybermen', and don't forget Susan. In stories set in Earth's future, humans seem to retain modern names, even by the fifty-first century (see 'The Invisible Enemy'). By the time of Earth's destruction in 'The Ark', some ten million years in the future, Earth names have become corrupted, but in 'Frontios', set in the same time period, the names are still 'modern'. On this basis it is not impossible for aliens to have Earth-like names; so the Kinda explorers are not necessarily from Earth.

Todd says 'our mother world is very over-crowded'. Deva Loka is being surveyed 'with a view to colonisation'. If they are from Earth, we could set 'Kinda' at the same time as 'Colony In Space', in 2472, a time when colonisation was a priority given that Earth was becoming over-populated. Incidentally, the explorers live in a pre-fabricated dome, as do the colonists in 'Colony In Space', which suggests that that form of structure was common to that time period. However, the actions of the survey team (taking hostages, for example), do not conform to practices seen in other Earth-based colony stories.

When he examines the Total Survival Suit (TSS), the Doctor says they are 'human or humanoid at the very least', but the explorers themselves twice refer to their own planet as Homeworld, but never as Earth: Sanders says they are 'a couple of parsecs off Homeworld', and the term is even used in the wording of the operations manual that Hindle reads: '... the security of Homeworld itself', which suggests that Homeworld is actually the name of their planet.

The fact that at the end of 'Snakedance' the Mara is completely destroyed and 'gone forever', means that 'Kinda' must be set prior to 'Snakedance', within the 500 years since the Mara was first banished to the Dark Places Of The Inside. Strong supporting evidence in 'Snakedance' sets that story in 1983. 'Kinda' would therefore be set prior to that date.

It is clear that the Mara in 'Kinda' is but only an aspect of the creature ('This world is free of it'), but in 'Snakedance' it is the complete Mara entity itself that is destroyed. If we indeed accept that 'Kinda' is set prior to 1983, that would mean that the expedition members aren't from Earth.

On the basis that 'Kinda' is set prior to 1983, we can use an earlier story to aid with the dating. Tegan still wants to get back to Earth at the end of 'Four To Doomsday'. On Monarch's ship, the TARDIS is only four days away from the planet, and the date is 28 February 1981. One would have thought that the Doctor would simply pilot the TARDIS to Earth to drop Tegan off. And yet they end up on Deva Loka. Of course, Adric does say in 'Four To Doomsday' that 'Nyssa never repaired the time curve indicator', which may have caused the TARDIS to miss Earth and land on Deva Loka instead – a journey in space only, and not in time.

Given the logic that 'Kinda' must be set in a time zone before 'Snakedance', and given the strong support for why 'Snakedance' is set in 1983, the first day of 'Kinda' must be set on 28 February 1981, the same date as 'Four To Doomsday', given that the opening TARDIS scene in 'Kinda' continues from where 'Four To Doomsday' ends, following Nyssa's fainting spell. Therefore, the Deva Loka survey team are not from Earth.

Based on the abundance of fallen leaves on the forest floor, I would say it was the Deva Lokan equivalent of autumn.

1583

The planet Deva Loka has been cursed by the Mara before, and, as it turns out, a very accurate prophecy – as narrated by Panna – has been built around the Mara's eventual return. The Doctor confesses to having 'heard the legends of the Mara'. The Mara has turned the wheel of time 'through the centuries' on Deva Loka. The fact that the Kinda seem to have knowledge of the structure of the double helix, the heart of the chromosome, implies that they once had a technically advanced civilisation that collapsed as a result of the Mara, similar to the events on Manussa: '[History is] beginning again … the great wheel … through the centuries … Wheel turns, civilisations rise … Wheel turns, civilisations fall … '. The Mara was created on Manussa in 1183 and banished to the Dark Places of the Inside in 1483 (see 'Snakedance'). We can assume that the Mara emerged temporarily from the Dark Places of the Inside via the unshared dream of one of the citizens of the earlier advanced Kinda civilisation. As a result, that civilisation fell, and centuries later another civilisation rose in its place, just as Panna narrates. Allowing for say a century for the Mara to be trapped in the Dark Places of the Inside, the time that the Mara began to influence Deva Loka would be around 1583.

1941
Sanders says this is his 'fourteenth' expedition, 'in forty years'. That would make his first expedition around 1941. Interestingly, Deva Loka is designated planet 'S14'; the number could represent the number of expeditions that Sanders has been on.

1962
Tegan recalls that she didn't like the taste of her ice cream when she was 'three'. Assuming Tegan is about 22 in 'Kinda', she would have been three in 1962.

1980
The survey team has been on Deva Loka for some time, and the mothership is not due to pick them up 'for six seasons'. This probably means another 18 months. We can assume that they've been there for less than a month, given that Roberts and the other two have only just vanished and the two Kinda hostages are only recent captives.

DURATION

⇨ **Day One (28 February) (Ep1)**
Hindle wakes in the morning. Nyssa spends the next '48 hours' in the TARDIS. Adric has 'breakfast' at the dome. Tegan falls asleep. The Doctor, Adric and Todd spend 'all night' locked up in the cage.

⇨ **Day Two (1 March) (Ep2-4)**
Sanders encounters Karuna and Panna the following morning. When Tegan wakes she has been asleep 'for nearly two days', so it is late afternoon. The Mara is destroyed later this day.

⇨ **Day Three (2 March) (Ep4)**
Nyssa has 'fully recovered' by the final farewell scenes. Given that she spent '48 hours peaceful sleep' in the TARDIS, it must be the third day.

THE VISITATION

+STORY LINK

'The Visitation' follows on immediately after the TARDIS has left Deva Loka in 'Kinda'. The Doctor and Adric are arguing about the incident with the TSS, while Tegan tells

Nyssa (who had been asleep) about being possessed by the Mara. With both 'Four To Doomsday' and 'Kinda' set within days of each other, the Doctor has been trying to get Tegan home. The trip from Deva Loka to Earth would therefore be in space only, with a short time jump back some 48 hours (from 2 March to 28 February) to ensure that Tegan gets 'back at the airport exactly on time for [her] flight, half an hour after [she] entered the TARDIS' (on 28 February 1981, see 'Logopolis'). However, 'the lateral balance cones' malfunction again, moving the ship off course in time by some 315 years.

OBSERVATIONS

- In 'Pyramids Of Mars', the Doctor, in conversation with Sarah, implies that he was once accused of starting the fire of 1666, but denies having had anything to do with it.
- In 'Black Orchid' the Doctor says the fire 'would have happened if we'd been there or not'. Considering the fire started when the Doctor drops his burning torch on to dry hay in the Pudding Lane bakery, it is hard to see how the fire could have started without his direct participation – see THE N-SPACE UNIVERSE.
- When he hears from Mace about the 'comet', the Doctor says 'you're not due for a comet for years'. The Doctor knows which century they are in, so he could be referring to Halley's comet, which was discovered and named in 1680 (1682 has also been noted as the date). In fact comet sightings are almost an annual occurrence, but in most cases these could not be seen without the aid of a telescope. The Doctor is probably referring to a comet that could be seen with the naked eye, as was the case with the Terileptil 'comet'. (Of note, Nemesis will be due to pass Earth again in 1688, but the Doctor can't be thinking of this comet given that he has forgotten about the statue since his third incarnation (see 'Planet Of The Spiders') and won't remember again until 'Silver Nemesis'.)

LANGUAGE

The Terileptils communicate with the villagers, and so must speak English. However, Tegan and Richard Mace are unable to read the Terileptil script, which Tegan likens to mathematical formulae. Nyssa reads a women's magazine, presumably one that Tegan had in her handbag when she first entered the TARDIS in 'Logopolis', unless it was one of Sarah's ...

TIMELINE DATES

1666, August
Mace says the comet was 'a few weeks ago', putting the arrival of the Terileptils in early August.

1666, September 1 – 2
The Doctor thinks the TARDIS has landed on 'Earth, Heathrow, 1981 ... where requested to be', but Adric reads the console and declares they are 'about three hundred years early', which suggests 1681. The Doctor later confirms the century when he is searching for electrical emissions – 'not something you'd expect to find on seventeenth century Earth'. Given the historical aspect of the story, we can use the historically recorded dates of 1st or 2nd September 1666 when the Great Fire of London started.

1666, August 30 – 31
Mace says he spent the 'last night or two' in the barn. He found the mind control bracelet in the loft 'last night', being August 31.

DURATION

⇨ **Day One (August) (Ep1)**
The Terileptils land at night, and kill the Squire and his family.

⇨ **Day Two (August) (Ep1)**
The Terileptils move into the Squire's house ...

⏲ **A few weeks pass ...**

⇨ **Day One (1 September) (Ep1-4)**
'A few weeks' later the TARDIS lands in the 'morning'. It is 'beginning to get dark' when the Terileptil leader leaves for his London base.

⇨ **Day Two? (2 September) (Ep4)**
A bell is heard chiming five times when the TARDIS lands in London, possibly signalling the time as 5 am (otherwise it is still the night of 1 September). The TARDIS leaves less than ten minutes later as the fire spreads...

BLACK ORCHID

Nyssa wonders if it is safe to leave the TARDIS 'considering what we've just done to London', which indicates that 'The Visitation' and 'Black Orchid' are consecutive. At the dance Adric says 'I didn't have any breakfast', so after leaving London 1666 the travellers had a period of rest in the TARDIS. It is the equivalent of 'morning' ship time when they land in 1925. Nyssa now wears her hair up, and Tegan has now decided she wants 'to stay with the crew for a while'. She tells the Doctor 'you can stop trying to get me back to Heathrow'.

OBSERVATIONS

- The policemen recognise the Doctor's TARDIS as a police box. In our history the model of police box adopted by the TARDIS wasn't introduced in England until 1932. But the policemen obviously know what it is from the fact that it has the words 'Police Public Call Box' written over the windows and on the telephone hatch.
- The Doctor is puzzled by the TARDIS's 'compulsion for planet Earth', something he has commented on before (see 'The Web Of Fear' and 'Fury From The Deep')

LANGUAGE

The Doctor opens one of Latoni's books and notes that it is written in Portuguese.

TIMELINE DATES

1925, June 10 – (14?) ·
When the TARDIS lands it is 'Three o'clock, June the Eleventh, Nineteen Hundred and Twenty-Five'. Digby was killed 'last night', which is 10 June.

The travellers stay for George's funeral. 11 June 1925 is a Thursday. The funeral may have been on the Saturday or the Sunday, allowing for time to make the necessary funeral arrangements.

1877
Lady Cranleigh says she was six when she got the doll. Assuming she is now 55, she was born in 1871.

1923 ▨ ▨ ▨ ▨ ▨ ▨ ▨ ▨ ▨ ▨ ▨ ▨ ▨
Lady Cranleigh says that George 'never returned from his last expedition two years ago'. It is not clear if she means he left two years ago, or he failed to return two years ago.

DURATION

⇨ **Day One (10 June)** ▨ ▨ ▨ ▨ ▨ ▨ ▨ ▨ ▨ ▨
Digby is killed at night.

⇨ **Day Two (11 June)** ▨ ▨ ▨ ▨ ▨ ▨ ▨ ▨ ▨ ▨
The TARDIS lands at 'three o'clock' (3.00 pm). The fancy dress ball is held after the cricket match, and continues for the rest of the afternoon.

🕐 **A few days (?) pass ...** ▨ ▨ ▨ ▨ ▨ ▨ ▨ ▨ ▨ ▨

⇨ **Day Four? /Five? (13/14 June?)** ▨ ▨ ▨ ▨ ▨ ▨ ▨ ▨
The travellers stay for the funeral.

EARTHSHOCK

+STORY LINK

The Doctor is reading the book *Black Orchid* presented to him by Lady Cranleigh, and Nyssa still has her hair tied back in the same way she has it in the previous story, which suggests that 'Black Orchid' and 'Earthshock' are consecutive. Nyssa says 'Oh, not again' when the Doctor reveals that they have landed on Earth.

The Doctor says that he and Adric have 'spent many hours discussing and debating endless topics'. Since the previous four stories ('Four To Doomsday', 'Kinda', 'The Visitation' and 'Black Orchid') are consecutive, these 'many hours' would have passed between 'Castrovalva' and 'Four To Doomsday', and also during the latter era of the fourth Doctor ('State Of Decay', 'Warriors' Gate', 'The Keeper Of Traken' and 'Logopolis'). Adric comments on how 'immature' the Doctor has become since his regeneration, which indicates that the time that has passed since 'Logopolis' is relatively short.

Given the close consecutiveness between the stories spanning 'Full Circle' to 'Time-Flight', Adric has been with the Doctor for what could only be a matter of months, certainly not years. In terms of direct story duration, this is only some 25 or 26 days, not taking into account short gaps between non-consecutive stories.

CYBERMAN LINK

As covered under CYBERMAN HISTORY, this is the ninth appearance of the Cybermen. And as noted under 'The Tomb Of The Cybermen' and 'Revenge Of The Cybermen', following Professor Parry's return to Earth, the Cybermen have been revived from their tombs on Telos and have amassed an army with which to attack Earth and its planetary allies. The Cybermen have allied themselves with Ringway, who has managed to get 15,000 Cybermen on board the Earth-bound freighter. Several crewmembers have been killed (and converted into new Cybermen?) during the flight from the pick-up point to Earth. Another group of Cybermen has managed to get to Earth to set up the bomb (some of whom are time scooped to Gallifrey by Borusa – see 'The Five Doctors'). The Cyber-leader in 'Earthshock' might even be one of the surviving Cybermen from Gallifrey, which is why he recognises the fifth Doctor ('So, we meet again, Doctor').

LANGUAGE

The Cybermen communicate with Ringway, so they must speak English. The Cybermen use 'minutes' and 'seconds'.

TIMELINE DATES

2526 ◆ ▬ ▬ ▬ ▬ ▬ ▬ ▬ ▬ ▬ ▬ ▬ ▬ ▬

The Doctor says they are in the 'twenty-sixth century', to which Adric adds, 'the year is two thousand, five hundred and twenty six in the time-scale you call Anno Domini'.

The freighter has been docked at the station for 'seven hours'. Ringway says three crewmen have disappeared 'in the last two weeks', which gives an indication as to how long they have been heading for Earth with active Cybermen on board (since the missing crewmen's bodies have not been recovered, we could assume they have been converted into Cybermen). It is not stated where the 15,000 silos containing the Cybermen came from, but we can gather that these Cybermen are from the Telos base; Ringway is certainly familiar with the planet.

Kyle says they were down in the caves for 'four weeks before the androids attacked'. This gives an indication as to how long ago the Cybermen and their androids set up the bomb and have been planning their attack. The conference has therefore been in planning for even longer.

65,000,000 BC ▪ ▨ ▨ ▨ ▨ ▨ ▨ ▨ ▨ ▨ ▨ ▨ ▨

The Doctor tells Nyssa that the dinosaurs died out almost overnight '65 million years' ago; and later he announces that the TARDIS has 'travelled backwards in time some 65 million years'.

Oddly, the landmasses seen on Earth are more like they are in the twentieth century, and not millions of years ago, which should show the land masses bunched together.

Nyssa comments that the storm created by the freighter's impact on Earth 'must have lasted for months'.

DURATION

(TARDIS) (Ep1) ▨ ▨ ▨ ▨ ▨ ▨ ▨ ▨ ▨ ▨ ▨ ▨

The Doctor reads *Black Orchid* while Nyssa shows Tegan some calculations. Adric is moping in his room.

⇨ **Day One (Ep1-4)** ▨ ▨ ▨ ▨ ▨ ▨ ▨ ▨ ▨ ▨ ▨

It is day outside the caves. The subsequent adventure takes place over several hours on Earth and in space. The freighter's ETA on Earth was between '22.1' and '19.8', as seen on the ship's main screen.

⇨ **Day One (Ep4)** ▨ ▨ ▨ ▨ ▨ ▨ ▨ ▨ ▨ ▨ ▨

The TARDIS and the freighter are in the past for a matter of minutes (see Duration 'Time-Flight').

TIME-FLIGHT

+STORY LINK

'Time-Flight' follows on directly from 'Earthshock'. The Doctor has rescued the surviving freighter crew and troopers from the life pod off-screen and returned them to 2526. Tegan and Nyssa are still grieving over the death of Adric. The Cyber-fleet has dispersed.

The TARDIS is stationary in the opening scene. The Doctor enters, having said his farewells to the freighter crew. He sets the coordinates for 1851, and then presses the dematerialisation switch. The TARDIS immediately buffets with the effects of the time contour – which reaches as far as 1981. Therefore the TARDIS has travelled from 2526 to 1981 in a split second.

MASTER LINK

When Kalid is revealed to be the Master, the Doctor says 'So, you escaped from Castrovalva. I should have guessed'. As covered in 'Castrovalva' above, the Master left Castrovalva and immediately arrived on prehistoric Earth, his TARDIS damaged so that it could not time travel, stranding him in the same time-zone, so there is little doubt that 'Castrovalva' and 'Time-Flight' are consecutive for the Master. The Master wants to transfer the Xeraphin sarcophagus to the centre of his TARDIS (into the Eye of Harmony? – 'Doctor Who (The TV Movie)'). He already has all the equipment he needs, such as the induction loop, and establishes an exponential time contour to the twentieth century in a bid to escape.

OBSERVATIONS

- It is not made clear why the Master disguises himself as Kalid, as surely there is no way he would be expecting the Doctor (or anyone else who would recognise him) to show up. Therefore, it could be that the Master isn't actually wearing a disguise, but that instead Kalid is a form into which his body has shaped itself. We know from 'Castrovalva' and 'The King's Demons' that the [Ainley] Master possesses the ability to change his outward appearance at will, but it has never been explained how he does this. It is possible that the Master's body is now actually composed of this malleable protoplasmic material, a side-effect perhaps of the Traken Keepership. In 'Doctor Who (The TV Movie)' the Master transforms into a snake-like creature made of some kind of gelatinous material. In 'Time-Flight' Kalid's features are also snake-like, and he 'bleeds' a protoplasmic substance when his link to the Xeraphin sarcophagus is broken, so there could actually be a connection; that the Master's form in 'Doctor Who (The TV Movie)' is simply the final stage in a slow mutation that has been developing ever since Traken, and which reached a transitional stage when he first arrived on prehistoric Earth ...
- Two of the components of a TARDIS are the temporal limiter and the time-lapse compressor, without which the TARDIS can only travel 'in this time zone'. It is possible that the temporal limiter is one of the circuits that help to govern the GRT of a TARDIS (see GALLIFREY HISTORY).

LANGUAGE

The Xeraphin apparently speak English. The Master says, '*Au revoir*, Doctor'.

TIMELINE DATES

140,000,000 BC ▸ ▧ ▧ ▧ ▧ ▧ ▧ ▧ ▧ ▧ ▧ ▧

The Doctor gives the date when the Concorde lands as 'some 140 million years ago … definitely Jurassic … we can't be far off the Pleistocene Era', to which Tegan asks, 'The Ice Age?' (The Jurassic Period was 170 – 140 million years ago. The Doctor is some 138 million years out with his reference to the Pleistocene Era, however, he is probably only joking.)

1981, February 26 – 28 ▸ ▧ ▧ ▧ ▧ ▧ ▧ ▧ ▧ ▧ ▧

Tegan comments that 'this is the 1980s, Nyssa' when they land inside the Terminal building. All other reference to the period are only ever given as 'the twentieth century' [as if a deliberate attempt has been made by the production team to keep the year undefined.] The Doctor knows the exact date from the newspaper he buys (and as noted under THE UNIT YEARS, he knows they are in a period years after his time with UNIT in the 1970s). The Heathrow section takes place over three days (see Duration).

The evidence of snow at the airport does suggest a winter month. On the other hand, the fact that the Doctor comments about the state of English cricket suggests it is summer, but this is at odds with all the snow. However, the English team could simply be playing overseas in Australia or New Zealand at the time so a winter/spring month can still apply.

I doubt that it is 1982, 1983 or 1984. It is clear in 'Arc Of Infinity' that after 'Time-Flight' Tegan resumed her normal life. However, if she had been missing for more than a year, Tegan would have had to explain to her employers where she had been since her disappearance. And the police were probably treating her disappearance as very suspicious; possibly even making her a prime suspect in the death of her aunt. But there is no indication in 'Arc Of Infinity' that Tegan has been through any such ordeal.

1981 is the best date, for the following reasons: Tegan was due to catch her very first flight on 28 February 1981 at 5.30 pm (see 'Logopolis' and 'Four To Doomsday'). Since then, the Doctor has been trying to get her back to that date, both 'Four To Doomsday' and 'The Visitation' being stories in which his efforts are emphasised but he misses the mark, either by location or by time.

The exponential time contour generated by the Master is his lifeline back to the twentieth century. But why would he try to reach that particular century? I would suggest that this was because 1983 is his GRT and he was trying to get to his own time, but falling short by 2 years. Another possibility is that the time contour links 140,000,000 BC with the last time zone the Master's TARDIS was in during the twentieth century. This was 28 February 1981 (see 'Logopolis' and 'Castrovalva'), which also happens to be the period that Tegan is from. This explains why it is not a coincidence that the Doctor's TARDIS just happens to be dragged back to the time period the Doctor had been trying to reach for so long.

When the Doctor reads the newspaper, he sees for the first time that they are back in Tegan's time. But why doesn't he say something to Tegan? Tegan would probably have gone off the minute she discovers what the date is. Of course, in 'Black Orchid' Tegan does tell the Doctor that there is no longer any need for him to try and get her back to 1981, so perhaps by now she had resigned herself to the fact that she really doesn't want to get home even if she was back in her own time; as seen at the end of 'Time-Flight', she had intended to resume her travels with the Doctor.

For Tegan's sake (and to a degree his own), the Doctor would want to get her back to the right date of 28 February 1981, so she could catch her plane. By doing so he would be able to prove once and for all to her that he was in complete control of the TARDIS.

If the date was shortly after 28 February, when Tegan walks through the Terminal, she realises she is in a time later than she had hoped for. She prefers to stay with the Doctor, but now back in 1981 she can slip back into her old life again, as she eventually does when she discovers she has been left behind.

If it was shortly before 28 February, the Doctor would have been concerned that if Tegan stayed behind in what was effectively her own past she ran the risk of deliberately attempting to meet her earlier self and trying to prevent herself from going to the airport on the 28th, therefore saving Aunt Vanessa's life, and by doing so altering her own past. In fact, the Doctor had early scolded Tegan and Nyssa about changing history when they asked if he could save Adric ('There are some rules that cannot be broken, even with the TARDIS. Don't ever ask me to do anything like that again!'). There was also the risk that if two Tegans met they could cause a time differential (like that which happened when the Brigadiers meet in 'Mawdryn Undead'). But as circumstances eventuate Tegan leaves that time period the next day to fly in the Concorde, so that potential risk cancels itself out.

Taking this a step further, if the date when they first arrived at Heathrow was before 28 February, but it is actually 28 February when they return from the past, then the risk factor has been diminished even further. The Doctor knows this, which is why he is not careful to ensure that Tegan is back in the TARDIS before dematerialising.

On this basis, I have set 'Time-Flight' from 26 – 28 February 1981. This means that Tegan is returned to Earth on the same day she first entered the TARDIS (in 'Logopolis'), making her now slightly out of sync with Earth relative to her time with the Doctor. But she is not the only companion who has been affected in this way: both

Ben and Polly become out of sync in 'The Faceless Ones', Jamie and Zoe in 'The War Games', and Jo Grant is out of sync in 'Colony In Space' and 'The Time Monster', so it is not as if this hasn't happened before to one of the Doctor's companions.

Of note, it is the morning of 28 February 1981 when Tegan leaves for Heathrow in 'Logopolis', and it is the morning of 28 February 1981 when the Concorde returns to Heathrow 24 hours after it left, so the Doctor has in fact succeeded in returning Tegan to her own time – precisely (in terms of the Durations of the stories so far, she has been with him for about 19 days since 'Logopolis').

2526 ▪ ■ ■ ■ ■ ■ ■ ■ ■ ■ ■ ■ ■ ■

The crew from the freighter from 'Earthshock' are 'returned to their own time' and the Cyber-fleet has dispersed. The Doctor activates the TARDIS controls for 1851, and as soon as he flips the switch, the TARDIS is caught in the time contour.

140,000,500 BC ■ ■ ■ ■ ■ ■ ■ ■ ■ ■ ■ ■

The Xeraphin came to Earth some time ago. The spaceship has 'been here a long time'. It has decayed by only a minimal degree, so only centuries as opposed to millennia can have passed since it crashed. I would say 500 years to be a maximum period, but that is highly arbitrary.

1851, May 1 ■ ■ ■ ■ ■ ■ ■ ■ ■ ■ ■ ■

Only Nyssa reads the year of the Great Exhibition off the TARDIS console; the Doctor wants to get there for 'opening day', which was in our history on 1 May 1851.

DURATION

⇨ **Day (2526) (Ep1)** ■ ■ ■ ■ ■ ■ ■ ■ ■ ■

The Doctor has collected the freighter crew and returns them to 2526.

⇨ **Day One (26 February 1981) (Ep1)** ■ ■ ■ ■ ■ ■ ■

The first Concorde to vanish was 'this morning's flight from New York', which vanishes as it approaches London that 'afternoon' (Capt Urquhart greets control with 'Good afternoon, London'). The Doctor greets the controllers with a 'Good afternoon, gentlemen' when he arrives at Heathrow.

⇨ **Day Two (27 February 1981) (Ep1)** ■ ■ ■ ■ ■ ■ ■

Capt Stapley greets a 'Good morning, Doctor' when they board the other Concorde, so it is now the next day.

⇨ **Day Three (28 February 1981) (Ep4)** ▦ ▦ ▦ ▦ ▦ ▦

It is morning when they return. They were 'only missing for 24 hours'.

⇨ **Day One (140m) (Ep2-4)** ▦ ▦ ▦ ▦ ▦ ▦ ▦

In terms of the Blinovitch Limitation Effect the travellers spend the latter part of the second day and the first part of the third day in the past, a duration of no more than 24 hours.

ARC OF INFINITY

STORY LINK

Nyssa is still wearing the same outfit she has worn in the last seven stories, which suggests that not a great deal of time has passed since 'Time-Flight'. The Doctor and Nyssa have spent time working on the TARDIS systems, about which the Doctor remarks: 'You put things off for a day and the next thing you know it's a hundred years later'. The Doctor refers to the Cybermen damaging the console (in 'Earthshock') as if it were only a recent event. Therefore, only a few months have passed since they last saw Tegan, although two years have passed for her since 'Time-Flight' (see below, and THE DOCTOR'S AGE).

GALLIFREY LINK

In 'The Invasion Of Time' the fourth Doctor's GRT was 1963. With the fifth Doctor's GRT now at 1983, 20 years have passed since his last visit home. There have been several changes since then: Borusa has regenerated and become Lord President. (But surprisingly, the Presidential codes to unlock doors have not been changed since the Doctor held the position!) There is a new Castellan (replacing Kelner). The Council's policy of allowing aliens on Gallifrey has changed; when the Doctor and Nyssa arrive on Gallifrey, Thalia greets Nyssa with 'You are welcome on Gallifrey, Nyssa'. This could possibly be due to Leela's influence; the fact that she is an alien who helped them against the Sontarans showed that there is a benefit to allowing the integration of aliens into Gallifreyan society. (Indeed, in 'School Reunion', the Doctor tells Sarah he couldn't take her to Gallifrey because 'in those days humans weren't allowed', which indicates that there has indeed since been a change in policy.) Reference is made to the Doctor failing to return Romana, as the Time Lords had requested at the end of 'Meglos' (although it is rather odd that Thalia refers to Romana with the shortened version of her name, the one the Doctor invented in 'The Ribos Operation', and not the proper full name Romanadvoratrelundar. Of course, Thalia could have been the Time Lord who sent the summons to the TARDIS in 'Meglos', and noted that Romana responded using an abbreviated form of her name).

The Doctor asks Damon about Leela. Damon replies that 'she's well and very happy', which again supports the view (see THE DOCTOR'S AGE) that the passage of time between 'The Invasion Of Time' and 'Arc Of Infinity' is only a few decades, and not centuries.

In 'The Five Doctors' the Doctor states that he has 'known the Castellan too long … any mention of the dark days filled him with dread'. Like Hedin and Damon, the Castellan must have been a friend of the Doctor's prior to his departure from Gallifrey.

OBSERVATIONS

- Omega has a functioning TARDIS, which is odd because when he first vanished into the anti-matter dimension (see 'The Three Doctors') the Gallifreyans had not yet developed time travel or TARDISes. It is unlikely that he built it himself, because in 'The Three Doctors' Omega's world was basically a solid illusion created by the effort of his will, so it is unlikely that he could create a fully functioning TARDIS by will alone, otherwise he would have done it in 'The Three Doctors'. Mind you, after the ship is damaged, he does says that he can always build another, but then when he says this he has already achieved transference, and is now free of his prison in the anti-matter Universe. As he tells the Doctor, 'expect me on Gallifrey – soon', so what he probably means is that he can build a new one there. Therefore, Hedin probably sent this TARDIS to him, and Omega converted it into anti-matter. This TARDIS is quite different to the Doctor's. It does have chameleon capabilities, but there is no readily visible control console (but then the control room that we do see on-screen isn't necessarily the console room). The fact that Omega uses the ship only to travel from his world to Earth means that there is actually no indication that it can time travel. In fact, there is no need for Omega to time travel because Earth and Gallifrey, as well as the Arc which is 'the gateway between the dimensions', are all in the same time zone. The Doctor is chosen for temporal bonding mainly because of 'time, present location, personality', not from any desire for revenge on Omega's part. In fact, the term 'present location' is quite telling. When the Doctor is first assaulted by Omega, the Doctor and Nyssa have just finished repairing the audio circuits. The ship is not time travelling; it is parked in space (and possibly quite 'near' the Arc of Infinity itself). The ship must therefore be in

GRT 1983, the desired time zone. In other words, if another Time Lord were parked in the 'present location', then they would have been the one attacked. To me it is quite clear that Omega cannot time travel. Besides, if he could, why doesn't he simply go back 10,000,000 years and prevent his own death, rather than bother with all this temporal bonding nonsense? (Of course, as noted under GALLIFREY HISTORY, the TARDIS safeguard usually prevents this, but it is clear that Omega has converted the machine.) On this basis, Omega's 'TARDIS' is probably just a travel capsule, and not a time machine. Another question that comes to mind is: what happens to Omega's TARDIS? It is damaged in the final explosion, but unless the Doctor disposes of it (by destroying it or sending it back to Gallifrey?) before leaving Amsterdam, it is still there in the crypt for someone to find ...

- The Castellan tells Maxil that the execution of a Time Lord has only ever 'happened once before' in their history. This could be a direct reference to Morbius's execution on Karn (see 'The Brain Of Morbius').

LANGUAGE

We see on the computer room screens on Gallifrey a series of numbers representing the Doctor's bio-data. Later we see on the same screen words in English. The TARDIS computer has information on the Arc of Infinity in English. However, all the signs in Amsterdam are in Dutch. Omega has a Ω symbol on his helmet: the upper case Greek letter Omega.

TIMELINE DATES

1983, May

'Arc Of Infinity' is set in a time after Tegan has been left behind on Earth in 'Time-Flight', and certainly prior to 1984, which is the current year for Tegan and her grandfather in 'The Awakening'. With 'Time-Flight' set in 1981, this means that Tegan has been back on Earth for two years. She has been able to fit back into her old life (but without her Aunt Vanessa). She recently 'got the sack'. Nyssa says 'I've missed you'.

The time of year could be early summer, with Colin and Robin touring Europe during the first weeks of the University summer break. The story was recorded in May [of 1982], so this month would seem more appropriate to match spring seasonal conditions.

With 'Mawdryn Undead' set in May 1983, 'Arc Of Infinity' can be the same month.

It is also May 1983 on Gallifrey. For more on the relationship between the Earth and Gallifrey in this story, see GALLIFREY HISTORY.

DURATION

There are two locations, Amsterdam and Gallifrey, but the events all take place simultaneously on the same 'day': and night falls on both locations at the same time.

⇨ Day One (Ep1)

The clock reads '3.31' (pm) in the opening scenes on Earth. Colin tells Tegan (on the telephone) he will see her at the airport 'tomorrow'. Colin and Robin spend the night in the crypt. It is night on Gallifrey when Talor is killed.

⇨ Day Two (Ep1-2)

The High Council is in session the following day. Robin goes to the hostel in the morning and learns that Tegan will now arrive 'tomorrow morning at 10.30' (a day later than she originally told Colin in Day One). The Doctor gets shot and spends the equivalent of the night resting in the TARDIS.

⇨ Day Three (Ep.2-4)

Robin meets Tegan at '10.59' (seen on the airport clock). The story ends later this day at both locations.

SNAKEDANCE

+STORY LINK

At the end of 'Arc Of Infinity', Tegan reports that Colin will be out of hospital 'in a couple of days'. We can assume that she, Nyssa and the Doctor stayed in Amsterdam until then before leaving in the TARDIS again. Given Nyssa's references to Omega in the opening scenes of 'Snakedance', the TARDIS has probably just left Amsterdam.

The Doctor has been teaching both Tegan and Nyssa how to read the star-charts, which suggests that the TARDIS has been travelling in space only (see Timeline Dates below). The Doctor comments that they're 'not where we're supposed to be', implying that they were heading for a specific destination. Tegan does ask if they are 'on Earth', and the Doctor replies 'No, we're not', which suggests that Earth was their intended destination, but because of Tegan's possession they are in the right time zone, just on the wrong planet (it's still 1983). Tegan is asleep, which suggests it is now the 'night' relative to the same day in which she rejoined the Doctor in the TARDIS.

Also, Nyssa changes in this story from her usual velvet trouser suit to a blue and white dress, and even makes a big show of it to the Doctor, but he fails to notice instantly. From this it is clear that she has never worn any clothes other than her velvet suit since 'Castrovalva' (with the exception of the ball gown in 'Black Orchid'), so I would say that the passage of time between 'Castrovalva' and 'Snakedance' is only a relatively short period of time, certainly no more than a few months (see also Story Link, 'Arc Of Infinity').

OBSERVATIONS

- The Great Crystal is blue, just like the crystals of Metebelis Three (see 'Planet Of The Spiders'), which suggests that all blue crystals have special properties that control the mind. The similarly-coloured numismaton gas on Sarn has special healing properties ('Planet Of Fire').

LANGUAGE

Nyssa reads from a large grey book, possibly one of the Doctor's time logs. Interestingly, the specifications of Manussa are recorded in terms of Earth readings, i.e. 'terra normal'.

TIMELINE DATES

1983, May

Manussa is the third planet of a three-planet Federation System. Although there is the phrase 'the human heart' in Dojjen's journal, the crystal is described a being 'man-made', and the female puppet is apparently called 'Judy', there is nothing else to suggest the Federation colonists are from Earth (as noted in THE N-SPACE UNIVERSE, the term 'human' only means humanoid). The history of the Federators does not conform in any way with Earth's future history as seen in other stories. The warrior uniform worn by Lon's ancestor at the time the Mara was defeated is hardly a futuristic Earth design, so this Federation is not the same as the Galactic Federation of 'The Curse Of Peladon' and 'The Monster Of Peladon'.

A strong date reference is provided in the opening TARDIS scene: the ship has already landed on Manussa. The Doctor announces 'we're not where we're supposed to be ... there are traces of anti-matter'. Nyssa wonders if this could be Omega, but the Doctor says it's 'highly unlikely he's still alive'. Significantly, he doesn't say 'we're not in the same time zone as Amsterdam' or words to that effect. Also, when the Doctor asks Tegan where they are, she replies 'Well, aren't we on Earth?', which suggests that she expected them to still be in Amsterdam in 1983.

The fact that the Doctor detects anti-matter on Manussa suggests that under the influence of the Mara, Tegan has unknowingly piloted the TARDIS spatially from Earth to Manussa. They are still in 1983, the setting of 'Arc Of Infinity', the anti-matter detected being residue from the Arc of Infinity which still spans across the galaxy from Earth to Rondel. On this basis, I am prepared to accept that 1983 is the date for 'Snakedance'. Of course, it is rather coincidental that they just happen to arrive on Manussa the day before the important once-every-ten-years ceremony is to take place!

1183

The Doctor says 'according to Chela this crystal is 800 years old'. The Mara subsequently ruled for 300 years.

1283

The Maran statue Lon toys with is '700 years old. From the middle Sumaran era'.

1483

It is stated on several occasions that the Mara was banished by the Federator '500 years ago'.

1883

Snakedancing was banned 'nearly one hundred years ago', according to Chela.

1965

When the Doctor hypnotises Tegan, she regresses back to a time when she was in her garden when she was 'six, silly'. As covered under 'Kinda' Tegan was aged 3 around 1962, so she is aged 6 in 1965.

1973

According to Chela, 'Dojjen hasn't been seen for ten years'.

DURATION

⇨ Day One (Ep1-2)

It is 'morning' when Ambril takes Lon and Tanha to the caves. It is night when Lon goes to Dugdale's booth and meets Tegan. The Doctor interrupts Ambril's dinner and is locked up overnight.

⇨ **Day Two (Ep3-4)** ▪ ▪ ▪ ▪ ▪ ▪ ▪ ▪ ▪ ▪ ▪
The Doctor is released the next morning. The ceremony takes places that 'afternoon'.

MAWDRYN UNDEAD

+STORY LINK

At the beginning of 'Mawdryn Undead', Tegan shares her concerns with the Doctor about whether or not she is free of the Mara. She says she is 'still having terrible dreams', which suggests that at least a few days have passed since 'Snakedance'.

Tegan says how much she hates transmats, and that she is always worried about coming out puréed. There is no story in which we see her using such a device, so it would appear she has had experience with one in an off-screen adventure.

OBSERVATIONS

- The transmat capsule makes its first trip to Earth on 7 June 1977 with Mawdryn on board. The capsule becomes invisible and remains on the hillside until 1983, when Turlough activates its camouflage screen by pressing the base of the urn. He takes the capsule up to the spaceship. Turlough and the Doctor then travel in the capsule from the ship back to the hill to switch off the transmitter. With the 1983 Brigadier, they take the globe back to the ship. The fifth and final trip is with the 1977 Brigadier on board, but in this case the capsule returns to the ship without going anywhere. Mawdryn explains that 'every seventy years the beacon guides us to within transmat distance of a planet', so we can assume that he is referring to the transmitter in the urn. One question remains: who placed the transmitter that guided the transmat capsule to Earth in the urn in the first place? The Black Guardian, as part of his trap for the Doctor, perhaps?
- An interesting loop-paradox concerning the TARDIS homing device occurs in this story: Tegan takes the homing device with her when she goes to the school. She gives it to the 1977 Brigadier, who as we clearly see places it in his pocket. Later, the 1977 Brigadier removes the homing device he finds in the transmat, so he now has two. Unless he loses one, or the Doctor takes one from his pocket when the Brigadier is returned to 1977, the Brigadier still has two in his pocket. The 1983 Brigadier returns one of the devices, which he has kept all those years to the Doctor, who uses it to guide the transmat capsule back to Mawdryn's ship. The 1977 Brigadier later takes this from the

transmat. He now has two. Unless he loses one, or the Doctor takes one from his pocket when the Brigadier was returned to 1977, the Brigadier still has two … ad infinitum.

- Is the crystal the Black Guardian gives to Turlough made of the same substance as the Key To Time? As noted under 'The Armageddon Factor', it has taken the Black Guardian 11 years to locate the Doctor for the Guardian to take his revenge …

LANGUAGE

Mawdryn speaks English when Nyssa and Tegan first find him in the capsule, so it is clear that it is his native tongue.

TIMELINE DATES

1977, June 7

The year '1977' is mentioned several times, and it is seen on the T-shirts worn by the students. The Doctor establishes the precise date that the Brigadier met Tegan during 'the Queen's Silver Jubilee' as being 'June the Seventh, 1977'.

The Brigadier says he is 'a new boy here myself', so he has only recently arrived at the school when Tegan meets him.

1983, May

The year '1983' is given numerous times for the date from which Turlough and the older Brigadier come.

Although Mawdryn's spaceship is said to be 'in a fixed orbit in time as well as space' the Doctor reads from the ship's console and states that 'if these readings are correct it's 1983 on Earth', and that the capsule first left the ship 'almost six years ago', in 1977. Turlough later confirms that he is from 1983. All the scenes set on Mawdryn's ship therefore take place in this year.

Mawdryn arrived on Earth in the capsule on 7 June 1977. The Doctor says this was 'almost six years ago', so the 1983 section must be set before June 1983. Some of the school boys are heard playing cricket, which is a summer sport, so it can't be much earlier than May 1983.

Interestingly, it is 1977 when Mawdryn first arrives on Earth, but because the TARDIS takes him back to the ship in 1983 only a few hours later, Mawdryn is six years 'younger' than the ship and the other mutants.

1017 BC

The Doctor reads from the spaceship's flight-log that it has been in orbit for 'three thousand years', which is around 1017 BC. One of the mutants says they 'have experimented for centuries' on their disability. It is not explained how the mutants managed to steal the metamorphic symbiosis generator from Gallifrey, given the Time Lords' embargo on alien beings visiting Gallifrey. Perhaps there was no such law at the time that Mawdryn visited thousands of years ago, and it was only because he stole Time Lord technology that that law was subsequently established. Also, the transmat capsule is dimensionally transcendental, like a TARDIS, so it is possible that the mutants stole this technology from Gallifrey too.

1929

Ibbotson gives the date for the Brigadier's car.

1946

When surveying the damage done to his car, the Brigadier says that 'in thirty years of soldiering' he has never seen anything more destructive than the British schoolboy. He retired from UNIT in 1976, which means he joined the army around 1946. In 'The Invasion' the Brigadier mentions that he served with Billy Rutlidge at Sandhurst, presumably soon after enlisting.

1953, June 1

The date in our history upon which Elizabeth II was crowned Queen. (See 'The Idiot's Lantern'.)

1976

Harry Sullivan was last seen in 'The Android Invasion', which is set in July 1975. The 1983 Brigadier knows that Harry was 'seconded to NATO' (a fact to which he would be privy under the Official Secrets Act), so this must have happened when the Brigadier was still with UNIT, making it some time between July 1975 and his retirement in 1976.

1976

The 1983 Brigadier tells the Doctor he left UNIT 'seven years ago', which is 1976. This would have been only a year after the events of 'The Seeds Of Doom'. Indeed, the Brigadier was in Geneva during that adventure, possible negotiating the terms of his early retirement.

398

1979 ▓ ▒ ▒ ▒ ▒ ▒ ▒ ▒ ▒ ▒ ▒ ▒ ▒ ▒
The Brigadier says Benton 'left the army in '79'.

1982 ▓ ▒ ▒ ▒ ▒ ▒ ▒ ▒ ▒ ▒ ▒ ▒ ▒ ▒
Since Turlough's name is not in the 1977 school register, he must have been exiled on Earth some time between 1977 and 1983. The way the Headmaster talks to Turlough about his refusal to join in any games at school suggests he has only been at Brendon for a short time, say since 1982 (see also 'Planet Of Fire').

DURATION

⇨ **Day One (7 June 1977) (Ep1-2 / Ep4)** ▒ ▒ ▒ ▒ ▒ ▒ ▒
All the 1977 scenes take place this single day.

⇨ **Day One (1983) (Ep1-4)** ▒ ▒ ▒ ▒ ▒ ▒ ▒ ▒ ▒
It is 'afternoon' when Turlough and Ibbotson have their accident. A bell can be heard chiming three times when the Doctor repairs the homing device, so it could be three o'clock at that point in the story. It is later the same day when the Brigadier is returned to 1983.

TERMINUS

+STORY LINK

This story follows on directly from 'Mawdryn Undead', with Turlough settling into the TARDIS; Tegan shows him his new room (Adric's old one) for the first time. At the end of 'Mawdryn Undead' the TARDIS crew dash back into the ship to rescue Turlough, whom they believe to still be on Mawdryn's ship. Since they find him safe in the TARDIS, there is no reason to believe that they leave 1983 immediately. After all, at the beginning of 'Mawdryn Undead', Tegan wants to go to Earth to get over the Mara trauma, and certainly the Doctor would want to spend some more time with the Brigadier. Therefore it is likely that they remain in 1983 for a few days. The Brigadier probably arranged with the Headmaster for Turlough to go with the Doctor, which is why Turlough shows no concern or surprise at seeing the Brigadier on Gallifrey in 'The Five Doctors'.

Since leaving Earth, Nyssa has begun work on synthesising an enzyme, a task with which Adric had helped with calculations, at some point prior to 'Earthshock'. As noted below, the TARDIS is not time travelling at this point, only moving through space.

OBSERVATIONS

- The Doctor states that the Terminus was once capable of time-travel, but does not establish where or when it came from. This suggests that the vessel is from the N-Space Universe, not another dimension or Universe, and that it had travelled backwards in time from the future to a point in time before the Universe existed. Perhaps that was the ship's intended flight-path; it is an explorer ship sent out to discover the secret of the origin of the Universe – only for the crew to discover that its very presence in that time zone creates the Universe. (Note: I have not placed in the TIMELINE the date from which the Terminus ship originated as it could be any time period.)

LANGUAGE

Signs on the liner and Terminus are in English (i.e. 'HAZARD'). The raiders, Vanir, Lazars, Garm and the computer all speak the same language. With Nyssa staying behind, she would have to speak their language too, as it is unlikely that the Time Lord 'gift' is permanent.

TIMELINE DATES

1983, May •

The Terminus is a spaceship that was boosted 'billions of years into the future' by the shock wave known as the Big Bang (aka 'Event One'). Olvir refers to the liner as 'a leper ship', leprosy being an Earth disease, and to 'the old plagues'. Bor quotes an Earth proverb ('a burden shared is a – '), which suggests that they are all of Earth descent. However, despite their origins in classical Norse mythology, the names of the Vanir and the raiders do not indicate an Earth origin (see THE N-SPACE UNIVERSE).

It has been suggested that the Lazar's disease is the same as the disease destroying Earth colonies in 'Death To The Daleks', setting Terminus around 3500. However, this is unlikely, given that the cure for that virus is processed parrinium, while the only known cure for Lazar's disease is a massive dose of radiation.

The Terminus itself is located 'at the exact centre of the known Universe', which in reality would be billions of light years away from Earth's galaxy. Given that intergalactic travel is developed around 2980 (see 'The Ribos Operation', 'Terror Of The Vervoids'), if the humans are from Earth, Terminus would need to be set at a time well after 2980, when travel through space by such distances to the centre of the Universe is possible. In 'Planet Of Evil', the Morestrans are capable of journeying to planets at the edge of the known Universe by the year 37,166. The Morestrans could be human colonists based on the mix of races in the crew. So, if humans can reach the edge of the known Universe by the 380th century, then in all likelihood they can also reach the centre.

Another possible date comes from the Doctor's comment about the TARDIS fail-safe: 'On impending break-up it seeks out and locks onto the nearest spacecraft'. This suggests that the TARDIS left Earth in 1983 (at the end of 'Mawdryn Undead') and is actually travelling in space only, without temporal displacement. The fact that it attaches itself to the nearest spacecraft supports this idea, as this seems to be a manoeuvre that would be extremely difficult if the TARDIS is travelling in the time vortex.

My own preference is that the humans in the story are not from Earth, and for setting Terminus in the same time zone relative to 'Mawdryn Undead'; the TARDIS is travelling spatially to its next destination. And on my assumption that the Black Guardian cannot time travel, the same date as used for 'Mawdryn Undead' has been selected.

13,000,000,000 BC

Scientists have estimated the Universe to be between 15 and eight billion years old. In 'Secrets Of The Stars' this is narrowed down to thirteen billion.

1978

Valgard says he served with Captain Periera 'for five tours'. Assuming a tour is a year, he started with the Captain in 1978.

DURATION

(TARDIS) (Ep1)

The TARDIS travels in space before docking with the liner ...

⇨ Day One (Ep1-4)

Several hours are spent on the liner and the Terminus station.

ENLIGHTENMENT

There is no mention of Nyssa, but when Tegan criticises Turlough's cowardly streak, he says 'I explained what happened on Terminus', as if it were a recent event. As this story is the final part of the Black Guardian trilogy, it is safe to consider that Terminus and 'Enlightenment' are consecutive. We can assume that the TARDIS crew stay on the Terminus for a while to help Nyssa settle in and to ensure that she is capable of synthesising hydromel.

Tegan and Turlough are playing chess, while the Doctor investigates the mysterious power drains caused by the White Guardian. As noted below, the TARDIS is not time travelling, which is how it is possible for the Guardian to locate the ship.

OBSERVATIONS

- The Doctor is not familiar with the Eternals, but he deduces that they are very powerful, and have the power to take beings 'from any planet, any galaxy, any time', and can 'pick the minds of more advanced beings from other galaxies'. The tenth Doctor is, however, more familiar with the Eternals, saying they call the Void between dimensions 'the Howling' ('Army Of Ghosts'). It was the Eternals who banished the Carrionites into the Deep Darkness ('The Shakespeare Code').

- If the ships in the race are created from the minds of the human crews, why doesn't the *Buccaneer* vanish when Wrack and Mansell are sent back to their own dimension? And what is the crystal of lights seen at the end of the race? Is it the domain of the Guardians? The fact that it is a crystal-like structure suggests that it is made of the same substance as the Key To Time and (possibly) Turlough's cube.

- After the Black Guardian vanishes in flames the White Guardian says 'While I exist he exists also – until we are no longer needed'. The question is, no longer needed by whom?

- The TARDIS console explodes quite spectacularly in Ep1. Although the Doctor later successfully pilots the ship from the *Shadow* to the *Buccaneer*, to Earth in 'The King's Demons' and then on to the Eye of Orion in 'The Five Doctors', we can assume that the Doctor builds the new console as seen in 'The Five Doctors' as a direct result of this damage.

LANGUAGE

The Eternals would presumably speak the language native to the respective human crews they control, since they get their inspirations directly from the minds of their crews, however the 'Vacuum Shield' on Wrack's Spanish-based ship is labelled in English and not Spanish.

TIMELINE DATES

1983, May ▸
The actual time period in which the race takes place is unknown. There are a number of different ideas in the offing:

1) 'Enlightenment' is best not set beyond the late twentieth century; the planets in Earth's solar system are the marker buoys for the race and the Eternals would risk attracting the attention of Earth's space fleet or network of space stations (see 'The Wheel In Space'), or even Space Corps (see 'Nightmare Of Eden'), as the fleet sails around Venus and the other planets.
2) The positions of the four planets of Earth's solar system around which the race passes are seen on the star maps. If we could pinpoint when this positioning is likely to occur or have occurred, we could set 'Enlightenment' in that time period.
3) The crew of the 'Edwardian England' racing yacht *Shadow* are, in chronological Earth terms, the latest to be taken by the Eternals, so the story could be placed relative to when the sailors were abducted, which was on 3 October 1901. They have been on the ship 'two days' so to them it is 5 October 1901.
4) Since the Guardians are controlling the outcome of the race (particularly the Black Guardian through Wrack; though why would he actually bother? What would he gain from it?), with both 'Mawdryn Undead' and 'Terminus' set in the same time period, and in my belief that the Guardians cannot time travel, 'Enlightenment' would have to also be set in May 1983.

My own preference is for option 4), with the race taking place in the same time zone as 'Mawdryn Undead'.

447 BC
The Doctor mentions 'the Athens of Pericles'. Pericles (c495 BC – 429 BC) was the Athenian statesman who made Athens the political and cultural focus of Greece. He oversaw construction of the Acropolis, begun in 447 BC.

1644
1912 ■ ■ ■ ■ ■ ■ ■ ■ ■ ■ ■ ■ ■ ■ ■
The Doctor mentions the 'Ch'ing dynasty' as being one of the time periods of the ships in the race. That dynasty lasted 268 years, from 1644 to 1912.

1650 ■ ■ ■ ■ ■ ■ ■ ■ ■ ■ ■ ■ ■ ■
The Doctor recognises the jewelled sword given to Critas by Wrack as 'Seventeenth century Spanish', which is the period of the Spanish pirates in our history, which is probably where Wrack's crew are from. 1650 is an arbitrary date.

1901, September 6
1901, September 7 ■ ■ ■ ■ ■ ■ ■ ■ ■ ■ ■ ■
The date on the newspaper read by the Doctor is 'September 7, 1901'. The launch would therefore have been the previous day. Jackson says the paper is 'two days old', which indicates that the crew were abducted the same day the paper was issued; he says they have been confined to quarters since arriving on board, which makes the relative 'present' date for the sailors 9 September 1901. (In our history, the first British submarine was actually launched on 2 October 1901.)

DURATION

(TARDIS) (Ep1) ■ ■ ■ ■ ■ ■ ■ ■ ■ ■ ■ ■ ■
The TARDIS travels in space only before landing on the *Shadow*.

⇨ **Day One (Ep1-4)** ■ ■ ■ ■ ■ ■ ■ ■ ■ ■ ■
The Doctor and Tegan share a meal with the *Shadow*'s officers. Later, on the bridge, Tegan says that she 'expected it to be daylight', which suggests that the meal was a luncheon. Wrack's reception is therefore probably in the 'evening'.

THE KING'S DEMONS

+STORY LINK

At the end of 'Enlightenment', Turlough asks to be taken to 'my planet. My home', and in 'The King's Demons' he confirms they 'were on our way to my planet, actually'. After they land on Earth in 1215 the Doctor says he did not set the coordinates for Earth. Tegan asks if this 'could be a Black Guardian trap?' With the Black Guardian defeated at the end of 'Enlightenment', we can assume that 'Enlightenment' and 'The King's Demons' are definitely consecutive. Since leaving the Guardian's domain, Tegan has changed her outfit (her hair has grown somewhat since 'Enlightenment').

MASTER LINK

At the end of 'Time-Flight' the Doctor sends the Master's TARDIS shooting off to Xeriphas in 1981. There, the Master finds Kamelion, who helps him escape. As the Doctor comments when Sir Gilles is unmasked to be the Master, 'You escaped from Xeriphas', there is little doubt that 'Time-Flight' and 'The King's Demons' are consecutive for the Master.

The Doctor considers the Master's plans to change history on Earth to be 'small-time villainy by his standards'. The Master reveals his ultimate goal to be 'with Kamelion's ability at my command, it's only a matter of time before I undermine the key civilisations of the Universe. Chaos will reign. And I shall be its Emperor!' Although history records otherwise, it is clear that the Master believes he can succeed. This indicates that being a Time Lord the Master possesses a kind of natural affinity with the nature of time (see THE N-SPACE UNIVERSE). Of note, the year 1215 is close to the Doctor's date of birth (1213 – see THE DOCTOR'S AGE). Could we therefore conclude that the Master has specifically selected 1215 as the year from which to launch his plan for Universal domination because it is his own (Relative Earth) year of birth?) (He's two years younger than the Doctor?)

OBSERVATIONS

- The Doctor and Tegan have an in-depth discussion about history being 'wrong'. Tegan is bored with it, and says 'Who cares?' The Doctor replies, 'I care!'

LANGUAGE

An early form of French was the native tongue of the lords and noblemen in this age; however it is odd that Sir Gilles (the Master) is the only one speaking with anything resembling a French accent. It is amazing that the Time Lord 'gift' is able to translate the King's song from French to English and still have it rhyme! It is assumed that Kamelion is the name used by the automaton, not a name given to it by the Master. It seems odd therefore that Kamelion's builders would name it after an Earth reptile, and one that presumably didn't exist 140,000,000 years ago.

TIMELINE DATES

1215, March 3 - 4 *

The TARDIS lands on Day Two (see Duration). The Doctor reads the date off the console: 'March the Fourth, Twelve Hundred and Fifteen'. Sir Geoffrey left London 'four hours' ago.

HISTORICAL COMPARISON

As the Doctor puts it, the events in 1215 are 'too well-documented'. The King is in London 'to take the cross as a crusader'. It is hard to accept that the Master would succeed in his plans to change history by having Kamelion impersonate King John and pre-empt the signing of the Magna Carta. That really is small fish compared to some of the other historical events he could have visited in which to demonstrate Kamelion's abilities. Besides, it is now believed that much of the 'official' history of the Magna Carta was fabricated around the seventeenth century.

1214, September

Ranulf comments that he previously gave money to the King 'but six months since', which makes this in September 1214.

1215, February 24

The King in London 'but a week since' summoned Geoffrey, which would be February 24.

1215, June 15

The Doctor comments that Magna Carta is 'still three months away'. This is the recorded date in our history.

1216

King John loses the crown jewels 'next year', in 1216.

1981, February 28

Kamelion is 'a tool of an earlier invader of Xeriphas'. It is not clear what the Master means by 'earlier'. The Doctor had sent him to Xeriphas on 28 February 1981 at the end of 'Time-Flight'. The Xeraphin had abandoned their planet after it was all but destroyed in crossfire during the Vardon/Kosnax war several millions of years earlier. Either Kamelion has been on the planet for over 140 million years (which seems unlikely on account of his name – see Language), or Kamelion's creators invaded Xeriphas more recently. But this makes nonsense of the use of the word 'earlier' – or is the Master suggesting that his arrival on Xeriphas was an invasion, and that Kamelion's creators had invaded shortly before his arrival?

DURATION

⇨ **Day One (3 March)**
The banquet for the newly-arrived 'King' is held at the castle that night.

⇨ **Day Two (4 March)**
The TARDIS lands in the morning during the tournament. Sir Geoffrey leaves London 'this morning' and arrives 'four hours' later, so it is on the afternoon of Day Two that the TARDIS leaves.

K9 AND COMPANY– A GIRL'S BEST FRIEND

NOTE: I have placed 'K9 And Company' here due to its continuity links with 'The Five Doctors'.

STORY LINK

At the end of 'The Hand Of Fear' the Doctor dropped off Sarah at her home on Hill View Road in South Croydon. Or so he thought – as it turned out it was actually Aberdeen in Scotland! (See 'School Reunion'). She continued working as a journalist, living in a flat in London, which was to where the Doctor delivered the crate containing K9 in 1978. But Sarah was abroad at the time. The crate was eventually relocated to the homestead in Moreton Harwood by her Aunt Lavinia in 1981.

Sarah has been abroad for the 'last fortnight'.

TIMELINE DATES

1981, December 5 – 6
Lavinia left for the States 'last Sunday week', which would have been the 6th.

1981, December 18 – 25
On the day that Sarah arrives at her aunt's house she tells K9 the 'Earth year' is '1981,

December 18th'. On 6 December Lavinia says that Sarah would be arriving 'Friday week', making the 18th a Friday, which matches the true calendar for December 1981. The other dates of the story can be determined from sections of dialogue.

1891

Sergeant Wilson says to George Tracey, 'There 'asn't been a human sacrifice since 1891.'

1978 *

K9 says 'the Doctor last spoke in One-Nine-Seven-Eight Earth years', which presumably means it was in 1978 rather than 1,978 years ago. He said, 'Give Sarah Jane Smith my fondest love. Tell her I shall remember her always'. Lavinia says the box has been in the attic at South Croydon 'for years'. Given that 'The Hand Of Fear' is set in 1976, two years have passed between Sarah leaving the Doctor and the delivery of K9.

As for when the Doctor builds and delivers K9 Mark Three, it is probably at the same time he builds K9 Mark Two, which is at the beginning of the nine-year gap between 'The Invasion Of Time' and 'The Ribos Operation'. Having created one new K9 model, he probably had enough spare parts to build a third. Not wanting to have a TARDIS filled with over-talkative robotic dogs he decides to leave K9 Mark Three on Earth with Sarah. However, due to her being abroad a great deal she does not get to open the crate for another three years.

1979

The story is set in 1981. Lavinia has been at Moreton Harwood for 'two years'.

1980

Bert Pollock moved into the eastern wing of Lavinia's house 'last year'.

1981, June

Peter Tracey was put on suspended sentence 'six months ago'.

1981, September

Bert Pollock speaks of 'last September' when the hailstorm struck.

1981, December 4

On 18 December Sarah says she has been 'abroad for the last fortnight'.

1981, December 29

Howard Baker says the Traceys and the other coven members will go on trial 'on the 29th'.

DURATION

⇨ **Day One (5 December)**
The coven meets that night and burns a photo of Lavinia.

⇨ **Day Two (6 December)**
Lavinia leaves for the United States.

🕐 **A week passes ...**

⇨ **Day Seven (11 December)**
Brendan breaks from school on this Friday.

🕐 **A week passes, Brendan stays on at the school ...**

⇨ **Day Fourteen (18 December)**
Sarah arrives that morning. She goes to the Bakers that evening, and while she is there, George and Peter Tracey attack Brendan.

⇨ **Day Fifteen (19 December)**
The damage caused by K9 the night before is checked. Brendan is kidnapped that night.

⇨ **Day Sixteen (20 December)**
Sarah discovers that Brendan is missing and goes to the police at '10.15 am' (as seen on the station clock). The coven initiates Peter that night. Sgt Wilson dies.

⇨ **Day Seventeen (21 December)**
The next morning Sarah finds that Bert is missing. Howard calls in at the police station at '4.16 pm'. Sarah and K9 begin searching the chapels. At '11.59.30' they save Brendan from being sacrificed.

🕐 **Three days pass ...**

⇨ **Day Twenty (25 December)**
Sarah and Brendan have Christmas Day dinner with the Bakers.

THE FIVE DOCTORS

+STORY LINK

At the end of 'The King's Demons' the Doctor sets the TARDIS's coordinates for the Eye Of Orion. The TARDIS is now on the planet. There is no mention or sign of Kamelion, who is presumably quartered in Tegan's room. The Doctor has spent some time reconfiguring the TARDIS console room and the console itself, presumably due in part to the damage sustained in 'Enlightenment'. But the console has only been altered cosmetically; the actual controls are still not functioning properly, and the Doctor has to thump the console to make it work (see also 'Doctor Who (The TV Movie)', where the console has once again been reconfigured but is still just as unreliable). Turlough is unaware that the Doctor has two hearts, so we can surmise that from his own personal time, he has been with the Doctor for only a short time, and a matter of weeks, not years, has passed since 'Mawdryn Undead'.

CYBERMAN LINK

As covered under CYBERMAN HISTORY, this is the eighth appearance of the Cybermen. See Timeline Dates below for details on the link to 'Earthshock'.

DALEK LINK

Although the Dalek recognises the Doctor, it is impossible to ascertain at what point in Dalek history this Dalek comes from. Given that all the Doctors and companions are time scooped from Earth, as well as the Cybermen, we can assume that the Dalek, too, has been time scooped from Earth. This could have been towards the end of 'The Dalek Invasion Of Earth' (in 2174), or 'The Chase', 'The Daleks' Master Plan', 'Day Of The Daleks', 'Resurrection Of The Daleks' or 'Remembrance Of The Daleks', or simply from an untelevised adventure.

GALLIFREY LINK

The Doctor's GRT is still 1983 (see THE DOCTOR'S AGE), so the events in 'The Five Doctors' take place only a matter of weeks since 'Arc Of Infinity' (which is also relative to the time that Turlough has been with the Doctor – see Story Link above).

Much has happened on Gallifrey in the few short weeks since the events of 'Arc Of Infinity'. The Castellan remarks to Borusa that 'your regeneration has not helped your stubbornness', so we can assume that Borusa has regenerated only recently. He even seems bitter by the fact that he is using up his incarnations quickly (this is his fourth incarnation in twenty years, since 'The Deadly Assassin' in GRT 1963), and always as an old man, which is why he has taken to seeking immortality. Borusa says 'You know how long I have ruled Gallifrey, Doctor? Both openly or behind the scenes … How long before I must retire … ', which hints that he has only ruled a short time (no less than 20 years), but desires to rule for much longer.

Assuming that Borusa has been in possession of the Black Scrolls of Rassilon and the Coronet since the events of 'The Deadly Assassin' (when the Eye of Harmony and the vaults dating from the Old Time are discovered), Borusa has been plotting to take control of the Time Lords for quite some time. His three premature regenerations could even have been brought about due to his secret meddling with the time scoop, trying to learn its secrets, furthering his twisted cause, and making him even more desperate to succeed given that he is probably nearing the end of his allotted number of lives.

Other changes on Gallifrey since 'Arc Of Infinity' include Maxil having been replaced as Guard Commander, and the other members of the High Council (except for the Castellan) have also been replaced. Two Time Lords had earlier been sent into the Death Zone, and never came back (possibly Maxil, Zorin or Thalia from 'Arc Of Infinity'). Flavia is now on the Council, a fact seemingly already known by the Doctor and the Master before they even arrive at the Capitol.

Curiously, Flavia says 'yet again it is my duty and pleasure' to inform the Doctor that he has been decreed the new President. But when was the previous time? Perhaps she was a Council member in 'The Invasion Of Time' at the time of the Doctor's induction? But the Doctor has no memory of that adventure …

MASTER LINK

There is no mention of the events of 'The King's Demons' (the Master does not mention the Doctor having stolen Kamelion from him, nor even ask after the robot); the Doctor sabotaged the Master's TARDIS by using the tissue compression eliminator on the directional controls, but in 'The Five Doctors' the Master arrives easily on Gallifrey after being summoned by the High Council. We do not see him arrive, so it is possible that he does not come in his own TARDIS but by other means of transport. It does seem somewhat strange that, despite the Master having caused the destruction of nearly half the entire Universe in 'Logopolis', the Time Lords do not mention this particular crime.

On the assumption that the TARDIS crew have stayed on the Eye of Orion for a few days (see Duration), then only a day or so has passed since the events of 'The King's Demons' for the Master as well.

The Master refers to one of the wars on Earth during which they used to drive sheep across minefields; the Master has read about, heard of, or even been to, that particular time period in Earth history to know that.

UNIT HQ – COUNTRY # 2

This is clearly the same building last seen in the previous multi-Doctor story, 'The Three Doctors', set in 1973. This means that UNIT has used this building on and off for 10 years. The sign out front is different to that seen in 'The Three Doctors': it now says:

MINISTRY OF DEFENCE
U.N.I.T. HEADQUARTERS
KEEP OUT

We see two rooms: the corridor outside and Crichton's office. The second Doctor comments upon the fact that there have been some changes made to the office ('I don't like it'), so he clearly remembers it from his previous visit.

OBSERVATIONS

- According to the Doctor, the legends of the Death Zone state that 'even in our most corrupt period our ancestors never allowed the Cybermen to play the game. Like the Daleks they played too well'. It is clear in 'The Tenth Planet' that the Doctor already knows of the Cybermen, so this knowledge most likely came from the legends. However, it is clear in 'The Daleks' that the Doctor has never heard of the Daleks before. It could simply be that the Daleks were not known by that name at the time that the Death Zone was in operation; the legends simply mentioned robot-like creatures. It is only after his subsequent travels and encounters with the Daleks that the Doctor has surmised that the creatures referred to in the legends were in fact the Daleks.
- The High Council is able to offer the Master 'a complete new life cycle' of regenerations. The fact that he accepts it proves that it is possible; they are not lying to him. The Master is clever enough to see through a deception. It has been stated on several occasions that a Time Lord can only regenerate twelve times (see 'The Deadly Assassin', 'The Keeper Of Traken', 'Mawdryn Undead' and 'Doctor Who (The TV Movie)'). (As noted under 'The Stolen Earth', it is likely that all Time Lords were provided with new regenerative life cycles during the Time War.)
- At the end of the story, the first, second and third Doctors and their respective

companions depart in what look to be copies of the Doctor's own TARDIS. But rather than the Doctor's time ship splitting off and being duplicated three times, it is more likely that the High Council materialised three other TARDISes inside the console room of the Doctor's ship, and their chameleon circuits adopted the shape of the police box exterior. And it was while the Doctors and companions were travelling back to the time zones and locations from which they were originally time-scooped that the High Council erased or blocked their memories of the adventure they have just experienced on Gallifrey; it is clear from 'School Reunion' that Sarah Jane Smith did not recall this adventure.

LANGUAGE

The second Doctor's ancient Gallifreyan nursery rhyme still rhymes when translated into English! The Doctor can read Old High Gallifreyan, which resembles Greek. The Doctor translates the script on 'the Harp of Rassilon', which is a series of Greek-like symbols.

TIMELINE DATES

1215, March 4 •

Despite originally trying to get Turlough home ('We were on our way to my planet, actually') the Doctor programs the ship for the Eye Of Orion at the end of 'The King's Demons', so the year could still be 1215. Turlough has also been to the Eye before, but that would have been relative to his own time stream. In the absence of contrary dates, I have the sequences at the Eye Of Orion on the same date as 'The King's Demons'.

1983, June •

Turlough says 'according to the [TARDIS] instruments we're nowhere in no time', but that is only because the force-field around the Death Zone has made the TARDIS inoperable.

The previous Gallifrey story, 'Arc Of Infinity', is set in May 1983, so 'The Five Doctors' needs to be set relative to THE DOCTOR'S AGE, with only a few weeks having passed since 'Arc Of Infinity'.

1984, March •

In terms of the Brigadier's time stream the UNIT reunion is after 'Mawdryn Undead', because he recognises Tegan, Turlough and the fifth Doctor. He has also grown a new moustache. The UNIT scenes were filmed in March [of 1983], so the same seasonal conditions can apply (the Brigadier is wearing a thick coat), but to take into account that 'Mawdryn Undead' is set in June 1983 it is most likely the following year, 1984.

The fact that *The Times* is published 'tomorrow' would mean that the reunion is a weekday or a Sunday.

The desk sergeant knows who the second Doctor is, which suggests he was with UNIT during the Cybermen invasion of 1970 ('The Invasion') or when the second Doctor 'visits' in 'The Three Doctors' (although no one except for those directly involved with the Omega problem actually see the second Doctor in that story).

1984, March +

Sarah obtained K9 in December 1981 (see 'K9 And Company'), so it is a few years later in her time stream. (She is now living in a modest house.) I have therefore set Sarah's time to be the same as the Brigadier's, March 1984, to match seasonal conditions. It is likely to be a weekday, as Sarah is heading off for work when she is abducted.

- For details of when and where the other Doctors are time scooped, refer to their respective eras in STORYFILE.

9,993,000 BC

As covered under 'The Trial Of A Time Lord' and GALLIFREY HISTORY, Rassilon came to power some 10 million years ago. We do not know how long he lived (as mentioned in 'The Five Doctors': 'no one really knows how extensive his powers were' / 'Immortality ... Rassilon achieved it. Timeless, perpetual bodily regeneration'), so he could have lived for thousands of years. As covered under THE DOCTOR'S AGE, the average life span for a Time Lord is around 6,700 years, so assuming that Rassilon lived his full term he was probably placed in his tomb around the year 9,993,000 BC.

2194

Susan leaves the TARDIS crew at the end of the Dalek Invasion in 2174 (see 'The Dalek Invasion Of Earth'). When he is time scooped to Gallifrey, the first Doctor has only aged a few years since Susan left him, however the time scoop means that they are not necessarily of the same GRT any more. Susan is clearly older [Carole Ann Ford is 20 years older], so we can assume that 20 or so years have passed for Susan, and that she is from 2194.

When she sees the Dalek, Susan automatically assumes she and the Doctor are on Skaro. Considering she is now (apparently still) living on post-Dalek invasion Earth, why doesn't she assume she is still on Earth, and that the Dalek is a survivor from the invasion? The Dalek does after all recognise the Doctor.

2526

The Cybermen seen in 'Earthshock' know a lot about TARDISes and the Time Lords. This information is probably something that they discover while on Gallifrey – perhaps after having tortured and killed the two Time Lords initially sent into the Death Zone, and whose remains the Master finds.

Since they are of the same design as those seen in 'Earthshock' and 'Attack Of The Cybermen', we can assume that these Cybermen come from around the same period. Since all the earlier Doctors and their companions had been time scooped from Earth, we can assume the same of the Cybermen. They have several bombs with them, so these Cybermen could have been part of the group that set up the bomb in the caves as seen in 'Earthshock' (set in 2526). Although most of the other Cybermen are destroyed by the Raston robot or by the booby-traps in the Dark Tower, the Cybermen attacking the TARDIS survive, and are probably returned to 2526 by the power of Rassilon, or maybe even the High Council of the Time Lords. They retain all the information they learned while on Gallifrey, which explains why the Cybermen in 'Earthshock' ('so, we meet again, Doctor') and 'Attack Of The Cybermen' know all about the Time Lords, when they have never possessed such information before (see also CYBERMAN HISTORY).

DURATION

⇨ **Day One**
It is day at the Eye Of Orion. The TARDIS has been there for as many days as it takes for the TARDIS console to be reconfigured.

⇨ **Day One**
The story takes place over one day on Gallifrey.

WARRIORS OF THE DEEP

STORY LINK

The Doctor is sporting a new haircut, and Tegan's hair is longer, so some time has passed since 'The Five Doctors'. There is no mention at all of their adventure on

Gallifrey (but the Doctor does say 'I should have changed [the TARDIS] for a Type 57 when I had the chance'). At the end of 'Enlightenment', Turlough asks the Doctor to take him to his home planet. But by 'Warriors Of The Deep' he has decided to stay with the Doctor ('I thought I would learn more if I stayed with you'). Turlough is putting on his tie, which suggests he has been getting dressed, after having been asleep, or maybe in the pool?

Tegan is wearing the same top she has on in 'The King's Demons', so that adventure is probably relatively recent. But as noted under Story Link in 'The Awakening' below, there should be at least a few months between these stories. This makes sense of the fact that Turlough has decided to stay with the Doctor; they have spent a lot of time – unsuccessfully – trying to get back to Trion.

The Doctor has 'promised to show Tegan a little of her planet's future'. It is not known what time zone they were bound for, but a fault with the TARDIS takes them 'too far advanced', so we can assume they were intending to reach somewhere in the first quarter or half of the twenty-first century. The planned destination might even have been to the period when the Gravitron became operational ('The Moonbase') or to a time when Salamander was in power ('The Enemy Of The World').

LANGUAGE

All the signs in the Base are in English. The Sea Base crew converse with the Silurians and Sea Devils even when the Doctor is not present. On the Sea Devils' helmets we can see strange symbols: these could be rank or other designation, or it is their own written language. There is no indication as to which of the two power blocs the Sea Base network is protecting. The crew appear to be a mixture of races and nationalities. Despite the non-English names of the top people in command, and Katrina and Dr Solow's Eastern-European accents, it should not be inferred that it is the Eastern bloc.

TIMELINE DATES

2084 ·
The Doctor has been on a Sea Base before ('If I remember rightly, the Command Centre is ... '), so when he discovers they are on a Sea Base, he says the date is 'around Two Thousand and Eighty Four', which is presumably the date of his previous visit to a Sea Base. This is not the same as saying that the year they are now in is 2084, but in the absence of other information this date is the best. The Doctor's previous visit could even have been only a matter of months earlier.

The Doctor knows about the Sea Base defences. He says 'there are still two power blocs, fingers poised, ready to annihilate each other'. In 'Warriors Of The Deep', when he sees canisters of hexachromite gas, the Doctor says 'I thought they would have banned it by now', which indicates that in this first visit to 2084 the Doctor probably experienced the dangers of the chemical first hand.

1584 ▨ ▨ ▨ ▨ ▨ ▨ ▨ ▨ ▨ ▨ ▨ ▨ ▨ ▨ ▨ ▨ ▨

Icthar says 'for hundreds of years our Sea Devil brothers have lain entombed, awaiting impatiently for this day'. He also states that the 'Elite Group One' force was to have been revived earlier but wasn't. This suggests that the Sea Devils were originally revived centuries ago, but went back into hibernation, some 500 years earlier.

2020 ✦ ▨ ▨ ▨ ▨ ▨ ▨ ▨ ▨ ▨ ▨ ▨ ▨ ▨ ▨ ▨ ▨

Icthar says 'twice we offered a hand of friendship to these Ape-descended primitives, and twice we were treacherously attacked, our people slaughtered'. This does not accurately describe the events of 'Doctor Who And The Silurians' and 'The Sea Devils'. Although it may have been the intention that Icthar is the Silurian Scientist the third Doctor met in 'Doctor Who And The Silurians', the fact that the Silurians look and sound different, and the Doctor knows more about Silurian technology and politics than he could have possibly discovered in those two previous adventures, I think we can safely accept that all this happened in an off-screen adventure. Indeed, Icthar says the Silurians and Sauvix's Sea Devils are 'blood related comrades', which suggests that these particular 'breeds' are different to those Silurians and Sea Devils seen previously.

In 'Doctor Who And The Silurians', set in 1970, the Silurian Scientist had 'set the controls to revive us in 50 years from now', which is 2020. The Young Silurian appointed the Scientist to be the new leader when they reawaken. So, in 2020 the Wenley Moor base reactivated, and the Scientist became leader. He contacted Icthar and the Silurian Triad, which was in another hidden base, and together they set in motion a strategy to ensure 'the apes are destroyed'. It is around this time that the Doctor arrives (the Doctor says he was 'in an earlier regeneration', and that it was 'a long time ago', so it was either the third or the fourth Doctor). The Doctor meets Icthar and the Triad, sees a Silurian Battle Cruiser and the Myrka. Despite the Doctor's best efforts to broker peace between the Silurians and the people of Earth, the Silurians are treacherously attacked and slaughtered. Icthar is wounded. The Doctor leaves, believing that Icthar had 'been killed'. Then some 64 years later, in 2084 when the political situation on Earth became unstable, Icthar reawakens Sea Devil Elite Group One, and attacks Sea Base Four ...

2084 ▪ ▬ ▬ ▬ ▬ ▬ ▬ ▬ ▬ ▬ ▬ ▬ ▬ ▬

The Doctor says he has previously visited this time period.

DURATION

⇨ **Day One (Ep1-4)** ▬ ▬ ▬ ▬ ▬ ▬ ▬ ▬ ▬ ▬

The story takes place over several hours on the Base. Michaels' replacement is due to arrive 'the day after tomorrow'.

THE AWAKENING

STORY LINK

The only connection with 'Warriors Of The Deep' is that Tegan wears the same dress. The Doctor has a new cricket outfit; he discarded the old one on Sea Base Four when it got wet.

In 'Warriors Of The Deep' the TARDIS is damaged after the attack by Sentinel 6, and the Doctor says it would 'take some time' to repair her, so presumably 'some time' is spent afterwards on Sea Base Four making the necessary repairs.

At the beginning of 'The Awakening', the TARDIS is affected by 'some time distortion'. Tegan then asks if they are still 'going to Earth'. Considering that 'Warriors Of The Deep' is set on Earth, it would appear that they have been to another planet (or planets) off-screen after leaving Sea Base Four. (Since 'The Awakening' is set in 1984, the time distortion could actually be from the Dalek time corridor that is operating in that time zone – see 'Resurrection Of The Daleks'.)

As noted under THE DOCTOR'S AGE, Tegan has been back with the Doctor for 14 months since they were reunited in Amsterdam ('Arc Of Infinity'). The majority of this off-screen time must have been spent between 'The Five Doctors' and 'Warriors Of The Deep'.

OBSERVATIONS

- There are strong continuity links with 'The Visitation': the Doctor explains to Jane Hampden 'the Terileptils mine tinclavic for more or less the exclusive use of the people of Hakol. That's in the star system of Rifta, you know.' The Malus was sent to Earth by the people of Hakol 'to clear the way for an invasion'. For reasons unknown (at least to the Doctor) the invasion never happened; the

Doctor said he didn't know why and that he would have to check the TARDIS computer to see if there was anything recorded about it. Interestingly, 'The Visitation' is set in 1666, which is only 23 years after the original battle in Little Hodcombe; the Terileptils had escaped from the very same tinclavic mines on Raaga.

- Andrew Verney is Tegan's grandfather. He is English, so we can assume that he is the father of Tegan's mother. Tegan's Aunt Vanessa ('Logopolis') is Australian, as is Tegan's cousin, Colin Fraser ('Arc Of Infinity'). Aunt Vanessa would therefore be either the sister of Tegan's father, or the wife of his brother. It is unlikely that she is Colin's mother, since there is no indication of this relationship in 'Arc Of Infinity'.

TIMELINE DATES

1984, July 13 ·

Turlough confirms the year: 'I checked the time monitor. It is 1984'. Tegan asks for the 'date, time and place' so that she could visit her grandfather. As covered under THE DOCTOR'S AGE 1984 must be Tegan's Earth Mean Time; it is doubtful that the Doctor would agree to let Tegan visit her grandfather out of sync with her own (if you'll excuse the pun) relative time stream. She first met the Doctor on 28 February 1981 (see 'Logopolis'). With the year now 1984, she has aged three years in the time she has known the Time Lord, but two of those years pass off-screen between 'Time-Flight' and 'Arc Of Infinity'.

Although the year for 'The Awakening' is specified, there are two choices available for the month:

a) Sir George says that 'on the Thirteenth of July Sixteen Hundred And Forty Three the English Civil War came to Little Hodcombe'. Since Hutchinson is re-enacting this event, it could be set on 13 July 1984 (341 years later). The story was recorded in July [of 1983], so the seasonal conditions can also be matched.

b) Tegan has been selected as the Queen of the May, and there is a May Day Pole in the village green. May Day is traditionally 1 May. It seems odd however that there would be a Queen of the May when the war was in July.

I would be inclined to take 13 July 1984 as the best date, based on the fact that the war games are being played to celebrate the original war of that date. Also, that means that Will Chandler emerges from the priest hole on the same date he first entered it, although he is now displaced by some 341 years. Of course, this now also means that Tegan returns to Earth at the end of 'Resurrection Of The Daleks' 23 days before the events of 'The Awakening' take place ...

1184

No dates are given for when the Malus first came to Earth, other than that it has been in the church 'for hundreds of years ... long before the Civil War started'. On the assumption that the church wasn't much older than 500 years at the time of the English Civil War, we can assume that the Malus arrived no earlier than 1184.

1643, July 13

Sir George Hutchinson gives the date for when the battle was fought.

1981

Andrew Verney says he has done 'years of research' into the legend of the Malus. Tegan doesn't know anything about this, so it seems that she hasn't seen him for several years, say three years.

1984, July 10

Andrew Verney 'disappeared a few days ago', say the 10th.

DURATION

⇨ **Day One (13 July 1984) (Ep1-2)**
The story takes place over one ('very hard') day.

FRONTIOS

STORY LINK

At the end of 'The Awakening', Tegan asks the Doctor if they could 'spend a little time' with her grandfather in Little Hodcombe. Turlough (whose clothes are left absolutely filthy at the end of 'The Awakening' but clean once more in 'Frontios') admits: 'I wouldn't mind staying for a while'. The Doctor agrees: 'All right, just for a little while'.

There is also the small matter of returning Will Chandler back to 1643. We can assume that while Tegan and Turlough stay a few days in Little Hodcombe, the Doctor takes Will home in the TARDIS. In order to take into account the awkward matter of

the Doctor ageing from 771 years old to 900 (see THE DOCTOR'S AGE), it is possible
that the Doctor and Will don't get to 1643 straight away (the TARDIS could still be
malfunctioning due to the same unexplained 'time distortion' that was affecting it at
the beginning of 'The Awakening'), and they have a series of off-screen adventures
for a few years. After eventually getting to 1643 and parting company with Will (they
may have even stayed in 1643 for a time), the Doctor travels for many more years,
and eventually gets back to Tegan and Turlough where he left them in July 1984, but
he is now 129 years older. Given that Kamelion is also a passenger in the TARDIS, it
is possible that the automaton is also involved in some of these 'missing' adventures.
The fact that the Master does not attempt to repossess the robot in 'The Five Doctors'
suggests that he has no real interest in getting Kamelion back then; it is not until
his accident prior to 'Planet Of Fire' (which is 130 years after 'The Five Doctors' for
the Master) that he needs Kamelion's assistance. Indeed, the Doctor seems rather
uncharacteristically concerned about maintaining Time Lord 'etiquette' and not
transgressing their 'normal sphere of influence', which hints that something happened
to him that has brought about this change of outlook.

'Frontios' opens with the TARDIS having drifted forwards in time 'too far into
the future'. Given that it takes the ship several hours to travel back billions of years
in 'Inside The Spaceship' and 'Castrovalva' and 12 million years in 'Image Of The
Fendahl', we can assume that it takes a similar length of time here. The Doctor has
been spending this time doing some tidying up in the TARDIS corridors.

Turlough tells Norna of the Arar-Jecks on the planet Hieradi, who built huge
underground shelters during the Twenty-Aeon war. This knowledge is either from
an off-screen adventure while travelling with the Doctor, or Turlough knows of the
war from his time on Trion, before his exile. He was exiled to Earth around 1982
(see 'Mawdryn Undead', 'Planet Of Fire'), so the war would have been prior to this
year. I have not placed the Twenty-Aeon war in the TIMELINE, as it is impossible to
establish when it was, as an aeon is such an undefined period.

Also, Turlough has a couple of two-corpira pieces, square-shaped alien coinage by
which one blows through the hole in the centre for luck. It is unlikely that these are coins
of Trion, given that he has never produced the coins 'for luck' before. (Turlough does
not appear to have any possessions when he moves into the TARDIS in 'Terminus'.)
It is more likely that he obtained the coins during an off-screen adventure prior to
'Frontios'. It is even possible that the two-corpira piece was obtained on Hieradi.

OBSERVATIONS

• The Gravis knows of the Time Lords, Gallifrey and TARDISes, and he
  apparently knows the Doctor 'at least by reputation' (but this last point could

simply be because Plantagenet tells the Gravis of the Doctor while a prisoner). If the Gravis does indeed know of Gallifrey, this suggests the Time Lords are still in power at this point in the distant future, which might be why the Time Lords of the Doctor's GRT deem this time period to be 'completely outside [their] normal sphere of influence' and why the TARDIS console reports 'BOUNDARY ERROR – TIME PARAMETERS EXCEEDED': even the Time Lords of Modern Gallifrey fear knowing their own future … Of course, it is possible that with Gallifrey long gone, the planet having been destroyed in the Time War, the influence of Time Lords from the past still echoes … (see 'Bad Wolf').

LANGUAGE

The Gravis is able to communicate with Plantagenet. The Gravis also calls the planet Frontios, and uses the term Veruna system, a name that would have been created by the humans. The TARDIS has records on the Veruna system.

TIMELINE DATES

10,000,040 ‣ ▪ ▪ ▪ ▪ ▪ ▪ ▪ ▪ ▪ ▪ ▪ ▪ ▪

The Doctor announces that the TARDIS 'has drifted too far into the future'. Turlough reads off the ship's computer: 'Fleeing from the imminence of a catastrophic collision with the sun, refugees from the doomed planet Earth … ', a description that matches the evacuation of Earth in 'The Ark', so the same year can be used for 'Frontios'. (Of course, as it turns out, the Earth did not perish – it was it seems rescued from its fiery destruction – see 'The End Of The World'.) 'The Ark' leaves Earth in the 57th segment of time, some 10 million years in the future, so this date can be applied to 'Frontios'. The colonists have been on Frontios for '40 years', so it is now 10,000,040. (It is curious to note that despite being millions of years in the future, humans have not really evolved much physically or technologically; for instance Mr Range wears glasses, and Brazen refers to waxworks.)

There are no Monoids here – perhaps they all died in the crash? An increasing number of colonists 'leave every week' to become Retrogrades. The bombardments 'have become more frequent over the last few weeks'.

9,995,000 ▪ ▪ ▪ ▪ ▪ ▪ ▪ ▪ ▪ ▪ ▪ ▪ ▪ ▪

The Gravis says 'only those who have been isolated for millennia truly appreciate the power of mobility', which suggests that the Tractators have been wandering without a home base for thousands of years, say 5000.

9,999,500

The Gravis says: 'We have been marooned out here on Frontios for nearly 500 years, as I'm sure the Time Lords already know'. The Tractators have existed for millions of years, because Turlough knows of them from his own planet's history; they invaded 'long ago, on my home'.

10,000,000
10,000,010

The colonists have been on Frontios for '40 years'. They had '10 years of clear skies' before the bombardments started. The first one came 'a little over 30 years ago'.

10,000,035

The quarry has 'been closed for years'; say five.

DURATION

⇨ **Day One (Ep1-4)**

The story takes place over one day on Frontios.

RESURRECTION OF THE DALEKS

+STORY LINK

At the end of 'Frontios', the TARDIS is pulled towards 'the middle of the Universe' by some unknown force. This is revealed to be the Dalek time corridor.

DALEK LINK

As covered under DALEK HISTORY, this is the Daleks' fourteenth appearance. The Daleks now have information about the Time Lords, Gallifrey, the High Council, and TARDISes. They probably got this information from the Master in 'Frontier In Space'. Presumably Gallifrey is one of the 'solar planets' they intended to conquer in that story, and in 'Planet Of The Daleks'.

The duplicator machine would appear to be a more advanced version of the reproducer machine seen in 'The Chase'.

Since the events of 'Destiny Of The Daleks', the Daleks have been locked in the 'impasse of logic' with the Movellans for a further 90 years. We can assume that the Supreme Dalek in 'Resurrection Of The Daleks' is the same as the one mentioned in

'Destiny Of The Daleks'. As part of the war effort the Daleks have set in motion several simultaneous plans including the destruction of Gallifrey and Earth. To invade the planet of the Time Lords, which is protected by the transduction barrier, the Daleks probably worked out that they would need a TARDIS. To achieve this, the Daleks set about to trap the Doctor. The time corridor is established as part of the lure to bring him to them.

It would appear that the destruction of Earth was the Daleks' ultimate aim, in order to weaken the only power that had proven to be a powerful enemy. The human duplicates were the means to this end. Meanwhile, the Movellan virus was beginning to take its toll, which means the Supreme Dalek has a new priority. The invasions of Earth and Gallifrey would have to wait. The time corridor is still active and the Doctor is drawn in as planned. The Daleks rescue Davros in order to find a cure. It is just a coincidence that just as the Daleks achieved this part of their plan, the Doctor appears on the scene.

OBSERVATIONS

- The Daleks' time corridor is a link between 4590 and 1984, however the corridor is also linked to other time periods, from which the duplicates come (Stien says 'not all the prisoners are from the same period'). That the Supreme Dalek has duplicates 'placed in strategic positions around the planet' suggests that 1984 is the earliest period in Earth history that the time corridor can reach; the planned 'collapse of Earth society' would not be as effective if the duplicates were placed in a time period before or after the late twentieth century.

- The Daleks plan to send duplicates of the Doctor, Tegan and Turlough to assassinate the High Council of the Time Lords on Gallifrey. The fact that the Doctor 'forgets' to recall Leela when he is under the duplicator machine suggests that he is deliberately blocking her from his mind in order to fool the duplicate, which will not recognise her when it gets to Gallifrey, alerting the High Council to the deception. Of course, Leela would be dead in the fifth Doctor's current GRT as well as in 4590, so it seems that the Daleks intend to send the duplicates back in time by several years. We know that the time corridor has been used by the Daleks to send their duplicates to Earth (as noted above). The fact that 1984 was also once the GRT of the fifth Doctor (around the time of 'The Five Doctors' – see THE DOCTOR'S AGE) could be relevant. Perhaps the corridor was set up to not only send human duplicates to Earth, but also to send the duplicate Doctor to Gallifrey in the same time zone. The defences around Gallifrey were probably weakened when the Eye of Harmony lost power thanks to Borusa's meddling in 'The Five Doctors'. Perhaps the Daleks wanted to exploit this. The duplicates would be sent to Gallifrey in 1984 along the same time corridor. The Daleks must have somehow been aware that the fifth Doctor, Tegan and Turlough were the TARDIS crew on Gallifrey at the time, which is why they were able to duplicate the TARDIS crew so easily without coming into direct contact with them. And the fact that the Daleks appear to be aware that the Doctor was the Lord President, the title bestowed upon him at the end of 'The Five Doctors', supports this idea.

- It is interesting the way in which relative time is portrayed in the narrative structure of this story. For example, Lytton (who is in 4950) says the Doctor's capture 'is imminent'. But the Doctor is in 1984, participating in events that in effect already took place 2,606 years in Lytton's past. But because the time corridor links the two time zones and Stien is from the future, Lytton perceives Stien's actions as happening in his 'present' time stream. A similar example occurs in 'Attack Of The Cybermen', in which the Cryons in 2530 perceive the arrival of Halley's Comet in 1986 as 'heading towards Earth at this very moment', when in actual fact it was 544 years earlier.

- Lytton and the two policemen duplicates remain on Earth, until December 1985, when the policemen are converted into Cybermen, and Lytton travels to Telos with the Doctor (see 'Attack Of The Cybermen').

LANGUAGE

The Daleks, Lytton and his troopers and the duplicates all speak the same language. Given that Lytton is later able to infiltrate the criminal underworld in 'Attack Of The Cybermen', he must be able to speak convincing English.

TIMELINE DATES

1984, June 20 ◆

Turlough establishes that the time corridor ends in 'twentieth century Earth, it seems'. Later the Doctor says the TARDIS's 'instruments are still affected by turbulence [from the time corridor], but I think it's 1984'. Given that Lytton is stranded on Earth, and he appears again in 'Attack Of The Cybermen', in December 1985, we can take it that the TARDIS instruments are correct, and that the year is indeed 1984, which also happens to be near to Tegan's Earth Mean Time.

The month of June comes from when the Earth scenes of 'Planet Of Fire' are set; the TARDIS does not travel temporally to Lanzarote, only spatially. The Earth-based scenes of 'Planet Of Fire' are established as taking place on 20 June 1984. Of course, this means that Tegan stays behind on Earth at least a month before the events of

'The Awakening'. She would have to be very careful not to contact her grandfather, Andrew Verney, for whom the events in Little Hodcombe have yet to happen. Short-term displacement like this has also happened to Jo (in 'Colony In Space') and Ben and Polly ('The Faceless Ones'). (Since she was reunited with the Doctor in 'Arc Of Infinity', Tegan has been with the Doctor for over a year.)

4590 ⋆ ▨ ▨ ▨ ▨ ▨ ▨ ▨ ▨ ▨ ▨ ▨ ▨ ▨
Davros is captured at the end of 'Destiny Of The Daleks', set in 4500, and taken to Earth to stand trial. He is imprisoned in suspended animation for '90 years of mind-numbing boredom', so 'Resurrection Of The Daleks' is set in 4590.

Mercer has 'only been here [on the station] three days'. Stien says he hasn't 'eaten since yesterday'.

1884 ⋆ ▨ ▨ ▨ ▨ ▨ ▨ ▨ ▨ ▨ ▨ ▨ ▨ ▨
The Doctor says 'a hundred years ago this place would have been bustling with activity'. In fact, the warehouses are located in the same area that the TARDIS lands in 1895 (see 'The Talons Of Weng-Chiang').

DURATION

(TARDIS) (Ep1) ▨ ▨ ▨ ▨ ▨ ▨ ▨ ▨ ▨ ▨ ▨ ▨
The TARDIS is pulled from the far future to 1984 through the Daleks' time corridor …

⇨ **Day One (1984)** ▨ ▨ ▨ ▨ ▨ ▨ ▨ ▨ ▨ ▨ ▨
Several hours pass on Earth.

⇨ **Day One (4590)** ▨ ▨ ▨ ▨ ▨ ▨ ▨ ▨ ▨ ▨ ▨
Several hours pass on the space station.

PLANET OF FIRE

+STORY LINK

The Doctor refers to the Daleks and says he misses Tegan ('We were together a long time'; he might even be including the 129 years between 'The Awakening' and 'Frontios'), which suggests that 'Planet Of Fire' follows directly on from 'Resurrection Of The Daleks'. Turlough is not wearing his necktie in the opening TARDIS scene, so this does not follow directly on from the last scene in 'Resurrection Of The Daleks', in which he is still wearing the tie. It is unlikely that the Doctor's reference to Daleks refers to an off-screen adventure he and Turlough have just had with the Daleks.

From the fact that Kamelion diverts the TARDIS soon after detecting the 'distress signal' from the Trion beacon that is on Earth, we can assume that it is during the Doctor's adventure with the Daleks that he first picks up the beacon's signal (see Observations below). Clearly the TARDIS is not travelling in time, since the distress signal is not a temporal signal.

MASTER LINK

The last time we saw the Master, he was being dematerialised by the power of Rassilon to answer for his crimes in 'The Five Doctors' ('his sins will find their punishment in due time'). As noted under 'Frontios' the Doctor is now 130 years older than he was in 'The Five Doctors', so to keep their GRTs in sync, the Master must also now be 130 years older. (He may have encountered the Doctor on many other occasions during this off-screen period.) In 'Planet Of Fire', the Master says he has 'travelled a billion light years through time and space' to get to Sarn. Therefore, at some point after 'The Five Doctors' he must have travelled that same distance away from the galaxy. This could even mean that the Master's billion light year round journey has taken him over a century to complete. The fact that he has a TARDIS with a console that looks the same as the Doctor's suggests that he has remodelled (one of?) his own based on the Doctor's, perhaps during an attempt to regain control full control of Kamelion again (the robot might even have relayed information about the Doctor's new console to the Master soon after 'The Five Doctors').

The Master has also built 'a new and more deadly version' of his tissue compression eliminator. Following an accident with the device ('a small design problem'), which reduced his size, he has travelled 'a billion light years through time and space' to find the Doctor's TARDIS in order to contact Kamelion and get to Sarn, the only place he knows where he could be cured. Kamelion feels the Master's pain at the moment of the accident with the TCE (which supports the idea that the Master and the Doctor still share the same GRT), due to Kamelion being 'remote paralleled with the Master's TARDIS'.

The Master says his feud with the Doctor ('our periodic encounters') has lasted a while; the events of 'Terror Of The Autons' were 450 years ago. The Master says 'over the years I have dreamed of a million exquisite tortures to accompany your final moments', so we can assume that during the 'missing' 130 years the Master has had plenty of time to think of ways to destroy the Doctor.

The Doctor says the Master's 'present body must be good for a few years yet'. It eventually decays in 'Doctor Who (The TV Movie)', some 69 years later.

OBSERVATIONS

- It is never explained what the purpose is of the Trion data core found by Howard Foster in the Greek shipwreck, nor how it got there. We know that Trions have been to the planet more recently, when they delivered Turlough, and there is a Trion agent currently posing as a solicitor in Chancery Lane, so it is likely that Trions had visited Earth thousands of years ago. The beacon was left behind, and eventually ended up on board the Greek ship. Kamelion pilots the TARDIS to Lanzarote close to the beacon soon after the Master has his accident. It is possible that the Master does not know where Sarn is, but programs Kamelion to seek out any Trion-based signals. Kamelion detects the closest signal, which is coming from Lanzarote, while the TARDIS is still in London (in 'Resurrection Of The Daleks'), and the android programs the TARDIS to fly to that location.
- Peri has an 'ecology project' to complete for her schoolwork, as well as having exams coming up. She displays her knowledge of botany in 'The Mark Of The Rani', 'Timelash' and 'Revelation Of The Daleks'.
- Peri's date of birth, as seen on her passport appears to be 'Nov 15, 1940'! The detail visible on-screen also gives her name as 'Sydney' and address as being 'New York'. The issue date for the passport reads 'Feb 10, 1972' and expiry date is 'Feb 19, 1977'. One of the stamps reads HOTEL SAN ANTONIO, RESERVED, 13 OCT 1983. This is the hotel at which the cast and crew stayed whilst filming on Lanzarote, and the date is the day they checked in. As it's clear that the passport is a hastily created prop not intended to be seen in any detail on-screen, I have not included the dates in the TIMELINE.

LANGUAGE

Howard Foster assumes the Doctor is English (from hearing his accent). Presumably the Sarns speak Trion, otherwise they will all have a communications problem when they get back to Trion. The Doctor leaves some alien-looking coinage (is it Gallifreyan?) on the table at the taverna. The keypad in the crashed Trion ship has the standard layout (including * and # keys) as on a regular push-button telephone.

TIMELINE DATES

1984, June 20 ›
Peri says 'I've still got three months of my vacation left'. She 'is due back at college in

the fall' (i.e. autumn). She has 'exams coming up'. From this we can assume that it is the start of the summer break from school, which in the States is usually from the third Monday of June to the first Tuesday in September. This places the events on Lanzarote to be somewhere between 18 to 22 June. We can say it is the 20th, which at least gives Peri and her mother a few days to get to the island where, presumably, Howard has been for some time already.

In 'Attack Of The Cybermen', the Doctor says 1985 and 1986 are in Peri's future. In 'Timelash' the Doctor threatens to set the TARDIS's coordinates for '1985' and take Peri home. Therefore, I have selected 1984 as the year; with 'Resurrection Of The Daleks' set in 1984, this means the TARDIS has only moved spatially, without temporal displacement, to Lanzarote. This is because Kamelion detects the Trion data core signal coming from Lanzarote while the TARDIS in London (see Observations).

2000 ›

I think it was intended that the events on Sarn were contemporaneous to those on Earth, i.e. 1984. However, when factoring in Malkon's age, this is an impossibility.

Turlough says that the crashed ship was 'the last Trion ship to come here [to Sarn] … Malkon was the only survivor. It must have been the ship my father was on … I know that [Malkon] would have been the only infant on board'. Malkon is Turlough's 'younger brother', who was 'found on the slopes of the volcano' when he was 'very young'. (By definition, an 'infant' is a baby, or a very young child of 3 to 4 years old.) At the same time, Turlough, for his sins, 'was sent by the regime to Earth' where he was incarcerated at Brendon school. It is clear from this that Turlough was sent to Earth at the same time that his father and brother were sent to Sarn. As established in 'Mawdryn Undead', Turlough arrived at the school some time between 1977 and 1983, so the crash on Sarn must have occurred at some point within these same years. The way the Headmaster talks about Turlough to the 1983 Brigadier in 'Mawdryn Undead', it seems likely he's only been there for about a year, say since 1982. Turlough is of school age (he is too young to have a driver's licence as established in 'Mawdryn Undead'), so he would have to be no older than 18.

Malkon too appears to be no older than 18. If he crashed in 1982 as a baby, the current year on Sarn would have to be at least 18 years later, around 2000.

If the Sarn sequences were set in 1984, then Turlough would have to have been exiled on Earth when he too was a baby. However, this seems unlikely, given that he is a Junior Ensign Commander (a rank that would hardly be given to a child, unless it is a hereditary title) and he knows all about the civil war on Trion and the fate of his father. Turlough also knows what proton missiles are ('Warriors Of The Deep'), of the Tractators (and possibly the Arar-Jeks) (see 'Frontios'), and has been to the Eye

Of Orion before ('The King's Demons'), so he cannot have been a baby when he left Trion. On this basis, the sequences on Sarn can't possibly be in the same year as the Earth sequences. Incidentally, due to the time travel factor, and taking into account that Turlough has been with the Doctor for about a year, Turlough is now only a year older than his younger brother. He is also now out of sync with his planet. Captain Lomand appears to know who Turlough is ('Still running away?'), although he can't be much older than Turlough himself. He is a more senior officer than Turlough's own rank.

350 BC •

Praxiteles lived 370 to 330 BC. The Doctor probably met him around 350 BC, when the artist was most prolific.

1545

Howard mentions the *Mary Rose*. This was an English vessel that sank in 1545. It was later found in 1836, and the only section of its hull still intact was brought to the surface in 1982. It contained valuable treasures.

1950

Timanov says he saw Logar when he 'was a boy', and 'since my father's time unbelievers have been sent to the flames'. The blue flame hasn't been seen on the mountain 'for many generations'. Timanov is about 60, so that would put this event about 50 years ago, in 1950.

1982

This is the estimated year that Turlough arrived on Earth, as covered earlier (see 'Mawdryn Undead').

DURATION

(TARDIS) (Ep1)

The Doctor and Turlough travel in the TARDIS for a while before landing on Lanzarote.

⇨ Day One (Earth) (Ep1-2)

It is 'afternoon' on Lanzarote. The TARDIS is there for a few hours.

⇨ **Day One (Sarn) (Ep.2-4)** ▨ ▨ ▨ ▨ ▨ ▨ ▨ ▨ ▨ ▨
One day passes on Sarn. The Doctor is there for several hours.

THE CAVES OF ANDROZANI

+STORY LINK

Peri is still wearing the same pink shorts and white top she has on in 'Planet Of Fire'. She says that the threat of mud-bursts on Androzani Minor 'makes a change from lava', which also suggests they have just left the volcanic planet Sarn. She also asks the Doctor about his celery, something one would expect her to do early rather than late in their relationship.

LANGUAGE

The Doctor criticises Peri when she uses an American figure of speech: 'Fall guys'. He says 'Do try and speak English, Peri'.

TIMELINE DATES

3983 ⁎ ▨ ▨ ▨ ▨ ▨ ▨ ▨ ▨ ▨ ▨ ▨
Morgus speaks of 'the golden visions of our glorious pioneers', and is himself 'descended from the first colonists', while Jek wonders if the Doctor and Peri are from Earth. Given that Androzani Major is one of 'the five planets ... in the Sirius system', which is the closest to Earth's own solar system, we can assume that the five planets are among the first to be colonised when warp-drive was developed in 2106 (see below).

The Doctor is not familiar with spectrox, despite it being 'the most valuable substance in the Universe', so clearly this is a time period that he has not visited before. Also, if spectrox is available throughout the Universe, then this must be a time period following the development of intergalactic travel, which was in 2980 (see 'Terror Of The Vervoids'). Assuming that spectrox is readily available on Earth, the Doctor has never encountered it during any of his visits there.

Chellak is 'commander of all Federal forces'. This suggests that Androzani Major is part of the Galactic Federation, seen in 'The Curse Of Peladon', which existed around 3225 to 3275.

In 'The Daleks' Master Plan', Mavic Chen has been Guardian of the Solar System for at least '50 years'. Given that spectrox offers 'at least twice' the normal human life span, we might assume that Chen is a regular user of the substance. This suggests placing

'The Caves Of Androzani' in the same time period as 'The Daleks' Master Plan', being the year 4000.

This is one of only a few stories which feature advanced android technology developed by humans (Jek says 'I was a doctor myself, once, before the study of androids took over my life'). The level of technology is vastly superior to that seen in 'The Robots Of Death', which supports that 'The Caves Of Androzani' is set in a time period much later than 2777.

The links to the Federation and Mavic Chen are highly tenuous, however I think that in order to explain Chen's incredible life span, we have to assume that he is a spectrox user. On this basis, I have set 'The Caves Of Androzani' relative to 'The Daleks' Master Plan', in 3983 using the Century Factor.

The troops have been fighting Jek for 'six months', but are failing because the android Salateen had been informing Jek of their plans.

The 84-year old President has been without spectrox 'for three weeks', and yet he still looks '50 at the most'.

1,000,000,000 BC

The Doctor says it's been 'about a billion years since there was any sea on Androzani Minor'.

2106

Jek wonders if the Doctor and Peri come from Earth, while Morgus claims to be 'descended from the first colonists'. The star we call Sirius is one of the closest to Earth, so the five planets 'in the Sirius System', including Androzani Major, would most likely have been some of the first planets to be colonised when warp-drive was developed in 2106 (see 'Nightmare Of Eden'). Sirius 3 and Sirius 4 are mentioned in 'Frontier In Space'; there is a gallery on Sirius 5 (mentioned by Romana in 'City Of Death'); and there was a Sirian colony mentioned in 'Destiny Of The Daleks', so we can assume that these are all part of the same group of colonies.

3978

Jek has spent 'these last lonely years' hiding in the caves, say five years.

DURATION

⇨ Day One (Ep1-2)

It is day when the TARDIS lands on Androzani Minor. The President visits Morgus 'at five'.

⇨ **Day Two (Ep.2-4)** ▨ ▨ ▨ ▨ ▨ ▨ ▨ ▨ ▨ ▨

The North Cawl copper mine is destroyed 'early this morning'. The story ends later that day.

(TARDIS) (Ep4) ▨ ▨ ▨ ▨ ▨ ▨ ▨ ▨ ▨ ▨ ▨

The TARDIS dematerialises from Androzani Minor. The Doctor regenerates while in flight.

THE TWIN DILEMMA

+STORY LINK

'The Twin Dilemma' follows directly on from 'The Caves Of Androzani', with the Doctor regenerating in the TARDIS after departing from Androzani Minor.

OBSERVATIONS

- The Doctor describes the process of regeneration as being 'a kind of violent biological eruption in which the body cells are displaced, changed, renewed and rearranged'. There is no acknowledgment of the fact that the Doctor now has the same appearance as Commander Maxil (see 'Arc Of Infinity').
- In other stories, when Time Lords meet, they always seem to be able to recognise one another, even when regeneration has occurred. We can assume that each Time Lord possesses a unique 'aura' that is identifiable regardless of the external physical features [similar to the way in which the Immortals of *Highlander* are able to recognise the presence of another Immortal]. In 'The Twin Dilemma' the Doctor does not recognise Azmael immediately, and vice versa. For the Doctor this could be down to post-regenerative trauma, his mind still not fully capable of identifying Azmael's 'aura' ('now there's a face that floats upon my memory'). As to why Azmael doesn't immediately recognise the Doctor, this could simply be down to the Doctor having newly-regenerated and, like his personality, his 'aura' is not fully stable, and Azmael is unable to 'focus' on who the Doctor is. Also, Azmael has just used the revitalising modulator, and so his own body and mind could still be in a state of mild confusion after using the device. (In the case of the Doctor not recognising the Master in 'Castrovalva', 'Time-Flight' and 'The King's Demons', this could be down to the method by which the Master disguises himself being capable of blocking the 'aura' from being read.)

- The twins' 'mathematical skill could change events on a massive scale'. It is this skill that Mestor wants to exploit. As demonstrated in 'Logopolis' and 'Castrovalva', mathematics and Block Transfer Computations can influence the structure of the Universe.
- The Doctor say Azmael was 'the finest teacher I ever had', and Azmael responds with 'You learned all I know, and much besides'. This exchange would seem to suggest that Azmael was the hermit guru that the Doctor mentions in 'The Time Monster' and 'State Of Decay', and who appears in 'Planet Of The Spiders', as it is unlikely the Doctor would have two such influential teachers. On the assumption that Azmael is 'K'Anpo/Cho Je', we can say that at some point after the events of 'Planet Of The Spiders', Azmael (presumably still in his 'Cho Je' incarnation) left Earth and took up the mantle of Master of Joconda. He regenerated for the final time (Azmael points out that he cannot regenerate anymore), and some years later he shared a happy time by the fountain with the fourth Doctor. That Azmael uses the name Professor Edgeworth when he abducts the twins suggests that, since he uses the names K'Anpo Rimpoche and Cho Jo while in two of his earlier incarnations, he creates a different 'name' for each of his regenerations; Edgeworth is therefore the adopted identity and name of Azmael's thirteenth and final regeneration ...

LANGUAGE

The controls on the bomb mechanism in the habitat on Titan Three are in English. The star-chart showing the Jocondan system is labelled with Earth numbers and alphabet. Presumably Azmael speaks Jocondan, the language of the Gastropods and English with the help of the Time Lord 'gift'. The Doctor corrects Peri's American pronunciation of the word Lieutenant ('loo-tenant' instead of 'leff-tenant').

TIMELINE DATES

2200, August

Lang says 'the X.V. class of freighter was never built for warp drive', but Azmael has modified the 773 so that he could cross 'galaxies' to abduct the Sylvest twins. The Interplanetary Pursuit A Squadron is equipped with fighter-ships also capable of warp-drive, which at least sets the story in a time after warp-drive is developed, which was around 2106 (see 'Nightmare Of Eden'), but before intergalactic flight, which was developed around 2980 (see 'Terror Of The Vervoids'). [In the novelisation (page 7) it is stated that the Sylvest home was built in 1810, some 500 years earlier, which sets the book in 2310, but there is nothing on TV to support that the Sylvest home is a Georgian building.] The freighter was 'believed destroyed eight months ago'. Last contact was established at '12-99', as seen on the computer at Interplanetary Pursuit HQ. If we assume that '12-99' is a month and year – i.e. December of '99 – that would set 'The Twin Dilemma' eight months later, in August of a year ending in '00'. If the story is set after 2106, it could be 2200, 2300, 2400, etc.

As seen in 'The Leisure Hive', by 2290 Earthlings are freely associating with aliens and the leisure planets in the galaxy, which shows clearly that by that time period the Earth does not fear contact with aliens. In 'The Twin Dilemma' the twins' father, the Minister and Commander Fabian all appear anxious and nervous about the possibility that aliens have abducted the twins. This common xenophobia may be as a result of the Dalek invasion of Earth of 2164 (see 'The Dalek Invasion Of Earth'); with the peoples of Earth becoming overly cautious of being invaded again, hence the pursuit taskforce. Therefore I suggest placing 'The Twin Dilemma' after the Dalek invasion but before 2290. This would make '12-99' December 2199, and thereby eight months later, August 2200.

2055 •

The Doctor and Azmael last met on Joconda when the Doctor was in his fourth incarnation ('I've regenerated twice since our last meeting'). 'The Twin Dilemma' is set in the Doctor's GRT of 2113. If we assume that the fourth Doctor met Azmael during the nine year gap between 'The Invasion Of Time' and 'The Ribos Operation', which was GRT 1963 to GRT 1972, say 1968 which is half-way, then no more than 145 years have passed for them both. Mestor must have seized control of the planet some time around 2055 Jocondan / Earth time.

2199, December

The date the freighter disappeared, as seen on the computer screen; see above.

DURATION

Although there are three different planetary locations in this story, the Duration is basically all the same day, given that there is no time-travel between the locations.

(TARDIS) (Ep1)

The Doctor and Peri travel in the TARDIS for a while before landing on Titan Three.

⇨ Day One (Earth) (Ep1)

Professor Sylvest goes out for the 'evening'. Azmael arrives when it is 'a bit late for social calls'. The Professor returns after 'two hours maximum' to find the twins gone.

Lang is dispatched soon afterwards.

⇨ **Day One (Titan Three) (Ep1-2)** ▨ ▨ ▨ ▨ ▨ ▨ ▨ ▨
It is day on Titan Three. The Doctor and Peri are there for a few hours at the least
(Hugo has 'an hour's rest' after the Doctor attends to his wounds).

⇨ **Day One (Jaconda) (Ep1-4)** ▨ ▨ ▨ ▨ ▨ ▨ ▨ ▨
It is day when the TARDIS lands on Joconda. The rest of the story takes place on this
day.

ATTACK OF THE CYBERMEN

+STORY LINK

At the end of 'The Twin Dilemma', the Doctor and Peri take the Sylvest twins home
(to 2200). At the beginning of 'Attack Of The Cybermen', the Doctor tells Peri that
'after the bleakness of Joconda' he is taking her to Earth – which is odd, as they have
just been to Earth to drop off the twins. This suggests that after leaving the twins they
returned briefly to Joconda, perhaps to check out how Hugo was getting on.

Peri reminds the Doctor that he has 'only recently regenerated', and later berates
him for calling her Tegan, Zoe, Susan, Jamie and Zodin, all 'in the past couple of days',
a period which would also include 'The Twin Dilemma', in which the Doctor does
indeed call her 'Tegan'.

The Doctor says: 'we've both spent too long in the TARDIS', and indeed he has spent
some considerable time repairing the chameleon circuit. This activity was probably
provoked by his comment in 'The Twin Dilemma' that the Police Box exterior of the
TARDIS was 'hideous, utterly hideous'. We can therefore place a few days between
'The Twin Dilemma' and 'Attack Of The Cybermen'.

GALLIFREY LINK

130 years have passed since 'The Five Doctors' (see THE DOCTOR'S AGE), so it is
doubtful that the Doctor is still President (but he doesn't know any differently). But
even if he is, the Time Lords are still manipulating him. Somehow Flast is aware that
the Time Lords have sent an agent to Telos. It is possible that the Time Lords became
aware of what the Cybermen are planning when they kept track of the Cybermen on
Gallifrey in 'The Five Doctors', and managed to trace them back to Telos. Also, the
Time Lords could have been monitoring the journey of Bates and Stratton's time-ship.

When it lands on Telos, the Time Lords fear that the Cybermen will use it to try and change 'the web of time'. Because the Doctor has had previous experience with the silver giants, the Time Lords ensure that the TARDIS is heading for Earth 1985 in time to pick up Lytton's distress signal ...

CYBERMAN LINK

As covered under CYBERMAN HISTORY, this is the Cybermen's tenth and chronologically final appearance.

In terms of continuity with the events of 'Earthshock', we can assume that the Cyber-fleet disperses (as is stated in 'Time-Flight') and returns to Telos, to discover that in their absence the Cryons have been systematically killing the dormant Cybermen. And with the loss of 15,000 units in 'Earthshock', the Cybermen once again face extinction. The alliance that is being planned in 'Earthshock' between Earth and other planets probably never happens, due to the Earth / Draconian war of 2526 (see 'Frontier In Space'), so it is possible that Cybermen numbers are reduced further during another war.

When the time-ship lands on Telos, the Cybermen see this as being the perfect way to prevent extinction. They decide that of all the events in their own history, the destruction of Mondas in 1986 is the most significant, so that becomes the historical event they plan to change. A squad of Cybermen is sent back in time to set up a base in the sewers, while the time ship is parked on the dark side of the moon ...

OBSERVATIONS

- The Cybermen originally went to Telos specifically to make use of the Cryons' ice cities for hibernation. The city seen in 'Attack Of The Cybermen' is deep underground. There are probably hundreds of these Cryon cities all over the planet. The hive-like tomb seen in 'The Tomb Of The Cybermen' is more likely to be a Cyberman construction, being merely a lure for humanoids to revive the dormant Cybermen in the hive. The remaining other tombs (previously part of the cities built by the Cryons before the Cybermen came to Telos?) would have been reactivated at some later point following the opening of the hive tomb (see also CYBERMAN HISTORY).
- The Doctor says he hasn't thought about Zodin 'for years'. The second Doctor mentions her in 'The Five Doctors' – which was 450 years ago in the Doctor's GRT.
- Lytton, trapped in 1984 following the Dalek defeat ('Resurrection Of The Daleks'), is able to send out a distress signal using stolen electronic equipment which is answered by the Cryons in the twenty-sixth century. How is this possible? One solution is that the Dalek time corridor is still open and Lytton

simply beamed the signal through to his own time zone in the hope that his fellow Riftans would rescue him. Since the Cryons contact him from 2530, it could be that his signal is not strong enough to reach 4590, when 'Resurrection Of The Daleks' is set. However, considering the duplicates in 'Resurrection Of The Daleks' are from different time zones, it is possible that Lytton and his men are from a period earlier than 4590, maybe 2530, which is why his signal is directed to 2530. The Cybermen know of Lytton's people ('a race of warriors'), so the Riftans exist in the time period that the Cybermen are from. It is clear that Lytton is of human descent (he speaks to Griffiths about 'our ancestors'), so he must be from an Earth colony.

- Lytton knows a lot about the Doctor and recognises the Doctor's handiwork with a sonic lance, and yet in 'Resurrection Of The Daleks' they are in the same room together for all of a few moments and never actually speak with one another.
- Bates and Stratton are two of the crew from the stolen time-ship. The Cybermen kills a third crewman during the first escape attempt. The other human slaves on Telos are probably also from the time-ship. The Time Lords have shown a dislike for any other race that develops time travel (see 'The Time Warrior', 'The Two Doctors'), so where are Stratton and Bates from? (They are not from Earth, because in 'The Ark' it is stated that time travel is never developed by humans.)

LANGUAGE

Lytton is able to pick up the Cybermen's transmissions from the moon, so clearly they speak English. He also communicates with the Cryons, who must also speak English. The panels in Cyber-control are labelled in English: i.e. 'READY', 'DETONATOR'.

TIMELINE DATES

1985, December •

The Doctor tells Peri they are 'in the year you would calculate as 1985'. On the basis that he doesn't say this is Peri's own time, 1985 must be her future (it is still 1984 from her relative point of time; see 'Planet Of Fire').

Griffiths gives the month: when told by the Doctor that Mondas will return in 1986, Griffiths says 'Next year? That's almost now', which suggests it is late December 1985.

It is a presumably a weekday, because the diamond exchange is open.

2530 ·

As noted under Observations, Lytton is in communication with Cryons on Telos. Also, Flast says the Cybermen plan to use Halley's Comet as a bomb, and that it is 'heading towards Earth at this very moment'. From a narrative point of view, these alone suggest that the events on both Earth and Telos are contemporaneous. However this is clearly not the case, given that 'Attack Of The Cybermen' must be set after 'The Tomb Of The Cybermen', which is set in the future. (Unless, we assume that when the Doctor says the Cyber-Controller was destroyed, he is actually referring to a different encounter with the Cyber-Controller, and not of the events of 'The Tomb of The Cybermen'.)

'Attack Of The Cybermen' is set after the events of 'The Tomb Of The Cybermen', which has been set in 2525; the Cyber-Controller 'was only damaged'. The Cybermen in 'Earthshock' do not refer to the events of 'Attack Of The Cybermen', so it is safe to assume that 'Attack Of The Cybermen' is set after 'Earthshock', which is set in 2526. Also, the Cybermen in 'Attack Of The Cybermen' are making a last effort attempt to stop themselves from dying out. According to the Cryons the attack on Earth 'is the only way their race can survive'. In 'Earthshock' the Cybermen have an army of 15,000 that they sacrifice on the freighter, which would explain why in 'Attack Of The Cybermen' they consider their numbers are reaching near-extinction. Therefore, I would set 'Attack Of The Cybermen' a few years after 'Earthshock', say 2530. This is an arbitrary period of years. With the loss of 15,000 in 'Earthshock', the Cybermen would need to act quickly after this latest defeat to ensure their survival.

Stratton says they have been mining the planet with high explosives for 'the past fortnight', which gives an idea as to at least how long the time ship has been on the planet.

Flast has been a prisoner for 'some time'.

1985, November

It is not clear when the Cybermen come to Earth and set up their base in the sewers. There was work done in the tunnels 'seven years ago', according to the workmen; the wall hiding the Cyber-base was not there then, so at least we know that the Cybermen arrived at some point between 1978 and 1985 (they cannot therefore be the same Cybermen seen in the sewers in 1970 in 'The Invasion'). I would say they have been there for not more than a month. They would have no need to stay there for longer, given that the comet would be closest to Earth in February 1986, which would be when the comet can be diverted for their purposes.

2113

With the Doctor now aged 900, his GRT is 2113. The Time Lords who send him on his mission to Telos are from this time zone (see Gallifrey Link above).

DURATION

(TARDIS) (Ep1)

The Doctor spends several hours working on the TARDIS circuits. He says he and Peri have 'both spent too long in the TARDIS'.

⇨ Day One (Earth) (Ep1)

It is day on Earth. All the scenes set on Earth probably last no more than a few hours in total.

(TARDIS) (Ep.2)

It takes a little time to travel from Earth to Telos in the TARDIS.

⇨ Day One (Telos) (Ep1-2)

It is day in all the scenes set on Telos. The Doctor spends several hours there.

VENGEANCE ON VAROS

+STORY LINK

'Attack Of The Cybermen' and 'Vengeance On Varos' are consecutive: Peri points out to the Doctor that 'since we left Telos, you've caused three electrical fires, a total power failure and a near collision with a storm of asteroids. Not only that: you've twice managed to get yourself lost in the TARDIS corridors, wiped the memory of the flight-computer, and jettisoned three quarters of the storage hold. You even managed to burn dinner last night … I was supposed to have a cold supper'. Peri's reference to 'last night' indicates that at least the equivalent of one day and a night has passed in the TARDIS since 'Attack Of The Cybermen'. The Doctor is still working on the TARDIS systems, as he was in that earlier story. (In 'Timelash', Peri seems to know about the Daleks and that they possess a time corridor, so we can assume that after the events of 'Attack Of The Cybermen', she asked the Doctor to tell her about Lytton, and he told her the events of 'Resurrection Of The Daleks'.)

OBSERVATIONS

- Sil says 'the engineers of every known solar system cry out for [Varos's] product [zeiton-7] to drive their space/time craft'. Given that the TARDIS needs zeiton-7 to line its transitional elements, this implies that other races have developed time-travelling machines like the TARDIS. But given the Time Lords' dislike of other beings developing time travel, it is possible that 'space/time craft' is simply Sil's terminology for faster-than-light vehicles.

LANGUAGE

Sil uses a (faulty) 'language transposer' in order to communicate with the Varosians, who appear to use English as that is seen on their screens, i.e. 'VOTE-VOTE', 'EXECUTION', 'YES', 'NO' buttons, and the numbers of votes. The Doctor criticises Peri's pronunciation: 'Zee? Oh, zed ... ', which suggests that the Gallifreyan pronunciation of 'Z' is the same as English. Peri finds the TARDIS manual (which is a larger book than the one in 'Four To Doomsday') in the workshop, propping open a vent. It has the words TARDIS TYPE 40 HANDBOOK printed on its cover. The Doctor says he 'started reading that once'.

TIMELINE DATES

2327 ⚬ ▨ ▨ ▨ ▨ ▨ ▨ ▨ ▨ ▨ ▨ ▨ ▨ ▨ ▨ ▨
Sil meets the Doctor for the second time in 'Mindwarp', which is set in 2379, so 'Vengeance On Varos' must be set at a time before that date.

In 'Vengeance On Varos', Peri tells the Governor and the First Officer that she's 'from another time, another century. Nearly three centuries before you were born I lived on another world'. Peri left Earth in 1984 (see 'Planet Of Fire'). Three hundred years from then is 2284. The Governor appears to be about 43 in human terms [based on actor Martin Jarvis' age of 43 when 'Vengeance On Varos' was made], which suggests the current year is around 2327.

Arak recalls how a blind man was trapped in the punishment dome 'last week'.

2027
2097 ▨ ▨ ▨ ▨ ▨ ▨ ▨ ▨ ▨ ▨ ▨ ▨ ▨ ▨ ▨
Varos was originally 'a colony for the criminally insane. The descendants of the original officers still rule'. The Governor reassures Sil that Varos's political situation 'has been stable for more than 200 years', say 230 years. The Galatron Mining Company has been exploiting Varos 'for centuries' / 'these many generations', say 300 years. With the current year being 2327, Galatron has been exploiting Varos since around 2027, and Varos has been stable since around 2097.

These dates make it impossible for Varos to have been an Earth colony. Although the Governor's torture device uses 'human cell disintegration bombardment', given the dates and the fact that Varos is in the distant constellation of Cetes. Any links to Earth are highly unlikely. As noted under THE N-SPACE UNIVERSE, the term 'human' is a generalisation for humanoids. In terms of humanity's space technology intergalactic travel is not developed until 2980 (see 'The Ribos Operation', 'Terror Of The Vervoids' and A HISTORY OF SPACE-FLIGHT). Also, when Peri explains where she is from, she says she comes from 'another world'; if she thought that Varos was an Earth colony surely she would have said she came from Earth, a planet that the Governor would know of?

DURATION

(TARDIS) (Ep1)

The Doctor and Peri have been in the TARDIS for at least the equivalent of a day. The Doctor has been working on the console for some time ...

⇨ Day One (Ep1-2)

Arak comes home from work. It is 'evening' when the Governor makes his first TV announcement. Jondar's execution is set for '8 o'clock' that night. The TARDIS lands around '19:58:32'. The rest of the story takes place over several hours from this point.

THE MARK OF THE RANI

STORY LINK

There is no indication that 'The Mark Of The Rani' follows directly from 'Vengeance On Varos'. The TARDIS is now working again thanks, presumably, to the zeiton-7 obtained from Varos. The Doctor is still annoyed, however, that the TARDIS isn't operating properly even 'after all the work I've done on it', which could be a reflection of his having given it an overhaul after leaving Varos, or perhaps simply a reference to the recent work he undertook on the ship in 'Attack Of The Cybermen'.

MASTER LINK

There are several references to the Doctor's last meeting with the Master in 'Planet Of Fire': 'He was burnt to a crisp the last time I saw him'. The Master says to Peri, 'When we last met you could have saved me, and you didn't', but there is no explanation given as to how he survived his apparent death in the blue flames on Sarn. The Master's TARDIS was still in the control room on Sarn as the room collapsed, so we can only assume that the Master got back into his ship before Sarn was destroyed. Due to these close references, the events of 'Planet Of Fire' must have taken place a matter of months ago from both the Doctor and the Master's perspective.

We do not see the Master's TARDIS, so we can only assume that it is parked near Killingworth. The Master tells the Rani that he 'dropped in on your little domain before following you here. Chaos. Complete mayhem'. Therefore, at some point after leaving Sarn, the Master made a brief stop at Miasimia Goria before heading for Earth to pursue his scheme to destroy the Doctor.

It is not explained how the Master was able to divert the Doctor's TARDIS from Kew Gardens to Killingworth. The Rani says that he 'forced the TARDIS off course ... Overrode the controls?'

OBSERVATIONS

- The Rani, the Master and the Doctor recognise each other almost immediately, even after only a very brief glimpse; the Master knows it is the Doctor despite his recent regeneration (see the note about a Time Lord's 'aura' under 'The Twin Dilemma'). The Rani is fully aware of the ongoing feud between the Doctor and the Master. In fact, it appears that she has been observing them: 'I thought that last mad scheme of yours had finished you for good ... No wonder the Doctor always outwits you'. The Master points out that Earth is the Doctor's 'favourite planet'.

- The Rani was exiled from Gallifrey following an experiment that turned 'mice into monsters'. One of the creatures ate the Lord President's cat and 'took a chunk out of him'. She has a fully operable TARDIS, which indicates that her exile was of mutual agreement. (Presumably she was exiled to the planet Miasimia Goria, over which she was subsequently able to take control.) The Master says he remembers the mice attack, which suggests he was an eyewitness. 'Pity it wasn't the Doctor,' he adds. This suggests that the Doctor was also there at the time (and knowing the Doctor he was probably the one who stopped the mouse from further destruction). The Doctor clearly knows the reasons for the Rani's exile too, so we can assume that this was before he left Gallifrey. The Rani says she has been visiting Earth 'for centuries', which we can assume is after her exile began, indicating that she has been in exile for several hundred years.

- The Master says the 'borrowed' box of maggots is 'Perfectly safe. Next to my hearts. Both of them'. It is clear in 'Earthshock' that Nyssa does not have two hearts, so the Master retained this aspect of his Gallifreyan physiology when he took over Tremas's body (see 'The Keeper Of Traken').

- This is the Master's second recent attack against Earth by attempting to change the course of history. He failed in 1215 (see 'The King's Demons'). Interestingly, the Doctor claims: 'I haven't changed the course of history. Indeed, I'm expressly forbidden so to do', which emphasises that it is indeed possible to change the course of history but only the written rules of the Time Lords forbid it (see GALLIFREY HISTORY).

- When he quotes Shakespeare, the Doctor says: 'Must see him again some time' (see 'Planet Of Evil' and 'City Of Death'). He eventually does, in 'The Shakespeare Code'.

LANGUAGE

One would assume that the Master and the Rani speak Gallifreyan when they are together. It jars to hear the Master say phrases such as 'Finito TARDIS'. The Rani is a self-chosen title, rather than a name: is it significant that she chooses an Earth word which is Hindu for queen? When the Master meets the mineworkers, one of them says he talks funny. The Doctor again takes delight in correcting Peri's English ('Who by?' / 'By whom').

TIMELINE DATES

1813, October •

Peri says 'I could have been stuck in the eighteen-hundreds for ever', which at least defines a century. There are many references to the Luddites, who were mainly active from 1811 – 1816. The actual date can be derived from real history.

HISTORICAL COMPARISON

In our history, George Stephenson actually did live in Killingworth, from 1804 until about 1824. Humphrey Davy, one of the invited guests on Stephenson's list, died in 1829, and the real Lord Ravensworth was given his title on 17 July 1821, which helps narrow the date down further. In the serial, Stephenson is still working on a steam engine; he would test the Rocket for the first time in 1829. His first engine, the Blücher, was constructed in 1813, and can be seen in a semi-complete state in Stephenson's workshop. 1813 is therefore the best year. The story was filmed in October [of 1984], so that month has been selected to match seasonal conditions.

The Rani has been in Killingworth for several weeks: after taking the phial of brain fluid from the Rani, the Master says 'I wonder how many weeks of work this represents'. It is noted that the attacks by the miners only started 'recently', while Josh has 'been missing for days'.

Stephenson's meeting with the scientific elite is to take place 'in less than two days'.

100,000,000 BC ▨ ▨ ▨ ▨ ▨ ▨ ▨ ▨ ▨ ▨ ▨ ▨ ▨

The Doctor guesses that the Rani 'popped back to the Cretaceous Age' to obtain her tyrannosaurus rex embryos. The Cretaceous period was 136 million to 65 million years ago in our history. 100 million is a rough guess for the time line.

The Rani says she's 'been coming to this wretched planet for centuries', and mentions the following historical events:

1210 BC ▨ ▨ ▨ ▨ ▨ ▨ ▨ ▨ ▨ ▨ ▨ ▨ ▨

The estimated time of the Trojan War in our history (see 'The Myth Makers').

300 – 1100 ▨ ▨ ▨ ▨ ▨ ▨ ▨ ▨ ▨ ▨ ▨ ▨

The time period in which the Dark Ages in Europe occurred in our history.

1775 – 1783 ▨ ▨ ▨ ▨ ▨ ▨ ▨ ▨ ▨ ▨ ▨ ▨

The years during which the American War of Independence occurred in our history.

1792 ▨ ▨ ▨ ▨ ▨ ▨ ▨ ▨ ▨ ▨ ▨ ▨ ▨

Lord Ravensworth says that Jack Ward has been working for him for 'over thirty years'.

DURATION

⇨ **Day One (Ep1-2)** ▨ ▨ ▨ ▨ ▨ ▨ ▨ ▨ ▨ ▨ ▨

The story takes place over one day. According to Luke, his father 'was perfectly normal this morning'. It wasn't until after he went to the bathhouse and was operated on by the Rani that Jack lost control, so I would guess that the story opens in the early afternoon.

THE TWO DOCTORS

STORY LINK

NOTE: Unlike 'The Three Doctors' and 'The Five Doctors', where the Doctors are deliberately removed from their time streams and brought together with the aid of Time Lord technology, the meeting between Doctors in this story is purely accidental. As the sixth Doctor explains to Peri: 'when you travel around as much as I do, it's almost inevitable that you'll run into yourself at some point'. Indeed, given that the second Doctor's TARDIS is not on Earth when the sixth Doctor lands, the TARDIS safeguards do not activate (see GALLIFREY HISTORY). Therefore, I have split the story in two. Details concerning the second Doctor's segments are covered under his stories in STORYFILE.

The fact that the sixth Doctor collapses in the TARDIS, similar to the fifth Doctor in 'The Five Doctors' (when his other selves are time scooped), might suggest that a time scoop is involved. But as is pointed out in both 'The Three Doctors' and 'The Five Doctors', to use a time scoop drains too much energy, so it is clear that the second Doctor is not being manipulated by Time Lords from a time period outside of his own GRT, i.e. 1984, the time zone in which that the story takes place, or 2113, which is the sixth Doctor's GRT. Details concerning the second Doctor are covered as part of his stories.

STORY LINK

There is no indication that this story follows directly on from 'The Mark Of The Rani'. Given that Peri originally intended to stay with the Doctor for only 'three months' (see 'Planet Of Fire'), we should accept that Peri has been with the Doctor for less than that length of time.

SONTARAN LINK

This is the fourth entry in the Rutan / Sontaran war saga. (Sontarans have also been active on Earth at some point in the mid-twentieth century, as Bea Nelson-Stanley mentions that her husband, Edgar, knew of the Sontarans in 'Eye Of The Gorgon'.)

Unlike in 'The Time Warrior' in 1274, by 1984 Earth is of strategic importance in the ongoing Sontaran war effort; the Ninth Sontaran Attack Group, of which both Group Marshal Stike and Field-Major Varl are members, is planning an attack on the Madillon Cluster, and Earth 'is conveniently situated' as a staging base.

The Sontarans have allied themselves with Chessene in order to gain control of the Kartz / Reimer time capsule. The Sontarans have long sought mastery of time travel. They already had limited time travel in the 13th century (see 'The Time Warrior'), and in 1963 they failed to invade Gallifrey ('The Invasion Of Time'). And as seen in 'The Sontaran Stratagem', the ATMOS devices are fitted with a one-second time protection field.

It could be that after failing to procure the Kartz / Reimer device, the Sontarans abandoned all further attempts to steal a time machine. It is clear from 'The Sontaran Experiment' that they still do not possess the secret of time travel, even 15,000 years in the future.

OBSERVATIONS

- The Doctor attended the opening of station Camera on behalf of the Time Lords during his first incarnation. This was at a time before he fell from favour with the Time Lords and became 'a pariah'. Given that the space station is in the future in terms of the first Doctor's GRT (prior to his departure in GRT 1610), it may have been only a few years since it was opened from Dastari's perspective; the first Doctor may have been quite young at the time, and still a novice Time Lord undertaking one of his first off-world missions.
- The second Doctor and Dastari discuss the nature of time travel. It is revealed that 'Time Lords possess a symbiotic link with their machines which protects them and anyone travelling with them from [molecular] de-stabilisation'. This system may also account for the protection of the occupants of the TARDIS from ageing faster than at their natural rate, hence they maintain their own Mean Time link with their own planet.
- The sixth Doctor slowly begins to feel the effects of the Androgum inheritance given to the second Doctor. Therefore, it should be accepted that the third, fourth and fifth Doctors all feel the change too, and have at some point acted oddly towards animals. Interestingly, the fact that a Time Lord can be turned into an Androgum suggests that a Time Lord can be turned into any species, even human. (See HALF-HUMAN? for more on this.)
- It seems to me to be rather too coincidental that the sixth Doctor, having collapsed in the TARDIS, suddenly decides to visit Dastari on Station Camera for medical assistance – this being the exact location from which his second self has only just been tortured and abducted (which itself is partially the cause of his collapse). The sixth Doctor is probably acting from some subconscious memory; his desire to see Dastari is nothing more than a subconscious 'unblocking' of this repressed memory from his second incarnation's life.
- There is no time differential explosion when the two Doctors touch, but there is between the two Brigadiers in 'Mawdryn Undead'. The fact that the two Doctors are two physically different aspects of the same person could explain why there is no time differential.

LANGUAGE

The Androgums speak and read English: Doña Arana asks if the invaders are English when she hears them talking, and Shockeye understands her cookbooks. The text on the computer screen on the Station is in English. The computer itself must also speak English: can the Time Lord 'gift' also work on a computer? A danger sign is seen written in Spanish. When Peri says 'I don't speak Spanish', the Doctor replies 'neither do they', meaning the Sontarans and the Androgums.

TIMELINE DATES

1984, August ◦

There are three locations in this story: Space Station Camera, the fishing hole, and Spain. The fact that the Sontarans go from the Station to Spain without time-travelling means those two locations are in the same time zone. And the fact that the sixth Doctor receives the second Doctor's 'mind slip' while still at the fishing-hole location suggests that it is also in the same time zone. It is most likely that because the sixth Doctor is in the same time zone as the second Doctor, that is why the sixth is the incarnation that receives the 'call' and goes to his second persona's aid; is it possible for a 'timeslip in the subconscious' to time travel, even on the astral plain? On this basis I will accept that all three are in the same time zone.

'The Two Doctors' was recorded in August [of 1984], so this is the month selected, to match seasonal conditions in Spain. Although there is nothing in the story itself to indicate the year for the Spanish portion, there are plenty of visual and verbal references to a 1980s setting: such as the modern [for 1984] telephone at the restaurant, modern vehicles (the truck hijacked by Shockeye and the Doctor has a Wynn's Oil sticker on it), and Oscar mentions 'credit cards', and says that 'nouvelle cuisine has yet to penetrate this establishment'. Oscar also mentions that his father 'was an air-raid warden in Shepton Mallet throughout the war'. Oscar appears to be about 35, which would mean he was born in 1949, after the war had ended.

'The Two Doctors' is usually set in the year of broadcast (1985) in other chronologies, but that is not necessarily the case. Peri joined the Doctor in June 1984 (see 'Planet Of Fire'), so we could just as easily set 'The Two Doctors' in August 1984. On the other hand, in the next story, 'Timelash', the Doctor threatens to take Peri 'to 1985', suggesting that that is now her current year. That Peri does not stay on Earth at the end of 'The Two Doctors' suggests that her three months are not yet up – or that she has since decided she would rather stay with the Doctor.

I prefer August 1984, as this still places 'The Two Doctors' within the three months that Peri originally intended to stay with the Doctor.

220 BC ◦

The Doctor has Archimedes's visiting card. The inventor lived c.290 to c.211 BC. The Doctor probably met him around 220 BC.

c1310 ⋆ ▨ ▨ ▨ ▨ ▨ ▨ ▨ ▨ ▨ ▨ ▨ ▨ ▨

The Doctor has Dante's visiting card. Danté was born in 1265 and died in September 1321. The Doctor probably met him towards the end of his life, say 1310.

1492, October 12 ⋆ ▨ ▨ ▨ ▨ ▨ ▨ ▨ ▨ ▨ ▨ ▨

The Doctor has Columbus's visiting card. Given that the Doctor makes a comment to Peri about Columbus's discovery of America, it is probably during this event, which occurred on 12 October 1492 in our history, that the Doctor met the explorer.

c1830 ⋆ ▨ ▨ ▨ ▨ ▨ ▨ ▨ ▨ ▨ ▨ ▨ ▨ ▨

The Doctor has a visiting card for 'Brunel'. We can assume this is Isambard Kingdom Brunel (9 April 1806 to 15 September 1859), rather than his equally famous father, Sir Marc Isambard Brunel (who, incidentally, is given a name-check in 'The Mark Of The Rani'). Isambard Brunel was a British engineer, his greatest claims to fame were building the Bristol docks and bridge (1830s), and constructing ships and railways (1833). The Doctor probably met him around 1830.

DURATION

This section of Duration covers only the sixth Doctor's involvement in the story.

⇨ **Day One (Ep1)** ▨ ▨ ▨ ▨ ▨ ▨ ▨ ▨ ▨ ▨ ▨ ▨

The sixth Doctor and Peri are at the fishing hole 'for hours'.

⇨ **Day One (Ep1-3)** ▨ ▨ ▨ ▨ ▨ ▨ ▨ ▨ ▨ ▨ ▨

The Doctor and Peri arrive on the station '10 or 12 days' after the second Doctor and Jamie landed there. They spend an hour or so wandering around before finding Jamie.

⇨ **Day One (Ep1-3)** ▨ ▨ ▨ ▨ ▨ ▨ ▨ ▨ ▨ ▨ ▨

It is around midday when the TARDIS lands in Spain. The augmented second Doctor and Shockeye go into town for lunch.

TIMELASH

STORY LINK

At the end of 'The Two Doctors' Shockeye wounds the Doctor in the leg. By 'Timelash' his limp is gone, which means that sufficient time has passed between the two stories for the Doctor's leg to completely heal. (His trouser leg displays no signs of a tear, so no doubt the Doctor has several pairs of the same yellow trousers in the TARDIS wardrobe.)

The Doctor is contemplating taking Peri to the Constellation of Andromeda ('I haven't been there recently'). Peri is aware that the Daleks operate a time corridor in space. She doesn't appear to recognise the Daleks in 'Revelation Of The Daleks', so she is at least familiar with them by name. The Doctor did mention the Daleks several times while talking about Lytton in 'Attack Of The Cybermen', so no doubt Peri later asked the Doctor to tell her about his earlier encounter with Lytton ('Resurrection Of The Daleks'). The Doctor has also at some point shown Peri photographs of Jo Grant.

The Doctor says to Peri 'perhaps you're trying to tell me you've had enough', and threatens to 'set the coordinates for Earth, 1985'. This suggests that by this time the 'three months' she had originally intended to stay with the Doctor (from June to early September 1984, see 'Planet Of Fire') is over, and her own Earth Mean Time is now 1985, meaning she has been with the Doctor for over six months.

As far as the Doctor is aware, he is still 'President of the High Council of Gallifrey' (he was elected 130 years earlier in 'The Five Doctors'). The Bandrils are aware of the Time Lords.

OBSERVATIONS

- Herbert George Wells uses his adventure on Karfel as the inspiration for several of his famous novels: the TARDIS, Vena and the Morlocks inspire *The Time Machine* (1895); *The Island Of Dr Moreau* (1896) is based on the Borad and the mutation of humans; *The Invisible Man* (1897) is based on the Doctor's trick with the Kontron crystal; *The War Of The Worlds* (1898), being the conflict between Karfel and Bandril. [In addition, the Bandril spaceship is based on the shape of the Martian warships in the 1953 movie version of *War Of The Worlds*.]
- When the Borad threatens to blind Peri, the Doctor says 'You can alter Peri's outward appearance, but you can't change the brain in her head'. These are twisted prophetic words indeed, given the later events of 'Mindwarp'.

LANGUAGE

Herbert is able to communicate with Vena in Scotland before the Doctor's arrival, so the Karfelons must also speak English. And just prior to Vena's arrival in his cabin, Herbert's Ouija board spells out her name V-E-N-A. Renis receives his instructions in a letter with the words 'To Maylin Renis' hand-written upon it. The Bandrils speak the same language as the Karfelons.

TIMELINE DATES

2113 ✦

A time tunnel by its very nature suggests there would be a time differential of any length between its two extremities across time and space: in the case of the Timelash this is Karfel and 1179 Earth, so the events on Karfel could be set in any time zone. Vena tells Herbert that she has 'come from beyond the stars' which, together with the Doctor's comment that the tunnel is 'in space', suggests there is no temporal difference between the two points and therefore Vena's time and 1179 are in fact contemporaneous (she doesn't know that she is not in 1179 when she arrives in 1885 Scotland), with the only temporal aspect of the space tunnel on account of the journey from Karfel to Earth being almost instantaneous, which is like travelling in time given the likely vast distance between the two planets. The crystals the Doctor removes from the Kontron tunnel have the power to send the android back in time by 'perhaps an hour or so', and also to project the Doctor into 'a 10 second time break'. It is only an assumption that the thousands of crystals in the tunnel are therefore capable of moving people greater distances in time.

The Doctor calculates Vena's journey. He says: '1179 AD. Add a time deflection co-efficient of 706 years. That is 1885. AD'. The key word here is 'add', which indicates she has travelled forwards 706 more years from 1179 to 1885. Therefore, the events on Karfel could take place in a time period earlier than 1179.

But as noted above, the Doctor tells the Bandril Ambassador he is 'in fact President of the High Council of Gallifrey. Destroy me and you'll have more than a petty war on your hands'. This suggests that the Doctor knows what time zone he is currently in – which is his own GRT, so it is 2113 (see THE DOCTOR'S AGE). And later, when it is believed the Doctor has been killed in the warhead explosion, the Bandril Ambassador says he will 'make our apologies to the High Council'. If the time zone is not the Doctor's GRT, it would be a rather embarrassing conversation between the Ambassador and the High Council, especially if the events on Karfel take place in the Doctor's distant past or future – the Time Lords wouldn't know what or who the Bandrils were talking about.

I would take this idea over the rather dubious spatial and temporal calculations posed above, and suggest that 'Timelash' is set in the Doctor's current GRT of 2113. Otherwise the comments about the Doctor and Gallifrey would be meaningless.

1885, July ◆ ▨ ▨ ▨ ▨ ▨ ▨ ▨ ▨ ▨ ▨ ▨ ▨ ▨ ▨ ▨

The Doctor calculates that Vena has gone to '1885. AD'. Herbert says he goes to his uncle's cabin 'every summer'. He also says 'I'm a teacher. Or will be next term', which suggests it is early summer, say July. In our own history, Wells (1866 – 1946) did in fact holiday in Scotland during summer school breaks. Presumably the Doctor was able to return Herbert to Scotland the same day on which he first met the young writer at the end of the story (Herbert has had 'nothing published yet').

1179 ▨ ▨ ▨ ▨ ▨ ▨ ▨ ▨ ▨ ▨ ▨ ▨ ▨ ▨ ▨ ▨

The Doctor describes the Kontron tunnel as being a 'time corridor in space', which ends on Earth in 'a period you call 1179, AD'.

2063 ◆ ▨ ▨ ▨ ▨ ▨ ▨ ▨ ▨ ▨ ▨ ▨ ▨ ▨ ▨ ▨

The third Doctor and Jo Grant visited Karfel some time ago. This visit has, 'until recently', been taught in the schools. Kendron says 'my father always talked of the Doctor's return'; Tekker says the Doctor has returned, 'after all this time', and he makes reference to 'the stories I have heard about you; the great Doctor: all-knowing, and all-powerful'. Katz has a locket containing a photograph of Jo Grant, which was 'given to my grandfather by the Doctor', so we at least know the visit wasn't more than two generations ago, say 50 years at the most.

Given the length of the third Doctor's hair and the style of his green jacket as is seen in the painting of him in the Council chamber, we can place this visit to have occurred between 'Planet Of The Daleks' and 'The Green Death'. When the Doctor and Peri emerge from the TARDIS, Tekker comments 'Only the two of you?' to which the Doctor replies 'Yes. Travelling light this time'. From this, it would seem that after returning to Earth following the events of 'Planet Of The Daleks', the Doctor, Jo and a third person – possibly the Brigadier, Benton or Mike Yates, or another member of UNIT – visited Karfel.

By 2379 ▨ ▨ ▨ ▨ ▨ ▨ ▨ ▨ ▨ ▨ ▨ ▨ ▨ ▨ ▨

The Borad says he has an increased intelligence (the Doctor comments that Karfel is 'centuries from such technology' as the Timelash), plus 'a life spanning a dozen centuries' (but how would he know this when it is clearly only less than 50 years since his accident?). The Borad is sent back to Scotland in 1179, where the Doctor says he will 'have somewhere to swim for the next … thousand years?' and will be seen 'from time to time', implying that the Borad is the Loch Ness Monster. This, of course, conflicts with the Skarasen being the monster ('Terror Of The Zygons'), but with so many sightings of the beast, there could in fact be two (or even more) 'monsters' living in the Loch. The fact that the Borad could live a further 1000 to 1200 years places the latest time of his death to be around no later than 2379.

DURATION

(TARDIS) (Ep1) ▨ ▨ ▨ ▨ ▨ ▨ ▨ ▨ ▨ ▨ ▨ ▨
The Doctor and Peri travel in the TARDIS for some time before entering the Kontron tunnel and arriving on Karfel.

⇨ **Day One (Karfel) (Ep1)** ▨ ▨ ▨ ▨ ▨ ▨ ▨ ▨ ▨ ▨ ▨
The rebels Aram, Gazak and Tyheer attack a storage chamber, but are captured.

⇨ **Day Two (Karfel) (Ep1-2)** ▨ ▨ ▨ ▨ ▨ ▨ ▨ ▨ ▨ ▨
The next day the councillors discuss the attack of 'last night'. There is a passing of 'perhaps an hour or so' between the appearance of the burning android in the caves in Ep1 and its initial destruction in Ep2. At the end of the story Vena says 'it's been a terrible day'.

⇨ **Day One (1885)** ▨ ▨ ▨ ▨ ▨ ▨ ▨ ▨ ▨ ▨ ▨
It is a bright summer's day in Scotland when Vena and the Doctor arrive. Vena is there for about half an hour before the Doctor arrives.

REVELATION OF THE DALEKS

+STORY LINK
Peri wears the same blouse and trousers she has on in 'Timelash'. Allowing for time for them to return Herbert to Earth in 1885, and for the Doctor to receive word (presumably through the TARDIS communications system) of Stengos' internment on Necros, only a short length of time has passed since 'Timelash'. Peri is having 'lunch' at the beginning of 'Revelation Of The Daleks'.

The Doctor confirms he is now 'a 900-year old Time Lord'.

DALEK LINK
As covered under DALEK HISTORY, this is the Daleks' sixteenth appearance. Since the events of 'Resurrection Of The Daleks', the Daleks have returned to Skaro (the Thals have left the planet; or have they all been exterminated?) There is no reference to

the Movellans, so we can assume that the threat of the virus has been ultimately dealt with. There is a new Supreme Dalek, the last one having been destroyed by Stien in 'Resurrection Of The Daleks'. Davros has now been declared an enemy of the Daleks. After setting a trap for the Doctor, these Daleks have exterminated the Master, whose remains have been secured by the Doctor, as seen in 'Doctor Who (The TV Movie)'.

Davros has attempted to create a new 'breed' of Dalek that answers solely to him. These Daleks will eventually become known as the Imperial Daleks – as seen in 'Remembrance Of The Daleks'.

OBSERVATIONS

- Davros has 'eliminated famine from the galaxy'. We can assume that the galaxy is Earth's. A President governs the galaxy.

LANGUAGE

The Daleks and Davros speak the same language as the Necrosians. The Time Lord 'gift' does not translate the Doctor's use of the Latin *herba baculum vitae*.

TIMELINE DATES

4600 ◆

Enough years have passed since 'Resurrection Of The Daleks', set in 4590, to allow Davros to set himself up as the Great Healer. Some of the Necrosians, such as Kara and Orcini, have heard of Davros, but none fear the Daleks. It is not clear if the Necrosians are from Earth (the D J's great-grandfather had visited Earth; Grigory says the brains in the lab are 'human'; Davros refers to 'humanoid life forms'). One of Davros's achievements is that he has 'conquered the diseases that brought their victims here'. The cure for Beck's Syndrome was found '40 years ago'. However, I doubt that 40 years have passed since 'Resurrection Of The Daleks', as Takis says 'I don't think things have been the same since the Great Healer took over' / 'This used to be a good place before you came. I enjoyed working here'; Takis cannot be much older than 45 himself, so clearly Davros arrived within Takis' working life time.

Assuming that Davros is brought to Necros shortly after escaping in 'Resurrection Of The Daleks', 'Revelation Of The Daleks' should be set no more than 10 years after 'Resurrection Of The Daleks'; 4600 is the best date.

The Great Healer notes that has been watching Tasambeker's 'progress these last few months'.

4560 ▪ ▪ ▪ ▪ ▪ ▪ ▪ ▪ ▪ ▪ ▪ ▪ ▪ ▪

The D J says the cure for Beck's Syndrome was found '40 years ago'.

4570 ▪ ▪ ▪ ▪ ▪ ▪ ▪ ▪ ▪ ▪ ▪ ▪ ▪ ▪

The Doctor has been to this time period before, which is when he first met Arthur Stengos. He also knows of the Knights of the Grand Order of Oberon, who also exist in this time period. He does not appear to know Natasha, Stengos's daughter, so it is possible that the Doctor's previous visit was before she was born. On the basis that Natasha is about 25, we can place the Doctor's first encounter with Stengos to be around 30 years earlier.

DURATION

⇨ **Day One (Ep1-2)** ▪ ▪ ▪ ▪ ▪ ▪ ▪ ▪ ▪ ▪ ▪

One day passes on Necros. The Dalek ship's ETA early in Ep2 'is approximately 57 minutes'. It lands towards the end of Ep2, so just over 57 minutes pass during this episode.

UNSEEN ADVENTURE THE MYSTERIOUS PLANET

NOTE: In *Timelink* the title 'The Mysterious Planet' relates solely to the factual events that occurred on Ravolox / Earth, and not the altered version seen at the Doctor's trial. Because we do not see the actual adventure – only an edited projection of it – it has been treated as an UNSEEN ADVENTURE.

STORY LINK

The Doctor is still 'only 900 years old', so a matter of only a few months has passed since 'Revelation Of The Daleks', in which he was also 900. The Doctor tells Peri 'You've been travelling with me long enough … ' In the intervening period the Doctor and Peri's relationship has mellowed (the Doctor is no longer abusive towards her), and her hair is much longer. In 'Revelation Of The Daleks' the Doctor promises to return Orcini's medals to the Grand Order of Oberon, so we can assume that he has done so. The Doctor has also obtained a new pocket watch (his other one having being broken by Peri on Necros). (This is unlikely to be the alarm watch he has in 'Silver Nemesis' because the design is different.) In 'Attack Of The Cybermen' Peri makes her first visit to London, however in 'The Mysterious Planet' she recognises Marble Arch underground station, which suggests that they have visited London again at some point between 'Attack Of The Cybermen' and 'The Mysterious Planet'.

The Doctor says he only decided to go to Ravolox 'yesterday', having read about the planet in 'the records on Gallifrey'. It is unlikely that he has been to Gallifrey to read this; more likely the records are old TARDIS computer files that he has been studying.

OBSERVATIONS

- Katryca says Glitz and Dibber 'are not the first to visit my village from another world'. We can assume that the other visitors include the original Time Lord explorers who first visited the planet and whose reports the Doctor had read, as well as, presumably, the Master, who came to retrieve the stolen secrets, but had to leave empty-handed because he could not shut down the black light converter and thus gain access to Drathro's castle.
- On reviving after being knocked out by the L-1 robot (in Ep3), the Doctor's voice temporarily reverts to that of his third incarnation when he says 'Ooh, my head hurts abominably, Sarah Jane'.

LANGUAGE

The Doctor says it's a 'billion to one chance' that the inhabitants of what he thought at the time was Ravolox wrote in English. The fact that Balazar could read the 'Books' indicates that English is still their language. Glitz and Dibber could communicate with the dwellers and the tribe. The fact that Drathro has a large '3' stamped on his chest, and the L-1 'Robot' is marked with 'L1', indicates that all three races (the tribe and Marb Station dwellers, Glitz and Dibber, and Drathro) all speak English. Glitz even speaks in Latin at one point. So much for the Doctor's calculation of chance!

TIMELINE DATES

2,000,000 (November?) ◂ ■ ■ ■ ■ ■ ■ ■ ■ ■ ■ ■

When asked by Peri 'what time are we in?', the Doctor dramatically examines his pocket-watch and says 'Ooh, a long time after your period. Err, two million years or more?' Clearly he is only guessing because his watch is not a chronometer, so this is only an estimated date arrived at probably by taking into account the rate of decay in the Marble Arch underground station (which is clearly a more advanced version of the station than the one in use in the present day). The Doctor certainly had no idea when he still thought the planet was just Ravolox. It certainly is not his own GRT period (see 'The Trial Of A Time Lord').

Peri says 'it reminds me of a wet November back on Earth', so we can use this as the month.

1985

There is nothing that indicates that Glitz and Dibber are from the same time period in which 'The Mysterious Planet' is set. In fact, given the events of 'Dragonfire', it is almost certain that Glitz is from a time relative to the twentieth century. And given that Glitz is in the employ of the Master, to obtain the secrets (as is later revealed in 'The Trial Of A Time Lord'), it would appear that Glitz and Dibber are delivered to the future time period in which Ravolox is located by the Master in his TARDIS (it is clear from 'The Trial Of A Time Lord' that Glitz has been inside the Master's time ship before), where they obtain the use of a spacecraft, and then travel to the planet. (It is likely that Glitz and Dibber's ship is a small two-man stealth craft, as opposed to the big clunky *Nosferatu*, a ship that the Tribe would surely have heard or seen landing.) 'Dragonfire' has been set in 1987, so Glitz would have to be a couple of years younger in 'The Mysterious Planet', say from 1985. Glitz says he is 'wanted in six different galaxies for crimes you couldn't even imagine'. In 'Dragonfire' it is revealed that there are twelve galaxies; so Glitz has certainly made a name for himself in half of them. Some of these crimes could be ones committed with the Master who, as is revealed in 'The Trial Of A Time Lord', 'is a business partner, so to speak. We've had a few nice little tickles together'.

1,999,500

The Doctor says the solar fireball struck Ravolox 'some five centuries ago'. Glitz later confirms that it was '500 years ago'. The Doctor knows of this disaster 'according to the records on Gallifrey', but is surprised to see that they are wrong ('I think somebody exaggerated, don't you'). Drathro states that the fireball only destroyed part of the planet, although the records on Gallifrey say the planet was devastated. Clearly the records had been falsified by the High Council to hide their secret.

In 'The Trial Of A Time Lord', the Doctor talks of Earth having 'an ancient culture', which suggests that the planet was fully inhabited when the Time Lords moved it, however there is no evidence of human civilisation on the surface of the planet in 'The Mysterious Planet', even 500 years later. (The only remaining relic from an earlier time period is the remains of Marble Arch station. The survival shelter has been built inside the existing London Underground tunnels.) This suggests that the magnotron not only moved Earth spatially, but also temporally, two million years into the future, but this is only speculation on my part. In the absence of contradictory evidence, I have set the time of the fireball relative to the present date of 2,000,000.

DURATION

⇨ **Day One (Ep1-4)**
The story takes place over one day.

UNSEEN ADVENTURES

Immediately before their adventure on Thoros Beta the Doctor and Peri meet with the Warlord of Thordon, who asks them to go to Thoros Beta ('Mindwarp').

UNSEEN ADVENTURE
MINDWARP

NOTE: In *Timelink* the title 'Mindwarp' relates solely to the real events that occur on Thoros Beta before the Doctor is taken out of time, and not to the altered version seen at the Doctor's trial. In this real version of history (which we don't actually see), Peri stays to become Yrcanos's queen, and does not die as seen in the (false) trial version of 'Mindwarp'. Because of this, the story has been treated as an UNSEEN ADVENTURE.

STORY LINK

The Doctor and Peri have come to Thoros Beta from the planet Thordon, where one of the Warlords, in his dying breath, asks them to go to Thoros Beta to collect 'more beams that kill'. Peri had a disagreeable 'encounter' with the 'dirty old Warlord'. There is no indication as to how long after the events in 'The Mysterious Planet' this is.

In 'The Mysterious Planet' the Doctor is 'only 900'. When he is 'taken out of time' from Thoros Beta to stand trial he is 'over 900'. Given that Peri doesn't appear to have aged very much, we can assume that the Doctor is now only a year older than he is in 'The Mysterious Planet'. With 'Vengeance On Varos' set in 2327, 55 years have passed for Sil between encounters with the Doctor and Peri (he says to the Doctor, 'age has not improved you since Varos').

OBSERVATIONS

- The purpose of Crozier's experiment is to 'transform the evolutionary process and conquer death ... I have altered the basis of all future life ... I can transfer the mental energy and consciousness ... into yet another body. He need never die'. This achievement 'would affect all future life in the Universe', something which the Time Lords could not allow. Perhaps they felt that Crozier's discovery was too close to an unnatural form of regeneration? (See also 'Paradise Towers', in which Kroagnon's possession of the Chief Caretaker's body is by way of a similar form of mind transference.)

LANGUAGE

The Mentors all wear language transposers. The text on Sil's warp-fold relay is in English, not Thoros Betan. Crozier is able to communicate with the Mentors, Thoros Alphans and Yrcanos without the aid of a translator.

THE ALIEN CONNECTION

One of the specimens seen in Crozier's laboratory is a chest-burster from the *Alien* movies, which are set in an unspecified time a few centuries in the future (the fourth film is set 257 years after the first movie). But as noted under 'Destiny Of The Daleks' and 'Remembrance Of The Daleks', I have elected not to include 'in-joke' references to other series in the *Doctor Who* canon. Ironically, actor Alibe Parsons, who plays Matrona Kani, appears as a Med-Tech on the GateWay station in *Aliens*, and Peri does a very good impersonation of a bald Sigourney Weaver from *Alien³*! In 'Dalek' the (stuffed?) head of an Alien is mounted in Henry Van Statten's collection of extraterrestrial artefacts, presumably a remnant from the events of *Alien vs Predator* or its 2007 sequel *Aliens vs Predator: Requiem*.

TIMELINE DATES

2379, July 3 •

The Valeyard announces that the events on Thoros Beta take place in 'the twenty-fourth century; last quarter, fourth year, seventh month, third day', which from an Earth reference would be 3 July 2378 or 2379. It is somewhat odd that the Valeyard would use an Earth date when it is clear from stories such as 'The Invasion Of Time' that the Gallifreyans have their own method for dating Earth's time periods (e.g. 'Sol 3 relative date 034143989').

It is more likely that the Valeyard uses the Earth form of dating because the images are coming from the Doctor's TARDIS, and that is how the ship has recorded the information, using the form of dating that is preferred by the Doctor. Given that Crozier's experiments are said to affect 'all future life' in the Universe, this indicates that the events on Thoros Beta are in Modern Gallifrey's future GRT, which is now 2114, some 265 years earlier.

And given that he constantly refers to Peri as 'the Earth woman', it is unlikely that Crozier is from Earth – although he does appear to drink tea. Crozier 'was brought to Thoros Beta' by the Mentors to help Kiv, but we do not know from where.

2359

Tuza says that Vern 'was 20 years old', so he was born in 2359.

2369

Crozier says he has finally achieved success 'after a decade of hard work'.

2379, June

Crozier says 'it's taken me weeks' to find a suitable body for Kiv. This would be since the beginning of June.

2380

The Doctor recalls that there were 'a great many wars around the Rim Worlds' during the '24th century' and that there would be space battle debris ready to salvage 'soon'; the following year?

DURATION

⇨ Day One (Ep5-7)

The TARDIS arrives during the daytime. Sil has 'lunch' during Ep1, so it is probably around midday at that point. Kiv gives Crozier 'one day' to cure him. It is still daylight when the Doctor interrogates Peri on the rocks, but it is now high tide.

⇨ Day Two (Ep7-8)

The operation on Kiv takes place during Ep3, so it is most likely the next day at this point in the story.

THE TRIAL OF A TIME LORD

NOTE: In terms of *Timelink*, the title 'The Trial Of A Time Lord' refers only to the Twenty-

Third Season as screened on TV, which consists of the full trial itself: the introduction, the 34 interruptions during Eps 1-12, the final confrontation in the Matrix in Eps 13-14 – as well as all the screenings of the 'altered' versions of the Doctor's other adventures: the tampered versions of 'The Mysterious Planet', 'Mindwarp' and 'Terror Of The Vervoids'.

+STORY LINK

The Doctor is taken 'out of time' by the Time Lords to the trial ship while he was still on the planet Thoros Beta. The UNSEEN ADVENTURE 'Mindwarp' and 'The Trial Of A Time Lord' are therefore consecutive.

GALLIFREY LINK

The last contact the Doctor has with his own people is when he is used as an agent for the Time Lords in 'Attack Of The Cybermen' (probably for the CIA rather than the High Council, since he was still President at the time). And subsequent to the Doctor's last direct visit to his home planet (in 'The Five Doctors'), he has been deposed as President for wilfully neglecting the responsibility of that great office. At the end of 'The Five Doctors' the fifth Doctor gives Flavia 'full deputy powers', so we can assume that she is given the Presidency in the Doctor's place.

Since then, the latest members of the High Council have learned the secret of Ravolox, and like the other Councillors before them, have maintained the secret (see Timeline Dates below). However, when news comes through that the Doctor has visited Ravolox, the Council plan to destroy the Doctor. The trial is set up by the High Council specifically to get the Doctor out of the way. The Valeyard notes that 'if the Doctor had not visited Ravolox then the whole chain of events we are witnessing would not have been set in motion'. One would have expected that as part of the cover-up, the Time Lords would have deleted the record of the Doctor's visit to Ravolox, and all record of the planet's existence, but in 'The Mysterious Planet' the Doctor mentions having read about the planet 'in the records on Gallifrey'. And it is somewhat remiss of them that this 'secret' is chosen as the leading example with which to prosecute the Doctor!

While the Doctor is being dragged from Thoros Beta ('Mindwarp'), the Inquisitor and the Time Lord witnesses at the trial view the events on the planet taking place in the Doctor's absence – the High Council's time bubble and Yrcanos's assassination of Crozier, Kiv, and presumably Sil. (However, as it transpires, these images are mainly the creation of the Valeyard. Peri survives the assassination attempt but presumably Crozier and the real Kiv are destroyed.) After the viewing, the Inquisitor moves to the court room, where the Doctor is waiting …

MASTER LINK

No explanation is given for how the Master escapes from the Rani's TARDIS which is sent zooming to the outer regions of the Universe with a rapidly growing tyrannosaurus rex at the end of 'The Mark Of The Rani'. Since he has his own TARDIS again in 'The Trial Of A Time Lord', we can only assume that once the Rani regained control of her ship, she returned the Master to Killingworth where he recovered his own TARDIS. The Master's TARDIS now has a remote control feature, so it would appear that the Rani gave this facility to him.

According to Glitz, the Master 'is a business partner, so to speak. We've had a few nice little tickles together'. The Master may even have started his association with Glitz prior to the events of 'The Mark Of The Rani'. It is clear that Glitz has been inside the Master's TARDIS before. What is also certain is that the Master sent Glitz to Ravolox to retrieve the Matrix secrets (and as covered under 'Dragonfire', Glitz is not from the future, but is a contemporary from the Master's GRT). We can therefore speculate on the events leading up to the Master's appearance at the trial.

The Master somehow obtains or makes a copy of the Key of Rassilon, which opens the Matrix and enables his TARDIS to physically enter the 'micro-universe'. His plan is to obtain the ancient Matrix tapes phases 3, 4, 5, and 6, and to sell Time Lord secrets to the highest bidder. (In 'The Mysterious Planet' Glitz tells Dibber the secrets included 'facts, my son. Figures, formulas. Travelling faster-than-light, anti-gravity power, dimensional transference. Scientific stuff like that. Worth a small fortune'.) However, the Master discovers that the original tapes he wants are missing (they have in fact been hidden by the Valeyard), but also that a copy has been made by aliens from Andromeda who 'had found a way to break into the Matrix' some 500 years previously. He traces their movements and discovers that they had, presumably by using some of the secrets contained in the tapes, travelled some two million years into the future to Earth. The High Council in office at the time, some 500 years ago, had also discovered this fact and had ordered Earth to be moved to cover their tracks. This secret has been kept 'carefully buried … for centuries' (for 500 years), and has been passed on down to each successive High Council. Armed with this information the Master leaves the safety of the Matrix and goes to Ravolox / Earth in the future. He is unsuccessful in closing down the black light converter because of the villagers, so he returns to his own time, where he renews his relationship with Glitz from the planet Salostophus. The Master gives Glitz and his associate Dibber a map of the Underground city (obtained from one of the villagers?) and hires them to obtain the tapes from Ravolox. He takes them into the future and leaves them to obtain their own transport to Ravolox. The Master then returns to the Matrix. He discovers that the Doctor has recently been to Ravolox and that current High Council are aware that the Doctor has unknowingly blundered upon their predecessors' long-buried secret. The Council puts in motion drastic steps to put the Doctor out of the way. Part of this plan involves dealing with the Valeyard (see WHERE DO THEY COME FROM?). The Master watches as the Valeyard adjusts the Matrix from within. He makes careful note of where the Valeyard has hidden his base (information he writes down on a slip of paper which he subsequently gives to Glitz, who later passes it onto the Doctor). The Master then continues to observe as the Doctor's trial begins ...

Following the second case for the prosecution the Master temporarily leaves the Matrix again to locate Glitz and Mel to bring them to the trial to act as witnesses ...

OBSERVATIONS

- The Doctor says he has 'been through several such inquiries before', a reference to his first trial in 'The War Games', the inquest following the President's assassination in 'The Deadly Assassin', and possibly also to other incidents, such as the Mini-scope affair (see 'Carnival Of Monsters').
- As part of their deal the High Council promised to give the Valeyard 'the remainder of the Doctor's regenerations'. We can assume that the process to transfer the Doctor's life force into the Valeyard's body is similar to temporal bonding as attempted by Omega in 'Arc Of Infinity', or like that attempted by the Master in 'Doctor Who (The TV Movie)' using the Eye of Harmony, an eye-rig helmet and reflector staffs. In fact, it is probably learning about the Valeyard's plans while in the Matrix that gives the Master the knowledge and idea he would later use to try and take the Doctor's lives in 'Doctor Who (The TV Movie)'.
- The images seen during the trial (the 'separate epistopic interfaces of the spectrum') come from the Matrix, 'the repository of all knowledge', which is 'fed constantly by the experiences of all Time Lords, wherever they may be ... the experiences of third parties can also be monitored and accessed if needed as long as they are within the collection range of a TARDIS' (the Doctor's TARDIS, although 'an old model', has since been fitted with 'the new surveillance system', presumably during the last time the Doctor was on Gallifrey in 'Arc Of Infinity'. However, as seen in 'The Wheel In Space', it would appear that the TARDIS always had this function, because the Doctor is able to project mental images of events at which he is not present when he shows Zoe images from 'The Evil Of The Daleks'). This explains where the images from Ravolox and Thoros Beta come from, but not of those from the *Hyperion III*, which is in the Doctor's future; from his point of view his TARDIS has not yet been on the liner, so the images seen can't have come

from the Doctor's 'experiences' or his TARDIS. We do know from 'Genesis Of The Daleks' and 'The Deadly Assassin' that the Matrix is capable of predicting the future, so is this what the images are, a prediction of the Doctor's future should he be acquitted? Of course, assuming that the Valeyard still has the TARDIS, then the record most likely comes from that source.

LANGUAGE

The Time Lord trial ship has large white numerals painted on it; we can see a '3', '5' and '6'. The Inquisitor berates the Doctor for calling the Valeyard the brickyard, backyard, knacker's yard, and so on. Given that the Time Lords would all be speaking Gallifreyan, is it not odd that both languages have a similar number of derogatory words ending in '-yard'? ('boat yard, graveyard, farmyard, scrapyard, knacker's yard, brickyard, rail yard, stack yard'). The Valeyard's hit list is written in English. The signs seen in, and the nursery songs heard within the Matrix landscape are all English ('Fantasy Factory' / 'London Bridge is Falling Down'). Glitz can understand Mel when they first meet on the trial ship.

WHERE DO THEY COME FROM? THE VALEYARD

The origin of the Valeyard will only ever be speculative, given that he is from the Doctor's future, a future that [at least in terms of the television series] is still unwritten, and may never be told. [Should the Doctor's television adventures continue right up until he reaches his final regeneration (as noted under 'The Stolen Earth' the Doctor may already have been given a fresh regenerative cycle during the Time War), will the Valeyard's existence be acknowledged by the production team? Only time will tell.]

All we know for sure is that the Valeyard is a future 'incarnation' of the Doctor (from a future in which Gallifrey, the Time Lords and the Matrix no longer exist, all having been destroyed during 'the last great Time War' that occurred during the ninth Doctor's GRT). What is also understood is that the Valeyard somehow travelled back in time to the sixth Doctor's GRT. So, who is the Valeyard, where did he come from, how did he get to Gallifrey, and what are his objectives?

WHO/WHAT: The Master tells the Doctor that the Valeyard 'is an amalgamation of the darker side of your nature, somewhere between your twelfth and final incarnation. And I must say you do not improve with age'. The use of the term 'final incarnation' could be important, as this does not necessarily mean the Doctor's thirteenth incarnation.

The Master also tells the Doctor that the Valeyard is 'the distillation of all that's evil in you, untainted by virtue. A composite of your every dark thought', although it's not made clear how the Master knows this. Indeed, it is possible the Valeyard exists only because 'his' Gallifrey no longer exists; with the planet and the Time Lords gone, the physical and written Laws of Time that kept paradoxes and temporal anomalies in check no longer apply. Also, without Gallifrey, the regeneration process might not function correctly. The Valeyard could be an unfortunate side effect of these combined factors.

It is clear that even the Valeyard considers himself to be an incomplete entity: he says 'how else can I obtain my freedom, operate as a complete entity, unfettered by your side of my existence. Only by ridding myself of you and your misplaced morality, your constant crusading ... Only by releasing myself from the misguided maxims that you nurture can I be free ... With you destroyed and no longer able to restrain me, and with unlimited access to the Matrix, there will be nothing beyond my reach'. This speech seems to indicate that the Valeyard's ultimate aim is not the death of the Doctor but to gain control of the Matrix. Destroying the Doctor and taking his remaining lives is merely a welcome bonus.

WHY: The whole point of the trial (or at least as I understand it) was a diversion so the Valeyard could gain unlimited access to the Matrix so he could attain full corporeality. Since the Matrix no longer existed in his own GRT, he had to access it in an earlier time period. (Why he chooses the sixth Doctor's GRT is not known; it's likely this is simply because of circular logic – the trial has already happened in his past during his sixth incarnation and so therefore must happen again in his future.) And to gain 'unlimited access' to the Matrix, the Valeyard must also have access to the Key of Rassilon, which is in the possession of the Keeper.

HOW: The Master had the ability to fashion realistic face masks ('Terror Of The Autons', 'The Claws Of Axos', 'The Sea Devils'). The Valeyard disguises himself as Mr Popplewick with a similar life-like mask, so it is possible the Valeyard has acquired the same mask-making skills. This suggests there is a real Valeyard, whose face and identity the future Doctor has assumed.

The real Valeyard might even have been instrumental in bringing the future Doctor to Gallifrey. A Valeyard is said to be a 'learned court prosecutor'. But 'learned' can be defined as having knowledge acquired by study, or used as a colloquial courteous description of a lawyer in certain formal contexts. Therefore to attain such a title, a Valeyard would have to hold that office on Gallifrey for quite some time. It's therefore highly unlikely the Doctor has been the Valeyard for any considerable time, so the idea that the current (and long-serving) Valeyard has been replaced does have some merit.

Let's suppose, the future Doctor (let's call him Doctor/V for convenience) was able to lure the real Valeyard from Gallifrey (of the sixth Doctor's GRT), and using the powers he had, took over the Valeyard's body and TARDIS, and travelled back to 'old' Gallifrey. He was able to make this journey unhindered by the usual safeguards because he is not a complete being. Alternatively, the body-mask of the Valeyard assisted with blocking the fail-safe. Or it could be as simply as with the walls between the dimensions surrounding the whole of creation and reality collapsing during 'The Stolen Earth' crisis, the Doctor/V was able to slip back in time to the sixth Doctor's GRT.

On reaching the sixth Doctor's GRT, the Doctor/V assumed the (now-dead) real Valeyard's office and set in motion his plans. (The fact that he is an incomplete entity, and wearing a body-mask also helps him to block his 'aura' from the other Time Lords, so they don't recognise him as being the Doctor/V.) He uses his new position and knowledge of past and future events to blackmail the High Council into framing the sixth Doctor and placing him on trial. It is only once everything has advanced too far that he reveals his true identity to them; they were already too deeply implicated to turn back. He tells them he wants the Doctor's remaining lives, but what he really wants is the Matrix. (The Master, who is on Gallifrey at this time, hiding in the Matrix itself, discovers the Valeyard's true identity and intentions.)

In order to cover his tracks and make his escape the Doctor/V sets up the maser inside the Matrix to kill everyone at the trial, including all the members of 'the Ultimate Court of Appeal, the Supreme Guardians of Gallifreyan Law' in attendance. The Doctor/V then rigs parts of the Matrix records so that during the trial the sixth Doctor will become suspicious that the Matrix has been tampered with, and the Keeper will be summoned to the court room, giving the Doctor/V an opportunity to seize the Key, which is his ultimate objective.

The events of 'The Trial Of A Time Lord' then take place as we seen then unfold on-screen …

WHERE DO THEY COME FROM? MELANIE

The Mel who is brought to the trial ship by the Master already knows who the sixth Doctor is, but not who Glitz is, so she must come from a time before 'Dragonfire'. The Doctor has not yet met Mel; he only knows of her from seeing the future images from 'Terror Of The Vervoids'. But where does Mel come from? There are two possibilities.

1) The Master brings Mel from her home in Pease Pottage to the trial ship; she has never met the Doctor. While she is travelling in the transport capsule, the Master places a series of hypnotic suggestions into her mind that contain all the facts she needs to know to help the Doctor, including recollections of their 'meeting in Pease Pottage', and of the *Hyperion III* adventure, all of which are completely bogus. Therefore, Mel and the Doctor never do meet in

Pease Pottage; they do in fact meet for the first time on the trial ship.

2) Alternatively, Mel's origins are somewhat more complicated than simply having had her memory adjusted. If we examine this from Mel's perspective: she meets the Doctor in Pease Pottage around 1986. They travel together, having the adventure on the *Hyperion III*. Then later, while she is still travelling with the Doctor, the Master abducts her and brings her to the trial ship, where she meets an earlier version of her Doctor, before he has met her in Pease Pottage. After the trial, the earlier Doctor returns Mel to the point in space and time from which she had been abducted, and she is reunited with her 'older' Doctor (the 'earlier' Doctor being very careful not to meet his 'older' self). Mel and the 'older' Doctor travel together, and eventually they crash on Lakertya (see 'Time And The Rani').

One problem with this second idea is the ease with which the Doctor is able to get Mel back to the point in time and space from which the Master abducted her. How did the Doctor avoid meeting his older self, and how did the TARDIS land in the same location as the 'older' TARDIS when the safeguard should prevent such a landing (see GALLIFREY HISTORY)?

Another problem with this idea is that there is nothing to support it. In fact, if we go solely by evidence seen on-screen, what happens is that soon after leaving the trial ship the Doctor and Mel crash on Lakertya: the next time [on television] we see her she is in the TARDIS in the opening moments of 'Time And The Rani', just before the Doctor regenerates. From an average TV viewer's viewpoint, it would appear that this is the same Mel, because she later recognises Glitz when they meet again in 'Dragonfire'. This indicates that soon after leaving the trial ship, the Doctor regenerates. But that would mean that he never actually meets Mel in Pease Pottage in terms of their original off-screen meeting preceding the events in 'Terror Of The Vervoids'. In fact, in 'Dragonfire' the Doctor says 'You're going … gone for ages … already gone … still here … just arrived … *haven't even met you yet*' (my emphasis), which suggests that even the Doctor is fully aware of the paradox surrounding their relationship.

There is no easy way to explain the paradox; we just have to rely on speculation to solve it. [What was needed in the last scene of 'The Trial Of A Time Lord' was the Doctor saying something along the lines of: 'Right, young lady, first I have to get you back to where you came from. We don't want to interrupt the web of time, now, do we … ?' Instead, all we get is Mel threatening to get the Doctor 'back on the exerciser' and drinking carrot juice, two things that he hasn't actually started doing yet.]

I would say that the Master did abduct Mel from a time after 'Terror Of The

Vervoids', because it would seem that he needed her to confirm the events seen from that adventure at the trial, although she never actually gets to do so. As noted under 'Terror Of The Vervoids' below, I have taken this option.

TIMELINE DATES

2114

There are two possible dates for the Doctor's trial:

1) The trial takes place contemporaneously to the time zone in which Ravolox exists, some 'two million years or more' in the future. Drathro states that he has heard of Gallifrey and the Time Lords, but this knowledge could have come from his masters, the Andromedan sleepers who stole the secrets from the Matrix. But, as noted, the Doctor is only guessing the time period they are in, so it almost certainly is not his own present GRT (which is 2114). Given that it has been established that Modern Gallifrey and twentieth century Earth are contemporaneous (see GALLIFREY HISTORY), this would mean that the sixth Doctor has been taken out of his own GRT into Gallifrey's far distant future. It is stated in 'The Three Doctors' that breaking the First Law of Time and removing a Time Lord from his own time stream is forbidden except in extreme emergencies. I doubt that the Doctor's trial is enough of an emergency to warrant breaking the law. Of course, if these Time Lords are from the future, it is possible that the First Law has since been changed. It is stated during the trial that the First Law of Time is the now the law of non-intervention in the affairs of other planets, so it would appear that this was the case.

   The problem with this scenario is that it means that the Master is now millions of years old – he certainly hasn't been scooped out of time – but this is impossible in terms of the events of 'Survival' and 'Doctor Who (The TV Movie)', which both happen after the trial. Also, if the Time Lords at the trial are from a time two million years in the sixth Doctor's own future, why is the Doctor so surprised that he has been deposed as President, and why would they offer him the Presidency again when he is not from their time? Also, the Valeyard refers to 'the latest surveillance methods' with which the Doctor's TARDIS is fitted. If the Time Lords at the trial are from two million years in the Doctor's personal future the surveillance system in his TARDIS could hardly still be considered 'the latest'.

2) The trial takes place in the sixth Doctor's present, in his own GRT. As covered under THE DOCTOR'S AGE, the Doctor is aged '900' in 'The Mysterious

Planet', but in Ep14 of 'The Trial Of A Time Lord', he says he is 'over 900'. In 'Time And The Rani' the Doctor is '953', so he has aged 53 years between 'The Mysterious Planet' and 'Time And The Rani'. Given that the Doctor is still with Peri when he was taken out of time, we can assume that only a year or so has passed between 'The Mysterious Planet' and 'The Trial Of A Time Lord', so he is probably only 901 at the time of the trial. That makes his GRT to be 2114.

The Time Lords offer the Doctor the Presidency again, and the Valeyard mentions the 'latest methods of surveillance', which supports that these Time Lords are his contemporaries.

I prefer the second option – the trial is in the sixth Doctor's present, GRT 2114. The Master is therefore still his contemporary. It is only the Valeyard who is from a different GRT. The 'hows' and 'whys' that make this possible are covered in more detail in WHERE DO THEY COME FROM? above. Therefore, the Andromedans, after having stolen the secrets from Gallifrey, must have time-jumped to Earth two million years in the future to hide, knowing that that time period is ostensibly beyond the scope of the Time Lords' surveillance (as seen in 'Frontios', even the Time Lords have time parameters that cannot be exceeded). But on tracing the leak to Earth, the Time Lords move the planet across space so the relief ship that is also time-jumping from Andromeda misses the planet.

1614

Glitz reveals that the Andromedans had been nicking stuff from the Matrix 'for years'. The sleepers were hiding on Earth two million years in the future (presumably having used some of the secrets they stole from the Matrix, such as 'dimensional transference', to travel into the future). The members of the High Council who were in office at the time used the magnotron to move Earth to a new location. Given that 500 years had passed relative on Earth between the solar fire-ball and the Doctor's visit to Ravolox, we can assume that the same length of time was also relative to Gallifrey, so the theft was discovered 500 years ago on Gallifrey, being 1614.

Coincidentally the Doctor had left Gallifrey only four years earlier (in 1610, see 'The Time Meddler'), which may explain why the Doctor was oblivious to this having happened. It is unlikely that there is a connection between the two events.

1985

When his ship the *Nosferatu* blasts off in 'Dragonfire', Glitz cries out, 'You can't leave me. Not after all these years'. He either had the ship at the time he was working for the Master in 'The Trial Of A Time Lord', or he acquired the vessel after the Time Lords

TIMELINK

at the end of the Doctor's trial had released him from the Master's TARDIS. With 'Dragonfire' set in 1987, I would say there are no more than two years between 'The Trial Of A Time Lord' and 'Dragonfire' from Glitz's perspective, which makes 1985 the year in which Glitz is working for the Master and subsequently brought by the Master to the Doctor's trial (see 'The Trial Of A Time Lord').

DURATION

⇨ **Day One (Ep1-14)**

The trial appears to last many hours, possibly most of one whole day: taking into account the actual time screening the two segments of the prosecution's evidence, which is about 3 hours. A gap of several hours needs to pass between the end of the screening of the segment relating to the events on Thoros Beta and the start of the Doctor's defence (between Eps 8 and 9), to allow him time to grieve over Peri's apparent death, and to examine all the available Matrix files to find a suitable 'adventure' with which to prepare his defence case. The Doctor must have previewed several adventures before selecting the Vervoid story. It takes about 90 minutes to show this. The Doctor then spends about an hour or so inside the Matrix battling the Valeyard. In all, the Doctor spends around a minimum of 12 hours on the trial ship.

UNSEEN ADVENTURES

At some point after his trial, the sixth Doctor meets Captain Tonker Travers and saves the Captain's ship. He also meets Investigator Hallet for the first time ('Terror Of The Vervoids'). The Doctor then meets Mel (again) but this is the 'first' time for her, presumably in Pease Pottage (he knows she has a garden), and they have several adventures together (she even appears to know of the Bannermen ('Delta And The Bannermen') so it is possible that they have an encounter with them).

UNSEEN ADVENTURE
TERROR OF THE VERVOIDS

NOTE: This adventure is seen at the Doctor's trial by way of a projection into the Doctor's future time line, so the real events might not occur exactly the same way as it seems during the trial – if at all. The fact that the Valeyard has tampered with some

470

of the evidence indicates that not all of what we see will actually happen that way. Therefore, the story has been treated as UNSEEN for that reason. (See BUT DID IT HAPPEN?)

STORY LINK

On the assumption that the events in 'Terror Of The Vervoids' do actually take place, from the Doctor's point of view 'Terror Of The Vervoids' is some 52 years after his trial (he is aged 'over 900' at the trial, and '953' in 'Time And The Rani').

At the end of the trial, the Doctor leaves with Mel, who is from his future; he hasn't actually met her properly yet. To avoid paradoxical complications, the Doctor returns Mel to the point in time and space from which the Master had taken her, so she can resume her travels with his 'older' self. The post-trial Doctor subsequently travels for some 52 years (alone?) until the day he lands in Pease Pottage in 1986 where he meets the younger pre-trial Mel. She joins him in his travels (as he knows she was destined to do), quickly putting him on a strict diet and harsh exercise programme. The Doctor's exercise is interrupted a short time later by Hallet's message … It is clear from 'Terror Of The Vervoids' that Mel has only been with the Doctor for a relatively short period of time. The events in 'Terror Of The Vervoids' therefore feature the post-trial Doctor and the pre-trial Mel.

OBSERVATIONS

- The Doctor previews this adventure in the Matrix during a recess period. Since the Doctor sees that he knows (or will come to know) two of the people who appear in this adventure – Travers and Hallet, whom he 'admired' – it is possible that he selects this particular story for his defence for the very reason that he can rely on the integrity of the Matrix information.
- Given that this is in effect the last sixth Doctor adventure [on TV], it is possible that this is also the sixth Doctor's last adventure prior to the TARDIS crashing on Lakertya (in 'Time And The Rani'). The Matrix probably has a restriction over what the Doctor is allowed to view, and as a consequence he was unable to watch any adventures that take place beyond his current incarnation's time stream (he could not view any future incarnations). On the basis that he was looking for evidence in which he 'improves', we can assume that he looked specifically at stories as late in his time stream as possible. Therefore, with the Matrix only allowing him to view events up to a certain point in his sixth time stream, the Doctor would be made aware that when he had the *Hyperion III* adventure, his sixth incarnation was near its end.

- The Vervoids were created to replace robots in the factories and farms on Earth, one of the few times in which it is stated that Earth has any form of robot technology.

LANGUAGE

The Mogarians have translators, one of the few instances in which such devices are used by alien races. The Vervoids definitely speak English. The text on the TARDIS screen is in English.

BUT DID IT HAPPEN?

At the time of his trial this adventure is in the Doctor's future. Given that he wins the trial and leaves with Mel, we can assume that the events on *Hyperion III* do subsequently take place; but not necessarily exactly how they are shown by the Matrix, because the Doctor knows the outcome and should be able to 'change' events to ensure that no one gets killed. This is not the same as changing history because it hasn't happened yet, and so events can be shaped (as noted in 'Pyramids Of Mars'; see THE N-SPACE UNIVERSE). There are several possible scenarios for what actually happens:

1) After leaving the trial, the Time Lords erase / adjust the Doctor's memory of these future events. The events then play out exactly as seen at the trial (bar the Valeyard-altered sequences), which is why the Doctor does not already know what is going to happen.

2) The events play out exactly as they are seen at the trial, but the Doctor, who does remember what is going to happen, chooses to 'forget' so as not to draw undue attention to himself until the last minute. As a Time Lord he is not able to change the tragic course of events. After all, he was twice put on trial for meddling …

3) The *Hyperion III* does not exist; the Valeyard had fabricated the entire 'adventure'. However, Mel must exist since the Master brings her to the trial after he sees her taking part in the *Hyperion III* adventure …

4) On arriving on the ship, the Doctor goes straight to Travers and informs him of the Mogarians and Rudge's hijack plans. Hallet does not die and completes his mission by arresting the 'traitor' Doland. As a result the Vervoids are never hatched, and the shells are destroyed when the ship reaches Earth.

5) The Doctor receives Hallet's signal, but chooses not to respond. As a consequence, the *Hyperion III* is hijacked by the Mogarians, but gets destroyed when Bruchner takes control and flies it into the Black Hole of Tartarus.

I would suggest that option (2) was the most likely, on the basis that Time Lords are forbidden to interfere even if they know the outcome of future events; the Doctor has simply not confided in Mel that he knows what will happen. This would explain why the Doctor is not at all surprised that there is a convenient shipment of vionesium on board.

TIMELINE DATES

2986, April 16 *

The Doctor says the date is 'the Earth year two thousand nine hundred and eighty six'. On a screen in the communications room the notation '16 4 2986' appears, which suggests the full date is 16 April 2986.

1986 *

Mel's knowledge of modern fitness techniques and aerobics shows that she is from the 1980s. I have chosen 1986, as she is almost certainly a contemporary of Ace, who left Earth in 1986 (see 'Dragonfire').

2980

The *Hyperion III* is an intergalactic liner (although on this particular flight it is not being used in that capacity), which establishes firmly that by 2986 humans have developed intergalactic flight, whereas before they were isolated solely to their own galaxy. In fact, the Mogarians see humans to be 'going through the Universe like a plague of interplanetary locusts'. I would say that intergalactic travel was developed round 2980 (see A HISTORY OF SPACE-FLIGHT).

2976 *

The sixth Doctor first met Travers when he was only a Captain; say 10 years earlier in Travers' relative time.

2981

Doland speaks of their 'years of scientific research'. The Vervoids were created on Mogar, so we can assume that Lasky, Doland, Bruchner and Ruth Baxter have been on Mogar for say five years.

2983

Old Mr Kimber says he and Hallet 'met three years ago on Stellar Stora'.

DURATION

⇨ **Day One (Ep9-12)**

The events on *Hyperion III* take place over several hours.

TIME AND THE RANI

STORY LINK

Mel is wearing an outfit different to that she wears in 'Terror Of The Vervoids'. The Doctor is wearing the same ensemble from 'Mindwarp', but with his original green pocket-watch chain (it is pink in 'The Mysterious Planet', 'Mindwarp', 'The Trial Of A Time Lord' and 'Terror Of The Vervoids').

From the Doctor's point of view, 'Time And The Rani' takes place some 52 years after his trial (he is aged 'over 900' at his trial, and is '953' in 'Time And The Rani'). As covered under 'The Trial Of A Time Lord', after the events of the trial, the Doctor returns Mel to her own time and place, travels for about 52 years (on his own), then meets the 'younger' Mel in Pease Pottage in 1986. Later they encounter the Vervoids on *Hyperion III*. Mel is then abducted by the Master but returned by the 'younger' sixth Doctor. Some time after that, the TARDIS is attacked by the Rani, using 'a navigational guidance distorter' ...

From her point of view, at the end of the trial the 'younger' Doctor returns Mel to the point in time and space from which she was taken by the Master and reunited with her 'older' Doctor. They resume their travels together, until the Rani forces the TARDIS to crash on Lakertya with the aid of her 'navigational guidance distorter' ...

'Time And The Rani' therefore features the post-trial Doctor and the post-trial Mel. Both versions of Mel have had the Doctor on a steady diet of carrot juice and working out on the exerciser, which can still be seen in the TARDIS console room.

OBSERVATIONS

- At the end of 'The Mark Of The Rani', the Master and the Rani are sent to the outer reaches of the Universe in her TARDIS, threatened by time spillage and an ever-growing tyrannosaurus rex. As noted under 'The Trial Of A Time Lord', after escaping from this, the Master is returned to Earth to recover his own TARDIS. 182 years later (see THE DOCTOR'S AGE) the Rani has set up her laboratory on Lakertya. She has 'swarmed the Universe plucking [the] geniuses out of time at the height of their powers'. She has recently returned from Earth (1929) with Albert Einstein (she says collecting him has 'put me behind schedule'). The lab and the rocket launcher were built with her Lakertyan slave labour force. She must have visited Tetrapyriarbus in order to collect her Tetrap servants prior to arriving on Lakertya. It is not stated how long she has been there. (The Doctor comments that the Rani's past is littered with the results of her 'unethical experiments'.)

LANGUAGE

A form of symbol script with Earth numerals appears on the Rani's console. It could be Gallifreyan, but the terms PHB and PES also appear, both being shortened forms of two Earth chemical names. The labels on the cabinets containing the geniuses are in English. The fact that the Lakertyans can read and spell the names suggests they also speak English; Sarn knows how to spell 'Einstein'. The Tetraps speak the language of whomever they are speaking with. The Brain speaks English despite the fact that the geniuses that are connected to it are from different planets. The countdown is given in English in the verbal readout, on the scanner and on the Rani's wristband control. The Rani understands – and corrects – all the Doctor's mixed English proverbs and metaphors. (With both the Doctor and the Rani present, the Time Lord 'gift' could be working overtime, but why does English appear to be in use before Mel appears?). Also, in the final TARDIS scene when the Doctor is speaking with the eleven geniuses, they all seem to understand him, despite all being from different species or Earth nationalities.

TIMELINE DATES

After 1929? ◆

The Rani has recently abducted Albert Einstein. He is placed in a cabinet next to Hypatia. On the other side of the doorway is the cabinet reserved for the Doctor, and next to that lies Louis Pasteur. The location in the citadel of the remaining eight geniuses is not known. Given that the Doctor and Einstein are next to each other, it is possible that the Rani has been collecting her menagerie in chronological historical order, with Einstein being the last. As noted below he is from 1929, so it is possible that 'Time And The Rani' is set some time after 1929.

410 ◆

In our history, Hypatia, who lived in Alexandria, Egypt (370 – 415), was the first important woman mathematician. If, like Pasteur and Einstein, she was taken 'at the height' of her power, then this would be late in her lifetime, say around 410. The Doctor must have returned her to the correct point in time and space.

1861 ◆ ▨ ▨ ▨ ▨ ▨ ▨ ▨ ▨ ▨ ▨ ▨ ▨ ▨ ▨ ▨

The Doctor says that Pasteur (1822 – 1895) 'will rid his world of a major scourge. He will save the lives of tens of millions'. Pasteur's chief claim was his discovery of the vaccine for rabies in 1885 (he inoculated his first patient on 6 July 1885). However, in 'Time And The Rani', Pasteur does not look old enough to come from this period in his life stream. His other achievement was his discovery in 1861 that bacteria were the cause of disease, so it is from this point in time that he was most likely taken. The Doctor must have returned him to the correct point in time and space.

1929 ◆ ▨ ▨ ▨ ▨ ▨ ▨ ▨ ▨ ▨ ▨ ▨ ▨ ▨ ▨ ▨

In our history Einstein (14 March 1879 – 18 April 1955) presented his General Theory of Relativity on 25 November 1915, his greatest achievement. As the geniuses were taken 'at the height of their powers', the Rani would have taken Einstein at some point around 1915, however, his appearance in this story puts him at about 50, so that would be 1929. The Doctor must have returned him to the correct point in time and space. The Doctor has met Einstein before (see 'The Stones Of Blood').

1984 ▨ ▨ ▨ ▨ ▨ ▨ ▨ ▨ ▨ ▨ ▨ ▨ ▨ ▨ ▨

The Doctor gives the year. In our history, Edward Witten, of the Institute For Advanced Study in Princeton, New Jersey, first proposed the existence of strange matter indeed in 1984.

DURATION

⇨ **Day One (Ep1-4)** ▨ ▨ ▨ ▨ ▨ ▨ ▨ ▨ ▨ ▨ ▨

One day passes on Lakertya.

PARADISE TOWERS

STORY LINK

At the end of 'Time And The Rani' the Doctor has to return the eleven geniuses abducted by the Rani to their correct places in time and space, which would take quite some time. The Doctor and Mel could therefore be going to the pool at 'Paradise Towers' in order to relax and cool off after all these journeys. The Doctor had to jettison the TARDIS pool because 'it was leaking'.

OBSERVATIONS

- When Kroagnon takes over the Chief Caretaker's body, the Chief's clothes also change and become silver, the insignia and badges larger. The Doctor refers to this as 'corporal ectoscopy', so he is familiar with the process. Certainly as a Time Lord he would be, as the process seems to be very similar to regeneration (in the same way that the Doctor's own clothes changed with his first and fourth regeneration (see 'The Tenth Planet'/ 'The Power Of The Daleks', and 'Logopolis' / 'Castrovalva')). Also, the process could be similar to that used by Crozier (in 'Mindwarp') to transfer minds from one body to another.

LANGUAGE

All the wall-scrawls and signs in the Towers, plus the writing on the coinage and on the Fizzade cans, are in English.

TIMELINE DATES

2040 *

The Doctor says to Mel: 'I am told [that 'Paradise Towers'] won all sorts of awards way back in the, ah, twenty-first century'; which suggests 'Paradise Towers' is set a century later than the twenty-first. Alternatively the Doctor and Mel have been travelling backwards through time and into the twenty-first from a later century (having finished returning the eleven geniuses from 'Time And The Rani', see Story Link). A third possibility is the Doctor is speaking relative to his own GRT. As covered in THE DOCTOR'S AGE, the Doctor is 953 at the time of his sixth regeneration. His GRT is now 2166, which is indeed the twenty-second century.

When the Doctor arrives at the Towers, he doffs his hat to a metal cylinder. This indicates that he does not expect the occupants of the Towers to be human. However, it would appear that the residents of the Towers are from Earth: Kroagnon refers to 'all the nasty human beings', 'the human garbage' and 'useless humanoid creatures'. The Language (see Observations) is English; there is a black Kang and a black Caretaker; Tilda and Tabby eat 'tea and crumpets' and have duck ornaments on their walls, as well as a pink parrot statuette, and there are rats in the Towers. Although, as covered under THE N-SPACE UNIVERSE, the term 'human' does not necessarily mean 'Earthling', on this occasion I think it is safe to say they are colonists from Earth.

The Kangs were only children when they were sent 'in the ship' to the Towers. According to Tilda they have been there 'for ever such a long time', and the war was 'such a long time ago'. The Doctor surmises that Kroagnon has 'had years to brood over what he wants to do'. The Kangs can be no older than 25. It was their parents who killed Kroagnon, so no more than 20 years could have passed since the Towers were finished. Although the Kangs are 'adults' now they still all act like five-year-old children because they have not had any parental influences to emulate.

Apart from the Caretakers and Pex, there are no men or any middle-aged women in the Towers. The 'Inbetweeners' all went off to fight 'in the war'. In terms of established continuity it is unlikely that this is the war in 'Warriors Of The Deep', set in 2084, given that Earth was only in a state of potential war at the time, with no actual fighting taking place.

As covered under CYBERMAN HISTORY the Cyber-War mentioned in 'Revenge Of The Cybermen' was fought in the early twenty-first century, from 2020 to 2025. If we use this, and set the events of 'Paradise Towers' 20 years after the war started, the date would be 2040. It is clear in 'The Moonbase' that there are off-Earth colonies in 2070, so this supports that 'Paradise Towers' could be one of these. The colony is not necessarily in another solar system or galaxy. Given that warp-drive is not discovered until about 2106 (see 'Nightmare Of Eden'), humans are still restricted to areas of space within or close to their own solar system. Given that we see shots of the Towers from the outside, and there is a sun, we could assume that the colony is somewhere in Earth's solar system, possibly one of the moons of one of the other planets, perhaps even in the asteroid belt, which had been explored by 2077 (see 'The Wheel In Space').

DURATION

⇨ **Day One (Ep1-4)**
Daylight is visible through all the windows and in all the scenes at the pool, so the story takes place over one day.

DELTA AND THE BANNERMEN

STORY LINK

There is no indication that this story follows directly on from 'Paradise Towers'. At the end of 'Paradise Towers', the Doctor is given a Red and Blue Kang scarf: 'I will be honoured to wear it', but he is not wearing it in the opening moments of 'Delta And The Bannermen'.

OBSERVATIONS

- According to Weismuller and Hawk, the missing satellite 'is history in the making', suggesting that it is America's first artificial satellite. In our history, the first American satellite was Pioneer I, sent up on 11 August 1958, a year earlier than in this story. The missing satellite could (secretly) be one of the first deep space probes, as mentioned by the Brigadier in 'Spearhead From Space'.

- The Doctor's notoriety has spread throughout the galaxy, because Keillor says 'You're the traveller in time they call the Doctor. Your death will make me richer still'. However, it is not indicated who 'they' are. In 'The Sun Makers', the Doctor says 'the Droge of Gabrielides offered a whole star system for my head once', so it is just possible that Keillor is a bounty hunter working for the Droge.

- Garonwy says he has seen 'lights in the sky'. If these lights were extra-terrestrial in nature, presumably Torchwood Three in Cardiff would have had an interest in them.

LANGUAGE

The Navarinos, the Tollmaster (the Tollport has a serial number which reads G715), Delta, and the Bannermen all converse with each other without the apparent aid of translators, so it would seem that all these races speak English. The Doctor, however, is clearly at a loss when Burton and Ray converse in Welsh.

TIMELINE DATES

1959, June (Wednesday-Thursday)

The Tollmaster gives the year when he declares the Navarinos are 'going back to 1959; the rock and roll years'. Murray is seen reading the 7 March 1959 cover dated issue of *Eagle* comic. This is not necessary the 'current' issue of the magazine, so the story does not have to be set in March. In Britain people go to holiday camps in the summer (being mid-June to mid-September). Patrons are still arriving at the camp, so it is most probably the beginning of the summer season. Accordingly, June has been selected as the month; the serial was recorded during June and July [of 1987], so at least seasonal conditions are matched. By the door to the dance hall is a notice board, announcing 'WEDNESDAY, DANCE NITE WITH THE LORELLS, 7.30 - 10pm'. With the story set over two days, the first is a Wednesday and the second a Thursday. In 1959, Wednesdays in June were 3, 10, 17 and 24 June.

???? *

The time zone in which Tollport G715 and the war on Delta's planet are set is not known. Gavrok says he has 'traversed time and space to find the Chimeron Queen', while the Nostalgia Tours are 'going back to 1959', which indicates it is in the future. On this note it is clear both the Navarinos and the Bannermen have time-travel capabilities, so the time period could be any time. The Tollport is in the same galaxy as Earth so it might be of Earth origin, being at a time when space travel is common, which was the case in the twenty-sixth century (see 'Frontier In Space'). Due to the uncertainty I have set the Tollport scenes in ????

1917

Burton hasn't used his sword 'in over 40 years', which would be probably during World War I, say 1917.

1928 / 1932 (summer)

Goronwy gives the dates for two jars of honey: '1932, a hot summer and abundant cherry blossom', and '1928, hibiscus blossom'.

DURATION

⇨ **Day One (Ep1)**
It is day on the Chimeron planet.

⇨ **Day One (Ep1)**
It is the Doctor's 'lucky night' at Tollport G715.

⇨ **Day One (Ep1-2) (Wednesday)**
Burton says that 'lunch is at one and supper is at six'. He then says 'I'll see you at lunch', so they have arrived shortly before 1pm. The 'Get To Know You Dance' is held that evening (the notice board gives the time for the dance as '7.30-10.30 pm'). The Doctor spends the night with Ray in the laundry room. The last scene at night is when Billy sees the Chimeron baby.

⇨ **Day Two (Ep2-3) (Thursday)**
Weismuller and Hawk meet Goronwy at dawn ('Good morning. What a beautiful morning'). The campers wake at 7.00 am (a clock can be seen on the office wall). The clock reads 9.35 when Burton orders the staff to evacuate. In Ep1 when they arrived at the camp, the Doctor said it would take 'about 24 hours' for the new quarb crystal to grow. The new crystal is ready by the time the Bannermen arrive, so it is 24 hours later, before 1pm. The Doctor and Mel leave later that day.

DRAGONFIRE

STORY LINK

There is no indication that 'Dragonfire' follows directly on from 'Delta And The Bannermen'. The Doctor says he has been 'picking up a faint tracking signal for some time' from the planet. This is either the tracking device on Glitz's treasure map (given to him by Kane), or it is part of Fenric's trap to lure the Doctor to Svartos to ensure that he meets Ace …

OBSERVATIONS

- Ace has on her jacket a variety of badges and patches. Between 'The Greatest Show In The Galaxy' and 'Battlefield' some new badges have been added. As noted under 'Dragonfire' and 'Battlefield', several badges are from real-life NASA space missions. Among the other badges are the smiley-face from the *Watchmen* comic; a blue and a silver awards badge from the TV programme *Blue Peter*; the comics character Rupert the Bear; Spiderman; a *Thunderbirds* badge, plus one from Fanderson, the fan club for Gerry Anderson, the creator of *Thunderbirds*.

LANGUAGE

All the signs in IceWorld are in English. Sondheim appears to be familiar with Plato, Kracauer knows what a dog is, and the alien is termed an 'aggressive non-terrestrial', which implies the colonists are from Terra (i.e. Earth). Ace is able to converse with the customers at the cafe. The map is labelled in English. The Doctor corrects Mel's pronunciation of the Scottish word 'Loch'.

TIMELINE DATES

1987 ◦ ▪ ▪ ▪ ▪ ▪ ▪ ▪ ▪ ▪ ▪ ▪ ▪ ▪ ▪ ▪

Despite the futuristic-looking setting of IceWorld ('a space trading colony … Space travellers stop there for supplies'), it is clear to me that 'Dragonfire' is set in the late twentieth century or early twenty-first century. At the end of the serial, Glitz offers to take Ace back to Perivale by 'the direct route'. It is very clear that Kane's ship does not have time-travel capabilities (otherwise Kane would have gone back in time to before his planet was destroyed), so in order for Glitz to be able to deliver Ace back to her home, the time zone must be relative to her own. And the Doctor is not concerned at all about Glitz's offer, nor Mel's decision to go with Glitz ('You Perivale-bound as well?'); if it is the future when Earth had colonised other planets throughout 'the Twelve Galaxies' (in 'The Daleks' Master Plan', set in 4000, Earth had relationships with at least ten galaxies), he would at least say something about the time differential. And Mel herself seems confident that she will eventually get back to Earth in her own time if she stays with Glitz, so she is also aware that she is in her own relative time.

Glitz is from the planet Salostaphus in the Constellation of Andromeda (as is established in 'The Mysterious Planet'). He has on board his ship some fluffy dice, a boomerang, a stolen Dutch masterpiece and a Stradivarius violin. He would most certainly have been to Earth in the twentieth century to have obtained these; would these items still exist millions of years in the future if 'Dragonfire' were set at the same time as 'The Mysterious Planet'? The fact that Glitz is working for the Master in 'The Mysterious Planet' suggests that he and Dibber were delivered two million years in the future in the Master's TARDIS, where they use a ship to then travel to Ravolox, so 'The Mysterious Planet' and 'Dragonfire' do not have to be set in the same time zone, i.e. two million years in the future.

Ace left Earth when 'a time storm' blew up from nowhere and whisked her 'up here'. In 'The Curse Of Fenric' we learn that Fenric was responsible for the time storm. Fenric was able to bring the Ancient Haemovore back in time from 500,000 years in the future to 1943, so it is therefore not impossible for him to have moved Ace from Earth to another time zone. However, although the term 'time storm' suggests time travel of a great distance, there is no reason why Ace's temporal displacement couldn't be a matter of months or years as opposed to centuries or millennia. And the term 'up here' suggests that she is aware that she has simply been moved from Earth to Svartos spatially and not temporally.

As covered under Language, some of the people at IceWorld appear to be Earthlings, although there is no reason to assume that the humanoid personnel and visitors are from Earth; there are plenty of alien species there also, including an Argolin (see 'The Leisure Hive'). Svartos is therefore not necessarily an Earth trading colony.

On the basis that Kane's ship is not a time machine, I would set 'Dragonfire' relative to Ace's time. The Archive recording gives the criminal history segment concerning Kane and Xana the label '93-12-0-3', but it is unlikely that this refers to 1993-December-3 because the Archive was recorded three thousand years earlier and they couldn't be using a dating system that didn't yet exist. Ace left Earth in 1986; I would say she was whisked forward about a year, to 1987.

Based on Mel's comment that Ace hasn't done the washing for 'a couple of months', we can ascertain that Ace has been on IceWorld for several months.

Glitz has been at IceWorld for some time, and has been 'burning holes in this treasure map for the last two days', according to Ace.

1013 BC
Kane has been a prisoner for 'three thousand years'.

13 BC
Proamon was destroyed 'a thousand years' after Kane was exiled, 'two thousand years ago'.

1487
The colony has existed for a few hundred years, because the Doctor says travellers claimed to have seen the dragon 'throughout the centuries', say 500 years.

1887 *
The Doctor had been to Perivale when it had a blacksmith.

1951
1967
The scar on Belazs's hand has been there for '20 years'. She says she was '16' when she joined Kane, which makes her 36 in 1987. She was therefore born in 1951.

1977, August 12 – October 26
Ace has an *Enterprise* badge on her jacket. These are the dates in our history when the space shuttle Enterprise was tested.

1986, January 28
Ace wears a *Challenger* badge on her jacket. At 11.39 am (Eastern Standard Time) on this date in our history, the *Challenger* exploded shortly after take-off.

1986, November
Mel tells the Doctor that Ace is 'from the twentieth century'. Ace has a patch with '1987' on her left shoulder, but this does not mean that she comes from 1987 itself. In 'Ghost Light', it is stated that she was 13 in 1983, which makes her year of birth 1969 or 1970. She is 'only 16' in 'Dragonfire', so the relative year is either 1985 or 1986. She can't have left in 1985, because she has a *Challenger* shuttle badge, so she must have come to Svartos no earlier than January 1986. The fact that she doesn't know what Cybermen are in 'Silver Nemesis' suggests she wasn't on Earth when they invaded in December 1986 (see 'The Tenth Planet'). Of course, 'The Tenth Planet' could easily be set in the last days of December, so it would not be impossible for Ace to get a badge for the following year.

Given the date for 'Survival', June 1987, Ace probably left towards the end of 1986, and not early 1987. We need to take into account that she was still at school when she blew up the art room (school terms start in September in England), and that she then worked as a waitress 'day in, day out' for a while before leaving Earth, say late November 1986.

DURATION

⇨ **Day One (Ep1-3)**

The story takes place over several hours on Svartos. In Ep2, Kracauer asks Belazs if she can't sleep, which suggests that it's night.

⇨ **Day Two (Ep3)**

In the final scenes Glitz says 'Good afternoon, shoppers', which suggests it is later the next day.

REMEMBRANCE OF THE DALEKS

STORY LINK

It is from 'Remembrance Of The Daleks' forward that the seventh Doctor begins to display the mysteriousness that becomes a major trait of this incarnation.

At the end of 'Dragonfire' the Doctor promises to take Ace back to Perivale via the more scenic route. However, by 'Remembrance Of The Daleks' it appears that getting Ace home is at the bottom of the Doctor's list of priorities. This suggests that during the gap between 'Dragonfire' and 'Remembrance Of The Daleks' the Doctor has surmised the truth about Ace's biological heritage – that she is a Wolf of Fenric ('I knew she carried the evil inside her' ('The Curse Of Fenric')). We can speculate that it is this discovery that leads the Doctor to redefine his priorities; he has forgotten all about Fenric and no doubt many other misadventures he has had long before he left Gallifrey. Ace's arrival on the scene prompts the recollection of not only Fenric but also of other things that he had intended to do centuries ago. He would later term these 'unfinished business' (see 'Silver Nemesis'). One of the first things he sets about to do is to return the Hand of Omega to Gallifrey, but first he has to prevent the Daleks, who have discovered its existence, from controlling the device …

The Doctor somehow discovers that the Daleks are after the Hand, and so he sets a trap for them. He tells Ace that the Daleks are 'following me'. She doesn't know about them. He doesn't say 'following us'; by his use of 'me' I am sure he is referring just to his current incarnation and not his first, the one who originally left the Hand on Earth, which suggests that the pursuit (and therefore his plan) started before he had met Ace. He is only expecting the Imperial Daleks, not the Renegade faction as well ('the wrong Dalek'). He tells Ace he wants the Imperial Daleks to have the Hand. This suggests that at some point before 'Remembrance Of The Daleks' the Doctor learns that the Daleks are looking for the Hand of Omega and are planning to use its power to become the new Lords of Time (perhaps Davros, having established that this device was used by the Time Lords to create time travel in the first place, and that it had disappeared, has been searching for it for some time). This is something the Doctor has to prevent at all costs. And the only way to achieve this is to let them have the Hand of Omega, but already program it to destroy Skaro. It is likely that he sends a signal to the Daleks giving them information about where and when the Hand is hidden, so they can follow him to Earth. The signal is also intercepted by the Renegade Dalek faction who also head for Earth, which upsets the Doctor's plan.

DALEK LINK

As covered under DALEK HISTORY, this is the Daleks' seventeenth appearance. Since the events of 'Revelation Of The Daleks', Davros has taken over Skaro with his Imperial Daleks, become the new Emperor, and banished the grey Daleks – the renegades – from the planet. The Black Dalek leader on Earth is probably the same Supreme Dalek mentioned in 'Revelation Of The Daleks'. As Emperor, Davros has established a new order on Skaro. He has also made further adjustments to his Daleks, this time fitting his creatures with cyborg attachments so they are now part-creature, part-machine. Their time technology has also progressed, giving them a time corridor that is capable of sending a whole ship back in time. But this is not enough for Davros. He wants now to make the Daleks the new Lords of Time. To do this he needs the Hand Of Omega, a device that he knows exists but not its whereabouts. A mysterious signal is detected, telling him to search in 1963 …

OBSERVATIONS

- The TV announcer declares that it is 'a quarter past five, and Saturday's viewing continues … ', and yet in the context of the episode it is still late morning, as everyone has just had breakfast, and later, they have lunch at the cafe at 3.20 pm. So what is being transmitted on the television? It may be a BBC test signal that has somehow been intercepted by the Dalek ship in orbit and beamed back to Earth, causing some television sets to pick up the transmission. Since most sets would not be switched on at the time in the morning the anomaly would generally remain undetected by the rest of the country.

- The Doctor proclaims that he is 'the Doctor – President-Elect of the High Council of the Time Lords, Keeper of the Legacy of Rassilon, Defender of the Laws of Time and Protector of Gallifrey'. We know from 'The Trial Of A Time Lord' that the sixth Doctor had been deposed as President, so why is the seventh Doctor still making this claim? Of course, 'The Invasion Of Time', the story in which the Doctor is appointed President, is also set in 1963 (see THE DOCTOR'S AGE), so in effect the Doctor is actually telling the truth!

- After it destroys Skaro's sun in 4663, the Hand of Omega returns to 1963 down the Daleks' time corridor. The Doctor says 'the Hand of Omega is now returning to Gallifrey'. The Hand itself is not capable of time travel (it was created before the Gallifreyans had the power of total time travel). Therefore, it returns to Gallifrey in GRT 1963 (presuming that the journey home doesn't take centuries!). If the journey is relatively short, in terms of Gallifreyan history the events of 'The Invasion Of Time' occur in GRT 1963, so the Hand returns some time after that particular adventure.

- It is worth noting that Davros escapes from the exploding Dalek mothership while it is still parked in orbit above 1963 Earth. Unless the escape pod has its own motive power and he leaves Earth's system, Davros is trapped on or near Earth. The evil creator is later rescued by other Dalek forces, and in time he partakes in the Time War, wherein his command ship is damaged during the first year of the War (see 'The Stolen Earth').

THE QUATERMASS CONNECTION

Allison and Rachel mention 'Bernard' and the 'British Rocket Group'. This implies that Britain has an advanced space programme in the early 1960s. This could be the precursor to the Mars Probe set-up in the late 1960s (see 'The Ambassadors Of Death' and A HISTORY OF SPACE-FLIGHT). Both are in-joke references to the four *Quatermass* television serials broadcast in 1953, 1955, 1958 and 1979, which implies that the continuity of those stories now also forms part of the *Doctor Who* canon. The British Rocket Group also makes an appearance in 'The Christmas Invasion', which is set in December 2006. However, as noted under 'Destiny Of The Daleks' and 'Mindwarp', I have elected to ignore 'in-joke' references to other programmes in terms of the *Timelink* analysis.

LANGUAGE

We see Dalek text (see also 'The Dalek Invasion Of Earth') in the shuttle and on their target-sights. The lower-case Greek symbol for Omega seen on the grave-stone (ω) is the same in English and Gallifreyan. The Doctor's calling card has a series of symbols on it, two of which are Theta and Sigma, which is his Academy nick-name ('The Armageddon Factor', 'The Happiness Patrol'). The '?' symbol appears on some of the Doctor's clothes and his umbrella, as well as his tattoo ('Spearhead From Space'), and his signature ('The Invasion Of Time').

TIMELINE DATES

1963, November 15 – (17?) *

Ace gives the year as '1963', and the month appears on the calendars displayed in Harry's Cafe and Ratcliffe's office.

In Ep2 the TV announcer says 'Saturday viewing continues … ', placing the story on a Friday and Saturday. Mike's funeral is presumably held on the Sunday.

There is no mention of American President John F Kennedy's assassination, so we can set the story in the week prior to that event, on Friday 15 November.

4663

The Doctor says the Daleks are 'from another planet in the distant future'. Later, he tells the Renegade Black Dalek that it is 'trapped, a trillion miles and a thousand years from a disintegrated home'. If we take the Doctor's comment completely at face value, then Skaro must be in orbit just beyond Pluto, and the Black Daleks come from 2963. This clearly cannot be correct, so we have to accept that the Doctor is being deliberately vague and evasive as part of his tactic to confuse the Black Dalek (or he is simply generalising the distance and location). In 'The Daleks' Master Plan', set in 4000, Skaro is still a base of operations. The time period the Daleks of 'Remembrance Of The Daleks' come from must be after 4000. 'Revelation of The Daleks' has been set in 4600. Given that the Daleks time travel to 1963, we could use the Century Factor and make the year 4663. This allows Davros 63 years in which to take over Skaro, build his new Imperial Dalek forces, and begin the search for the Hand Of Omega.

10,000,000 BC *

This is the date given in 'The Trial Of A Time Lord' (see also GALLIFREY HISTORY) for the age of the Time Lords, which I understand to be when Omega used the Hand of Omega to detonate a sun.

While it is not explicitly stated that it was the first Doctor who left the Hand on Earth in 1963 (all we know is that the Doctor was 'an old geezer with white hair', which could just as easily be a description of the third Doctor), I think we can generally accept that it was indeed the first, as that was the intention of the writer.

It is not known how the Hand of Omega came to be in the Doctor's possession. The popular fan theory is that he took it when he first left Modern Gallifrey, but there is nothing at all on-screen to support this. The Hand has only one function – to create supernovas – so it is doubtful the Doctor took it with him for that purpose. In fact, circumstances in '100,000 BC' indicate that it was found elsewhere. His arrival in 1963 with Susan (see '100,000 BC') was many years after his departure from Gallifrey, so why did he only decide to bury it then and not before? He's been to Earth many times and visited many different time periods, so why not leave it in one of those locations? There is nothing significantly special or different about 1963 that makes that time period more suitable over any other. And why send the Hand back to Gallifrey if he had stolen it from there in the first place?

The fact that the first Doctor has arranged for a grave marked with the lower-case Greek symbol for Omega at the cemetery ('ω') indicates clearly that he was not overly concerned with keeping the location of the Hand completely hidden; the gravestone being a rather blatant signpost. If burying it were of such vital importance to the Doctor, he wouldn't have just left Earth when Ian and Barbara stumbled on board the TARDIS ('I had to leave suddenly'). No, he would have found some other means to ensure their silence. Of course, his desire to return the two schoolteachers to 1963 could also be for his own benefit, but then we must ask why the Doctor didn't accompany Ian and Barbara back to 1965 in the Dalek time machine in 'The Chase', and then slip back to 1963 to bury the Hand before returning to Mechanus. He doesn't, so burying the Hand can't possibly be the totally urgent matter that we think it is.

Although unsupported, I prefer to think that the Doctor came into possession of the Hand during the 'adventure' immediately prior to his and Susan's arrival on Earth in 1963 (as suggested in MORE THAN A TIME LORD? the Doctor found the abandoned Hand adrift in space in the year 10,000,000 BC, shortly after it was used to detonate Omega's supernova). Although he succeeded in communicating with the device, it was too powerful for him to control, so he decided to hide the Hand because he didn't want to keep it in the TARDIS. The next point of landing was Earth 1963. Alternatively, the Hand might have interfered with the TARDIS' navigational controls, forcing the ship to land on Earth (which is why the Doctor is out looking for a replacement filament in '100,000 BC'). This could explain why the Doctor and Susan stayed for five months in London; in '100,000 BC' the Doctor is anxious about staying 'in one place too long', but he needed to find a suitable hiding place for the Hand.

The Doctor has the opportunity to return to Shoreditch to check the Hand after the events of 'The War Machines', during the four days before he leaves London with Ben and Polly, and of course during his exile on Earth. However, had he done so, he would have found the Hand no longer there. He would have quizzed Reverend Parkinson, who could only tell him that someone calling himself 'the Doctor' came to bury the Hand in 1963. The fact that Parkinson is blind (a very convenient plot-device!) means that he could not describe what 'the Doctor' looked like, so the Doctor is unable to identify who this was. It is not until his seventh incarnation, when he discovers the Daleks' plan to obtain the Hand, that the Doctor realises the truth behind the Hand's 'disappearance', and that he is (will be) the other 'Doctor' that Reverend Parkinson knew.

1963, October (before 15th) *

Reverend Parkinson says the 'grave's been ready for a month', being October. See '100,000 BC'.

1963, October (late)

The Renegade Daleks arrive on Earth using the time controller, and have been there for some time prior to the Doctor's arrival in order to set up the battle computer at Ratcliffe's. The Imperials land their shuttle at the school and set up the transmat in the cellar (presumably killing the caretaker, whose position is being advertised when the Doctor and Ace first call at the school). We can only assume that this was weeks, certainly no more than a month, beforehand, say late October.

It is not clear why one Renegade is at Totter's Lane. Perhaps the Daleks detected the Doctor's TARDIS in the area and one was sent to the junkyard to investigate, only to witness the TARDIS dematerialising (as in '100,000 BC'). It stayed on guard in the yard on the chance that the Doctor will return (which he does do, the following month).

1963, November *

The Doctor knows that Harry's wife gives birth to twins. This knowledge is either from an earlier visit to this time period, or the Doctor simply returned to Shoreditch and looked Harry up during his later visit to London in 1966 in 'The War Machines', or during his period of exile, 1969 to 1971.

DURATION

⇨ Day One (Friday 15 November)

The story opens near the end of the school day (the Doctor greets the Headmaster with 'Good afternoon'). Ace spends the night at Mike's while the Doctor returns to the cafe (the sign in the cafe window shows the opening times as '7-10', so presumably this means 10.00 pm). The last night scene is of a Dalek materialising on the transmat in the school cellar.

⇨ **Day Two (Saturday 16 November)**
In the very next scene it is morning; the Doctor goes to the funeral home ('Good morning'). A late 'lunch' is had at the Cafe at 3.20 pm (as seen on the clock). The final battle occurs later that same day.

⇨ **Day Three? (Sunday 17 November?)**
The Doctor and Ace stay for Mike's funeral. This is either the next day – a Sunday – or it could in fact be later in the week.

THE HAPPINESS PATROL

STORY LINK

The Doctor tells Ace he has 'been hearing disturbing rumours about Terra Alpha, so I decided to look in some time … Rumours of something evil, and we're going to get to the bottom of it'. This information could have come to hand at any time prior to 'The Happiness Patrol', not necessarily after 'Remembrance Of The Daleks'. It is not clear how he comes to 'hear' these rumours; presumably on one of the planets he has recently visited in this time zone.

Just prior to landing, the Doctor tells Ace about his encounters with dinosaurs (specifically from 'Invasion Of The Dinosaurs').

LANGUAGE

The Pipe People speak English, or at least pick up Ace's slang – 'Gordon Bennett!'

TIMELINE DATES

2788 •
The Doctor tells Ace that Terra Alpha is 'an Earth colony, settled some centuries in your future' (she is from 1986, see 'Dragonfire'). The name Terra Alpha suggests that it is one of the first colonies established after warp drive is discovered, around 2106 (see 'Nightmare Of Eden'). The Doctor says he hasn't 'met a Stigorax since I was in Birmingham in the twenty-fifth century'. On the assumption that Stigoraxes came to Earth and its colonies in that time period, then 'The Happiness Patrol' would be set

after the twenty-fifth century.

There is no indication as to the age of the colony on Terra Alpha. It is overcrowded; hence Helen A's drastic measures for population control. Galactic Centre is undertaking six-monthly census readings, which suggests this is a time when humanity has spread out into most of the galaxy, if not all of it, and there is fear of vast overcrowding throughout the systems. According to Trevor Sigma Earth is a 'miserable sort of place', which seems to tie in with the description of Earth in 'The Mutants' (set in 2971). Using the Century Factor, 'The Happiness Patrol' could be set in 2988. Of course, there is no indication that Earth's Empire is in decline at this stage, which suggests a date prior to the thirtieth century. Half way between the two suggested dates is 2738. Using the Century Factor, I have selected 2788 as the date for 'The Happiness Patrol'.

Trevor was last on Terra Alpha 'six months ago', after which Helen A initiated her extreme culling programme. Six months later she has overseen the deaths of some 500,000 people.

1677

The Doctor mentions this date. He has probably read Dr John Wallis's paper on sympathetic vibrations. Wallis lived 23 November 1616 to 28 October 1703. The Royal Society was founded in 1662.

2110

As covered above, Terra Alpha is probably colonised soon after warp drive was developed.

2450 •

The Doctor says he was in Birmingham 'in the twenty-fifth century'. This is an arbitrary date.

2787 •

As noted in Story Link, the Doctor has to have been in this time period before in order to have picked up the rumours about Terra Alpha; rumours that spread in the previous six months, following Trevor Sigma's census. Although 'The Happiness Patrol' is set in 2788, it makes sense that the previous visit was in the preceding year.

DURATION

⇨ **Day One (Ep1-3)**
It is early evening when the Doctor and Ace arrive. The story takes place over one

'night'; it is still dark at the end of the adventure ('It's been a long night').

SILVER NEMESIS

STORY LINK

The Doctor has made a new cassette deck for Ace since 'Remembrance Of The Daleks'. There is no indication that 'Silver Nemesis' follows directly from 'The Happiness Patrol'. Ace is wearing Flower Child's earring on her jacket, which she does not actually obtain until the next adventure, 'The Greatest Show In The Galaxy'. [This 'error' occurred because the original story order for Season Twenty-Five was 'Remembrance Of The Daleks', 'The Greatest Show In The Galaxy', 'The Happiness Patrol', 'Silver Nemesis'. On the basis that Ace does have the earring, we could consider that the televised order of the stories does not matter, and that the intended continuity of the stories should be taken into precedence. I have elected however to retain broadcast story order.]

CYBERMAN LINK

As covered under CYBERMAN HISTORY, this is the Cybermen's third appearance on Earth. The surviving Cybermen from 'The Invasion', now based on Planet 14, observe the destruction of Mondas in 1986 ('The Tenth Planet'). Two years later they detect the return of Nemesis (which they had previously encountered way back in 1638), and realise its potential as the tool with which to make Earth 'the new Mondas'. Certain of success, the entire Cyber-fleet is sent to Earth. A squad is sent to the landing site in Windsor to prepare for the statue's retrieval ...

OBSERVATIONS

- The Doctor and Ace travel to Lady Peinforte's house three times during the story [four times in the extended video], each time being after the previous visit. It is the same day that Lady Peinforte and Richard leave, because the candles and the fire are still burning when the Doctor and Ace arrive. If the Doctor had miscalculated the coordinates, it could have proved disastrous had he arrived at a time when he was already there – meaning he would meet himself. [In the extended video, when the Doctor and Ace go to Lady Peinforte's house for the second time, they note that the mathematician's body has disappeared and that 'somebody has moved the chess pieces']. On the second visit in the TV version [the third in the video] the body is still missing.

The Doctor again studies the chessboard, and moves several pieces. It is at that point that he realises Fenric's involvement in recent events (as he reveals in 'The Curse Of Fenric'). This could mean that Lady Peinforte is one of the Wolves of Fenric, and it would appear that she has been attempting to solve the chess puzzle set for Fenric by the Doctor centuries before. The Doctor moves some of the pieces on the board probably to ensure the solution to his puzzle is not discovered. All this suggests that it is a time storm generated by Fenric that enables Peinforte and Richard to travel to 1988, which Peinforte believes was black magic. During this visit to 1638 Ace takes the bag of gold. She is also seen to be holding the parchment with the mathematician's calculations. She is still holding this when she moves away from the desk, so presumably she takes the paper into the TARDIS with her. Given that this is supposedly the same document as seen on Karl's desk in the opening scenes, how does it come into de Flores' possession?

- Richard, stuck in 1988, wonders 'How shall I live now? Stranded. A stranger in this time', to which the Doctor replies, 'I know how you feel'. This could be a reference to the Doctor's exile.
- On 23 March 1989 in our history, an asteroid 800 metres in diameter passed some 800,000 kilometres from Earth.

LANGUAGE

When he meets the Cybermen, de Flores speaks English with them, not German. They understand him.

NEMESIS IS LAUNCHED

'Silver Nemesis' is the sequel to an untelevised adventure set in 1638. From Lady Peinforte's perspective, only a month or so has passed since she lost the statue (see Timeline Dates). For the Doctor, hundreds of years have passed – when his alarm goes off, the Doctor says he 'probably arranged it centuries ago'; he is speaking from his own personal relative time. At first he forgets what he set his alarm for ('obviously the arrangements were made in rather a hurry'), but he soon recalls what is about to happen after he goes to the TARDIS to check his instruments. The watch had been set to go off at a pre-arranged time so the Doctor could 'change course for another destination', but the Doctor confesses that he had 'forgotten' what it was for. The fact that the Doctor intended to 'change course' when the alarm went off clearly indicates that he had a working TARDIS at the time. The seventh Doctor is now at least 953 years old (as stated in 'Time And The Rani'), so it all happened centuries ago in an earlier incarnation.

Before she has even seen the seventh Doctor Lady Peinforte refers to the Doctor as 'that predictable little man … the nameless Doctor whose power is so secret'. The reference to 'little man' would appear to rule out the third, fourth, fifth and sixth Doctors who were all relatively tall. Therefore it would appear to be either the first or the second Doctor who first encountered Lady Peinforte. However, given that the Doctor's frequent references to 350 years seem to be relative not only to Earth and Nemesis but also to himself, it appears that all this happened when the Doctor was around 603 years old. According to THE DOCTOR'S AGE chart, this would be during the 196-year gap between 'The Monster Of Peladon' and 'The Five Doctors' / 'Planet Of The Spiders', which is the third Doctor's era. This does not conform to Lady Peinforte's description of the Doctor being a 'little man'. In that case, I would suggest that when Peinforte refers to the Doctor being 'little' it is not a slight on his height but on his insignificance. It is clear that she knows a lot about the Time Lords, so it is therefore not unlikely that she is familiar with the concept of regeneration, which would explain her unquestioned acceptance of the seventh Doctor as being the same man she had encountered months earlier.

The whole Nemesis matter hinges around the Doctor's watch alarm going off at the pre-set time in 1988. Given that the previous Doctors are never seen to wear the pocket watch, it is easy to see how the Doctor could forget. It does, however, seem rather coincidental that the Doctor just happens to be wearing his watch and be on Earth on the very day of – and only hours away from – Nemesis's return to Earth. But perhaps it wasn't a coincidence at all? Perhaps the TARDIS itself was responsible and deliberately landed on Earth on 23 November 1988 because it 'knew' that the Doctor had forgotten.

The following is a theoretical backstory to the sequence of events leading up to the statue's return to Earth in 1988:

Validium is sentient, and it knows the secret of the Time of Chaos (whatever that may be – see MORE THAN A TIME LORD?). Given that the validium knows all about the event, this is probably the last thing it is involved in before it departs from Gallifrey.

How it leaves Gallifrey is not known. When Ace asks 'who brought validium to Earth in the first place?' the Doctor ignores her but he has a knowing expression on his face, which suggests that he was the one responsible. The fact that the statue knows the Doctor's secret indicates that he and the validium have 'met' before (probably even several times before). But if the Doctor wasn't directly responsible, we can assume that he does know who was, or how it happened.

The validium therefore must have left Gallifrey after the Time of Chaos, and it either travelled for millions of years before crashing on Earth in 1638, or it was released into space in a later time period relatively close to the 1638 time zone. The Doctor left Gallifrey in GRT 1610, so it is even possible that there is a closer connection between the two events and dates, given that there is only a 28-year difference.

Given the spatial distance between Gallifrey and Earth, I assume that it still takes the validium fragment some time to reach Earth. The fact that Lady Peinforte uses the silver arrow to time travel to 1988 also suggests that validium possesses the ability to time-travel (which is boosted by Fenric for Lady Peinforte's own time journey), so its journey might have been reduced by temporal displacement.

During its flight through space from Gallifrey to Earth, the validium causes chaos on many planets as it flies past ('the Nemesis generates destruction that affects everything around it'). One of the planets it passes is Mondas, which is currently on its way back to its own solar system. The Cybermen launch a ship to follow it, seeing it as a potential weapon that they could use.

The lump of validium falls to Earth in 1638, where Lady Peinforte fashions it into a statue of herself. The third Doctor, travelling alone in the TARDIS, lands in 1638, and discovers the validium (which, depending if he was responsible or not, he presumably thought was still adrift in space). Knowing what it knows, the Doctor has to get rid of it. When the Doctor appears, the statue tells Lady Peinforte who the Doctor is, that he is a Time Lord, as well as other secrets. The Cybermen arrive. They observe the subsequent altercations between the Doctor and Lady Peinforte (which is why the Cybermen in 1988 know who the Doctor is, who Lady Peinforte is and of what validium is capable).

Realising the threat the statue poses to Earth, the Doctor breaks the statue into three parts 'to try and stop Lady Peinforte ... or anyone else ... from ever putting the three bits together', and places the main body into a rocket-sled that he has specially built. His plan is to launch 'the largest piece into space', in order to 'draw the Cybermen so [he] could wipe them out'. The Doctor tells the statue to 'reform' after the fleet is destroyed. The statue asks him if he will need it in the future. The Doctor replies 'I hope not'. The Doctor then tells the statue it won't have its freedom until he says so – things are still imperfect.

The Doctor is rushed with his calculations because Lady Peinforte and a regiment of Roundheads are approaching. He unknowingly mis-programs the rocket-sled, and after it is launched it misses the Cybermen and flies into deep space. The Cybermen are denied their prize and return to Mondas. Later, realising that he 'got [his] sums wrong', the Doctor calculates that Nemesis will pass Earth again every 25 years, until it crashes again in 1988. The Doctor leaves the bow in the care of King Charles I, giving the King precise instructions not to let it out of Windsor Castle. The Doctor then leaves 1638.

Lady Peinforte arranges for a mathematician to calculate and plot the return of Nemesis, and less than a month later, with the assistance of black magic (provided by Fenric?), and the silver arrow, she and Richard time-travel to 1988 …

Meanwhile, the Doctor attempts to time-jump ahead to Windsor in 1988, but three temporal barriers prevent the TARDIS from landing there. Firstly, the ship detects the presence of a TARDIS from a future GRT in the vicinity. The signature of this TARDIS is very familiar, so the Doctor concludes that his future self is already there. Secondly, given that the validium is a Gallifreyan life-form, the TARDIS fail-safe would not allow the Doctor to cross the validium's GRT – there is now a 350-year time differential between them. The third factor is the Blinovitch Limitation Effect.

To prevent a potential temporal short-circuit, should he land in 1988, the third Doctor resumes his travels, safe in the knowledge that he will indeed encounter Nemesis again. But just to be sure, he sets his watch alarm to go off in 350 years' time relative, to remind himself to complete his 'unfinished business' …

The third Doctor eventually returns to UNIT HQ in 1975 (as noted before, the adventure in 1638 occurs during the 'missing' period between 'The Monster Of Peladon' and 'The Five Doctors' / 'Planet Of The Spiders'). The Doctor realises that it will be 1988 in 13 years relative to Earth time, but he is uncertain what will happen should he travel to Windsor and try to meet with the statue at that time. The Doctor never finds out the answer, because shortly after his return to 1975, he regenerates. Probably as a side-effect of the regeneration, the Doctor forgets about Nemesis (as well as his study into ESP, as seen in 'Planet Of The Spiders'), and takes off in the TARDIS again. During the next three centuries the Doctor regenerates three more times and never regains the memory of the statue's return ('I've been busy'). He also stops wearing the pocket-watch. It is not the one broken by Peri in 'Revelation Of The Daleks'. He has a new one in 'The Mysterious Planet', but the chain is not the same, so that could be a different one again. He starts wearing the silver watch in 'Paradise Towers'. As programmed, the watch goes off, now 350 years later. At first the Doctor can't remember why ('Well, I probably arranged it centuries ago'), but he eventually rediscovers that the alarm was to remind him to change course for Earth in 1988, and the events as seen in 'Silver Nemesis' take place.

The fact that Mondas is destroyed two years previously, in 1986 (in 'The Tenth Planet'), makes the Cybermen more determined to obtain the validium, so they can turn Earth 'into our base planet. The new Mondas'. The seventh Doctor realises he has to complete his original 'unfinished business' of destroying the Cyber-fleet as he had originally intended back in 1638. If he does not succeed, this time the Cybermen will use the validium to destroy Earth …

TIMELINE DATES

1988, November 22 - 23 *

The date '22nd November 1988' appears as a caption on-screen for the first day. The main story takes place the next day, the 23rd, a date that is also mentioned by the mathematician and by Karl.

1638, November 12 *
1638, December *

It is not a matter of simply setting the date that the Doctor launched Nemesis into space as 23 November 1638, the year given on-screen, because there are several date anomalies in the structure of the story that need to be considered.

The Doctor says that he has known that the statue would return to Earth 'since November the 23rd 1638', and that by 1988 the statue has 'been in orbit for exactly 350 years'. The mathematician has calculated correctly that 'the comet Nemesis will circle the heavens once every 25 years … its trajectory, however, is decaying … it will circle ever closer until finally it once again strikes the Earth at the point from which it originally departed. In the meadow outside … on the 23rd day of November in the year of our Lord nineteen hundred and eighty eight'. This means that the statue has travelled in a very precise orbit to land in the same field where it left and on the very same date 350 years later (of course, Earth is no longer in the same spatial position). However, the statue should have landed on 3 December 1988: in the seventeenth century the Julian calendar was still in use in Britain. In 1582 Pope Gregory XIII revised the Julian calendar by 'shortening' the year by eleven days to put the seasons back into sync (the calendar went from 3 October, 4 October, 15 October, 16 October, and so on). This new calendar wasn't adopted by England until 14 September 1752, some 114 years after Lady Peinforte's time, with the eleven-day discrepancy adjusted in September (the calendar for that year went 2 September, 3 September, 14 September, 15 September, etc). However, since Lady Peinforte has knowledge of 'rudimentary time travel' (and may have been guided to 1988 by Fenric, see Observations), she may have been aware of the change in calendar and advised the old man to adjust his calculations accordingly. [In the extended video, there is an extra scene in which the Doctor removes a page of notes from the desk and burns it in the fire, saying the mathematician 'needed a little help to get started'. This suggests that the Doctor himself assisted the mathematician to obtain the correct date.] It is possible that Fenric may have enabled Peinforte and Richard to bypass the incorrect date. But even if this was the case, or the mathematician was able to adjust his calculations to the new calendar, this would only have assisted Lady Peinforte and Richard in travelling to the correct date; how did the statue know the dates had changed? Its 350-year orbit from 23 November 1638 would still have landed it on 3 December 1988. One answer is to bring the date of the launch forward; the Doctor launched the statue not on 23 November 1638, but on 12 November. With the change in calendar, the Nemesis still lands on 23 November 1988, but as far as it is concerned the date is 12 November 1988. It is this version of the dates that I have selected.

A further problem that extends from the date of the launch, regardless of whether it was the 12th or the 23rd, is the amount of time that has elapsed between when the Doctor first launched the statue and when Lady Peinforte and Richard travel to 1988. When landing in Lady Peinforte's study in 1638 for the first time, the Doctor tells Ace that 'in the matter of months since I was last here, [the mathematician] has calculated the exact time and date' of Nemesis's return. This means that the mathematician started his calculations soon after Nemesis was launched in November 1638, but the Doctor's reference to this being 'months' ago should set the date that Lady Peinforte travelled to 1988 as being in early 1639. This would be acceptable if it wasn't for the fact that the caption setting the date for the first Peinforte scenes reads '1638', and that the Doctor gives the year as 1638 on several occasions. In this case, we would have to accept that the Doctor was only generalising when he says 'months'. To make sense of the 1638 date, I have set the Lady Peinforte scenes as being only a month after Nemesis was launched, say late in December. (See the Nemesis Is Launched section.)

Before 10,000,000 BC

Validium was created 'as the ultimate defence for Gallifrey back in early times ... by Omega ... and Rassilon ... ' for 'one purpose – destruction'. As covered under GALLIFREY HISTORY, Omega died about 10,000,000 BC, which was before the Time Lords came into being, so the time that validium was created must have been several years prior to that. I have not stated a precise date, other than that it was 'before' 10 million BC. It does seem odd that a material of which the only purpose was for 'destruction' was used for the defence of a planet.

After 10,000,000 BC

As covered under GALLIFREY HISTORY, the Old Time was less than 10,000,000 years ago, after the period that the Time Lords were created. If the Doctor has visited 'the Time of Chaos', he could have been the one who launched the validium fragment from Gallifrey in the first place – possibly because it had discovered who he was, and he needed to protect his identity.

1070 ▪ ▪ ▪ ▪ ▪ ▪ ▪ ▪ ▪ ▪ ▪ ▪ ▪ ▪

The Doctor says the last time he was in Windsor 'they were building the place'. In our history the castle was built in 1070 by William the Conqueror shortly after his victory at Hastings (see also 'The Time Meddler'). As seen in 'The Time Meddler', the Doctor only knew a little of the history of the time period, so his other visit to Windsor during the castle's construction must have been after his adventure in 'The Time Meddler'.

1509 ▪ ▪ ▪ ▪ ▪ ▪ ▪ ▪ ▪ ▪ ▪ ▪ ▪ ▪

The castle guide says the 'gargoyles have been there for about 500 years. They were built in 1509 originally. And the castle was already 400 years then … '

1606
1657, November 2 ▪ ▪ ▪ ▪ ▪ ▪ ▪ ▪ ▪ ▪ ▪

Richard's tombstone reads 'Here Lyeth the Body of RICHARD MAYNARDE departed this Life ye 2ND November 1657 in the 51st yeare of his Age. "He saw worlds end and begin"'. He was therefore born in 1606. He is 32 in 'Silver Nemesis'.

1621 ▪ ▪ ▪ ▪ ▪ ▪ ▪ ▪ ▪ ▪ ▪ ▪ ▪ ▪

Mrs Remington and Lady Peinforte discuss the year of Dorothea's death.

1663, November
1688, November
1713, November
1738, November
1763, November
1788, November
1813, November
1838, November
1863, November
1888, November ▪ ▪ ▪ ▪ ▪ ▪ ▪ ▪ ▪ ▪ ▪ ▪

Nemesis passes Earth in November 'every 25 years'. The bow 'mysteriously disappeared in 1788'.

It is not revealed how the mathematician's calculations and the bow came to be in de Flores' possession. When Ace asks if the same person who stole the bow also stole the calculations, the Doctor ignores her, which suggests that the Doctor was responsible. With 'exactly 350 years' between 1638 and 1988, the asteroid must pass Earth in this regular cycle. We might assume that Nemesis was responsible for triggering several wars during these periods. Known conflicts include: 1663 – The Austro-Turkish War; 1688 – the Glorious Revolution; 1713 – War of the Spanish Succession; 1788 – The Swedish-Russian War; 1838 – The Durban Massacre; 1863 – The Japanese Civil War; 1888 – The Arab uprising in East Africa. I have not included any of these events in the TIMELINE.

1913, November
1938, March 12
Both years and events, the eve of the First World War and the annexation of Austria by Nazi Germany, are discussed by the Doctor and Ace. March 12 is the date this occurred in our history, which is some eight months outside Nemesis's orbit.

1938
De Flores says that their leader had predicted the coming of silver giants (the Cybermen). [In the extended video, de Flores says it was '50 years ago' that he stood with the Führer on their first steps to power, which is 1938.] Hitler became Chancellor of Germany in 1933, so I have elected to use the date from the video.

1963, November 22
The date in our history on which John F Kennedy was assassinated. The Doctor only mentions the event as happening in '1963', but with Nemesis passing Earth in November every 25 years, this date is suitable. See also 'Remembrance Of The Daleks'. The ninth Doctor was in Dallas on that day (see Rose).

1988, November 20
The Doctor says the electricity has been 'drained over the last few days', so the Cybermen first arrived around the 20th.

DURATION

⇨ Day One (1638)
It is day when Lady Peinforte and Richard leave 1638. The Doctor and Ace arrive later that same day (the candles are still burning). They later return for a second time.

⇨ Day Two (1638)
Richard is returned to his time. The Doctor and Ace stay a while.

⇨ Day One (22 November 1988)
The Germans prepare to leave for England on this day.

⇨ **Day Two (23 November 1988)**
The Doctor and Ace listen to the jazz that 'afternoon'. The rest of the story takes place this day.

THE GREATEST SHOW IN THE GALAXY

STORY LINK

There is no reason to assume that 'The Greatest Show In The Galaxy' follows immediately on from 'Silver Nemesis'. Ace is searching for her rucksack at the beginning of the story; and yet it was blown up with the Cyber-ship in the previous story. The Doctor has been teaching himself how to juggle. Ace has found an old scarf of the Doctor's plus Mel's blue top from 'Paradise Towers'.

OBSERVATIONS

- The Doctor says he has 'fought the Gods Of Ragnarok all through time', and yet this is the first he has ever mentioned them. Perhaps he is speaking metaphorically? It would appear that the Gods' dark circus is capable of travelling through space (and time as well?), because the Doctor finds a piece of broken blade from a sword belonging to a (Roman?) gladiator who fought and died in their circus ring.

LANGUAGE

There are many different cultures present on Segonax, all of whom communicate with one another without difficulty, which suggests they all originated from the same planet. Even Mags and Cook communicate; the Whizzkid and the Stallslady; Nord and Cook, and so on. The Gods of Ragnarok must therefore also speak English. The Ringmaster's rap rhymes in English, and he even has an American accent. The advertisement satellite speaks in English. All the signs and posters at the landing port, fruit stall, circus and bus are in English.

TIMELINE DATES

3000 +

Although there is no on-screen evidence either way, we can date 'The Greatest Show In The Galaxy' if we accept that the Psychic Circus, the Whizzkid, and Captain Cook are Earthlings. The bus, hearse, and Bellboy's clothes all seem to point that way. And if we take into account the notes under Language, I think it is safe to assume that, given the space satellite, transmat landing port, Morgana's Tarot cards and the robot clowns, 'The Greatest Show In The Galaxy' is set in a future Earth period.

Of significance, Captain Cook is 'the eminent intergalactic explorer', and the circus is 'an intergalactic success', which would place the story at a time after intergalactic space travel has been discovered by humans, around 2980 (see 'Terror Of The Vervoids'). Cook is probably one of the first explorers to another galaxy, hence his widely-known reputation. He was famous during the Whizzkid's lifetime, which would be about 18 years. All the planets visited by the Circus as seen on the posters would therefore be Earth colonies.

There is no indication as to how long the Circus has been on Segonax. The Whizzkid says he 'had a long correspondence with one of the founder members, too, soon after it started'. Again using the Whizzkid's age as a guide, and given the ages of the members, the Circus would therefore be about 10-15 years old. When he sees the bus, the Doctor thinks it was left there 'perhaps millennia ago', however given the subsequent course of events, he is clearly mistaken.

On the basis that both the Circus and Cook would have begun their exploits between 15 and 20 years previously, and both would have begun fairly soon after the development of intergalactic flight, I would set 'The Greatest Show In The Galaxy' 20 years after 2980, in the year 3000.

2980

Cook must have begun his exploration of other galaxies soon after intergalactic flight was developed, which was around 2980 (see 'Terror Of The Vervoids').

2990

The Psychic Circus began during the Whizzkid's lifetime, which is probably about 10 years ago.

DURATION

(TARDIS) (Ep1)

The Doctor and Ace travel in the TARDIS for some time before arriving on Segonax.

⇨ Day One (Ep1-4)

It is a 'good afternoon' when the Doctor and Ace arrive on Segonax. They stay on the planet for several hours.

BATTLEFIELD

STORY LINK

There is no indication that 'Battlefield' follows directly on from 'The Greatest Show In The Galaxy'. The Doctor says he and Ace have come 'quite a distance, as it happens' to Earth. Indeed, Segonax is in another region of the galaxy.

OBSERVATIONS

- When cradling the apparently deceased Brigadier, the Doctor cries that the man is 'supposed to die in bed'. Is this just the Doctor wishing for a better death for his friend, or does he really know the Brigadier's final fate? (Sir Alistair has been knighted, and is still alive in 2009 ('The Sontaran Stratagem').)
- The battle between Morgaine and Arthur's forces was witnessed by the peoples of England at the time. The mythology of the characters entered into the legends and became 'real'. In our history, legend has it that Arthur will one day return to help the people of Britain.
- The knights know of the Doctor as Merlin. The seventh Doctor has never met these people before, but the evidence of the Doctor's letter to himself, the spaceship, and the runes all indicate that the Doctor will meet them in what he says is 'my personal future'. With this knowledge, the Doctor knows he will not die in this present incarnation. Ancelyn knows that Merlin has a 'ship of time ... being larger within than without' (the TARDIS), and that he can change his appearance, which implies that he has seen this happen or has heard of it happening second-hand. Therefore, at least two or three successive future incarnations of the Doctor become involved with Morgaine and Arthur. According to Mordred, Morgaine sealed Merlin in 'the ice caves for all eternity'. It is not clear if these ice caves are on Earth or in the knights' sideways dimension. We can only assume that the future Doctor eventually escapes from the caves if the Doctor is to become the Valeyard (see 'The Trial Of Time Lord'). More of this future Doctor is explored in UNSEEN FUTURE ADVENTURES at the end of this DOCTOR WHO STORYFILE section.

LANGUAGE

Mordred reads the words on the tombstone at the church, and Morgaine reads the commands on the missile launch control computer, so they can read and speak English. The Doctor's message to himself, 'Dig Hole Here', is written in his own handwriting, but in a series of symbols.

OBSERVATIONS

- How did the Brigadier know about gold plated bullets 'for you-know-who'? Presumably this vital information came from Harry Sullivan who, after his return to Earth, would have fully briefed UNIT on his recent encounter with the Cybermen (in 'Revenge Of The Cybermen').

TIMELINE DATES

1992, May +

The trees in the Lethbridge-Stewarts' garden are in full blossom, and the plant shop contains spring foliage, so the month of recording, May [of 1989], has been selected. The Doctor tells Ace it is 'a few years in your future'. Ace comes from 1986 originally (see 'Dragonfire'), so the early 1990s would seem likely. [The novelisation and other sources have suggested the year is 1999, but there is no evidence on-screen to support this.] The Brigadier has retired from teaching, so it is now some time since 'Mawdryn Undead' and 'The Five Doctors'. [Nicholas Courtney was born in 1931, which if applied to Lethbridge-Stewart makes him aged 61.]

Of course, since the story was made the real-time political climate of Earth has changed: the Cold War ended in 1990, the Union of the Soviet Socialist Republic ceased to exist on 25 December 1991, and Czechoslovakia was no longer a communist country by late 1989, so the Czech members of UNIT as seen in 'Battlefield' would not be wearing red stars.

The best dating tool comes from Sergeant Zbrigniev. He says, 'When I served under Lethbridge-Stewart we had a scientific adviser called the Doctor ... He changed his appearance several times ... The word was he changed his whole physical appearance'. This suggests that Zbrigniev was with UNIT when the Doctor acted as scientific adviser (from 1970, see 'Spearhead From Space'), and was serving when the third Doctor regenerated in 1975 ('Planet Of The Spiders', 'Robot'). The fact that he knows the Doctor changed his appearance 'several times' suggests that he was there at the time of the second Doctor's involvement during the Cybermen invasion, which was also 1970 (see 'The Invasion'). Zbrigniev does not appear to be much older than 40, so if 'Battlefield' is set in the late 1990s, say 1999, he would have been 11 in 1970 and 16 in 1975! I prefer to set 'Battlefield' no later than 1992, which gives Zbrigniev the more likely age of 18 in 1970, and 23 in 1975.

Alternatively, if we work on the basis that Zbrigniev joined UNIT in the mid-1970s, and only ever knew of the third and fourth Doctor (he could have learned of the second Doctor's appearance from files pertaining to the Cyberman invasion in 1970), then we can age him at 19 in 1975. This would now make the date for 'Battlefield' to be 1995 or 1996.

However, setting 'Battlefield' in a year after 1995 does not conform with the Doctor's comment that it is 'a few years' in Ace's future; if it were 1996, wouldn't he have been more specific and said 'ten years in your future'? 1992 is the best year to set 'Battlefield'.

792

Mordred says Morgaine 'has waited twelve centuries' to face Merlin again. The Doctor says that the concrete tunnel to the spaceship 'was built in the eighth century', and that Arthur 'died over a thousand years ago', which places the time of the battle as being no later than AD 792. Peter Walmsey dates the scabbard as 'eighth century AD', but the Doctor says 'it's been waiting around longer than that', which is nonsensical given the references to 792 above. One assumption we get from this comment is that the sword is indeed much older – and was originally the Doctor's; he brought it with him in the TARDIS when he first arrived in the 'sideways' Universe dimension; which would have been a number of earlier than 792.

1684

The mantelpiece at the Gore Crow Hotel has '1684' carved on it, presumably the date the hotel was built.

1982

Peter Walmsey says he has been working on the dig 'about ten years so far', progressing only one centimetre a year.

1988

The Brigadier knew Doris back in 1964 (see 'Planet Of The Spiders'). He doesn't appear to be married in 'Mawdryn Undead', so he must have married Doris at some point after 'Mawdryn Undead', say in 1988? (The Brigadier apparently appears briefly in 'Silver Nemesis' as one of the tourists at Windsor Castle; perhaps he and Doris are on their honeymoon?)

1985, November 26

Ace has an *Atlantis* shuttle badge on her jacket. This is the date of the launch in our history.

DURATION

(TARDIS) (Ep1)
The Doctor and Ace are in the TARDIS for some time before landing on Earth ...

⇨ **Day One (Ep1-2)**
Lethbridge-Stewart is recalled by UNIT that afternoon, and arrives in London that night. The Doctor and Ace spend the night at the Gore Crow. Morgaine arrives that night.

⇨ **Day Two (Ep.2-4)**
The Brigadier leaves London at 'sunrise'. The final battle takes place that day.

⇨ **Day Three? (Ep4)**
It appears to be a day later than Day Two. It is a weekday; the girls leave to go shopping, promising to be back in time for 'supper'.

GHOST LIGHT

STORY LINK

There is nothing to indicate that 'Ghost Light' follows directly from 'Battlefield'. At the end of 'Battlefield', the Doctor agrees to cook supper. We can assume that he and Ace stay with the Lethbridge-Stewarts for a while before setting off in the TARDIS again. Ace has told the Doctor of her 'thing about haunted houses', so he takes her to the only one that she knew. The Doctor has made a new key for the TARDIS.

OBSERVATIONS

- Control notes of the Doctor: 'Something tells me you are not in our catalogue. Nor will you ever be'. Even the Doctor appears to refer to his 'powers' when he says 'Even I can't play this many games at once'.

LANGUAGE

It would appear that even Light speaks English. The mathematical symbols consist of familiar Earth symbols.

TIMELINE DATES

1883 (pre-August) ↟

Mackenzie first came to Gabriel Chase 'in 1881', which 'was two years ago'. Ace reveals that she burned down Gabriel Chase 'in 1983', which the Doctor confirms will be 'in a hundred years' time', which gives us 1883.

Gwendoline talks of sending people 'to Java'. If the story was set after August 1883, then perhaps those people she says that to (who don't necessarily cotton on to what she really means) would comment about the fact that Krakatoa had erupted and that passage by ship to the island would be impossible. Since there's no mention of the eruption, then 'Ghost Light' is best set before the eruption.

140,000,000 BC

On coming to Earth Light says he 'once spent centuries faithfully cataloguing all the species there. Every organism from the smallest bacteria to the largest ichthyosaur'. Ichthyosaurs lived during the Jurassic period, some 140 million years ago, and died out 65 million years ago (see 'Earthshock'). Light later wonders 'how many more millennia' must he suffer Control's company, which implies the survey went on for quite some considerable time. He is concerned about 'centuries of work wasted'.

98,000 BC (winter) ↟

Light takes Nimrod as the 'last specimen of the extinct Neanderthal species'. In our own history, the Neanderthal is believed to have become extinct around 35,000 years ago. However, in 'The Dæmons', the Doctor says the Neanderthal died out 100,000 years ago, thanks to the Dæmons.

Nimrod remembers first seeing Light when 'at the season when the ice floods swamped the pasture lands, we herded the mammoths sunwards to find new grazing'. This suggests that is was at the approach of winter.

The Doctor produces from his pocket a fang of the cave bear, so the Doctor has clearly been to Nimrod's time zone before.

1871, November 10

The date in our history on which Stanley found Livingstone.

1881

The Doctor tells Ace that Mackenzie 'was sent here in 1881 to investigate the disappearance of Sir George Pritchard'. There is no indication as to when Survey evolved into Smith, but it is most likely to be the same year. And while it is not directly stated on-screen, this is also probably when Light's ship 'landed' under Gabriel Chase – i.e. the Chase was not built on top of the already buried spaceship. Redvers Fenn-Cooper says 'we're two weeks out from Zanzibar', which may be an indication of how long he has been in the house.

1912, April 13
The Doctor tells Ace that the name for the Royal Flying Corps 'wasn't thought up until 1912'. In our own history the RFC was named on 13 April 1912.

1970
1983
Ace says she burned down Gabriel Chase 'in 1983' when she was '13', which means her year of birth was either 1969 or 1970. I have chosen 1970 (see also 'Dragonfire' and 'The Curse Of Fenric').

DURATION

⇨ **Day One (Ep1-2)**
The grandfather clock reads '5.50 pm' when the story starts. It is 5.55 pm when the TARDIS lands.

⇨ **Day Two (Ep2-3)**
When Ace escapes from the stone spaceship the clock reads 4.35. Mrs Pritchard says 'It's almost first light' so it is now the next day. Ace does not wake until it is 'all of five o'clock'. The Doctor moves the clock forward from 5.45 pm and stops it at 6.00 pm in Ep2. He restarts the clock again at the end of Ep3. Several hours have elapsed in the interim.

THE CURSE OF FENRIC

STORY LINK
There is nothing to suggest that 'The Curse Of Fenric' immediately follows 'Ghost Light', although Ace does confide in Kathleen Dudman that she doesn't like dark buildings: 'There was one in Perivale. Old empty house. Full of noises. Evil. Things I didn't understand. Undercurrents.' This appears to be a reference to at least one of Ace's visits to Gabriel Chase – in 1883 or 1983.

OBSERVATIONS

- Fenric explains that he engineered the time storm that takes Ace to Svartos (see 'Dragonfire'), and that he was responsible for moving the chess pieces in Lady Peinforte's study. This suggests that Lady Peinforte is one of the Wolves of Fenric (see 'Silver Nemesis').
- It has been suggested that, like Fenric, the Doctor is also a being from 'the Dawn of Time', but there is no evidence in this story to support this idea. (See MORE THAN A TIME LORD? in the Appendices.)

LANGUAGE

The Russians initially speak their own language (and there are English subtitles on screen). They then switch to speaking English, even when at the point of death. The Doctor can read Russian script and speaks the language. Despite being from the future and living under the sea for thousands of years, the Ancient One speaks English.

TIMELINE DATES

1943, April (Saturday – Sunday) *

Ace says 'I didn't know they had personal stereos in 1943'. No month is given, but Nurse Crane makes the comment that down in the crypt 'it's like winter', so it is not the winter months.

The story was recorded in April [of 1989] so I have selected that month to match seasonal conditions. Wainwright holds a service on the second day of the story, which makes it a Sunday, so it is a Saturday when the Russians land at the beach. Therefore the dates that could apply to 'The Curse Of Fenric' are 3/4 April, 10/11 April, 17/18 April, or 24/25 April.

BEFORE 15,000,000,000 BC *

As covered under 'Terminus', the Universe was created 15 billion years ago. This was when the intelligence known as Fenric existed: 'The Dawn of Time. The beginning of all beginnings. Two forces only, good and evil. Then chaos. Time is born, matter, space. The Universe cries out like a newborn. The forces shatter as the Universe explodes outwards. Only echoes remain. And somehow, somehow, the evil force survives. An intelligence. Pure evil'. (It is possible that the Doctor was there to witness this 'birth', see 'Destiny Of The Daleks'.)

243 *

Fenric says the Doctor 'left me in the shadow dimensions. Trapped for seventeen centuries', which would be since AD 243. The second set of runes that appear in the crypt are said by Judson to be 'more than a thousand years old', which ties in with them being 1700 years old. According to the Doctor, his encounter with Fenric was 'so long ago' in terms of his own time stream, so presumably this was the first Doctor when he was younger.

1743
The Doctor asks Wainwright to search the parish records for details about 'the descendants of the early Viking settlers, about two hundred years ago'. Wainwright confirms that the records 'go back as far as the eighteenth century'.

1809, April 8
1820, July 3
1872, February 3
1898, January 12
1898, March 4
1898, March 17
These dates all appear on the family tombstone at the church.

1895
Wainwright's grandfather translated the runes 'at the end of the last century', so we could place this to be around 1895.

1918
Millington says that Judson's accident happened 'over twenty years ago'. I have placed it 25 years earlier, in 1918, just before World War I ended. This is based on the idea that Judson was injured during the War, with Millington being responsible, and while Millington stayed in the forces, Judson took up science.

Millington tells of an event 'many years ago' in which he had to sacrifice the lives of several crewmen trapped in a burning hold, which probably also happened during World War I.

1942, October
Sorin mentions the event of the dead rising, which happened 'six months ago'.

1943 ∗
The Doctor recognises that Millington's office is an exact replica of the German naval cipher room in Berlin, so it would appear that he has actually been there.

1970

Sorin says Ace will be born 'in thirty years' which, from 1943, makes Ace's birth year to be 1973, but it has previously been established in 'Dragonfire' and 'Ghost Light' as being in 1970.

500,000 +

The Doctor says he has seen the Earth, 'thousands of years in the future. The Earth lays dying, the surface just a chemical slime. Half a million years of industrial progress'.

DURATION

⇨ **Day One (Saturday)**

The Russians and the TARDIS arrive very late in the afternoon. It is nightfall by the time the Doctor and Ace arrive at the bunkhouse. Ace sleeps in the bunkhouse while the Doctor goes out for a walk. Petrossian is killed in the last scene set at night.

⇨ **Day Two (Sunday)**

Ace meets the girls at St Jude's the next morning. The rest of the story takes place during this day.

SURVIVAL

STORY LINK

There is nothing to suggest that this story follows on from 'The Curse Of Fenric', other than that Ace is still wearing Captain Sorin's Russian Star badge. She does try to telephone her mother (but there's no-one home), so this could mean that she wants to reconcile with her mother – something she wanted to do at the end of 'The Curse Of Fenric'.

MASTER LINK

When last seen in 'The Trial Of A Time Lord', the Master was trapped by a limbo atrophier in his own TARDIS. At the end of his trial the Doctor tells the Time Lords 'you can do what you like with the Master'. As covered under GALLIFREY HISTORY, it is possible that the Master is from a different GRT to the Doctor, on the basis that they both arrive on the Cheetah world by means other than TARDIS, so there is nothing to govern a cross-GRT meeting. However, I would suggest that they are still close to the same age. The Doctor is 52 years older than he was at his trial, so the Master must also be 52 years older. This suggests that he is kept a prisoner for many years by the Time Lords following the events of 'The Trial Of A Time Lord'. The Master is released or escapes. He also obtains a new wardrobe. From what we can gather, he landed his TARDIS on a planet being hunted by the kitlings. He is transported to the planet of the Cheetah people, without a means to return to his ship. He slowly becomes part of the planet whilst being able to control the Cheetahs.

LANGUAGE

The Master uses his Time Lord 'gift' to communicate with the Cheetah people. Karra speaks with Ace.

TIMELINE DATES

1987, June 7 (Sunday) •

It is a 'Sunday afternoon'. One of the old posters at the youth club advertises a bout between British heavyweight boxer Frank Bruno and James 'Butch' Tillis for 'Tuesday 24th March '87', so the date cannot be earlier than that.

Ace asks 'How long since I was here?' The Doctor responds with 'You've been away for as long as you think you have', and Ace replies, 'I feel like I've been away for ever'. Patterson tells Ace: 'Your Mum had you listed as a missing person' and that 'four kids have gone missing just this month', which suggests that Ace left Earth (via Fenric's time-storm) only recently from Patterson's perspective, if he thinks she was one of those missing. Ace left Earth around November 1986 (see 'Dragonfire').

Ace and the Doctor are in Perivale at her request so she can see 'what my old mates were up to'. When she meets up with her friends again, they don't appear overly concerned about her having been absent, so it really can't have been more than a year since she left. Also, Squeak appears to know who Ace is; she is only about five or six years old. If Ace had been away for more than two years, would the small child still recognise her? Given that, like Tegan in 'The Awakening', the Doctor wouldn't have deliberately let Ace return home out of sync with her own Mean Time – in case she decided to stay behind with her mother – the date is relative to the time that Ace has been away from Earth in total. She was on IceWorld for several months (see 'Dragonfire') and she has been with the Doctor for certainly no more than a year, so it is most likely to still be only 1987. 'Survival' was recorded in June [of 1989], so this would be June 1987.

June 7th has been derived from the information given about the various disappearances: Midge tells Ace that Derek has been on the Cheetah planet for 'three weeks', which is the longest of them all. Midge and Stevie 'went last month'. This means that Derek also disappeared last month. With 'Survival' set in June, Derek, Midge and Stevie all vanish in May. Shreela went 'last week'. This means that Derek left in the third week of May, Midge and Stevie in the last week of May, and Shreela in the first week of June. That sets 'Survival' on the first Sunday of June, which is the 7th.

1987, May
1987, June ▨ ▨ ▨ ▨ ▨ ▨ ▨ ▨ ▨ ▨ ▨ ▨
As mentioned above, Derek has been on the Cheetah planet for 'three weeks', which is since May. Derek, Midge and Stevie all vanish in May too. Shreela went 'last week'. This means that Derek left in the third week of May, Midge and Stevie in the last week of May, and Shreela in the first week of June.

▨▨▨▨▨▨ DURATION ▨▨▨▨▨▨
Both locations in this story are contemporaneous.

⇨ **Day One (Sunday) (Ep1-3)** ▨ ▨ ▨ ▨ ▨ ▨ ▨ ▨ ▨
Dave is called in for 'dinner' (lunch) by his mother. The clock in the gym reads 4.47 when Paterson returns to the youth club.

⇨ **Day One (Ep1-3)** ▨ ▨ ▨ ▨ ▨ ▨ ▨ ▨ ▨ ▨
One day is spent on the planet of the Cheetah people.

UNSEEN ADVENTURES

At some point after 'Survival', Ace leaves the Doctor.

DOCTOR WHO (THE TV MOVIE)

NOTE: This was the final adventure covered by the original version of *Timelink*. With the advent of the new 2005 series, and in order to fit 'Doctor Who (The TV Movie)' with all the new continuity, I have heavily revised my conclusions about this story. In order to make sense of the many inconsistencies – such as the Doctor's (supposed) half-human heritage, his unusual ability to 'predict' future events, his inexplicable search for the beryllium chip, the TARDIS's Gothic appearance and odd behaviour, the unclear purpose and function of the Eye of Harmony, etc – I have come to the conclusion that much of what the Doctor and Master and/or the TARDIS say and do during 'Doctor Who (The TV Movie)' is directly attributed to the malfunction of a particular component of TARDIS technology, namely the perception filter, which was first introduced in 'Human Nature'.

STORY LINK

Some time has passed since 'Survival'. Ace is no longer travelling with the Doctor. He has constructed a new sonic screwdriver and a new TARDIS key, similar to the one he had during his third and fourth incarnations, a copy of which he keeps in a secret compartment on the roof of the TARDIS's outer police box shell. The TARDIS interior is also significantly different (but some of these aesthetic changes can be attributed to the perception filter – see below). The Doctor has obviously been cleaning out some of the storage holds (see 'The Invasion Of Time', 'The Creature From The Pit' and 'Castrovalva'), and moved some of his furniture and collectibles into the now much larger console room. (As noted under THE DOCTOR'S AGE as many as 16 years have passed since 'Survival'.)

Off-screen, the seventh Doctor has received – presumably directly from Gallifrey – a message that the Master has been taken prisoner by the Daleks on Skaro and that the Master has requested that the Doctor collect his remains. However, the Doctor, obviously suspicious that it might merely be a trap by the Daleks to lure him to Skaro to kill him, devises an elaborate plan by which he can land on Skaro, enter the Dalek city and, assuming the Master was there and still alive, allow both of them to escape undetected and unharmed.

To this end, the Doctor presumably returns to Gallifrey. To prevent the Daleks or the Master from seizing control of the TARDIS, the Doctor requests a number of modifications made not only to the TARDIS, but also to himself: to prevent the ship from being taken over by the Daleks or the Master, the TARDIS's perception filter is boosted and extended to the interior of the ship. This booster is powered by the ship's central power source, the Eye of Harmony, which is relocated to the cloister room. (The Eye has not been opened for 700 years, ever since the Doctor took his first flight in the TARDIS.) The Time Lords may have even secretly rigged the Eye so that should it be forced open by the Daleks, it would activate a gravitational shift that would pull Skaro inside out…

One unfortunate 'side-effect' of this booster is that it turns the Eye into a highly dangerous gravitational force that could pull a planet inside out if it is forced and left open for too long. But the interior perception filter has the added effect of blocking from any occupant of the ship the true function of the Eye of Harmony, and its now destructive powers. And as an extra precaution, to prevent the Daleks or the Master using it as a weapon, the Eye is fitted with special locks that can be opened only with a human eye. (What neither the Doctor nor the Time Lords foresaw was that the TARDIS would end up on Earth, the only place in the Universe where the Eye could in fact be opened, thus making that planet vulnerable in the event of the Eye being opened...)

The final phase of the stealth mission is to have the Doctor undergo conversion through a chameleon arch-like device (like that used by the Doctor in 'Human Nature' to render him as a complete human) to convert his Time Lord body so it was 'half human'. This is for two reasons: firstly so the Daleks would not detect his arrival on Skaro – as they'd be expecting a Time Lord – and secondly to prevent the Doctor himself from opening or being forced to open the Eye of Harmony. The process changes the retinal structure of his eye, but retains his two hearts and non-human blood type. Before departing, the Doctor also changes his clothes into something more suitable for the mission to Skaro. (An unexpected side effect from the combination of the boosted perception filter and chameleon arch is the Doctor's warped memory of his early life on Gallifrey and the history of 1999, the functions of the TARDIS, and the psychic ability to perceive the future of people he comes into contact with.)

With the ship protected by the perception filter, and the Doctor now 'half-human', the TARDIS ultimately arrives on Skaro. As planned, the Doctor enters the Dalek stronghold. However he witnesses the Master's execution by the double-crossing Daleks but manages to acquire the Master's remains, and escape in the TARDIS. All the Doctor has to do is return to Gallifrey with the Master, then once back home, have the Eye of Harmony removed, and then be turned back into a full Time Lord...

However, when the Master escapes his bonds and damages the console, the ship makes an 'AUTOMATIC EMERGENCY LANDING' on Earth, the last planet the Doctor wants to be on given the nature of the locks around the Eye of Harmony (hence his reaction of 'oh, no' when there is a 'TIMING MALFUNCTION'). And when the Doctor regenerates, part of the chameleon arch process and residue from the perception filter cause confusion within his mind, making him forget who is he and giving him a somewhat scrambled and confused memory of his real life on Gallifrey and that created by the chameleon arch, such as the memories of his father, and that for a time he believes he might actually be 'half human'.

MASTER LINK

It has been suggested that the Master is the [Delgado] incarnation that was working for the Daleks in 'Frontier In Space'. And following his failure to start a war between

Earth and Draconia the Daleks execute him. The third Doctor is called in to collect his remains, but it is the seventh that instead shows up on Skaro. Then, following the events of 'Doctor Who (The TV Movie)', the Master escapes from the Eye of Harmony undetected by the Doctor, and makes his way to Tersurus, where his partly digested form is found by Goth, who takes him back to Gallifrey. The Master, having failed to use the Eye of Harmony in the Doctor's TARDIS to trigger a new life-cycle, then sets about to use the real Eye of Harmony on Gallifrey to restore his life. The events of 'The Deadly Assassin' take place... While this idea has some merit, it simply does not work because of the following points:

- The eighth Doctor confirms that the Master is in his 'final incarnation', which means this is the [Ainley] Master, last seen in 'Survival', rather than being the Master from an earlier point in time, such as the [Delgado] Master, whom the third Doctor encountered on numerous occasions.
- If the Master's near-death state in 'The Deadly Assassin' is as a direct result of the events of 'Doctor Who (The TV Movie)', why does the [Ainley] Master set about to subsequently destroy the Doctor on several occasions, particularly in 'Castrovalva', when by doing so would mean changing the course of events in the Doctor's future which are already in the Master's distant past?
- From a GRT perspective, the Master on Gallifrey in 'The Deadly Assassin' cannot be from the seventh / eighth Doctor's GRT.

Since this idea does not work, then clearly the Master in 'Doctor Who (The TV Movie)' is also from a period long after 'Survival'. As covered above, 16 years have passed for the Doctor since 'Survival' – the same number of years have therefore also passed for the Master. The Doctor also confirms that the Master is in his 'final incarnation'.

It is hard to see the face of the Master before he is executed on Skaro, but we do see his eyes, which appear to have retained the cat-like shape they were on the planet of the Cheetah people, as seen at the end of 'Survival'. As that planet disintegrates the Doctor is transported 'home' to his TARDIS, so we can only assume that the Master is also transported back to his own 'home', either his own TARDIS, or another location.

It is worth noting that the snake-like protoplasm that the Master turns into in 'Doctor Who (The TV Movie)' is very similar to the substance that he 'bleeds' in 'Time-Flight' when he is disguised as the snake-like Kalid. The fact that the post-Traken Master has the power to change his form (as seen in 'Castrovalva' and 'The King's Demons') suggests that this malleable protoplasmic substance is partly a side-effect of taking on the Traken Keepership. (An alternative is that the Master has existed in this protoplasmic state for far longer, perhaps even as far back as before the events of

'The Deadly Assassin', and this glutinous state is how the Master is able to transfer his essence from one form to another. Is the Master's burnt-out body seen in 'The Deadly Assassin' an unfortunate side-effect of the latest transference having gone wrong?)

So, in the years long after escaping from the destruction of the planet of the Cheetah People ('Survival'), the Master somehow ends up on Skaro (either in his own TARDIS, by teleportation, or he is taken there by the Daleks). He wants to lure the Doctor into a trap, to which the Daleks agree. The Master plans to seize control of the Doctor's TARDIS and take over the Doctor's body. The Master knows that the Doctor will see through the charade of a trial but that his curiosity will get the better of him, and he will not be able to resist the invitation to investigate. An open broadcast is transmitted into time and space, giving the location and temporal coordinates, which the Time Lords receive. However, the Daleks double cross the Master and blast him anyway, their intention all along being to hijack the TARDIS and kill the Doctor. But the execution does not kill the Master, and instead turns his part-Traken / part-Gallifreyan / part-Cheetah Person / part-whatever else body into a protoplasmic snake-like form, which the Doctor is able to recover.

When the Master damages the TARDIS console, the ship makes an emergency landing on Earth, unfortunately the one planet in the cosmos where the Eye of Harmony could be turned into a weapon. After he possesses the human form of Bruce the paramedic, the Master breaks into the TARDIS, where he remains for several hours before Chang Lee enters the ship and finds 'Bruce' there. During those hours, the Master attempts to gain control of the ship and open the Eye of Harmony, but the ship won't respond, and the perception filter is clouding his mind. But the Master is intelligent enough to see through some of the conditioning of the perception filter, and discovers how to open the Eye of Harmony. He needs a human eye. To his delight, he sees Chang Lee outside with the TARDIS key, and lets him enter…

When the Eye shows him images of the Doctor's eye, the Master says 'the Doctor is half human, no wonder' in realisation as to how the Doctor was able to escape from the Daleks.

GALLIFREY LINK

At the conclusion to the Doctor's last direct contact with Gallifrey (in 'The Trial Of A Time Lord'), the High Council had been deposed, and insurrectionists were running amok. The Doctor suggested to the Inquisitor that once order was restored, she should stand for the Presidential office. Whether or not she did is unknown. We can assume that the Master contacted the Time Lords on Gallifrey directly from Skaro, and they in turn contacted the Doctor. In terms of the Doctor's age, the GRT is now 2182.

DALEK LINK

These Daleks are still based on Skaro, so the Master's 'trial' must be set and 'Remembrance Of The Daleks' prior to the destruction of Skaro. It's unlikely that Davros has been returned to Skaro at this point in Dalek history, so the best placement of this event is between 'Resurrection Of The Daleks' and 'Revelation Of The Daleks'. This is their fifteenth appearance.

OBSERVATIONS

- The Doctor reports on the Master's trial and says 'they say he listened calmly as his list of crimes was read and sentenced passed'. But who are 'they'? It cannot be the Daleks; if anything the comment suggests that there are other witnesses on Skaro who later report on what they saw, reports that the Doctor later heard or read, which is unlikely. One way of interpreting this line is to say that the signal sent from Skaro received by the Time Lords contained images of the 'trial' as proof of the Master's imprisonment – the 'they' are the Time Lords. (And presumably the Doctor's narration at the start of the TV Movie is from his debrief by the Time Lords after the Doctor had returned to Gallifrey.)
- The Eye of Harmony is described by the Master as being 'the heart of the [TARDIS] structure. Everything gets its power from here'. In 'Inside The Spaceship', 'Boom Town' and 'Bad Wolf' the heart of the TARDIS is said to be under the main control console. Other than that little else is revealed about the Eye. It is clear that this is not the same Eye that is on Gallifrey. Until the events of 'The Deadly Assassin' the Eye of Harmony was considered to be only a myth. Therefore the Time Lords must have thought the large silver globe in the heart of each TARDIS to be simply an independent power source that never ran out or required maintenance, because they could never open them. Then, after the events of 'The Deadly Assassin', the Time Lords discover there is a link between the real Eye and the TARDIS power globes, and so they give the globes a new name. Opening the Eye in a TARDIS is a difficult process (the Doctor says 'I haven't opened the Eye before' / 'In 700 years no one has managed to open the Eye'). The Doctor deduces that the Master wants the Eye open so he can take over the Doctor's body. This implies that one of the functions of the Eye is to allow transference between two Time Lords when something goes wrong with regeneration. In 'Castrovalva', during his wandering through the TARDIS, the Doctor notes 'there are strong dimensioning forces deep in the TARDIS. Tend to make one giddy', and that 'we must be close to the main TARDIS drive now'. I would suggest that he is referring to the Eye of Harmony power source. As demonstrated

in 'Mawdryn Undead', the TARDIS environs – not just the zero room – are capable of stabilising a regenerative crisis, so the Eye must in some way be an important part of the process. The fact that the special eye-rig and harness are still on board the Doctor's TARDIS supports this.

- The TARDIS goes into 'Temporal Orbit', and as a result Earth is returned to the state it was in before the Eye was opened. This is similar to what happened in 'The Sound Of Drums', where one whole year was erased when time rewinds when the Paradox Machine is destroyed. The Doctor says he has never opened the Eye before, and why would he need to? I would guess that a Temporal Orbit is only possible when the Eye is in its opened state. Therefore, the Doctor has never used the TARDIS to turn back time before, because he has never been able to and it is therefore unlikely that he will do so again in the future, on the basis that the Eye is too dangerous even when opened under controlled conditions. (And as I have noted above, if the Eye is powering the protective devices installed to prevent the Daleks from taking control of the ship, this might explain why an entire planet (as note above, possibly intended to be Skaro?) could be sucked into the Eye.) The Doctor manages to close the Eye with the help of the circuit from the atomic clock, but by that time the damage has already been done and Earth is still threatened with destruction. The Doctor says the only way to fix the situation is to go back to before the Eye was opened or before the TARDIS has arrived. To do this by conventional methods, such as programming the ship to travel back one day, would not be possible in terms of the Blinovitch Limitation Effect, because the TARDIS is already there: the TARDIS lands in the alley around 9.00 pm on December 31st and is still there at 11.55 pm. It cannot go back and land there between 9.00 pm and 11.55 pm, because it is already there (a Time Ram would result, see 'The Time Monster'). It would be possible for the TARDIS to land in the alley prior to 9.00 pm but it could not stay beyond 9.00 pm because it will be due to land there at 9.00 pm for the first time (another Time Ram would occur). Also, it is hard to see how that would reverse the problem with the Eye. I think the word 'reverse' is very important here. What the Doctor probably means is that the open Eye enables the TARDIS to enter a Temporal Orbit, a specific form of time-travelling which literally winds time backwards around the ship, effectively erasing everything that happens from the point the Orbit commences. (This is similar to rolling time backwards, as Whitaker and Grover attempted to do in 'Invasion Of The Dinosaurs', and Scaroth in 'City Of Death'.) This is a function of which a TARDIS has always been capable, but which is not actively promoted by the Time Lords for fear that too many Time Lords would abuse the function and cause untold damage to the web of time. So, by going into Temporal Orbit, the TARDIS reverses time on Earth from midnight on 31 December 1999 back to 29 December 1999. The way it probably works is this: the TARDIS enters Temporal Orbit. Time outside the ship is spun into reverse, but neither the TARDIS nor the Doctor is affected by the time reversal (being a Time Lord, he is immune, which is why he doesn't change back into his seventh self). As the Doctor states, they did go back far enough, which is why Grace and Chang are still alive ('I don't believe in ghosts'). The fact that Grace has a future beyond 1999 that the Doctor knows about indicates that she does not actually die, but is merely in a state of deep 'unconsciousness' that can only be reversed by the process.

- As I have noted under Observations for 'Planet Of The Spiders', the fact that K'Anpo gives the Doctor a boost of energy to help him to regenerate could be linked to the energy issued by the Eye Of Harmony which brings Grace and Chang Lee back to life, this being some Time Lord / TARDIS power which is used to aid problematic regenerations. You could almost call it a 'state of temporal Grace'.
- Refer also to the Appendices, for further exploration as to whether or not the Doctor is HALF-HUMAN.

LANGUAGE

The TARDIS scanners show all text in English. The fact that Grace says the Doctor is 'British' indicates that his Gallifreyan accent is similar to a British accent. The Master corrects Grace's grammar. The Doctor says 'vacation' instead of 'holiday'.

TIMELINE DATES

1999, December 29 – 2000, January 1 ⋅

The year '1999' is first given as a caption on-screen. The full date is given by Chang Lee and Bruce in the ambulance: 'What's the date?' / 'December Thirtieth' / '1999' (Chang writes the date on the hospital admission form as 'DEC, 30, 1999'). The Doctor regenerates between 1.00 am and 1.14 am on the morning of December 31.

The TARDIS enters a Temporal Orbit and travels back to 'December 29', as seen on the TARDIS console. The ship then returns to December 31 materialising as midnight strikes again. The final scene takes place during the first minutes of 1 January 2000, the new millennium.

<<2000, January 1>>

The Doctor sets the coordinates for 'one minute past midnight' and glimpses an alternative future in which the Earth no longer exists beyond 31 December 1999. This is merely a temporal projection, possibly from the time scanner the Doctor used in 'The Macra Terror' to predict the future with the Macra (see Alternative Time, THE N-SPACE UNIVERSE).

4595 ✦

The Master is 'executed' on Skaro clearly at a time before the planet is destroyed in 4663 (see 'Remembrance Of The Daleks').

As covered under DALEK HISTORY, the Daleks do not openly reveal that they know of the Time Lords and Gallifrey until 'Resurrection Of The Daleks', in 4590, so it appears that the trial is set after that which is why they know of the Time Lords and Gallifrey.

When the Master interferes with the TARDIS controls, the ship has to 'Instigate Automatic Emergency Landing'. It lands on the nearest planet, in this case being Earth in 1999. This indicates that the TARDIS is travelling from Skaro to Gallifrey in GRT 2182 (see THE DOCTOR'S AGE), with the ship exiting from the vortex into normal space near Earth in 1999. This suggests that the TARDIS is travelling forwards in time, so Skaro might be in the distant past, prior to 1999. The fact that after leaving Skaro the Doctor has time to listen to music, brew and drink a cup of tea, and read a few chapters of his book, indicates that the flight time from Skaro to Gallifrey is quite long. (The Doctor tells Grace that to travel from Earth to Gallifrey is 'a good ten minutes in this old thing'. It was going to take the TARDIS '32 minutes' to travel in space only from Earth to Gallifrey in 'Full Circle'.)

As noted under DALEK HISTORY, the best placement for Skaro is between 'Resurrection Of The Daleks' and 'Revelation Of The Daleks', which is the arbitrary date of 4595.

1206

Genghis Khan (1162 – 1227) was named 'Universal Ruler' in 1206; his greatest achievement was his invasion of Asia between 1206 and 1216. This is most likely to be the time being referred to by the Master.

1449 ✦

The Doctor says 'in 700 years no one has managed to open the Eye'. Assuming that the Eye was closed for the last time when the Doctor first got the TARDIS – which was in GRT 1449 (see THE DOCTOR'S AGE) – then it has actually been 733 years ago, we can assume that the Doctor is only generalising when he says it was 700 years.

1911 ✦

Marie Curie lived from 7 November 1867 to 4 July 1934. She met her future husband, Pierre, in 1894, and they married on 25 July 1895. Pierre died in April 1906, and

Marie remarried in 1926. Being a gentleman, the Doctor wouldn't have known Marie 'intimately' while she was married, so we might assume that his meeting(s) with her were prior to 1895, or between 1906 and 1926. She was awarded her first Nobel Prize in 1903, and her second in 1911. Interestingly, in 'Pyramids Of Mars' the Doctor says that 1911 was one of his favourite years. Perhaps this was when he knew Marie?

1924, November 29 ✦ ▨ ▨ ▨ ▨ ▨ ▨ ▨ ▨ ▨ ▨ ▨
Giacomo Puccini was born on 22 December 1858 and died on 29 November 1924. The Doctor says he was 'with Puccini before he died', when the composer was writing the opera *Turandot*. I am assuming the Doctor is referring to the same day as the composer's death.

1930 ✦ ▨ ▨ ▨ ▨ ▨ ▨ ▨ ▨ ▨ ▨ ▨ ▨
Sigmund Freud was born 6 May 1856, and died 23 September 1939. The Doctor knows him 'very well', presumably towards the end of his life.

2000, December 25 ✦ ▨ ▨ ▨ ▨ ▨ ▨ ▨ ▨ ▨ ▨
While dreaming in 'The Mind Robber' the Doctor says he has 'been in the year 2000'. The Doctor warns Chang Lee not to be in San Francisco 'next Christmas'; clearly he knows what happens then. It could be that given his knowledge of Gareth's work on predicting earthquakes that the 'Big One' hits San Francisco in 2000. It could even be something much simpler; it is possible that this is the date Mandragora returns to Earth (see 'The Masque Of Mandragora').

2009 ✦ ▨ ▨ ▨ ▨ ▨ ▨ ▨ ▨ ▨ ▨ ▨ ▨
The Doctor knows that 'ten years from now' Gareth will lead a seismology unit of the UCLA and devises a way of accurately predicting earthquakes. (This may have been due directly to the 'disaster' of 25 December 2000.) (See also 'The Enemy Of The World' – it is possible that Gareth's research was used a few years later by Salamander to create earthquakes.)

I would suggest that it was during this visit to San Francisco that the Doctor also gained knowledge of the atomic clock.

It is curious to note that at the end of the adventure, the eighth Doctor asks Grace to come with him in the TARDIS, even when he already knows that Grace 'will do great things' in her future beyond 1999. If she did go with him, wouldn't that change her future?

2182 ▨ ▨ ▨ ▨ ▨ ▨ ▨ ▨ ▨ ▨ ▨ ▨ ▨ ▨
The TARDIS scanner reads:

DESTINATION
GALLIFREY
LOCAL DATELINE
5725.2
RASSILON ERA

The rotating wooden 'blocks' on the console also give the destination as 'Rassilon Era – Gallifrey', but with the month, day and time displayed as 'December 30 – 22.47'. The year cannot be seen. This shows clearly that the day and month of the destination year on Gallifrey (5725.2) is relative to 10.47 pm on 30 December (year unknown) on Earth. As covered under THE DOCTOR'S AGE, the Doctor's GRT is now Earth year 2182.

DURATION

(TARDIS)
The Doctor spends some time in the TARDIS after leaving Skaro …

⇨ **Day One (30 December 1999)**
The Doctor lands in the alley, probably around 9.00 pm, given that it is 9.20 pm when Grace arrives at the hospital, and his 'time of death' is '10:03' pm, allowing for the time needed to get him to hospital and to be operated upon.

⇨ **Day Two (31 December 1999)**
It is '12.48' am on the alarm clock at Bruce's house. It is '1.00 am' when the Doctor's body is delivered to the morgue. He regenerates and walks the morgue corridors at '1.14 am', as seen on the wall clock. It is 3.41 in the afternoon when Grace leaves the hospital. It is 4.30 when the Doctor and Grace arrive at her house. The rest of the adventure takes place that day. It is '8.59.59' when the Doctor announces that the planet will be destroyed in three hours' time, at 'midnight'. The Doctor is chained up in the cloister room at '11.55' (pm). The Earth is apparently destroyed as midnight strikes.

⇨ **Day Three (1 January 2000)**
The Doctor departs in the early hours of the morning as the New Year is welcomed in.

(TARDIS)
The TARDIS travels in a Temporal Orbit, going backwards in time as far as 29 December 1999 …

UNSEEN ADVENTURES

RETURN TO GALLIFREY?

Presumably the Doctor would have returned to Gallifrey ('LOCAL DATELINE 5725.2') to have the perception filter adjusted and the TARDIS reverted back to the way it was, to have his biology returned to that of a full Time Lord, and to have the Master's body removed from the Eye of Harmony. (This later point would explain how the Time Lords were able to later resurrect the Master to fight in the Time War, as stated in 'The Sound Of Drums'.)

A SECOND FAMILY?

We know that the first Doctor had a family when he lived on Gallifrey, long before he took the TARDIS and fled with his granddaughter, Susan. But did the Doctor have a second family in his later life?

It is significant that, when the Doctor was on Gallifrey during high-profile events that affected or threatened Time Lord society (such as in 'The Deadly Assassin', 'The Invasion Of Time' and 'Arc Of Infinity'), at no stage during those visits did he mention, or have contact with, any relatives or members of an immediate family. Therefore, it would seem that the Doctor did not have any relatives living on Gallifrey at the time.

The Doctor often recalls the Time War, and in many of those recollections, he refers to the grief he has suffered at the loss of his family and friends. Is he merely speaking of his fellow Time Lords, or is he in fact referring to a wife and children?

In the following quotations, I have emphasised those words that clearly suggest that the Doctor is referring to his own immediate family:

DOCTOR: My entire planet died. *My whole family.* Do you think it never occurred to me to go back and save *them*?

- 'Father's Day'

DR CONSTANTINE: Before this war began, I was a *father* and a *grandfather*. Now I'm neither. But I'm still a doctor.
DOCTOR: Yeah, I know the feeling.

- 'The Empty Child'

DOCTOR: I could save everyone. I could stop the war.

- 'School Reunion'

DOCTOR: *I was a dad once.*

- 'Fear Her'

DOCTOR: There was a war. A Time War... Everyone lost. They're all gone now: *My family. My friends.*

- 'Gridlock'

DOCTOR: I could imagine *they* were alive, under a burnt orange sky.

- 'Gridlock'

DOCTOR: I'm rubbish at weddings. *Especially my own.*

- 'Blink'

DOCTOR: If I could go back and save *them* I would. But I can't. I can never go back. I can't. I just can't. I can't.

- 'The Fires Of Pompeii'

DOCTOR: Donna, I've been a *father* before.
DONNA: What?
DOCTOR: *Lost all that a long time ago.* Along with everything else.

- 'The Doctor's Daughter'

DOCTOR: When I look at her now I can see *them*. The hole *they* left, all the pain that filled it ... When *they* died, that part of me died with *them*.

- 'The Doctor's Daughter'

From these quotations, can we take it that some time after 'Doctor Who (The TV Movie)', the eighth Doctor returned to Gallifrey (specifically to be reverted back to have the temporary half human aspects removed, and to have the Master freed from the Eye of Harmony), and decided to stay? Did the Doctor spend most of his eighth incarnation on Gallifrey? Could that be why there are no further recorded adventures or appearances of the eighth Doctor beyond 'Doctor Who (The TV Movie)'? (As noted in THE DOCTOR'S AGE, there seem to be 167 years unaccounted for between the eighth and ninth Doctors.)

And while on Gallifrey, did the Doctor fall in love and get married (the Doctor refers to his wedding in 'Blink') and have a family? And was it while that family was still young that the Daleks declared war on Gallifrey? And during the Time War, when the Daleks attacked Gallifrey, the Doctor's family was killed…

THE TIME WAR

The Time War is a significant event in the ninth Doctor's life. A conflict of, by, through, inside, outside, beyond, within, without, under, over and beside Time itself, shrouded in myth and legend. But it happened – a great battle waged across time and space, Dalek against Time Lord. Little is known about how it started; more is revealed about how it ended. And it ended with the destruction of Gallifrey.

The Daleks' last appearance was in 'Remembrance Of The Daleks', at the end of which the Dalek home planet, Skaro, was destroyed. Was the destruction of Skaro the spark that triggered the War? Did the Daleks who survived the destruction retaliate? And had the Daleks also discovered that the Time Lords had previously tried to prevent their creation by sending the Doctor back in time to the moment of their birth? ('Genesis Of The Daleks')

In terms of when the War broke in Gallifrey history, it must have been relative to the Doctor's GRT. As covered under THE DOCTOR'S AGE, the eighth Doctor was around 969 in 'Doctor Who (The TV Movie)', and the ninth was possibly 1136 in 'Rose', which leaves 167 years unaccounted for. The Time War would have taken place during that period.

Another important factor that has yet to be revealed is how the Doctor survived. Was this because he was protected in some way (by a force field?) or was it luck? Design? Was he removed from the War by a third party or outside force? (Or was it because he was half-human? Or more than a Time Lord? See those chapters in the Appendices for future discussion.)

When thinking of what a Time War could be, one calls up mental images of thousands of Dalek ships and battle-TARDISes zooming across time, shooting at each other like the X-Wing and TIE fighter dog-fights of *Star Wars*, but applied on a four-dimensional level; a Battle-TARDIS in the year AD 2526 could fire its temporal weapons upon and destroy a Dalek cruiser in the year 50 BC.

The following are all the leading quotations regarding the War:

DOCTOR: [You] go to bed, eat chips, watch telly. While all the time underneath you there's a war going on.

– 'Rose'

As stated by the Gelth (see below), the Time War was invisible to smaller species.

Given that Earth was not directly affected by the conflict, we must assume that humans belong to the 'smaller species' category.

DOCTOR: I was there! I fought in the War. It wasn't my fault! I couldn't save your world. I couldn't save any of them!

- 'Rose'

The Nestene's protein planets were just some of many planets caught in the crossfire during the War. It's hinted that the Nestene came to Earth directly after the loss of its food supply using warp-shunt technology, a term which does not suggest time travel. From the Nestene Consciousness's viewpoint the War had only just ended relative to March 2005, the setting for 'Rose'. Taking this and the other quote from 'Rose' above, can we take this to mean that by 2005, the Time War had already ended?

JABE: ... It refused to admit your existence. And even when it named you, I wouldn't believe it. But it was right. I know where you're from. Forgive me for intruding but it's remarkable you even exist. I just want to say how sorry I am.

- 'The End Of The World'

This story is set in the year five billion; Jabe's people, from the Forest of Cheem, must be classed as higher forms.

DOCTOR: My planet's gone. It's dead. It burned. Like the Earth. Before its time … There was a war and we lost.
ROSE: A war with who? What about your people?
DOCTOR: I'm a Time Lord. I'm the last of the Time Lords. They're all gone. I'm the only survivor. I'm left travelling on my own 'cos there's no one else.

- 'The End Of The World'

GELTH: We face extinction
DOCTOR: Why? What happened?
GELTH: ... the War came.
DICKENS: War? What war?
GELTH: The Time War. The whole universe convulsed. The Time War raged, invisible to smaller species, but devastating to higher forms.

- 'The Unquiet Dead'

The term 'higher forms' may refer to time sensitive races such as the Tharils

('Warriors' Gate'), or beings that possess a conscious awareness of events occurring within the temporal spectrum. The Gelth have crossed from the other side of the Universe, emerging in Cardiff, 1869. The War resulted in their physical forms being destroyed.

> DOCTOR: Your race is dead. All burned. All of you. Ten million ships on fire. The entire Dalek race wiped out in one second.
> DALEK: You lie.
> DOCTOR: I watched it happen. I made it happen!
> DALEK: You destroyed us?
> DOCTOR: I had no choice.
> DALEK: And what of the Time Lords?
> DOCTOR: Dead. They burned with you. The end of the last great Time War. Everyone lost.
> DALEK: And the coward survived.
>
> - 'Dalek'

Although it's not stated as being so, it's tempting to think that using a delta wave (as seen in 'Bad Wolf') was the 'final solution' that the Doctor was forced to engineer to destroy the Daleks, and with Gallifrey caught in the aftermath. It would certainly explain his reticence to use it once he had built it… And the rather scary impression one gets from the 'I made it happen' line above is that it was the Doctor himself who pressed the button…

The mention of 'the last great Time War' implies that there was more than one Time War. It could be there were numerous specific conflicts during the War, and that each was given a name (the fall of Arcadia for instance – see below), in the same way that certain conflicts fought during the Second World War are known in that manner – such as the Battle of Britain. The Last Great Time War (with capital letters) is therefore probably the name applied to the all-consuming final conflict that resulted in the destruction of Gallifrey and, the Doctor had believed, every Dalek.

> DOCTOR: It must have fallen through time. The only survivor.
> GODDARD: You talked about a war.
> DOCTOR: The Time War. The final battle between my people and the Dalek race.
> VAN STATTEN: But you survived.
> DOCTOR: Not by choice.
>
> - 'Dalek'

This Dalek was the first survivor from the Time War that the Doctor encountered; he would later discover that the Dalek Emperor ('Bad Wolf'), the four members of the Cult of Skaro and a prison ship containing millions of Daleks ('Army Of Ghosts'), and Davros ('The Stolen Earth'), had also survived.

DOCTOR: The Daleks destroyed my home, my people. I've got nothing else …
Oh, Rose, they're all dead.

- 'Dalek'

ROSE: The Dalek survived. Maybe some of your people did too?
DOCTOR: I'd know. {taps head}. In here. Feel's like there's no one.

- 'Dalek'

DOCTOR: My entire planet died. My whole family. Do you think it never occurred to me to go back and save them?

- 'Father's Day'

DOCTOR: There used to be laws stopping this kind of thing from happening. My people would have stopped this. But they're all gone. And now I'm going the same way.

- 'Father's Day'

'Father's Day' is set in 1987. The fact that the Reapers break through to sterilise the wound in time, a task usually under the jurisdiction of the Time Lords, suggests that Gallifrey was destroyed long before 1987.

THE EDITOR: The last of the Time Lords and his travelling machine.

- 'The Long Game'

This story is set in 200,000. As it transpired, the Editor was but a puppet under the control of the Dalek Emperor who, along with his new Dalek army, was lying hidden at the edge of space, so the Editor may have known about the Doctor's role in the War from his masters.

DR CONSTANTINE: Before this war began, I was a father and a grandfather. Now I'm neither. But I'm still a doctor.
DOCTOR: Yeah, I know the feeling.

- 'The Empty Child'

The Doctor's reference to his 'family' is covered in the earlier section, A SECOND FAMILY?.

> JACK: That's impossible. I know those ships. They were destroyed.
> DOCTOR: Obviously they survived.
>
> — 'Bad Wolf'

> JACK: One minute they're the greatest threat in the universe, the next minute they vanish out of time and space.
> DOCTOR: They went off to fight a bigger war. The Time War.
> JACK: I thought that was just a legend.
> DOCTOR: I was there. The war between the Daleks and the Time Lords, with the whole of creation at stake. My people were destroyed but they took the Daleks with them. I almost thought it was worth it. But now it turns out they died for nothing.
>
> — 'Bad Wolf'

Jack is from the fifty-first century, and although Jack is an ex-Time Agent and could time-travel, it's clear that he is referring to the Daleks vanishing from the viewpoint of his own personal timeline – therefore we could assume that the Time War started prior to the fifty-first century. Assuming the War was in part the result of the Doctor's actions in destroying Skaro in 4663 ('Remembrance Of The Daleks'), then from the Daleks' timeline the War started during the 300 or so years between 4663 and 5000.

> DOCTOR: So tell me. How did you survive the Time War?
> DALEK EMPEROR: They survived through me.
>
> — 'Bad Wolf'

> DALEK EMPEROR: You destroyed us, Doctor. The Dalek race died in your inferno, but my ship survived. Falling through time. Crippled, but alive.
>
> — 'Bad Wolf'

The Dalek Emperor was the second Dalek survivor encountered by the Doctor. The 'inferno' mentioned here is also referenced in 'The End Of The World' and 'Dalek'. The mental imagery this invokes, is that of ten thousand Dalek ships descending on Gallifrey, and the planet disintegrating in a fiery conflagration, engineered by the Doctor, that spreads out and engulfs the entire Dalek fleet.

RODRICK: There aren't any Daleks. They disappeared thousands of years ago.

- 'Bad Wolf'

'Bad Wolf' is set in 200,100. Rodrick's statement implies that the final War took place thousands of years in the past.

DOCTOR: I lived. Everyone else died.

- 'School Reunion'

LASSAR: And what of the Time Lords? I always thought of you as a pompous race. Ancient, dusty senators. So frightened of change and chaos… They're all but extinct.

- 'School Reunion'

LASSAR: The Paradigm gives us power, but you could give us wisdom. Become a god, at my side. Imagine what you could do, think of the civilisations you could save. Perganon, Ascinta, your own people, Doctor. Standing tall. The Time Lords, reborn.

- 'School Reunion'

DOCTOR: I could save everyone. I could stop the war.

- 'School Reunion'

'School Reunion' has been set in January 2007. It seems unlikely that the Krillitanes possess time travel capabilities, so in order for Brother Lassar to know that the Time Lords were extinct suggests that – as with 'Father's Day' (set in 1987) above – the final conflict in which Gallifrey was destroyed took place in Earth's distant past. To know of the War, the Krillitanes must be higher forms – or at least have acquired that level from one of the many species they had conquered and assimilated over the generations.

DOCTOR: When the Time Lords kept an eye on everything you could pop between realities, and be home in time for tea. And they died. Took it all with them. Walls of reality closed. The worlds were sealed.

- 'Rise Of The Cybermen'

In this story, the TARDIS fell through a crack between realities and onto a parallel Earth. As with 'Father's Day' and 'School Reunion' above, the fact that this happens in the mid-2000s implies that the worlds were sealed long before the twenty-first century.

THE BEAST: The killer of his own kind.

- 'The Impossible Planet'

The Beast has been imprisoned for billions of years, and is presumably one of the higher forms, and as such was fully aware of the Time War during its long incarceration beneath the surface of the planet Krop Tor.

DOCTOR: ... in the Time War, the Daleks evolved so they could use it [background temporal radiation] as a power supply.

- 'Army Of Ghosts'

DALEK: How did you survive the Time War?
DOCTOR: By fighting. On the front line. I was there at the fall of Arcadia. Someday I might even come to terms with that. But you lot ran away.

- 'Army Of Ghosts'

Arcadia is presumably the name of a planet, a significant strategic victory for one of the warring sides.

DOCTOR: At last! The Cult of Skaro! I thought you were just a legend.

- 'Army Of Ghosts'

The Cult of Skaro was established by the Dalek Emperor to think and plan strategies during the War. The four Daleks were each given a name: Caan, Jast, Thay, and their leader, Sec. Towards the end of the War, a Time Lord prison vessel, containing millions of Dalek prisoners, was seized by the Daleks, and along with the Cult this 'Genesis Ark' was secured within a Void Ship which was dispatched into the Void between realities to ride out the War. The Void Ship eventually emerged through a breach between the dimensions that had opened over London in the mid-2000s. (This is yet another hint that the War ended in Earth's past.)

DOCTOR: My home planet is far away and long since gone.

- 'The Runaway Bride'

DOCTOR: There was a war. A Time War. The last great Time War. My people fought a race called the Daleks. For the sake of all creation. And they lost. They lost. Everyone lost. They're all gone now. My family. My friends. Even that sky.

- 'Gridlock'

DALEK: My planet is gone. Destroyed in a great war.

- 'Daleks In Manhattan'

Skaro was destroyed in 'Remembrance Of The Daleks', long before the War started. The Daleks may have established a new home base. Later in the same story, one of the Daleks says 'Planet Earth will become the new Skaro'.

The other implication is that Skaro was, like Gallifrey, removed from time, and therefore never existed.

DOCTOR: They always survive. While I lose everything.

– 'Daleks In Manhattan'

DOCTOR: The final act of the Time War was life.

- 'Utopia'

DOCTOR: They died. The Time Lords. All of them, they died
JACK: Not if he was human.

- 'Utopia'

Jack's response is open to interpretation: did the Daleks have a weapon that targeted Time Lord biology, and the Master was able to survive the attack because he had become human?

MASTER: Where is it, Doctor?
DOCTOR: Gone.
MASTER: How can Gallifrey be gone?
DOCTOR: It burnt.
MASTER: And the Time Lords?
DOCTOR: Dead. And the Daleks, more or less. What happened to you?
MASTER: The Time Lords only resurrected me because they knew I'd be the perfect warrior for a Time War. I was there when the Dalek Emperor took control of the Cruciform. I saw it. I ran. Ran so far. Made myself human so they would never find me. Because I was so scared.
DOCTOR: I know.

MASTER: All of them? But not you. Which must mean -

DOCTOR: I was the only one who could end it. And I tried. I did. I tried everything.

MASTER: What did it feel like, though? Two almighty civilisations burning. Tell me. How did it feel?

DOCTOR: Stop it!

MASTER: You must have been like a god.

DOCTOR: I've been alone ever since. But not any more. Don't you see. All we've got is each other.

- 'The Sound Of Drums'

What is the Cruciform? A weapon? A being? A ship? Was it of Time Lord or Dalek origin? It was clearly a significant victory for the Daleks, given that it was what drove the Master to run and hide.

Given that the Master is able to regenerate in 'Utopia', we can assume that he was given a full new regeneration cycle (as had been offered to him in 'The Five Doctors'). In fact, it's more than likely that all Time Lords were given a new cycle, and even Gallifreyans who were not initiated into the Academies, were also given Time Lord status and powers because so much was at stake, and the Time Lords would need every able-bodied Gallifreyan to fight in the War.

The implication derived from the Master's question 'How can Gallifrey be gone?' is that the planet no longer exists – at all, in any time. Has Gallifrey been removed from time altogether so that it never existed?

Gallifrey was known to the Collector in 'The Sun Makers', set in 25,000 and to the Gravis ('Frontios') in 10,000,040, which suggests the Time War took place in the far future. Or is this a paradox side-effect of a War having been fought outside of time? Can a planet exist in the future and in the past (that is, the fourth and fifth Doctor's past), but no longer exist in the present (the ninth and tenth Doctor's present)?

Maybe the multi-temporal nature of the Time War created a paradoxical anomaly that affected only those who were actually present within the War, so that even though Gallifrey itself has been destroyed and no longer exists in any future timeline, it still existed within the Doctor's own relative past: all the TV Gallifrey stories – 'The War Games', 'The Deadly Assassin', 'The Invasion Of Time', 'Arc Of Infinity', 'The Five Doctors', 'The Trial Of A Time Lord', etc – still 'exist' but only in terms of the Doctor's own past timeline. Therefore as far as his past-selves are concerned, within their own relative timelines the future Gallifrey still exists – just as it does in the fourth Doctor's future as seen in 'The Sun Makers'; and in the fifth's, as stated by the Gravis in 'Frontios'. In other words, when the fourth Doctor travelled to the year 25,000 in

'The Sun Makers', Gallifrey existed in that future. But if the tenth or a later incarnation travels to the year 25,000 Gallifrey won't exist.

And with Gallifrey gone and the Doctor's Time Lord contemporaries all destroyed he is not only 'last of the Time Lords' he is also the only Time Lord in existence, which further adds significance to Jabe's comment: 'I know where you're from … it's remarkable you even exist'.

DOCTOR: A few years ago I was sort of made, well, sort of homeless.
- 'Voyage Of The Damned'

The Doctor is 903 when he says this (but see THE DOCTOR'S AGE for a different take on this comment). He was 900 in 'Rose', which indicates that the War had only recently ended.

DOCTOR: If I could go back and save them I would. But I can't. I can never go back. I can't. I just can't. I can't.
- 'The Fires Of Pompeii'

GENERAL STAAL: Legend says [the Doctor] led the battle in the last great Time War. The finest war in history, and we weren't allowed to be part of it.
- 'The Sontaran Stratagem'

Here we have yet another inference that the final War occurred in Earth's distant past: 'The Sontaran Stratagem' is set in 2009, and it is clear that these Sontarans do not possess time travel. The fact that the Sontarans were aware of the War indicates that they would be, it has to be said, regarded as being higher forms.

DOCTOR: You're an echo. That's all. A Time Lord is so much more. A sum of knowledge. A code. A shared history. A shared suffering. Only it's gone now. All of it. Gone forever.
JENNY: What happened?
DOCTOR: There was a War.
JENNY: Like this one?
DOCTOR: Bigger. Much bigger.
JENNY: And you fought? And killed?
DOCTOR: Yes.
- 'The Doctor's Daughter'

DOCTOR: Donna, I've been a father before.
DONNA: What?
DOCTOR: Lost all that a long time ago. Along with everything else.

- 'The Doctor's Daughter'

DOCTOR: When they died, that part of me died with them.

- 'The Doctor's Daughter'

SHADOW ARCHITECT: Time Lords are the stuff of legend. You belong to the myths and whispers of the higher species. You cannot possibly exist.

- 'The Stolen Earth'

The Architect's statement that the Time Lords are 'legend' again supports the idea that Gallifrey, and therefore the Time Lords, have been totally removed from existence.

We can assume that the Shadow Proclamation vessel that the Doctor and Donna go to is in the 'present day' (i.e. 2009), as the Shadow Architect has been monitoring the disappearance of the first 24 planets from across the Universe. Again, here we have reference to Gallifrey's destruction being something that happened long ago in the distant past rather than the present or future.

DOCTOR: But you were destroyed. In the very first year of the Time War. At the Gates of Elysium. I saw your command ship fly into the jaws of the Nightmare Child. I tried to save you.
DAVROS: But it took one stronger than you. Dalek Caan, himself.
CAAN: I flew in the wild and fire. I danced and died a thousand times.
DAVROS: Emergency temporal shift took him back into the Time War itself.
DOCTOR: But that's impossible. The entire War is time-locked.
DAVROS: And yet he succeeded. Oh, it cost him his mind, but imagine, a single, simple Dalek succeeded, where Emperors and Time Lords have failed.

- 'The Stolen Earth'

The fact that the Time War had a 'first year' suggests that the conflict lasted for many years, possibly even centuries. (At the beginning of this section, I offered the possibility that the Doctor had aged 167 years between 'Doctor Who (The TV Movie)' and "Rose". Did the Time War last for over 150 years?)

DOCTOR: [Dalek are] experts at fighting TARDISes.

- 'The Stolen Earth'

DAVROS: The rage of a Time Lord who butchered millions.

- 'The Stolen Earth'

The above quotations are listed in story order. From these it is possible to construct a likely order of events, from the start of the War to its conclusion.

THE LAST GREAT TIME WAR

Following the destruction of Skaro (and their discovery that the Time Lords had previously attempted to prevent their creation), the Daleks declare war against the Time Lords. The boundaries of the War stretch out to encompass the whole of time, every corner of the Universe, back into the distant past and to the farthest reaches of the future. The whole of creation at stake. The War itself becomes time-locked, with Gallifrey and Skaro, from past to future enclosed in the time bubble, both planets effectively ceasing to exist as far as the rest of the universe knew.

The Doctor (presumably in his eighth incarnation) joins the conflict. In the first year of the War, at the Gates of Elysium, Davros's command ship flies into the jaws of the Nightmare Child. The Doctor is unable to save him. (But Dalek Caan, who has re-entered the War from outside of time, rescues him, and they hide in the Medusa Cascade, where they build the Crucible...)

As the War continues, the aftershocks ripple out across the whole of time, causing the Universe to convulse.

Over time the Daleks evolve, and use background radiation as a power source. The Dalek Emperor appoints four Daleks to become the Cult of Skaro strategists.

Planets caught in the crossfire include Perganon, Ascinta, the Nestene feeding planets and the Gelth homeworld. Higher forms become aware of the conflict, but smaller beings, such as humans, remain completely oblivious. The Sontarans are denied entry.

Time Lord casualties are high. The Master is resurrected and given a new regeneration cycle. (Presumably all other Time Lords – including the Doctor – undergo this process.) But when the Dalek Emperor takes control of the Cruciform, the Master flees into the distant future ('Utopia').

The Time Lords take millions of Daleks prisoner. When the Daleks' new base planet is destroyed, the Daleks capture the prison vessel. The Emperor dispatches the Cult of Skaro into the Void with the vessel, which they have named the Genesis Ark, to wait out until the end of the War.

The Doctor is there at the fall of Arcadia, a major defeat for the Daleks. A lone Dalek falls through time and arrives on Earth ('Dalek').

Towards the end of the War, a fleet of ten thousand Dalek ships descends upon

Gallifrey. The Doctor's family is killed. Left with no alternative, the Doctor (now in his ninth incarnation) engineers an inferno that wipes out the entire Dalek fleet, but also destroys the planet below. The Dalek Emperor's ship escapes the conflagration and although crippled it vanishes through time...

Gallifrey is gone, the Doctor and his TARDIS are the only survivors from his planet.

The following were known to have escaped the War:

- The now-gaseous Gelth come to Earth through the Rift, emerging in Cardiff in 1869 ('The Unquiet Dead').
- A lone Dalek falls through time, crashing on Earth in the mid-twentieth century, and ending up in Henry Van Statten's private museum beneath Utah in the early twenty-first century. The Dalek ultimately destroys itself ('Dalek').
- The Dalek Emperor's ship falls through time, emerging within Earth's solar system some 200,000 years in the future. Abducting humans from Earth, the Emperor builds a new hybrid Dalek army, which attacks Earth in 200,100. Rose, imbued with the power of the time vortex itself, reduces the Dalek army to dust ('Bad Wolf').
- The Cult of Skaro emerges from the Void (in which they had been hiding during the War), coming through a breach that had been opened within Torchwood Towers of London in 2007. The millions of Daleks taken prisoner by the Time Lords are released from the Genesis Ark, but all are sucked back into the Void ('Army Of Ghosts'). The Cult of Skaro make an emergency temporal shift, arriving in New York, 1930 ('Daleks In Manhattan'). The other three Daleks destroyed, Dalek Caan makes a further emergency temporal shift...
- Caan emerges back within the Time War itself, where he saves Davros's command ship. Davros, Caan, and the Dalek Supreme, hide within the Medusa Cascade, and from Davros's own flesh, create a new Dalek army ('The Stolen Earth').
- The Master, having become human and adopting the persona of Professor Yana, flees to the Silver Devastation, some 100 trillion years in the future ('Utopia'). The Master regains his memory, regenerates, and escapes in the Doctor's TARDIS to Earth, where he becomes Harold Saxon. He ultimately dies in the Doctor's arms ('The Sound Of Drums').

A short while after the end of the War (a matter of only weeks or months relative to his own personal timeline), the Doctor discovers that the Nestene Consciousness has sought out a new breeding ground, and follows its trail to Earth...

ROSE

STORY LINK

Prior to 'Rose', the ninth Doctor has a number of adventures, and these off-screen adventures (in date order) include:

- 1223 – an encounter with the hordes of Genghis Khan
- 1883 – swimming to Sumatra the night Krakatoa exploded
- 1912 – meeting the Daniels family in Southampton (and maybe also sailing on the *Titanic*)
- 1963 – a visit to Dallas at the time of the Kennedy assassination

It might be argued that the Krakatoa, Southampton and Dallas adventures take place some point after 'Rose', but the fact that neither Rose nor Jack Harkness appear in the photos suggests the Doctor had not yet met them. (The Doctor disappears in the TARDIS briefly at the end of 'Rose', before returning to offer Rose a trip in his 'time' machine so it is possible he had several off-screen adventures – including visits to 1883, 1912 and 1963 – during this period, before returning to Rose after he realised he wanted her to be his travelling companion. In 'The Empty Child', it appears the Doctor knows that Rose got a red bicycle for Christmas when she was twelve, so it's possible he has spent some time finding out things about her before returning to offer her a trip in the TARDIS. Of course it's just possible he learnt about the bike from Jackie or Mickey during the events of 'Aliens Of London' ...)

The Doctor has a new sonic screwdriver, which acts as an Auton detector / deactivator, and is capable of opening all types of locks rather than just electronic ones as was the case previously (except for locks with a deadlock seal). It is also used as a medical / biology scanner, and to repair cut wire in 'The Empty Child'. The Doctor has also acquired some psychic paper (presumably from the fifty-first century, as this handy tool is also used by Jack Harkness and Professor River Song ('Silence In The Library') who both hail from that century.)

Sometime before the events of 'Rose', the ninth Doctor is embroiled in the 'last great

Time War' between the Daleks and the Time Lords. See UNSEEN ADVENTURES above.

AUTON LINK

In 'Spearhead From Space' and 'Terror Of The Autons', the Nestene Consciousness is seen and described as being a 'cephalopod', or like 'an octopus'. And yet in 'Rose' it is described as being a creature composed of 'living plastic' that can be killed with 'anti-plastic'. So, not only does the creature have power to control anything made of plastic, it appears to have now evolved into something actually made of the same material. Of course, there night be a number of different types, forms and species (?) of Nestene, and the one in 'Rose' is simply a less-organic variation.

During the Time War, the Nestene Consciousness's home world and protein planets are destroyed. The Doctor says 'it wasn't my fault, I couldn't save your world. I couldn't save any of them'. Since the War, the entity has returned to Earth to 'overthrow the human race' and destroy it, and feed on the 'smoke and oil ... toxins and dioxins in the air' since 'its food stock was destroyed in the War – all its protein planets rotted'. The Doctor has followed the Consciousness bringing with him a phial of anti-plastic (which presumably he has used on the Autons before as he is confident it will work).

It's not clear for how long the Nestene Consciousness has been in London (it used 'warp shunt technology' to travel to Earth). It is a living plastic creature without any limbs, so obviously it needed human help and a considerable amount of time (e.g. months) for everything to be set up, to have the relay installed in the roof of Henrik's, and to establish the base beneath the London Eye Millennium Wheel (the structure being selected due to its radial shape being ideal for the Nestene's purposes). Also, the Auton window dummies had to have been manufactured and installed in the Queen's Arcade shopping centre (and other locations around London) several months prior to the start of the invasion. There are also many spare mannequins in the shop basement. In 'Spearhead From Space' and 'Terror Of The Autons', the Autons were constructed with the aid of a humanoid agent – Hibbert and the Master respectively. Presumably the latest invasion force was built up and placed in the windows with the assistance of at least one human agent, who also had a hand in installing the Henrik's relay. This was probably Wilson, the store's chief electrician, who is missing when Rose goes looking for him in the basement. The Doctor believes him to be dead.

Alternatively, the Autons in Henrik's are dormant left-overs from the first invasion in 1970 ('Spearhead From Space'), missed by the UNIT clean up operation overseen by Captain Yates (as mentioned in 'Terror Of The Autons'), and when the Nestene Consciousness arrived on Earth in 2005 the dummies were reactivated with its 'thought control', and Wilson, who was nearby, was taken over and controlled by the Consciousness to assist with its invasion plans, before being killed once his purpose had been served.

OBSERVATIONS

- The TARDIS console room has changed, this time looking almost organic. The changes to the ship's interior configuration were probably undertaken to make the ship more functional during the Time War. All TARDISes would have had to be functioning properly, with pinpoint accurate guidance and navigation. Although it's clear the ship does not always land in the intended destination ('The Unquiet Dead', 'Aliens Of London', for example) the Doctor makes five pinpoint-accurate landings during the course of 'Rose', The wardrobe room is now located some distance from the control room (in 'The Unquiet Dead' he tells Rose the room is 'first left, second right, third on the left, go straight ahead, under the stairs, past the bins, fifth door on your left'). It appears the state of temporal grace that prevents weapons from being fired within the ship is broken or has been disconnected, since in 'Bad Wolf' Jack blasts the Dalek that the TARDIS materialises around.
- When the Doctor looks in the mirror at the Tylers' he says 'Could have been worse. Look at the ears!' It is highly unlikely this is his first glimpse of his new face, as there are many shiny and reflective surfaces in the TARDIS control room (and he must have also shaved at some point). Indeed, Clive has visual evidence recording the ninth Doctor's presence in 1883, 1912 and 1963 (see Timeline Dates). These three adventures may have all taken place prior to the events of 'Rose'. So the Doctor has not necessarily regenerated only just recently. From the angle the Doctor holds his head in the reflection, it seems that from the 'could have been worse' line he is commenting on his short hair – maybe he's recently had it cut, and is still unsure about it as it makes his ears stick out.
- Clive refers to accounts of the Doctor's activities ('the Doctor is a legend woven throughout history') recorded in 'political diaries, conspiracy theories, even ghost stories'. He has recorded the ninth Doctor's presence in 1883, 1912 and 1963 (see Timeline Dates). Clive has clearly read of previous Auton invasions (specifically 'Spearhead From Space') because when he sees the window dummies come to life he says 'It's true. Everything I read; all the stories. It's all true!' He also refers to the ninth Doctor as 'your Doctor' when he shows Rose his collection of sightings, which suggests he is aware that there are 'other' Doctors.

LANGUAGE

The Nestene Conscious speaks but not in English, although the Doctor can understand it. The only English it does utter are the words 'Time Lord'. Mickey says the creature can speak, so presumably the Consciousness spoke to him in English, or it's just that creature made the noises that he identified as being a language.

TIMELINE DATES

2005, March 4 – 6 *

A calendar can be seen pinned to the wall of Jackie Tyler's bedroom, but the dates cannot be read.

When Rose accesses the Searchwire internet search engine, one of the index pages contains the notation 'Contents Copyright © 1995 – 2004', so it is no earlier than 2004. The road user tax disc on Mickey's car expires on '31.03.05'. Both these dates hint at it being early 2005. In 'The End Of The World', the Doctor briefly stops the TARDIS 'ten thousand years in the future. Step outside it's the year twelve thousand and five', which suggests the date of their departure was 2005. Based on these clues, 2005 is the best date.

While shopping, Clive speaks of spending 'summer money in winter months', so it appears to be winter, which supports it being no later than March.

In 'Aliens Of London', the Police Appeal Missing Person posters give the date of Rose's disappearance as '6th March 2005', which suggests this was the date Rose left with the Doctor. However, 6 March was a Sunday, and the shops were open late on the day Rose left in the TARDIS, so Day Two (see Duration) can't possibly have been a Sunday.

Since Clive's son is home when Rose calls by to see him, it could be a weekend, so Day Two could therefore be a Saturday, 5 March. However there are wheelie-bins being put out for collection on Clive's street, which implies it is not a weekend. It is possible Clive's son is home from school for some reason – maybe he is sick, or it is actually later in the day that it appears and he is already home from school?

A person is not legally deemed to be missing until they have been absent for at least 48 hours. After the events of Rose, Jackie could have returned home, and gone to bed expecting Rose to return home sometime the following day. In 'Aliens Of London' Rose says 'it's not the first time I've stayed out all night', so Jackie would not be overly concerned that Rose wasn't at home when she woke. Jackie would only begin to worry that she hadn't heard from Rose by late that evening. Jackie would have spent that night and the following day looking for her errant daughter, getting in touch with Rose's friends Shareen and Mickey (although he couldn't tell her the truth about Rose's departure).

If 6 March was the date for when Jackie last had contact from Rose, this would be the short phone call Rose makes before she leaves in the TARDIS. This was therefore shortly after midnight, the morning of Sunday 6 March. Therefore Rose takes place on three days – 4, 5 and 6 March 2005.

1223

The Doctor says 'the assembled hordes of Genghis Khan couldn't get through [the door of the TARDIS] – and believe me, they've tried'. In 'The Dæmons' the Doctor says he has met Genghis Khan, which I've placed as being around 1223. It's not necessarily the same visit, though; the ninth Doctor seems to imply explicitly that the hordes tried to break through the TARDIS doors as they exist in their present configuration, which would mean a recent adventure, set just prior to the events of 'Rose'.

1883, August 26 •

Clive records the ninth Doctor's arrival in '1883 … on the coast of Sumatra on the very night that Krakatoa exploded', which was on 26 August 1883 in our history. The drawing of the Doctor shows him in his usual jacket. The first or second Doctor was also on Krakatoa at the time, as mentioned by the third Doctor in 'Inferno'. The fact that Clive describes the Doctor as having 'washed up' on the coast of Sumatra suggest he did not arrive on the island in the TARDIS. (The eruption of Krakatoa also released the Xylok crystal; see 'The Lost Boy'.)

1912, April 9 •

Clive shows Rose a picture of the ninth Doctor and tells of his presence at Southampton in 'April, 1912 … the day before [the Daniels family was] due to sail to the new world on the Titanic'. In our history the Titanic set sail at noon on 10 April 1912, so the Doctor was there on the 9th (see also 'The Invasion of Time'.) In 'The End Of The World', the Doctor infers he was actually on the ship when it struck the iceberg, so it is possible these events are part of the same 'adventure'. Of note, the photo shows the ninth Doctor wearing clothes that look to be very similar to those worn by the eighth Doctor. Is this simply a costume worn by the ninth Doctor while he was in 1912, or is it perhaps one initially worn by the ninth soon after his regeneration, but which he discarded in favour of a less cumbersome leather jacket?

1963, November 22 •

The full date is given by Clive. The ninth Doctor was photographed in the crowd lining the streets of Dallas, Texas, as President Kennedy's motorcade drove towards Dealey

Plaza, just moments before the President was assassinated (see also 'Silver Nemesis'). He does not appear to be wearing his 'usual' jumper and leather jacket, but instead a green polo neck sweater.

2004 ■ ■ ■ ■ ■ ■ ■ ■ ■ ■ ■ ■ ■ ■
Clive says he obtained the photo of the Doctor in Dallas 1963 from the Washington public archive 'just last year'.

DURATION

⇨ **Day One (4 March)** ■ ■ ■ ■ ■ ■ ■ ■ ■ ■ ■ ■
It is '7.30' am when Rose wakes. She meets the Doctor shortly after closing hours – 6pm or 7pm, but certainly not any later than 8pm since Rose is home when the '20.45' (8.45pm) TV news item reporting the explosion at the store is aired.

⇨ **Day Two (5 March)** ■ ■ ■ ■ ■ ■ ■ ■ ■ ■ ■ ■
Rose wakes again at '7.30' am. The Doctor arrives around 12.45 (as indicated by the clock on the mantelpiece), having spent 'this morning' tracking the Auton arm. The story ends on the night of this second day, some time after '10.30pm' (as can be seen on the clock face of Big Ben). However this would mean Queen's Arcade was open for much later than most shops in London; this could be a special late-night closing due to all the (end of season?) clearance sales that are being advertised in the window displays. (This would also account for why night buses are operating; they don't usually begin their services until after midnight.)

⇨ **Day Three (6 March)** ■ ■ ■ ■ ■ ■ ■ ■ ■ ■ ■ ■
It is shortly after midnight (early Sunday morning) when Rose leaves in the TARDIS …

THE END OF THE WORLD

+STORY LINK

'The End Of The World' begins with Rose running into the TARDIS, as seen at the end of 'Rose'.

OBSERVATIONS

- The destruction of Earth in this time zone contradicts the events seen in 'The Ark' (and alluded to in 'Frontios') in which the Earth collides with the sun in the Fifty-Seventh Segment of Earth life, some ten million years in the future. However it's possible the planet didn't fall into the sun at all (we don't actually see this on-screen in 'The Ark' – all we get is a shot of the smouldering planet). So, taking 'The Ark' and 'Frontios' into account, the course of events was probably something along these lines: in ten million years time, life on Earth is threatened when the planet's orbit moves it closer to the sun. The space Ark and other colony ships are launched (as seen in 'The Ark' and 'Frontios'). The planet, although not destroyed but now orbiting closer to the sun, is rendered uninhabitable, a condition in which it remains for, presumably, millions of years. The planet eventually becomes viable again, a few billion years later, and new live evolves. (It's also possible that humans from colony worlds return to the ancestral planet.) In time, the National Trust takes custody of the planet and the land masses (in 'Bad Wolf', it is the Daleks who change the land-masses when they bombard the planet in 200,100) are realigned to reform 'Classic Earth'. Then billions of years later, the planet is once again threatened but this time with destruction, and so the National Trust sets up the sun barriers to save the planet. However, by this time the new human race has already abandoned the planet; the National Trust then decides to switch off the sun shields on the five billion year anniversary of the human calendar ...

- During the final five billion years, new life evolves on the planet such as the trees from which Jabe's race is descended, as well as the new (long-lived?) humanoid species that Cassandra is from. Five billion years is after all a very long time; the Earth is already over 10 billion years old (see 'Inferno'). Cassandra says 'I don't look a day over two thousand', which indicates the new species of human that she is of has a much longer lifespan. She mentions 'new humans', 'proto-humans' and 'digi-humans' (she considers them all to be 'mongrels'); it is possible these are a new species of human that evolved on Earth in the second five billion years phase of life on Earth following the abandonment of the planet in 'The Ark'.

- Given that the Face of Boe, who organised the viewing of Earth Death from Platform One, is Captain Jack, and that the Doctor is in a way ultimately responsible for Jack's fate in becoming Boe, it could be inferred that the Doctor is therefore indirectly responsible for everything that happens on Platform One. And Boe might also be a member of the National Trust who has been preserving 'Classic Earth' for billions of years, and who has now turned off the shields keeping the sun at bay, so the Doctor could be said to be responsible in some way for Earth Death, too! So much for Earth being his favourite planet.

LANGUAGE

All the aliens on Platform One – bar the little blue attendants (who speak in a high-pitched twitter) – speak English, and the written language, such as on the keypads, is English. The 'coat-check' receipt the Doctor is handed is adorned with alien symbols that also appear to be in English. The Doctor explains to Rose the reason the aliens 'all speak English' is because the TARDIS's 'telepathic field gets inside your brain and translates'. Cassandra speaks English. Indeed, her name, despite this being five billion years in the future, is still very 'modern'.

TIMELINE DATES

2005, March 2 (?)

When Rose rings her mother, Jackie says it is 'the middle of the day' and it's a 'Wednesday'. The fact that Jackie thinks Rose is at work and asks her to put a quid in the lottery syndicate clearly indicates this day is not after the events of 'Rose', in which the department store was destroyed. It must be either some time prior to 'Rose', or it might even be two days prior to 'Rose' (which is set on a Friday and Saturday). Jackie is wearing the same top she wore on Day One of 'Rose', but this does not necessarily mean it is the same day: she is doing the laundry when Rose phones, so in all likelihood she does another load at some point prior to 'Rose'.

An interesting anomaly arises because of this phone call: Jackie asks Rose to put a quid into the store's lottery syndicate, and says she will pay Rose back. But the Rose she is speaking with is from her near 'future' and not 'her' Rose. 'Her' Rose doesn't have this conversation, and therefore wouldn't have put any money into the syndicate on Jackie's behalf. So, when Jackie goes to reimburse her daughter, Rose wouldn't know what the money was for, and would deny having spoken with Jackie. One can only just imagine the argument that followed!

Presumably the Doctor fixes this temporal 'fault' with the phone, so that the next time Rose rings home, Jackie receives the call relative to the time that Rose has been away (as in 'Love & Monsters', in which Rose says she'll be home 'soon'), otherwise Rose could ring Jackie out of sync relative to the passage of time for Jackie. It certainly seems that when the Doctor later adjusts Martha's phone in '42' that Martha always rings home relative to her own time. (See also 'The Sontaran Stratagem' and 'The Stolen Earth' for additional notes about ringing the TARDIS with a mobile phone.)

2005 (after March) ▸ ▩ ▩ ▩ ▩ ▩ ▩ ▩ ▩ ▩ ▩ ▩

After leaving Platform One, the Doctor takes Rose back to London. We can assume that this is contemporary to her own time period as the Doctor wants to show her a familiar place. Given that a whole year has passed when they return to London again in 'Aliens Of London', this brief landing could be set at any time between March 2005 and March 2006. They stay there long enough to buy and eat chips.

2105 ▸ ▩ ▩ ▩ ▩ ▩ ▩ ▩ ▩ ▩ ▩ ▩ ▩

Rose wants to go 'one hundred years' into the future; which from 2005 (see above) is 2105. The TARDIS lands in that time zone (does it also shift its location?), but the Doctor says 'the twenty second century; it's a bit boring, though', which is a rather strange comment for him to make considering all the adventures he has had in that century! (e.g. 'The Dalek Invasion Of Earth'). On the assumption that the TARDIS has travelled exactly 100 years to 2105, then this is around the time that T-Mat was in use ('The Seeds Of Death'), as well as the beginnings of early warp-drive capability ('Nightmare Of Eden') – hardly a boring time period!

12,005 ▸ ▩ ▩ ▩ ▩ ▩ ▩ ▩ ▩ ▩ ▩ ▩ ▩

The next time jump is to 'ten thousand years in the future. Step outside it's the year twelve thousand and five, the New Roman Empire'. As established in 'The Ark In Space' and 'The Sontaran Experiment', in the year 15,000 the surface of the planet Earth had been devastated by solar flares, and it's stated that 'no one's set foot [on Earth] for thousands of years', which I have taken to mean ten thousand years. This would seem to counter any idea that a second Roman Empire has been established on the planet. However in 'The Sontaran Experiment', Vural says while the Nerva people slept his people established 'bases all across the galaxy now… We made an empire'. It is therefore possible that the 'empire' he speaks of is also known as the New Roman Empire.

5.5/apple/26 ▸ **(5,000,000,000)** ▩ ▩ ▩ ▩ ▩ ▩ ▩ ▩ ▩ ▩

The Doctor tells Rose 'this is the year five point five slash apple slash twenty six. Five billion years in your future.' It's not clear what the 'slash apple slash' signifies, but it could be some form of abbreviation for the six zeros, which could make the full date something like 5,500,000,026. The planet is uninhabited (the Doctor says 'it's empty; all gone, all left'). The fact that he says 'I know exactly where to go', and takes the TARDIS to Platform One on the precise day this event occurs, suggests he has been to this very time zone before.

The fact that he specifically says it is the year five billion (a date he and Rose later confirm in 'Aliens Of London') suggests that this is indeed the actual year. Of course, given the number of times in which the Earth has been abandoned and re-colonised during this time (see 'The Ark', 'The Ark In Space' / 'The Sontaran Experiment', 'The Sun Makers', 'Frontios', The Mysterious Planet), one then has to accept but at a bit of a stretch that the Gregorian calendar is still recognised and unaltered for these five billion years!

Of course, it is highly likely that the date of Earth Death has specifically been scheduled to take place on the five billion milestone date – a legacy that has been maintained by the National Trust (at the behest of the Face of Boe?) for quite some time – as it is a nice round number on which to switch off the energy fields holding back the sun. On this basis, I am prepared to accept that it is indeed the year 5,000,000,000, rather than, say 5,500,000,016.

In 'Colony In Space', the Doctor says Earth's sun would explode in 'ten thousand million years' time', however in that instance he is referring to the death of the sun, whereas in 'The End Of The World' it is merely its expansion at least as far as Earth's orbit.

1912, April 14 – 15 ♦

The Doctor tells Jabe he was once on board an 'unsinkable' ship and ended up clinging to an iceberg ('it wasn't 'alf cold'). While it is not actually named as such, the inference is that this is the *Titanic*. The ninth Doctor met the Daniels family on 9 April (see Rose), so if it was also the ninth Doctor who was on board the ship, then it's possible he sailed on the *Titanic* two days later. (Did he save the family so he could use their tickets?) The fourth Doctor mentions the *Titanic* in 'Robot' (and again in 'The Robots Of Death'), making it the first, second or third Doctor who was in that time period – or who at least acquired knowledge of the disaster. And the newspaper glimpsed in 'The Invasion Of Time' could have been purchased by any one of the first four Doctors. Therefore, at least two – possibly even three – different Doctors were present before, during and after the *Titanic* disaster!

5.4/cup/16 (5,400,000,016?)

The Steward says that teleportation devices were banned in the year 'five point four slash cup slash sixteen'.

DURATION

(TARDIS)

The Doctor and Rose spend a few minutes in the TARDIS before landing on Platform One …

⇨ **Day One** ▪ ▪ ▪ ▪ ▪ ▪ ▪ ▪ ▪ ▪ ▪ ▪
The TARDIS arrives on Platform One around 15.07 – there are just over 'thirty minutes' until Earth-Death, which 'is scheduled for 15.39'. The rest of the story plays out almost in real-time, with Earth's destruction occurring some 27 minutes later.

⇨ **Day One (2005?)** ▪ ▪ ▪ ▪ ▪ ▪ ▪ ▪ ▪ ▪ ▪
The Doctor and Rose return to (presumably 'present day') London.

THE UNQUIET DEAD

+STORY LINK

Having taken Rose to the far future (and then back to 2005 for chips), the Doctor wants them to 'have a look at the past'; 'The End Of The World' and 'The Unquiet Dead' are therefore consecutive. For Rose, in terms of her own time it is probably well past midnight, and yet she shows no sign of being tired. It is possible that after their brief stopover in London, Rose has had a short nap prior to arriving in Cardiff 1869; she is wearing the same clothes she wore in 'Rose' and 'The End Of The World'.

While Rose is dressing in the TARDIS wardrobe, the Doctor takes the opportunity to change his jumper (from crimson to dark blue), and also to put some money in his pocket, which he didn't have when they returned to Rose's time in the coda to 'The End Of The World'. (Thinking they were in Naples, the Doctor would have stocked up on some lira, and yet he purchases the Cardiff paper with (presumably) the correct currency, which indicates he also stocked up with other forms of currency.)

OBSERVATIONS

- The Doctor says he saw 'World War Five'. No dates are known for when this took place. World War Six was nearly trigged towards the end of the fifty-first century (circa 5000 AD), as mentioned by the Doctor in 'The Talons Of Weng-Chiang', which means World War Five (plus Wars Three and Four) occurred some time between 1945 and 5000.
- When talking with Rose, Gwyneth 'sees' into Rose's mind and gains impressions of the future; not only modern-day London, but also 'the Big Bad Wolf', and 'the darkness'. With regard to this latter vision of the darkness, is Gwyneth perhaps 'seeing' Rose's participation in the events seen in 'The Stolen Earth' at which a future distant relative of Gwyneth's is also present?

LANGUAGE

The Gelth speak English as well as through Gwyneth's mouth.

TIMELINE DATES

1869, December 24 ✦
The full date appears as 'Friday, December 24th, 1869' on the poster in Charles Dickens's dressing room at the Taliesin Lodge, and is also confirmed by the newspaper the Doctor buys. (The Doctor was actually heading for 1860, and thought they had landed in Naples on 'December 24th, 1860', a date he reads from the TARDIS instrumentation.)

1188 BC ✦
The Doctor mentions being there during 'the fall of Troy' – an event he did indeed witness in 'The Myth Makers'.

1773, December 16 ✦
The Doctor says he 'pushed boxes at the Boston Tea Party', an event which took place on this date in our history (see also 'The Dalek Invasion Of Earth'). The raiders of the three tea ships in Boston harbour were disguised as Indians, so presumably the Doctor was dressed likewise!

1783
Mrs Redpath 'was 86' in 1869, so she was born in 1783.

1848
The Rift is 'a weak point in time and space ... a connection between this place and another ... [on] the other side of the Universe'. Note the use of the word 'place' rather than 'time'. (In 'Boom Town' and numerous *Torchwood* episodes, it is said the Rift runs 'through the middle of the city'.) The Rift has probably been there for many years; Mr Sneed says stories of hauntings go back 'generations', and which as he says is probably one of the reasons why he got the house so cheap. Gwyneth, who is about 26, 'grew up on top of the Rift', ever since she was 'a little girl'. She says Angels (the Gelth) have 'been singing to me since I was a child'; Gwyneth first heard the voices when she was say about 5. The Doctor says she is 'part of it ... the key'. The disembodied Gelth have probably been seeking a solution to their plight for many years, which suggests the affects of the Time War devastated their planet as early as the 1850s, if not earlier. They only succeeded in making the journey through the Rift in 1869 once conditions to do so became suitable.

1855

Gwyneth says she lost her 'mum and dad to the flu when I was 12'. Assuming she is about 26 in 1869, her parents died in 1855. Although Gwyneth has no children of her own, she must have aunts, uncles and cousins – and it is due to what the Doctor calls 'spatial genetic multiplicity' in 'The Stolen Earth' that Gwen Cooper of Torchwood Three looks like Gwyneth.

1869, September

Mr Sneed says the dead first started getting restless 'about three months back', which is around September – so this must be when the Gelth first journeyed through the Rift to Earth; presumably the approaching winter months and the increased use of gas at this time suited their purposes. However they have obviously made (limited) contact with Gwyneth many years prior to this – see 1855 above.

1870, June 9

The Doctor says Dickens will die in '1870'; this was on 9 June 1870 in our history.

DURATION

⇨ Day One (24 December 1869)

The TARDIS lands in the evening of 24 December 1869. The Doctor and Rose depart a few hours later on the same night just before midnight. (Dickens refers to all the things he's learned 'tonight'.)

ALIENS OF LONDON
WORLD WAR THREE

+STORY LINK

Since the events of 'Rose', the Doctor believes they have been gone for 'about twelve hours'. Rose tells Mickey 'It's only been a few days for me. It's just a few days since I left you'; in that time she was on Platform One for just over half an hour, stopped in London for chips ('The End Of The World'), and then visited Cardiff for a few hours in 1869. The rest of the time was presumably spent in transit in the TARDIS. Rose is wearing the same clothes she had on when she entered the TARDIS in 'Rose', so she has changed back into them since the recent adventure in Cardiff ('The Unquiet Dead'). The Doctor had on a crimson jumper in 'Rose' and 'The End Of The World', but changed to a dark blue one in 'The Unquiet Dead'; he is still wearing it in 'Aliens Of London'.

Rose refers to being the only person on Earth who knows about 'aliens and spaceships and things'. It is not clear when she would have seen 'spaceships' – there is certainly no clear moment for this to have occurred in 'The End Of The World', although there are some hovering outside Platform One. So, unless she is explicitly referring to the Earth-Death observers' spacecraft, there must have been an off-screen adventure before 'Aliens Of London' in which she saw such vessels.

OBSERVATIONS

- Unless the Doctor deals with it during the off-screen period prior to leaving with Rose ('I'll be a couple of hours'), the Slitheen ship is still where it crashed in the Thames when the Doctor and Rose depart in the TARDIS. The other Slitheen ship is in the North Sea. It is possible therefore that the military seized both vessels to study the technology, and from this they develop the *Valiant* ('The Sound Of Drums'), deep space rockets, orbital space stations, moonbases and other hardware such as that seen in 'The Moonbase' (2070), and 'The Wheel In Space' (set in 2080), etc. When Blon Fel Fotch Slitheen escapes to Cardiff (see 'Boom Town'), she certainly does not take any opportunity to recover either ship. (And the Slitheen in 'Revenge Of The Slitheen' and 'The Lost Boy' also do not mention the lost ship.)
- It is not readily clear why the TARDIS jumps ahead one year when returning Rose to her home. It does not have the same problem when returning Martha Jones or Donna Noble home within their own respective relative timelines. A likely answer lies in the fact that the events seen in 'Bad Wolf' required Rose to return home in order for her to become Bad Wolf. It was the effect of the Bad Wolf influence that pulled the TARDIS forwards one year, so 2006 would become Rose's 'present day', so when she was sent home by the Doctor, the TARDIS would land in its new default year of 2006 rather than Rose's correct year of 2005 in order for the Bad Wolf to be created.
- The Doctor says Harriet Jones will be a future Prime Minister, and 'elected for three successive terms', becoming 'the architect of Britain's Golden Age'. However, Jones is deposed in 'The Christmas Invasion', having, it seems, served only a few months of her first term. As noted under POLITICALLY INCORRECT, it's possible Jones called early elections during 2006 to take advantage of her popularity, and therefore had two successive terms in the space of half a year.
- The Doctor claims to be '900' years old. This is covered in more detail under

THE DOCTOR'S AGE.

- The Doctor gives Mickey a CD containing a virus that will erase all record of the Doctor from the internet. In 'Love & Monsters' Victor Kennedy refers to a 'Bad Wolf virus', which has corrupted Torchwood's files on the Doctor. It's possible the Bad Wolf virus is the one the Doctor created.

- The unnamed medic who performs the autopsy on the dead 'space pig', turns out to be Toshiko Sato from Torchwood Three in Cardiff. She recalls the 'space pig' incident in 'Exit Wounds'. Originally Dr Owen Harper was supposed to attend to the autopsy but was suffering a hang-over, so Toshiko went in his place. It's unclear why one of the team from Cardiff would be sent to London, when presumably Torchwood One would have its own qualified personnel who could be assigned. Tosh refers to the Doctor by name in 'Aliens Of London', and yet in later *Torchwood* episodes, when Jack refers to his Doctor ('the right kind of doctor'), Tosh does not display any sign of making a connection. It seems odd that Tosh finds the existence of aliens hard to accept, although this might simply be pretence on her part, since she does not know who the Doctor is.

- The Albion Hospital is chosen as the place to take the body from the crashed spaceship as it is the one 'closest to the river'. However, as we see in 'Smith And Jones', the Royal Hope Hospital is in fact closer, being adjacent to the London Eye, which is next to where the spaceship crashed. We can assume from this that the Royal Hope did not exist in March 2006, but that it was built and completed by June 2008, the setting for 'Smith And Jones'. The Albion Hospital is also the hospital that the gas-mask zombies were taken to during the 1941 Blitz in 'The Empty Child'.

LANGUAGE

The Slitheen speak English; and even more curiously they still speak with the voice of the human they were disguised as even when not wearing the human 'skins'.

TIMELINE DATES

2006, March 6 – 7 ⁜

A whiteboard in the infirmary at Albion Hospital displays a number of dates, one of which is '31/01/04'. In context it's not clear what this date represents [the location filming in July 2004 was at a functioning hospital, so this date is a Production Factor].

The Doctor discovers that he and Rose have been away from London for '12 months', and tells her she's 'been gone a whole year'. They left on 5 March (see 'Rose') so, taking into account their '12 hours' in the TARDIS (Rose certainly thinks it's the next day: 'it's not the first time I've stayed out all night'); it is now 6 March 2006 ('a whole year'). This means Rose is out of sync with her own relative time (as had previously happened with Jamie and Zoe in 'The War Games', Jo in 'Colony In Space' and 'The Time Monster', Tegan in 'Time-Flight' and 'Resurrection Of The Daleks', and Turlough in 'Planet Of Fire'.) She continues to be one year out of sync every time she returns to Earth ('Boom Town', 'Bad Wolf', etc). In 'The Christmas Invasion' she even tells Mickey she's 'out of sync'.

218 BC

The Doctor and Harriet Jones know about Hannibal, who marched across the Alps in 218 BC (See also 'Marco Polo', 'The Dalek Invasion Of Earth' and 'Robot'.)

1730 (+?)

It seems the Doctor has met Mr Chicken ('a nice man'), who was the original owner of 10 Downing Street in '1730'. (In our history Mr Chicken moved out in 1735, when Sir Robert Walpole became the first Prime Minister to take up residence.)

1796

The Doctor knows the location of the Cabinet Room in 1796.

c1920 *

The Doctor says Lloyd-George 'used to drink me under the table'. In the context of the name-drop and the Doctor's follow-on comment 'Who's the Prime Minister now?', the Doctor presumably met David Lloyd-George (born on 17 January 1863, died on 26 March 1945) during his term as Prime Minister, which was from December 1916, at the height of the First World War, until 1922. The first Doctor and Susan were in London during the 1917 Zeppelin raids ('Planet Of Giants'), but it's unlikely the Doctor would have been drinking-buddies with Lloyd-George during this visit, or indeed whilst in his first incarnation, as he once said 'I never touch alcohol' ('The Gunfighters'). The Doctor met Dame Nellie Melba circa 1920 ('The Power Of Kroll'), so it is possible he met Lloyd-George during the same visit to London.

1991 (+?)

The Doctor knows that the security shutters around the Cabinet Room were 'installed in 1991'. Was he there at the time?

2005, December (?)

The Doctor says the Slitheen have 'been here for a while' (the ship was in the North Sea), although there is no indication as to exactly how long in terms of days, weeks, months or years. Given the complexity of their scheme, it would obviously have taken the Slitheen months just to assess the situation, devise the plan, and begin the infiltration of the various key positions in the British government and authority. Then they would have to capture and complete the augmentation of the pig, etc. It is therefore not unreasonable that the Slitheen have been on Earth for three or more months.

2005, December 31

Jackie says she has a bottle of wine left over 'from New Year's Eve'. Mickey mentions that Jackie does a conga when she gets drunk. Rose had been missing for nine months by that time.

2006, March 3

The Doctor says the satellite detected the radiation blip beneath the North Sea 'three days ago'.

DURATION

⇨ **Day One (March 6) (Ep1-2)**

It is early morning when the TARDIS lands. The spaceship crashes into Big Ben at 9.58am. [Although it is clear that the footage of the smashed clock-face has been reversed, and the time of the crash should be 2.02pm, I have taken the on-screen position of the clock's hands as being the more correct.] Harriet Jones was left waiting at 10 Downing Street, some hours after her '3:15' appointment with the now-missing Prime Minister, so several hours pass. When the crash is reported 'LIVE' on the TV news, the hands of Big Ben read 6.10pm. The clock on the mortuary wall reads '10.46' when the Doctor materialises the TARDIS in Albion Hospital later that night, and it reads '10.55' when the dead pig is examined. When Jackie Tyler rings the alien help-line number, the TV news gives the time as '23.08'.

⇨ **Day Two (March 7) (Ep1-2)**

It is '3 o'clock in the morning' when Jackie and Mickey access the UNIT website. At 'midnight' in New York (which is 6am in the UK in March) the UN convenes. The missile is launched as day breaks. After the threat is over, the Doctor takes 'a couple of hours' to sort things out. That evening Jackie wants to cook 'tea', but Rose and the Doctor depart in the TARDIS ...

DALEK

STORY LINK

At the end of 'Aliens Of London' Rose packs a bag of clothes and belongings. The Doctor has tempted her with a trip to see 'a plasma storm brewing in the Horsehead Nebula' but there's no indication in 'Dalek' that they have done this. Although Rose is wearing the same Punky Fish sweater she had on at the end of 'Aliens Of London', she has a distinctively different hair-style in 'Dalek', so it would appear she's had time (off-screen) to get it waved and restyled. The Doctor now sports a green jumper.

In 'Boom Town', Rose tells Mickey of her visit to the planet Woman Wept, which was 'a while back'. Presumably this adventure on the frozen sea took place early on in her travels with the Doctor, so it probably took place between 'Aliens Of London' and 'Dalek' (almost certainly before she met Adam). Therefore, we can assume they left Earth, saw the plasma-storm, eventually arrived on Woman Wept (where Rose also had her hair done?), then some time after that the TARDIS is drawn off course by the Dalek's distress signal …

DALEK LINK

This is the eighteenth appearance of the Daleks – see DALEK HISTORY. During the Time War this lone warrior Dalek falls 'through time' …

… and crashes on Ascension Islands on Earth around 1960, and is found 'three days later'. For over 50 years it is sold at private auction, moving from one collection to another, eventually coming into the possession of Henry Van Statten. (Although it's not clear why no one knows what the creature is, despite numerous appearances of Daleks on Earth over the years…). All this time it has been transmitting a distress signal to other Daleks seeking orders, but the message goes unanswered … until the TARDIS detects the signal in 2012 …

OBSERVATIONS

- Included in the exhibits of Van Statten's museum is the head of an Alien from the film series. Presumably this is a remnant from the events seen in the film *Alien vs Predator*, which is set in the early twenty-first century. See also 'Mindwarp' for more on links between *Doctor Who* and the *Alien* series.
- The Slitheen arm in Van Statten's museum is not necessarily from one of the creatures destroyed when 10 Downing Street blew up in 'Aliens Of London', or killed during 'Revenge Of The Slitheen' or 'The Lost Boy'. Indeed there's no reason why it has to be a Slitheen – it could simply be that of another

Raxacoricofallapatorian who had visited Earth prior to 2012.

LANGUAGE

The Dalek is silent while it is in Van Statten's museum. It does not speak until it comes face to face with the Doctor; presumably its language is translated into English by the TARDIS telepathic circuit / Time Lord gift.

TIMELINE DATES

2012 ·

The Doctor tells Rose the year is 'two thousand and twelve'. At the time of transmission, this date was accepted without question, but in light of subsequent stories, a 2012 setting becomes harder and harder to rationalise.

The main problem lies in the fact that no one at the Geocomtex base knows what the Dalek is, despite widespread Dalek activity on Earth prior to 2012: such as in 'The Chase', 'Day Of The Daleks', 'Army Of Ghosts', 'Daleks In Manhattan' and 'The Stolen Earth'. And for a man of Van Statten's standing and influence, not to forget being a collector of alien artefacts, he must be known to UNIT and Torchwood, and in turn know of them and presumably their past dealings with Daleks.

The second problem lies in Adam's comments to Rose about the existence of aliens – 'I'm almost certain it's from the hull of a spacecraft'. He says 'thing is, it's all true – everything the United Nations tries to keep quiet. Aliens, spacecraft, visitors to the Earth. They really exist ... I know it sounds incredible. But I honestly believe the whole universe is just teeming with life'. This is an odd statement to make when by 2012 the Earth had been invaded several times, all of which were witnessed on a global scale (and often reported on American TV by AMNN news anchor Trinity Wells): in 2006, the Sycorax spaceship ('The Christmas Invasion', in which the Doctor says 'No denying the existence of aliens now. Everybody saw it'); 2007, the Cybermen ('Army Of Ghosts') and the Racnoss ('The Runaway Bride'); 2008, the Toclafane ('The Sound Of Drums); the Adipose ('Partners In Crime') plus all those Daleks themselves in 'Army Of Ghosts' (2007) and 'The Stolen Earth', which was only three years earlier (2009) [and also all those likely 'aliens invade present day Earth on a global scale' stories still to come in the post-2009 (and particularly the 2012?) series of *Doctor Who*].

Here are three plausible solutions to get around the continuity and dating problems:

1) 'Dalek' is not set in 2012; the Doctor got the date wrong again, just as he did two journeys earlier: taking Rose to 1869 Cardiff rather than 1860 Naples

('The Unquiet Dead'); and to March 2006 rather than 2005 ('Aliens Of London'). Indeed, there are no other indications as to the year from which Adam comes; in 'The Long Game', he says the year 200,000 is 198,000 in his future, which is a general rounding down by 2000 years. [In the DWM Series One Companion, Russell T Davies says the original 2010 setting was changed to 2012 for 'no good reason, I think it just sounded better', so the date was not exactly essential to the story.] We could actually shift 'Dalek' (and in turn the final scene in 'The Long Game') back a few years, say to mid to late 2006, prior to 'The Christmas Invasion', which was when the existence of aliens become globally accepted. The Slitheen arm could have been salvaged from 10 Downing Street ('Aliens Of London').

2) 'Dalek' takes place in 2012, but when the Daleks invade Earth in 'Army Of Ghosts', 'Daleks In Manhattan' and 'The Stolen Earth' [and TV Dalek adventures still to come], Earth's timeline is changed to the degree that the events of 'Daleks' play out in a different way (the main alteration being that Van Statten knows what the Dalek is) if ever at all. This would presumably mean that Van Statten is still alive and head of Geocomtex, and Adam never travelled in the TARDIS. Do Adam's memories change following the events of 'The Stolen Earth', or is he protected from these changes because he has travelled in the TARDIS? And how far does any change extend? With 'Fear Her' also set in 2012, did Chloe Webber and her mother experience the events of 'The Stolen Earth', or did this not happen in their timeline? When we try to factor in alternative futures like this, even when we take into consideration what the Doctor calls the infinite temporal flux ('The Shakespeare Code' – see ALTERNATIVE TIMELINES), we are always crossing very dangerous grounds as it has often been said by the Doctor himself that parallel worlds, and altered and/or alternative timelines and the like, are all closed off, so how could the TARDIS have travelled into this and the altered version of history?

3) Taking 2) a step further, if time is 'in flux' ('The Unquiet Dead'), at the time of 'Dalek', the Doctor has yet to meet Queen Victoria in 1869 and thus the events that lead to the creation of Torchwood ('Tooth And Claw') haven't yet taken place in the past. Since Torchwood does not exist in this version of history, the Cult of Skaro never emerges from the breach in the Void that Torchwood opened in 2007 ('Army Of Ghosts'). The Cult of Skaro therefore does not make an emergency temporal shift to 1930s New York ('Daleks In Manhattan'), from which Dalek Caan makes a further fateful jump back into the Time War (from which Van Statten's Dalek had originally fallen through Time), which itself ultimately results in the events of 'The Stolen Earth'. In

a yet-to-be-revealed (off-screen?) event between 2009 and 2012, something must happen that brings this circular 'paradox' around again back to the events as seen in 'Dalek', in which no one knows what the Metaltron is…

4) It is the year 2012, but somehow everyone at Geocomtex is suffering from mass memory block, and as such do not know what the Dalek is. This might be caused by one of the many alien artefacts held in the underground complex. It's possible that it is the Dalek itself that is (unknowingly?) radiating some form of psychic perception filter (just as the Master had done on a far bigger scale through the Archangel Network in 'The Sound Of Drums') that can cloud people's minds, and remove from it any recognition of what the Dalek is, even when they – and it – access the internet, which should have reports on past sightings of Daleks on Earth. And it has been generating this block ever since it crashed on Earth, which is why all the others who owned the 'Metaltron' prior to Van Statten also can't have identified what the creature really was. The block must also have affected Adam in a different way, which explains his unusual conversation with Rose about aliens, and why he failed to recognise what the alien musical instrument and other artefacts he was cataloguing (such as the 'hair-dryer') really were. The Doctor is of course immune to the block, and once he becomes aware of the Dalek's name, Van Statten too becomes 'immune'. And once the Dalek is destroyed, the effects of the block eventually wear off, so Adam and Goddard would in time remember what had been blocked from their minds.

5) The timelines (and therefore people's memories) have been affected by some external force or influence.

[And as I said earlier, if *Doctor Who* runs for a further four years, and a full series screens in 2012, it's possible there will be a reference to this adventure, and perhaps there will be an 'official' explanation for the contradictions between 'Dalek' and 'The Stolen Earth'.]

1700s

Goddard says extraterrestrial technology 'has been falling to Earth for centuries', so we can assume this has been happening since around the 1700s.

1908, June 30

Van Statten refers to the cultivation of bacteria taken from 'the Russian crater'. This is presumably the one at Tunguska in Siberia, believed to have been caused by a single large meteor that exploded over the Tunguska River valley on this date in our history. (The Tunguska Basin is also where the Tunguska Scroll was found - see

'Enemy Of The Bane'.)

1947, July 4 (+?) ▨ ▨ ▨ ▨ ▨ ▨ ▨ ▨ ▨ ▨ ▨ ▨
The Doctor recognises 'the mileometer from the Roswell spaceship'. The 'crash' is documented as having occurred on 4 July 1947 (around 11.30pm) in our history, with the military arriving on the morning of 5 July. The Doctor might have been there. Van Statten developed broadband from the alien technology found at the crash site.

1960 ▨ ▨ ▨ ▨ ▨ ▨ ▨ ▨ ▨ ▨ ▨ ▨ ▨ ▨
Goddard says the Dalek has 'been on Earth for over 50 years'; so it fell to Earth around 1960. It crashed on Ascension Island where it lay buried, screaming in pain 'for three days'. Curiously, if its distress signal has been transmitting ever since the crash, why didn't Daleks detect or act upon the signal when they were on Earth at various points between 1963 and 1984, as seen in 'The Chase', 'The Evil Of The Daleks', 'Day Of The Daleks', 'Resurrection Of The Daleks' and 'Remembrance of the Daleks'? One answer is that since this is a Dalek from a time zone far in the future from those of the other stories noted above, we could assume that the distress signal is simply not compatible with the technology used by the Daleks from those earlier time periods in Dalek history. This would be rather like someone transmitting a colour digital television signal in 1960 – no one would have the equipment to receive, decode and play the transmission.

2010 ▨ ▨ ▨ ▨ ▨ ▨ ▨ ▨ ▨ ▨ ▨ ▨ ▨ ▨
Amongst the exhibits in Van Statten's museum is the helmet of a Cyberman of the design that appeared in 'Revenge Of The Cybermen'. Although the events of that story have seen set in the year 2525 this Cyberman could quite easily come from a time period prior to the original Cyber-War of 2020 – 2025. [Of note, the label on the display cabinet says 'Extraterrestrial Cyborg Specimen Incomplete / Recovered From Underground Sewer / Location: London, United Kingdom / Date: 1975'. The inference is that this is a Cyberman from 'The Invasion' – 1975 being the year the head was found rather than the date of the actual invasion, which was in 1970 – and yet the helmet design is very different from the Cybermen in that earlier story. Since the text on the label is not visible on-screen, I have dismissed using it as a dating tool.] Therefore, with the Cyber-War commencing in 2020, it is not inconceivable that several decades or so prior to the start of the War a scout ship crashed on Earth, from which the head was recovered. (See 'Revenge Of The Cybermen' for more on this War.)

2011

Van Statten says 'just last year' his scientists cultivated bacteria (from the Russian crater – see 1908 above) that would cure the common cold.

DURATION

⇨ **Day One**

Just before leaving in the TARDIS, the Doctor tells Adam there is time for him to catch the next flight to Heathrow, which leaves at '1500 hours', so it is some time prior to 3pm. The Doctor and Rose are in the Geocomtex underground complex for a couple of hours at least, so they probably arrived around midday.

THE LONG GAME

+STORY LINK

Adam entered the TARDIS at the end of 'Dalek'. He is wearing the same clothes in 'The Long Game'. Rose is wearing different clothes, so only a short period of time has elapsed in the TARDIS between departing 2012 and landing on Satellite Five. The Doctor still has on his green jumper. (Adam had a bag with him when he entered the TARDIS, but presumably this gets left on board since the Doctor doesn't return it to Adam when he gets dumped back home.)

Of note, after leaving Earth following their encounter with the Dalek, is it coincidence that the TARDIS's next landing is not only to the year 200,000, a time period in which a hidden fleet of Daleks was amassing on the edge of the solar system, but also to the satellite station where, in 100 years time, the Doctor would face that same Dalek army?

OBSERVATIONS

- Adam is left on Earth in 2012 with future technology fused to his brain. While he only glimpsed some of Earth's future history from the Satellite Five computer (learning that the redundant microprocessor is replaced by single molecule transcription in 2019, and might be in a position to exploit that knowledge) it is also possible that he retained more of the download he received through the implant …

LANGUAGE

The Mighty Jagrafess of the Holy Hadrojassic Maxarodenfoe speaks in an alien language that the Editor can understand. Although the signage on Satellite Five is in English, there are alien symbols on the screens in the Editor's control room. Despite transmitting news to the entire Empire, which includes aliens, the Satellite only broadcasts in English. Certainly, 100 years later ('Bad Wolf'), the TV broadcasts are all still in English.

TIMELINE DATES

200,000 ✦

The Doctor gives the year as 'two hundred thousand'. He has been to this time period before because he says 'my history's perfect' and knows this to be the time of the 'Fourth Great and Bountiful Human Empire' (and even has a cashpoint card with unlimited credit so he must have a bank account there), but later realises 'this technology's wrong' and that 'humanity has been set back about 90 years'. (He discovers the truth behind this distortion of history in 'Bad Wolf'.) Suki gives her (faked?) date of birth as 'one-nine-nine-apostrophe-eight-nine' (199'89) but if this is supposed to mean 199,089, then that would make her only 11 years old! (As in 'The End Of The World', it appears that dates now include words starting with the letter 'a' – i.e. 'apple'.)

The Fourth Great and Bountiful Human Empire stretches across a million planets, a million species. Earth is the centre, with a population of 96 billion. There are now five moons. If this indeed is the Fourth Empire, then there must have been a First, Second and Third. The Second Great and Bountiful Human Empire of the forty-second century encompasses at least three galaxies, as seen in 'Planet Of The Ood' (set in 4126).

2012 ✦

'Dalek' is set in 2012, so we can assume that this is the same time period that Adam is returned to. According to his mother he has been away for 'six months' (if 'Dalek' is set early in 2012, then he could have left home in 2011). In 'The End Of The World', when Rose spoke to her mother on her mobile phone, for Jackie it was a few days earlier than the events of 'Rose' – in other words the Doctor's initial 'jiggery pokery' with Rose's mobile means that calls made from the phone backwards through time would be a few days out of sync with the caller's relative time. So when Adam returns home, the Doctor probably steered the TARDIS to follow the telephone messages Adam had left on the answering machine, therefore possibly arriving a day or so 'earlier' than Adam's actual relative time.

2019

From the station computer, Adam learns that the microprocessor was made redundant 'in the year 2019' and replaced by single molecule transcription.

199,909

From his knowledge of this time period, the Doctor estimates that 'humanity's been set back about 90 years'. Cathica confirms that Satellite Five started broadcasting 'ninety one years ago', which is 199,909. The Editor says the Mighty Jagrafess of the Holy Hadrojassic Maxarodenfoe has being ruling humanity 'for almost a hundred years'. The Jagrafess has a lifespan of 'three thousand years', but there is no indication as to the age of this particular specimen. The Jagrafess was installed under the aegis of the Daleks, who have been controlling Earth's Empire for 'centuries' (since around 199,000?) ('Bad Wolf'). It's not clear where the Jagrafess came from and why the Daleks should use that particular kind of creature to control the station, especially given its rather restrictive life support requirements (e.g. heat-extraction). It's not a Dalek creature or mutant like the Slyther ('The Dalek Invasion Of Earth') as the fact that it has such an elaborate name implies it comes from another civilisation. Of course the name could be part of the deception to ensure the Editor is kept none-the-wiser of the true purpose of Satellite Five or the true nature of his Dalek masters.

199,997

Cathica says she has been applying for promotion to Floor 500 'for three years'.

DURATION

⇨ **Day One**

The TARDIS is on Satellite Five for about an hour; they arrive shortly before a meal break (lunch?). Adam's surgery takes '10 minutes'.

⇨ **Day One**

The TARDIS arrives in Adam's home during the day.

FATHER'S DAY

STORY LINK

There is no mention of Adam. The Doctor now still wears his green jumper from

'Dalek' and 'The Long Game', but Rose is wearing clothes different from those she had on in 'The Long Game', so these two stories are not necessarily consecutive. Rose's desire to see her father was obviously one she has had for some time – in 'The Unquiet Dead' Gwyneth comments that Rose had been thinking about her father 'more than ever' recently, so the thought has been with Rose as early as that, and may even have been a motive behind why she agreed to travel with the Doctor once she found out the TARDIS was a time machine.

OBSERVATIONS

- There is a paradox in this story: in the first flashback scenes Jackie tells a young Rose that her father, Pete Tyler, died alone, a hit and run victim. It is because he died alone that 19 year old Rose asks the Doctor to take her back to 1987, so she can be with her father when he died. But on the second attempt, Rose saves her father from that fate. Later, Pete sacrifices himself to repair the resulting 'wound in Time', and Rose is with him when he dies. But in the closing flashback Jackie tells the younger Rose her father died in the presence of an unknown girl; history has been changed, a history that Jackie remembers (since Rose mentions it to her mother in 'Bad Wolf'). This means that when 19 year old Rose meets the Doctor in 'Rose' she would know only the 'second' story of her father's death, and so she wouldn't nurse the same desire to be with her father – therefore Rose would not interfere and the events seen in 'Father's Day' would not take place, and therefore Pete Tyler does die alone, the victim of a hit and run driver … and the cycle continues ad infinitum in this continual loop. There is also the awkward fact that the Doctor and Rose who are on Jordan Road the first time seem to vanish when Rose saves Pete on the second visit. Where do they go? What happens to their TARDIS? Does it vanish too, or is it still there in 1987? We can only assume that once Pete died and the 'wound in time' that had been created through Rose's interference was healed, the 'first' Doctor and Rose reappeared back on Jordan Road and everything else clicked back into its proper place. The only changes to the timeline were Pete's time and place of death, and the memories of Jackie and Rose. As the Doctor puts it 'everybody here forgets what happened'. This must also include Rose. In other words, at the start of 'Father's Day', Rose knew her father died alone, but at the end she knew he died holding her hand. Rose's memory therefore changes. In 'Bad Wolf' Rose reminds her mother about the girl being with him: 'That was me. You saw me!' so the 'second' version of history is now the 'real' version for both of them – she 'forgets' the old version of her timeline. It is not clear from Jackie's initial disbelief and reaction whether this is because she does remember seeing Rose in 1987, or simply that she disbelieves her daughter's claim. Depending on how we interpret Jackie's reactions, this might go so far as to provide an explanation for the paradox issues that exist within the 'Father's Day' narrative. Only the Doctor remembers that there were two 'versions' of that history. In 'The Unquiet Dead' the Doctor says 'Time's in flux, changing every second. Your cosy little world can be rewritten like that [snaps fingers]. Nothing is safe ... Time isn't a straight line – it can twist into any shape'. This speech is as good as any explanation as to why the paradox mechanics and events in 'Father's Day' are confusing and somewhat nonsensical. (See also THE N-SPACE UNIVERSE.)

- It's apparent that the events of 'Father's Day' take place in an alternative bubble of time. This bubble is 'created' at the moment that Rose saves her father from his death. The bubble continues to exist for several more hours, until the moment of Pete's death when it kind of merges with the path of the original timeline, overwriting certain elements, such as people's memories of how and where Pete died. Taking each step in turn, the Doctor and Rose arrive in 1987. The TARDIS is parked on Walterley Street, which is walking distance from Jordan Road. The Doctor and Rose see Pete killed. This is the original timeline (Timeline A). Rose asks if she can 'try again'. The TARDIS lands again on Walterley Street as it had before. There must now be two TARDISes parked there. The Doctor and Rose see their earlier selves (Doctor1 and Rose1) standing on the footpath. When Rose saves Pete, the bubble is created – this is Timeline B. When the new Timeline is created, Doctor1 and Rose1 appear to vanish because they have not moved into Timeline B as they need to remain in Timeline A to make the second journey, which they do (they don't see the 'second' TARDIS when they return to the ship as it is no longer there, it having moved into Timeline B). And it is probably on account of there having been two TARDISes occupying Timeline A, that the 'second' ship is split in half, with the empty exterior moving into the new Timeline, but now without its interior dimensions, which are still locked onto Timeline A and thrown out of phase. The car that killed Pete is also locked onto both Timelines, moving back and forth between the two. The Reapers arrive and begin to consume the time bubble, as that is their function – to eat wounds in time. Trapped in the church the Doctor attempts to merge the two separated aspects of the TARDIS. A few hours later (Pete speaks of the extra hours he has had with his daughter), Pete is killed outside the church. Time is now fixed; Timeline B merges into Timeline A. The separated TARDIS interior locks back onto its exterior. Timeline A continues along its original path, with the only major change being everyone's memory of how and where Pete died. Only the Doctor remains aware of the alternative timeline, and Pete's 'other' death.

TIMELINE DATES

1981, July 29

This is the date in our history on which the Royal Wedding took place – see below.

1984 ⁕

No date is given for when Pete and Jackie are married, but she alludes to 'Lady Di' stumbling with her words during her vows; Lady Diana Spencer and Prince Charles married on 29 July 1981, so the Tyler wedding was some time after that. Rose was born in 1986, so the Tylers therefore got married sometime between 1981 and 1986. In fact, we can pinpoint it down to 1984, because the parallel Pete and Jackie ('Rise of The Cybermen') were married for '20 years'; that story is set in 2007, which dates the year of their wedding as 1987. Taking into account the three year shift between those two worlds, then Rose's parents married in 1984. (As noted under 'Rise Of The Cybermen', Rose's mum was 23 when she married Pete (who was 30) whereas the parallel world Jackie married when she was only 20.)

1986

How old is Rose? The baby seen in 'Father's Day' appears to be less than one year old. The Doctor says Rose is 'only 19' in 'The Unquiet Dead'. And in 'Dalek', the Doctor says 'she was only 19', while Rose herself says she would be 26 in 2012. With 'Rose' set in 2005, both references place her birth year as 1986.

But there are contradictions regarding her age in other stories: Rose has been missing for a whole year in 'Aliens Of London', so she would have had her birthday during that time, and yet the 'Where is Rose Tyler?' posters say she is still '19 YEARS OLD', whereas from Jackie's viewpoint she would be nearly 20. If Rose did turn 19 in 2006, that makes her birth year 1987. This year is supported in 'Rise Of The Cybermen' when the Doctor reminds Rose that her father died when she was 'six months old' – Pete died on 7 November 1987, which places her birth in May 1987. This would make her two months shy of turning 18 in 'Rose'.

Further complications arise in 'Army Of Ghosts' wherein Rose says 'in the first 19 years of my life nothing happened' before she met the Doctor, and she later tells Jackie that she's 'had a life with you for 19 years'. But by this time she has been travelling with the Doctor for at least a year, which would make her closer to being 20 in 'Army Of Ghosts'.

The majority of these clues point to Rose having been born in 1986. We simply have to accept that the Doctor got the estimation of how old she was wrong in 'Rise Of The Cybermen', and that she was at least a year, not just six months old, when her father died.

1987, November 7 *
<<1987, November 7>> * ▨ ▨ ▨ ▨ ▨ ▨ ▨ ▨ ▨ ▨
In 'The Unquiet Dead', Rose says her father 'died years back'. In 'Father's Day' Rose asks to be taken back in time to the day her dad died, which is given as '1987. Seventh of November' by Jackie, and 'November the seventh' by Rose. (7 November 1987 was a Saturday.)

1991
<<1991>> ▨ ▨ ▨ ▨ ▨ ▨ ▨ ▨ ▨ ▨ ▨ ▨
In the 'flashbacks' of Jackie showing family photos to a very young Rose, Rose looks to be of pre-school age, say four, so it is around 1991. (There are two different 'versions' of this 'flashback' – see Observations above.)

1876, March 10 (+?) ▨ ▨ ▨ ▨ ▨ ▨ ▨ ▨ ▨ ▨ ▨
This is the recorded date in our history that Alexander Graham Bell (1847 – 1922) made the first telephone call. The Doctor is familiar with this event, and may even have been there, as was hinted at in 'The Android Invasion'.

1954, September 15 ▨ ▨ ▨ ▨ ▨ ▨ ▨ ▨ ▨ ▨ ▨ ▨
The full date on which her father was born is given by Rose.

1987, November 20 ▨ ▨ ▨ ▨ ▨ ▨ ▨ ▨ ▨ ▨ ▨
A poster announces a concert by Energizer to be on '20.11.87'. One of these posters is adorned with 'Bad Wolf' graffiti.

▨▨▨▨▨▨▨▨ **DURATION** ▨▨▨▨▨▨▨▨

(TARDIS) ▨ ▨ ▨ ▨ ▨ ▨ ▨ ▨ ▨ ▨ ▨ ▨ ▨
The Doctor and Rose spend a few minutes in the TARDIS before she asks him to take her to 1987 …

TIMELINK

⇨ **Day One (1984?)** ▨ ▨ ▨ ▨ ▨ ▨ ▨ ▨ ▨ ▨

The Doctor and Rose attend Pete and Jackie's wedding.

⇨ **Day One (1987)** ▨ ▨ ▨ ▨ ▨ ▨ ▨ ▨ ▨ ▨

The Doctor and Rose spend a few hours in 1987. Pete makes the comment that he has had 'all these extra hours' of life to spend with Rose.

UNSEEN ADVENTURES

In 'Boom Town' Rose tells Mickey about the places she has seen – including Platform One ('The End Of The World'), Justicia, and 'the glass pyramid of San Kaloon'. It is possible these last two adventures took place between 'Father's Day' and 'The Empty Child'.

THE EMPTY CHILD
THE DOCTOR DANCES

STORY LINK

The Doctor is now wearing a purple/dark blue jumper. Rose has once again changed her clothes and hair style. There is no mention of the events of 'Father's Day'. Indeed, Rose does not exhibit any sign of emotional trauma despite the events she experienced in 1987. I would suggest 'The Empty Child' takes place months after 'Father's Day' – see UNSEEN ADVENTURES above.

The Doctor has been following the Chula medical transporter across the 'time tracks' for some time at beginning of the story. He later exhibits his frustration that the TARDIS has landed on Earth again.

OBSERVATIONS

- As noted under 'Everything Changes' and 'Captain Jack Harkness', Jack is posing as the real Captain Jack Harkness. According to the official records, 'on the morning of January the 21st Captain Jack Harkness failed to report for duty. Never seen again'. However, the truth behind Harkness's disappearance was that his plane was shot down by Messerschmitts during a training exercise. 'Jack' falsified the official records to make it seem that

Harkness was still alive (presumably the destruction of his plane was not witnessed). The real Harkness was last seen in Cardiff, so 'Jack' set up his operation at a London RAF base, befriending Algy while awaiting the arrival of the ambulance – and a gullible victim – in a couple of weeks time... And when Jack later became head of Torchwood Three, he presumably later altered the records further, so that when Gwen Cooper ran a background check on a 'Captain Jack Harkness', she would not find any evidence that he existed after 1941.

TIMELINE DATES

1941, February 12 ·

The Doctor deduces that the year is '1941', and this is confirmed by Jack Harkness, who tells Rose 'it's 1941, the height of the London Blitz, the height of the German bombing campaign'. In our history, the Blitz began on 7 September 1940 (London was bombed for 57 consecutive days), with the onslaught ending on 11 May 1941. Nancy and the other children are dressed for winter.

In 'Everything Changes' and 'Captain Jack Harkness', we learn that Jack assumed the identity of the real Captain Jack Harkness, who was killed on the morning of 21 January 1941.

There is a full moon the night Rose and the Doctor arrive in London. The January 1941 full moon occurred on the 13th, and the February one was the 12th. We learn that the Chula ambulance fell to Earth 'about a month ago' (see below). We can assume that Jack has been posing as Harkness since the ambulance first fell, which would be on or around but certainly not before 21 January. A month or so later, on the night of a full moon, the Doctor and Rose arrive – 12 February, which is three weeks after 21 January.

AD 79, August 24 – 25

Jack refers to a scam he used to pull in Pompeii, which was destroyed on these dates ('Volcano day!') in our history (See also 'The Brain Of Morbius' and 'The Fires Of Pompeii'.)

1921

The Doctor guesses that Nancy is 20 or 21 ('older than you look, yes?'), so she was born around 1921.

1937 ▩ ▩ ▩ ▩ ▩ ▩ ▩ ▩ ▩ ▩ ▩ ▩ ▩ ▩

Jamie was a '4 year old', born when Nancy was 15 or 16, so he was born around 1937.

1941, January 21 – 28 ▩ ▩ ▩ ▩ ▩ ▩ ▩ ▩ ▩ ▩ ▩

The Doctor says the Chula medical transporter pod landed in London 'about a month ago'. As noted above, this would have been on or around but not before 21 January, as that was the date on which Jack assumed the identity of the real Captain Jack Harkness.

Dr Constantine tells the Doctor that the capsule infected Jamie first, and 'by the following morning' all the doctors and nurses who treated him were infected; 'by the morning after that' all the patients in the ward were affected, then the whole hospital 'within a week', which takes the date to 28 January.

1998, December 25 (+?) ▩ ▩ ▩ ▩ ▩ ▩ ▩ ▩ ▩ ▩ ▩

It is implied that the Doctor knows Rose got a red bicycle at Christmas when she was '12'. (She was born in 1986 – see 'Father's Day'.) He might have learned of this from Jackie or Mickey during 'Aliens Of London', or he may have spent some time doing some research on Rose before offering her a trip in the TARDIS at the end of 'Rose'.

5001 – 5100 (The 51st Century) + ▩ ▩ ▩ ▩ ▩ ▩ ▩ ▩

Jack Harkness is an ex-Time Agent, from 'the fifty-first century'. The Doctor has been to that time period before, when he destroyed the weapons factories at Villengard; there is a banana grove there 'now', so the Doctor must have returned to that time period at a later date. The Doctor was with the Filipino army when they attacked Reykjavik (as given in 'The Talons Of Weng-Chiang'), so we might assume the weapons factory was destroyed during the same visit to 5000. The Time Agents were known to Magnus Greel, who thought the Doctor was one that had pursued him to the nineteenth century in 'The Talons Of Weng-Chiang'.

▩▩▩▩▩▩▩▩▩▩▩▩ **DURATION** ▩▩▩▩▩▩▩▩▩

(TARDIS) ▩ ▩ ▩ ▩ ▩ ▩ ▩ ▩ ▩ ▩ ▩ ▩ ▩

The Doctor and Rose spend some time in the TARDIS following the ambulance pod to 1941 ...

⇨ **Day (21 January?) (Ep1)** ▨ ▨ ▨ ▨ ▨ ▨ ▨ ▨ ▨ ▨
The Chula ambulance crashes to Earth…

⊕ **'About a month' passes…** ▨ ▨ ▨ ▨ ▨ ▨ ▨ ▨ ▨

⇨ **Day One (12 February) (Ep1-2)** ▨ ▨ ▨ ▨ ▨ ▨ ▨ ▨
The TARDIS arrives in London at night. The clock on Big Ben reads '9.30pm' while Rose is with Jack Harkness (although the hands never change position despite Rose being there for some time). There is a full moon. The German bomb that destroys the Chula capsule is due to fall 'in two hours', so the story ends shortly after 11.30pm that same night.

(TARDIS) ▨ ▨ ▨ ▨ ▨ ▨ ▨ ▨ ▨ ▨ ▨ ▨ ▨
The Doctor and Rose follow Jack's ship in the TARDIS, and bring him on board.

BOOM TOWN

STORY LINK

The Doctor now wears his crimson jumper again (see 'Rose'). Jack asks the Doctor about the TARDIS looking like a Police Box, and the Doctor explains how the 'chameleon circuit' works (and refers to '100,000 BC' when he recalls how it got stuck in the shape of a Police Box in the 1960s), so it is clear Jack has been with them only a short time since 'The Empty Child'. The TARDIS lands over the Cardiff Rift scar for refuelling, the last series of landings presumably having drained the ship's power supplies.

OBSERVATIONS

- The Rift which runs 'through the middle of the city' was 'healed' in 1869 (see 'The Unquiet Dead') leaving a 'scar' that 'generates energy', over which the TARDIS can 'soak up the radiation' and refuel. Indeed, in 'Time-Flight' the Master attempted to use the Xeraphin sarcophagus to power his TARDIS which had become stranded when the ship's dynomorphic generator had exhausted, while the Doctor needed zeiton-7 ore to repair the TARDIS in 'Vengeance On Varos', so it is clear that all TARDISes can draw power from and be refuelled by external sources.
- When the Rift opens, it causes significant damage to Roald Dahl Plass, beneath which is Torchwood Three's Hub. Presumably Jack and the other

members of Torchwood Three had already vacated the Hub during this story, since 'older' Jack already knew the Rift was going to be active on that date. (He would also have been careful not to be around at the time thus avoiding accidentally meeting his 'earlier' self.) Of note, the usual Information Office entrance to Torchwood is not there when Mickey and Rose pass by the wall during their walk along the promenade. This suggests that that particular entrance wasn't established until some time after 'Boom Town', as presumably the original hidden entrance/s to the Hub had been damaged or blocked. It's also worth pointing out that the TARDIS is parked some distance from the water tower, and yet in 'Everything Changes', the perception filter effect apparently left by the TARDIS affects one of the stones situated at the base of the water tower.

- Just prior to the missile striking 10 Downing Street at the end of 'Aliens Of London', Blon Fel Fotch Pasameer-Day Slitheen uses a one-person teleport device to escape the explosion, and ends up in a skip on the Isle of Dogs. From there she makes her way to Wales, and still in her disguise as Margaret Blaine, over the subsequent six months is able to stand for and be elected as Mayor of Cardiff. This is very difficult to accept, given that the real Margaret Blaine was an MI5 agent killed by the Slitheen. Harriet Jones would have made a full statement and disclosed vital information regarding which humans had been impersonated by the Slitheen, including Blaine. It's hard to accept that not one person in high authority in London discovered that the supposedly dead Margaret Blaine was running for the mayoralty in Cardiff. Although Blon Fel Fotch does say no one in London cares about Cardiff, the fact she had authorised the building of a nuclear power plant in the middle of Cardiff should have set off a few alarm bells in London!

- Blon Fel Fotch has a tribophysical waveform macrokinetic extrapolator device with which she plans to escape Earth. Clearly this means the Slitheen spaceship that crashed in the Thames plus the other one in the North Sea are not accessible by her, otherwise she would have escaped by using one of those two vessels.

- Blon tells the Doctor she was forced to make her first kill 'at 13'. I've not included this event in the TIMELINE since we don't know Blon's current age.

LANGUAGE

The 'Margaret Blaine' Slitheen talks with the same voice regardless of whether or not she is wearing the human skin. A banner gives the name of the nuclear power project in English and in Welsh – 'The BLAIDD DRWG Project – Prosiect Y BLAIDD

DRWG' – and yet the English meaning of Blaidd Drwg ('Bad Wolf') is not translated. The Doctor confirms that the TARDIS is telepathic, and 'translates alien languages'.

TIMELINE DATES

2006, September

The Doctor says it is 'the early twenty-first century'. No dates are given other than an on-screen caption following a montage of clips from 'Aliens Of London' that reads 'SIX MONTHS LATER'. This is after the events of 'Aliens Of London', set in March 2006, so it is now September 2006.

The Doctor says the TARDIS will be parked on the Rift to refuel for 'a couple of days', and then later says it 'should take another 24 hours'. Therefore the TARDIS has been sitting on the Rift for 24 hours already, so it must have landed in Cardiff the day before; Rose must have phoned Mickey who then caught the first available train the following day (he had probably already sold the yellow VW he had in 'Rose'). (In 'Bad Wolf', Jack says he got his denims at 'a little place in Cardiff' – The Top Shop – so he must have had time to do some shopping before Mickey arrived.) The press conference for the Blaidd Drwg project in 'Blaine's' office must have been held earlier that same morning; a photo taken of the mayor at this event appears in the afternoon newspaper the Doctor sees later on ('and I was having such a nice day'). Later that night, 'Blaine' refers to her meeting with Cathy Salt as being 'just today'.

Cathy Salt says Mr Cleaver was killed 'recently'. We see his death in the opening moments of the episode (it is night, as lit street lights can be seen through the window); so it is not necessarily the day before the events of 'Boom Town'. It may even have been a week or so earlier.

1986, April 25 – 26

Reference is made to Chernobyl, where a Russian nuclear power station went into meltdown. This disaster occurred in our history on 25-26 April 1986.

1996

Blon reveals that the Slitheen family was tried in its absence 'many years ago', say ten years earlier.

2006, October 19

Cathy Salt tells 'Margaret' that she and her boyfriend Jeffrey are getting married 'next month' on 'the nineteenth', which would be 19 October. She is 'three months' pregnant.

DURATION

⇨ **Day** ▨ ▨ ▨ ▨ ▨ ▨ ▨ ▨ ▨ ▨ ▨ ▨ ▨
Mr Cleaver is killed at night …

🕐 **A few days to a week pass** … ▨ ▨ ▨ ▨ ▨ ▨ ▨ ▨

⇨ **Day One** ▨ ▨ ▨ ▨ ▨ ▨ ▨ ▨ ▨ ▨ ▨ ▨ ▨
It is early morning when Mickey arrives in Cardiff and finds the TARDIS (which arrived yesterday). The press conference is held that morning. Mickey joins the TARDIS team for a late meal (it has to be afternoon at this point in order for there to be sufficient time for the article and photo of the Mayor taken earlier that day to be printed in the newspaper). The Doctor has a late meal with 'Margaret' that evening. The story ends later that night.

BAD WOLF
THE PARTING OF THE WAYS

STORY LINK

At the end of 'Boom Town', the Doctor sets course for Raxacoricofallapatorius to place Blon Fel Fotch Pasameer-Day Slitheen's egg 'in the hatchery' so she can start life anew, raised by a better family than the Slitheen. At the beginning of 'Bad Wolf', the Doctor (now sporting a dark-coloured jumper) says after leaving Raxacoricofallapatorius 'we went to Kyoto … Japan, in 1336'. Soon after leaving Japan, the ship is brought by the Controller (using time technology?) to Game Station in 200,100; the TARDIS is housed in the Archive Six room, while the Doctor, Jack and Rose are each transported into different levels on the Station.

The tribophysical waveform macrokinetic extrapolator that Blon had in 'Boom Town' is still on board the TARDIS (and later proves indispensable in the battle against the Daleks). At some point prior to 'Bad Wolf', the Doctor added to the sonic screwdriver a remote control activator for the TARDIS and recorded his Emergency Programme One hologram message to Rose (the hologram is wearing the same dark jumper the Doctor wears in 'Bad Wolf').

DALEK LINK

See DALEK HISTORY – this is the Daleks' nineteenth appearance. The Doctor believed he had destroyed all the Daleks in an 'inferno' at the end of the last great Time War (and that the sole survivor was destroyed in 2012 – see 'Dalek'), however the Emperor Dalek also survived; its ship 'falling through time, crippled but alive'. It waited 'in the dark space, damaged but rebuilding'. During this time the Emperor went mad, believing it was a god. It created a new Dalek army: the Emperor tells the Doctor that 'centuries past, and we quietly infiltrated the systems of Earth, harvesting the waste of humanity', filleting and refining the carcasses into new Daleks. The Controller of the Game Station says her masters (the Daleks) have been 'hiding in the dark space. Watching, shaping the Earth. So, so, so many years. They've always been there. Guiding humanity. Hundreds and hundreds of years'. The Doctor says 'someone's been playing a long game, controlling the human race from behind the scenes for generations', and later 'they're insane, hiding in silence for hundreds of years, that's enough to drive anyone mad'. Despite these references, it's not clear exactly how long the Daleks have been manipulating the destiny of humanity. The Jagrafess itself was only installed in 199,909 (see 'The Long Game'), but it's clear the Daleks have been there for much longer – see Observations below.

OBSERVATIONS

- The 'duration' of the Doctor's ninth incarnation (from 'Rose' to 'The Parting of the Ways') amounts to what can be only a few months in total. Of note, this is the fourth time (at least on-screen) in which the Doctor regenerates in the TARDIS (see 'The Tenth Planet', 'The Caves Of Androzani', and 'Time And The Rani'), but it is also the first time the Doctor regenerates standing up!
- When the TARDIS returns Rose to her own time, it materialises on the same street on which her father was killed in the original Timeline A (see 'Father's Day'). [This is because the same location on Louden Square was used in both 'Father's Day' and 'Bad Wolf', both of which were directed by Joe Ahearne.]
- In one round of *The Weakest Link* questions, one of the contestants is asked 'The Great Cobalt pyramid lies on the ruins of what ancient institute?', to which the correct answer is 'Torchwood'. Given that the Face of Boe exists in this time zone (200,100), and is also named in one of the questions, can we assume that Jack had a hand in preserving the name of Torchwood even this far into the future?

LANGUAGE

The Daleks speak English. Despite transmitting to the whole planet, the Game Station appears to be broadcasting only English programmes. The Doctor refers to 'billions' of languages.

TIMELINE DATES

2006, November?
When Rose returns to her own time, it is some time after the events of 'Boom Town' (Rose reminds Mickey of the Slitheen 'the last time I saw you'); say a month or two later? Mickey is pleased to see Rose, so we can assume that he is no longer dating Trisha Delaney. He has had his hair cut, and has a new car – he had a yellow VW in Rose, but is now driving a black mini. Since he got the train to Cardiff rather than driving in 'Boom Town' he must have bought the new car after the adventure in Cardiff.

200,100 *
'The Long Game' was set in the year 200,000; in 'Bad Wolf', the TARDIS returns to Satellite Five '100 YEARS LATER' according to an on-screen caption, and the Doctor, who says it's 'a hundred years exactly. It's the year two zero zero one zero zero'. (In 'Utopia', Jack names the year 'two hundred one hundred'.) Satellite Five is now called the Game Station.

Strood says he has been in the house for 'all nine weeks', so the game itself is drawing to a close with only three contestants left before the Doctor is transmatted into the house.

1336 *
The Doctor says they visited Kyoto, Japan in '1336'. From an historical perspective, in that year the Warlord Ashikaga Takauji captured Kyoto, and overthrew the Minamoto shogunate. Presumably the Doctor, Rose and Jack were witness to this.

199,000
The Emperor Dalek fell 'through time' – which I understand to mean backwards in time – and has been manipulating humanity's destiny for 'centuries', although it is not immediately clear as to how long this is. The Jagrafess had been controlling Satellite Five since 199,909 ('The Long Game'), so we can assume the Daleks were in the dark place for hundreds of years prior to that, say 1000 in total, which places the year the Emperor emerged from time as being around 199,000.

200,000 – 200,100
Davidge Pavel says rumours of secret transmissions 'go back decades' / 'been going on for years'. Lynda says Satellite Five was renamed 'a hundred years ago', and everything went wrong then – which was when the Doctor visited in 'The Long Game' and

destroyed the Jagrafess, resulting in 'one hundred years of hell' (the Doctor realises 'I made this world!').

200,075

The Controller was installed in the Game Station 'when she was five years old' and she hasn't been human 'for years'. It's difficult to determine what age she is now, but assuming no more than 30, then she has probably been in control since 200,075.

200,080

Lynda says 'the Great Atlantic Smog Storm' has 'been going 20 years'.

200,102

The next solar flare is due 'in two years time'.

THE TiME WAR +

In terms of Dalek history, the War would have begun after the events of 'Remembrance Of The Daleks', set in 4663.

DURATiON

⇨ **Day One (Ep 1-2)**

The Doctor arrives in the *Big Brother* house 'five minutes' before the next eviction. Rose plays *The Weakest Link* for half an hour – given the commercial breaks in between each round, the live show must run for 30 minutes in total. The Doctor and Jack find her at the end of the final round. The solar flare activity in Delta Point Seven is due in 'ten' minutes while Rose plays the game, and these flares strike when the Doctor confronts the Controller – she uses the flares to temporarily block the transmissions. When the Daleks attack in Ep2 events appear to play out in real time … with the Daleks destroyed less than an hour later.

⇨ **Day One (2006) (Ep2)**

Rose is on Earth for a few hours; she, Mickey and Jackie have lunch (?) at a fried chicken restaurant. Jackie says the truck she borrows to break into the TARDIS has to be back at '6 o'clock'; so it must be mid-afternoon.

(TARDIS)

The Doctor and Rose are in the TARDIS for a few minutes, as the Doctor regenerates while the ship is in flight…

THE CHRISTMAS INVASION

+STORY LINK

'The Christmas Invasion' picks up from where 'Bad Wolf' left off, with the Doctor having just regenerated – it's no later than 15 hours since this happened. Presumably the TARDIS set course for Earth 2006. [As far as *Timelink* is concerned, the short *Children In Need* special mini-episode, in which the Doctor makes the course correction for Earth on Christmas Eve, is not canonical, and is therefore not included in this section.]

From Jackie and Mickey's perspective, it has been at least a month since they last saw Rose, and helped her get the TARDIS working in 'Bad Wolf'.

Big Ben is surrounded by scaffolding as it undergoes reconstruction following the Slitheen spaceship crashing into it in March (see 'Aliens Of London'). These repairs will be completed by the middle of the following year, as the scaffolding has been removed by the time of 'Army Of Ghosts'.

OBSERVATIONS

- The main continuity problem with 'The Christmas Invasion' is that it states the Martian Guinevere One probe is Britain's first major space exploration vehicle, and yet as seen in 'The Ambassadors Of Death' and 'The Android Invasion' it is clear that Britain already had an advanced space programme, with at least seven trips to Mars, and one to Jupiter, during the 1970s. (Had Guinevere One been bound for one of the outer planets, such as Pluto or one of the newly-discovered dwarf planets, this continuity contradiction would not exist.)

- There is a photo of Queen Elizabeth II on Harriet Jones's desk, and the PM refers to 'Her Majesty'. (Yvonne Hartman cites doing her duty for 'Queen and country' in 'Army Of Ghosts'.) This contradicts the Brigadier's comment in 'Battlefield' about a King being on the throne (see THE UNIT YEARS). We might have to accept that Lethbridge-Stewart was probably being facetious (or might have been referring to Elvis Presley).

- The Doctor refers to Arthur Dent ('there was a nice man'). As I've noted under 'Destiny Of The Daleks', *The Hitchhiker's Guide to the Galaxy*'s 'Universe' does not conform to the *Doctor Who* Universe, so this must be accepted as being a joke.

- The pilot fish are revealed to be robo-forms in 'The Runaway Bride'. It remains unanswered how and why the robots dress as Santas, and where they get the deadly musical instruments and Christmas tree. Also, they demonstrate knowledge of the Christmas carol 'God Rest Ye Merry Gentlemen'. One way to explain this is to accept that the 'pilot fish robots' have been to Earth before, and used the Santa disguises and instruments in the past, and were already near Earth when the Sycorax arrived, perhaps even already in the pay of some alien creature planning to use Christmas as a smoke screen for whatever chaos they were planning. Then once that scheme had past, the 'pilot fish robots' still in the guise of deadly Santas detected the Doctor and stayed near Earth to take advantage of that. And then after leaving Earth, they hung around maybe thinking they could use the Christmas disguises again. A year later the Racnoss arrived in orbit so the 'pilot fish robots' offered her their services...

LANGUAGE

UNIT has a language translator software programme that can be uploaded to portable hand-held units. The Sycorax, however, only speak the Sycoraxic language. Once the Doctor has revived, and re-attuned himself to the TARDIS translator, everyone is able to speak and hear in 'English'. However, after making his challenge to the Sycorax leader, the Doctor shouts something in Sycoraxic that is not translated. But whatever he says, it certainly riles the leader...

TIMELINE DATES

2006, December 24 – 25 +

There is an open calendar pinned to the wall of the kitchen in the Tylers' flat, but while the month appears to be December, the year cannot be read clearly. It's Christmas Day, 25 December, on the second day of the story, so the TARDIS crash lands late afternoon/ early evening on 24 December. No year is given, but it's clearly soon after the events of 'Bad Wolf', so it's 2006. (This 'date' is near enough confirmed in 'School Reunion' and 'Love & Monsters'; Elton says the Sycorax spaceship arrived at '7.45am'.)

From Mickey and Jackie's perspective, a month or so has passed since they last saw Rose in 'Bad Wolf'. Mickey has a (full time/part time?) job at a mechanic's (unless he's just helping out at a friend's garage?). Jackie has been dating Howard from the market for 'a month or so'. Rose refers to the fact that travelling in the TARDIS has made her 'out of sync' with Mickey and her mother.

2006, November

Jackie says she has been seeing Howard for 'about a month'. Presumably this was soon after she stopped seeing Rodrigo, from whom she borrowed the yellow truck in 'Bad Wolf'.

DURATION

⇨ **Day One (24 December)**
The TARDIS crash-lands around late afternoon.

⇨ **Day Two (25 December)**
The Sycorax ship arrives at 7.45am (given in 'Love & Monsters'). It is destroyed later that day. The Doctor, Mickey and the Tylers enjoy Christmas dinner. (At some off-screen point after this, the Doctor goes to Trafalgar Square, and is photographed by Ursula Blake ('Love & Monsters').)

NEW EARTH

STORY LINK

With 'School Reunion' being set in early January 2007, the Doctor and Rose must leave Earth soon after 'The Christmas Invasion', most likely during the week between Christmas and New Year. Of note, the TARDIS is parked in a playground rather than the forecourt of the Powell Estate, where it was at the end of 'The Christmas Invasion', at the end of which the Doctor and Rose choose a direction in which to travel next. There is also no presence of 'snow' (ash from the destroyed Sycorax ship), so either it's been cleared up, or none of it fell to the playground. But since the TARDIS has moved, then it's possible Rose and the Doctor have already made a trip off-screen. Indeed, in 'Love & Monsters', Ursula shows Elton photos she took of the Doctor at Trafalgar Square on Christmas Day, so it's clear the Doctor popped in to the centre of London at some point off-screen at the end of 'The Christmas Invasion'. The Doctor and Rose may have had any number of off-screen adventures during this time (some of them likely observed by Victor Kennedy).

It would seem that the Doctor received the Face of Boe's message while on Earth, as he and Rose are specifically heading for New Earth ('further than we've ever gone before') in order to answer that secret summons.

OBSERVATIONS

- The Doctor has been to New New York on New Earth before; presumably this was when he bought the facsimile edition of *Death in the Clouds* he has in 'The Unicorn And The Wasp'.

LANGUAGE

All the creatures in the hospital speak the same language. The signage in the hospital is in English.

TIMELINE DATES

2006, December (28?)

With 'School Reunion' set in the first week of January 2007, and to keep Mickey's timeline relative to both stories, the Doctor and Rose's departure for 'New Earth' must take place only a few days after Christmas, say 28 December.

As noted above, the Doctor and Rose might have had a couple of off-screen adventures since 'The Christmas Invasion'.

4,999,998,000

The Doctor and Rose take Chip/Cassandra back to an earlier time when Cassandra was still human, to the Ambassador of Thrace's reception. There is no indication as to when this was date-wise, but it was intimated in 'The End Of The World' that she was over 2000 years old, so it is earlier than 4,999,998-something.

5,000,000,023

The Doctor gives the date as 'the year five billion and twenty three', so it's 23 years after the events of 'The End Of The World'. Of note, he doesn't use the 'slash apple slash' description that he did previously. New Earth itself is in the distant galaxy M87.

For Cassandra, she has spent the last 23 years or so hidden in the sublevels of the hospital, keeping tabs on the Sisters' actions. Only her brain and eyes survived her 'death' in 'The End Of The World', while a new 'body' was created from the remaining skin taken from her back.

5,000,001,023

The Doctor says a cure for petrifold regression won't be found for 'a thousand years?'. Does he know this because he's been to that time period before, or is this merely an educated guess?

DURATION

⇨ **Day One (2007)**
It is day when the Doctor and Rose depart in the TARDIS.

⇨ **Day One (5 Billion 23)**
The Doctor and Rose arrive in the morning, and leave later, early evening, the same day (it is falling dark when the NNYPD officers arrive to arrest the Sisters).

⇨ **Day One (4.99 Billion)**
It is evening when the Doctor takes Cassandra/Chip into the past, back to the moment that Cassandra watched on the film recording earlier.

TOOTH AND CLAW

STORY LINK

When she and the Doctor left New Earth with Cassandra (in Chip's body), Rose's hair was straight. But when they delivered 'Chip' at Cassandra's party, Rose's hair is tied up. In 'Tooth And Claw', Rose's hair is now frizzy. There is no mention of the events on 'New Earth', so a non-stated amount of time has passed since they left galaxy M87.

The TARDIS is bound for the 'late 1970s' so the Doctor can show Rose the punk era. The specific target is Sheffield, 21 November 1979, to see Ian Dury and the Blockheads in concert.

LANGUAGE

Queen Victoria's native language was German; she had only limited English, and yet here she speaks perfect English.

TIMELINE DATES

1879, November 28 – 29 *
The TARDIS was bound for 21 November 1979, so the Doctor and Rose could attend an Ian Dury concert in Sheffield, but it arrives instead in '1879 – same difference'. We might assume that the TARDIS overshot by exactly 100 years, and it is November 1879. Indeed, there is a full moon the night of the adventure, and the November 1879 full moon occurred on 28 November. Did the TARDIS therefore also overshoot by a week?

49 BC, January 10

The historic event of 'Caesar crossing the Rubicon' occurred on this date in our history, whereupon Julius Caesar led an army north towards Rome across the river, which marked a provincial border.

1540

Sir Robert says the story of the wolf 'goes back three hundred years'. Later, the book found by the Doctor dates the arrival of the creature as 'in the year of Our Lord 1540 under the reign of King James the Fifth, an almighty fire did burn in the pit'. Rose says this was 'over three hundred years ago'. A new Host is found 'every generation'. If we assume a generation is 25 years (as given by the Doctor in 'Four To Doomsday'), then there have been at least 13 Hosts previous to the current one. The Doctor knows what a lupine-wavelength-haemovariform is.

1805, October 21

The Battle of Trafalgar was fought on this date in our history.

1979, February 17 – March 16

Dates in our history for the Sino-Vietnamese conflict, referred to by the Doctor.

1979, May 3

On this date in our own history, Margaret Thatcher became Britain's first female Prime Minister. The political environment in the *Doctor Who* Universe rarely reflects that of the real world, as it is established in 'Terror Of The Zygons' that there was a female PM in office as early as 1975. Thatcher's term in office is explored in more detail in POLITICALLY INCORRECT.

1979, July 11 ·

Debris from the Sky Lab space station (launched into orbit in 1973) fell to Earth on this date in our history as the station broke up on its re-entry into the Earth's atmosphere (with a 'little help' from the Doctor, who nearly lost his thumb in the process!).

DURATION

⇨ **Day One (28 November)**

The monks arrive at the House late afternoon. It is 'almost nightfall' / 'almost dark' when the Doctor and Rose meet Queen Victoria's entourage. They 'dine at seven' (7.00pm). There is a full moon that night. The clock in the mistletoe-lined library later reads 10.10pm.

⇨ **Day Two (29 November)** ▬ ▬ ▬ ▬ ▬ ▬ ▬ ▬ ▬ ▬

The Doctor and Rose are knighted the following morning (the Doctor and Queen both refer to 'last night'). That evening (the moon is again full), Queen Victoria announces her intention to set up the Torchwood Institute.

SCHOOL REUNION

STORY LINK

There's no indication as to how long after the events of 'Tooth And Claw' this is. Mickey has contacted the Doctor and Rose (via her mobile phone) a few days earlier. From his viewpoint, it is probably only a few days after the Doctor and Rose left at the start of 'New Earth'. He has been investigating recent UFO sightings in the area from 'three months ago', which was also when Finch and co arrived at Deffry Vale High School. The Doctor and Rose have already been at the school for a day (the story starts on their 'second day'). They must have arrived back home at least a few days prior to that in order to be briefed by Mickey, and get everything set up, such as getting Rose the job in the kitchen, getting the winning lottery ticket (the Doctor must have zipped ahead in the TARDIS to get the winning numbers for that week's upcoming lottery draw) and delivering it to the lucky teacher, so the Doctor could be assigned as the supply science teacher. Presumably the psychic paper also came in handy to establish the Doctor's 'teaching' credentials.

As noted below, the Doctor and Rose were probably videoed by Victor Kennedy during this mission 'set-up' period.

Between the Doctor and Rose's departure in 'New Earth' and (off-screen) return for 'School Reunion', the Archangel Network has gone online, and Harold Saxon has made his first public appearance ('The Sound Of Drums'). In 'Rise Of The Cybermen', Mickey refers to 'Tony Blair'. Blair's identity is explored further in POLITICALLY INCORRECT.

Since the events of 'K9 And Company', Sarah has continued her work as a journalist; she is currently working for *The Sunday Times* newspaper. Over the past 25 years, K9 has become rusty and his components have started to decay and fail.

OBSERVATIONS

- The Doctor says to Sarah he has regenerated 'half a dozen times since we last met', whereas in fact he has regenerated only five times since 'The Five Doctors'. Sarah says 'I thought you'd died. I waited for you, you didn't come back. And I thought you must have died'. She later says 'You never came back for me. You just dumped me', so which the Doctor replies 'I was called back home. In those days humans weren't allowed'. From this, it is clear that Sarah doesn't remember 'The Five Doctors' (her mind was altered by the Time Lords when she left Gallifrey), and her last experience with the Doctor was 'The Hand Of Fear'; the Doctor has indeed regenerated six times since then.
- The Krillitanes know that the Doctor is the last of the Time Lords. This would seem to place the end of the Time War – or one aspect of it, at least – in the recent past.
- It is odd that the Doctor refers to K9 Mark Three as 'old friend', when in actual fact, this K9 never travelled with the Doctor. (As I've noted under 'K9 And Company', Mark Three was probably built at the same time as the Mark Two model, and delivered to Sarah's flat soon after the events of 'The Invasion Of Time'.)
- After K9 Mark Three is destroyed, the Doctor builds and programs a new and improved Mark Four model. The Doctor must have at some point (perhaps whilst undertaking the repairs in the café?) made a back-up copy of K9's Mark Three's memory circuits, fearing that this model was on its last legs (or wheels?). And when he made the Mark Four version he was able to transfer the 'old' K9's memories to the 'new' one, along with much more, such as schematics for a sonic device (the sonic lipstick that is introduced in 'Invasion Of The Bane'), as well as the TARDIS's base code (which proves to be an invaluable asset in 'The Stolen Earth'). But how and when did the Doctor make Mark Four? There is no clear moment within the narrative for him to have done so. Does the Doctor perhaps have a ready supply of empty K9 shells somewhere in the TARDIS? Did he build a number of additional models, based on the original which was still on Gallifrey, to help in the Time War? Could the shell of K9 Mark Four actually be that of Mark One, saved by the Doctor from the destruction of Gallifrey, but kept in storage?)

LANGUAGE

The Krillitanes speak English, a language they must have adopted when assuming the human form. Alien symbols are painted on the vats containing the Krillitane oil. An alien text appears on Finch's office computer screen.

TIMELINE DATES

2007, January 8 – 10 *

The Doctor and Rose left in the TARDIS in 'New Earth' the week after Christmas 2006 ('The Christmas Invasion'). With 'Rise Of The Cybermen' set in early February, despite it not looking remotely like mid-winter, 'School Reunion' must also be set in January 2007. The story is set over a three day period. There is a full moon on the night of the second day: the January 2007 full moon occurs on Thursday, 4 January. However, schools are shut for the Christmas break, reopening on Monday 8 January. Assuming the Doctor and Rose started work at the school on the first day of term, the story is set between Monday 8 January to Wednesday 10 January 2007.

2006, October

Mickey says army records document 'three months ago massive UFO activity. They logged over 40 sightings – lights in the sky – all of that'. It was also 'three months ago' that Finch arrived as the new Headmaster of Deffry Vale High School. Presumably these UFOs were Brother Lassar and his twelve fellow Krillitane arriving on Earth. 'The next day' half the staff got flu, with seven teachers, four dinner ladies and one nurse all being replaced by Finch. With the story set in the first week on January, Finch and co must have arrived at sometime during the first term of the new school year. If it is exactly three months, then it would be in the first or second week of October 2006.

2007, January 4? *

With 'School Reunion' set from 8 – 10 January 2007, the Doctor and Rose must have arrived back on Earth the week before, which is a week or so after they had initially left in 'New Earth'. They would need this time set up everything so they would infiltrate the school when it reopened after the Christmas break, in the second week of January. (In 'Love & Monsters', Victor Kennedy has footage of the Doctor and Rose entering the TARDIS: it's possible this recording shows the Doctor and Rose soon after their return to Earth, and moving the TARDIS to the store room behind the gymnasium at Deffry Vale High School.)

DURATION

⇨ Day One (8 January)

The Headmaster kills the girl when 'it's nearly time for lunch'. (The Doctor and Rose are at the school this day, but are not seen on-screen.)

⇨ **Day Two (9 January)** ▨ ▨ ▨ ▨ ▨ ▨ ▨ ▨ ▨ ▨ ▨

The Doctor enters the class room ('good morning, class'). He meets up with Rose in the canteen at lunchtime. (This is their 'second day' – they've been at the school for 'two days'.) The Doctor meets Sarah Jane Smith. That night, the Doctor, Rose and Mickey break into the school. The Doctor is properly reunited with Sarah. They spend the night in the café. (There is a full moon.)

⇨ **Day Three (10 January)** ▨ ▨ ▨ ▨ ▨ ▨ ▨ ▨ ▨ ▨

When the school opens the following day, the Doctor and his friends return to the school. The story ends later that afternoon. (The Doctor has had time to slip away to build a new K9.)

THE GIRL IN THE FIREPLACE

+STORY LINK

'The Girl In The Fireplace' takes place immediately after 'School Reunion'. The landing on the SS *Madame de Pompadour* is Mickey's first journey in the TARDIS (he's delighted to get 'a spaceship on my first go!'). Mickey is wearing the same yellow t-shirt he had on at the conclusion to 'School Reunion', but Rose is now wearing a different blue shirt, and her hair is once again frizzy (it was straight in 'School Reunion'). 'School Reunion' and 'The Girl In The Fireplace' are the only two adventures of Series Two that are definitely consecutive.

It must have been during the off-screen flight, that the Doctor told Mickey about his meeting with 'Cleo'. (The Doctor also mentions his meeting with Cleopatra in 'The Masque Of Mandragora'.)

OBSERVATIONS

- More is revealed about the Doctor's past life on Gallifrey, specifically that he had 'such a lonely childhood', and was 'such a lonely little boy' (see LIFE ON GALLIFREY).
- The Doctor has previously demonstrated an attraction to France, notably the French Revolution period being a favourite of his (as stated in 'The Reign Of Terror'), and he has twice mentioned knowing Marie Antoinette ('Pyramids Of Mars' and 'The Robots Of Death'). His knowledge of Madame de Pompadour is presumably an off-shoot of this. He (jokingly?) says 1757 is 'one of my favourites. August is rubbish, though'. As I've noted under 'The

Massacre Of St Bartholomew's Eve', there are clear similarities between the courts of French nobility and Time Lord society.

LANGUAGE

Mickey is surprised to discover that he can now speak French. Rose explains to him how the TARDIS translates. When the Doctor meets young Reinette for the first time, she twice calls him 'Monsieur'. She pronounces 'Paris' as it is in English, rather than the French "Pah-ree". The servo robots must be multi-lingual as they also speak French, unless this 'ability' is only available to them once the Doctor 'becomes part of events'. One thing that is not clear is why one of the robots speaks with a female voice and actually dresses accordingly.

TIMELINE DATES

1727 (pre-August) ›
1727, August ›
The young Reinette says the year is 'seventeen hundred and twenty seven'. (Which the Doctor says is one of his favourites, but that 'August is rubbish, though' – presumably he was there at the time). On their third meeting, Reinette says she has known the Doctor 'since I was seven years old'; but with the first meeting being in early 1757, she would have been only six years old.

1727 (winter) ›
Reinette says her first meeting with the fireplace man 'was weeks ago. That was months'. It is now winter; it is snowing. This is the first period in Reinette's life that the servo-droids travel to.

1740 ›
On the third meeting, Reinette is a young woman. No dates are given, other than she has known the Doctor 'since I was seven year old' (actually six – see above). In recorded history, Reinette was married in 1741 (aged 19). Given that she does not appear to have a husband in this scene we can set it the year before, 1740.

1744 (summer) ›
The next time window brings the Doctor to the grounds of the palace at Versailles. The King's current mistress, Madame de Châteauroux, 'is close to death'. She died on 8 December 1744 in our history. It appears to be summer, so it is a few months prior to the death.

1745, February 25 ⋆ ▨ ▨ ▨ ▨ ▨ ▨ ▨ ▨ ▨ ▨ ▨

It was 'the night of the Yew Tree Ball' (on 25 February 1745 of our history) that Reinette and the King meet. The Doctor tells Reinette 'you're 23, and for some reason that means you're not old enough'.

1753 ▨ ▨ ▨ ▨ ▨ ▨ ▨ ▨ ▨ ▨ ▨ ▨ ▨ ▨ ▨

Rose tells Reinette the robots will 'be here in five years… sometime after your thirty seventh birthday. I can't give you an exact date'. Reinette's birthday is 29 December, so she turns 37 in 1758, which makes it 1753. We can assume the robots attack the very night of her birthday, given the importance to them of her reaching that vital age.

1758, December 29 ⋆ ▨ ▨ ▨ ▨ ▨ ▨ ▨ ▨ ▨ ▨

Reinette turns 37 on 29 December 1758. The night the robots attack (this is the first time she has seen them since 1727) is presumably the night of a masquerade ball to celebrate this occasion. Or it is early 1759. (It does seem odd that the robots are suitably attired for such an occasion, despite them not knowing the year she would become 'compatible'.)

1764, April 15 ⋆ ▨ ▨ ▨ ▨ ▨ ▨ ▨ ▨ ▨ ▨ ▨

The King says Reinette was 'only 43 when she died'. Of the Doctor, it has been 'so many years since I saw you last' (which was 1758, six years ago). The portrait gives the year only, '1764'. In our history she died on 15 April 1764, and her funeral was on 17 April.

5058 ⋆ ▨ ▨ ▨ ▨ ▨ ▨ ▨ ▨ ▨ ▨ ▨ ▨ ▨ ▨

After the first scene set in 1758, an on-screen caption over the spaceship says '3000 YEARS LATER', which infers a setting of around 4758. But the Doctor tells Rose and Mickey they've travelled 'about three thousand years into your future, give or take' and that it's the 'fifty-first century'; they left Earth in 2007, which suggests a date around 5007. But this is just a guess on his part, an assumption he's made based on a cursory examination of the ship's technology, which as we later discover is 37 years old. In the 2006 podcast commentary for this story, author Steven Moffat notes the caption is wrong and that it should be 'three thousand three hundred – roughly'. If we take this into consideration, that makes the year around 5058. From this we can subtract 37 years for the age of the ship, giving us 5021 for when the ship was built. And subtracting from that the year in which the TARDIS left Earth – 2007 – we get 3014, which is, as the Doctor says 'about three thousand years into your future, give or take'. The scenes onboard the SS *Madame de Pompadour* therefore take place in 5058.

1721, December 29 ▨ ▨ ▨ ▨ ▨ ▨ ▨ ▨ ▨ ▨ ▨ ▨ ▨

The year of Madame de Pompadour's birth is given as '1721' on the frame of the portrait onboard the spaceship named of her. This is the full date in our history when Jeanne-Antoinette Poisson was born.

1745 ▨ ▨ ▨ ▨ ▨ ▨ ▨ ▨ ▨ ▨ ▨ ▨ ▨ ▨

Reinette says she had the fireplace moved 'many years ago'. Presumably this was soon after she moved into the Palace, which was in 1745.

5021
5057 ▨ ▨ ▨ ▨ ▨ ▨ ▨ ▨ ▨ ▨ ▨ ▨ ▨ ▨

The Doctor says 'this ship is 37 years old' and hasn't moved 'in over a year', which gives us the timeframe for when the crew were killed and the droids created the time windows.

The early fifty-first century is the time of the solar flares when Earth was abandoned (see 'The Ark In Space'). Of course, the ship is 'three and a half galaxies' away, so is actually distant enough not to be affected by or concerned with the conflicts taking place on Earth at the time.

I have accepted a dating of 5058 as the main setting, with 5057 for when the ship was damaged, and 5021 for when it was built.

DURATION

We see eight different 'days' from Reinette's life through the time windows, a period spanning 37 years. This Duration is ordered to reflect her timeline:

⇨ First Day (1727) ▨ ▨ ▨ ▨ ▨ ▨ ▨ ▨ ▨ ▨ ▨ ▨ ▨

It is night when the Doctor first meets Reinette. He is there for a few minutes only ('Goodnight, Monsieur').

⇨ Second Day (1727, winter) ▨ ▨ ▨ ▨ ▨ ▨ ▨ ▨ ▨

It is 'weeks ago… Months' later that the Doctor meets Reinette again, whereas only moments have passed for him. It is snowing that night.

⇨ Third Day (1740) ▨ ▨ ▨ ▨ ▨ ▨ ▨ ▨ ▨ ▨ ▨ ▨ ▨

It is day for the third very brief meeting.

⇨ Fourth Day (1744) ▨ ▨ ▨ ▨ ▨ ▨ ▨ ▨ ▨ ▨ ▨ ▨

It is day when the Doctor sees Reinette in the grounds of the Palace at Versailles.

⇨ **Fifth Day (1745)** ▨ ▨ ▨ ▨ ▨ ▨ ▨ ▨ ▨ ▨ ▨

The 'night of the Yew Tree Ball' and when Reinette meets the King. The Doctor and Reinette share minds.

⇨ **Sixth Day (1753)** ▨ ▨ ▨ ▨ ▨ ▨ ▨ ▨ ▨ ▨ ▨

Rose visits Reinette to tell her the robots will arrive 'in five years'. The clock reads '5.38pm'. (Reinette steps into the spaceship, and hears herself in 1758.)

⇨ **Seventh Day (1758)** ▨ ▨ ▨ ▨ ▨ ▨ ▨ ▨ ▨ ▨ ▨

Reinette is 37. The robots attack that night. (This is the moment also seen in the pre-titles, and heard again when Reinette steps into the ship from 1753.)

⇨ **Eighth Day (1764)** ▨ ▨ ▨ ▨ ▨ ▨ ▨ ▨ ▨ ▨ ▨

Although the Doctor is away for no more than 'two minutes', six years have past. Reinette's body will reach Paris 'by six' (6.00pm).

⇨ **Day One (5058)** ▨ ▨ ▨ ▨ ▨ ▨ ▨ ▨ ▨ ▨ ▨

While 37 years pass for Reinette, it is eight or nine hours for the Doctor, Rose and Mickey: the Doctor is 'gone for flippin hours' when he goes to 1745 and returns 'drunk'; when the Doctor returns from 1758, Rose and Mickey have been waiting 'five and a half hours'.

RISE OF THE CYBERMEN / THE AGE OF STEEL

STORY LINK

Quite some time seems to have passed since 'The Girl In The Fireplace' – Mickey's hair is much shorter, while Rose's is no longer frizzy. It's clear they've not visited a parallel Earth before.

The Doctor and Rose reminisce about an encounter on an asteroid with 'a weird Munchkin lady with the big eyes. Remember the way she looked at you, and then she opened her mouth and fires comes out!' We can assume this was during Rose's time with the ninth Doctor, as there is little room between 'The Christmas Invasion' and 'Rise Of The Cybermen' for this off-screen adventure to have taken place. At least 'half an hour' has passed in the TARDIS, all the while Mickey has been needlessly holding down a button on the TARDIS console.

When the Doctor and Rose return to the Powell Estate at the end of 'Rise Of The Cybermen', Jackie asks 'where's Mickey?', so presumably from her perspective it is soon after the events of 'School Reunion', although it's not clear how Jackie knew Mickey was with the Doctor and Rose as there is no on-screen moment in 'School Reunion' in which they contact her, so they must have phoned her soon after leaving Earth.

Rose refers to 'Sir Doctor, Dame Rose', which is from when they were knighted by Queen Victoria in 'Tooth And Claw'.

OBSERVATIONS

- The TARDIS falls through 'a crack in time' into the parallel Universe. Although it's not stated as being such, this 'hole' may be the same breach that Torchwood in London has been experimenting with. This might be one of the earliest tests, from before the arrival of the Void Ship and the ghosts that followed. (The Doctor does say he has closed the breach; while this is likely the case at the time, presumably the breach is re-opened by Torchwood – and the Void Ship comes through. It is even conceivable that the Void Ship was drawn to Earth simply because the TARDIS had crossed its path…)
- In the parallel world, the mobile phone network is owned by Cybus Industries. In Rose's world, its equivalent is the Archangel Network, which went online in January 2007 ('The Sound Of Drums').

TIMELINE DATES

2004 = <<2007, February 1>> ∗

Mickey finds a newspaper that gives the date as 'First of February this year. Not exactly far flung, is it'. The parallel Jackie celebrates her 40th birthday, and Rose confirms that 'February the first' is also her mother's birthday (in 'Army Of Ghosts', Jackie confirms she is 40), so the newspaper is the current day's edition. For Mickey and Rose it is 2007, so presumably this is the (unseen) year on the newspaper masthead. The fact that 1 February is a very near future date, indicates that their departure from their Earth was January 2007, the chosen setting for 'School Reunion'.

At one point, Ricky says 'Pete Tyler's been working for Lumic since Twenty Point Five'. If this is a date – the year? – it's clear that the measurement of dates and time is different in this world. The Preachers' van has a tax sticker that reads '30.04.06' [a Production Factor?], the clocks all have a 24 hour movement, and people speak of 'hours', 'weeks', 'months', and 'years'. (Given that the Preachers are rebels, they probably haven't renewed their tax for at least two years, which would explain the expired road tax sticker.)

In 'Army Of Ghosts', Pete reveals that it took the Cybermen 'three years' to cross from that world into the 'real' Universe, which suggests that the parallel runs at a different temporal velocity. In 'The Stolen Earth', the Doctor confirms that Rose's new home is 'running ahead of this Universe'. The parallel is a few days ahead in 'Rise Of The Cybermen' (it's February rather than January), three years ahead in 'Army Of Ghosts' (it's only three months on the real Earth), and if the speed is constant, with two years passing between 'Army Of Ghosts' and 'The Stolen Earth', as many as 36 years should have elapsed, but Rose, Mickey and Jackie are if anything only a few years older.

One way of explaining the difference between the two worlds is that assuming movement between the two realities in both directions is constant, then although the parallel is 'ahead', is it always the same number of days ahead, in this case three years. But for the TARDIS to have fallen through the crack between the two realties, it must have done so at a time relative to the parallel's 'present day', which is February 2007. Therefore it must have been February 2004 when the ship fell through the crack. In other words, the calendar in the parallel is three years 'out'. The TARDIS was bound for 2007, but it slipped back three years to 2004 as it fell through the crack, into a parallel world, where the calendars read 2007. Therefore, 'three years' pass on both worlds – 2007 to 2010 in the parallel and 2004 to 2007 in Rose's.

2007, January

The coda where the Doctor and Rose return home must be set relative to when they left Earth in 'School Reunion', so it is still January, but presumably a week or so later. Given that Jackie's birthday is on 1 February, it's likely that the Doctor and a very distraught Rose stayed on Earth until after that date.

1964 = <<1967, February 1>>
1985 = <<1988, February 1>>

Jackie celebrates her '40th' on 'February the First' 2007, so she was born in 1967. Pete recalls her 'twenty-first' ('a cider at the George') which would have been in 1988, the year after they were married.

1984 = <<1987>>

The parallel Pete and Jackie have been marred for 'twenty years', which would have been in 1987. Jackie was only 20 years old. (If her own parents also married in 1987, by implication, Rose would have already been born by then. However, since it has been established that the parallel world was running three years 'ahead' of the N-Space Universe, Rose's parents were married in 1984, which still equals 1987 in the parallel variant, the only common event shared by both Tyler couples to have taken place at the same time rather than three years apart. This means that the parallel Tylers married when Jackie was 20, but that Rose's mum and dad married when Jackie was 23.

2002 ▨ ▨ ▨ ▨ ▨ ▨ ▨ ▨ ▨ ▨ ▨ ▨ ▨ ▨ ▨

Rose says Mickey's grandmother died 'about five years ago now. I was still at school'. With the year 2007, the death would have been in 2002.

2002 = <<2005>> ▨ ▨ ▨ ▨ ▨ ▨ ▨ ▨ ▨ ▨ ▨ ▨

Ricky says Pete has been working for Lumic 'since Twenty Point Five'. If this means the year, then presumably this is a shorthand for 2005.

2003 = <<2006, November>> ▨ ▨ ▨ ▨ ▨ ▨ ▨ ▨ ▨

Jake says the disappearances have being 'going on for months', presumably since November 2006.

2004 = <<2007 January>> ▨ ▨ ▨ ▨ ▨ ▨ ▨ ▨ ▨

Pete says he moved out 'last month'.

▨▨▨▨▨▨▨ DURATION ▨▨▨▨▨▨▨

⇨ Day One (<<1 February>>) (Ep1-2) ▨ ▨ ▨ ▨ ▨ ▨ ▨

The TARDIS lands late morning – the time on Rose's phone reads '11.35am' when she connects with the Cybus Network. It later reads '14.40pm'. Lumic is due to arrive at the airfield 'by five o'clock'. Jackie's 40th birthday party is held that night. After the Cybermen crash the party, the Doctor says it will take the crystal 'four hours' to recharge. (It has done so by the end of the story, which means at least four hours pass from this point on.) When Crane is killed, the clock in the base reads '8.30pm'. It is '10.10pm' when the Doctor arrives at the base. The cancellation signal is sent at '10.20pm'.

⇨ Day Two (<<2 February>>) (Ep1-2) ▨ ▨ ▨ ▨ ▨ ▨ ▨

It is after midnight by the time the Doctor and Rose leave in the TARDIS.

⇨ Day One (2007) (Ep2) ▨ ▨ ▨ ▨ ▨ ▨ ▨ ▨ ▨ ▨ ▨

It is day when the TARDIS lands in the Tyler flat. (Jackie is in her dressing gown making a cup of tea.)

THE IDIOT'S LANTERN

STORY LINK

It would appear that some time has passed since the events of 'Rise Of The Cybermen'. The Doctor and Rose must have stayed a while at the Tyler flat to get over the loss of Mickey. And since 1 February was Jackie's 40th birthday, they probably stayed on for a couple of days to celebrate that before moving on again. (They might even have been spotted by Victor Kennedy at this time – see 'Love & Monsters'.) They are bound for New York to see Elvis Presley perform on *The Ed Sullivan Show* (on 28 October 1956).

Both the Doctor and Rose are now 'infected' with Void-radiation, which comes into play in 'Army Of Ghosts'.

LANGUAGE

The Wire speaks English, in the voice of the real-life television presenter whose form the Wire takes on. Bishop uses the French term *'sans visage'* ('without face').

TIMELINE DATES

1953, April (late)

Bishop says they first started finding people *'sans visage'* 'about a month ago'. This would have been soon after Magpie began selling his cheap television sets, which itself would have been at least a week or so after the arrival of the Wire.

1953, June 1 – 2 ✦

The Doctor says 'Oh! Is this 1953?', to which Magpie replies 'Last time I looked'. The full date is never stated, but the Doctor and Rose arrive the day before the official coronation of Queen Elizabeth the Second, which in our history was on 2 June 1953. Although it's a fine day in the episode, in reality it poured with rain!

1956, October 28

The day on which Elvis Presley performed live on *The Ed Sullivan Show*.

DURATION

⇨ **Day (April 1953)**

It is raining the night Magpie encounters the Wire. This is soon after closedown of broadcasts from the BBC.

🕘 **About a month passes**... ▨ ▨ ▨ ▨ ▨ ▨ 🕘 ▨ ▨ ▨

⇨ **Day One (1 June 1953)** ▨ ▨ ▨ ▨ ▨ ▨ ▨ ▨
The TARDIS lands in the afternoon. It is night when the Doctor and Rose meet the Connelleys. The Coronation is 'tomorrow'. The Doctor is interrogated by Bishop during the night.

⇨ **Day Two (2 June 1953)** ▨ ▨ ▨ ▨ ▨ ▨ ▨ ▨
'The big day dawns' when the Doctor is released by Bishop. (In our history, the live television broadcasts of the Coronation day began at 10.15am). The Doctor battles the Wire a few hours later. The Doctor and Rose stay for the post-Coronation street party.

THE IMPOSSIBLE PLANET
THE SATAN PIT

STORY LINK

There is no mention of any recent events, so any amount of time could have passed since 'The Idiot's Lantern'. Presumably the Doctor and Rose made it to *The Ed Sullivan Show* on 28 October 1956 to see Elvis Presley perform, their original destination at the start of 'The Idiot's Lantern'.

As noted under 'Love & Monsters' below, the Doctor's encounter with the Elemental Shade, which killed Elton's mother in 1967, might have occurred between the events of 'The Idiot's Lantern' and 'The Impossible Planet'. The Doctor notes that the TARDIS is feeling 'queasy'.

OBSERVATIONS

- The Doctor says TARDISes 'were grown, not built', which contradicts earlier revelations (see 'The Chase', 'Warriors' Gate', 'Arc Of Infinity') that TARDISes were manufactured. Of course he could be referring just to the outer plasmic shell rather than the interior. The Doctor says 'my people practically invented black holes. Well, in fact, they did', which supports Omega's claim in 'The Three Doctors'.
- Captain Zachary Cross Flane says he is 'representing the Torchwood Archive'. Given that he would be alive in this time zone, presumably Jack Harkness

has something to do with preserving the name of Torchwood this far into the future. (Was Jack in any way involved with sending the mission to the planet?)

LANGUAGE

The Doctor says the ancient language of the people who imprisoned the beast is 'Very old. Impossibly old' – in fact it's so old even the TARDIS can't translate it.

TIMELINE DATES

4043 • (43/K/2.1)

No dates are given. Jefferson refers to an 'Empire'; the Base crew are from Earth. The Doctor later says Earth is 'that way – turn right, keep going for about, um, five hundred years? And you'll reach Earth'. This comment implies that it's 500 years after Rose's time – around the year 2500. When the crew of Sanctuary Base personnel are killed, the same entry is made in the log: 'Deceased Forty Three K Two Point One'. It's not clear if this is a date. If so, then it might indicate the year to be as late as 43,000. But given that in 'Planet Of The Ood', the creatures are released from 200 years of slavery in 4126, 'The Impossible Planet' can only be set between 3926 and 4126. The Empire mentioned by Jefferson is therefore 'the Second Great and Bountiful Human Empire' mentioned by the Doctor in 'Planet Of The Ood'.

If 'Forty Three K Two Point One' is a date, we might interpret the first two digits to represent a year ending '43' – which gives us two options, 3943 and 4043 – with the other number and letters denoting a code for the month and day. I have taken 4043 as the preferred date.

Before Time

The Beast says it is from 'Before time... Before the cataclysm – before this Universe was created', a concept that the Doctor finds hard to accept: 'That's impossible. No life could have existed back then'. The Universe was created some 15 billion years ago (see 'Terminus' and 'The Curse Of Fenric').

Toby says the planet supported life 'aeons ago'. The possessed Ood declare the Beast 'has woven himself in the fabric of your life since the Dawn of Time... Some may call him Abaddon. Some may call him Krop Tor. Some may call him Satan or Lucifer or the King of Despair. The Deathless Prince. The Bringer of Night'. (Abaddon, who is the son of the Beast, is trapped beneath the Rift in Cardiff, and is released in 'End Of Days'.)

The Doctor knows of devil imagery on many planets, such as Earth ('The Dæmons' and 'The Awakening'), Draconia ('Frontier In Space'), Vel Consadine, Daemos ('The

Dæmons'), and as the Kaled God of War ('Genesis Of The Daleks').

Billion Years BC

The Scarlet System was the home of the Pallushi, a mighty civilisation 'spanning a billion years'.

4023

Ida says Scooti was '20 years old', so she was born circa 4023.

DURATION

⇨ Day One (Ep1-2)

This adventure takes place over several hours. Rose has a meal with the Base crew. The Doctor and Ida have only '55 minutes of air left' when they are trapped in the pit. Ida is nearly dead when the Doctor rescues her in the TARDIS.

LOVE & MONSTERS

NOTE: Given that this episode is told in the first person by Elton, and punctuated with some unusual visuals (such as the cartoon-like corridor chase scene in the warehouse between the Doctor, Rose and the Hoix), it can't be taken for granted that all the events Elton narrates actually occurred exactly in the way he says they did. Elton might be embellishing certain elements of the story to some degree to make it all sound more exciting and believable. It's therefore possible that Ursula did not actually survive the attack by the Abzorbaloff at all. Her survival as a paving stone might be a figment of Elton's imagination.

STORY LINK

Elton's narration jumps around all over the place, but we can place the Doctor and Rose's travels in some form of chronological order based on what we see and hear: Ursula first saw the Doctor at Trafalgar Square on Christmas Day 2006 (an off-screen event from after the closing moments of 'The Christmas Invasion'). Victor Kennedy shows LINDA footage of the Doctor and Rose entering the TARDIS, which is another off-screen adventure (possibly from their arrival back on Earth a few days prior to 'School Reunion'). Given that Rose's hairstyle is different each time she appears during this episode, a considerable amount of time probably elapses between all these various coming and goings. Weeks later (in March – see Duration) Elton locates the TARDIS and encounters the creature (named as a Hoix in 'Exit Wounds') in the deserted warehouse. He sees the Doctor and Rose for the first time. Rose (who is 'so far away') rings Jackie the night that Elton calls round and gets the pizzas. Rose has told her 'she'll be home soon'. We can probably place this call soon after the events of 'The Impossible Planet'; Rose tried to ring Jackie when they were trapped on Sanctuary Base Six, but there was no signal. Presumably she rang home at the first opportunity she had once she was back in the TARDIS. The Doctor and Rose return (off-screen) the next day to find a very distraught Jackie; they set off to locate Elton, and find him with the Abzorbaloff in the alley.

From Jackie's perspective, this is soon after the Doctor and Rose returned to the flat at the end of 'Rise Of The Cybermen'. Jackie tells Elton of Mickey, who has 'gone now'. It's not clear how long the Doctor and Rose stayed. (Since 1 February was Jackie's birthday, we might assume that the Doctor and Rose stayed on Earth until after that date.) It would seem that Jackie is no longer dating Howard (see 'The Christmas Invasion'), hence her sudden attraction to and flirtation with Elton.

There is also the Doctor's encounter with the Elemental Shade to factor in. Although Rose is not seen in the flashback, she was with the Doctor at the time; since the Doctor seemingly recognizes the older Elton, we might assume that the Doctor's encounter with the Shade occurred recently, possibly just prior to the events of 'The Impossible Planet'.

In summary, the various Doctor and Rose montages might fit within the rest of the stories like this:

- 'The Christmas Invasion'
  The Doctor is seen in Trafalgar Square by Ursula Blake on Christmas Day
- 'New Earth' / 'Tooth And Claw'
  The Doctor and Rose are called back to Earth by Mickey. Victor Kennedy videos the Doctor and Rose with the TARDIS
- 'School Reunion' / 'The Girl In The Fireplace' / 'Rise Of The Cybermen'
  The Doctor and Rose return home; they stay for a few days
- In 1977 the Doctor stops the Elemental Shade, but Elton's mother is killed
- 'The Idiot's Lantern'
  The Doctor and Rose are seen by Elton with the Hoix
- 'The Impossible Planet'
  The Doctor and Rose return home, and meet Elton and the Abzorbaloff

OBSERVATIONS

- Bridget shows documentary evidence of sightings of the Doctor and the TARDIS throughout history, including etchings and bas-reliefs. Given the vagueness of the time periods of these, I have not attempted to date or place them in the TIMELINE.
- It's not clear how the Doctor was able to zero in the TARDIS to where Elton was. Elton did touch the TARDIS when he saw the Doctor and Rose with the Hoix. And the Doctor might have realised how and why he recognized Elton at the warehouse based on Jackie's description. The Doctor then programmed the TARDIS to locate Elton's presence from his hand print on the TARDIS exterior.
- The term Abzorbaloff is given to the creature by Elton ('ooo, I like that'). Given that we know so very little about the planet Clom (even the Doctor expresses having no knowledge of it) there's no reason to not assume that Victor Kenney is the creature's real name. He even has the initials VK monogrammed onto his briefcase.
- Victor Kennedy is reading the *Daily Telegraph*, which headlines the news that 'Saxon leads the polls with 64 per cent' in the 'ELECTION COUNTDOWN'. A secondary headline reads 'Four months of government stagnation'. The significance of these headlines is explored further under 'The Sound Of Drums'.
- At the end of 'Aliens Of London' the Doctor gives Mickey a CD containing a virus which would remove all record of the Doctor from the internet. In 'Love & Monsters' Victor Kennedy refers to a 'Bad Wolf virus', which has corrupted the Torchwood files that he has obtained. It's possible that the two viruses are one and the same; did Mickey perhaps name 'his' virus the 'Bad Wolf virus' as that was the name that had been painted on the side of the TARDIS at the time?

LANGUAGE

The Abzorbaloff creature speaks with an accent in its natural state, but with a different accent and voice in its human guise.

TIMELINE DATES

1973
1977 ⁕ ▦ ▦ ▦ ▦ ▦ ▦ ▦ ▦ ▦ ▦ ▦ ▦

Elton was 'three or four years old' when his mother died. [Actor Marc Warren was born in 1967. In a deleted scene from this story, Elton says he was born in 1973. Of note, Elton's surname is never given on-screen; it is given as Pope in the script.] Elton's mother was killed by the Elemental Shade, and he saw the Doctor for the first time 'in the middle of the night'.

2005, March 5 ✦ ▨ ▨ ▨ ▨ ▨ ▨ ▨ ▨ ▨ ▨ ▨
Elton refers to shop window dummies coming to life in London 'two years ago'. This is established as being 5 March 2006 in 'Rose'.

2006, March 6 ✦ ▨ ▨ ▨ ▨ ▨ ▨ ▨ ▨ ▨ ▨ ▨
Elton refers to the events of 'Aliens Of London', which was 'twelve months later', after the events of 'Rose'. This was 6 March 2006.

2006, December 25 ✦ ▨ ▨ ▨ ▨ ▨ ▨ ▨ ▨ ▨ ▨ ▨
Elton mentions the arrival of the Sycorax spaceship at 'quarter to eight in the morning' on 'Christmas Day', in 'The Christmas Invasion'.

2006, December 25
2006, December 27
2006, December 29
2006, December 30 ▨ ▨ ▨ ▨ ▨ ▨ ▨ ▨ ▨ ▨ ▨
Parts of Elton's narrations refer to events that occur after Christmas, such as the internet going into meltdown with all the online conspiracy theories after the Christmas Day spaceship (presumably the night of 25 December); his discovery 'one day' of Ursula Blake's 'My Invasion Blog'; the fact that one night it is snowing (or could it still be falling ash from the destroyed Sycorax ship?) (on December 27?); his meeting with Ursula in the park (December 29?); Ursula saying that the photo of the Doctor was taken on 'Christmas Day' at Trafalgar Square 'that night'; and him taking Ursula to see his old house, and filming with his 'brand new camera' (which he got at Christmas?) on, say December 30. Both he and Ursula (who his holding the camera) are wearing gloves, so it is still winter.

2007, January
2007, February
2007, March
2007, April ▨ ▨ ▨ ▨ ▨ ▨ ▨ ▨ ▨ ▨ ▨
(See DURATION below for more detail on the spread of actual dates)
Elton attends the first meeting of The Inner Sanctum (later renamed LINDA) on a Tuesday in early 2007, shortly after the events of 'The Christmas Invasion'; this would

probably be Tuesday, 2 January 2007.

A number of weekly LINDA meetings are depicted, and factoring in the different shirts Elton is wearing in them, LINDA meet for at least nine weeks before Victor Kennedy enters their lives, which Elton says was 'that Tuesday night in March', which is the tenth week. Several weeks then pass as they work for Kennedy, investigating reported sightings of the Doctor. Elton sees the Doctor and Rose with the Hoix in the third week of March.

A calendar showing 'MARCH' is visible in the laundrette when Elton first meets Jackie. He meets her again on eight subsequent occasions, presumably on a daily basis. Since he tells the others about this at the next meeting seven days later, we have to assume that two of these eight visits take place on the same day, despite the fact that Elton is mostly wearing different shirts throughout the montage. This takes the story into April. It is on 2 April that Jackie discovers the truth about Elton the night he goes to get the pizzas. The following day, Tuesday 3 April, Victor Kennedy reveals his true colours, and Elton finally meets the Doctor and Rose.

2007, January 4? •

Victor Kennedy records the Doctor, Rose and the TARDIS. Presumably this is from around the time they were called back to Earth by Mickey in 'School Reunion'.

2007, April 4 – 7

Going by his changes in clothing, Elton makes four separate 'to video' recordings, describing the events we've seen via flashback; spanning the first week of January to the first week of April. We can assume that he makes the first of these the day after Ursula was 'killed' by the Abzorbaloff. He doesn't have a remote control zoom to start, but by the fourth entry he has bought one. See Duration below for a complete day by day breakdown of the episode.

DURATION

'Love & Monsters' is made up of 32 separate 'events' in the life of Elton; 28 flashbacks and four to-video narrations. The bulk of the story spans a period of four months – January to April. Since we do not see the story unfold in strict chronological order, the following DURATION breaks down the events into order of occurrence rather than the order as seen on screen: [FB: Flashback, VN: Video Narration]:

⇨ FB (1977)

Elton remembers happy times with his mother (various scenes, in the kitchen, in the park)… Elton's mother is killed 'in the middle of the night', and young Elton sees the

Doctor in the living room with his mother's body, which is presumably the same night as the flashbacks of his mother when she was alive.

⇨ **FB (5 March 2005)** ▓ ▓ ▓ ▓ ▓ ▓ ▓ ▓ ▓ ▓
Elton sees shop window dummies coming to life ('Rose').

⇨ **FB (6 March 2006)** ▓ ▓ ▓ ▓ ▓ ▓ ▓ ▓ ▓ ▓
Elton sees the spaceship crash into Big Ben ('Aliens Of London').

⇨ **FB (25 December 2006)** ▓ ▓ ▓ ▓ ▓ ▓ ▓ ▓ ▓
At 'quarter to eight in the morning' (7.45am) Elton sees the Sycorax spaceship hovering over London ('The Christmas Invasion'). The Doctor is photographed by Ursula in Trafalgar Square that night. Elton reads about the sightings on the internet.

⇨ **FB (27 December 2006?)** ▓ ▓ ▓ ▓ ▓ ▓ ▓ ▓ ▓
Then 'one day', Elton finds Ursula's 'My Invasion Blog'. (Snow/ash falls that night.)

⇨ **FB (29 December 2006?)** ▓ ▓ ▓ ▓ ▓ ▓ ▓ ▓ ▓
Elton meets Ursula (they are dressed for winter).

⇨ **FB (30 December 2006?)** ▓ ▓ ▓ ▓ ▓ ▓ ▓ ▓ ▓
Elton shows Ursula his childhood house, where he first met the Doctor 'all those years ago'.

⇨ **FB (Tuesday, 2 January 2007)** ▓ ▓ ▓ ▓ ▓ ▓ ▓ ▓ ▓
Elton attends his first meeting with The Inner Sanctum; they meet 'every week' on Tuesdays. {Elton wears a blue sweater}

⇨ **FB (Tuesday, 9 January 2007)** ▓ ▓ ▓ ▓ ▓ ▓ ▓ ▓ ▓
Second meeting; Mr Skinner shows his diagrams {blue denim shirt}.

⇨ **FB (Tuesday, 16 January 2007)** ▓ ▓ ▓ ▓ ▓ ▓ ▓ ▓ ▓
Third meeting; Bridget shows her slides {red polo shirt}.

⇨ **FB (Tuesday, 23 January 2007)** ▓ ▓ ▓ ▓ ▓ ▓ ▓ ▓ ▓
Fourth meeting; Bliss shows her sculpture {green t-shirt}

⇨ **FB (Tuesday, 30 January 2007)** ▦ ▦ ▦ ▦ ▦ ▦ ▦ ▦
Fifth meeting; Elton suggests the new name LINDA {blue sweater}

⇨ **FB (Tuesday, 6 February 2007)** ▦ ▦ ▦ ▦ ▦ ▦ ▦ ▦
Sixth meeting ('after a while'); Bridget demonstrates her cooking skills {sweater}

⇨ **FB (Tuesday, 13 February 2007)** ▦ ▦ ▦ ▦ ▦ ▦ ▦ ▦
Seventh meeting; Mr Skinner reads from his novel {short sleeved shirt}

⇨ **FB (Tuesday, 20 February 2007)** ▦ ▦ ▦ ▦ ▦ ▦ ▦ ▦
Eighth meeting; Bridget tells of her missing daughter {grey shirt}

⇨ **FB (Tuesday, 27 February 2007)** ▦ ▦ ▦ ▦ ▦ ▦ ▦ ▦
Ninth meeting; the sing-a-long ('Brand New Key') {blue sweater}

⇨ **FB (Tuesday, 6 March 2007)** ▦ ▦ ▦ ▦ ▦ ▦ ▦ ▦
Tenth meeting; the group play ELO; Victor Kennedy arrives 'that Tuesday in March', and shows them a video of the Doctor and Rose (from the time of 'School Reunion'?). He tells them to 'meet back here, this time next week'. Bliss is absorbed.

⇨ **FB (Tuesday, 13 March 2007)** ▦ ▦ ▦ ▦ ▦ ▦ ▦ ▦
The following week they meet up, and ask where Bliss is.

⇨ **FB (Tuesday, 20 March 2007)** ▦ ▦ ▦ ▦ ▦ ▦ ▦ ▦
The following week, Mr Skinner reports on a sighting of the TARDIS in Woolwich. Elton sees and touches the TARDIS, encounters the Doctor and Rose with the Hoix (as seen in the pre-credits sequence). He reports back to the others. Kennedy shows them pictures of Rose from the Torchwood files (corrupted by the Bad Wolf virus) and tells them to search for the girl.

⇨ **FB (Wednesday, 21 March 2007)** ▦ ▦ ▦ ▦ ▦ ▦ ▦ ▦
The next day (?) Elton locates and meets Jackie in the laundrette (there is a 'March' calendar on the wall). He fixes her washing machine. She tells him about Mickey (he's 'gone now'). The clock on the mantelpiece reads '5.00pm'.

⇨ **FB (Tuesday, 27 March 2007)** ▦ ▦ ▦ ▦ ▦ ▦ ▦ ▦
At the next meeting, Elton tells of his encounter with Jackie. Kennedy assigns 'this week's homework' to Elton – to keep tabs on Jackie Tyler. Bridget is absorbed. Elton

goes to Jackie's and fixes the wiring. {short blue shirt}

⇨ **FB (Wednesday, 28 March 2007)** ▨ ▨ ▨ ▨ ▨ ▨ ▨
Elton puts up shelves. {long blue shirt}

⇨ **FB (Thursday, 29 March 2007)** ▨ ▨ ▨ ▨ ▨ ▨ ▨
Elton puts up more shelves. {blue polo shirt}

⇨ **FB (Friday, 30 March 2007)** ▨ ▨ ▨ ▨ ▨ ▨ ▨ ▨
Elton mends the wiring. {long green shirt}

⇨ **FB (Saturday, 31 March 2007)** ▨ ▨ ▨ ▨ ▨ ▨ ▨
Elton mends more wiring. {long blue shirt}

⇨ **FB (Sunday, 1 April 2007)** ▨ ▨ ▨ ▨ ▨ ▨ ▨ ▨
Elton mends more wiring {blue polo shirt} and attends to the sink pipes. {long blue shirt}

⇨ **FB (Monday, 2 April 2007)** ▨ ▨ ▨ ▨ ▨ ▨ ▨ ▨
Elton fixes the fuses. Jackie spills wine over Elton's shirt. Rose rings to say she will be home 'soon' (for Rose, this might be soon after leaving 'The Impossible Planet'). Elton goes to get pizzas, but Jackie discovers his true motives. {long blue shirt}

⇨ **FB (Tuesday, 3 April 2007)** ▨ ▨ ▨ ▨ ▨ ▨ ▨ ▨
At the next LINDA meeting, Elton tells about his week with Jackie. Mr Skinner gets absorbed, and Elton and Ursula discover the truth about Victor Kennedy. Ursula gets absorbed. Elton finally meets the Doctor and Rose in the alleyway.

⇨ **VN 1 (Wednesday, 4 April 2007?)** ▨ ▨ ▨ ▨ ▨ ▨ ▨
Elton begins his video diary. He doesn't have a remote zoom. He starts with the encounter with the Doctor, Rose and the Hoix, and ends with the spaceship on Christmas Day. {blue sweater}

⇨ **VN 2 (Thursday, 5 April 2007?)** ▨ ▨ ▨ ▨ ▨ ▨ ▨ ▨
(It looks like sunset through the window) Elton makes an addition to his video diary, namely his obsession with ELO; he dances around his room to 'Mr Blue Sky'. {blue t-shirt}

⇨ **VN 3 (Friday, 6 April 2007?)** ▨ ▨ ▨ ▨ ▨ ▨ ▨ ▨
Elton continues his video diary, picking up where he left off with the spaceship at Christmas, and ending with his meeting with the Doctor. {grey long shirt}

⇨ **VN 4 (Saturday, 7 April 2007?)** ▨ ▨ ▨ ▨ ▨ ▨ ▨ ▨
Elton completes his video diary (he now has a remote zoom). {blue sweater}

FEAR HER

STORY LINK

The Doctor mentions meeting cats 'in a nun's wimple', a reference to the events of 'New Earth'. In 'Dalek', the Doctor and Rose visited the USA in 2012, but they make no reference to this here. Any amount of time could have passed since the events of 'Love & Monsters'. The Doctor has deliberately brought the TARDIS to 2012 as he had a 'passing fancy' ('only it didn't pass, it stopped') to visit the 'near future'. (He may have been to the 2012 Games previously, as he knows the outcome of the Papua New Guinea shot-putting event.)

OBSERVATIONS

- The Isolus take 'thousands and thousands of years to grow up', and live for over 'a thousand' years.
- With 'Fear Her' set in 2012, this is three years after the events of 'The Stolen Earth', in which the Daleks move Earth into the Medusa Cascade. Therefore Chloe, her mother and the other residents of Dame Kellie Holmes Close (not to mention the rest of the planet!) all experienced the events of that story, and yet in 'Fear Her' they seem rather oblivious to the possibility of alien intervention. Did the Daleks change future events, so that from 2009 onwards history is changed?

LANGUAGE

The Isolus speaks through Chloe Webber, using her voice and presumably language, although since the Isolus 'speaks' only when the Doctor is present, its speech might be being translated through him.

TIMELINE DATES

2012, July 21
The Isolus arrived 'six days ago', which would be on 21 July. Danny was the first of three children to disappear 'in the last six days'.

2012, July 27 *
The street banner reads 'LONDON 2012', which the Doctor declares is 'the Thirtieth Olympiad'. [In our history the Games are to be held from 27 July to 12 August 2012.] The radio announcer says it is 'a lovely summer's day'. Dale Hicks is the boy who vanishes in the opening moments, and the missing child poster put up later that day says he has 'not been seen since July 27 2012', which is in fact the same day. Five cars have broken down on the Close 'today'. This has been happening 'all week', which is ever since the Isolus landed.

1948, July 29 **
The Doctor says he saw the opening ceremony of the Games at Wembley in 1948, which opened on 29 July in our history. He loved it so much he went twice!

2000
Chloe is 'a 12 year old girl', so she was born in 2000.

2011
Chloe's father 'died a year ago'.

2012, July 23
The date that Jane McKillen disappeared is seen on the poster: 'Missing: 23-Jul-12' and 'missing since July 23 2012'.

2012, July 26
Chloe says she drew the picture of her father in the wardrobe 'yesterday'.

2012, August *
The Doctor knows the outcome of the shot-put (Papua New Guinea wins), so he may have been there towards the end of the London Games.

DURATION

⇨ **Day (27 July 2012)**

The Isolus arrives, and its pod is buried in the hot tar. It takes possession of Chloe Webber.

🕐 **'Six days' pass...**

⇨ **Day One (27 July 2012)**

Dale Hicks vanishes that morning. The Doctor and Rose arrive later that day. The opening ceremony is 'tonight'. The story ends that same night, after the opening ceremony.

ARMY OF GHOSTS DOOMSDAY

+STORY LINK

The Beast said that Rose 'will die in battle so very soon', so from Rose's perspective, 'Army Of Ghosts' takes place shortly after the events of 'The Impossible Planet'. We see a short montage of various off-screen adventures: the Doctor and Rose running along a street (London?); on an alien world with manta-ray-like creatures wheeling in the sky. These could have taken place at any point between 'New Earth' and 'Army Of Ghosts'.

Rose has 'loads of washing', and gives Jackie a bazoolium barometer they got from an asteroid bazaar.

CYBUSMAN LINK

In the wake of the events of 'Rise Of The Cybermen', the Cyberman factories on seven other continents have been destroyed by Mickey and other resistance groups. But moralists demanded that the Cybermen not be destroyed. The Cybermen seized control of Torchwood, then vanish when the Void opened. It took 'three years' for five million Cybermen to travel through the rift between dimensions and emerge as ghost-like images in the 'real' Universe. (As pointed out below, there is not a temporal divergence between the Cybermen's Universe and the 'real' Universe; the 'three years' differential is due only to the calendars being 'out' by three years.)

DALEK LINK

The Void Ship contains the four members of the legendary Cult of Skaro, Sec, Jast, Thay and Caan, who have in their possession the Genesis Ark, a Time Lord prison ship containing millions of captured Daleks. At the end of the Last Great Time War they took the Ark and vanished into the Void presumably to ride out the War but became trapped. It wasn't until there was a breach in the Void, some 600 feet above London, that they emerged, into a holding room near the top of Torchwood Tower, a building in London's docklands, also known as Canary Wharf. The breach in the Void also releases the Cybermen who had travelled through a crack between realities. It's not readily clear how long the Void ship has been within Torchwood, but given that the 'ghosts' had been appearing for 'two months', we can assume that the Ship also came through at roughly the same time. The Ship itself has presumably been lost within the Void for decades, certainly for longer than however many years it has been since the Time War ended.

In 'Daleks In Manhattan', Dalek Sec says 'my planet is gone, destroyed in a great war'. He can't be referring to Skaro as that was destroyed by the Doctor in 'Remembrance Of The Daleks'. This would imply that the Daleks – or just the Cult? – had acquired a new homeworld prior to the outbreak of the Time War.

OBSERVATIONS

- When he arrives in Torchwood, the Doctor says 'All those times I've been on Earth, I've never heard of you'. It does seem rather unlikely given that a lot of other people seem to know of them. The biggest difference between them and UNIT is that UNIT is a military organization with a philosophy to defend and protect against alien menace, whereas Torchwood's agenda is to exploit alien technology and aliens for their own personal gain. This may be why the government keeps close tabs on Torchwood but turns a blind eye because the government benefits from Torchwood's activities, whereas UNIT answers to the Ministry of Defence and has limited powers.
- If anything, this story creates the greatest number of problems with reconciling the established continuity of both DALEK HISTORY and CYBERMAN HISTORY. The Cybermen invade Earth en masse in 2007, and yet in stories like 'The Moonbase' and 'The Wheel In Space' no one seems to have heard of them. More significantly, in 'Dalek' no one at Van Statten's base knows what a Dalek is. Given that Van Statten has been collecting alien artefacts for years, we can assume that he only started doing so after Torchwood One in London was destroyed, otherwise Yvonne Hartman and her team would have been monitoring or at least

been aware of Van Statten's activities.

- The Doctor shouldn't be at all surprised to see the Daleks – in many previously encounters with the Daleks or Cybermen he has encountered one or the other very soon after – 'The Tenth Planet' and 'The Power Of The Daleks'; 'The Evil Of The Dalek' / 'The Tomb Of The Cybermen'; 'Genesis Of The Daleks' / 'Revenge Of The Cybermen'; 'Resurrection Of The Daleks' / 'Attack Of The Cybermen'; 'Remembrance Of The Daleks' / 'Silver Nemesis'; and again in 'The Stolen Earth' / 'The Next Doctor'.

- The Doctor refers to the Void being the 'space between dimensions… There's all sorts of different realities around us, different dimensions. Billions of parallel Universes all stacked up against each other'. The Doctor has visited some of these parallel Universes before, as in 'Inferno' and 'Rise Of The Cybermen', and is aware of a 'sideways' dimension in 'Battlefield' where he is known as Merlin.

- Rose gives Jackie a gift from an alien bazaar in 'Army Of Ghosts,' presumably just one of many such items Rose has given to her mother on each (off-screen) return visit. When Jackie is one of the 'declared dead', presumably the authorities would search the now-abandoned Tyler flat. If they found all these alien objects, we can assume Torchwood, UNIT or other organisations (or even private collectors like Henry Parker ('A Day In The Death')) would procure them.

- Rose says 'According to the papers, they've elected a ghost as MP for Leeds'. This happened on account of the long period of political upheaval covered under 'The Sound Of Drums'.

- When Rose uses her mobile phone it does not connect to the Archangel Network, which had been operating since January 2007 (also 'The Sound Of Drums'). This is either because the Doctor's 'universal roaming' setting overrides the system, or her particular model is not compatible with the network.

LANGUAGE

The name of the Norwegian beach where the Doctor contacts Rose is called 'Darlig Ulv Stranden', which is not automatically translated into English. But given that the TARDIS is not there, and the Doctor is only a hologram, that would explain why the translator is not translating. And since Rose has been away from the TARDIS for seven months, any residual effects of the telepathic circuits may have long since worn off. When the Doctor uses the 'Allons-y' catch-phrase, it is not translated from French into English equivalent 'Let's go!' The Daleks use the time measurement 'Rels'.

TIMELINE DATES

2007, May 27 *
2007 = <<2010, May 27>> * ░ ░ ░ ░ ░ ░ ░ ░ ░

Rose says in 'the first nineteen years of my life, nothing happened' and then she met the Doctor. She also later says she had a life with Jackie 'for nineteen years'. She was born in 1986, but has been travelling with the Doctor for nearly a year by now, so for Rose, the 'current year' would be 2006. But she 'lost' a year between 'Rose' and 'Aliens Of London', so in actual fact, the current year for Jackie is 2007. This date is supported by Jackie's comment that Pete died '20 years ago', which was on 7 November 1987, as seen in 'Father's Day'.

Taking into account the dates for 'Love & Monsters' (January to April 2007), 'Everything Changes' and the Ianto flashback in 'Fragments', 'Army Of Ghosts' must take place no earlier than April 2007 and no later than July 2007. The last week of May 2007 is the best date. On the day that Rose and the Doctor arrive in time for the midday ghost-shift, there are a number of children playing in the Powell Estate courtyard, so we can assume that it is the weekend. Jackie shows the Doctor a scene from an episode of *EastEnders*; this can't be a week day edition, as those play in the evening, so it must be the afternoon Sunday Omnibus edition; the best day to place 'Army Of Ghosts' is Sunday 27 May 2007.

As noted under 'Rise Of The Cybermen', the events on the two parallel Earths are in sync with each other (i.e. movement between the two realities is spatial only; there is no temporal shift), but the calendars are three years 'out', so while it's 2007 on Rose's Earth the calendars on what the Doctor playfully calls 'Pete's World' would read 2010.

In the three years since 'Rise Of The Cybermen', one Harriet Jones has been elected as the new President. This means that as well as the calendar being three years 'out', the political environment is also very different to Rose's Universe.

The repair work on Big Ben has been completed, and the scaffolding seen in 'The Christmas Invasion' has been removed.

2007 = <<2010, December 22>>
2007 = <<2010, December 23>>
2007 = <<2010, December 24>> * ░ ░ ░ ░ ░ ░ ░ ░ ░

Since Donna is getting married on 24 December ('The Runaway Bride'), and she travels to the TARDIS spatially and not temporally, then the beach goodbye between the Doctor and Rose must also take place on 24 December.

Rose's dream is at night. The scene with her telling the others of her vision must be the following night (she says the dream was 'last night'). In the beach scene, Mickey, Jackie and Pete are all wearing the same clothes they have on when they left the house, which was presumably on the night of 23 December, which means it took them all day to drive from England to Norway. While some seven months have passed for Rose, we can assume that a similar period would have also passed for the Doctor, as this would account for his now having aged another year (see THE DOCTOR'S AGE).

Jackie is already 'three months' pregnant by 24 December, so she must have conceived in late September.

1967, February 1

Jackie says she's '40'; her birthday was on 1 February, as given in 'Rise Of The Cybermen'.

1988
1991

According to Yvonne Hartman Torchwood had been getting warning signals 'for years'. Torchwood Tower was constructed in order to reach the breach that had opened 600 feet above the docklands district of London. In our history, construction of the 50 floor tower, known as One Canada Square, was started in 1988 and completed in 1991. (If Torchwood One moved into the Tower on its completion in 1991, we can assume that its previous headquarters was, like Torchwood Three in Cardiff, situated underground.)

1997

Rose says Granddad Prentice 'died, like, ten years ago ... His heart gave out'.

1997

Yvonne Hartman says the Jathaa Sun-Glider was shot down off the Shetland Islands 'ten years ago'. It was stripped bare, and its weapons used to shoot down the Sycorax 'on Christmas Day' 2006 ('The Christmas Invasion').

2007, April

Jackie says the ghosts first appeared 'about two months ago ... Woke up one morning and there they were'. (There was no sign of the Doctor). There is no mention of the 'ghosts' in 'Love & Monsters', so we can assume that the first ghosts appeared soon after that, which would be the second week of April. The fact that Jackie says 'almost' probably means she is counting all of April and all of May as being 'two months', so it is not necessarily into June.

2006 = << 2009, December>>
Pete Tyler says the temperature began to rise 'six months ago'. As note elsewhere, the current calendar in this Universe reads 2010. Harriet Jones is the new President.

DURATION

⇨ **Day One (Sunday, 27 May) (Ep1-2)**
The TARDIS lands shortly before the midday ghost shift at 'ten past' (12.10pm); this lasts 'a couple of minutes', and at 'twelve minutes past' they vanish. The next shift is at 'quarter to' (12.45pm). The decorative clock in Yvonne Hartman's office reads '1.15pm' when the shift is activated, and the Cybermen (5 million of them) materialise across the globe. The clock reads '4.29pm' when the Doctor and Rose return to open the breach. Rose is trapped when the breach closes...

🕐 **Seven months pass...**

⇨ **Day One (22 December) (Ep2)**
That night, Rose dreams of the Doctor...

⇨ **Day Two (23 December) (Ep2)**
Rose tells her family of her dream 'last night'. They set off into the night...

⇨ **Day Three (24 December) (Ep2)**
The following day they arrive at Bad Wolf Bay in Norway, and Rose is reunited briefly (for little more than 'two minutes') with the Doctor.

THE RUNAWAY BRIDE

+STORY LINK

While the Doctor is in orbit around a supernova, speaking with Rose at Darlig Ulv Stranden in the alternative world's Norway, as seen at the end of 'Army Of Ghosts', Donna is pulled to the TARDIS. 'The Runaway Bride' is therefore consecutive to 'Army Of Ghosts'. (And at the same time that this is happening, Owen is watching Diane fly off in the Sky Gypsy, as seen in the *Torchwood* story 'Out Of Time'.)

OBSERVATIONS

- When the Doctor browses the web with the mobile phone he borrows at the reception party, a number of sites flash up, including: a UNIT site; Torchwood House ('Tooth And Claw'); Geocomtex – Support Site & FAQs ('Dalek'); Deffry Vale School ('School Reunion'); British Rocket Group ('Remembrance Of The Daleks', 'The Christmas Invasion').
- The fact that Donna worked for H C Clements, which was owned by Torchwood, means that all of the Doctor's latest companions have at some point worked for or been associated with Torchwood in some way: Jack Harkness became leader of Torchwood Three; Rose Tyler took up a position with Torchwood One in the parallel Universe; Martha Jones's cousin Adeola worked at Torchwood One and was killed in 'Army Of Ghosts'; and now Donna herself.
- The Racnoss was hibernating 'at the edge of the Universe'. It's possible it awoke on account of the Time War – as did the Carrionites ('The Shakespeare Code'), Weeping Angels ('Blink') and the Beast ('The Impossible Planet'), all of which are beings from the dawn of time that emerged from hiding in last four or so hundred years.
- While the Doctor surmises that Donna was pulled into the TARDIS because she was being drawn by the residual Huon particles contained within the ship, as seen in 'The Stolen Earth' it was actually Dalek Caan who was somehow directly manipulating these events in order to fulfil the prophecy that he had foreseen.

LANGUAGE

The Empress of Racnoss speaks English with Lance long before the Doctor appears on the scene.

TIMELINE DATES

4,600,000,000 ⟶ ▨ ▨ ▨ ▨ ▨ ▨ ▨ ▨ ▨ ▨ ▨ ▨

The Doctor says he and Donna travelled back 'four point six billion years'. 'I've always wanted to see this', he says. 'We're going further back than I've ever been before'. He has clearly forgotten travelling back to Event One ('Castrovalva'), which pre-dates the creation of Earth by some 400 million years. (See also 'Inside The Spaceship'.)

Huon particles haven't existed 'for billions of years', since 'the dark times'. The Time Lords were responsible for destroying the particles. The Fledgling Empires then went to war with the Racnoss, wiping them out (except for one ship, the *Sacred Heart*, that hid within the centre of the newly-forming planet Earth), and forcing the Racnoss Empress to go into hiding, 'hibernating at the edge of the Universe'.

2007, June 26

Donna started at H C Clements 'six months' ago, which would be in June 2007. In 'Turn Left' it is stated that her job interview was on 'Monday the 25th', which is indeed June 2007. (Going by the different dresses she is wearing, we see at least five different days during the flashback sequence where Donna tells the Doctor how she met and was 'proposed to' by Lance.)

In the alternative Universe see in 'Turn Left' Donna did not get the job at H C Clements, didn't meet the Doctor, and instead her life was very different.

2007, December 24 ▸

No year is given (the poster on the door of one of the taxis reads 'CHRISTMAS IN LONDON 200-' but the last numeral cannot be seen clearly). The tax discs on all the vehicles seen are all inconveniently covered by the windscreen wipers. But taking into account that the Doctor refers to the spaceship that appeared 'last Christmas' ('The Christmas Invasion'), and the dating for *Torchwood*, the year must be 2007. Donna is getting married on 'Christmas Eve'. The Big Ben clock tower is clear of the scaffolding that covered it the previous year ('The Christmas Invasion').

The sales advertised in the shop windows start on 'BOXING DAY'. One sign says 'SALES START TUESDAY'. In 2007, Boxing Day fell on the Wednesday, so the sign probably refers to a sale that starts on New Years Day. [This is an example of the Production team overlooking THE YEAR AHEAD RULE.]

Donna's grandfather, Wilfred Mott, is not at the wedding, having fallen to a bout of Spanish flu ('The Sontaran Stratagem'). He does, however, meet the Doctor the following Christmas in 'Voyage Of The Damned'.

1984

The Torchwood Institute bought out H C Clements '23 years ago', which from 2007 is 1984. Presumably this acquisition was on account of the H C Clements building being closest to the Thames Flood Barrier, beneath which Torchwood was drilling into the centre of the Earth, a task that would have taken a considerable length of time.

It was their reaching the centre and exposing the *Sacred Heart* vessel that drew the Empress of Racnoss to Earth. And when Torchwood One fell on 28 May 2007, Clements and Lance continued with the task started by Torchwood, but under the control of the Racnoss. A few days later, one Donna Noble started at the firm as a temp...

2005 – 2007

Donna says she spent 'the last two years' working at a double-glazing firm.

2007, May 26 - 27 ■ ■ ■ ■ ■ ■ ■ ■ ■ ■ ■ ■
Donna says she was skin diving in Spain and did not see the Cybermen invading in 'Army Of Ghosts'. Presumably she was away for the whole weekend.

DURATION

⇨ **Day One (24 December 2007)** ■ ■ ■ ■ ■ ■ ■ ■ ■
Donna's wedding is at '3pm'. It's '3.30pm' on Donna's wristwatch when the Doctor rescues her from the taxi. Night has fallen by the time the Web-Star descends. The Doctor leaves late on Christmas Eve, after making it snow.

SMITH AND JONES

STORY LINK

There are no direct references to 'The Runaway Bride'. In that, Donna told the Doctor he needed someone to 'stop' him (an event that was key to the creation of the parallel world in 'Turn Left'). It would seem that he has travelled on his own for some time. The Doctor is now wearing a light blue suit in place of his brown suit. The Doctor says he 'was just travelling past... just wandering... not looking for trouble', when he detected that plasma coils around the Royal Hope Hospital in London had been 'building up for two days now', and thought it his duty to investigate, and had himself admitted with 'severe abdominal pains'.

The Doctor seems to have grown out of his phobia of hospitals (in 'New Earth' he says 'I hate hospitals. They give me the creeps'; possibly in reaction to what happened to him in 'Doctor Who (The TV Movie)'?) Later, he notes that the hospital has a little shop; but surely he would have seen that when he was admitted?

OBSERVATIONS

- When Maratha asks whether the Doctor has a brother, he replies 'Not any more'. The Doctor's family is discussed under LIFE ON GALLIFREY.
- The Doctor seems to have a supply of sonic screwdrivers in the TARDIS; or several days may have passed since he last saw Martha during which time he made another, and decided to return and offer her the chance to travel with him.
- Martha Jones refers to her cousin Adeola. In 'Army Of Ghosts', Adeola's surname was given as Oshodi on her computer monitor. She is therefore the daughter of Martha's father's married sister, or Martha's mother's brother or married sister.

- In the alternative history seen in 'Turn Left', this adventure takes place several months later (in September 2008), and Sarah Jane, Luke Smith, Maria Jackson and Clyde Langer are killed when the Judoon take the hospital to the moon. [This makes it an episode of *The Sarah Jane Adventures*, in which case it is Sarah Jane who is the 'Smith' of the title!]

LANGUAGE

The Judoon have devices which, after a language is 'assimilated', can translate their guttural speech into English and *vice versa*. The Plasmavore can speak English.

TIMELINE DATES

2008, June 2 (Monday) •

No direct dates are given. Martha refers to the events of 'Aliens Of London' and 'The Christmas Invasion' as being 'a few years ago'. Later, in 'Utopia', Martha mentions an earthquake in Cardiff 'two years ago' (being the events of 'Boom Town'), which has been set in September 2006. In 'Daleks In Manhattan', Martha says 1930 is 'nearly eighty years' before her own time. Therefore, from Martha's perspective, it is now 2008. A notice to doctors and nurses announcing the sizing for new uniforms is taped to the door of the X-Ray room [that is seen very briefly and can be best seen using a precise freeze-frame], and gives the dates as: 'Mon 22 Sep – Fri 26 Sep' / 'Mon 29 Sep – Fri 3 Oct'. This calendar structure does apply to 2008, which suggests the story is set several months prior to September.

In 'Turn Left', Sarah Jane Smith, her son Luke and his friends Maria Jackson and Clyde Langer are killed when the hospital is taken to the moon. In 'Revenge Of The Slitheen', Luke and Maria don't meet Clyde until the start of the new school term in September 2008. This suggests that 'Smith And Jones' (and therefore 'The Sound Of Drums') is also set in September. However a September setting is at odds with the detail given regarding the Master and Harold Saxon; the Master has been on Earth already for 18 months in 'The Sound Of Drums', for which a September 2008 setting would make his point of arrival around March 2007. However, Saxon was already pulling ahead in the political polls by early April, as seen in 'Love & Monsters'. A September setting also does not sit well with 'To The Last Man', which is set in June 2008.

Of course, the events in the 'Turn Left' parallel don't necessarily have to mirror exactly those in the N-Space Universe. As I have noted under 'Turn Left', it's possible the Plasmavore and the Judoon didn't arrive on the parallel Earth for several months later on account of the opening of the new Royal Hope being delayed three or so months on account of the closure of the Thames following the river being drained at Christmas 2007. (The Royal Hope Hospital did not exist in 'Aliens Of London', as after crashing to Big Ben the space pig was taken to the nearest hospital, which in March 2006 was the Albion. The Royal Hope, which is across the river from Big Ben, seems to be fairly new and very modern – the MRI scanner is state of the art – which suggests it is only a few months old.)

'The Sound Of Drums' has been set in June 2008. Martha met the Doctor 'four days' before the Election, which we can assume took place on the traditional Thursday. I have set the second day of 'The Sound Of Drums' on Saturday 7 June 2008. Therefore, 'Smith And Jones' takes place on Monday 2 June 2008. While a June setting might contradict the dates on the new uniforms notice, the flyer could simply be giving the hospital staff three months advance warning regarding the forthcoming wardrobe changes. (And if Royal Hope is a brand new hospital, the uniforms might reflect a change in uniform policy within the hospital service.) Another possible contradiction lies in the fact that there is a full moon the night of Leo's party. In June 2008, the full moon appears on the 19th. However, in the scenes on the moon, when Earth can be seen in the night sky, the angle of light and shadows places the sun in the wrong position for there to be a full moon visible from Earth at that time. On this basis, I'm prepared to overlook the brief shot of the moon seen in the puddle.

(The span of the 'present day' stories covering 'Smith And Jones' to 'The Sound Of Drums' is one week – see CALENDAR JUNE 2008 below.)

1752, June 15 *

This is the supposed date upon which Benjamin Franklin conducted his experiments using a kite.

1903 *

During the women's suffragette movement, Emmeline Pankhurst and her followers would chain themselves to the fence railings outside Parliament. Presumably she used the Doctor's sonic spanner to bind (or later undo) the locks on the chains. 1903 is an arbitrary date for when the 'cheeky woman' met the Doctor.

1983

Francine (nee Oshodi? – see Observations) marries Clive Jones. They are married for '25 years', but have separated in 2008.

1987, June 2

Leo Jones is born. His '21st' is held on the night of Monday, 2 June 2008.

2008, May 26

Florence has been at the hospital 'the past week', so she probably arrived around Monday June 26.

2008, June 1 (Sunday) ♦ ▓ ▓ ▓ ▓ ▓ ▓ ▓ ▓ ▓ ▓ ▓
The Doctor was admitted to the hospital 'yesterday'. See STORY LINK above.

DURATION

⇨ **Day One (Monday, 2 June 2008)** ▓ ▓ ▓ ▓ ▓ ▓ ▓ ▓ ▓
It is 'early' in the morning when Martha first bumps into the Doctor on Chancellor Street while on her way to work. Mr Stoker greets the Doctor with 'a very good morning to you' during his rounds. The Royal Hope Hospital is transported to the moon 'at lunchtime', around '12.30pm', going by the wall clock at the hospital. Leo's '21st' buffet dinner is at 'seven thirty' that night. Martha leaves with the Doctor later that evening. There is a full moon.

CALENDAR JUNE 2008

As I've established under 'Smith And Jones', 'The Lazarus Experiment', the 'present day' segments of '42', and 'The Sound Of Drums', the best month in which to set this run of stories is June 2008. And after factoring in the *Torchwood* episodes 'Captain Jack Harkness' and 'End Of Days', the structure for when the various episodes relate to one another can be shown in this table:

CALENDAR JUNE 2008						
SUN	MON	TUE	WED	THUR	FRI	SAT
1 The Doctor arrives at the hospital	2 Smith And Jones	3 The Lazarus Experiment	4	5 (Election Day) 42	6 The Sound Of Drums	7 The Sound Of Drums
8 The Sound Of Drums	9	10	11	12	13 Kiss Kiss, Bang Bang	14 Kiss Kiss, Bang Bang
15	16 Sleeper	17 Sleeper	18	19	20 To The Last Man	21 To The Last Man
22	23	24 Meat	25 Meat	26	27	28 Adam arrives
29	30 Adam	1 Adam				

THE SHAKESPEARE CODE

'The Shakespeare Code' follows on from the end of 'Smith And Jones'; this is Martha's first trip ('one trip and one trip only') in the TARDIS. The Doctor is wearing his brown suit, which he had changed into after leaving the hospital. Martha is wearing the same clothes she had on at the end of 'Smith And Jones'. The Doctor has a new sonic screwdriver 'which needs road-testing'. (The implication is that he built it soon after leaving the hospital, which may have taken several days to complete, before he decided to return to offer Martha a trip 'to say thanks'.) It's clear that the Doctor did not pick 1599 as the destination, so it's a purely random destination for the TARDIS. Intriguingly, when the TARDIS returns Martha to her own time in 'The Lazarus Experiment', the Doctor ends up in Southwark Cathedral, which is near to where the TARDIS lands in 'The Shakespeare Code'. This might suggests that the TARDIS had chosen this particular location if not the actual date deliberately. (The ship does a similar thing in 'Gridlock' and 'Daleks In Manhattan' by landing first in 'New New York' and then back in time to 'Old New York'.)

OBSERVATIONS

- Shakespeare has not met the Doctor before. The fourth Doctor says he met Shakespeare in 'Planet Of Evil', and later in 'City Of Death' the Doctor declared that he helped the Bard write *Hamlet*, which was circa 1599 to 1601. We can assume that the Bard may have known who the Doctor was at that time, but did not mention anything about the events of 'The Shakespeare Code' to the Time Lord.
- The Carrionites' power to manipulate structure through words is akin to the Logopolitans' ability to shape and manipulate reality using mathematics and Block Transfer Computations ('Logopolis'). The Doctor was 'resurrected' in 'The Sound Of Drums' by using the word 'Doctor' broadcast worldwide through the fifteen Archangel Network satellites (which is one more than the fourteen walls of the Globe Theatre).

LANGUAGE

Although they have been imprisoned for billions of years, it is English, a language that didn't exist when the Carrionites were banished to the deep darkness, which contains the structure code required to release them.

TIMELINE DATES

1599 *

An on-screen caption reads 'LONDON 1599'. The Doctor also determines it is 'Fifteen Ninety Nine', and that it's 'Elizabethan England' from the architecture. No month is indicated. There is a full moon visible both nights of the story. The Doctor says the Globe Theatre is 'brand new, just opened'. The exact date of the opening is not known from an historical perspective. Peter Streete went mad 'a month after' completing the theatre.

DAWN OF THE UNIVERSE

The Doctor says the Carrionites 'disappeared – way back at the dawn of the Universe'. They were banished 'into the deep darkness' by the Eternals ('Enlightenment').

1599 *

Queen Elizabeth I recognises the tenth Doctor as her 'sworn enemy', so this 'previous/ future' meeting must have been earlier in 1599, or in a previous year. The Queen seemingly only recognises the Doctor but not Martha, which suggests that this 'future' adventure takes place at a time when Martha is no longer travelling with the Doctor. Or it could simply be that the Queen never met Martha. (The first Doctor glimpsed the Queen on the time/space visualiser in 'The Chase', and the third Doctor mentioned her 1559 coronation in 'The Curse Of Peladon'.)

1596, August

11 August 1596 is the recorded date for when Hamnet Shakespeare was buried. It was the writer's grief that enabled the first three Carrionites to be escape from their prison. It has therefore taken them over three years to prepare themselves and put into motion their plans by which to release the rest of their kind. Part of this included inspiring Peter Streete to build the Globe with fourteen sides.

1598

The Doctor links with Peter Streete's mind: 'go into the past… one year ago', which was when the Globe was being built.

2007, July 21 *

The Doctor says he cried when he read 'book seven' in the Harry Potter series (*Harry Potter and the Deathly Hallows*), which was published worldwide on 21 July 2007. Martha is familiar with the phrase 'Expelliarmus!' from the stories, but she may only have seen the film adaptations rather than read the books.

DURATION

(TARDIS)

The Doctor and Martha travel for a brief time in the TARDIS before arriving in 1599.

⇨ Day One

That evening, Lilith kills Wiggins. The Doctor and Martha arrive in London soon after, and attend a moonlit performance at the Globe. They stay the night at the Elephant inn. Martha later sees Lilith flying a broomstick across the face of the full moon.

⇨ Day Two

Shakespeare wakes the following morning (a cock crows). A bell can be heard ringing about eight times (signalling it to be 8am?). Later that day, the Doctor visits Peter Streete in Bedlam. The first (and only) performance of *Love's Labours Won* is that night, and the Carrionites are released from their prison.

⇨ Day Three

The Doctor and Martha depart the following day, making a hurried departure following the arrival of Queen Elizabeth I.

GRIDLOCK

+STORY LINK

The Doctor promises Martha 'one trip into the past, one trip into the future', so this is her second trip in the TARDIS. He is still wearing his brow suit, and Martha her red leather jacket. When he exits from the TARDIS, the Doctor removes the arrow that was fired into the ship's door by one of the Queen's soldiers at the end of 'The Shakespeare Code'. As Martha notes, the Doctor seems to be following the same pattern of past/future journeys as he had taken Rose (in 'The End Of The World' and 'The Unquiet Dead', but with the past/future order reversed to future/past for 'New Earth' and 'Tooth And Claw').

The Doctor said he would place the crystal globe containing the Carrionites in the

TARDIS 'attic', but as can been seen in 'The Unicorn And The Wasp', he has stored them in a chest marked with the letter 'C' under the metal floor grating of the control room.

OBSERVATIONS

- Thomas Kincaid Brannigan and his wife Valerie have a litter of kittens, who are only 'two months old'. In 'The End Of The World' Cassandra spoke of 'new humans', 'proto-humans' and 'digi-humans', whom she considers to be 'mongrels'. Presumably Valerie is one of these 'mongrel' species, who is capable of procreating with cat-kind.
- The Doctor encounters the Macra in 'The Macra Terror'. He says they were the scourge of this galaxy, but that over the last few 'billions of years' they have de-evolved 'down the years'. We can assume that the unnamed planet that the Macra controlled in 'The Macra Terror' is also in galaxy M87 – it's unlikely the creatures would have intergalactic travel capabilities (unless they had been transported from planet to planet by humans?). It is also possible that that colony planet of 'The Macra Terror' later becomes New Earth.

THE FACTS OF BOE

The Face of Boe has made five direct appearances in the series, four of these in the flesh. When we place these into chronological rather than story order, we get:

- 'The Long Game' (200,000)
- 'Bad Wolf' (200,100) [mentioned in a Weakest Link question]
- 'The End Of The World' (5Billion)
- 'New Earth' (5Billion23)
- 'Gridlock' (5Billion53)

The following quotations provide us with important 'facts' about the Face of Boe:

STEWARD: Our friend from the Silver Devastation, the sponsor of the main event, please welcome the Face of Boe.

- 'The End Of The World'

CATHICA: Over on the Bad Wolf channel, the Face of Boe has just announced he's pregnant.
[Caption: 'BAD WOLF TV: Face of Boe expecting Baby Boemina']

- 'The Long Game'

ANN-DROID: Rose, the oldest inhabitant of the Isop Galaxy is the Face of what?
ROSE: Boe! The Face of Boe!

- 'Bad Wolf'

NOVICE HAME: He's thousands of years old. Some people say millions. Although that's impossible.

- 'New Earth'

NOVICE HAME: The rest of Boekind became extinct. Long ago. He's the only one left. Legend says the Face of Boe has watched the Universe grow old.

- 'New Earth'

DOCTOR: Legend says the Face of Boe has lived for billions of years. Isn't that right?

- 'Gridlock'

BOE: Everything has its time. You know that, old friend, better than most.
BOE: I have seen so much. Perhaps too much. I am the last of my kind, as you are the last of yours, Doctor.
BOE: But know this Time Lord. You are not alone.

- 'Gridlock'

JACK: What happens if I live for a million years? ... When I was a kid, living in the Boeshane Peninsula, tiny little place, I was the first one ever to be signed up for the Time Agency. They were so proud of me. The Face of Boe, they called me.

- 'The Sound Of Drums'

If what Novice Hame says about the Face of Boe is indeed mainly 'legend', the fact that the Face of Boe is millions or billions of years old might not be altogether the whole truth. A legend by definition often means the story has over a period of time become distorted and lost its intent in Chinese Whisper-fashion. And let's not forget that if Jack does live to be millions of years old, then we can't rule out the likelihood that at some point during that lifespan he re-acquires the ability to time travel. So, while Boe might have existed for billions of years throughout history, he might not actually be billions of years old.

Taking these statements at face (!) value, we can construct a possible sequence of events that might explain how the human Jack became the non-human Face of Boe.

- *Jack lives for millions of years as a human*
  It's preferable that Jack stays as a humanoid for most of his extended life. That he lives as the Face of Boe in a smoke-filled tank that requires assistance and maintenance for millions if not billions of years doesn't ring true. He probably lived on Earth for thousands of years, leaving only when interplanetary and intergalactic space travel had been developed, and he set off to see more of the Universe. (He may even have re-acquired his ability to time travel. Did he obtain this from the Time Agents? Did older Jack perhaps meet his younger past self? Is that why Jack lost two years of his memories?)

- *While visiting the Isop Galaxy, Jack's body grows to gigantic proportions and he develops telepathy*
  Given the size of Boe's head, I prefer that this gigantism occurred first, rather than being something that happened to the head after the loss of its body. And knowing that Boe is the oldest living inhabitant of the Isop Galaxy, where gigantism among insects has already established (as seen in 'The Web Planet') does tie in nicely with the notion that Jack became a giant while he was living there. I would also suggest that this was when Jack developed the telepathy which he later uses as the Face. (It's possible that size-gain mutation is caused by certain solar properties within this galaxy.)

- *Giant Jack is decapitated, and while the body dies, the head lives, and is placed within a life support unit by well-meaning aliens*
  Someone or something had to assist Jack and build the life-support unit. (One immediately gets the image of the severed heads in glass domes as seen often in the SF comedy animated series *Futurama*.)

- *On account of the life preserving smoke, Jack's head mutates into its new form. He adopts the name 'the Face of Boe', taken from his old childhood nickname*
  If Jack was decapitated while still human, the 'mutant' look of the Face of Boe must have occurred at a much later stage. Again, it makes sense that the title 'The Face of Boe' was also adopted at this point, rather than before he became a giant head in a tank.

- *Boe travels back in time, to long before 200,000, and over time becomes so well-known that he is worthy of inclusion in a TV quiz show*
  The fact that the events of 'Bad Wolf' are set in 200,100, and Boe is known in that time zone (and also in 200,000 – 'The Long Game'), time travel is

the only way to explain this, otherwise it means Jack became Boe after only living less than 200,000 years, which does not ring true. And given that the Game Station is where Jack was originally killed by the Daleks and brought back to life by Bad Wolf Rose cannot be passed as mere coincidence. Did Boe travel to the Fourth Great and Bountiful Human Empire for a reason? Was it because he knew the Doctor was / had been there? Did he go there seeking a cure for his condition?

- *The mutation causes Boe to spawn Baby Boemina, the announcement of which appears on Bad Wolf TV in the year 200,000*
  Novice Hame refers to the extinct 'Boekind'. We can assume that these Baby Boemina are the earliest 'children' born of this new species, which ultimately becomes extinct millions of years later. It makes sense that in order for Boekind to have existed, Jack was their originator.

- *After the birth of Boekind, Boe travels ahead billions of years, settling in the Silver Devastation*
  The Silver Devastation is where Boe is said to have come from in 'The End Of The World'. It is also where the Master sought refuge after fleeing from the Time War, as given in 'Utopia'. Is there a connection? Was Boe responsible for assisting the Master, and perhaps even creating his new persona as Professor Yana? This would certainly explain why Yana's name was an acronym for 'You Are Not Alone', Boe's dying words to the Doctor in 'Gridlock'. Was Boe merely giving a little push to future events that he had already been witness to in his own past?

- *During his travels forwards in time, Boe makes the odd stop along the way*
  Making appearances now and then would maintain the legend that the Face of Boe has lived for billions of years.

- *In 5 Billion, Boe arranges the Earth-Death viewing on Platform One*
  During 'The End Of The World', we hear that the Face of Boe's suite has no hot water, Boe discusses the 'Bad Wolf Scenario' with the Moxx of Balhoon, and is seen having the glass of his tank wiped down by Platform One attendants. And he is certainly present in the main hall when the Doctor and Rose are there. Since Earth was his adoptive home during most of his early life, it's reasonable to assume that this was the main reason why Boe was the sponsor for the Earth-Death event. And if it is the National Trust that owns Earth, is Boe a member of this Trust? Was he responsible for preserving the 'Classic

Earth' appearance of the continents? Did he know the Doctor and Rose would be there? Rose does mention Platform One while in ear-shot of Jack in 'Boom Town', but would Jack still remember that after so many years?

- *In the belief that he is dying, Boe goes to New Earth, and sends a psychic message back through time to summon the Doctor so he could impart his 'secret'*
  It's clear that the 'WARD 26 PLEASE COME' message that the Doctor received was sent back through time, which supports my suggestion that Boe possesses some form of time travel. (Jack has his own psychic paper in 'The Empty Child', so he certainly knows how to use it.) I like to think that Boe sent the message for the Doctor and Martha, as it was she who was there when the Master was reborn on Malcassairo, but when he saw Rose at the hospital on New Earth, Boe had to leave, but said he would meet the Doctor again.

- *Boe dies, saving New Earth, and tells the Doctor the final secret*
  Jack tells the Doctor the secret he has been carrying for millions of years, ever since the events of 'The Sound Of Drums'.

It's clear that in dropping the hint that Jack becomes the Face of Boe writer Russell T Davies had overlooked some of the history that he had already established for Boe, especially Boe's appearance in 'The Long Game' and that Boe was just one of an entire species, the Boekind. But by giving Boe time travel, we can at least circumvent some of the minor continuity discrepancies.

LANGUAGE

As seen in 'The End Of The World', in the year five billion, the spoken and written language of New Earth is a hybrid of familiar words, numbers and Greek symbols: Milo and Cheen are in car 'four-six-five-diamond-six', and the other car identity numbers consist of digits and symbols, such as 4-5-Δ-7-1, 3-6-3-Δ-2, 1-5-9-¥-7, and 3-1-7-α-1.

TIMELINE DATES

5,000,000,053 ◆

The Doctor gives the date as 'the year five billion and fifty three'; 30 years have passed since 'New Earth' (and 53 since 'The End Of The World'). Of note, like in 'New Earth' the date is not given as 'five point five billion slash slash slash' as it was in 'The End Of The World'. Does this mean that the dating used by the ninth Doctor in 'The End Of

The World' was merely a result of the TARDIS translator malfunctioning, or that in the years since the events on Platform One the dating standard has been changed to reflect those of 'classic Earth'?

The litter of kittens is only 'two months old'. Cheen had a pregnancy scan 'last week'.

1969 ◆
The Doctor says he was given his brown coat by Janis Joplin. Joplin was at the height of her popularity in the late 1960s. She died tragically aged 27 on 4 October 1970.

5,000,000,029
Novice Hame says the City died 'twenty four years' ago. The virus killed everyone in 'seven minutes flat'. An automatic quarantine that lasted 'one hundred years' was initiated.

5,000,000,030
May and Alice Cassini have been driving together for '23 years'. If this is accurate, they therefore set off the year after the Bliss virus had struck down the Senate.

5,000,000,041
Brannigan and Valerie have been driving for '12 years', starting out when they were newly-weds. They have moved all of five miles in that time.

5,000,000,048
Junction Three has been closed 'for five years'.

DURATION

(TARDIS)
The Doctor and Martha travel for some time before arriving.

⇨ **Day One**
Sally Calypso announces the time to be 'ten fifteen'. It is daytime when the TARDIS lands in the undercity ('the sun is blazing high'). It is still daytime when the cars are released from the motorway. The events of this story take place over several hours of this single day.

DALEKS IN MANHATTAN
EVOLUTION OF THE DALEKS

+STORY LINK

Having visited New New York on New Earth, the TARDIS lands at the foot of the Statue of Liberty in the real New York. The Doctor says their detour 'just got longer', which suggests he did not set the coordinates for this destination. Martha is still wearing the same clothes she had on in 'Gridlock', but the Doctor is now wearing his blue suit. The Doctor had previously offered her two trips: one to the past and one to the future. It's not clear if the arrival in 1930 was planned or accidental; although the Doctor has a certain degree of control over the ship, it still from time to time does arrive in the wrong place and time, as witnessed in 'Tooth And Claw'.

Interestingly, while the trips to the past and future are similar to those on which the Doctor took Rose ('The End Of The World', 'The Unquiet Dead') – a fact which Martha was very quick to notice and point out to him in 'Gridlock' – of the four adventures experienced by the Doctor and Martha, three of them almost mirror a sequence of adventures by the second Doctor, Ben and Polly: specifically a trip to the moon ('The Moonbase'), an encounter with the Macra ('The Macra Terror'), followed shortly by an encounter with the Daleks, who are undertaking experiments in Earth's recent past ('The Evil Of The Daleks').

DALEK LINK

During the Battle of Canary Wharf ('Army Of Ghosts'), Dalek Sec activates an 'emergency temporal shift' and vanishes. The other three members of the Cult of Skaro also vanish, but off-screen. It's not clear if the Cult of Skaro arrive in New York directly after their temporal shift in 'Army Of Ghosts', or whether they arrive elsewhere and shift to New York in order to take advantage of the Empire State Building after they detect the gamma-flare build up. The Doctor notes that the temporal shift must have 'roasted up [their] power cells', effectively stranding them in this time zone, although Dalek Caan is able to affect another temporal shift (which takes him back into the Time War – see 'The Stolen Earth').

One of the Daleks notes that 'versions of this city stand throughout history'. A group of Daleks had previously visited New York City and the Empire State Building in 1966 whilst pursing the TARDIS in 'The Chase'. Presumably New York was also a target of the Daleks during their occupation of Earth in the twenty-second century, in 'The Dalek Invasion of Earth'. The Daleks attack the USA in

200,100 in 'Bad Wolf'. They were probably aware that there had been at least fifteen other New Yorks.

If the spheres attached to the Daleks' lower panels are explosives (as seen in 'Dalek'), why are some of those panels attached to the Empire State Building masthead? Surely they would explode when the gamma-flare hits? (Or do the balls on the casings of the non-combatant Cult of Skaro Daleks serve an entirely different function?)

Dalek Sec says the Daleks were created 'thousands of years' ago.

LANGUAGE

The Daleks speak English with Mr Diagoras. They use 'Rels' as a measurement of time (which is the equivalent of a second). As noted elsewhere, the TARDIS translator doesn't seem to be able to translate values.

TIMELINE DATES

1930, October 18?
Tallulah says Laszlo disappeared 'two weeks ago'. They discuss her meeting his parents on 'Sunday', so it's probably Saturday, 18 October. The story starts 'two minutes' before curtain.

1930, November 1 (Saturday) +
The date 'Saturday, November 1st 1930' appears on the copy of the *New York Record* newspaper, and also repeated by Martha. She says it is 'nearly eighty years ago' from her own time (which is 2008).

1917
Solomon says he fought in the Great War 'thirteen years ago', which would be 1917.

1929, March 29
The Doctor says Herbert Hoover became President 'a year ago', which is in 1929, the same year as the Wall Street crash, which is mentioned by Martha. It was on 4 March 1929 that he took office in our history; and he held office until 4 March 1933.

1930, September
Mr Diagoras was merely a foreman, but became the boss 'a couple of months ago'. We can assume that this was when the Cult of Skaro arrived in this time zone.

DURATION

⇨ **Day (Saturday, 18 October?) (Ep1)**
Laszlo vanishes one evening (Sunday is a future day, so it's possibly a Saturday)

🕐 **'Two weeks' pass...**

⇨ **Day One (1 November) (Ep1-2)**
The TARDIS arrives on Liberty Island. The gamma-flare strike is due at '11.21' that evening (when the time reaches 'eleven fifteen' (11.15pm), the strike is still 'six minutes' away). The Doctor notes that it has 'gone midnight' ...

⇨ **Day Two (2 November) (Ep2)**
The final confrontation in the theatre takes place shortly after 'midnight'. The Doctor and Martha leave New York later that day.

THE LAZARUS EXPERIMENT

+STORY LINK

The Doctor (still in his blue suit) tells Martha the TARDIS has brought them 'back to the morning after we left. So, you've only been gone about twelve hours.' In fact, Martha has spent the equivalent of nearly four days away – she spent two nights in 1599 ('The Shakespeare Code'), several hours in New New York ('Gridlock'), and one night and part of a day in 1930 ('Daleks In Manhattan'). Martha is now several days out of sync with her own relative time (as had previously happened with Ben and Polly, Tegan, and Rose). She mentions all the things they've done: 'Shakespeare, New New York, Old New York', which indicates that these are the only three trips she has made in the TARDIS, which the Doctor says they did 'all in one night'.

OBSERVATIONS

- The Doctor says the creature that Lazarus mutates into is a genetic throwback to 'millions of years ago'.
- Francine Jones is warned by Saxon's representatives that the Doctor was not to be trusted. Did they tell Francine that the Doctor was partly responsible for the death of her niece Adeola? ('Army Of Ghosts')

TIMELINE DATES

2008, June 3 (Tuesday) ✦
No dates are given, other than it being the day after 'Smith And Jones': Tish says it's been 'two nights out in a row for Martha', and Francine says 'you saw me last night' at Leo's birthday dinner. As noted under CALENDAR JUNE 2008 above, it is now the Tuesday of that same week.

1807 ✦
The Doctor says he used to 'hang around with Beethoven'. Ludwig van Beethoven's most famous piece, the Fifth Symphony, was complete in this year.

1917
The recorded year in which New Zealand-born Ernest Rutherford split the atom, an event mentioned by Lazarus.

1932
Lazarus says he is '76 years old'; if the year is 2008, then he was born in 1932.

1940
Lazarus recalls the bombing of London in '1940', when he was 'just a child'. The Doctor says he was there – which was in 1941; see 'The Empty Child'.

1969, July 21
Lazarus mentions Armstrong standing on the moon, which was on these days in our history. See also 'Blink'.

1998
Lazarus says he has been working on his genetic manipulator 'for so many years'; say ten. He has only been able to complete his research thanks to funding from Mr Saxon (who has been on Earth since late 2007). The reasons for the Master's keen interest in Lazarus's work are revealed in 'The Sound Of Drums'; he wanted to develop a genetic manipulation weapon to use against the Doctor.

DURATION

⇨ **Day One (Tuesday, 3 June 2008)**
The TARDIS lands in Martha's flat that 'morning'. The Lazarus event takes place that

evening. The Doctor and Martha depart again later that night.

STORY LINK

Since leaving Martha's flat at the end of 'The Lazarus Experiment', the Doctor has changed out of his tuxedo (which he wears again in 'Voyage Of The Damned') and into his blue suit, and Martha has changed from her evening dress into a more practical outfit. If they had a specific destination in mind, that trip is intercepted by the distress signal from the SS *Pentallian*. The Doctor adjusts Martha's mobile phone (which bears the Archangel Network logo – see 'The Sound Of Drums') for 'universal roaming'. (When he did the same with Rose's phone in 'The End Of The World', he did this by fitting in a small device inside the phone, whereas here the Doctor simply places his sonic screwdriver against the LED screen.) At least 24 hours must have passed for them (during which they probably had a long deserved rest, since Martha has in effect been awake for over twenty hours) given that when Martha rings her mother it is now 'Election Day', which is Thursday, 5 June 2008. The 'universal roaming' must work relative to the passage of time on Earth, otherwise Martha could ring home and find it's a week later or months earlier.

OBSERVATIONS

- The technology that enables Martha's mobile phone to be used temporally, must be channelled through the TARDIS. Is this the same methodology that enables Boe to communicate across galaxies and millions of years through the Doctor's psychic paper? But does it work in relative time? By that I mean, when Martha rings home it is Election Day (which is the Thursday, see CALENDAR JUNE 2008 under 'Smith And Jones'). But Martha has only been away from Earth for what can be only a matter of hours since leaving in 'The Lazarus Experiment' and yet a whole day has passed for Francine. How does the TARDIS determine the time differences between the caller and the other person? What would happen, say, if Martha phoned home but the call was answered a year earlier? I would say the TARDIS takes into account the internal biological clock of the caller, and factors in the passage of time between current ship's time and the time zone of the other phone. In that case, for Martha to have left Earth on Tuesday evening and her subsequent call to reach Francine on Thursday afternoon, then one full day must have passed off-screen for Martha and the Doctor. The same temporal relativity must also apply in 'The Sontaran Stratagem', when Martha calls the Doctor a year after she left the phone with him at the end of 'The Sound Of Drums'.

LANGUAGE

The living sun communicates through the crew and the Doctor.

TIMELINE DATES

2008, June 5 (Thursday)

It is 'Election Day' when Martha rings home ('three calls in one day'). Francine says she has voted, so it's probably some time in the afternoon. Traditionally, General Elections in the UK are held on Thursdays. In terms of the June 2008 calendar, it is Thursday, 5 June 2008. As noted in Observations, in terms of Martha's relative timeline, a whole day has passed since she left with the Doctor at the end of 'The Lazarus Experiment', otherwise any of Martha's calls back home using the 'universal roaming' function added to her phone by the Doctor might connect with a past or future date on Earth.

4137 *

No dates are given. It is the Torajii system. Although it's not stated as such on-screen, the technology of the SS *Pentallian*, particularly the spacesuits, is very similar to that of Sanctuary Base 6 in 'The Impossible Planet'. Since there are no Ood on board the SS *Pentallian*, we might conclude that this story is set after the Ood were released from their two centuries of slavery in 'Planet Of The Ood', which is set in 4126. A setting within the forty-second century [a possible deliberate double-meaning of the title '42'] does seem incongruous when we take into account the references to Elvis and The Beatles and musical downloads, all of which would be expected to have faded into obscurity this far into the future. In 'The Chase', Vicki mentions the Beatles, and she is from 2493, some 200 years earlier. But in 'The Unicorn And The Wasp', the Doctor has a year five billion printing of Agatha Christie's *Death In The Clouds*, which indicates that some aspects of twentieth-century popular culture and art can survive across the centuries.

Therefore, applying an arbitrary Production Factor of 2130, I have set '42' in the year 4137, which is eleven years after 'Planet Of The Ood'.

4126

Kath and Korwin have been married 'eleven years'.

DURATION

(TARDIS)

The Doctor and Martha travel for some time before arriving on the SS *Pentallian*.

⇨ **Day One (4137)**

The TARDIS lands on the SS *Pentallian* 'four minutes' after the engines went dead. The ship's computer announces impact with the sun is in 'forty two minutes, twenty seven seconds'. Martha rings home at '00:29:48' till impact. Erena is killed at '00:24:53'. The escape pod is released at '00:17:07'. It is '00:12:57' when the Doctor enters the airlock. Impact is averted as the chronometer reaches '00:00:02'.

⇨ **Day One (Thursday, 5 June 2008)**

It is 'Election Day' when Martha phones her mother, so it's Thursday. Francine has already voted, so it's probably around midday or the early afternoon when Martha rings.

HUMAN NATURE
THE FAMILY OF BLOOD

STORY LINK

At the end of '42', the Doctor suggests they try ice-skating on the mineral lakes of Kurhan. 'Human Nature' opens with the Doctor (back in his brown suit) and Martha in mid-adventure somewhere, making a hurried return to the TARDIS with the Family of Blood on their trail. (It's possible this off-screen adventure takes place in the year 2007 – see below.)

Martha says she met the Doctor 'not even that long ago'. She has been travelling with him for at least 'two months' by this stage.

OBSERVATIONS

- When activating the chameleon arch, the Doctor says 'I never thought I'd use this. All the times I wondered'. As I've covered under 'Doctor Who (The TV Movie)', the Doctor may have used a similar device to make himself 'half human'.
- John Smith's manuscript contains black and white sketches showing images of the Doctor's past adventures: these include gas-mask zombies ('The Empty

Child'), Daleks, the Moxx of Balhoon ('The End Of The World'), Autons ('Rose'), a werewolf ('Tooth And Claw'), K9 ('School Reunion'), clockwork robots ('The Girl In The Fireplace'), Cybermen, and the Slitheen ('Aliens Of London', 'Boom Town'), as well as images of Rose. There are also sketches of some of his previous incarnations, specifically the first, fifth, sixth, seventh, and eighth Doctors.

LANGUAGE

The Family of Blood speak English even before they take over their human host.

TIMELINE DATES

1913, November 10 - 12 +

At the start of the story, Martha gives the date as 'Monday, November 10th, 1913', and we see the same date on a newspaper's masthead. The 'Annual Dance' takes place the following day, 'Tuesday November 11th 1913', according to the posters.

1918

When he and Hutchinson are fighting in the trenches, Tim Latimer refers to the events from 'all those years ago', so it is probably closer to the end of the war – 1918 – rather than the beginning.

2007

At the start of the story, John Smith tells Martha about last night's dream, which 'took place in the future – in the year of Our Lord two thousand and seven'. However, this does not necessarily mean that Martha comes from 2007. (This may be an example of THE YEAR AHEAD RULE being overlooked.)

2008, November 11? +

When the Doctor and Martha attend the Remembrance Day ceremony on 11 November, it is presumably in line with the other 'present day' landings, so it is probably 2008.

1815, June 16

The date of the Battle of Waterloo is seen written on the blackboard in John Smith's class room as '16th June 1815'. (See also 'Day Of The Daleks'.)

1900, January 23 – 24
Joan says her husband Oliver was killed at Spion Kop. I've adopted the date in our history when this battle was fought during the Boer War campaign.

1913, September ✦
Joan says she has known John Smith 'for all of two months', so it was September, presumably near the start of the new school year, when the Doctor and Martha arrived in Farringham.

1914, June 28
The Doctor refers to the assassination 'in June 1914'. This event was on 28 June 1914 in our history. The Family passed through this period in their hunt for the Doctor.

DURATION

(TARDIS) (2007) (Ep1)
The Doctor and Martha take off in the TARDIS. The Doctor activates the chameleon arch…

⇨ **Day (September 1913)**
The Doctor and Martha arrive in Farringham…

🕐 **'Two months' pass…**

⇨ **Day One (Monday, 10 November 1913) (Ep1)**
The Doctor wakes from his dream. It is '7.29' when Martha brings John Smith his breakfast and 'this morning's paper'. The clock reads '3.00pm' when Joan attends to Smith's injuries. The Family of Blood land in the woods that night. (A clock is heard chiming at least eight times when the possessed Baines returns to the school.)

⇨ **Day Two (Tuesday, 11 November) (Ep1-2)**
The following day, Martha returns to the TARDIS. The normal school day passes. The teachers prepare for the dance at '7.00pm'. The rest of the story takes place over this night. The hands on John Smith's fob watch read '10.31' when Baines opens it.

⇨ **Day Three (Wednesday, 12 November) (Ep2)**
The Doctor deals with the Family of Blood. He and Martha depart.

⇨ **Night (1918) (Ep.2)** ▨ ▨ ▨ ▨ ▨ ▨ ▨ ▨ ▨ ▨ ▨

It is 'one minute past the hour' (7.01) when Tim Latimer and Hutchinson survive the bombing.

⇨ **Day (11 November 2008?) (Ep.2)** ▨ ▨ ▨ ▨ ▨ ▨ ▨ ▨ ▨

The Doctor and Martha attend the Remembrance Day memorial service.

BLINK

STORY LINK

Since the Doctor and Martha's scattered appearances in 'Blink' are observed in 'order' from Sally Sparrow's [as well as the viewer's] perspective, but 'out of order' from their own, there is no certainty that the Doctor's first encounter with Sally, when she hands him the envelope at the end of the episode, takes place after the events of 'Human Nature'. The red hatching 'adventure' could have occurred between '42' and 'Human Nature'. But given that the televised story comes after 'Human Nature', that is the best placement for when the Doctor first meets Sally in 2008. The Doctor's chronology might run in this order:

- 11 November 2008 – The Doctor and Martha attend the Remembrance Day service at the end of 'Human Nature'...
- After several journeys in the TARDIS (including seeing the moon landing four times) they eventually arrive in February 2008. There, they must deal with the migration of the red hatching (which is 'four things – and a lizard'), happening in 'twenty minutes'. The Doctor meets Sally Sparrow, who gives him the folder containing all the facts and details about her adventure in February 2007.
- After dealing with the red hatching, the Doctor reads the file.
- February 2007 – The TARDIS lands in Wester Drumlins (randomly, or did the Doctor take the ship there on purpose?). The Doctor leaves the TARDIS key behind, and the Weeping Angels send the Doctor and Martha back in time to early 1969... The TARDIS is found at the house and relocated to the police station.
- Stranded in early 1969, Martha has to get a job to support them. The Doctor builds his timey-wimey device, and they locate Billy Shipton. With Billy's help, the Doctor prepares and sets in place all the elements detailed in Sally's folder, such as making the recording for Billy to place years later onto the

DVDs. The Doctor and Martha return to Wester Drumlins, where the Doctor writes the warnings on the walls and papers over them. They wait for the TARDIS to arrive…

- The TARDIS arrives in 1969, and the Doctor and Martha depart.
- Some time later, the Doctor lands the ship in Cardiff to refuel the TARDIS at the Rift…

OBSERVATIONS

- The Doctor says he is rubbish at weddings, adding 'especially my own'. As noted under UNSEEN ADVENTURES, the (eighth) Doctor may have returned to Gallifrey long after 'Doctor Who (The TV Movie)' and got married prior to the outbreak of the Time War.

TIMELINE DATES

1920, December 5
The *Hull Times* gives the date as '5th December 1920'.

1969 (early) *
The Doctor says the year is '1969'. The Doctor tells Billy 'you've got the moon landing to look forward to', so it is some time prior to July 21.

2007, February 6 – 7
The year 2007 is given four times: Kathy's letter (and accompanying voiceover) refers to her being 'in 2007'; Kathy died '20 years ago', and her gravestone carries the dates '1902-1987'; the Doctor says 1969 was '38' years ago.

The letter Kathy wrote shortly before her death is dated 'Feb 7th 1987'. We might therefore assume that the letter was written specifically on that date in order to convince Sally of its authenticity, as that was also the day in 2007 on which Kathy disappeared.

2008, February 7 (?)*
An on-screen caption reads 'ONE YEAR LATER', so it's February 2008. There are no visible VOTE SAXON posters; the Election is four months away (on 5 June), so it might be too early for election posters to be displayed.

DAWN OF THE UNIVERSE
The Doctor says the Weeping Angels 'are as old as the Universe. Or very nearly'. These

creatures are yet another in a great number of beings that existed from the dawn of time that the Doctor has encountered before (or at least knows of), and that have recently resurfaced: the Beast ('The Impossible Planet'); the Racnoss ('The Runaway Bride'); the Carrionites ('The Shakespeare Code'). Are they returning to the Universe now that the Time Lords are no longer there to hold them in check? Or is something else manipulating their resurrection?

There are four Angels in Wester Drumlins. Presumably, each Angel sends people to one specific year, which is why Billy ends up in 1969 with the Doctor and Martha. Another Angel must send people to 1920, like Kathy.

1897
1962
These dates are seen on Ben's headstone: '1897-1962'.

1969 (earlier) *
The Doctor and Martha have been stranded in 1969 for several weeks (or months) by the time they meet Billy.

1969, July 21 ****
Martha says 'we went four times' to the moon landing ('back when we had transport'). We can assume she means 'went' literally, and that they were actually on the moon at the time. Armstrong is mentioned by Lazarus in 'The Lazarus Experiment'.

1987, February 7
Kathy's letter to Sally is dated 'Feb 7th 1987'. Kathy says she has been living in Hull since 1920, which is 'over sixty years'.

2005
Billy tells Sally the abandoned cars were all found outside Wester Drumlins 'over the last two years'. The owners of these vehicles presumably ended up in 1920, 1969 or one of two other eras. This is presumably when the Weeping Angles first arrived on Earth.

DURATION
The story Duration is ordered in terms of Sally Sparrow's timeline.

⇨ Day One (6 February 2007)
Sally visits Wester Drumlins that night. She rings Kathy at 'one in the morning'.

⇨ **Day Two (7 February 2007)** ▨ ▨ ▨ ▨ ▨ ▨ ▨ ▨

Sally and Kathy return the following day to the house. Sally notes one of the statues has moved 'since yesterday'. Malcolm Wainwright delivers the letter 'on this date, at this exact time'. Sally meets and is reunited with the dying Billy later that same day ('It's the same rain'). He refers to this being 'the night I die', and she stays with him till then. Sally and Larry return to the house later that night. The TARDIS is sent back to 1969.

⏱ **A year passes...** ▨ ▨ ▨ ▨ ▨ ▨ ▨ ▨ ▨

⇨ **Day (8 February 2008)** ▨ ▨ ▨ ▨ ▨ ▨ ▨ ▨

'ONE YEAR LATER', the shop clock reads '10.10am' when Sally meets the Doctor.

⇨ **Day (1969)** ▨ ▨ ▨ ▨ ▨ ▨ ▨ ▨ ▨ ▨

It is night when the Doctor and Martha meet Billy Shipton.

UTOPIA

NOTE: Although 'Utopia' ends with a cliff-hanger leading into 'The Sound Of Drums', it is treated as a separate story in *Timelink*.

STORY LINK

There is no direct link to 'Blink'. The Doctor and Martha had been stranded in 1969 for several months, but get the TARDIS back thanks to the efforts of Sally Sparrow. It's possible the ship was already running low on power, and the pit-stop in Cardiff is the first port of call after leaving 1969. The Doctor is still in his brown suit.

MASTER LINK

The Master was last seen being sucked into the Eye of Harmony within the Doctor's TARDIS in 'Doctor Who (The TV Movie)'.

In 'The Sound Of Drums', the Master says 'the Time Lords only resurrected me because they knew I'd be the perfect warrior for a Time War. I was there when the Dalek Emperor took control of the Cruciform. I saw it. I ran. I ran so far. Made myself human they would never find me. Because I was so scared'. We can assume that the Doctor returned to Gallifrey soon after 'Doctor Who (The TV Movie)' to have the Master released from his imprisonment in the Eye. The Master's body may have reverted back to its protoplasmic form (Bruce's body having disintegrated in the Eye), and was kept in that state (in some form of suspended animation?). He was then 'resurrected' and given a new body to serve with the War effort.

The Master may have got the idea of turning himself into a human from the Doctor's example in 'Doctor Who (The TV Movie)'. He escaped the War, and using chameleon arch technology changed his biology, and fled (using some form of time travel other than a TARDIS) some 100 trillion years into the future. (We must assume that the Time Lords gave the Master a whole new regenerative cycle (as in 'The Five Doctors'), which is how he was able to regenerate when he was shot by Chantho. (It's possible that all Time Lords who fought in the Time War, including the Doctor, were given additional regenerative powers during the War…))

Professor Yana's earliest memory is of being 'an orphan in the storm. I was a naked child, found on the coast of the Silver Devastation'. But it's not clear how much of this memory was created by the chameleon arch process, and how much was what actually happened. It's inferred from the comment about his being a 'child' that the newly-resurrected Master was merely a boy, which would explain partly why he was scared and ran from the Time War, as that is what a child would do. And over the next six to seven decades, he lived as Yana. (But if the Master was resurrected as an adult, it was in the form of a much older man.)

Assuming that the Master was resurrected as a child, then the story of moving from refugee ship to refugee ship might in fact be true. Some 70 or so years later, now calling himself the Professor (which he says is an honorary title), he eventually ended up on Malcassairo, where for the next '17 years', he works with Chantho on perfecting the footprint impeller system on the refugee spaceship, ready to take the survivors, who had been drawn to the planet, to their salvation on Utopia. (A thought on the possible origin of the name Yana is given below.)

OBSERVATIONS

- In 'Gridlock', the Face of Boe tells the Doctor 'You Are Not Alone', which in acronym form is YANA, the name adopted by the Master when he became human after using the chameleon arch process. Professor Yana says he came from the Silver Devastation, which is also where the Face of Boe had lived (as given in 'The End Of The World'). This can't be a coincidence; indeed, perhaps it was deliberate: when Jack became the Face of Boe, he settled in the Silver Devastation, carrying with him the memory of his meeting with Yana on Malcassairo, and also that Martha mentioned the name 'Face of Boe'. He knew there was a connection but not the actual nature of this connection; but he felt he was in part responsible for what had happened on Malcassairo all those years ago in the future. Knowing that the Master would arrive in the Silver Devastation in 100 trillion years time, Boe travelled there (as covered under 'Gridlock', Boe most likely has regained some form of time travel capability) to await the arrival of the Master, and manipulate events so the name he would be given by his guardians was Yana.

- It's not clear why Jack left the Hub via the Information Office entrance, rather than taking the lift that ascends through the base of the water tower. Jack must have run up the emergency stairs (which has 105 steps) because Owen, Tosh and Ianto were descending in the passenger lift, as he didn't want to risk using the tower lift in case the TARDIS was parked on top of or blocking the stone that concealed the hidden entrance.

LANGUAGE

Chantho speaks using the prefix 'Chan' and suffix 'Tho' in every sentence. To not do so is considered to be akin to swearing. And despite trillions of years of evolution, the Futurekind still speak English. The keyboard on Yana's computer uses the standard QWERTY layout, but with keys also bearing characters that look like Chinese. The countdown clock for the spaceship uses standard numerals: '101', '100', '99', etc.

TIMELINE DATES

2008, March 28 ·

The TARDIS landing at the Rift in Cardiff is a direct continuation of the last scene of 'End Of Days', with Jack hearing the arrival of the TARDIS. This I have dated as 28 March 2008. Martha refers to the 'earthquake in Cardiff a couple of years ago', which is from the events of 'Boom Town' set in September 2006, which supports the 2008 dating. The Doctor notes that the Rift has been active recently, which is in all likelihood on account of the events seen in 'Captain Jack Harkness' and 'End Of Days'.

100,000,000,000,000 ·

The Doctor gives the date as 'the year one hundred trillion' / 'we're going to the end of the Universe' / 'not even the Time Lords came this far'. A trillion is a million million. In 'Frontios', the Doctor makes a similar comment about the temporal limitations of the Time Lords' influence ten million years in the future.

Yana speaks of the Science Foundation that created the Utopia project 'thousands of years ago' to preserve Mankind. He also says there hasn't been such a thing as a university for 'over a thousand years', and that he has spent his life going from one refugee ship to another. It's not clear how truthful these claims are; they might simply be false memories created by the chameleon arch process. However one thing that is true, is that Yana has worked with Chantho for 'seventeen years;', which gives us a possible time frame for how long the Master has been in hiding.

1869

Jack says he arrived on Earth 'in 1869'. His Time Agent vortex manipulator burnt out after the temporal journey from the year 'two hundred one hundred' (i.e. 200,100; see 'Bad Wolf'). (Presumably he went down to Earth from the Game Station first before making the trip through time, as he may not want to risk materialising in orbit above the planet!) He lived through 'the entire twentieth century', eventually basing himself near the Cardiff Rift, to await the Doctor.

And if he then spent the next 139 years waiting for the Doctor, but also travelling to Europe and the States during that time, how many other near misses or close calls meeting with the Doctor were there?

(It might be a stretch, but on 24 December 1869, the Cardiff Rift opened, through which came the Gelth ('The Unquiet Dead'). Given the Rift's later importance in his life, might we assume that the opening of the Rift in that year is what also pulled Jack back to 1869? It's very tempting to think that Jack might even have been in Cardiff during 'The Unquiet Dead'.)

1892

Jack says he discovered he was immortal in '1892' when he was fatally wounded on Ellis Island. It wasn't until after he experienced several other 'deaths' that Jack realised his fate, and he headed for Cardiff, knowing that in time the Doctor would visit the Rift to refuel.

1991 – 1999

Jack says he went to the Powell Estate 'in the nineties, just once or twice' to watch Rose growing up. It's tempting to think that when Rose went missing in March 2005 ('Rose'), by pulling a few strings as leader of Torchwood Three, it was Jack who was responsible for ensuring that Mickey, who was the number one suspect, was exonerated from suspicion surrounding her disappearance ('Aliens Of London').

2006, December 25

The Doctor refers to 'Christmas Day', when he lost his hand 'in a sword fight' ('The Christmas Invasion'). Somehow the hand came into Jack's possession, and he used it as a 'signal' device to detect the Doctor's presence.

It's not stated how Jack knew it was the Doctor's hand. We can assume that with

Torchwood One being directly responsible for destroying the Sycorax spaceship that day, Jack may have been involved in the subsequent clean up operation. And discovering from Harriet Jones' people that the Doctor had been there, and what had happened to his hand during the fight with the Sycorax leader, Jack searched for and found the severed limb.

Millions of Years
The Doctor speaks of how the human race spent 'a million years evolving into clouds of gas, and another million as downloads', before reverting back 'to the same basic shape'.

99,999,999,999,983
Chantho says she has been working with Professor Yana on Malcassairo for 'seventeen years'.

DURATION

⇨ **Day One (28 March 2008)**
The TARDIS refuels over the Cardiff Rift for '20 seconds', before departing again, with Jack Harkness clinging to the exterior...

⇨ **Day One (100 Trillion)**
It appears to be night, when the Doctor, Martha and Jack arrive on Malcassairo. They are there for a couple of hours at the most.

THE SOUND OF DRUMS
LAST OF THE TIME LORDS

+STORY LINK
This story is a direct continuation of 'Utopia', with the Doctor, Martha and Jack escaping from Malcassairo in 100,000,000,000,000 and travelling back to Earth in 2008 with the use of Jack's Time Agent's vortex manipulator, which has been modified by the Doctor. But rather than returning to their exact point of departure (Cardiff in March 2008 – see 'Utopia') they have instead arrived in London, three months later, in June.

MASTER LINK

At the end of 'Utopia', the Master regenerates, and takes control of the Doctor's TARDIS, the coordinates of which the Doctor has fused, locking them 'permanently', which means the ship could travel only back and forth between 'the year one hundred trillion and the last place the TARDIS landed, which is right here, right now'; actually the last place was on top of the Cardiff Rift in March 2008, but with a little leeway of 'eighteen months, tops', the ship could have overshot, and landed in London around September 2006.

During his time on Earth, the Master is busy, putting into effect a plan to create a new Time Lord Empire by bringing five billion Utopia humans back in time and wiping out their distant ancestors on Earth, thus creating a paradox, which he controlled and kept in check by converting the TARDIS into a Paradox Machine. As Harold Saxon, he infiltrates the British government, and eventually rises to the top seat of Prime Minister, giving him power and influence – and the *Valiant*, UNIT's flagship vessel.

When Vivien Rook tries to tell Lucy Saxon the truth about her husband, Rook holds up a newspaper clipping announcing 'Archangel in the Heavens… Harold Saxon announces launch of British satellite breakthrough'. The text of the article goes as far as to name Saxon as 'Minister of Communications'. It's not clear if the word 'launch' means the actual launch of the satellites into space, or just the activation of the system. I prefer it to mean the latter. Also, it's not clear if 'launch' in this context means it has been launched or that it will be launched. I think it's the former, since it's made clear by Rook that Saxon only came into existence when the signals from satellites started broadcasting. And is there any connection to the fact that Archangel was launched soon after Christmas? The sinister blonde woman who is at the Jones' house listening in on their telephone calls in '42' and 'The Sound Of Drums', seems to be an Archangel employee (if only for that fact that her notebook computer bears the Archangel logo). The Master probably took over the running of Archangel once he had become Harold Saxon, and had subjugated its staff.

Another major plot point is Rook's statement 'that's when it all started, when Harry Saxon became Minister in charge of launching the Archangel Network'. But it is important to note that it is never explicitly stated that Saxon designed or built the Archangel Network, only that he was there when it was launched, and that was when Saxon first appeared on the scene. I read this to mean that Archangel was an independent global communications project that was already underway long before the Master arrived on Earth, and that he merely hijacked the satellites to carry his hypno-signal devices – and once the signal activated, *et voila* – 'Hello, I'm Harold Saxon, I'm Minister of Communications' – and no one disbelieved him.

Rook says 'Eighteen months ago, he became real. This is his first honest-to-god appearance, just after the downfall of Harriet Jones. And at the exact same time they launched the Archangel Network. The downfall of Harriet Jones was in January 2007.

Jack also knows about Saxon's ministerial duties, saying Saxon was 'former Minister of Defence. First came to prominence when he shot down the Racnoss on Christmas Eve'. (Jack also knows the Doctor was involved in this – see 'The Runaway Bride'.)

As noted, the Doctor says Master can travel from 'the last place the TARDIS landed, which is right here, right now'. But this can't be correct, given that they are in London in June, and the last TARDIS landing was Cardiff in March. Therefore, the 18 months referred to by the Doctor really is only a guess.

On first impression, the Master's plan seems very complex: to became Harold Saxon, work his way up through the political ranks to Prime Minister, bring the Toclafane to Earth, launch missiles across the Universe and create a new Time Lord Empire – all of which takes him two and a half years! But the problem with accepting this at face value is that the story narrative simply doesn't support that he came up with that plan and then implemented it all within a very short time of arriving on Earth after leaving Malcassairo in 'Utopia'. And as for his having the patience to wait over two years…

One way to reinterpret the Master's scheme is to consider that there are in fact two plans being implemented. Plan A is the creation of a New Time Lord Empire by taking control of Archangel, becoming Harold Saxon, infiltrating the government, becoming Prime Minister, and using that power to launch the missiles to create the New Time Lord Empire. And it was while all that was happening, the invasion by the Toclafane became an afterthought – Plan B. (I like to think it was after the events of 'Army Of Ghosts', when he saw how the world reacted to an alien incursion, that the Master formulated the idea to bring to Earth another alien race (just as he had done in 'Terror Of The Autons' and 'The Claws Of Axos'), and he got the idea to use the surviving 'Utopia' humans as his guinea pigs when he took Lucy on a trip into 100 Trillion to show her the end of the Universe …)

The following is a summary of how I think the Master spent his months between his arrival on Earth and the Election, paying particular attention to overall continuity within *Doctor Who* and *Torchwood*, and how his actions may have influenced events in other stories:

- 2006, September/November: The Master arrives on Earth, the TARDIS skipping back no more than 18 months from its last landing location, which was the Cardiff Rift in March 2008. (Interestingly, September 2006 was when the Rift was active in 'Boom Town'; is it possible the Rift was responsible for pulling the ship off course, given that it was recently active in 2006 and 2008?) He soon discovers the ship will travel only between the year 100 Trillion and Earth 2006, always arriving at the same permanently locked time zones at either end of the journey. He also attempts to locate Gallifrey, but there is nothing; the planet has vanished. Resigned to being stranded on Earth, he devises Plan A, which is to infiltrate the British government, gain influence and power along the way, with an aim to create a New Time Lord Empire. To this end, he creates the persona of Harold Saxon.

- 2006, December: The Master prepares to use the Archangel Network, which is due to be launched later that month (the fifteen satellites have already been sent up during the year), to carry the hypno-signal he has created which, when transmitted through the orbital satellites, will send out a pulse that will hide his presence from the Doctor, and also make the world susceptible to suggestion.

- 2006, Christmas: The events of 'The Christmas Invasion'. The Doctor, still suffering from post-regenerative trauma, does not detect the presence of the Master – who might actually have been away from Earth and in 100 Trillion at that time, to keep his existence hidden from the Doctor: he may have heard Harriet Jones's TV broadcast plea for the Doctor, and deliberately left Earth.

- 2007, January: Harriet Jones is deposed. (The TV reports in 'The Christmas Invasion' declare 'PM HEALTH SCARE Unfit for duty?', HARRIET JONES 'UNSTABLE AND FAILING FAST'. She states a 'vote of no confidence is completely unjustified'.) Her replacement is 'Tony Blair' (refer to the chapter POLITICALLY INCORRECT). Archangel goes on line, the Master's hypno-signal activates – and the world is introduced to Harold Saxon, Minister of Communications. The Master's presence is now shrouded, and the Doctor remains unaware that the Master is on Earth in 'School Reunion', and all subsequent visits to present day Earth ('Rise Of The Cybermen', 'Love & Monsters', 'Army Of Ghosts', 'The Runaway Bride', 'Smith And Jones', 'The Lazarus Experiment' and 'Utopia'). In 'Rise Of The Cybermen', Mickey implies a dislike towards Tony Blair, whose policies are already creating political unease, perhaps partly due to Saxon's influence as he begins to rise within the government.

- 2007, April: As the political environment becomes more and more unstable (the headline on the *Daily Telegraph* newspaper seen in 'Love & Monsters' (set in April) is 'ELECTION COUNTDOWN. Four more months of government paralysis. Fourth minister resigns – so who's running the country?'), Saxon's popularity rises, and he 'leads polls with 64 per cent'. The Election is set for four months' time, July. The first 'ghosts' begin to appear around the world...

- 2007, May: As the 'ghosts' begin to become accepted as part of everyday life, one is elected MP of Leeds (in a By-Election?). And then the world is plunged into chaos as the 'ghosts' are revealed to be Cybermen; the events of 'Army Of Ghosts' take place.
- 2007, June: In the aftermath of the Cybermen invasion, the July Election is postponed. The Master makes particular note of how the planet reacted and responded to the threat of a worldwide alien incursion. Saxon gets appointed as Minister of Defence. He assists with the design of UNIT's new vessel, *Valiant*. Plan B begins to form in his mind...
- 2007, August: In 'Greeks Bearing Gifts', Jack rings the PM to discuss why 'Torchwood operations have become part of [his] security briefings to the leader of the opposition'. The PM is more than likely being influenced by the Master, who is fully aware of the Doctor's association with Torchwood and relationship with Jack.
- 2007, Christmas: The Racnoss Web-Star is shot down on 'orders from Mr Saxon'. (Jack says Saxon was 'Minister of Defence. First came to prominence when he shot down the Racnoss on Christmas Eve'.)
- 2008, January: By this time, the Master has met Lucy. He takes her on a trip in the TARDIS to 100 Trillion, to show her the fate of the Utopia humans, and they see the Universe 'collapsing around them'. Another factor of Plan B falls into place. Saxon contributes funding for Richard Lazarus's genetic experiments, applying the scientist's findings to building a molecular weapon that could be used against the Doctor should the need arise ('The Lazarus Experiment').
- 2008, February: Saxon splits from the government and forms his own party, influencing others to leave their parties to join him. (Jack says Saxon was 'former Minister of Defence'.) He and Lucy are married.
- 2008, March: With the Election three months away, VOTE SAXON flyers are posted around the country. Jack and Tosh investigate the Ritz dancehall ('Captain Jack Harkness'). Jack is injured by Abaddon, but awakes from his coma days later ('End Of Days'). The TARDIS lands in Cardiff to refuel, and Jack is reunited with the Doctor ('Utopia'). And so it all begins...
- 2008, April: With Plan B underway, the Master builds the Paradox Machine.
- 2008, May: The *Valiant* is completed. Plan B is now ready to be activated. Saxon makes his final journey to 100 Trillion, to prepare the Utopia humans for their journey back in time. He takes four of the spheres back to Earth with him. The TARDIS is taken to the *Valiant*, and the Paradox Machine is completed.

- 2008, June: Sunday, the Doctor arrives at the Royal Hope Hospital. On Monday, the hospital is taken to the moon (the Master may have even seen the TARDIS parked outside the hospital, as it was across the river from the Houses of Parliament) ('Smith And Jones'). On the night of Lazarus's final experiment, Francine Jones is approached by Saxon's representatives, who warn her about the Doctor. The following day, Tish is offered a new job at Downing Street. On Election Day (Thursday), Saxon's people monitor Francine's telephone calls. Saxon wins the Election…

OBSERVATIONS

- Why did the Master choose the name Saxon? Is it a deliberate anagram of Axons? (He does mention them at one point.) And did he chose the first name Harold from 'Hark, the Herald Angels', as in Archangel?
- The design on the Master's ring is the logo of Lazarus Labs ('The Lazarus Experiment'). Given that Lazarus Labs provided the technology used to build the Master's sonic laser, and develop its ageing capabilities, it's also possible the Master used the labs for research into life extension, hence why the ring has some significance to the unseen woman who picks it up after the Master's body is cremated. Does the ring contain the Master's genetic code, or perhaps it is a chameleon arch container like the fob watch?
- At the start of the second episode, a message saying 'Space lane traffic is advised to stay away from Sol Three, also known as Earth. Pilots are warned, Sol Three is now entering Terminal Extinction. Planet Earth is closed'. This is not a message being broadcast from Earth, but about Earth – but broadcast by whom? Given that in 'Voyage Of The Damned' Earth is referred to as 'Sol Three – also known as Earth', we might conclude that the message was being broadcast from Sto, and was perhaps directed towards the *Titanic*, which would have been on its way to Earth in the original timeline.
- The Doctor's 'resurrection' by his name being called at the same time all around the world is similar to the process used by the Carrionites in being brought back into existence through specific words recited within the Globe Theatre.
- The Doctor tempts Martha to travel with him again, and considers a meeting with Agatha Christie: 'I'd love to meet Agatha Christie. Bet she's brilliant'. He gets his wish in 'The Unicorn And The Wasp'.
- In the alternative 'Turn Left' Universe, the events of 'The Sound Of Drum' never happen. With the Doctor dead, he couldn't travel to Malcassairo, and the Master would never be reborn. No Master, no Saxon. No Saxon, no Election, etc.

2008, June 6 (Friday) – 7 (Saturday) ↑
2008, June 7 (Saturday) – 8 (Sunday) ↑ ▓ ▓ ▓ ▓ ▓ ▓ ▓

When he, the Doctor and Martha arrive on Earth, Jack says 'twenty-first century, by the look if it'. Saxon refers to events from 'a few years ago', specifically the destruction of Big Ben ('Aliens Of London'), March 2006; the Sycorax spaceship ('The Christmas Invasion'), December 2006; metal men ('Army Of Ghosts'), May 2007; and the Christmas Star ('The Runaway Bride'), December 2007. Martha says Saxon's 'been around for years', and Jack says he's 'been around for ages'.

Given that Martha's global crusade spans '365 days' rather than 366, 'The Sound Of Drums' must occur after February, on account of 2008 being a Leap Year. When Martha rings Tom Milligan at the end of the story, we see a patients' statistics board on the wall behind him with columns headed for the months 'JFMAMJJASOND', with all the columns up to October filled in. The November and December columns are both empty. This suggests the story is set in or around October. However, the first column has the words 'Act 2004' on them; this might stand for Actuals 2004, in which case it's a past year and meaningless as a dating tool. It's possible the 2004 is not a date but a figure, being the column total. Without knowing the purpose of the chart – it might be a record of 2004's statistics, it could be a list of projections for the coming months, or it could be statistics up to October of the previous year – we can't use it as an accurate dating tool.

General Elections in Britain are traditionally held mid-year (in our history, past Elections were held in April (in 1992), May (1979, 1997, 2005), and June (1970, 1983, 1987, 2001)). (There were two elections in 1974, February and October, but that was during a period of intense political turmoil.) According to Vivien Rook, Saxon appeared on the scene 'just after the downfall of Harriet Jones'. This was in the aftermath of the events of 'The Christmas Invasion' (24 – 25 December 2006); she was probably removed from office around the first week of January 2007. That was 'eighteen months ago', so the Election must be taking place no later than June 2008.

Elections are also traditionally held on Thursdays. Martha notes they've arrived on 'the day after the Election. That's only four days after I met you', which places 'Smith And Jones' on the Monday, 'The Lazarus Experiment' on Tuesday, the Election on Thursday (Martha rings Francine on the Election day in '42'). 'The Sound Of Drums' therefore starts on the Friday, and runs into Saturday, with the Paradox Machine reaching critical at 8.02am.

The story 'To The Last Man' is set from 20 – 21 June 2008, and is when Jack has rejoined his team at Torchwood Three in Cardiff, so the Election must have been held prior to 20 June. With 'Kiss Kiss, Bang Bang', 'Sleeper', and the fact that Gwen, Owen and Ianto had to get back from Nepal, where Saxon says he has sent them on a wild goose chase, all to be factored in, the best dates for 'The Sound Of Drums' are Friday, 6 June to Saturday, 7 June.

We can assume that it is on the Saturday night that the Doctor burns the Master's body. The next sequence is when Martha gives Professor Docherty the flowers. This is probably the Sunday, following the pyre scene. It appears that Docherty is in Cardiff, as Martha meets her by the Cardiff Town Hall (the clock reads '2.10pm'). The next scene is Jack's farewell near the Hub entrance. Martha is wearing the same clothes as in the Docherty scene, so again, this is probably the same day. The Doctor, Jack and Martha must have travelled to Cardiff by train since the TARDIS was probably still out of commission on account of the destroyed Paradox Machine. Presumably the Hub is empty when Jack returns to the base. He may have spent some time on Flat Holm island (see 'Adrift'), as he had been away for a whole year, and he rejoins his team in 'Kiss Kiss, Bang Bang' a few days later.

The Paradox Machine is gone when Martha makes her farewells to the Doctor; it's possible this is a later day, although Martha is wearing the same clothes she had in the Cardiff scenes. (Leo was in Brighton when Martha's flat was blown up on the Friday, and he is back in London in this final scene.) I'll accept that this is all the same day; removal of the Paradox Machine is probably a few hours' work for the Doctor. Martha telephones Tom Milligan at the hospital to check that he is all right. (Although she rings off before he can say anything, she does make contact with him again off-screen, and within a few months they are dating ('A Day In The Death'), and by early 2009, they are engaged ('The Sontaran Stratagem').)

<<2009, June 7 – 8 >>

When Martha returns to England at night, an on-screen caption reads 'ONE YEAR LATER', and Martha confirms that she has been away for 'three hundred and sixty five days. It's been a long year'. She left on Saturday, 7 June 2008, so it is now Sunday, 7 June 2009. In the lead up to the attempted coup on board the *Valiant*, we see a digital clock with the display showing '1 1 SA', which might stand for the day, month and day of week – i.e. 1 January SATURDAY. [This might be a Production Factor; with the set dressers fixing the scripted time of 15.00 on the clock, but not bothering to adjust the clock's '1/1/SA' defaults for the other settings.]

It is Monday, 8 June 2009 when the Paradox Machine rewinds times; the Doctor notes that they've gone back 'one year and one day', which would be to Saturday,

7 June 2008, the day President Winters was killed. (With the Master winning the Thursday election, and dying that Saturday morning, as far as history records him, he was Prime Minister for all of one day, making him one of if not the shortest-serving PM in history!) Presumably Archangel was still transmitting its hypnotic signal so the people of the world were not fully aware of what was happening on the *Valiant*. Of note, when the President is killed, the *Valiant* is hosting not only his bodyguards and attaches, but also UNIT personnel, members of the press and a television crew. Obviously they aren't on the *Valiant* when time rewinds, so it is anyone's guess what happened to them. To them, they were on the *Valiant* filming the arrival of the Toclafane one minute, the President is blasted, and then everything kind of goes fuzzy at '8.02', and then – well, who knows… We can assume that the Doctor informed UNIT of what had happened, and instructs them to deactivate the Archangel network. Once that is done, the population comes out from the trance.

The Members of Parliament who aren't killed during the Friday cabinet meeting, presumably form a new party and choose a new leader to replace the deceased Saxon. As noted in 'Revenge Of The Slitheen' (set in September 2008) there is a new Prime Minister in office.

1221 ✦
The Doctor would have been 'eight' when he was initiated into the Time Lord Academy, which is GMT 1221 – see THE DOCTOR'S AGE.

1968
President Winters says 'First Contact policy was decided by the Security Council of 1968'. This is the Security Council of the United Nations, and was most likely set up partly on account of the Yeti invasion in 1967 – 'The Web Of Fear' (see THE UNIT YEARS).

Beyond 100,000,000,000,000
The Toclafane humans come from a point in time possibly many generations after the humans who had left Malcassairo arrived on Utopia, which was in 100,000,000,000,000. The Master took Lucy to this point in time to show her the future of the human race, and also made various trips there on his own to broker the arrangements to bring the Toclafane back in time to 2008.

DURATION

⇨ **Day One (Friday, 6 June 2008) (Ep1)** ▨ ▨ ▨ ▨ ▨ ▨ ▨

It is the day after the Election, so it's Friday. (Martha notes that they've 'missed the Election'.) Saxon has returned from the Palace. Saxon declares 'tomorrow morning' the Toclafane will arrive; everything ends 'tomorrow'. The Doctor, Jack and Martha are declared fugitives, and hide out in the warehouse that night. They receive Vivien Rook's email video at '22.00' (10.00pm). Air Force One lands that night. They later go to the airfield as the US President arrives. Saxon says they will reach the *Valiant* 'within the hour'. The Doctor and co teleport to the *Valiant*...

⇨ **Day Two (Saturday, 7 June 2008) (Ep1)** ▨ ▨ ▨ ▨ ▨ ▨

... and arrive on board as 'dawn' breaks (the vessel is in orbit above Norway). The broadcast starts at '7.58'. The US President is killed at 8.00am. The Paradox Machine reaches critical precision at '8.02 precisely'. The Toclafane arrive; the Machine activates – and everything goes fuzzy....

🕑 **A year passes within the time bubble ('365' days)...** ▨ ▨ ▨ ▨

⇔ **Day 366 Y (<<Sunday, 7 June 2009>>) (Ep2)** ▨ ▨ ▨ ▨ ▨

Martha arrives on the coast of England in the early hours of the morning, after being away for '365 days'. The Master announces Launch Day will be 'in 24 hours'. Later that day, Tom Milligan shows Martha the missile silos. At '15:00:00' the Doctor and the other rebels attempt a coup on the *Valiant*. That evening, Martha, Tom and Professor Docherty capture a Toclafane. Martha and Tom hide out in the house.

⇔ **Day 367 Y (<<Monday, 8 June 2009>>) (Ep2)** ▨ ▨ ▨ ▨ ▨

It is 'almost dawn' when Martha is captured by Saxon, and fully day when she arrives back on the *Valiant*. The Master starts the countdown at '180' seconds. The Doctor is revived. Jack destroys the Paradox Machine...

🕑 **Time reverses – 'one year and one day'** ▨ ▨ ▨ ▨ ▨

⇨ **Day Two (Saturday, 7 June 2008) (Ep2)** ▨ ▨ ▨ ▨ ▨ ▨

Time is reversed back to the start of Day Two, at 'two minutes past eight in the morning... Everything back to normal... None of it happened'. The Master is shot.

The Doctor burns the Master's body that night. An unidentified person takes his discarded ring.

⇨ **Day Three (Sunday, 8 June 2008) (Ep.2)**
Martha meets Professor Docherty. Jack is taken back to the Hub in Cardiff. Later that day, Martha rings Tom Milligan, and leaves the Doctor.

VOYAGE OF THE DAMNED

+STORY LINK

In the moments after dematerialising from outside the Joneses' house the TARDIS in March 2008, the prow of the spaceship replica *Titanic* smashes through the weakened TARDIS wall, as was seen at the end of 'The Sound Of Drums'; the Doctor having 'left the defences down'. This suggests that the TARDIS has moved forward in time by six months to December. But it's possible that the two ships collide while the *Titanic* replica is still *en route* to Earth, and is still some six months away, and when the Doctor materialises the TARDIS on board the replica, that is when the time differential shift to December occurs.

OBSERVATIONS

- When cornered by the Host, the Doctor says 'Take me to your leader. I've always wanted to say that!' But the ninth Doctor said it in 'Aliens Of London', and the fourth in 'The Face Of Evil'. The fifth Doctor also uttered 'Take me to your leader' in 'Four to Doomsday'.
- When set adrift, the TARDIS is programmed to lock onto the nearest centre of gravity. A similar thing happened in 'Terminus', when the TARDIS attached itself to the spaceship.

LANGUAGE

The passengers and crew are from the planet Sto (the one exception being Bannakaffalatta, whose planet of origin is not stated), and they can speak and read English. Mr Copper has studied Earth history ('Earthonomics'), but has never been to the planet before. The signs onboard the ship are in English. They use Earth numerals: '6-7'. The people of Sto use 'hours' and 'minutes' to measure time.

TIMELINE DATES

2008, December 24 – 25 ⁕

No direct year is given. The 'CAROLS IN CAMDEN' poster on the side of Wilf's booth says 'CHRISTMAS IN LONDON 200-' but the last digit is blurred. Wilf says 'Christmas before last we had that big bloody spaceship, everyone standing on the roof, and then last year that Christmas Star electrocuting all over the place, draining the Thames'. The first describes the events of 'The Christmas Invasion', which was set in December 2006, and the latter 'The Runaway Bride', was December 2007, which places 'Voyage Of The Damned' at Christmas 2008. As noted in Story Link above, the TARDIS has moved forwards in time by six months. (It's possible the initial impact between the TARDIS and the *Titanic* was in June while the ship was still *en route* to Earth, but that when the TARDIS materialised on board it had then moved ahead in time when the *Titanic* was closer to Earth in December.)

Mr Copper establishes the 'Mr Copper Foundation', through which Harriet Jones, ex-Prime Minister, later develops the Subwave Network with which she contacts Torchwood, Sarah Jane, Martha and the Doctor in 'The Stolen Earth'.

In the alternative Universe seen in 'Turn Left', with the Doctor having died on 24 December 2007, the *Titanic* crashes, destroying London. Donna and Sylvia Noble, and Wilf, are all evacuated to Leeds.

4 BC ⁕

When he says 'I was there', the Doctor is inferring that he was in Bethlehem when Mary and Joseph came to the Inn, but he took 'the last room', meaning that the couple had to take accommodations in the nearby stables. It is commonly accepted that this event occurred around 4 BC.

1832

Max Capricorn says he has spent '176 years' running the company, the last few 'years' he has hidden his deformity from the company board of directors.

DURATION

⇒ Day One (24 December 2008)

The TARDIS materialises on board the *Titanic* on 24 December. The clock on the wall of the main ballroom reads 11.52 as the meteors approach. (Presumably the ship's clocks are synchronised with Greenwich Mean Time (given that the original *Titanic* was a British vessel), which would explain why the ship was attuned to the date and time in England rather than one of the other 23 World Time Zones, and why the teleport beamed the shore party to the centre of London.) As the survivors make their way across the chasm, Mr Copper announces it is now 'Christmas Day'.

⇨ **Day Two (25 December 2008)**
The *Titanic* plunges towards London 'as dawn rises over Great Britain'. The rest of this day passes off-screen; the Doctor bids farewell to Mr Copper at night. Despite London being deserted, all the lights of the city are on.

UNSEEN ADVENTURES

The Doctor probably has his encounter with the insane computer that had abducted Charlemagne around this time ('The Unicorn And The Wasp').

PARTNERS IN CRIME

STORY LINK

From the Doctor's perspective, it is some time after the events of 'Voyage Of The Damned'. He has been alone since Martha left ('The Sound Of Drums').

Having been on Earth recently, he has begun investigating Adipose Industries, although it is not clear why this is. He has built a detection device to trace the parthenogenesis residue.

In terms of Donna's timeline, it is after Christmas 2008 (she refers to the 'hoax' of the 'replica of the *Titanic* flying over Buckingham Palace on Christmas Day' ('Voyage Of The Damned'). Since 'The Runaway Bride' she spent a little time travelling, going to Egypt for 'two weeks', but other than that her life has been ordinary; she had a job in health and safety that lasted 'two days', and now unemployed again she has moved in with her mother and grandfather (who have moved to a new house from their previous house seen in 'The Runaway Bride'; in 'The Sontaran Stratagem' Sylvia refers to their 'new mortgage'). Donna's father, Geoff, has we can assume died. Donna has spent some time looking for the Doctor again, investigating anything weird knowing that the Doctor might also be there. She mentions 'UFO sightings, crop circles, sea monsters' and the disappearing bees (also mentioned in 'Planet Of The Ood', and 'The Unicorn And The Wasp'). It come across as odd that she doesn't mention anything to do with the disappearance of Harold Saxon, or that the sun turned blue ('Revenge Of The Slitheen'), Earth had a near miss with a meteor ('Whatever Happened To Sarah Jane?'), or that the moon nearly crashed into the planet ('The Lost Boy'), and not forgetting all the weird goings on in Cardiff (numerous *Torchwood* stories).

OBSERVATIONS

- The taxi that Stacey orders bears an ATMOS sticker on its windscreen. See 'The Sontaran Stratagem'.
- The Doctor refers to cat-flaps ('Survival', 'Rose') and 'cat people' ('New Earth').
- Adipose 3, the breeding planet of the Adipose children, has been lost. The Doctor wonders 'how do you lose a planet?' Other lost planets include Pyrovillia ('The Fires Of Pompeii'), and the moon of Poosh ('Midnight'). This is the work of the Daleks (see 'The Stolen Earth').
- It's not readily clear how long Adipose Industries has been established on Earth. They have been selling the pills in Britain for at least 'two weeks' (Roger has been taking them for that long; he is woken at 'ten past one' every morning), and the whole of the Adipose Industries office tower has been fitted with the inducer, which would have taken months – assuming the device was added later rather than when the building was under construction. It's also clear that the Adipose operations are based only in London, as Miss Foster declares they are ready to go nationwide shortly; she says England is 'a beautifully fat country. Believe me, I've travelled a long way to find obesity on this scale', so it's clear she had not even considered America as a base of operations. (In the 'Turn Left' parallel world, with London destroyed by the crash of the *Titanic*, the Adipose instead set up their operations in the United States, and ultimately kill over 60 million people.)

LANGUAGE

Matron Cofelia of the Five-Straighten, Classabindi Nursery Fleet selected her name deliberately as she is the foster mother to the Adipose. She speaks English.

TIMELINE DATES

2009, August 18 – 19 •

No year is given. Miss Foster refers to it being 'the twenty-first century'. In 'The Sontaran Stratagem' Wilf recognises the Doctor from their brief meeting when the passengers from the *Titanic* beam down to London at Christmas (December 2008) in 'Voyage Of The Damned', so for Wilf that meeting was fairly recent; it is now 2009.

In 'The Fires Of Pompeii', Donna says 'you saved me in 2008; you saved everyone'. The way she structures this sentence (she doesn't say 'you saved me this year') indicates that 2008 is a past year for her. She's not referencing 'Partners In Crime', and it's not likely she means 'Voyage Of The Damned', as she had previously said she thought the *Titanic* must have been a hoax. (Unless the Doctor told her about this off-screen while they travelled in the TARDIS *en route* to Italy.) 'The Runaway Bride' was in December 2007, so it's unlikely she is referring to that, unless she is generalising and saying that by his saving her in December 2007, which was only a week out from the start of 2008, the Doctor metaphorically saved her in 2008 as well. (She did some overseas travel in 2008 (to Egypt for 'two weeks'), as the Doctor suggested she ought to do.) It's also possible she is referring to the events of 'The Sound Of Drums' (set in June 2008), an adventure the Doctor may have told her about off-screen. Regardless of what Donna means when she speaks of '2008', the overriding continuity of past 'present day' stories means that the year must be 2009. (See THE YEAR AHEAD RULE.)

On the first night, Stacey says she started taking the pills 'on Thursday', and it's now 'five days later', which makes it Tuesday. On the second day, Sylvia mentions her 'Wednesday girls' meeting, so the story takes place over these two days.

I have set 'The Stolen Earth' on 12 September 2009. There is a period of a few days between 'Partners In Crime' and 'The Sontaran Stratagem', and possibly three weeks between 'The Sontaran Stratagem' and 'The Stolen Earth' (if we take into account Rose's comment to Donna in 'Turn Left' that Donna is going to die in 'three weeks'), and there is a six week gap between 'The Last Sontaran' and 'The Day Of The Clown', which is set in early October; therefore, I have set 'Partners In Crime' on 18 to 19 August 2009.

1974 (Summer?)

Wilf reminds Donna of the time that Donna caught a bus to Strathclyde when she was 'six years old'. Assuming Donna is in her early 40s [Catherine Tate was born in 1968], this was 1974. It was probably in the summer, since the reason for the solo excursion was because there was to be no family holiday that year.

DURATION

⇨ **Day One (Tuesday)**

It is '11.30am' ('Good morning') when the Doctor and Donna interview the staff at the Adipose Industries call centre. Donna returns home later that night.

⇨ **Day Two (Wednesday)**

The Doctor and Donna arrive at Adipose at '9.30am' ('Morning!'), and stay hidden until '6.09pm' (as seen on the clock). The story ends later that same night.

THE FIRES OF POMPEII

+STORY LINK

There is no mention of the events of 'Partners In Crime', but given the Doctor's 'welcome on board' at the end, we can assume this is Donna's first trip in the TARDIS. Donna has had time to change her dress, just one of the many she packed in her suitcases; the Doctor still wears his brown suit. The Doctor has set the TARDIS for 'ancient Rome', but the ship instead arrives in Pompeii. (With 'Partners In Crime' set 18 to 19 August 2009, the TARDIS has slipped back in time by exactly 1,930 years, almost to the exact date!)

OBSERVATIONS

- The Doctor mentions that he has been to Rome before: 'Ages ago. And before you ask, that fire had nothing to do with me. Well, a little bit. I hadn't had the chance to look around properly'. All this refers, of course, to 'The Romans', set in AD July 64. The Doctor was aged around 446 then (see THE DOCTOR'S AGE).
- In 'The Empty Child', Captain Jack tells the Doctor and Rose that Pompeii was a perfect place to run a self-cleaning con (he refers to this as 'Volcano Day', a term which the tenth Doctor utters when he realises where they are, so it's likely that the Doctor was remembering what Jack had said). There is no sign of Jack, nor any direct reference to him in 'The Fires Of Pompeii'. We do not know the exact nature of his Volcano Day con, nor how it worked, but if he is there Jack is most likely parked safely in his invisible Chula spaceship watching as events unfold. He might even have seen the TARDIS in the market place – he would have at least detected its arrival – and thinking it

might have been a Time Agent on his trail, might have slipped away. Of note, Jack readily recognises the tenth Doctor in 'Utopia', so it's possible he had indeed seen the tenth Doctor in Pompeii.)

LANGUAGE

Much is made of the fact that the TARDIS translates Latin speech and written text into English, and even makes some speakers have an accent. But when Donna deliberately speaks Latin ('*veni vidi vici*') to the Pompeiians it sounds as if she is speaking Welsh / Celtic.

TIMELINE DATES

AD 79, August 23 – 24 ·

The Doctor gives the date of Day One as '79 AD, twenty third of August, which makes Volcano Day tomorrow'. The eruption of Vesuvius is recorded in our history as being on this date (see also 'The Brain Of Morbius' and 'The Empty Child').

AD 80, February

A caption reads 'SIX MONTHS LATER', so the final scene set in Rome is in February AD 80.

5000 BC

The Pyrovile had been dormant in the mountain for 'thousands of years', say five thousand.

AD 62

There was an earthquake 'seventeen years ago', which was when the Pyrovile were awakened from their millennia-long slumber. (They had been dormant 'for thousands of years'.) And it was on awakening that they discovered that Pyrovillia was 'lost'. (It had been removed from time and space by the Daleks in 'The Stolen Earth', and although the Doctor saved the planet, it must have been returned to a different time period, probably relative to 2009.)

DURATION

⇨ Day One (23 August)

It is late in the afternoon when the TARDIS lands in Pompeii (Lucius is expected at the villa 'this afternoon'). It is night when the Doctor and Quintus visit the Sisterhood's temple.

⇨ **Day Two (24 August)** ■ ■ ■ ■ ■ ■ ■ ■ ■ ■

Caecilius announces 'Sunrise… A new day'. Later that same day the family watch from the hillside as Pompeii dies.

⇨ **Day One (February)** ■ ■ ■ ■ ■ ■ ■ ■ ■ ■

It is daytime in the SIX MONTHS LATER scene.

PLANET OF THE OOD

+STORY LINK

Donna says 'history's one thing, but an alien planet…', which indicates this is her second trip in the TARDIS. The TARDIS has been set 'to random'. Both the Doctor and Donna have changed clothes (the Doctor is now in his blue suit).

OBSERVATIONS

- The Doctor says his visit to the Sense-Sphere was 'Years ago. Ages'. For him it was some 693 years (THE DOCTOR'S AGE), whereas in terms of history was 1,362 years ago – 'The Sensorites' is set in 2764.
- Donna asks if the Doctor has met Houdini. Although he doesn't reply, the answer is yes – see 'Planet Of The Spiders' and 'Revenge Of The Cybermen'.

LANGUAGE

The Ood speak English with the aid of the translators that were surgically implanted after their secondary hind-brain is removed. The Doctor speaks Italian ('*molte bene*' and '*delissimo*') without it being translated, which proves that certain phrases or words can be suppressed from being translated if the Doctor so wishes.

TIMELINE DATES

4126 ⋆ ■ ■ ■ ■ ■ ■ ■ ■ ■ ■ ■ ■

The Doctor says it's the 'forty-second century', and later 'the year forty one twenty six, that is the Second Great and Bountiful Human Empire', which has spread itself across at least three galaxies. (The Fourth Great and Bountiful Human Empire is in the year 200,000 – see 'The Long Game'.)

3926

The Ood Brain was found in the glacier 'centuries ago'. The Ood themselves have been slaves for 'two centuries now' / 'two hundred years', which makes it 3926 when the Ood Brain was first discovered. It does seem odd that while the Doctor has been to all sorts of times and planets, he has never encountered the Ood before (especially since they are in servitude across three galaxies). Of course, they have only been in slavery for 200 years, so it's possible he's simply missed that particular span of time.

4116

Halpen says he hasn't been in Warehouse 51 in 'ten years'. The first time he visited the odorous facility was when he was 'six'. Dr Ryder says it has taken him 'ten years' to infiltrate Ood Operations.

4121

Halpen says 'five years ago I had a full head of hair', so he has been taking the 'hair tonic' for at least that long.

DURATION

⇨ **Day One**

The story takes place across several hours. Halpen requires sales figures 'by nineteen hundred' (i.e. 7.00pm).

THE SONTARAN STRATAGEM
THE POISON SKY

STORY LINK

Since leaving the Ood-Sphere ('Planet Of The Ood'), the Doctor (still wearing his blue suit) has been teaching Donna how to fly the TARDIS ('you're getting a bit too close to the 1980s'). Martha's phone has been left sitting on the TARDIS console. When Donna returns home, she remembers events from 'Partners In Crime', 'The Fires Of Pompeii' and 'Planet Of The Ood', but no other, so we can assume that these are the only three adventures she has had with the Doctor. However in 'The Doctor's Daughter', Donna says she has seen 'some amazing things... whole new worlds', which suggests she has been to more than just one alien planet. If this is the case, then these occurred off-screen between 'Planet Of The Ood' and 'The Sontaran Stratagem' (but not seen in the flashback montage when Donna returns home in 'The Sontaran Stratagem').

Following 'The Sound Of Drums', Martha has been head-hunted by UNIT with the Doctor's (off-screen) help. She is now a fully qualified doctor (she says 'UNIT rushed it through, given my experience in the field'). In late 2008 she was brought in by Jack Harkness to assist Torchwood Three with a medical crisis in 'Reset', with Martha staying on for three days to assist Owen Harper in 'Dead Man Walking' and 'A Day In The Death'. She returned to her UNIT duties at the end of 'A Day In The Death'. In the time since then she has become engaged to Dr Tom Milligan although he is currently in Africa. Although the Doctor never met Tom in 'The Sound Of Drums', Martha must have told the Doctor about him off-screen, as he seems to know who she is talking about when she mentions Tom's name.

In 'The Stolen Earth', Martha says the Doctor's number (07700-900461) 'calls anywhere in the Universe. It never breaks down'. Martha gives the Doctor her phone in 'The Sound Of Drums', some twelve months earlier. As noted in '42', the telephone signal must be sent in real time, which means that the same relative time has passed on Earth (in terms of Martha's time frame) as well as for the Doctor since he and Martha parted in June 2008. Given that Donna has been away for what her mother says is 'days', there must be a long off-screen period for the Doctor between 'Voyage Of The Damned' and 'Partners In Crime'. Presumably the time differential between when Martha left her phone with the Doctor and when she rings it again must be relative to that, so over twelve months must have also passed for the Doctor. Most of this time passes off-screen, with the majority occurring between 'Voyage Of The Damned' and 'Partners In Crime'. (As covered under THE DOCTOR'S AGE, he would be 904 in this story.)

SONTARAN LINK

This is the sixth chronological appearance by the Sontarans, their last being in 'The Two Doctors', set in 1984. General Staal refers to the Doctor as being a known 'enemy of the Sontarans. A face-changer... Legend says he led the battle in the last Great Time War'. Staal also knows the Doctor is 'the last of the Time Lords', and that the TADIS is the Doctor's 'infamous vessel'. He also gloats that 'we are the first Sontarans in history to capture a TARDIS'. Clearly Staal does not consider the Sontarans' failed invasion of Gallifrey ('The Invasion Of Time') as a success. The last time the Sontarans were active on Earth was in 1984 ('The Two Doctors') in which they were actively planning to use stolen time technology to help with their war effort. Staal refers to Earth as the Doctor's 'precious Earth', so he certainly knows a lot about the Doctor's past. The Doctor refers to the Sontarans as being 'the finest soldiers in the galaxy', which confirms that the Sontaran / Rutan conflict (which as been waging for 50,000 years) is confined to Earth's galaxy.

These Sontarans have developed teleport technology. They also have a form of advanced time technology in that the ATMOS units are shielded by a two-second time displacement field.

OBSERVATIONS

- The Doctor says he worked for UNIT a 'long time ago. Back in the seventies. Or was it the eighties?' Mace tells him he is technically still on staff, as he never resigned. In *Timelink*, I have evaluated that it was definitely the former. (See THE UNIT YEARS.)
- It's not known how long Colonel Mace has been with UNIT. He is not mentioned in 'The Christmas Invasion', in which Major Blake was in charge of UNIT operations during the Sycorax event.
- At some point after 'Battlefield', Brigadier Alistair Gordon Lethbridge-Stewart is knighted. It's unlikely this would be for his work for UNIT, as that is a covert organisation. It's possible this knighthood was given due to other merits, perhaps charity work with Doris? Mace says 'Sir Alistair' is stranded in Peru. In 'Enemy Of The Bane' it is said he was there acting as 'UNIT's special envoy'. He returns home a few months later, and is waiting to be debriefed on his 'mission to Peru' when he is reunited with Sarah.
- The Doctor seems very excited and pleased to see the *Valiant* again, despite his having spent a whole year as the Master's prisoner onboard her during 'The Sound Of Drums'.

LANGUAGE

The Sontarans speak English; in 'The Time Warrior' it is revealed that Sontarans use translation devices, but there is no mention of such devices in use here.

TIMELINE DATES

2009, August 22 – 23 ·

No direct dates are given. Luke Rattigan is '18' years old. According to UNIT's file on him, Luke attended his local primary school from '1990 – 1992'. Assuming Luke was at least two or three years old at that time, that makes the current year no later than 2007. Another screen of the same file brings Luke's activities up to date, and is headed '2006 – Present', which confirms that the current year is a few years after 2006. It's possible the first recorded date, '1990' is his year of birth, and that he first attended primary school on the second, in '1992'. That would make the current year no earlier than 2008 or 2009. As noted by other stories and the chapter THE YEAR AHEAD RULE (2005 TO 2009), the date must be 2009. This means that the child prodigy was one or two years old when he first went to primary school in 1992.

Wilfred mentions his encounter with the Doctor at 'Christmas' 2008 ('Voyage Of The Damned'), so it is 2009. Sylvia recalls meeting the Doctor 'at the wedding' in 'The Runaway Bride'. Wilf was ill with Spanish flu, and couldn't be there. (There is no mention as to what has happened to Donna's father, Geoff, who was also at the wedding.)

Sylvia wonders where Donna has been 'these last few days', and a neighbour says she hasn't seen Donna 'for days', so it is still the same month, if not the same week as 'Partners In Crime' (Sylvia mentions 'that silly little trick with the car keys'). The second day of that story was a Wednesday. On the first day of 'The Sontaran Stratagem', Donna passes a boy playing with a football. On the second day, after the crisis has past, Sylvia comments that she has seen 'kids on bikes' everywhere. Does that indicate it is now the weekend, and that the events of 'The Sontaran Stratagem' take place over the Saturday and Sunday of that same week? Or is it already the summer school holiday break? Sylvia is not at work for either of the two days, so it is not unreasonable to set 'The Sontaran Stratagem' over a weekend.

The gutters along the streets are full of dead leaves which suggests that it is early autumn, giving a range of months from September to November [the story was filmed in October/November of 2007] to match seasonal conditions.

In the opening scenes set at night, Jo Nakashima mentions the people who all died in their cars 'yesterday'. Colonel Mace later tells the Doctor how 52 people died 'yesterday'. Assuming that Nakashima was investigating the same 52 deaths, then her own death occurs in the early hours of that same day rather than the previous day. The death reported in the UK occurred at '5am'. Other deaths include France ('6am'), Moscow ('8am') and at '1pm in China'.

In the parallel world of 'Turn Left', on the night in which the members of Torchwood Three are killed destroying the Sontarans, Rose tells Donna that she is going to die 'in three weeks'. If we accept this to mean there is a period of 'three weeks' between 'The Sontaran Stratagem' and 'The Stolen Earth', then 'The Sontaran Stratagem' takes place as least three weeks prior to 'The Stolen Earth', which I have set on 12 September 2009; so it is late August 2009. If the story takes place over a weekend, then the likely dates are 22 and 23 August.

As noted in Story Link above, this means that over a whole year has passed since Martha last saw the Doctor (in 'The Sound Of Drums').

(Kaagh, a Sontaran Commander, survives the destruction of the Sontaran command ship, and is stranded on Earth in 'The Last Sontaran', and returns in 'Enemy Of The Bane'.)

48,000 BC

The Doctor says the Sontaran/ Rutan was has been waging for 'fifty thousand years'.

1990

Luke Rattigan is born – the date appears on the UNIT file.

1992

Luke Rattigan attends primary school. The date is seen on the UNIT file.

1996

The data and dates concerning Luke Rattigan are seen on the UNIT file. He invented the Fountain Six search engine when he 'was six years old' and became a millionaire overnight. Assuming he was born in 1990 (see above) this event was in 1996.

2005, September

According to the UNIT file, 'September 2005' was when Luke Rattigan was given an IQ rating of 174 by Mensa experts. There are seventeen ATMOS factories across the globe, and at least half of the 800 million cars on Earth have been fitted with the AMTOS device, which indicates that the Sontaran Stratagem has been underway for quite some time, certainly many months if not years, but there is no indication as to how many. It was only since the 52 simultaneous deaths 'yesterday' that UNIT thought to investigate ATMOS, and when Martha called for the Doctor's help.

DURATION

⇨ **Day One (Saturday?) (Ep1-2)**

It is in the early hours of the morning when Jo Nakashima crashes her car. The Doctor and Martha arrive around ten o'clock in the morning: the clock in UNIT Mobile HQ reads '10.15' when the Doctor is introduced to Colonel Mace. The clock reads '1.20' (pm) when Donna leaves the TARDIS, which has been taken onboard the Sontaran ship. The main story therefore takes place over a period of no more than three to four hours.

⇨ **Day Two (Sunday?) (Ep2)**

The story ends on the morning of the following day. When Sylvia returns from the shops, she is greeted with 'Morning' by a neighbour.

THE DOCTOR'S DAUGHTER

+STORY LINK

'The Sontaran Stratagem' ends with the TARDIS being pulled off course, with the Doctor, Donna and Martha onboard. The start of 'The Doctor's Daughter' is a direct continuation from this moment. The Doctor still carries the stethoscope he has in 'Daleks In Manhattan' and 'Planet Of The Ood'.

OBSERVATIONS

- Jenny is not a Time Lord in the full sense of the term. She could, however, be classified as being a Gallifreyan, on account of her possessing two hearts. This would be why she did not fully regenerate; her coming back to life could be akin to a form of rejuvenation, maybe even similar to the rejuvenation process that the Minyans had perfected ('Underworld'), that she has inherited from her 'father'. And as I have speculated elsewhere, if the Doctor has been given a second regenerative cycle, the ability to rejuvenate without changing form (as seen in 'The Stolen Earth'), may be part of the process.

LANGUAGE

The Hath don't speak but do communicate through the water apparatus attached to their mouths. It appears that Martha is able to understand some of what they say, certainly the meaning if not the actual words themselves. Presumably the TARDIS telepathic circuits are unable to cope with such a complicated method of communication. What appears to be Hath writing is visible on the walls of the Hath base.

TIMELINE DATES

601.207.24 [2009, August 23?] ▸ ▦ ▦ ▦ ▦ ▦ ▦ ▦ ▦ ▦ ▦

Donna interprets the digital display (and the numbers stamped on the walls) as being 'the date. Assuming the first number is some big old space date… you've got the year, month, day. It's the other way round like it is in America'. The Doctor remembers this is 'the new Byzantine calendar' – but is this 'new' as in terms of it being an amended calendar per the original Byzantine calendar in use on Earth from 988 to 1453, or is 'New Byzantine' actually the name of the colonists' planet of origin? Although they are called 'human', and the Doctor identifies the 'Source' as being a 'terra-former', there is nothing given to suggest that the humans on Messaline are actually from Earth. The fact that the humans and Hath are co-colonising the planet suggests they are from the same planet of origin, when means it cannot be Earth, even in the future. [The existence of a UNIT logo on one of the control panels can be accepted as being a production gaffe, rather than a dating clue.] Therefore, the calendar doesn't necessarily mean it is the Earth date 24 July 6012.

Of note, if the colonists are not from Earth, it is entirely possible that the story takes place contemporary to August 2009, with the TARDIS moving to Messaline spatially only. This is supported by the fact that the Doctor's severed hand, which has been wired into the TARDIS circuits since the end of 'The Sound Of Drums', detects and reacts to the presence of another Time Lord (Jenny), which is understandable in spatial but not temporal terms – if so, why had the hand not detected Jenny before?

The Doctor says 'Jenny was the reason for the TARDIS bringing us here. [We] just got here too soon. We then created Jenny in the first place. Paradox. An endless paradox'. This is not a 'paradox' in the true sense of the word, but is an example of an endless linear event circling back on itself. (A true paradox is when events turn back on themselves but there is no clear reason for them doing so.) Let's examine the course of events from the Messaline timeline: Jenny emerges from the progenation machine at what we can call 12:00. Presumably it is at that very moment that the Doctor's severed hand reacts to her presence through the TARDIS's spatial circuits. The ship travels to Messaline, the journey taking approximately 10 minutes. But the ship lands on Messaline at 11:50; the TARDIS has to land at an earlier time point to avoid colliding with itself and causing a Time Ram (see 'The Time Monster'). Jenny is 'born' at 12:00 – and the TARDIS on Earth detects her presence... So in effect, it was the TARDIS that was directly responsible for putting into motion the sequence of events that leads to Jenny's creation.

Given that Jenny's presence is detected in August 2009 on Earth, this must be relative to the date on Messaline.

Martha is returned to her London flat presumably only a few hours after she left in 'The Sontaran Stratagem'. Her old flat was destroyed by the Master in 'The Sound Of Drums'; she has either moved in with Tom, or this is her new flat. Although her fiancé Tom Milligan is in Africa, Martha seems overly keen to get back home.

60120711 [2009, August 10?] ▪ ▪ ▪ ▪ ▪ ▪ ▪ ▪ ▪ ▪

The corridor outside the Source chamber was completed on 60120712. Presumably this was soon after the colonist ship arrived on Messaline.

60120717 [2009, August 16?] ▪ ▪ ▪ ▪ ▪ ▪ ▪ ▪ ▪ ▪

This is the stamped date for when the main hall was completed by the construction drones. If the Doctor's summation is correct, this was also the day on which the war started, all of 'seven days' ago. The war started following the death of the mission commander, when an agreement could not be reached between the humans and Hath as to who should assume leadership, and so the two species divided into factions.

Other dates indicated by the stamps are as follows [I have not included these in the TIMELINE]:

60120712 ▦ ▦ ▦ ▦ ▦ ▦ ▦ ▦ ▦ ▦ ▦ ▦ ▦
The stamped date for when the corridor outside the Source chamber was completed by the construction drones.

60120713 ▦ ▦ ▦ ▦ ▦ ▦ ▦ ▦ ▦ ▦ ▦ ▦ ▦
The date stamped for when the 'laser beam' corridor was completed by the construction drones.

60120714 ▦ ▦ ▦ ▦ ▦ ▦ ▦ ▦ ▦ ▦ ▦ ▦ ▦
The date stamped for when the corridor was completed by the construction drones.

60120716 ▦ ▦ ▦ ▦ ▦ ▦ ▦ ▦ ▦ ▦ ▦ ▦ ▦
The stamped date for when the cell area was completed by the construction drones.

DURATION

⇨ **Day One** ▦ ▦ ▦ ▦ ▦ ▦ ▦ ▦ ▦ ▦ ▦ ▦ ▦
Shortly after the TARDIS lands and Jenny is 'born', the progenation machines are powered down for 'the night shift'. General Cobb later announces that 'come the dawn, we march', so the story takes place over a few hours during the equivalent of the 'night'. Indeed, it is still dark when Martha and Hath Peck venture onto the planet surface.

⇨ **Day Two** ▦ ▦ ▦ ▦ ▦ ▦ ▦ ▦ ▦ ▦ ▦ ▦ ▦
When Jenny leaves in the shuttle, the sun is rising over the newly terra-formed world.

THE UNICORN AND THE WASP

STORY LINK

There is no direct link between 'The Doctor's Daughter' and 'The Unicorn And The Wasp'. The Doctor certainly shows no sign of grief following the 'loss' of his 'daughter', and the wound on the back of his hand caused by the progenation machine has fully healed. Indeed, the Doctor (in his brown suit) and Donna could have experienced any number of adventures together after returning Martha to her flat in London. Donna refers to 'planet Zog', which might refer to their intended destination. Intriguingly, meeting Agatha Christie was one of the delights the Doctor wanted to show Martha at the end of 'The Sound Of Drums' (the Doctor says to Agatha 'I was talking about you the other day', although this was clearly a lot longer than a few days from the Doctor's personal timeline – at least well over a year. It is possible that the TARDIS deliberately homed in on 3 December 1926 on account of Martha's recent presence in the TARDIS.

OBSERVATIONS

- The chest kept under the TARDIS control room floor grating contains a Cyberman chest piece, the Carrionite globe ('The Shakespeare Code'), and a bust of Caesar, as well as a facsimile copy of *Death in the Clouds*.

LANGUAGE

The Vespiform creature was able to communicate with Lady Eddison in India.

TIMELINE DATES

810

Agatha says Charlemagne 'lived centuries ago'. Charlemagne (born 742, died on 28 January 814), was crowned first Emperor of the Holy Roman Empire in 800, reigning until his death in 814. We can assume that he was 'kidnapped by an insane computer' during his time as Emperor, say 810.

1885

Lady Eddison says she met Christopher 'forty years ago in the heat of Delhi', which would be 1886. She later says it was in '1885'. There was a full moon that night. She saw Christopher again the following day, which was when she fell pregnant to him. He was killed in the flood.

1886

'Forty years ago', shortly after returning home from Delhi, and after 'six months' locked in her room, Lady Eddison gives birth to her son. He is '40' years old in 1926.

1926, November 25

With the story set on Friday, 3 December, the break in at the church was 'last Thursday night' rather than 'last night', which means it was the Thursday of the previous week, 25 November.

1926, December 3 – 4 ‧

The Doctor says 'it must be the 1920s', based on the period cars. He later sees a newspaper, and although he doesn't state the date, he does say 'it's the day Agatha Christie disappeared'. Later, he says it is '1926', and that year is given a couple more times. In our history, Agatha Christie disappeared on Friday, 3 December 1926 (the day 'Friday' can be seen in one of the spinning newspapers reporting Christie's disappearance).

Although the 'afternoon' garden party suggests it is the height of summer, as it is still broad daylight when cocktails are served at 4.30pm (Greeves said they are to be served 'from half past four'), Christie's disappearance and discovery ten days later is an historical fact, so those dates should still be applied.

The Doctor says Christie's car 'will be found tomorrow morning'; the story ends in the early hours of Saturday morning.

1926, December 14 ‧

Agatha Christie disappeared, and is later found at the Harrogate Hotel in a dazed state (ten days later in our history, 14 December), with no memory of the events of the night of 3 December, although some memories will bleed through from her subconscious, and provide inspiration for her future novels.

1899, October 13 – 1900, May 17

The Colonel refers to Mafeking ('terrible war'), which began on 13 October 1899, and ended 17 May 1900 (see also 'The Daleks' Master Plan' and 'The Invasion Of Time').

1918, March – 1920, June

The Colonel says he has been an invalid since the flu epidemic 'back in 18', which would be the Spanish flu outbreak of March 1918 that ended in June 1920 in our history.

1935
5,000,000,000 ‧

The Doctor possesses a facsimile copy of *Death in the Clouds*, which carries the copyright dates: 'Facsimile of the 1957 Earth edition (Sol 3) Published in the year 5,000,000,000

"Death in the Clouds" first published in Great Britain in 1935'. Presumably the Year 5 Billion facsimile was published on New Earth.

Christie's books are still very popular in the year 2986; Professor Lasky is seen reading *Murder on the Orient Express* in 'Terror Of The Vervoids'.

DURATION

⇨ **Day One (1885)**
It is night (there's a full moon), when Lady Eddison sees the falling star.

⇨ **Day Two (1885)**
Lady Eddison meets Christopher the following day. He gives her the firestone.

⇨ **Day (Thursday, 25 November 1926)**
The break in at the church was 'last Thursday night'.

⇨ **Day One (Friday, 3 December)**
The story takes place over one day and night: Professor Peach is killed at 'quarter past four' (4.15pm) (although for December it is still very light at that hour). Cocktails are served at '4.30', soon after the TARDIS lands. Dinner is served at '10.10pm'.

⇨ **Day Two (Saturday, 4 December)**
It is '12.42am' (on the clock in the dining room) when the Vespiform reveals its true self, and it is destroyed less than an hour later. The Doctor takes Agatha onboard the TARDIS…

⇨ **Day Three**
… and delivers the concussed Agatha to the Harrogate Hotel (she is wearing the same clothes she had on the 'previous' night) where she will be found in ten days' time.

SILENCE IN THE LIBRARY FOREST OF THE DEAD

STORY LINK

Donna makes a passing comment about their going to a 'beach', but the Doctor later says his passing fancy to go to The Library was actually on account of his receiving the unsigned message to go to 'The Library – Come as soon as you can x'. The Doctor also refers to 'wasps'.

OBSERVATIONS

The Doctor's relationship with Professor River Song, strongly hinted at in 'Silence In The Library', presents a few revelations about the Doctor's future. River Song appears to be in her mid-40s [actress Alex Kingston was born in 1963]. She has known the Doctor for a number of years. The last time she saw him was only a few days before her arrival at The Library. This was when he gave her his sonic screwdriver, now modified with a red setting and dampeners. It was during the 'four days' travelling to The Library that she sent a message to 'her' Doctor's psychic paper asking him to meet her there, but the message arrived accidentally at an earlier point in the Doctor's time stream, and it's the tenth Doctor who arrives. It takes River a while to realise that this man is the Doctor.

River has a very full diary recording her travels in the TARDIS and experiences with the Doctor:

- 'Crash of the Byzantium, have we done that yet?'
- 'Picnic at Asgaard? ... Very early days, then'.
- 'Early days yet ...'
- 'You're young ... You're younger than I've ever seen you'.
- 'We go way back, that man and me. Just not this far back'.
- 'He hasn't met me yet. I sent him a message. But it went wrong. It arrived too early. This is the Doctor in the days before he knew me'.
- 'I do know the Doctor. But in the future. His personal future'.
- 'I trust that man to the end of the Universe. And actually, we've been'.
- 'He hasn't met me yet'.
- 'You're hard work when you're young'.
- 'He came when I called, just as he always does. But not my Doctor. Now, my Doctor, I've seen whole armies turn and run away and he'd just swagger back to his TARDIS, and open the doors with a snap of his fingers'.

From the way River describes her travels with the Doctor, one gets the impression that she met up with him periodically over a number of years, rather than her being a full-time travelling companion in the TARDIS. She would call for him (via his psychic paper?) and he'd arrive. But the last time she saw him, it was in the final days of her life:

RIVER: This means you've always known how I was going to die. All the time we'd been together, you knew I was coming here. The last time I saw you, the real you – the future you, I mean – you turned up on my doorstep, with a new haircut and suit. You took me to Darivium to see the singing towers. What a night that was. The towers sang, and you cried. You wouldn't tell me why. But I suppose you knew it was time. My time. Time to come to The Library. You even gave me your screwdriver. That should have been a clue.

The reference to a new haircut and suit strongly implies that she knew a different incarnation (or incarnations?) of the Doctor.

RIVER: If you die here, it'll mean I never met you.
DOCTOR: Time can be rewritten.
RIVER: Not those times. Not one line. Don't you dare ... It's okay. It's not over for you. You'll see me again. You've got all of that to come. You and me. Time and space. You watch us run.

On one of River's previous meetings with him, the Doctor did something he has never done before:

DOCTOR: You know my name. You whispered my name in my ear. There's only one reason I'd ever tell any one my name. There's only one time I could.

It's not clear when the Doctor acquired River's communicator chip containing her 'data ghost'; we don't see what happened to River's body or spacesuit, and the Doctor does not (at least on-screen) retrieve her chip. The Doctor might have the chip with him when he leaves The Library, and which he keeps in a very safe and secure place to await the time he needs to use it, which can only mean that River's 'data ghost' signal must last for quite some time before decaying, unless the Doctor keeps it somewhere so it is safe and protected from the passage of time. Another possibility is that moments after he and Donna leave The Library the post-River a future incarnation of the Doctor's arrives to collect the chip from River's body. That Doctor places the chip in the sonic screwdriver, and then goes to see River for the final time...

TIMELINE DATES

5008 •

The Doctor says it is the 'fifty-first century'. (He is certainly very familiar with this time period, as seen in 'The Empty Child' and 'The Girl In The Fireplace'. It appears that he's been to The Library before, but that would have been before it was sealed off, or if his previous visit was also in the fifty-first century, it would have been after it had been reopened and cleared of the Vashta Nerada.) There is no indication as to when between 5001 and 5100 this story is set. The space suits worn by the expedition team are akin to those worn in 'The Invisible Enemy', which is set in 5000.

I have therefore taken the arbitrary date of 5008 (a Century Factor of 3000 years).

4908

The Library was abandoned 'a hundred years ago'. It has taken the Lux family 'three generations' to decode the seals that have locked The Library. It's even possible that many of the books contained within The Library were deposited there as a preservation measure due to the impending crises about to strike Earth – a second Ice Age ('The Ice Warriors', 'The Talons Of Weng-Chiang'), and solar flares ('The Invisible Enemy', 'The Ark In Space').

DURATION

⇨ **Day One (Ep1-2)**

It is late in the day when the Doctor and Donna arrive in The Library. The sun sets and the moon rises during Ep2. (Donna spends 'seven years' within the CAL construct.)

⇨ **Day Two (Ep2)**

It is daylight again at the end of the story when the 'saved' people are brought back.

MIDNIGHT

STORY LINK

There are no direct links to 'Silence In The Library'. The Doctor is wearing his brown suit.

OBSERVATIONS

- Dee Dee refers to writing a paper on 'the lost moon of Poosh'. This is one of the 27 planetary bodies taken by the Daleks to the Medusa Cascade to power their Reality Bomb ('The Stolen Earth'). With 'Midnight' set in the future, and 'The Stolen Earth' in 2009, the moon would have been removed from its location in time as well as space but subsequently returned to a point in time long after the setting for 'Midnight' (if at all), otherwise it would no longer be lost in Dee Dee's past.

LANGUAGE

When the Doctor speaks French ('Allons-y') and Italian ('molto bene') it is not translated into English and the other passengers hear it exactly as spoken. The Doctor is probably speaking in English, because the creature is able to predict and speak his words.

TIMELINE DATES

3008 *

There is nothing to indicate a date or time period. The passengers on board Crusader 50 appear to be human; they all wear clothing akin to Earth styles from the twentieth or twenty-first centuries. They react to the Doctor's use of 'John Smith'. Jethro knows 'knock knock'/ 'who's there?'. Driver Joe says 'as they used to say in the olden days, wagons roll', and the entertainment system plays 'retro-vids of Earth classics', all of which indicate the Leisure Palace is of Earth origin.

A number of leisure planets are named in 'The Leisure Hive', which is set in 2290. Skye speaks of being jilted by her lover, who moved to a 'different galaxy'. Intergalactic travel was developed in the late 2900s (see 'Terror Of The Vervoids'). The Palace on Midnight may have been established in the early days of intergalactic travel. I have therefore set 'Midnight' in the arbitrary date of 3008, a Century Factor of 1000 years.

DURATION

⇨ **Day One**

The tour was initially going to be an eight hour round trip (the outward trip 'estimated at four hours'), a distance of '500 KLIKS', with the Doctor telling Donna he would be back in time 'for dinner'. The Doctor and the others have been talking by the time they've travelled '98 KLIKS' (which is about 49 minutes). The tour vehicle stops shortly after it has travelled '251 KLIKS' (which is about two hours, half way into the outward trip). The rescue truck is 'an hour' away. '20 MINUTES' after Sky and the hostess are killed, the rescue vehicle is 'three minutes' away. The Doctor is reunited with Donna a few hours later.

TURN LEFT

STORY LINK

There are no direct links to 'Midnight'. The Doctor does, however, refer to The Library when he says to Donna that parallel worlds seem 'to be happening a lot – to you'. In 'The Stolen Earth', the Doctor says he took Donna 'a thousand million light years away'. This might be a reference to 'Planet Of The Ood', 'Silence In The Library', 'Midnight', 'Turn Left' or even 'The Stolen Earth' itself. It could also refer possibly to an off-screen adventure.

OBSERVATIONS

- The Doctor refers to the Trickster, who is the sightless being that removes Sarah Jane from time in 'Whatever Happened To Sarah Jane?' and 'The Temptation Of Sarah Jane Smith', thus creating an alternative timeline.
- Rose's brief appearances in 'Partners In Crime', 'The Sontaran Stratagem' (on the TARDIS monitor), and 'Midnight' (on the Crusader 50 screen), and her four separate encounters with Donna in the parallel world ('Turn Left') are not necessarily displayed in order. She says she's 'crossed far too many realities' to reach Donna. A likely sequence of events is this:
  - In Rose's universe, which is three years 'ahead', they (presumably their version of Torchwood) watch as the stars begin dying and the walls of reality begin to collapse – a precursor to the events in 'The Stolen Earth'. They build a dimension cannon so Rose can be sent back to find the Doctor...
  - Rose attempts indirect contact with the Doctor but fails ('The Sontaran

Stratagem' and 'Midnight').

- Rose uses the dimension cannon to reach the Doctor, but due to the collapsing timelines converging on Donna (although they are not aware of this yet), Rose is instead pulled into Donna's parallel world, where the Doctor has been found dead: 'I shouldn't even be here... This is wrong. This is so wrong'; Rose meets Donna for the first time (the equivalent of 'The Runaway Bride'). Rose returns to her own Universe.

- Back in her own world, Rose undertakes research on Donna, and discovers that she is the epicentre of the collapse.

- Rose goes for a walk, and is pulled back into Donna's world (Rose says 'I was just walking along; that's odd', which means it was accidental rather than planned). But Rose knows more about Donna now from her research (especially the raffle ticket) and tells Donna to get out of London at Christmas...

- Rose makes another trip across the dimensional barrier, but this time she arrives in the *real* Universe, not the parallel, and meets the real Donna. Since this is the 'wrong' Donna, a very sad Rose crosses back to her own dimension... ('Partners In Crime'). (It's not clear why Rose doesn't attempt to contact the Doctor while she is there; it's possible she is operating to a tight schedule, and has to return to her own universe at the appointed time.)

- Off-screen, Rose makes another trip into the parallel, this time contacting UNIT, who have the TARDIS in their possession, informing them of what is happening and how the TARDIS can be used to help prevent the collapse.

- Rose makes another trip ('I've been pulled across from a different Universe'), arriving in the parallel shortly before the Sontaran ship is destroyed, and she warns the parallel Donna about the coming 'darkness'. Rose tells this Donna she will die 'in three weeks'...

- Three weeks later, Rose takes Donna to the warehouse where she has been assisting UNIT with tapping into the dying TARDIS to power the time portal through which Donna is sent across the dimensional barrier and back in time to Monday, 25 June 2007...

- Rose travels back to 25 June herself, and passes on a message for Donna to give to the Doctor...

- Eventually, Rose succeeds in crossing over to the real Earth via the cannon, and is reunited with the Doctor... ('The Stolen Earth').

TIMELINE DATES

2007, June 25 (Monday)

Rose says that the 'moment of intervention' was 'Monday the twenty-fifth, at one minute past ten in the morning'. Donna said this was 'six months' before the events of 'The Runaway Bride', which was 24 December 2007. The only month in 2007 on which the 25th falls on a Monday is June, which is indeed six months prior to Christmas 2007.

The events leading up to 'Army Of Ghosts', from April to May 2007, are referenced when Donna recalls how her friend Alice saw 'the ghost of Earl Mountbatten at the boat show'. In 'The Runaway Bride' Donna says she was skin-diving in Spain when the Cybermen appeared on Earth. Although neither Donna nor Sylvia mention this trip, Donna must have taken the advantage of going to Europe for a few days before starting to look for a new job, possibly because she thought she might not get the chance of taking another break before she started work.

<< 2007, June 25 (Monday) to 2009, August >>

The 'great big parallel world' that Donna experiences spans a period of 27 months – from June 2007 (see Duration below) to at least September 2009 (see 'The Sontaran Stratagem' and 'The Stolen Earth'). Rose says 'It [the beetle] feeds off time, by changing time, by making someone's life take a different turn'... 'The whole world just changed around you'... 'It seems to be in a state of flux'... 'Reality's bending around you'). From a temporal mechanics perspective, Donna is still physically seated in the fortune teller's tent, and yet she is also undergoing the experience of living a whole other life. The very fact that Donna's clothing does not change when she is in the tent proves that for her, the parallel is more of a mental than a physical experience. It's likely that Donna is mentally 'seeing' what her parallel double (Donna2) really is experiencing inside the time bubble. So, while Donna has not travelled back in time, she still experiences the whole 24 month period while seated in the fortune teller's tent. And when Donna2 is sent back in time to Little Sutton Road, she travels back not to Donna's 'turn left / turn right' moment but to Donna2's own equivalent of the same moment.

This Dual Time Line is erased the moment that Donna2 'dies'. Donna wakes back in the real world, but retains the full memory of that 24 month-long second life she experienced in what was really only a matter of just minutes.

In the parallel world, the Doctor2 never meets Donna2, and without her there to stop him, he is killed when the Thames is flooded after he destroys the Empress of Racnoss (as seen in 'The Runaway Bride'). The repercussions of the Doctor2's death ripple out further down the timeline: the following stories take place in the new parallel, but since this timeline is mostly created from Donna's memory, the events do not necessarily occur in exactly the same way as in her 'real' Universe:

- 'Smith And Jones': The Nobles are now living in their new house. Mr Chowdry says the Thames has been closed 'for the past few months ever since that Christmas thing' ('The Runaway Bride'). If only a few months have passed since Christmas then it is probably only March, some three months earlier than in 'Smith And Jones' of the real Universe, which I have set in June 2008. The TV news reports on the disappearance and return of Royal Hope Hospital refer to Martha Jones, Sarah Jane Smith, her son Luke and his friends Maria Jackson and Clyde Langer, all of whom are believed to have been killed. However, a dating of March or even June 2008 is too early for *The Sarah Jane Adventures*, as Maria does not meet Clyde until the start of the new school term in September 2008. One explanation is that the Bane arrive on this Earth much earlier than in the 'real' Universe, and the equivalent events of 'Invasion Of The Bane' and 'Revenge Of The Slitheen' all happen one year earlier, in 2007. Another possible explanation is that this adventure takes place in September, some three months later than in the 'real' Universe. It's clear that Royal Hope is a new hospital; in 'Aliens Of London', the 'space pig' is taken to the nearest hospital, which in March 2006 was the Albion, but Royal Hope is situated across the river from Big Ben where the pig's ship had crashed, and therefore would be the closest. Therefore we can assume that Royal Hope did not exist in March 2006. If it took two years to build, then Royal Hope could be open and running by early 2008. The fact that the Thames river is closed off since Christmas might have affected the completion and opening of Royal Hope by several months. Therefore in this Universe, the Plasmavore might not have arrived on Earth, pursued by the Judoon, until September. (It might have taken up residence in the Albion hospital in June, then moved to the Royal Hope three months later as it had a better supply of blood.) And it is Sarah Jane Smith, with Luke, Maria and Clyde, who all met the first day of the new school term in September, who investigate the presence of the plasma coils around the hospital. [Curiously, this means the Smith of the title is Sarah rather than the Doctor!]
- The Doctor and Martha's deaths in this world must have a flow on effect in relation to the events of stories set in Earth's past, such as the equivalents of 'The Shakespeare Code', 'Daleks In Manhattan' and 'Human Nature'. Clearly these events would have some impact on how events play out in the twenty-first century, which could also explain why the dating of this world's equivalent of 'Smith And Jones' is seemingly out of sync with the same events

in the 'real' N-Space Universe.

- 'The Sound Of Drums': With the Doctor and Martha both dead, they never travelled to Malcassairo, and therefore the Master never came to Earth and became Harold Saxon. This has the flow-on effect in that the events of 'The Lazarus Experiment' never take place, since Saxon was providing funding for Lazarus's experiments.
- 'Partners In Crime': With London destroyed in December 2008, Miss Foster instead sets up her Adipose operation in the United States, resulting in 60 million deaths. With a larger population to exploit, and more pills probably distributed much faster, the activation of the Adipose may have occurred much earlier than it did in Donna's reality (in April rather than June?).
- 'The Sontaran Stratagem': With little petrol available in the dystopian Britain, the Sontarans have instead concentrated their activities in Europe, China and South Africa. It is Torchwood Three who deal with the invaders, resulting in the deaths of Gwen Cooper and Ianto Jones, while Captain Jack Harkness is transported to the Sontaran homeworld.

<<<< 2007, June 25 >>>>

There is also a third timeline glimpsed in this story. In the original timeline, Donna turns left; in the parallel, it is Donna2 who turns right. When Donna2 travels back in time within her own timeline and dies, it is now Donna3, on account of the traffic jam that is not present in the other two parallels, who turns left…

????

There is no indication as to when the scenes set on Shan Shen take place – it might be a future Earth colony based around Oriental culture, or it could be just one small localised sector of the planet. As it does not have any actual bearing on the story, I have placed it in the ???? section of the TIMELINE.

2007, June 26

Presumably Donna starts her new job at H C Clements the day after her interview on the Monday.

DURATION

⇨ Day

It is day on Shan Shen. The Doctor and Donna are there, presumably for only a few hours at the most.

Apart from the scenes set on Shan Shen, this story takes place within a parallel Universe (marked B) spanning a period of 27 months (25 June 2007 to September 2009), although for Donna this lasts only a matter of minutes. We see nine separate moments experienced by the parallel Donna2. The events that Donna sees and witnesses within this parallel Universe do not necessarily reflect exactly the same events that occur in her 'real' world (A) – see Observations above:

⇨ **Day A1 (25 June 2007)**
At 'one minute past ten' Donna turns left...

⇨ **Day B1 (25 June 2007)**
At 'one minute past ten' Donna2 turns right...

⇨ **(26 June 2007)**
Donna2 begins her new job at Mr Chowdry's...

🕐 **Six months pass...**

⇨ **Day B2 (24 December 2007)**
On 'Christmas Eve' Donna2 sees the Christmas Star, and meets Rose for the first time.

🕐 **Months later...**

⇨ **Day B3 (2008)**
Mr Chowdry gives Donna2 the sack. The Royal Hope Hospital vanishes, only to return a few hours later 'this afternoon'. Donna2 meets Rose for a second time that night.

⇨ **Months pass...**

⇨ **Day B4 (24 December 2008)**
Donna2, Sylvia2 and Wilf2 arrive at the posh hotel on Christmas Eve.

⇨ **Day B5 (25 December 2008)**
Shortly before '10am' on Christmas Day, the *Titanic* explodes destroying London.

🕐 **Three months later...**

⇨ **Day B6 (March 2009)** ▬ ▬ ▬ ▬ ▬ ▬ ▬ ▬ ▬

After 'three months' housed in a hostel, Donna2, Sylvia2 and Wilf2 are relocated to Leeds.

⇨ **Day B7 (April? 2009)** ▬ ▬ ▬ ▬ ▬ ▬ ▬ ▬ ▬

Reports come in from America that 60 million are dead when their fat comes to life.

⇨ **Day B8 (August 2009)** ▬ ▬ ▬ ▬ ▬ ▬ ▬ ▬ ▬

After a sing-a-long, and witnessing soldiers attacking the runaway ATMOS devices on their trucks, Donna2 takes a walk, and meets Rose for a third time. She tells Donna2 about the Sontarans, Torchwood, the approaching darkness – and that in 'three weeks' Donna2 is going to die…

🕐 **Three weeks pass…** ▬ ▬ ▬ ▬ ▬ ▬ ▬ ▬ ▬

⇨ **Day B9 (September 2009)** ▬ ▬ ▬ ▬ ▬ ▬ ▬ ▬ ▬

The Colasantos are taken to a labour camp. That night, Donna2 and Wilf2 see the stars going out. Rose returns, and takes Donna2 to the UNIT warehouse. Donna2 is sent back in time to 25 June 2007

⇨ **Day B1 (25 June 2007)** ▬ ▬ ▬ ▬ ▬ ▬ ▬ ▬ ▬

… Donna2 arrives at '9.57'. She is killed shortly before '10.00'…

⇨ **Day C1 (25 June 2007)** ▬ ▬ ▬ ▬ ▬ ▬ ▬ ▬ ▬

At 'one minute past ten', because of the traffic jam, Donna3 turns left…

THE STOLEN EARTH
JOURNEY'S END

+STORY LINK

'The Stolen Earth' takes place straight after 'Turn Left', with the TARDIS landing on Earth soon after leaving Shan Shen. Both the Doctor and Donna are wearing the same clothes they do in 'Turn Left'. Wilf says the last time Donna phoned home, she was on the planet Midnight (which is one of the locations at which Rose tried to contact the Doctor – see 'Midnight').

Jack, Gwen and Ianto appear in 'The Stolen Earth'. When confronted with a Dalek in the Hub, Gwen shouts she wants to 'go out fighting, like Owen, like Tosh', both of whom died recently in 'Exit Wounds'. (Gwen rings Rhys to check that he is all right.) Jack knows about Project Indigo, having learned about the device from a UNIT soldier he met in a bar. (This would have been shortly after 'The Sontaran Stratagem').

Jack tells Sarah he's been 'following your work. Nice job with the Slitheen', so from her and Luke's viewpoint, this is after 'The Lost Boy'. The Verron soothsayer that gave Sarah the warp star crystal also gave her the memory box in 'Whatever Happened To Sarah Jane?' Clearly the soothsayer knew of what was going to happen to the Earth later that year. (Luke phones Maria, who is in Cornwall with her father, Alan; Clyde is home with his mother.)

DALEK LINK

Davros was last seen making an exit in his escape pod in 'Remembrance Of The Daleks' in November 1963. (Davros recognises Sarah, whom he recalls seeing on Skaro 'all these years' ago in 'Genesis Of The Daleks'; for him this was some 4,363 years ago.) Davros must have been rescued by Daleks loyal to him, and over time he has been given a new mobile life-support unit and mechanical arm. In the first year of the Time War, his command ship flew into the jaws of the Nightmare Child at the Gates of Elysium. The Doctor was there, but is unable to save Davros. The Doctor is unaware that Davros is saved by Dalek Caan, who had emerged back into the War after having made an emergency temporal shift from 1930…

At the end of 'Daleks In Manhattan', Dalek Caan makes an emergency temporal shift. But the mechanism is damaged, and he emerges into the midst of the time-locked Time War, specifically the first year of the War; he 'flew into the wild and fire' and 'danced and died a thousand times'. At the Gates of Elysium, he rescues Davros's command ship as it fell into the jaws of the Nightmare Child. Although he had been driven insane, Caan acquires prophetic abilities, and has seen the Daleks' ultimate future: 'I saw the Daleks. What we have done throughout time and space. I saw the truth of us… And I decreed no more'. To this end he tricks Davros into growing a new Dalek army from his own flesh, as well as creating the Crucible and the Reality Bomb. And through his manipulation of the timelines, he brings the Doctor and Donna together (as seen in 'The Runaway Bride') to fulfil the destiny that he has foreseen, that of 'The Threefold Man' (the Doctor, the other Doctor, and the Doctor/Donna) who would bring about the destruction of the Daleks.

The 27 planets selected by the Daleks to power the Reality Bomb include Earth; Callufrax Minor (not necessarily related to the similarly spelt planet Calufrax seen in 'The Pirate Planet'); Jahoo; Shallacatop; Woman Wept (visited by the ninth Doctor and Rose some time prior to 'Boom Town'); Clom (home of the Abzorbaloff ('Love &

Monsters')); Pyrovillia ('The Fires Of Pompeii'); Adipose 3 (the nursery planet of the Adipose – 'Partners In Crime'); and the moon of Poosh ('Midnight').

OBSERVATIONS

- The Doctor seemingly uses one his regenerations but doesn't change form because the process is interrupted when the Doctor siphons off the excess energy into his severed hand. This raises the question, when is a regeneration not a regeneration? A Time Lord has only twelve regenerations, therefore thirteen lives. But surely even if a regeneration begins but doesn't go full term, the fact that the process itself has started must mean that whatever organ or gland that initiates the process must now be less one of the twelve triggers that it controls? (If one suppresses a sneeze, the body has still initiated the muscular contractions that cause one to sneeze.) But given the events of the Time War, it's entirely possible that the Doctor is already the recipient of a new regenerative cycle – and perhaps even an unlimited one. The fact that the Master was able to regenerate in 'Utopia' and suppressed his ability to regenerate in 'The Sound Of Drums', indicates that he possesses a new regenerative cycle, given to him when he was resurrected by the Time Lords to fight in the Time War. If this was the case, then it's entirely likely that all Time Lords and other Gallifreyans who fought in the War were given permanent regenerative cycles, given that the rate of casualties would be high, and the Time Lords would need to have a continual 'supply' of soldiers who had unlimited regenerations. If the Doctor was there during the first year of the War, he would have been one of the first to receive this new cycle. This might also explain how it was possible for the Doctor's severed hand to re-grow 15 hours after his regeneration, the replacement of lost limbs being an additional benefit. Of note, the Master is able to suspend the Doctor's 'capacity to regenerate', and forces the Doctor to live '900 years', eventually emerging as a wizened dwarf-like figure. Is this a side-effect of this new regenerative process? Do the new cycles last for only 900 years? (This is explored in more detail under THE DOCTOR'S AGE.)
- It's worth noting that the Doctor's severed hand is actually one year older than he is. The Doctor was 900 when he lost the hand in 'The Christmas Invasion'. The hand is in Jack's possession from late December 2006 to mid-March 2008 (nearly 15 months). The Master takes it when he steals the TARDIS and leaves Malcassairo in 'Utopia', and keeps it with him while he is on Earth – from September 2006 through until the June 2008 Election (21 months). From December 2006 to March 2008 there are 'two' hands on Earth. The hand is on

the *Valiant* during the year that the Master rules over the Earth (12 months). That's 48 months in all, making the hand 904 years old. The Doctor reclaims the hand at the end of 'The Sound Of Drums', by which time he is three years older than he was when he first lost it – 903 (see THE DOCTOR'S AGE). The Doctor keeps the hand in the TARDIS between 'The Sound Of Drums' and 'The Stolen Earth', during which time he ages another year; he is '904' in 'The Stolen Earth', the hand is therefore 905.

- The Daleks remove 27 planetary bodies, three of which, Adipose 3, Pyrovillia and the lost moon of Poosh, are also taken from time (two from the past and one from the future). It's not clear why the Daleks should need to take these planets out of time when they should exist in the present. It's possible they have been destroyed or perhaps lost size or mass by 2009. And since these planets were the only known and accessible specimens with the precise size and mass needed by the Daleks to power the Reality Bomb, they had no option but to remove the three planets from time as well as space. At the end of the story when all the planets are returned, in the case of Pyrovillia, Adipose 3 and the moon of Poosh, they would have to be sent into time zones different from that which they had originally come otherwise they would never have been missing in the first place; specifically Pyrovillia, which had been missing for 'two thousand years', and the moon of Posh, which was still 'lost' in the year 3008.

- On a similar note, when Earth is returned to its orbit, it must have been a precision operation, given that the planet would have to be positioned exactly to the correct orbital tilt, angle of rotation, day/night cycle, and with the moon positioned correctly to its correct lunar cycle so tides are not affected. There is also the fact that the Earth has some 3,000 satellites in orbit around it – were these moved with the planet? (See 'The Last Sontaran' for more on this problem.)

- The Doctor erases from Donna's memory all traces of him and the TARDIS; but what of her mobile phone? The phone had 'universal roaming' installed on it, while the sim card and recent calls menu would record all calls made to and from the ship. Did the Doctor erase those menus as well? If so, he must have done it off-screen… And what of all the suitcases and clothes that Donna brought on board the TARDIS in 'Partners In Crime'? Would she wonder where they had all gone?

- With 'Invasion Of The Bane' set in August 2008 and 'The Stolen Earth' in September 2009 (see below), that means K9 has been inside the safe sealing the black hole for at least 30 months…

- With swarms of Dalek ships sweeping over the skies of New York, and Daleks patrolling the streets of London, and across the hills of central Europe, how is it that three years later, in 2012, Henry Van Statten and his staff at the Geocomtex base in Utah do not know what the 'Metaltron' really is? Or is it because time is in flux, and with only certain events in history fixed (see 'The Fires Of Pompeii'), the Daleks have successfully changed history by invading Earth in 2009? (See 'Dalek' for more on this.)

LANGUAGE

The Daleks use 'Rels' as a measurement of time, which seems to be the equivalent of a second. When the Doctor arrives at the Shadow Proclamation ship, he speaks to the Judoon troopers in their own language. The size of the missing planets is measured by the Shadow Proclamation in units of 'kelix', while mass is measured in 'gaats'. Atmosphere is measured by 'olb'. The Daleks speak German when they invade Germany. Martha understands the woman when she speaks German.

TIMELINE DATES

2009, September 12

When Rose arrives on Earth, she observes chaos and rioting in the streets of London. A poster on a shop wall advertises 'DANCE NIGHT' on 'FRIDAY 25TH July', which is 'CAMDEN'S SUMMER ALL NIGHTER'. 25 July falls on a Friday in 2008. But the year must be 2009 – see 'Fragments', 'Exit Wounds' and 'Partners In Crime' (and THE YEAR AHEAD RULE (2005 TO 2009)). [We can assume that it was intended to set this story around July of the 'present day', but that the props department forgot the 'year ahead' rule, and put the wrong date on the poster. In terms of my A/1, B/2 reliability scale, we have to accept that this poster is an old one, and has been on the wall since July of the previous year. Maybe the shop sells old posters, and these ones from the previous year are simply display items?]

Pinpointing 'The Stolen Earth' down to a specific month is reliant on a number of factors: Harriet Jones develops the Subwave network from work created by the 'Mr Copper Foundation', presumably referring to same elderly *Titanic* survivor who stayed on Earth at the end of 'Voyage Of The Damned'. But when did he set up the Foundation, and for how long has it been operating? If it is some sort of trust fund financing scientific development, it would require far more than the one million pounds that Copper had available on his credit card account. In reality, such a foundation would take years to set up.

Gwen Cooper refers to her fallen comrades, Tosh and Owen, who were killed in 'Exit Wounds'. But how long has Torchwood Three been down two vital members?

Would Jack really have waited several months before finding suitable replacements? The fact that he seemingly offers Martha Jones a job with Torchwood does beg the question of why has not previously offered her the position. (Or is it that with her being reassigned to New York he did not know how to contact her?)

Another factor to be taken into account is Project Indigo, a one-person experimental teleport device 'salvaged from the Sontarans', presumably following the events of 'The Sontaran Stratagem'. Martha has been promoted to Medical Officer in charge of the project, and she is now based in UNIT New York. One would think that Project Indigo would have taken several months if not years of research and development to even reach the stage of a functioning workable model. When Martha tries to ring the Doctor in the TARDIS, she rings him relative to the same amount of time that has passed on Earth as well as in the TARDIS. (See '42' and 'The Sound Of Drums'.)

The bees disappearing also needs to be taken into consideration; this is a recent phenomenon, one that started shortly before 'Partners In Crime', and the nature of which is directly related to the events in 'The Stolen Earth'.

Luke Smith is said to be '14' in 'Revenge Of The Slitheen' (set in September 2008; he was 'born' in August 2008), and in 'The Stolen Earth' Sarah says Luke is 'only 14', which places that story no later than August 2009 – otherwise Luke would be 15.

When the Doctor erases Donna's memory of him, he would have to delete everything that she did from 'Partners In Crime' to 'The Stolen Earth', which bridges several days between 'Partners In Crime' and 'The Sontaran Stratagem', and however many days or weeks between 'The Sontaran Stratagem' and 'The Stolen Earth', but in such a way that Donna wouldn't question why she has no recollection of the past few days, weeks or months; and given that her friends would probably at some stage talk about the Adipose, the Sontarans, the *Titanic*, and that the Earth had been 'stolen' while in her company, she would not be able to recall why she did not witness any of these events.

Finally, we also need to factor in 'The Last Sontaran' and 'The Day Of The Clown', in which it is established that the months are August and October, with a gap of no less than 'six weeks' between the two. 'The Last Sontaran' itself is set shortly after 'The Sontaran Stratagem'.

So, taking all of these clues onboard, 'The Stolen Earth' is probably set a month or so after 'Partners In Crime'. We have to accept that Project Indigo was ready within a very short period of time, and that Torchwood has been without any new members for five or so months. In the absence of contradictory evidence (Luke's age is still a bit of an anomaly), I have tentatively set 'The Stolen Earth' in September 2009. The milkman confirms that it is 'Saturday'; Saturdays in September 2009 are the 5th, 12th, 19th and 26th; of these, and taking into account everything noted above, the best date for 'The Stolen Earth' is Saturday, 12 September 2009.

2009 = <<2012, September>>

The Doctor says Rose's Universe is 'running ahead of this Universe', and as a result they've 'seen the future' (which means they've seen the stars dying, the first stage of the Reality Bomb wavelength breaking through the rift at the heart of the Medusa Cascade and destroying all the other dimensions and parallels). As covered under 'Rise Of The Cybermen', movement between the two Universes must always remain at a constant, so while two years have passed since 'Army Of Ghosts' and it's 2009 on Donna's world, two years have also passed on Rose's world, making it 2012 there. (Presumably Harriet Jones is still the President of Great Britain in that world.) Jackie and Pete's son, named Tony, must be two years old. Jackie says Pete is on the nursery run, which confirms that Tony is only a very young child. And to further support that only a few years have elapsed, Mickey says his gran 'spent her last years living in a mansion'.

DURATION

⇨ Day One (Ep1-2)

It is a 'Saturday' morning at 'eight o'clock' when Earth is taken to the Medusa Cascade (at the 'exact same moment' as the 26 other planets). The story takes place over several hours (the dimension jumpers that Jackie and Mickey use take 'half an hour' to recharge). It is later that same day that the Earth is returned to its orbit. The Doctor bids farewell to his friends. It is night when the Doctor takes Donna home.

THE NEXT DOCTOR

STORY LINK

Any amount of time (days, weeks, months) could have passed since the Doctor left Donna at the end of 'The Stolen Earth'. He mentions her in passing, when reflecting about his companions leaving: 'some of them forget me', which also applies to Jamie and Zoe ('The War Games').

CYBUSMAN LINK

The Cybermen and Daleks were sucked back into the Void in 'Army Of Ghosts'. In 'The Next Doctor', the Doctor surmises that the two factions probably battled within the dimension before everything in the Void perished, following the events of 'The Stolen Earth'. The Cybermen stole from the Daleks a cache of info-stamps (one of which contained a book of knowledge about the Doctor) and a dimension vault. But 'as the walls of the world weakened, the last of the Cybermen must have fallen through the dimensions, back in time', emerging in London, 'out of the sky in a blaze of light', three weeks prior to Christmas. The first humans they encountered were Jackson Lake, his wife Christine and young son Frederic... In a three week period, and with Miss Hartigan's help, they secretly constructed a Cyber-King Dreadnought Class vessel (with a Cyber factory within its chest) beneath the Thames. All they needed was a work force to power the machine. (Presumably one of their number was assigned the rank of Leader soon on arrival, and painted black accordingly, as no Cyberman was seen in 'Army Of Ghosts' with this particular insignia.)

OBSERVATIONS

- Despite the fact that much of central London near the Thames was flattened beneath the feet of the Cyber-King, there is no historical record of this incident. Interestingly, when the Cybermen of the N-Space Universe invade Earth in 1970, they walk down steps near St Paul's Cathedral, which was one of the buildings spared from destruction by the Cyber-King in 1851...

TIMELINE DATES

1851, December 24 – 25 *
The date is given by the youth the Doctor meets in the street: 'Christmas Eve ... Year of Our Lord, 1851'. The Cyber-King rises in the early hours of Christmas Day.

1851 *
The Doctor has been to 1851 before – he says 'Nice year, bit dull'.

1851, December
Jackson Lake says he and his family came to London 'three weeks ago'. This would be the first week of December. The Cybermen had also only just recently arrived in this time period at that time.

Jackson says he has been hunting the Cyber-shades 'for a good fortnight, now'.

DURATION

⇨ **Day One (24 December 1851)**
The Doctor arrives on 'Christmas Eve'. The funeral is at 'two o'clock'. Big Ben strikes 'midnight'...

⇨ **Day Two (25 December 1851)** ▨ ▨ ▨ ▨ ▨ ▨ ▨ ▨ ▨

It is in the early hours of Christmas morning ('the Cyber-King will rise tonight' rather than 'at dawn' as was planned) that the Cybermen are defeated. The Doctor is invited to a celebratory meal with Jackson Lake.

2009 OVERVIEW

The bulk of *Timelink* covers the televised stories of *Doctor Who* and its two spin-offs as broadcast to the end of 2008 only. This brief overview summarises some of the continuity highlights of the four additional specials that screened between April 2009 and 1 January 2010, taking the coverage up to the end of the tenth Doctor's era.

DOCTOR WHO

'PLANET OF THE DEAD'

The story is set at Easter. Mention is made of planets in the sky, which is a reference to not only 'The Stolen Earth' (set in 2009) but also 'The End Of Time'. Depending on whether 'The End Of Time' is set at Christmas of 2009 (the same year as 'The Stolen Earth') or 2010, then this is Easter of 2010 or 2011. I favour setting 'The End Of Time' in 2009, so 'Planet Of The Dead' is Easter 2010. Easter Sunday of 2010 fell on 4 April. The story is set over one evening, presumably in the week prior to the Easter holiday weekend. The Cup of Athelstan is also referred to in 'Mona Lisa's Revenge'.

'THE WATERS OF MARS'

The date 21 November 2059 is given in dialogue and by on-screen visuals. Captain Adelaide Brooke is said to have been 10 when she saw the Dalek, which places the events of 'The Stolen Earth' no earlier than 2009, and yet, the onscreen biographical profile of the Captain states that the Dalek invasion was in '2008', an example of The Year Ahead Rule not being applied correctly. We could explain the 'error' by saying that the computer record was written long after the fact, and that the accuracy of the dates in the record had become corrupted over time.

'THE END OF TIME'

Set on 24 and 25 December (although Rassilon incorrectly claims that the whole world was waking up to Christmas on the day that Gallifrey returned, when in actual fact those countries west of the International Date Line were celebrating Boxing Day on 26 December). The year is not given. If this is the Christmas following the events of 'The Stolen Earth', then it's 2009. But if it's the Christmas following 'Planet Of The Dead', then it's December 2010. The reference to 'planets in the sky' in 'Planet Of The Dead' can just as equally apply to either of those other two stories. I tend to favour it being Christmas 2009, as that means it has been only three months - rather than 15 - since Wilf last saw the Doctor...

Lucy Saxon has therefore been in prison for well over a year since the 'The Sound Of Drums', which was set in June 2008. Rose encounters the tenth Doctor on 1 January 2005, which now firmly cements the dating for 'Rose' and confirms that The Year Ahead Rule begins in 2006.

Barack Obama is the President of the United States of America. He is presumably still in office in election year 2012, and is therefore the incumbent of whom Henry van Statten expressed his dislike (see 'Dalek').

The Doctor is now aged 906. He was 903 in 'Voyage Of The Damned', meaning that very long inter-story gaps exist between 'Voyage Of The Damned' and 'Partners In Crime'; 'The Stolen Earth' and 'The Next Doctor'; 'The Next Doctor' and 'Planet Of The Dead'; and 'Planet of the Dead' and 'The Waters Of Mars'. The Tenth Doctor's other (off-screen) encounter with Queen Elizabeth I takes place between 'The Waters Of Mars' and 'The End Of Time'. The Doctor's reunion with his old companion Sarah (in 'The Wedding of Sarah Jane Smith') probably takes place between 'Planet Of The Dead' and 'The Waters Of Mars'.

An observation regarding Gallifrey: it breaks free from the time-lock during the ninth Doctor's timestream (he was 900), but the planet's emergence is during the tenth Doctor's timestream, some six years later.

Despite 100 years having passed since 'Planet Of The Ood', Ood Sigma still wears his Ood Operations overalls!

Donna's forthcoming wedding is in the 'spring'; the year would therefore be 2010. The appearance of Midshipman Frame at the space bar indicates that the brief scene with Jack must take place relative to Frame's timeline – sometime after 'Voyage Of The Damned', which is December 2008. Jack left Torchwood in March 2010 ('Children Of Earth'); the Doctor deactivated his vortex manipulator's time-travel capabilities in 'The Sound Of Drums', but it can still be used spatially, so it is probably 2010. The fact that a battle-dressed Hath also appears in the bar supports my placement of 'The Doctor's Daughter' in the present day rather than the future.

Sarah and Luke see the Doctor again, which must be after his appearance at her 'wedding' ('The Wedding Of Sarah Jane Smith'). This short scene takes place a day or so after Christmas.

When the tenth Doctor begins regenerating, it is his right hand that displays the first bursts of regenerative energy. This is odd given that that hand is actually 15 hours younger than the rest of this body - his original right hand having been cut off by the Sycorax Commander in 'The Christmas Invasion'.

2010 OVERVIEW

The adventures of the eleventh Doctor, as played by Matt Smith, began in 2010.

THE ELEVENTH DOCTOR

All the present-day adventures of the Eleventh Doctor's debut season take place on or around 25 and 26 June 2010.

THE DOCTOR'S FUTURE

BEYOND THE ELEVENTH...

As previously noted, it's possible that the Doctor had been given a whole new regeneration cycle during the Time War, and therefore he is not necessarily restricted to the previously dictated limitation of only thirteen lives...

THE TIME OF MERLIN

In 'Battlefield', we learn that a future incarnation of the Doctor calling himself Merlin, lives for a time in a 'sideways' dimension (arriving there a number of years prior to the Earth year AD 792). That Doctor still has the (or a) TARDIS because Ancelyn knows 'the ship of time' is 'larger within than without'. Morgaine knows that 'Merlin' has 'worn many faces', which implies that the Doctor regenerates at least twice in that dimension, or it was due to her great mental powers that she senses that the Doctor has lived a number of previous lives.

'Merlin' is often defeated at chess by Morgaine. It is at the battle of Baden, that 'Merlin' casts down Morgaine 'with his mighty arts'. The 'Merlin' Doctor is eventually tricked by Morgaine and sealed 'into the ice caves for all eternity', but not before secretly placing Arthur's body in a spaceship at the bottom of a lake on Earth in the Earth year 792, and leaving secret messages for his seventh self to find...

If the 'Merlin' Doctor is a much later incarnation, say the eleventh or twelfth, it might even have been spending untold centuries bound in the ice caves that drives the

Doctor into becoming the Valeyard...

THE LORD OF A TIME TRIAL

The Valeyard is described by the Master as being an amalgamation of the Doctor's darker sides of his nature, somewhere between his twelfth and final incarnation. If the Doctor *has* been empowered with a second regenerative cycle, then the period from which the Valeyard originates could potentially be hundreds of years along the Doctor's future time stream...

But if the Doctor has got only two regenerations left (assuming he didn't waste one in 'The Stolen Earth') then the time of the Valeyard is drawing nearer...

STORY ORDER

If you are keen to watch *Doctor Who* stories on video – or read the novelisations – in the same order as presented in the TIMELINE chapter, the following is a quick guide to that order.

KEY

STORY TITLE IN UPPER CASE
When a story is split between more than one time zone, I have used an UPPER CASE story title to represent the date in which the greater portion of the whole story is set. The figures in brackets indicate the episode/s in which that the time zone features.

STORY TITLE IN LOWER CASE
When a story is split between more than one time zone, I have used a Lower Case font to represent the date in which lesser portion of the whole story is set. The figures in brackets indicate the episode/s in which that the time zone features.

In terms of the Dalek stories that use time travel, such as 'The Chase' and 'The Daleks' Master Plan', UPPER CASE story titles are positioned according to when the time travel *originated* in terms of Dalek history.

15 BILL BC	Castrovalva (1-2)		79	THE FIRES OF POMPEII
5 BILL BC	INSIDE THE SPACESHIP		300	GENESIS OF THE DALEKS
4.6 BILL BC	The Runaway Bride		900	THE DALEKS
400 MILL BC	City Of Death (4)		1066	THE TIME MEDDLER
140 MILL BC	CASTROVALVA (2-4)		1191	THE CRUSADE
			1215	THE KING'S DEMONS
140 MILL BC	TIME-FLIGHT (1-4)		1274	THE TIME WARRIOR (1-4)
65 MILL BC	Earthshock (4)		1289	MARCO POLO
12 MILL BC	Image Of The Fendahl (4)		1450	THE AZTECS
100,000 BC	100,000 BC (2-4)		1492	THE MASQUE OF MANDRAGORA
2700 BC	The Daleks' Master Plan (9-10)		1505	City Of Death (2-3)
1527 BC	The Time Monster (2-3/5-6)		1572	THE MASSACRE ...
1188 BC	THE MYTH MAKERS		1599	THE SHAKESPEARE CODE
27	Torchwood: Exit Wounds		1638	Silver Nemesis (1/3)
64	THE ROMANS		1663	The War Games (10)

1665	Colony In Space (1)	1951	SARAH JANE ADVENTURES: THE TEMPTATION OF SARAH JANE SMITH
	THE THREE DOCTORS (1-4)		
1666	THE VISITATION	1953	THE IDIOT'S LANTERN
1672	THE SMUGGLERS	1959	DELTA AND THE BANNERMEN (1-3)
1727	The Girl In The Fireplace		
1745	The Girl In The Fireplace	1962	THE DEADLY ASSASSIN
1746	THE HIGHLANDERS	1963	UNDERWORLD
1753	The Girl In The Fireplace		THE INVASION OF TIME
1758	The Girl In The Fireplace		100,000 BC (1)
1794	THE REIGN OF TERROR		REMEMBRANCE OF THE DALEKS
1813	THE MARK OF THE RANI	1964	PLANET OF GIANTS
1851	THE NEXT DOCTOR		Sarah Jane Adventures: Whatever Happened To Sarah Jane?
1866	The Evil Of The Daleks (2-6)		
1869	THE UNQUIET DEAD		
1872	THE PIRATE PLANET	1965	The Massacre (4)
	The Chase (3)		The Daleks' Master Plan (7/8)
1879	TOOTH AND CLAW	1966	The Chase (3)
1881	THE GUNFIGHTERS		THE WAR MACHINES (1-4)
1883	GHOST LIGHT		THE FACELESS ONES (1-6)
1885	Timelash (1)		The Three Doctors (1)
1892	THE TALONS OF WENG-CHIANG		The Five Doctors
			The War Machines (4)
1902	HORROR OF FANG ROCK		The Faceless Ones (6)
1911	PYRAMIDS OF MARS		The Evil Of The Daleks (1-2)
1913	HUMAN NATURE	1967	THE WEB OF FEAR
1917	THE WAR GAMES (1-9)	1970	THE DOMINATORS
1925	BLACK ORCHID		THE MIND ROBBER
1926	THE UNICORN AND THE WASP		THE INVASION
			SPEARHEAD FROM SPACE
1929	The Daleks' Master Plan (7)		DOCTOR WHO AND THE SILURIANS
1930	DALEKS IN MANHATTAN		
1935	THE ABOMINABLE SNOWMEN		THE AMBASSADORS OF DEATH
1941	Torchwood: Captain Jack Harkness	1971	INFERNO
			TERROR OF THE AUTONS
	THE EMPTY CHILD	1972	The Ribos Operation (1)
1943	THE CURSE OF FENRIC		

	THE ARMAGEDDON FACTOR
	THE MIND OF EVIL
	THE CLAWS OF AXOS
	Colony In Space (1/6)
1973	THE DÆMONS
	DAY OF THE DALEKS (1-2/4)
	THE SEA DEVILS
	The Mutants (1)
	THE TIME MONSTER (1-4/6)
	The Three Doctors (1-2/4)
	CARNIVAL OF MONSTERS
1974	THE GREEN DEATH
	The Time Warrior (1)
	INVASION OF THE DINOSAURS
	The Five Doctors
1975	PLANET OF THE SPIDERS (1-6)
	ROBOT
	TERROR OF THE ZYGONS
	THE ANDROID INVASION
	THE SEEDS OF DOOM
1976	THE HAND OF FEAR
1977	Mawdryn Undead (2-3/4)
1978	THE STONES OF BLOOD
	IMAGE OF THE FENDAHL (1-4)
1979	CITY OF DEATH (1-4)
	The Five Doctors
1980	The Leisure Hive (1)
1981	Time-Flight (1/4)
	WARRIORS' GATE
	THE KEEPER OF TRAKEN
	FOUR TO DOOMSDAY
	KINDA

	LOGOPOLIS
	Castrovalva (1)
	K9 AND COMPANY
1983	MEGLOS
	FULL CIRCLE
	ARC OF INFINITY
	SNAKEDANCE
	MAWDRYN UNDEAD (1-4)
	TERMINUS
	ENLIGHTENMENT
	THE FIVE DOCTORS
1984	Resurrection Of The Daleks (1-2)
	Planet Of Fire (1)
	THE AWAKENING
	THE TWO DOCTORS
1985	Attack Of The Cybermen (1)
1986	THE TENTH PLANET
	The Power Of The Daleks (1)
1987	DRAGONFIRE
	SURVIVAL
	FATHER'S DAY
1988	SILVER NEMESIS (1-3)
1992	BATTLEFIELD
1995	FURY FROM THE DEEP
1996	The Chase (4)
1999	DOCTOR WHO (THE TV MOVIE)
2000	PLANET OF FIRE (1-4)
2004	RISE OF THE CYBERMEN
2005	ROSE
2006	ALIENS OF LONDON
	BOOM TOWN
	Bad Wolf
	THE CHRISTMAS INVASION
	New Earth

2007	Love & Monsters
	SCHOOL REUNION
	Rise Of The Cybermen
	BLINK
	LOVE & MONSTERS
	ARMY OF GHOSTS
	Turn Left
	TORCHWOOD: EVERYTHING CHANGES
	TORCHWOOD: DAY ONE
	TORCHWOOD: GHOST MACHINE
	TORCHWOOD: CYBERWOMAN
	TORCHWOOD: SMALL WORLDS
	TORCHWOOD: COUNTRYCIDE
	TORCHWOOD: GREEKS BEARING GIFTS
	TORCHWOOD: THEY KEEP KILLING SUZIE
	TORCHWOOD: RANDOM SHOES
	TORCHWOOD: OUT OF TIME
	Army Of Ghosts
	THE RUNAWAY BRIDE
	TORCHWOOD: COMBAT
2008	Blink
	Torchwood: Adrift
	TORCHWOOD: CAPTAIN JACK HARKNESS
	TORCHWOOD: END OF DAYS
	Utopia
	SMITH AND JONES
	THE LAZARUS EXPERIMENT
	42

	THE SOUND OF DRUMS
	TORCHWOOD: KISS KISS, BANG BANG
	TORCHWOOD: SLEEPER
	TORCHWOOD: TO THE LAST MAN
	TORCHWOOD: MEAT
	TORCHWOOD: ADAM
	SARAH JANE ADVENTURES: INVASION OF THE BANE
	SARAH JANE ADVENTURES: REVENGE OF THE SLITHEEN
	TORCHWOOD: RESET
	TORCHWOOD: DEAD MAN WALKING
	TORCHWOOD: A DAY IN THE DEATH
	TORCHWOOD: SOMETHING BORROWED
	SARAH JANE ADVENTURES: EYE OF THE GORGON
	TORCHWOOD: FROM OUT OF THE RAIN
	TORCHWOOD: ADRIFT
	SARAH JANE ADVENTURES: WARRIORS OF KUDLAK
	SARAH JANE ADVENTURES: WHATEVER HAPPENED TO SARAH JANE?
	SARAH JANE ADVENTURES: THE LOST BOY
	VOYAGE OF THE DAMNED
2009	TORCHWOOD: FRAGMENTS
	TORCHWOOD: EXIT WOUNDS
	PARTNERS IN CRIME

	THE SONTARAN STRATAGEM		2113	TIMELASH (1-2)
	THE DOCTOR'S DAUGHTER		2114	THE TRIAL OF A TIME LORD
	SARAH JANE ADVENTURES: THE LAST SONTARAN		2116	THE CREATURE FROM THE PIT
	THE STOLEN EARTH			NIGHTMARE OF EDEN
	Sarah Jane Adventures: Secrets Of The Stars			THE HORNS OF NIMON
	TORCHWOOD: CHILDREN OF EARTH		2120	THE POWER OF THE DALEKS
	Sarah Jane Adventures: The Last Sontaran		2150	THE SPACE PIRATES
	SARAH JANE ADVENTURES: THE DAY OF THE CLOWN		(2173)	Day Of The Daleks (1/3-4))
			2174	THE DALEK INVASION OF EARTH
	SARAH JANE ADVENTURES: SECRETS OF THE STARS		2200	THE TWIN DILEMMA
	SARAH JANE ADVENTURES: THE MARK OF THE BERSERKER		2215	THE CHASE (1-2)
			2290	THE LEISURE HIVE (1-4)
	SARAH JANE ADVENTURES: THE TEMPTATION OF SARAH JANE SMITH		2324	VENGEANCE ON VAROS
			2378	THE ANDROIDS OF TARA
			2379	MINDWARP
	SARAH JANE ADVENTURES: ENEMY OF THE BANE		2472	COLONY IN SPACE (1-6)
			2494	THE RESCUE
2010	Torchwood: Children of Earth		2525	REVENGE OF THE CYBERMEN
2012	FEAR HER		2526	THE TOMB OF THE CYBERMEN
	DALEK			EARTHSHOCK
2017	THE ENEMY OF THE WORLD			Time-Flight (1)
2040	PARADISE TOWERS		2530	ATTACK OF THE CYBERMEN (1-2)
2070	THE UNDERWATER MENACE		2540	FRONTIER IN SPACE
	THE MOONBASE			PLANET OF THE DALEKS
2080	THE WHEEL IN SPACE		2764	THE SENSORITES
2084	WARRIORS OF THE DEEP		2777	THE ROBOTS OF DEATH
2096	THE SEEDS OF DEATH		2788	THE HAPPINESS PATROL
			2929	STATE OF DECAY
			2973	THE MUTANTS
			2975	THE BRAIN OF MORBIUS
			2978	THE POWER OF KROLL

2986	TERROR OF THE VERVOIDS	5008	SILENCE IN THE LIBRARY
3000	THE GREATEST SHOW IN THE GALAXY	5058	THE GIRL IN THE FIREPLACE
3008	MIDNIGHT	6000	THE FACE OF EVIL
3010	THE RIBOS OPERATION (1-4)	15,000	THE ARK IN SPACE
3065	THE SPACE MUSEUM		THE SONTARAN EXPERIMENT
3225	THE CURSE OF PELADON	25,000	THE SUN MAKERS
3275	THE MONSTER OF PELADON	37,166	PLANET OF EVIL
3418	Planet Of The Spiders (3-6)	200,000	THE LONG GAME
3500	DEATH TO THE DALEKS	200,100	BAD WOLF
3550	The Chase (5-6)	2 MILL	THE MYSTERIOUS PLANET
3567	THE MACRA TERROR	10 MILL	THE ARK (1-2)
3983	THE CAVES OF ANDROZANI	10 MILL 40	FRONTIOS
4000	THE WEB PLANET	10 MILL 700	The Ark (2-4)
	MISSION TO THE UNKNOWN		THE CELESTIAL TOYMAKER
	THE DALEKS' MASTER PLAN (1-6/8/11-12)	FAR FUTURE	THE SAVAGES
4043	THE IMPOSSIBLE PLANET	5 BILL	THE END OF THE WORLD
	GALAXY 4	5 BILL 23	NEW EARTH
4066	THE EVIL OF THE DALEKS (6-7)	5 BILL 53	GRIDLOCK
4126	PLANET OF THE OOD	100 TRILL	UTOPIA
4137	42		
4500	DESTINY OF THE DALEKS	????	THE KEYS OF MARINUS
4590	RESURRECTION OF THE DALEKS (1-2)		The Daleks' Master Plan (8) Tigus
4595	Doctor Who (The TV Movie)		THE KROTONS
4600	REVELATION OF THE DALEKS		The Three Doctors (1)
5000	THE ICE WARRIORS		The War Games (10) ocean/space/swamp
	THE INVISIBLE ENEMY		The Five Doctors (Orion)
			TIME AND THE RANI
			Delta And The Bannermen (1)
			TURN LEFT

ABOUT THE AUTHOR

One of Jon Preddle's earliest memories of *Doctor Who* is from November 1969, watching the regeneration from William Hartnell into Patrick Troughton. This was when he was a five year old in Auckland, New Zealand. Although he began collecting the Target novelisations in April 1979, it wasn't until December 1981 that he could recite all the known *Doctor Who* story titles off by heart. In June 1982 he took delivery of his first issues of Marvel's *Doctor Who Monthly*. The following month the family's first VCR arrived, just in time for him to record – and then watch on a daily basis for the next two weeks – episode four of 'Logopolis'. Now afflicted with the fan bug, Jon began a long obsession with clocks, calendars, contradictions, canon and continuity. The fruits of this obsessive research, *Timelink – An Exploration of Doctor Who Continuity*, was self-published in 2000 (and which won Jon the Sir Julius Vogel best fan writer award in 2001), and has now been fully revised and updated to include the relaunched series of *Doctor Who* as a volume for Telos Publishing Limited.

Jon is a prominent figure within the New Zealand Doctor Who Fan Club, which celebrated its twentieth anniversary in 2007, and is a regular researcher / writer for the internationally highly regarded fanzine *TSV* (Time / Space Visualiser). He reached the semi-finals in the New Zealand edition of the television quiz *Mastermind* in 1988, the silver anniversary year, with *Doctor Who* as his specialist topic. He has contributed to a number of genre publications, including *Doctor Who* Magazine, the *In Vision* 'making of *Doctor Who*' series, and was one of the panel reviewers in J. Shaun Lyon's books, *Back to the Vortex* and *Back to the Vortex: Second Flight*, also published by Telos. Jon considers himself a fan of practically everything to do with film and TV SF. He lives in Hamilton, New Zealand, and works for a major retail bank.

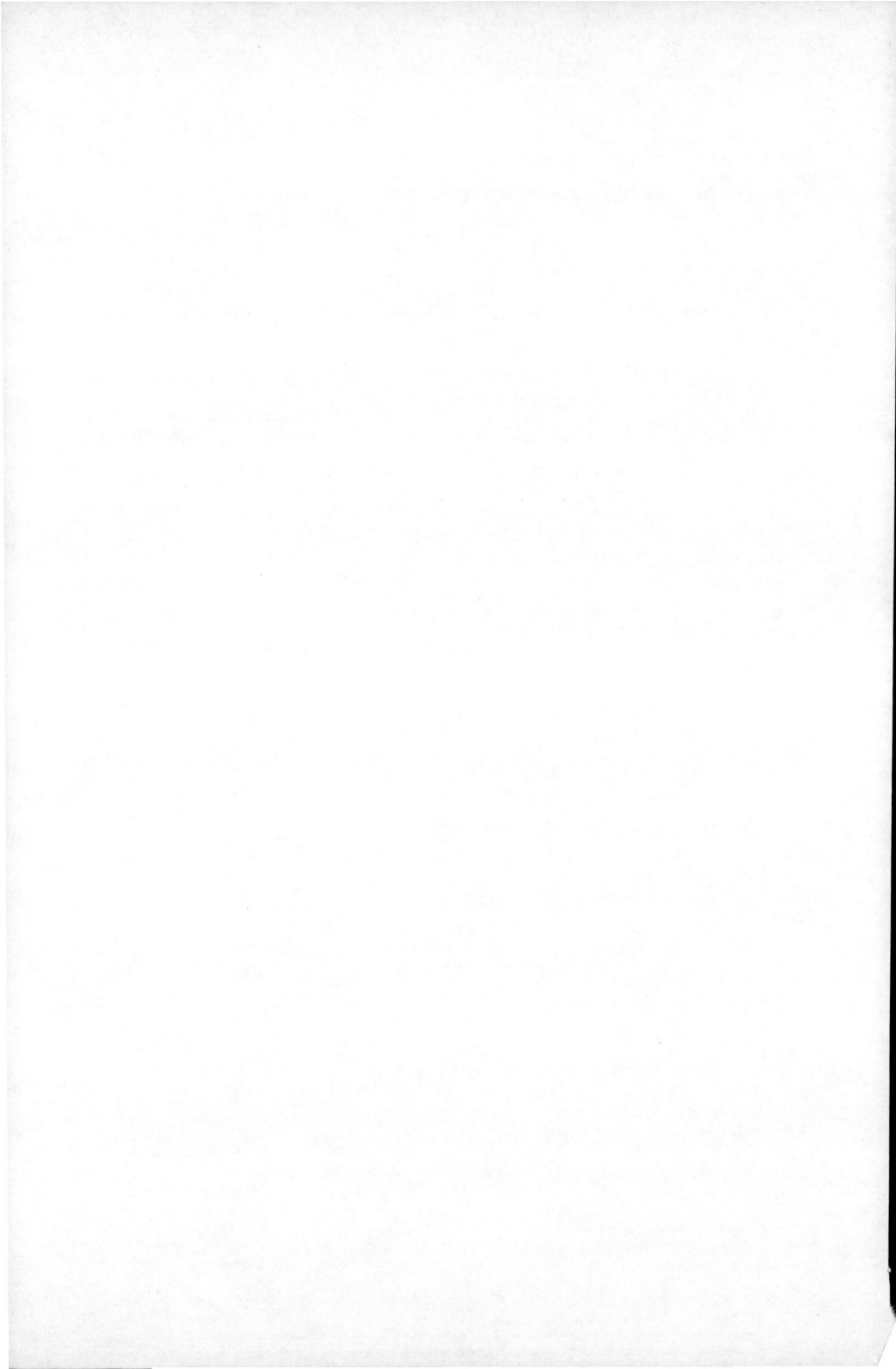